A Queen of Atlantis

&

The Devil-Tree of El Dorado

A QUEEN OF ATLANTIS

&

THE DEVIL-TREE OF EL DORADO

Frank Aubrey

COACHWHIP PUBLICATIONS
Landisville, Pennsylvania

A Queen of Atlantis (Frank Aubrey, 1898)
The Devil-Tree of El Dorado (Frank Aubrey, 1897)
  [Frank Aubrey was a pseudonym of Frank Atkins]
  Cover illustrations by D. Murray Smith, from *A Queen of Atlantis*

Copyright © 2009 Coachwhip Publications
Coachwhipbooks.com

ISBN 1-930585-74-8
ISBN-13 978-1-930585-74-4

Contents

THE DEVIL-TREE OF EL DORADO

A Queen of Atlantis

A Romance of the
Caribbean Sea

1
Dreams and Fancies

"Dear little boat! Gallant, saucy, little ship! Splendid, dashing, *Saucy Fan*! Isn't this glorious?"

The words were spoken in tones of high enthusiasm by a girl of nineteen or twenty years of age, who stood on the high stern of the brig, *Saucy Fan*, which was reeling and tossing on the Atlantic rollers nearly half-way out on her voyage from Liverpool to Rio de Janeiro.

"This boat, to-day," the speaker went on, with a hand on the rail, and swaying easily with the tumbling vessel, "puts me, somehow, in mind of a little thoroughbred mare I used to have in our home in the Argentine. I called her 'Romping Chit.' She was such a lovely creature! Without whip or spur she would carry you till she dropped, and she seemed to glory in it all the while. And the *Saucy Fan* is just the same. She keeps on her way unceasingly, untiringly; struggling up and down the swirling waves just as 'Romping Chit' would canter all day long over the green, rolling pampas. She never showed a sign of fatigue, and was just as full of fun, just as ready to break into a romping gallop at the end, as at the beginning, of the day's work. Don't you enjoy a day like this, Mr. Wydale?"

Owen Wydale, the person thus addressed, was a well-built, fine-looking young fellow of some twenty-five years. He had a handsome, bronzed face, with dark hair, eyebrows, and moustache; and very clear, steady, grey eyes. His sturdy, well-set figure betokened somewhat of a military training; while the manner in which he managed to keep his balance, with hands quietly clasped behind him, showed that he was not unaccustomed to the sea.

11

"Just my feeling, Miss Dareville," he replied. "This sort of thing has always had a great fascination for me."

Since, however, he looked, while speaking, at his companion, it was not quite clear which "sort of thing" he referred to;—the blue sky, the rocking vessel, and the white-crested waves, on the one hand, or the dainty, captivating face and form beside him, on the other.

Nor could it be much wondered at if he thought just then most of the latter, for Vanina Dareville was one of those who seem to have been born to tantalise and drive to distraction the soul of any male mortal upon whom they turn their glance.

She had a rather tall, but exquisitely-moulded figure, such as a sculptor would have chosen as a model for Diana; and a face and head that had a charm, a witchery that were unique. It was not merely, however, that she was beautiful; it was not only that she possessed lustrous brown eyes, and delicately chiselled features; all these gifts, charming and attractive as they are, were immeasurably enhanced by a most unusual, captivating expression; rather, it should be said, expressions. These came and went upon her face, each in turn seeming more seductive, more irresistible than the other. In the pouting lips, round which, as they curled one from the other, dainty little dimples played about, there was a coquettish roguishness that was inexpressibly bewitching. Yet, with all these was sometimes mingled a suggestion of queenly pride and dignity that conveyed a warning; it would not be well, it seemed to intimate, to incur the look of contempt and scorn with which those same lips could curl, and those large eyes could flash, on those who should be rash enough to merit it. To-day, the eyes were flashing only with innocent mirth; and, with her glowing colour, and the little white teeth that the lips at times disclosed, and that wondrous, inimitable smile that was all her own, made up a startling picture. And it was a picture that held Owen Wydale captive, bound in chains more hard to break than ever were fetters of hardened steel.

She was standing upon a piece of board that raised her just high enough from the deck to keep her feet out of the water which washed it every now and then, and with one hand on the rail she swayed freely to and fro with the motion of the brig; every turn, every pose, replete with rare and exquisite grace.

And her companion, noting all her winsomeness, found it no easy matter to turn his glance away from her to look upon the scene around them which had called forth her expressions of delight; while, she on her side, remained all unconscious of the admiration she inspired, her thoughts and interest being entirely given up to the enjoyment of the moment.

"Look, Mr. Wydale! Look at the water and see how daintily the *Saucy Fan* dips into one wave and then glides up gracefully over another. Oh! if every day at sea were such as this, I should never wish to go ashore again!"

For some minutes the two stood silently watching the great white-crested billows as they darted past, hissing, and seething, and dashing, and surging against the vessel's sides, and finally following one another into the line of foam that marked her wake. The strong, warm, invigorating breeze that whistled through the rigging, and whirled the particles of spray into the face, seemed to bear with it a feeling of exhilaration and elation. At intervals, as though in very sport and mischief, and bent upon justifying her name, the *Saucy Fan* would bury her head in the snowy crest of some soaring, foam-crowned billow, sending up a shower of spray that reflected all the colours of the rainbow, and sparkled in the sunlight before it fell with a crash upon the fore-deck. Then, poising for a moment on the summit of the wave, she would give a coquettish shake, a sort of tremor, before taking the great plunge into the hollow below, mounting the side of the succeeding one with one of those swinging leaps that all true lovers of the sea know so well, and so delight in. Indeed, the pretty brig, to-day, seemed bent upon a game of romps with the great Atlantic rollers that came sweeping up to her; almost, one might think, in imitation of a school of porpoises that were indulging in fantastic antics not far away. Some distance astern a solitary ship could be discerned, that rose and fell, and bobbed and nodded as though making friendly signs and salutes to its sister-bark in front. Otherwise, there was nothing to be seen on any side but the blue sky and glaring sun above, and the palpitating, heaving bosom of the marine expanse below.

On deck there were only the man at the wheel amidships, the burly skipper who walked to and fro beside him, and a man in oil-skins, who lounged in the bow. While the vessel lurched and pitched and the sails strained at their fastenings, the cordage creaked and grated in a wild kind of harmony with the wind that whistled shrilly through the rigging, and, every now and then came the dull, hollow "boom-ff" when a wave struck the bow, followed by the sound of the salt shower that fell pattering upon the deck.

Suddenly Vanina cried, "Look out!" and, with a merry laugh, dexterously ducked under a small canvas awning, just in time to escape a mass of water from a larger wave than usual. It had leaped up suddenly and unexpectedly, just where they were standing, and came rattling on the deck with the patter of a hail-storm. The squall carried away Wydale's hat, which disappeared over the bulwarks.

A moment afterwards a young boy, clad in waterproofs, emerged from the head of the companion that led down into the main cabin, and came towards them. He was a bright-eyed, curly-headed, good-looking youngster of about thirteen or fourteen years of age, and he looked at the two with a bright smile as he approached. Vanina extended a hand to him, and pushed him well under the shelter of the scanty awning.

"You had better keep close there, Georgy," she remarked; "we have just had a sea break over us."

"I know, sister," the boy replied. "We heard it down in the cabin, and Sydney sent me up to say he thinks the wind is freshening, and that you should come down."

"I, too, fancy it is getting rougher," put in Wydale. "Don't you think we should all do well to seek some better shelter, Miss Dareville?

"Not I," the lady answered, with vivacity. "I love it! I think I was born with a love for the sea. But, as for you," she went on to Wydale, with another merry laugh, "you'll never make a sailor if you don't learn to keep a better look-out. You were fairly caught that time, and, if I hadn't called out, you would have been thrown upon the deck and been wet through. You should keep a sharper eye to windward. You had better go and find another hat."

"I've got one," Wydale answered, pulling a waterproof cap out of his pocket, and composedly putting it on his head. "The fact is," he went on, "I was too much engaged—after what you said just now about your little mare—in thinking of you—of how you would look—"

"Well—what?" she asked archly, when he hesitated.

"On horseback—dressed as—as—as an Indian huntress, or—as—a warrior queen," he went on, laughing.

"Do you mean in a circus?" she demanded, a little stiffly.

"Oh, no, no! In real life—such as it used to be ages and ages ago," he returned hastily. "In the days when warrior princesses used to carry sword and shield, and ride in their chariots or on their war-horses, into the thick of the battle—and—and cheer on their soldiers—and—all that sort of thing, you know," he finished up—a little weakly, as he felt.

She looked earnestly at him, and drew a long, deep breath.

"Ah!" she said presently, "it is singular you should have such thoughts. That's how I feel myself sometimes. What put that into your head?"

"I scarcely know; something in your manner at times. You have the face—aye—and the figure, too, for it."

"I hope, all the same, that I don't look like an Amazon," she said. "For me, that kind of character has no attraction."

"No; Diana—or rather, perhaps, say, Boadicea."

"Leading a horde of savage 'Ancient Britons' clad in rough skins! No, thank you! I don't think that would suit me either."

"*Jeanne d'Arc*, then! Surely you will not object to that suggestion?"

"Yes, yes! The very thing!" young George put in, with strong approval.

"I'm not good enough," she answered simply. "I fear I should never make a *Jeanne d'Arc*."

"You don't know what you can do till you try," George suggested hopefully, and it was asserted in a tone of such conviction that the others laughed.

"We are talking no end of nonsense," Vanina presently declared; "I wonder what put such ideas into your head?"

"I'm sure I can't quite explain," responded Owen; "but it must, I think, as I said just now, be something in your face, or manner, or general air. Now I come to think about it, it is rather an odd notion; yet such ideas seem always to suggest themselves when I look at you."

Vanina gazed dreamily out upon the waters, and seemed to be musing. And, for a space, there was unbroken silence.

"It is curious," she said slowly, after a pause, "but I too, have very strange thoughts at times; and dreams—especially dreams."

"What dreams?" asked Owen.

"Dreams," she went on, still slowly, as though recalling them one by one, "of martial hosts, of armoured knights, and men in mail; of clashing swords, and flashing spears. And often I seem, just as you have suggested, to be myself clad in mail, brandishing a sword or spear, and urging my followers on to battle. And it is all as in the times of long, long ago, ages ago, when there were no cannons, no pistols, no fire-arms of any sort or kind. I often fancy I must have had ancestors, chieftains who lived and fought in those ancient times, and that they visit me in my dreams, and in them re-enact the scenes in which they bore a part. What strange days those must have been!"

"Perhaps better to think of, and read, and talk about, than to experience in their grim reality," Owen observed.

"I don't know; at least the men of those days were brave; or those who were not were soon found out. Men met one another face to face, foot to foot. They did not hide behind shelters, and shoot at one another from places a mile or two apart. How strange it would be for us, if we were unexpectedly thrown back into those old times? How should we act? If we were suddenly to find our-selves back in the midst of such a world, what sort of figure should we cut, I wonder? A poor one, I am afraid, men and women too. Our women of to-day would lack the pluck and endurance of those old-time heroines, and, as for the men—how would they fare if their lives depended upon their skill with sword, and shield, and lance?"

Just then another young fellow came up the companion and called out:

"I want to have a word with you, Wydale. Do you mind coming down for a few minutes?" Then he turned and disappeared; and Wydale, with a brief word of apology to the young lady, followed him.

There came now a sort of lull, and the brother and sister remained for a while silently watching the waves that were racing past. Vanina's thoughts returned to their former channel.

"I was telling Mr. Wydale, Georgy," she said to her young brother, "how much I enjoy being at sea on a day such as this, and on board a boat like the *Saucy Fan*. How splendidly she goes through it! Almost like a well-found, well-behaved yacht!"

"Ah!" returned the boy in a low tone, and with a serious face, "that is all very well, sister, when you are a passenger; but you cannot picture to yourself how very different this same vessel appears to you if you are a poor beggar of a cabin boy, as I was once here, you know. You can scarcely believe what a place they made it for me!"

Vanina took his hand, and pressed it tenderly.

"I know, poor boy," was her reply. "They must have ill-used you indeed, to drive you to—"

"It was just such a day as this," he went on dreamily, "when I crawled out beyond the bowsprit yonder, the seas breaking over me every minute, to escape from the mate; and when Mr. Wydale came out after me and brought me back. It was a plucky thing for him to do, I can tell you. No one else on the whole ship would have risked it; and that ugly-faced skipper over there, and his mate—who are so meek and mild to you to-day—stood looking on, and would have let the two of us drown for all they cared."

Vanina shuddered.

"I know, Georgy, dear," she said fervently. "But let us not talk about it now. It makes me turn quite sick. Certainly I feel we can never, any of us, be sufficiently grateful to Mr. Wydale for what he did for you that day. He must be very brave, and very kindhearted too."

"Brave? He's more than that! He's—he's—" and the boy hesitated, and cast about for a simile; then wound up with, "he's a regular brick!"

Meanwhile, the subject of this little talk was seated in the cabin of the brig, in close conference with the elder brother of the two, one Sydney Dareville. He was a well-built, good-looking man of nearly thirty; had been at one time a sailor, and at another had seen service as an officer in one or other of the endless civil wars that are ever breaking out in the volcanic regions of South America. A little thinner than Wydale, and a little taller, he also exhibited somewhat more of the swagger and dash that characterise the ex-soldier adventurer. Ordinarily, one could read in his laughing eyes something of the merry, boyish good-humour of his young brother, mingled with the roguish high spirits that characterised his sister. To-day, however, he was grave, and evidently disturbed in mind.

"Fancies or no fancies," he was saying, "I cannot put aside these feelings of vague suspicion and distrust that have laid hold of me. In my father's time all our vessels were manned by honest, decent men. How has it come about that my precious step-father and his present partner should send old and tried servants packing, to put in their places rascals like Durford, our cheerful skipper here, and Foster, his scoundrel of a mate, and the rest of our hang-dog looking crew? Can you explain that to me?"

"That they are a bad lot—at least, with the possible exception of Peter Jennings, the ship's carpenter—I have good reason to know," Wydale agreed.

"Still—"

"And what is that vessel behind us?" the other interrupted. "And why does she follow us as she has, taking in sail again and again, as I have seen with my own eyes, to keep in our wake when she had been overhauling us?"

"That may be but a fancy on your part; they may have feared foul weather. It has been squally and unsettled for some days. Of course, I can see what you are hinting at, but really cannot understand what anyone would have to gain by such a crime. The cargo is ours, or ours and your friend Casella's jointly. The brig itself is partly yours—"

"Aye, this brig carries all I have left in the world to call my own," Dareville interrupted gloomily.

"—And the insurance is made out in your joint names. Where, then, would be the gain to those you have in your mind?"

Sydney Dareville regarded his companion for a moment fixedly, then with a dry smile replied:

"What have they to gain? Nothing much on the ship and cargo, truly; but—if my sister and young brother were to die before coming of age—my respected step-father would come into—fifty thousand pounds."

Wydale started, and looked incredulously at the speaker.

"I never heard of that," he murmured; you never told me. "I had no idea that your sister was—that is, that your brother and sister were—" He hesitated.

"You didn't know that Vanina was an heiress," Dareville answered, with a hollow laugh. "Yes, very much so, my friend. And now you can understand why it would suit certain persons very well indeed if the three of us went to Davy Jones's Locker, as the outcome of this voyage. And you know now why I am distrustful and uneasy, and want you to be watchful and to help me to keep a sharp eye upon all that goes on. Now I must go up and fetch those two young people down. I can hear that the wind is getting up again." With that he rose and went on deck.

And Owen Wydale, turning over in his mind all that had been said, could not help recalling the talk he had had on deck concerning Vanina Dareville's dreams."

"Well, *they*, at least, were but dream-fancies," he at last id to himself. "Heaven send that these misgivings of Dareville's may turn out to be fancies, too."

2
Left to Die in the Sargasso Sea

Owen Wydale's presence on board the *Saucy Fan* this voyage had been brought about in a somewhat curious way. On her last voyage, which had been from the Cape to Liverpool, he had shipped at Cape Town as the only passenger, and had had very unpleasant experience of the character of her skipper and crew. He was returning to England after an absence of some years, during which he had knocked about the world a good deal, and had seen life under many varying phases. He had served for a year in the Cape Mounted Rifles, and seen some fighting; he had shot lions and other "big game" in the depths of the African forest and out on the "veldt," and had, in one place and another, met with many strange adventures and hair-breadth escapes. His mother he had never known; his father had died a few years before, leaving to him—his only child—just enough to get along with and no more, and he had lost some of his capital by injudicious speculations in African mines. Hence, at the time referred to, when he was returning to England with a vague idea of "settling down" to some sort of occupation, motives of economy had induced him to take passage in a small sailing vessel instead of in a steamer.

He had been not long at sea, however, before he found cause to regret having chosen the *Saucy Fan*; not on account of any fault to be found with the vessel herself, but by reason of the behaviour of the majority of those on board. The skipper, Joseph Durford, and his chief mate, Steve Foster, showed themselves to be blustering bullies, cruel and unscrupulous towards those whom they thought it safe to subject to ill-usage. In particular, they seemed to find a

special delight in ill-treating two young boys who had the misfortune to form part of the ship's company. One—the younger of the
two—was deaf and dumb; but even that affliction did not avail to
save him from the brutalities of his tormentors. Wydale soon saw
that the vessel was manned by a ruffianly crew, and that, while the
skipper and his mate bullied everybody all round, the two lads included, many of the men joined in against the latter to wreak on
them, in turn, the revengeful feelings they durst not show towards
those above them. The elder of the two boys strenuously tried his
utmost to help and shield the younger. Many a blow did he receive
that had been aimed at the other; but this chivalrous conduct, so
far from exciting sympathy, as one would have expected, would
only bring upon him further blows and thrashing. This was especially noticeable in the case of the mate, Steve Foster, who seemed to
pass no inconsiderable portion of his time in devising petty cruel-
ties and malicious torments against the two helpless lads.

Wydale viewed these proceedings with indignation and disgust,
and had more than one stormy passage with both skipper and mate
in consequence. He soon discovered that the two boys had been
delicately nurtured; they had, indeed, run away from home, and
hidden themselves as stowaways in the brig, just before she had left
Rio de Janeiro for the Cape. They, or rather George, the elder—for
the other could not speak—obstinately refused to give any account
of themselves; and this was one thing—so he said—that excited the
ire of the skipper. He grudged, moreover, every mouthful the
youngsters ate—he worked on a profit-sharing arrangement with
the owners, it appeared, and would lose considerably by their being
on board. These, at least were the statements he repeated, again
and again, to Wydale; but the latter subsequently found reason to
regard them with some doubt. At last, one morning, the little deaf
and dumb boy was missing. He had jumped overboard in the night,
leaving a pitiful note behind him addressed to his brother saying
that he could bear his life no longer, that he was going to join their
"dear dead mother," and concluding with a touching expression of
hope that his brother would get on better without him. "Perhaps
they will be kinder to you without me, dear brother," the poor, ill-
used little fellow wrote, "because I am so stupid, and I cannot hear

what they say, and do things quick enough." And so he had slipped over the vessel's side in the darkness, and gone for ever from the view alike of those who loved him and those who had made his short young life a burden too great for him to bear.

Over this pathetic tragedy a stormy scene took place between Wydale and the skipper and his mate that almost ended in blows. Wydale's indignation led him roundly to accuse the two of deliberate murder or what amounted thereto; and he declared his intention of laying information against them for that crime, or manslaughter, so soon as he got ashore. The skipper retorted by threatening to put him in irons, if he did not mind his own business, and refrain from interference between him and those under his control.

One would have thought that the miserable end to which the little stowaway had been driven would have earned for the survivor surcease of ill-usage and it did for a few days, but for no longer. Then the old persecutions, the tormentings, the ropes-endings began again, as bad as, even worse than, ever. One thing was now noticeable, however; Foster, the mate, was almost alone in the matter. The others had, to some extent at least, felt sufficiently impressed by what had occurred to refrain from further brutal violence. But Foster seemed possessed by an almost insane hatred of the lad; it looked, indeed—as Wydale bluntly told the skipper—as if the man were deliberately trying to drive the boy to follow the example of his unhappy brother.

One day the lad, to escape from his enemy, climbed out beyond the bowsprit on to the jib-boom, where he clung in imminent peril of being washed off, loudly declaring he would drop into the sea, unless a promise were given to ill-treat him no more. Wydale, at great personal risk, climbed out after him and brought him back, just when he was on the point of dropping into the sea. He had, in fact, already fainted, and would have fallen, but that one arm had become jammed between the spar and the foretopmast-stay. In this dangerous position—the seas rising and breaking over him from time to time—the rescuer received aid from one man only, Peter Jennings, the ship's carpenter; the skipper, his mate, and several of the men standing about looking on and grinning.

After this episode, Wydale took the lad entirely under his protection, paying—though he could ill-afford it; his passage money as a first-class passenger; and thenceforth the boy was no more molested.

Leaving Wydale for the moment, and turning to the three Darevilles, it should be stated that they were the daughter and sons of an Englishman, now dead, who had settled in South America many years before, and had been partly a ship-owner, partly a rancher, with considerable estates in Brazil and Argentina. At his death, Mrs. Dareville—to her sorrow, as it afterwards turned out—married Mr. William Blane, a man of whom little was known beyond the fact that he had made some money in Australia, and had joined the ship-owning firm of Dareville, Armitage, & Co., shortly before Mr. Dareville's death. After a year or two of unhappiness with her second husband, Mrs. Blane died, leaving to his care her three children by her first husband, *viz.*, Vanina, and two boys, George and Fred, the latter being deaf and dumb. Sydney Dareville, the eldest son, having no great liking for his step-father, and having inherited from his father a sum of money and a small share in the ship-owning business, had left home some time before, and gone away to seek fortune or adventure, as the case might be. Some of his interest in the firm he sold, retaining only a small share.

Vanina was sent to England to finish her education. She would be entitled, when of age, to a small fortune, her father having left a sum to each of his children on their attaining their majority, with the proviso that the shares of any dying before that event were to go to the survivors. The reason given by her step-father for sending her to England was that she might be educated so as to fit her for the position she would have to fill. But Sydney Dareville declared curtly, when he heard of the arrangement, that Blanc merely wished to get her out of the way.

While away she received very unhappy letters from her two younger brothers, complaining of the unkind treatment they met with at the hands of their stepfather and a woman to whom he had confided them, and culminating in the announcement that after the tender affection of their mother, his unkindness was more than they could bear, and that they had resolved to run away.

Thus it came about that these two little unfortunates, by some strange chance—if there is such a thing in this world—hid themselves away in the first vessel that opportunity supplied, and this happened to be one of those partly owned by their dreaded stepfather. But of that they had no knowledge. They had lived all their lives on the ranch, and had never seen a ship before; and, if they had heard that their late father had been a ship-owner, it had conveyed but the vaguest notion to their young minds. When afterwards they had to face the skipper, they, or rather George—for the other could only speak by the deaf and dumb alphabet—said that their name was Simmons. Beyond that, they obstinately refused to give any account of themselves or of their friends or relatives. How they fared—how the poor little waifs fell out of the frying-pan into the fire—has been told above.

Shortly after the two boys ran away, Sydney Dareville, tired of soldiering, came to Rio and called at the offices of the firm there to see his step-father. He had resolved to sell out a further share in the firm, and invest the proceeds in a trading venture in partnership with a friend who had a commercial connection in the Argentine. He was informed by the Rio agent that Mr. Blane had gone to Liverpool, partly upon business, and partly to arrange for his (Dareville's) sister to return home. It being part of Dareville's plan to go, in any case, to England, to select and purchase a ship-load of miscellaneous goods, he followed him by next steamer, instead of going to their home; thus he failed to hear that his two young brothers had levanted, the agent being unaware of it.

Thus also it came about that, when Owen Wydale, with his young protégé—concerning whom he felt very much perplexed, feeling that he could not well afford to take the boy's whole future upon himself—arrived in Liverpool, the lad's relatives were already in the town. Yet would he probably have missed them had he not gone to the office of the owners' agent, a Mr. Ridgway, to lay his complaint against the skipper and his mate. George had told his new friend his real name, and such other particulars as he knew about himself; but they were not clear enough to lead Wydale to suppose that the boy's step-father was one of the present owners of the vessel, even if he had known or remembered the name of the firm, which he did not. His relations with the skipper had not been such as to lead to much talk between them during the latter part of the voyage. When, therefore, Wydale, accompanied by George, entered Mr. Ridgway's office, their astonishment was great at finding there Mr. Blane himself. That gentleman looked anything but pleased to see his step-son, and listened but coldly to Wydale's account of what had happened. In reply to it he merely said he would think the matter over, refunded him the amount he had paid Durford for the lad's passage, and added that he would take future charge of him himself. George's terror at this was so extreme that Wydale hesitated as to what he ought to do; but when, a minute or two later, the boy heard that his brother and sister were in the town, he quickly brightened up, and Wydale then formally handed him over to his step-parent's custody, and returned to his hotel.

There, next day, came George, bringing Sydney and his sister, who thanked him in very different fashion from Mr. Blane's for his kindness to their brother, and quickly all became on friendly terms.

The two young men had many tastes in common; both had had some military training, and seen actual fighting; each had knocked about the world and met with adventures. Small wonder, therefore, that they soon became not only fast friends, but eventually partners in Dareville's projected trading venture. It appeared that all Dareville had left of his former interest in the firm consisted of a half share in the *Saucy Fan*, and this he had been unsuccessfully endeavouring to sell to his step-father. Therefore he was in a quandary, not having sufficient capital to pay for his share of the cargo. When Wydale was informed of this, he readily offered to join and go or with him, to seek fortune in the *Saucy Fan*, by which vessel Dareville had already arranged to take his cargo and his sister out together. Wydale expressed some reluctance to sail again with the present skipper and crew, but Dareville laughed, declaring that he would either keep them in their places, or know the reason why. In any case, he said, he had not the power to interfere with the manning of the vessel; so Wydale reluctantly gave up the point.

But a short time before, he could hardly have conceived it possible that he could have been induced to take another voyage in such company; now he would have made almost any sacrifice to sail in the same ship with Vanina Dareville, whose bright eyes and winning smiles had made a captive of him.

Thus the four young people had embarked together; and at first all had gone on as well as could be hoped for in the circumstances. The skipper gave up the chief cabin entirely to them, and lived in a deckhouse. They had but little occasion to speak either to him or to his mate; but, when they did, those worthies showed themselves exceedingly deferential towards their passenger-part-owner, and those with him. Yet the good little ship had not been long at sea before Sydney Dareville, as has been seen, began to entertain misgivings. Moreover, just before sailing, at a time when it was altogether too late to alter their arrangements, he had come across an old friend who had expressed grave doubts of Durford and "his gang," as he called them, hinting at dark doings in their former history. But Dareville at the time had kept this to himself, and only mentioned it to Wydale now, because other incidents—each of little moment in itself, yet in the aggregate importing much—had occurred to make him feel uneasy.

This was his state of mind when he left the cabin to fetch the two on deck. He met them already on their way to join him, for the skipper had warned them that a "dirty" squall was coming up, and the crew were already shortening sail. But, when it came, it proved to be much more than a squall; and it struck the gallant little ship before she was prepared to meet it, threw her, for some minutes, on her beams-ends, and quickly stripped from her some of the canvas she still carried. For two days, a heavy gale was raging, and the brig drove before the wind under almost bare poles, and going whither, no one in the cabin knew. Scarcely one of them, in fact, stirred out of it. Fortunately, their respective sleeping cabins opened into it; as well as several tiny rooms used as store cupboards, in which were kept a few articles handy for use, such as potted meats, bread and biscuits, a cask of water, and so on. Else might the little party have been starved; for no one came near them, save once or twice the skipper, who shouted down some unintelligible words about the hatchway, and forthwith went away. Once or twice, too, Owen or Sydney would venture on deck to take a look round; but, since nothing was to be seen but a wild waste of tumbling waters and driving spray, they returned quickly to the shelter of the cabin.

On the afternoon of the third day the weather began to moderate, and Wydale and Dareville were able to pass a short time on deck. But the outlook was still dark and gloomy, they reported, on their return; and night closed in on a still raging sea. But most curious—so Dareville thought—there astern, could still be seen the vessel that had seemed to dog them. She must have somehow followed them even through the hurricane.

"I am glad to say," observed Dareville to his sister, when they had rejoined her, "that I think we shall all be able to take a good rest to-night. The sea is evidently going down, though slowly; and in the morning you should be able to get out of this stuffy place, and be on deck again."

"That will be a glad change, indeed," returned Vanina. "I had no idea the cabin of a ship could become so hateful to one. A few days more of this would go far to cure me of my fondness for the sea. I would much rather be on deck and face the weather."

Presently there were some knocks on the hatch above, and, on going to see the cause, Owen found the ship's cook bearing a pot filled with steaming coffee.

"Cap'en thought as maybe ye'd like a cup o' coffee apiece," he said shortly. "Couldn't boil nothin' afore; the sea kep' puttin' out the galley fire. You've got cups and saucers."

And with that brief explanation the man handed over the coffee-pot and disappeared.

"H'm! It's little enough civility Durford has shown us," Dareville commented, with a laugh; "so I suppose we ought to think the more of this unexpected piece of politeness. Anyway, a cup of coffee's welcome."

But its flavour failed to satisfy their expectations. It was only partly drunk, and voted disappointing, and fully half of it was thrown away. Shortly after the four retired to their respective sleeping berths, to take the first spell of unbroken rest they had enjoyed since the storm began.

In the morning Owen woke suddenly, and with a strange sensation of uneasiness. Almost immediately he heard Dareville's voice calling and asking whether he was awake. He had not taken off his clothes, so he stepped out at once, and both went into the main cabin. Everything was strangely quiet. The vessel scarcely moved; she merely rose and fell on a slight swell, as though at anchor in a sheltered harbour. But beyond the soft plash of ripples against her side, and a scarcely perceptible creaking of the cordage, no sound was to be heard. No voices, no footsteps on the deck, nothing whatever to denote the presence of human beings. Wydale and Sydney stared blankly at each other; then, with a common impulse, made a rush up the companion and tried to open the hatch. It resisted all their efforts. Plainly the hatches had been fastened down upon them!

"What devil's-trap is this we have fallen into?" exclaimed Dareville, in mingled fear and anger—fear for his helpless younger brother and sister more than for himself, and wrath at the trick that had been played upon them. Then came a staggering thought. Had the wretches deserted the vessel, having first scuttled her, and left them there to die, stived up in the cabin like caged animals? Even now, while they were wasting precious moments, the vessel might be slowly filling through holes made by the scoundrels!

"Where's my rifle—and my revolver?" Dareville cried. "If they are within shot when we get on deck, I'll give them something to remember this business by!"

But, when he went to look for his arms, he found they had disappeared; so had Wydale's; and every cartridge with them.

Just then Vanina joined them. She read in their averted eyes that something serious had happened. Owen would have said a word to reassure her, and sent her away, perhaps, but Dareville interposed.

"This is no time for mincing matters," he declared, "and she must know directly; for we must break our way somehow out of here, and my sister is no weak-minded simpleton."

So he briefly explained what had occurred.

She fully justified his confidence, for she scarcely so much as winced, and her colour never changed. She drew herself up with one of the proud flashes that at times would dart forth from her eyes, as though rebuking Wydale for his anxiety on her account, and said quietly:

"I see. I understand. If you think you can break open the hatch, do so at once. I will go in and talk to George." And she turned and left them.

Dareville could not repress a gesture of admiration, or of conscious pride, at the behaviour of his sister.

"Told you so," he muttered, with a glance at Wydale. "She's a girl in a thousand for pluck." Then he went on, looking round: "And now, how to get that beast of a doorway open! And be on the look-out! For all it seems so quiet, some cowardly scoundrel may be lurking up there with a pistol to shoot us down the moment we show our heads. I've heard of such things before."

"So've I," said Wydale, between his teeth. "We've been two fools, Dareville, and ought to have known better, especially with a lady and a young lad in our charge. Two of us to look after them, and, with all, to fall into such a clumsy trap as this."

The other made no reply, and they both set to work, though cautiously. It took some time, and they had to break up some of the fitted furniture in the cabin to use as battering-rams before they made much impression. However, no one interfered, and they heard no sound, and, after a time, they were able to raise the hatch a little way, and take a careful look round. Then they pushed it open and emerged on to the deck. Plainly the vessel was deserted; both the boats had gone. There had been three before the storm, and all had now disappeared.

Sydney called to Vanina, who soon appeared, leading by the hand her brother, looking, as was but natural, very pale and scared.

"Confound their impudence!" exclaimed Dareville, gazing around him in astonishment. "What are they up to in all this? What in the name of all that's diabolical is their little game?"

The air was misty, and they could see no great distance whichever way they looked; but, so far as the view extended, there was nothing but one great field of green; they were surrounded on every side by a mass of seaweed.

Dareville stepped forward and tried the pumps. In a few minutes he came back, looking very thoughtful and perplexed.

"It's very odd," he said, "but the vessel's all right. Seems to be sound as a bell. At any rate, there's no water to speak of in the

hold. They haven't even tried to scuttle her—so far as I can make
out."

"Then what in the name of all that's damnable," asked Owen,
"is the meaning of this trickery?"

But Sydney Dareville had had a twelvemonth on board ships
some years before, and knew more about the sea of that part of the
world than Wydale did, and already an idea was forming in his
mind that nearly froze his heart with horror.

Turning to the other two, he said lightly:

"Well, you two will have to play at being cooks now, while we
look after the ship. So, go down and see what you can find for breakfast. It's clear there is no immediate danger."

Thus reassured, Vanina and her younger brother descended
into the cabin and busied themselves in setting it to rights, and
doing their best to prepare a meal.

But no sooner had they gone than Dareville took Owen by the
arm and led him into the bows of the vessel, so as to be well out of
hearing; then he turned and looked at him, his face all white.

"No immediate danger," he repeated, in a hard, bitter voice.
"No; but may the great God above help us!"

"Why," Owen exclaimed, alarmed, "what do you mean? Where
are we?"

"Where are we?" repeated the other between his teeth. "Why,
hard and fast in the Sargasso Sea!"

"The Sargasso Sea. But what is that?" asked Wydale wonderingly.

"It is," said Dareville, in a despairing tone, "a vast tract of ocean
adjacent to the Caribbean Sea, a region that has been called—and
for only too good reason—the maritime graveyard of half the world.
It is a gigantic trap, of such tenacity, that, if a vessel once gets
caught in it, never will it let her go. Here, on all sides of us—if it
were but clear enough to see—are untold scores of ships that have
been caught and imprisoned, and have lain rotting for long ages;
and here shall we also be held fast, to starve to death, and then lie
and rot, as many and many another doomed wretch has starved,
and died, and rotted here."

3
A Marine Graveyard

In the midst of the Atlantic Ocean, in the region lying between the Caribbean Sea and the Gulf of Mexico on the west, and the west coast of Africa on the east, is a vast expanse, never traversed by ship or steamer, and known as the Sargasso Sea. It would scarcely interest the reader, perhaps, to give here a detailed explanation of the curious system of ocean-currents to which, according to some scientists, the phenomenon owes its existence. Suffice it to say that here is a region extending over an area of many hundreds—some even estimate thousands—of square miles, so choked with seaweed that no vessel or boat can sail, steam, or row in it; and few who once get entangled in it ever return to tell the tale. There are, indeed, accounts of some who have attempted to explore this unknown waste, but none have succeeded in penetrating very far from the outer edge or fringe, and these adventurers experienced such difficulty in regaining the open waters as effectually to deter them from making any further expedition of the kind. In more than one such case, indeed, the explorers almost gave up the hope of ever escaping from the weed's fatal embrace. These adventurers describe the region as unique in its strange isolation and oppressive silence and stagnation. Here no waves ever foam or tumble, no spray ever leaps into the air, flashing and glittering in the sunlight; no raging sea disturbs the everlasting calm. But the calm that reigns unchallenged here is like unto the silence of the grave; it is, indeed, a veritable graveyard for unknown legions of the vessels of all nations. Abandoned at sea, hundreds, thousands of miles away, after years of lonely drifting from all quarters of the world, they find here their final resting-place. In every direction it is a scene of unutterable desolation, shunned, it is said, even by the sea-birds. No doubt the greater part of the hulks here entangled are abandoned vessels—derelicts; no doubt, also, if they could be approached and boarded, they would repay the adventurers with almost untold wealth. Those who abandoned them could not have carried with them the cargoes, scarcely even any of the treasure they were freighted with. Those were indeed fortunate who escaped with life, for terrible tales are told—and with only too much probability—of vessels held fast in the tenacious grasp of the clinging weed, having still on board unhappy creatures whose fate one cannot contemplate without a shudder.

Such being the reputation borne by this dismal tract of weed-strewn ocean, it is small matter for wonder that Sydney Dareville, in spite of the ready courage that was one of his foremost qualities, felt appalled at their position. Speculation as to the cause, and what had become of the skipper and crew, became a matter of but slight interest, compared with the grim fact of the hopelessness of their condition. Nor needs one feel surprised that he should have felt too utterly crushed, for the time being, to give his mind to plans for their escape. But Owen Wydale, of tougher stuff, would not abandon hope. His was one of those sturdy, British spirits of whom it has been said that they never know when they are beaten; and his brain was already busy studying the situation in all its bearings.

While talking, the two were startled by hearing a deep-drawn breath behind them, and, looking round, saw Vanina standing near, with a face that was both pale and anxious. Yet, though her cheeks blanched when she grasped the danger they were in—for she had heard what had been said—the steady look in her candid eyes showed that she had no thought of breaking down beneath the trial.

"You here, Vanina?" exclaimed Dareville. "I thought you were—"

"I came up to ask you a question—but it does not matter now. I heard what you said. Can it be true? Is there nothing to be done?"

"I can see—can think of—nothing," he answered wearily, almost listlessly. "It is a cruel—an inconceivably cruel—cowardly business. If we had a full crew, and boats, and a good wind, even then it

would be an almost hopeless undertaking to try to get out from
here into the open sea. Situated as we are, you can judge for yourself."

Here Wydale, who had been looking very hard in one direction, turned to go below, saying he "would be back directly." After
an absence of a few minutes he returned, carrying a pair of binocu-
lar glasses and a telescope.

"The murdering, thieving hounds missed these, anyhow," he
observed shortly, and fell to studying the scene before them, at
one time through the glasses, at another through the telescope.

The position of the brig was this. She was surrounded on all
sides by the tangled masses of weed, but, not far away in front of
her—straight, that is to say, from her bows—was an open channel
of clear water. Up this she had doubtless drifted, and then, through
a turn in the channel, had been thrown, either by the wind or her
own impetus, into a sort of backwater; and this once entered, the
weed had closed round her and held her fast. The channel of open
water was but a dozen yards or so away; but, in her present plight,
she was as hopelessly shut off from it as though the distance had
been a mile, or as though imprisoned in a great iron cage. This
channel stretched away with a curve to left and to right, and was
finally lost in each direction in the haze. A dull, moaning noise in
the distance indicated that the open sea was within hearing, and
that waves were there breaking, probably upon some rocky reef;
but the sound was so faint it was difficult to determine the side
from which it really came.

Wydale had observed attentively all these points, and he now,
as stated, studied the outlook carefully and patiently through the
instruments he had hunted out. Then he laid them down, and again
disappeared into the cabin.

The others took up the glasses, and through them viewed the
expanse of green by which they were surrounded. Then Vanina gave
a little cry.

"See!" she exclaimed. "See! What is that over there? 'Tis a ship
in full sail! We can surely attract her attention."

Dareville turned his glass in the direction indicated, then laid
it down with a gesture of despair.

"It is, as you say, a ship in full sail," he answered, with a shrug; "but she moves not, nor will she ever sail again. Judging by what I can make out, she has been standing thus, in full sail, for many a long day; only in this cursed sea of deadly calm no hurricane has ever come to blow her poor old sails away. If you look around, you will see other miserable wrecks, mostly old, battered, decaying hulks. As well expect help from them as from yonder 'ship in full sail!' Even such a breeze as you can now feel, slight as it is, is a novelty—according to what I have heard—in this hope-forsaken region."

And Vanina felt her heart sink while she listened to his words; and she laid the glasses down, infected, too, with his feeling of dull, cold despair.

Meantime Wydale had returned, carrying an armful of the broken pieces of furniture with which they had forced their way out of the cabin. These pieces of wood he began to throw energetically overboard, sending them far enough to fall beyond the weed into the open channel. Then he snatched up a pair of glasses, and attentively watched them. Suddenly he uttered an exclamation.

I thought so!" he cried out. "See, Dareville! Look! Those pieces are floating away. Not fast; but you can see they are moving along. There is a current there. I thought just now I could detect it; but it runs so smoothly I could not feel certain. Now, however, you can see it clearly enough. See where that first piece has floated to? It's going faster now that's because there's more current out in the middle. Jupiter! If we could but get out into that channel!"

Dareville laughed.

"What then?" he asked. "Firstly, we can't get there; secondly, do you think we could sail and tack the brig in a waterway thirty or forty feet wide, and with but two of us to manage her, too?"

"Don't you see," urged Wydale, disregarding his half-contemptuous manner, "that that current *must* lead somewhere, and where to, if not the open sea? With but the least bit of 'way' on her, and this wind behind her, we might keep her in the middle of the channel; and that may be all we need do. I fancy the wind must have changed since she drifted in here. It blew her in here then; now it would take her back into the current."

"But how can we get her there?" said Dareville, looking over the vessel's side at the tangled weed. "If we only had a boat in that open water, now, and a live—"

"Let's get some sail on her, any way, and try," Wydale interrupted curtly. "The wind's the right way, and her head's lying the right way. If we can get her to move at all, it may not be so difficult."

Unfortunately, to bend a sail of any sort seemed just what could not easily be done. Many of the higher sails had been blown away; other lower ones seemed to have been deliberately cut away. There were none within reach that could be utilised.

"Where are the spare sails kept, I wonder?" Wydale asked, as he realised all this. Then an idea occurred to him.

"Why, of course! George knows! Where's George? Call him up!" And George, who was below, soon put in an appearance. He had, under one arm, a bundle of wood which he had chopped up to make a fire with, and in the other hand he carried an axe he'd found.

When informed of what was wanted, he entered into the business with alacrity, and, throwing what he was carrying into a corner, quickly showed them where the spare sails and tackle were to be found.

But it took an hour and a half to get even a couple of moderate-sized sails hung out, in very unseamanlike fashion, on the lower yards. But the effect was small. The wind had freshened a little, and the brig yielded slightly to the pressure; but she made no decided way.

Wydale and Dareville got long poles and pushed desperately at the weed in an attempt to clear her bows, but they made no impression on it.

"If we could but get those royals out!" Wydale exclaimed, looking up aloft. These sails had been securely furled before the squall struck the vessel and had escaped damage. "There's more wind up there."

"I believe we could do it," George declared.

"You!" Vanina exclaimed, in alarm. She had been carefully watching all that was going on, and helping where she could. Breakfast had been long before forgotten; no one now thought of eating. Only water had been called for, for the day, though not sunny, was close and hot.

"I've had to do it before to-day in a rough sea," said George. "Surely I can do it now when she's as steady as a telegraph post! I believe it can be done."

"By Jove! but you're right, George," Dareville joined in. "Come on; I'll help, lad! We'll do it between us

And in the result, after many patient attempts and much tugging and pulling, and many exclamations, "not loud but deep," from Sydney Dareville, followed by good-tempered laughs from the boy, the sails floated out and were soon hauled taut, amid a little cheer from the two aloft, very heartily taken up by the anxious watchers on deck.

"She's moving!" Vanina cried out, in excitement. "Come down and help here now!"

The two "reefers" came scrambling down, and Dareville took up a pole and set to work to clear the rudder from the weed that clung about it, while Owen worked away with perspiring energy to clear the bows, and George and his sister together took in hand the management of the helm.

And slowly, inch by inch at first, but moving faster as she gathered way, the *Saucy Fan* crept, with a soft, brushing sound, through the greasy masses of weed, and finally, amid the breathless anxiety of those on board, emerged from it into the open channel!

"Hurrah! hurrah! Now, quick! Put her helm over—no, not that way—the other way!" cried Wydale.

"Starboard—no, I mean 'port!' Quick! Pull for your lives!" yelled Dareville.

Amidst these shouts and contradictory directions, the rudder was somehow got into its right direction, and the brig sailed freely and easily along the open channel.

"So far, so good," said Wydale, with a glance of triumph at Dareville. "This is better than sitting down and twirling our thumbs and waiting for starvation."

"Yes," Dareville assented, "you had the right ideas there, my friend. But now the question is, where are we going to? And if we get to the open sea, how do you suppose we two are going to manage a brig that needs a crew of eight or ten hands?"

"Let us hope—and pray—for the best," said Vanina gravely. "Surely Heaven, that has helped us so wonderfully thus far, will not desert us now!"

4
The Mysterious Island

The brig sailed on smoothly, easily, with a silent, gliding motion, past endless fields of weed on every side, past many lonely wrecks and forsaken, rotting hulks of what had once been stately, swift-sailing, white-winged ships. These forlorn relics were of all sizes, of all nations, and of every fashion of build known and unknown to those who looked upon them. And the farther they sailed, the older became the type of vessel, till they came to what they took to be old Spanish galleons, and, later, to vessels of still more ancient build. Scattered about were great beams and spars, and numerous small boats, and in the latter—as well as on the decks of some of the larger craft—could be seen, every now and then, little white heaps—all that was left, it was but too painfully obvious, of the bleaching bones of hapless victims of the dread Sea of Sargasso.

Inexpressibly sad, terribly solemn and impressive, were these relics, as they came quietly into view, and passed, silent and ghostlike, away out of sight.

Never, perhaps, has human eye gazed upon scenes more awfully desolate or more eloquent in their weird stillness and slow, unfailing decay. But soon the attention of the watchers was, perforce, drawn away from these mute memorials of an unknown past to the question that now forced itself upon their minds, "Where were they drifting to?"

Wydale had observed, first with growing surprise, then with alarm, the fact noted above, *viz.*, that the rotting wrecks around them became of a more and more ancient type the further they proceeded. Then he and Dareville happened to glance at one another, and with that the same thought struck each: "Did it not appear as though they were journeying steadily, not to the open sea—as they had fondly hoped—but towards the very heart of this dreary wilderness of weed?"

It had been long after noon when they sailed out into the channel. It was now within an hour of sunset. They could not go on like this in the dark! What was to be done? But just when Wydale, who was steering, called Dareville to him for a whispered consultation, fresh surprises broke upon them. First, the channel along which they were sailing began to widen; then the mist began to clear, and soon they saw dim shapes that rose high in the air straight ahead; these gradually took forms resembling the lofty towers of some mighty castle glistening in the evening sunlight. Slowly, for a while, the mist lifted, then suddenly cleared quite away. At the same time, the channel ended, opening into a large expanse of water that spread out for a mile in front of them, and for two or three miles to their right and left. And now they saw that what they had taken for Titanic towers were the lofty peaks and cliffs of an island, that lay sleeping and smiling, with its green woods and sandy shore, in the ruddy gold gleams of the setting sun

A wondrous scene! A fascinating, an enchanting scene! And the four on the deck of the gliding vessel gazed upon it as though spellbound, too astonished, too enraptured, to utter so much as a single word.

Before them was a bay shut in by towering, precipitous rocks that, at each end, came down almost straight into the sea. But, towards the centre, they receded, forming a natural amphitheatre with a wooded ravine in its midst that mounted up, terrace upon terrace, towards the cliffs that rose still higher in the background.

In front of the woods, and in strong contrast to their deep olive tone, was seen the vivid green of a wide strip of greensward, and, in front of this again, a broad belt of tawny-coloured sand.

Through the wood tossed and foamed a torrent of rushing water, while, from the cliffs around, leaped foaming cascades, all finding their way, eventually, into the waters of the bay. Perhaps the most remarkable feature of all this fairy scene was the castellated rocks that reared themselves in stately fashion high above the hanging

woods. These shone as though of glass—or crystal, and, in the setting sun, glittered and sparkled with tints of dazzling brightness.
But all was still upon this island; save for the distant murmur of
the falling water, and the lap of tiny ripples against the sides of
the brig, not a sound was to be heard, and no sign of human presence was to be seen.

"Well!" said Dareville presently, drawing a long breath, "we've
got somewhere at last, anyway! And it strikes me that, unless we
mean to run down this charming island (as I suppose it is), and
sink it beneath the sad sea waves, before we've had time to over-
haul it, we'd better take in sail—or let go the anchor—or 'bout ship—
or—Oh, hang the sea slang! What I mean is, we shall be ashore
directly, if we don't do something to stop her!"

"We shouldn't hurt much, if we did run ashore on that sand,"
said Wydale. "However, as we don't know what sort of people live
here, and what kind of reception they might give us, perhaps we'd
better try to anchor out here for the night. Then we can see about
landing in the morning. The breeze has died away; we might let
the anchor go first, and take in the sail afterwards—or leave it as it
is all night for the matter of that," he added, with a laugh. "We
can't possibly hurt here, if we get a good anchorage."

With some trouble they let the anchor go, and the cable ran
out with a rattle that was echoed again and again from the opposite rocks, almost like distant thunder. The sound somewhat
startled them, and they gazed anxiously along the shore to see
whether the noise had caused any movement in the place to show
it was inhabited. But, though they looked closely and carefully
through the glasses, they saw no trace of a living creature.

The anchor held, and the brig swung easily at the cable end,
about a quarter of a mile from land.

"What place can it be?" asked Wydale, much perplexed, while
they leaned on the rail, and watched the scene that was growing
dimmer in the fast deepening twilight. "Can it be, do you think, that
this is one of the West Indian Islands, and that, after all, it was the
Caribbean Sea—not the Sargasso Sea—that we came through?"

"Shooh! No, man!" returned Dareville. "I've been through the
Caribbean Sea—and more than once. There's weed there, but nothing

like what we've come through to-day. Besides, there are no wrecks lying about *there*. This is the region they call the Sargasso Sea, right enough; but what this place in the midst of it can be passes my wit to understand."

"What place—what island can it be?" Vanina asked, in growing wonder.

Suddenly George clapped his hands. A reminiscence of his *Lemprière* came into his mind.

"I know!" he burst out. "I know! It must be so!"

"What?" queried his sister.

"Atlantis! The lost Island of Atlantis!" he declared enthusiastically.

At this they all laughed heartily, and, it being now nearly dark, they turned slowly to go below to light the cabin lamp, and, at last, get something to eat.

In these latitudes there is but little twilight such as we are accustomed to in England. So soon as the sun goes down, almost instantly it is dark. By the time they reached the cabin stairs they had to grope their way.

"I think," suggested Wydale, "it would be as well to stuff something into all these ports, and so show no light. If there should be any hostile natives watching us, and thinking of coming off in canoes, it will be more difficult for them to find us in the dark."

"Don't," cried Vanina, with a shiver. "You upset me again; just, too, when I had got over our terrible fright of the morning."

"It's only a reasonable precaution, though," said Dareville; and the idea was carried out. This work done, he turned to his sister with the words, "We're not out of the wood, yet, you know. Other things apart—if, that is to say, there are no disagreeable inhabitants here, and we don't starve—we don't want to live on a forsaken, desert island all our lives. And for us, unaided, to work this brig out, and back to a port, is a simple impossibility."

This being obviously true, the reminder once more depressed the spirits of the little party, so that they ate their scanty meal almost in silence. Presently, when it was finished, George, full of boyish curiosity, stole quietly up the companion to take a look round. A minute later, his voice was heard calling to the others to come up; and in a few seconds all were again on deck.

"Look, look!" cried the boy excitedly. "The whole place is on fire!"

It was not exactly that; but it certainly looked like it. All around, the water was brilliantly phosphorescent; every tiny ripple was a glowing wavelet of light, that turned the whole area of water into a lake of fiery, waving lines, fringed, where the ripples lapped the shore, with brighter bands. Not only so, but some of the cascades tumbling from the cliffs above seemed to be alight also, and fell like streams of fire, the spray that splashed from rock to rock resembling glowing sparks. And above it all, through the dark sky, appeared, every now and then, darting lurid flashes like the "Northern Lights," as seen in higher latitudes.

"Whatever does it all mean?" Vanina whispered, in an awe-struck voice.

"The stagnant water," Dareville began oracularly, "in this sea of weed, is full of animalculae, and is strongly phosphorescent. That's—"

"Ah, yes! *that* we can understand," said she, cutting short his intended speech, "I have read it somewhere in a book. But I never heard of such a thing with falling water like this. Besides, you see it is only the case with one or two. The other streams are like ordinary water, quite different from those extraordinary fiery torrents. And those flashing lights, too, what can they be? Is the whole island a volcano in eruption?"

But against this suggestion there was the fact that there were none of the phenomena that go with such eruptions—no noise, no sign of ashes, smoke, or escaping sulphurous gases. Save for the murmuring of the falling water, the whole scene was as still as when they first looked upon it by daylight.

But before any theory or explanation could be advanced by any one of them, their attention was drawn away from the shore by a sound in the opposite direction. It was at first only perceptible as a slight distant rushing and splashing in the water.

Gradually it increased in volume, until it became a kind of low, dull roaring, like the advance of an immense wave; and, mingled with other sounds, could now be heard snorting and strange noises as of a whale, or some such ocean creature, swimming or struggling,

in violent fashion, along the surface of the water. Moving quickly
to the opposite side of the deck, the watchers could see a veritable
fiery fountain advancing down the channel along which they had
sailed earlier in the day. It soon became clear that some great deni-
zen of the deep was making its way towards them, with much tumbling and splashing, and many violent plunges, which sent the
phosphorescent water leaping in showers into the air, to fall back
in glittering drops upon the gleaming waves around. In a little
while, the cause of the disturbance had come out of the channel
into the open water, and approached so close to the vessel that it
was possible for those on board to make out what was going on.
And this is what they saw:—

A great sword-fish, of extraordinary bulk, though armed with
a terrible-looking "sword" of at least five feet in length, was struggling in the grasp of a gigantic cuttle-fish. The latter had two of its
arms twined like lithe snakes round the body of the fish. Every
now and then the latter would leap into the air, endeavouring to
fall back (sword-first) upon the body of its enemy, after the manner in which, as is well known, sword-fish will attack and kill the
largest whale. But the grasp of the arms around it always threw
out its aim, so that it fell back each time into the water between
the curling arms of the monster, and well away from its body. And
soon the combatants came almost alongside the brig, and, in their
furious struggles, even sent the spray up on to the deck. The four
onlookers were too much surprised and fascinated by the spectacle
to move or even speak. While they watched, they could see that
the sword-fish was growing weaker; and that gradually more of
the arms of the cuttle were coiling round it. Several of these arms
rose in the air, covered with the glittering particles, twisting, with-
ing, darting to and fro, like horrible fiery serpents, and one by one
they fastened with their tenacious grasp upon their plunging victim.

Suddenly, a new sound was heard of some other great body tearing through the water, and another immense cuttle-fish rushed
across the bay to the assistance of its mate. It came shooting along
the surface, leaving a brilliant path behind it, like a rushing rocket,
and launched itself into the fray with a ferocity fearful to behold.

To assist its attack it threw two or three of its great arms round the stern-post of the brig, and, with the purchase thus obtained, it laid hold, with the other arms, of the struggling sword-fish, and dragged both the antagonists bodily towards it, shaking the vessel from stem to stern in its exertions. Gradually, the struggles of the victim ceased, and one of the cuttles raised its body out of the water. When its great bulk, with the monstrous, gleaming eyes, as large as saucers, rose above the surface, Vanina, horrified, yet too frightened to move, could not repress a scream. This seemed to awake Wydale and the others almost as from a trance. With a vague idea that she was in danger, the former rushed forward, picking up the axe which he knew George had that morning laid down near the fo'castle, and returned quickly with it to her side. And he was only just in time. The other two had started from the bulwarks out of sight; but Vanina seemed fascinated by the awful hideousness of the creature, and remained staring over the side. Evidently the monster had caught sight of her and scented further prey, for, like a flash—more quickly even than the python seizes upon the swift-footed antelope—a long, dark, writhing "tentacle" darted over the rail and twined round her body. But even before the cry that rose to her lips was heard, Owen's axe had fallen upon the slimy limb and severed it just where it crossed the bulwark; the next moment the part that had taken hold upon her fell, now harmless, on to the deck. Another tentacle flashed across with lightning quickness, this time aimed at Wydale, coiling round his arms in such a manner as to pinion them and prevent his using the axe. Immediately he was, in his turn, dragged against the bulwarks, and he felt himself, despite his struggles to release himself, being lifted irresistibly off his feet then other arms of the monster were put forth, stretching out ravenously to seize him. Fortunately, Dareville saw his friend's great peril, and retained his presence of mind. He snatched the axe from Wydale's now powerless hand, and, with a swing, brought it down, as Wydale had but a minute before, cutting through the second tentacle. The severed portion fell limp and motionless beside the other piece, and the two great cuttles, with a loud splash and a mighty plunge, made off, carrying with them the captured sword-fish.

When Wydale turned to thank his friend, he saw that he was, assisted by George, already half-leading, half-carrying his sister towards the cabin; so he slowly followed them, without stopping to examine the hideous trophies of the encounter that lay on the deck.

5
A Deserted City

It was a gloomy, almost silent, little party that sat down to breakfast the following morning in the chief cabin of the *Saucy Fan*. The two young men had had little sleep, having passed the night, for the most part, in whispered consultation. Ostensibly they were supposed to be keeping watch and sleeping by turns, while Vanina and her younger brother slept on undisturbed; but, as a matter of fact, they carried out this arrangement only when the night was three-parts spent.

Naturally they were anxious and depressed, though, be it said, more on account of the other two than on their own. Had they but been alone, the spirit of daring and adventure that animates most young Englishmen would have caused them rather to rejoice in than to regret the chance that had placed them in so strange a situation. But placed in an unknown part of the world, inhabited, perhaps, by savage tribes, as it certainly was by grim and ferocious monsters, what chance had they, without firearms, of being able to protect themselves and those with them, if attacked? And then there was the question of food.

Of arms they had practically none; and the reliance of civilised man, in these days, upon firearms is so universal that it is astonishing how helpless he becomes without them, when the need arises to defend himself. Prehistoric man, thrown upon a desert island without his accustomed weapons, and with only his hunting knife in his girdle, probably immediately set to work to manufacture bow, arrows, and spears, after his own fashion; and, if unmolested for a while, was soon as well fitted out for the battle of life as if he had

been equipped from one of the primitive arsenals of his own country. Nowadays things are different indeed, for when the unarmed,
civilised man is cast upon the desert island, amongst uncivilised
foes, the latter are more at home in more senses than one, and
have very much the best of it, without counting numbers.

No wonder, therefore, that the two on whom the safety of the
whole party rested felt oppressed by the sense of their own helplessness. If they were not to starve to death, the food they already
had in the brig must be supplemented by supplies of some kind
from the land and sea around them; that was clear. But to obtain
these exploration was essential; and to explore an unknown country without arms is about as severe a test of the civilised man's
courage and resource as they can well be subject to. Both Wydale's
and Dareville's thoughts ran continually upon the difficulty they
had here to face, for both knew there were no arms amongst the
cargo.

Presently, while they sat at breakfast, Vanina broke the silence
with a little laugh. The others looked up in surprised inquiry.

"I was thinking," she explained, "how very much I must have
fallen in Mr. Wydale's estimation last night. He said once he
thought I had the face and figure of an Amazon—"

"Not at all," Owen hastily interrupted. "I did not say 'Amazon';
I said 'Warrior Queen.'"

"Ah, well, it's the same thing here. I fear I did not show more
pluck or spirit than the proverbial woman confronted by a mouse."

"The occasion was exceptional," Wydale returned gravely. "It
was something more than a mouse that attacked you. Many a man
so situated would have given way to panic. You, at least, did not do
that; and you did not faint. You behaved extremely well, I think."

"I'm glad to hear you say so," she replied more seriously. "I
feel we shall have many dangers to face here; and this is no time
for a woman to give way to 'nerves.' You shall find me different in
future—at least I hope so. But, you see, last night the incident was
so sudden, the sight of the horrid monster so unexpected, and it
looked doubly, trebly ghastly lighted up so fitfully and strangely
by the beams from the splashing water. Ugh! I can see it even now."
And she shuddered, and passed her hand before her eyes as if to

shut out the sight. After a pause, she went on: "But in future I mean
to be brave."

"It will only be your natural spirit, sister, if you are," George
interrupted. "Don't you remember that time when the rattlesnake—"

She interrupted him quickly in her turn. "Never mind that now,
George. We have something else to think of. Are there then no arms
amongst the cargo?"

Sydney Dareville sighed disconsolately.

"No," he said, with a troubled look, "that's the worst of it. There
are none at all."

"None—absolutely *none?*" Vanina repeated.

"None, I am sorry to say. You see—"

"But what *is* in the cargo?" then she went on. "Most of it belongs to you and your friend, you told me—and Mr. Wydale saw it
all put in. Are you *sure* there may not be a case of revolvers and
cartridges?"

Sydney shook his head. "I feel more vexed and upset about it than
you can think," he explained; "for it is my fault that there are none;
at least," he added, hesitating, "it was more Ridgway's than mine."

"Ridgway's!" exclaimed Vanina, in surprise.

"Why, yes; this was how it was. Mr. Cassella gave me a list of
articles I was to be sure to ship. As to others, he left that to my
discretion. Well, I thought of a lot of other things sure to sell well out
there, and amongst them firearms of different kinds. But, when I
spoke to Ridgway, he advised me not to take anything in that line. He
said they were themselves sending a consignment, and that therefore it would not be worth our while. So I struck out the firearms."

"But how were they sending them?" Wydale asked.

"That I can't say," replied the other, and then paused thoughtfully.
"Do you know," he went on, after a short space, "I couldn't understand Ridgway at all. I am half inclined to think he was playing some
game of his own, that even the partners in the firm knew nothing of."

"How do you mean? what sort of a game?"

"Ah, that I do not know. But there was something mysterious
in connection with the *Saucy Fan* before the cargo was stored in
her; and strange to say, I don't think Blane was in it. That Blane is
a scoundrel, a would-be, cold-blooded murderer—it's no use mincing

the fact, Vanina—we all know too well; and I don't believe much in either Armitage or Ridgway. But what I really fancy is that, while the other two were planning a deep and wicked game of their own, Ridgway was busy on another of *his* own. Those mysterious hints that I received, I am convinced they were well founded, in the light of what has since occurred."

"I see—or at least I, I think, begin to understand—a little," said Vanina musingly. "That there must have been a plot is clear. You think there may also have been an underplot of Ridgway's. I wish I could think better of my step-father; but I cannot. But no more on that score now; what I want to know is, what *is* the cargo? You forget you haven't told me yet."

"We have lists of everything," replied her brother, laughing, "and it will amuse you to hear what that consists of. Never, I should say, if you except firearms—was a more comprehensive list of articles, useful and the reverse, carried by any ship that ever sailed."

"Let us know first what 'useful' things you have," Vanina said. "The rest can wait."

"I'm afraid I can't; they're all so mixed up in the lists." Dareville pulled out a pocket book. "See here, for instance. This is only one short list. It relates to a few articles for a customer of Mr. Cassella's —a showman—keeps what they call in America, a 'Dime Museum.' I suppose the novelty of his show was wearing off, and the dollars were not pouring in quite so fast; so he asked us to send him out a few waxworks of celebrities who, though tolerably well-known in Europe, would attract out there; and anything else we thought might draw. Here are some of his consignments:—penny-in-the-slot-machines, with working models, and so on; a few fireworks; some stuffed animals from Africa, magic-lanterns, and dissolving views apparatus with a case of slides; Mary Queen of Scots—"

"Mary Queen of Scots!" Vanina cried. "What's that? Now you are laughing at me, Sydney."

"Upon my honour, no. He wanted some new waxworks, you must know, and was very particular that we should include Mary Queen of Scots and Lucretia Borgia. You know Lucretia Borgia has been whitewashed—'

"Lucretia Borgia whitewashed?"

"Certainly! Haven't you read all about it? Every historic villain gets whitewashed nowadays. Anyway, it's the case with her; and it's roused up a new interest in the lady over there. But, besides Mary Queen of Scots, there are, amongst the waxworks, a model of 'The Sleeping Beauty,' and some of the kings and queens of England— a few old ones, I believe, to take the place of some that have got damaged. There's King John, and Richard Coeur de Lion; and Boadicea, the famous British Queen, resplendent in a suit of mail, with a helmet on her head, and brandishing a spear, *à la* Britannia—"

Here Wydale glanced with a mischievous smile at Vanina, who flushed up.

"Oh, leave that, and go on to other things," Vanina interposed.

"Very well," agreed Sydney, glancing down his list. "Here are some more of the items. First, there are some pianos and musical instruments of various kinds, including musical-boxes; then come cutlery—knives and forks and so on—and crockery; there are umbrellas, and boots, and shoes; paint boxes and cameras, and photographic, as well as chemical, apparatus; telephones and phonographs; a large collection of mounted photographs of objects and places of interest in Europe; there are rat and mouse traps, and watches and clocks; opera and field glasses, and telescopes; there are reaping and mowing machines, and an ice-making machine—"

"I wish we could put it into use and have some ice here," sighed George.

"You can't get at it; it's half-way down in the hold. Then there's a case of stationery, pens, paper, ink, a large number of books of various kinds, and even a small hand-printing press; there's a portable steam-engine and boiler, and a steam launch—"

"A steam launch; can't we get at that?"

"By and by. If we can find anything to feed it with, it may be useful. Either coal or petroleum can be used as fuel. There are diving dresses, and some wood-cutting machinery. There are harpoons and 'tubes' to shoot them from—but useless without powder; a large quantity of oiled silk—intended for the construction of a war-balloon, I fancy, and some life-saving rockets. These last are packed away at the very bottom, else we could get them out. They might be useful on occasion instead of firearms."

When he had finished, Vanina remained silent a while. Then she observed:

"As you said, a curious collection. And to think that amongst it all we have no arms!"

"Yes; and no clothes either," George put in.

"You're right, Georgy," agreed Sydney. "Ah! it's a great over-sight; almost as bad as the absence of arms. If, for instance, this island should prove uninhabited, and we have to spend here the remainder of our lives—or even a few years—what on earth shall we do for clothes? To be sure, there are the dresses of the wax figures. But it would be funny, wouldn't it? Fancy Wydale and myself, for instance, strutting about in this lonely island, dressed as King John and Richard Coeur de Lion, and—you—Vanina as—as—"

"As Boadicea, the warrior queen," edged in Wydale, laughing, and looking at Vanina. "It'll have to come to that, after all, I do believe! It's fated. Many a true word's spoken in jest, you know."

And Vanina coloured up, and rose hastily from the little table. Then the "council " broke up, and they set seriously to work to solve the problem that lay first before them—how to get ashore to explore the land around, without running the brig aground. In the absence of a boat it was not an easy matter to accomplish. However, they managed to shift the anchor nearer the shore and get the vessel close in at the very end of the cable. Thus they would be able to pull her out into deeper water, if occasion should arise, by simply winding in the cable. Then they set to work to make a raft, and on this Wydale and Dareville made their way to the shore, taking with them a stout line attached to the brig's stern. This, when they had landed, they proceeded to make fast round a great boulder that lay on the beach. This sufficed to hold the vessel steadily in the position that was most convenient to them in the circumstances, and also enabled trips to and fro on the raft to be more easily made, since they had only to ferry themselves across by holding on to and pushing against the rope.

By the time this work had been completed, they were well into the afternoon, and it was clear that very little more could be done that day. It was deemed advisable, however, to take a look round the bay; in particular, to search about for signs of natives. A hunt through the brig for arms had brought to light only two more axes and an old, half-rusty cutlass. They discovered also a small keg of gunpowder, brought, no doubt, for use with the brass carronade that was carried in the bows. All other ammunition the crew had taken away.

"Just enough powder for a few charges, I reckon but no shot of any kind," muttered Dareville, in disgust. "We might cast some rough shot possibly—we've plenty of lead on board —and thus we might find the little cannon of some use, if there are savages here. But we can't carry it about with us."

In the end, the piece was loaded with powder only; a few pebbles of the most appropriate shape obtainable were selected and put aside to be used as shot, if needed. For signalling purposes the explosion of the powder only would suffice.

Owen and Dareville drew lots to decide which should start first upon the work of exploration. It fell to the latter, and it was agreed that he should take up the task that day and the next, and that then, should occasion call for it, Wydale should devote a day or two to going still farther afield.

In the trips to and fro on the raft, a sharp look-out was kept for the dreaded cuttles; but no more was seen of them.

Just before sunset Dareville returned, bringing with him a number of oranges he had found growing wild. He had traversed the bay from end to end at each point, being prevented from going farther by the rocks that ran out into the sea. Then he had ascended the ravine by the side of the watercourse which flowed down it, and, after a stiff climb over the cliffs at the top, had obtained a view of an extensive country lying beyond in a sort of basin. He had also seen a lake in the distance, and what looked like buildings beside it. But it having been agreed that he should return before dark, he had then retraced his steps to the shore. Of inhabitants he had come across no sign.

"But," he observed, "the place either is inhabited or *has* been. It may now be deserted by those who once lived here; but I am confident that the way by which I ascended was once a path and made by man. There are groves, too, as of trees that had been carefully planted and tended in former years, but now it is all overgrown and gone to ruin. It was there I gathered the oranges; they are only half wild. There were other fruits, too, which I could not reach, and were quite new to me. To-morrow I propose to start at dawn and go to the lake I saw, and ascertain whether there are really any buildings there. It may have been a mirage. All that we know is this: we are here on a tropical island in the midst of the Sargasso Sea, an island whose existence has never been suspected, an island, too, that has been, and may be still, inhabited. Therefore I advise that we all stick closely to the ship so far as may be possible, till we know more about the place."

"What makes those cliffs up there shine and sparkle so?" Vanina asked.

"Ah! I forgot that. The rocks are almost wholly crystal; some quite clear and white, others coloured—transparent as glass—some opaque and semi-opaque; but all beautiful in the extreme. I have never seen anything like it."

"And the falling water that is luminous at night; what of that?" asked Owen.

"I could not get to it; it falls from an orifice in the face of a precipice of the crystal rock, at the back of a deep fissure."

"And you saw no animals, small or large?"

"Well, yes, some small ones; rabbits, or something of the kind. I saw some snakes, too. These and some birds were the only signs of life."

The night passed without incident, and at dawn— which broke a little before six o'clock—they were all astir; and then Sydney, after an early meal, prepared to start upon a further journey of discovery. This time he slung a bag over his shoulders, and in it placed some provisions for the day.

"And it will be useful," observed Vanina, referring to the bag, "to bring back some more oranges in. Mind you fill it; those you brought us last night were delicious."

"Yes," Wydale added. "And, if you could only knock over two or three rabbits, or some birds, or something to provide us with a little fresh meat, it would be better still. Oh, for a fowling piece!"

During the day Wydale and the others occupied themselves in many ways. With some of the spare sails they rigged up an awning

over the deck. Then they started fishing, and caught a good supply, a few of which they cooked, when finding them good to eat,
they captured some more to be ready for a meal for Sydney when
he returned. Next they went along the shore in search of oysters,
and returned laden with as many as they could carry.

In the afternoon, Owen and Vanina found themselves sitting,
somewhat tired, under the awning, watching George, who was still
hunting about for oysters in the water, with bare legs and feet, a
short distance away.

"Do you think," Vanina laughed, "that we shall really have to
pass the remainder of our lives out here, as Sydney was so dis-
mally prophesying yesterday?"

Owen shook his head and sighed.

"Who can say?" he answered. "It may turn out so. It needs no
special knowledge to see that the difficulties for working the brig
out are practically insuperable. Still, we sha'n't starve, that is now
clear. And, since that is so, I would not, myself, very much care, if
only—" He paused and sighed again.

"If only—what?" Vanina asked, glancing at him with the roguish
look that, at times, came into her eyes.

"If only I knew how much you liked me," he returned impulsively.

"You are bold, Mr. Wydale," said his companion, looking down
in a thoughtful way. But she did not seem displeased, so Wydale
thought, and he felt encouraged to go on.

"Bold or desperate—call it which you will," he said, with sudden passion. "You must well know how I feel towards you. From
the moment I saw your portrait in the hands of your young brother,
the day I first took charge of him, I have been madly in love with
you, and every day since has made me—"

"Hold!" she said, lifting up her hand. "You must not say such
words to me. And you talk foolishly, too. You declare you—well,
say—liked me since first you happened to see my portrait, and you
assert that I must 'know' it. But how could I possibly know anything of the kind?"

She spoke softly, and gazed dreamily across the bay at the green
woods and cool-looking stream that lay smiling in the sunlight.

"Know?" repeated Wydale, seizing her hand in his. "Ah! you know only too well. You saw it the first time I fixed my eyes upon you. You have seen it ever since, in every look I have given you, every word I have spoken, every—oh, Miss Dareville—Vanina— speak to me—say something to end this suspense—tell me—tell me—do you—do you—like me a little?"

He had passed an arm round her and drawn her closer, she not resisting. George had gone up out of the water to the shade of some trees further away, where he was busy putting on his shoes and stockings. Screened as they were by the bulwarks, he could not see how they were engaged.

Owen drew her closer, and still she did not resist. She could even feel his breath upon her cheek; it blew about a few stray hairs, and she knew he was gazing at her with eager eyes; but she avoided meeting them.

"Of course I *like* you," she replied, looking down and toying with the end of a rope that hung from the rail. "Who could help doing so, after what you did for Georgy? We are both grateful, and—"

"For Heaven's sake, Vanina, do not trifle with me!" Owen burst out. "Grateful! Do you suppose I am talking now about gratitude? You know I am not. Still," he went on more calmly, and with sadness in his voice, "I know that perhaps I have no right to address you thus. I am poor, and you, I have been told, are rich; and it might seem wrong of me to speak, only that we are thrown here into a strange place, and may never see the old countries again. That seems to me to alter matters greatly. It was that that made me speak," he added rather apologetically, "and if I have offended you—"

She turned to him with a flushed face, and one of her wonderful smiles.

"No," she said, "you have not offended me. One who acted as you did towards Georgy could hardly do that. But don't you think you are acting very foolishly, and—prematurely? We don't know what may be before us, what perils may be in store for us. Is this a time and place to talk in such a style, dear friend? Cannot we be close friends—*dear* friends even, if you will—without talk of love?"

She looked so charming, so enticing, that Owen could not resist a sudden impulse.

"Be it so for the present," he said gaily, "we will be friends—
dear friends—but you will seal the bargain with a kiss?" and he
drew her face to him and kissed her.

Up sprang Vanina, but what she was about to say remained unsaid; for just then they heard George's voice, and saw him get up
and come towards the shore in the direction of the ship.

"Here is Georgy," Vanina said, looking at Wydale reproachfully,
and with a flushing face.

"'The meeting then broke up in some confusion,'" he quoted,
looking at her mischievously, "and it hereby stands adjourned,
until—"

But she had moved away, and was calling out to George, who
had now come within speaking distance. And so it was that no date
was fixed upon for the resumption of this important conference.

Towards evening, Dareville returned, and he brought back startling news; he had discovered a deserted city beside the lake he
had seen in the distance on the previous day.

"It is a wonderful place," he told them, "simply wonderful! Full
of ancient temples, and palaces, and buildings that must once have
been of great magnificence and beauty, but now are falling into
ruins. They look, nevertheless, as if they had been abandoned in
quite modern times; perhaps but a few years ago. I saw traces of
ornamental gardens, of parks, groves and fields, and meadows. On
all sides there are evidences of former careful cultivation, but none,
that I could detect, of living people."

"Where, then, can they have gone to—and when?" Vanina wondered.

The question could not be answered. But it afforded ample food
for speculation for the remainder of the evening.

6
The Vampire

When, the following morning, Owen prepared to set out on a further reconnoitering expedition, according to the arrangement that had been come to, George begged very hard to be allowed to bear him company. At first this was refused, but, after some discussion, leave was granted. They had now all come to the conclusion that the place was uninhabited; that there was, therefore, no danger to be apprehended from hostile natives. An hour after dawn they started, Wydale taking with him—as Dareville had the day before—only an axe, the old cutlass by way of arms, the marine glasses, and some bags containing food.

They mounted, without much difficulty, the rough path beside the water-course, and found their way over the cliffs at the summit. It was somewhat arduous work: more by reason of the heat than from the difficulties of the road itself. These would have been greater but for the track which had been constructed at some former time. They thus found their way directly enough to the heights; and there the path led them through a pass, flanked on each side by still higher rocks of glittering crystal, that led to the edge of the plain or basin that lay beyond. Here an extensive prospect opened out before their eyes, and far away they could see the lake that had been described, glistening like a sheet of burnished silver in the sunlight. It lay far below, and the road to it—which was still fairly clear, and easy to follow—skirted the margin of a stream that tumbled and foamed as it leapt from rock to rock. The heat increased as the sun rose higher in the heavens, and the two were often glad to make a halt under trees on the river bank to rest, and enjoy draughts of the clear, cool water, or to eat one of the oranges they had plucked upon their way; for of this fruit there was a plentiful supply. As they drew nearer to the lake, the ruined buildings of the deserted city came more clearly into view, and, after a march of nearly three hours from the time of leaving the shore, they reached them.

It certainly was, as Dareville had described it, a wonderful place. Once upon a time it must have been a flourishing, populous and wealthy city; but there was more than this to be deduced from an attentive study of the buildings, and more particularly of the interiors of the great palaces and temples. The magnificence of those—faded, falling to ruin, yet always grand and impressive in the story that they told—astonished Wydale, and excited his ever-increasing wonder, as he made his way about them.

There were exquisitely carved bas-reliefs, statues and pillars; and coloured frescoes, too, depicting battles, pictures of the sea with quaint, old-world, little ships, and other scenes, all telling of a white race—now apparently vanished—that had peopled the land in former times; a race that must have had their armies, their horse-men and chariots, their war fleets, and their trading ships, their battles by land and sea, their triumphs, and their slaves and cap-tives—all this and more was depicted on those walls with wondrous artistic skill, and in colours that were even now distinct and even brilliant.

Though partly prepared by Dareville's description, Wydale was utterly astonished at all he saw; and, so fascinating did he find the study of those surprising relics, that the hours slipped by almost unnoticed. Even his young companion was impressed and inter-ested, though he could not altogether grasp the true significance of all around him.

They sat down in the grateful shade of a group of cedars that stood near the edge of the lake, it had probably once been the fair garden of a stately pile that raised its towers and massive walls close by. There they made a light meal upon the food they had brought with them, and then resumed their exploration of the ruins.

They wandered by marble mausoleums and sculptured tombs, that spoke of the mighty dead of a mysterious past; and so on through palace courtyards and broad terraces with wide flights of steps that extended to the water's edge, till they came to the outskirts, where green fields and groves of fruit-bearing trees took the place of the deserted buildings.

Here Owen, looking round, saw at some distance the heights that, presumably, shut off the valley they were in from the sea to the south.

"We had better climb yonder rocks, George," he now said. "From there we should be able to get a view of the line of coast on this side. Do you think it will be too tiring for you? Remember, we shall have to go all the way back."

But the boy protested that he felt quite equal to the exertion, and accordingly the two proceeded in the direction of the heights.

Wydale's thoughts were full of the scenes he had just left, and of all kinds of quaint fancies they had evoked. To most minds such ruins must ever possess a solemn and profound attraction, suggesting thoughts of the past that sadden, while they interest. In the present instance the feeling of melancholy, hard to repress when it comes over one, was heightened by the strange apparent loneliness and isolation of the whole island itself. They had seen many gruesome monuments of a forgotten past in the poor deserted hulks that had lain along their route to the island; but these had seemed almost an appropriate feature in that desolate, silent wilderness of weed. Here, where smiling, murmuring streams ran from the hillside into the sleeping lake, where the whole landscape spoke of walks, and groves, and gardens that had once been the delight of the few who walked in them and the envy of the many who gazed upon them from afar, where soaring edifices and towering palaces told of wealth, of pomp, of pride, of power—the contrast suggested by its present utterly forsaken condition was at once more startling, more impressive, more awe-inspiring.

Occupied by thoughts and feelings such as these, and having no watch to refer to, Wydale noticed neither that the afternoon was fast wearing on nor that a dull haze was creeping over the landscape.

The two continued on their way towards the heights, but as the ground began to rise, the journey became steeper and more difficult at almost every step. Road or path there was none; huge masses of rock that had fallen from above were scattered here and there in wild confusion, necessitating detours; while their direct route would be obstructed at other times by deep gullies or fissures. While they were thus absorbed in picking their way with no more definite idea than that of reaching the ridge and looking beyond it, the mist crept up to them, and soon shut out from sight every object around them, save those almost within reach. And even these at last disappeared. The mist, indeed, soon became so dense, that it seemed to wrap them round as with a cloak, and overhead it hung like a sombre, threatening cloud. And now they found themselves in considerable difficulty. It was alike impossible either to proceed, or to return. It was, indeed, dangerous even to move, for at any moment they might be precipitated into one of the fissures that they knew were all around them.

Owen looked about him in some dismay.

"I fear there is nothing to be done, but to sit down and wait for this mist to clear," he observed ruefully. "And that may mean passing the whole night here. I was wrong to have ventured so far in face of the gathering fog."

"Well, it isn't cold, Mr. Wydale," George returned philosophically. "And, as there's no one about to interfere with us, we can't hurt much."

"No, but they will be anxious—alarmed, on board the brig," reminded Owen.

"But they will understand that we couldn't get back through such a fog as this," the optimist consolingly suggested.

But to proceed was quite impossible, so the two sat down on a ledge of rock to wait with such patience as they could command. They made a little meal upon what they had left, obtained with some difficulty a draught of water from a rivulet they could hear trickling close at hand, and then Wydale filled his pipe and smoked in contemplative silence. As is often the case with mountain mists, there was light enough to read by, though it seemed dark and gloomy compared with the glare of the sun in the earlier part of the day. So George took out a little book to read. He had found it— several, in fact—in the seamen's quarters on board the *Saucy Fan*.

Being chiefly concerned with tales of pirates, sea-thieves, and other desperadoes, it naturally had an irresistible attraction for the finder. He had carried the whole batch off to his own cabin, and afterwards had always kept one in his pocket for reading in his spare moments.

How long they remained thus silent neither could afterwards exactly say. Wydale had lost himself in a day-dream with which George's sister had probably much to do. George had reached a most exciting point in the story he was reading—when the hero, a boy of thirteen, spits a few burly ruffians, half-a-dozen or there-abouts, on his cutlass at one thrust—when, in the stillness around them, they distinctly heard the sound of voices.

In an instant Wydale was on the alert, and had put a firm grasp on the shoulder of the boy as a warning to be silent. Then they sat still and listened.

Again the voices could be heard, this time a little nearer, but not near enough for them to distinguish what was said. Only one thing was clear to Wydale's mind. There were two or more men close to them in the fog; therefore there must be people on the island after all! At the same moment another idea came into his mind. Might not these people be foes in search of them? Perhaps, while he and his companion had deemed themselves unseen, some-one living farther away might have marked them down, noted the direction they had taken, and might be now furtively following and seeking them with hostile purpose. If so, the sudden mist had, in reality, been a boon, for it had hidden them in friendly fashion from lurking foes.

He signalled to George to be absolutely silent, and to get up. Then both rose and stood listening and peering anxiously through the fog. It was very dark now and very quiet, and for a space they heard not a sound. Then the voices were once more heard, this time a little nearer and somewhat raised. Apparently the speakers were engaged in a dispute.

Suddenly Wydale heard a faint rushing sound as of a wind or strong current of air. It grew rapidly louder, and seemed to be approaching them; and now it could be heard almost close at hand like unto the mighty wings of some unseen monster of the air, of a size far beyond any known earthly bird. Most strange of all, a cold, sickly horror seized upon the two. It was a feeling of nausea such as might be caused by an aroma of intolerable foulness, and with it the sensation of repulsion and disgust that a human being has for a loathsome, unclean thing. It was the feeling that might be roused in one who, lying awake and still in the middle of the night, suddenly feels the cold, slimy touch of a snake, of whose size or nature he is ignorant, slowly creeping over or winding round him. And, under the influence of this deadly feeling, both Owen and his young companion found themselves fast held as in a vice.

All power of motion, of speech, almost even of thought, seemed gone from them. They could only wait and listen helplessly for some greater horror which they instinctively divined was yet to come, against which they were powerless even to struggle. And, during a space that seemed like hours, but was measured only by seconds, the rushing sound came nearer and nearer, and seemed to be almost upon them, when all at once it ceased.

Then there arose on the heavy air a cry, a shriek, so appalling, so full of utter, hopeless agony and horror that it struck to the very hearts of the two listeners, almost like a stab from an actual dagger. Still they had no power to move, and only could stand motionless, and wait and listen.

The cry was not repeated, and for a while all was silent; but presently could be heard low, indistinct sounds, the nature of which Wydale could but dimly guess at. But in his own mind he could only compare them to the rending of flesh by claws or beak, or both.

George turned upon Wydale a face of ghastly whiteness, and sank helpless to the rock he had just been seated on, and Wydale, with an effort, roused himself and caught the lad before he fell. He laid him gently down and knelt beside him, too dazed and still too sick and faint to be able to gather his own thoughts, and quite unable to cast off the paralysing spell that had seized upon his faculties.

And thus the minutes passed. To the two hapless listeners the time seemed an eternity; but it was brought to an end by the lifting of the mist. Slowly at first, but swiftly a little later, it grew thinner,

then drifted away before a light breeze that had sprung up. Then
Owen, gazing with straining eyes in the direction from which had
come that awful cry, saw dimly a monstrous shape raise itself on
wings almost colossal, and sail heavily away on the breeze into the
receding mist, as might a gigantic, gorged vulture after one of its
loathsome feasts. Then the paralysing grasp that had laid hold of
his very heart-strings was relaxed, the blood resumed its normal
course, and he was able to think, to act, to rouse himself.

George also, who had lain like one dead, revived, and, lifting
his head, gazed wonderingly around them. Owen put his finger on
his lips, and, drawing from his pocket a small flask of brandy he
had brought with him for emergencies, poured a little between his
lips, and then took some himself.

The mist had now nearly disappeared, and the setting sun was
shining brightly when the two finally got upon their feet. Wydale
now saw that the rocks beyond were almost perpendicular. The only
way out from the *cul de sac* in which they were lay in the direction
whence they had heard the voices and that blood-curdling shriek.
Now, however, all seemed still around, and he resolved to leave
their rocky labyrinth at once, lest the darkness should prevent
them.

Cautiously they moved forward, but had gone only a few steps
when, turning the end of a boulder, they came upon a fearful sight.
On the ground, right in their path, lay the motionless body of a
man. He was on his back, with a great gaping wound in the breast,
which looked as though it had been torn open by some ravening
beast. To his astonishment, when he examined him more closely,
Owen saw that the body was that of one of the ruffian crew of the
Saucy Fan. He could recognise the face, too, though now distorted
and set in such a look of ghastly horror as he had never seen before, and earnestly hoped he might never see again. He would have
prevented George from looking at it, but they had to step right over
it. Stooping down for a moment to ascertain whether the man was
dead, he was attracted by the glitter of something hanging from
the trousers' pocket, and he recognised, in another glance, the gold
seal on his own watch-chain. He took hold of it, and drew out from
the man's pocket his watch and chain together. Glad as he was to

recover them, he could scarcely repress a shudder when he noticed that there was blood upon the seal. He wiped it clean, and, slipping it into his own pocket without comment, hurried on after the boy, who had passed on without a pause.

Just when Wydale caught him up, a man crept out from behind a boulder a little way ahead of them. His face was white and haggard, and his eyes were bloodshot; but they recognised at once, even in the now waning light, Steve Foster, the brutal mate of the *Saucy Fan*. Evidently he at first scarcely knew what he was doing, but he pulled himself together, and, raising a hand holding a revolver, he called in a hoarse voice to the two to halt.

7
Monella

For some moments Foster and the other two gazed silently upon each other; the former was the first to speak.

"If yer comes any further, I shoots," he stuttered. "Ah, yes"— when they halted— "I've got yer at last, 'ave I? Now I guess we can square accounts atween us. I don' know how you got 'ere from the place where we left the *Saucy Fan*—we thought she was safe enuff— but, howsomedever, it won't help you much, 'cos if yer thinks yer've 'scaped, why, yer 'aven't, that's all. I've got a long score to settle wi' you two, an' I mean t' settle it now, to-day, when there's no-body to see or interfere."

Wydale could see the villain was like one drunk, partly with mingled fear and rage, no doubt, but partly, also probably, from strong drink. So unsteady was the hand that held the pistol, and so constantly did the man sway about, that Wydale would have closed with him and risked the consequence had he been alone. But the fear that George might be injured by a stray shot in the scuffle held him back. Meantime the scoundrel gradually pulled himself together, and seemed somewhat to recover his self-con-trol.

"I don' know how you came 'ere," he repeated, "an' I don' care; but it's so much the worse for you —both of you. For I am goin' to kill yer both; now, straight away, dead. I wanted to do it afore we left the brig, only t'others wouldn't let me. Now I've got my chance I'm not agoin' t' let it slip, I tell yer. So say yer prayers, if yer've got any ter say, an' look sharp. I shall count twenty, an' then bang! and good-bye to the two of yer. With your own pistol, too—my, but

64

that's a good un! Yer'll be killed with yer own pistol." For the wretch held in his hand Wydale's own stolen revolver.

While Owen quickly but despairingly turned over in his mind all kinds of plans, and narrowly watched his enemy, seeking an unguarded moment in which he might rush upon him with some hope of success, the other went on

"Yer said I killed t' boy, which were a lie, 'cos he killed hisseif; howsomedever, I mean t' pay yer out now by kiln' t'other young varmint and yerself, too. I dessay, besides, ye've 'ad some hand in kiln' my mate over there. There's been some hanky-panky business about it, and I 'spects you had a hand in it, so that's another good reason for my kiln' on yer."

All that he said was interlarded with low, blasphemous oaths and vile slang, and Owen knew it was useless to answer him, or to attempt to bandy words with such a merciless wretch.

"Now, I'm goin' to begin ter count," Foster went on. And he began "One, two, three," and so on up to twelve, when he suddenly stopped. "No," he grinned, struck by a new idea in the way of fiendish cruelty, "I won't kill yer; I shall just shoot yer in the legs, so's you can't get away. Then you'll lie 'ere alongside my pal till that flyin' beast comes back and makes a meal of yer. That's a bully thought. Now then, 'ere goes. Right leg first—"

But, just then, something came whizzing through the air, and the next moment his arm was hanging useless from the shoulder, with a large arrow through it. The revolver was dropped with a shriek of pain from his grasp, and fell to the ground, and his watchful antagonist rushed in and picked it up. Foster found himself now covered, in his turn, by the pistol. But of this he seemed to take but little notice. His attention was too much taken up with his wounded arm and the pain it caused him. He sat down on a rock close by, and, amid a perfect volley of oaths and curses, made futile endeavours to withdraw the arrow, each effort calling forth a fresh howl of agony and renewed cursings.

Seeing that he was, for the time at least, reduced to harmlessness, Wydale looked round to learn where the friendly arrow had come from, but the gathering dusk had already begun to render the rocks around him indistinct. His glance, was, however, quickly guided by hearing a rattling and jangling, as of steel accoutrements, and, looking in the direction whence it came, he saw, advancing towards him, a strange figure indeed.

A man of gigantic stature had come down a side path from a rock above. From head to foot he was clad in shining armour, and upon his helmet was a plume of white feathers. In one hand he carried an enormous bow, in the other a long spear of unusual size and weight; and slung over one shoulder was quiver filled with arrows. By his side was a great sword of a size proportionate to the other weapons, and to the wearer's powerful frame. He moved towards them with a long, easy stride, and behind him came three others of ordinary stature, clad also in suits of armour even more peculiar in appearance. These had no bows or quivers, but carried spears, swords, and shields. Beside them marched one who seemed to be shield-bearer to the first comer; he carried also—not without some apparent difficulty—another heavy spear, probably a spare one for his chief. The shield-bearer and some of the others had also lighted lanterns.

The newcomers marched onwards with military precision till within eight or nine yards, when they halted, and their leader addressed the astonished Wydale in English.

"I am glad to think, sir," said the stranger, in a full, sonorous voice, and with an air of dignity, "that I have been of some assistance to you, and saved you from the tender mercies of this miscreant, who proclaimed, as I overheard from yonder rock, his intention to shoot you with your own pistol."

This was spoken in clear, unmistakable English; the accent was perfect, so that no one could have doubted that the speaker was an Englishman. Yet there was a certain old-world air, a stateliness and gravity, both of tone and manner about him, and with it a bearing so majestic, that Wydale felt at once he was in the presence of no ordinary man. And, in his surprise, he scarce could find words in which to make reply.

Certainly, he had cause for wonderment. Here was an apparition, a figure of a knight of the olden times, with sword and bow and spear, with waving plume and chivalrous mien—a figure, too, of such stature as is rarely seen nowadays—attended by retainers as strangely attired as himself, yet addressing him, in casual fashion, in plain, every-day English!

It is scarcely matter for surprise that Owen felt thoroughly bewildered. He hesitated and stammered and seeing this, the other went on:

"It is growing dark, and it is not good to be abroad in this part in the darkness. If you will trust yourselves to my guidance, I will see you conducted to a safer place."

Wydale roused himself at last to speak.

"Sir," he now returned slowly, and almost unconsciously imitating the other's gravity and old-world speech, and with instinctive respect, "if it was you who sent that arrow to its mark, we have, indeed, reason to be grateful, and your offer places us under a still further obligation. Since you have so clearly proved your friendliness to us, I shall have no hesitation in accepting your advice and proffered help. We know nothing of the country here, having only drifted in by chance on an abandoned vessel."

The stranger nodded curtly, as if he quite understood or already knew the position of Wydale and his companion. Then he strode over to the wounded man, who had ceased his cursings and lamentation to listen and stare in astonishment as great as Owen had shown.

"You do not deserve mercy, for you would have shown none," the stranger thus addressed him sternly; "but I shall let you go this time; beware, however, how you conduct yourself in future. Let me see to your wound."

He handed his weapons to the shield-bearer, and, stepping up to the mate, examined his arm and deftly withdrew the arrow; not, however, without causing the sufferer to give vent to a howl of pain. Calling to his attendant in a tongue unknown to the others, he was handed a handkerchief or scarf, with which he bound up the arm in a manner that showed him to be well skilled in surgery.

"We may as well see what other stolen property the scoundrel has on him, before we let him go," the stranger observed to Wydale.

He turned to his men and spoke to them as before, in a foreign language; whereupon they went up to the man, and, despite his protests, made a careful search of him, the shield-bearer holding up a lantern to assist them. Then they vent to the dead body and searched that also. What they found they handed to their chief, who passed them on to Wydale.

"This cartridge belt is mine," said Wydale, "and the other revolver and cartridge belt taken from the dead man belong to my friend. So also do this watch and chain." The last-mentioned articles had been found on Foster.

"Then take them," said the stranger briefly. And, turning to the mate, resumed, "Look you, sirrah! Take my advice and get back into that hole you were hiding in just now; you will be safe there for the night. In the morning you can go where you please; but remember, if you offend again, and you fall into my hands, I shall not let you off so easily. And now, friends," he added, turning to Wydale and his companion, "let us be going. My people like not to trust themselves abroad here in the dark—nor would you, if you knew their reasons. They will give you the benefit of the lights; for myself, I know my way blindfolded."

He spoke with a grave yet easy courtesy; it was the courtly grace of a king wishing to put his guests thoroughly at their ease, yet, in doing so, to call forth in them a sentiment of homage and respect.

When he had finished speaking, he inclined his head and made way for them, and the two, returning the bow, followed the men with the lanterns.

They ascended a steep, winding path, and soon arrived at a broad ledge of rock that overlooked the scene of their encounter with the mate. Peering down, Owen thought he could dimly discern the man leaning against a rock and looking after them. And he could not help a passing feeling of pity for the wretch left thus, alone and wounded, in a strange place, exposed to unknown dangers; and near at hand was the dead body of the other upon whom had fallen some awful fate, the exact nature of which they did not even then understand.

Following his guides, he now saw before him, in the face of the perpendicular rock, a sort of gateway, within which could be seen the forms of men moving about with lights. These illuminated the opening with a glow that, mingled with a clanging and clashing of arms and armour, made the place appear a cheerful refuge from

the darkness and loneliness of the silent plain below, with its deserted ruins and its hinted terrors.

When they entered, men, all in armour, as were their guides,
formed in two lines and saluted with respect; and immediately they
were well inside, a great barred gate behind them clanged to with
a bang and an obvious haste that somewhat surprised Wydale, and
made him start.

The tall stranger looked round with the semblance of a smile.

"They like not to have these gates open at night," he said. "Indeed, it had fared ill with you, if I had not been here; for, though
they heard and saw all, and would have been glad to help you, yet
none would have ventured forth, either alone or in a crowd."

Wydale would fain have put many inquiries that rose in his
mind, but there was that in the manner of their newly-found friend
that seemed to forbid questioning him. He spoke only that which
pleased him; such was the feeling he inspired.

So Owen held his peace, and patiently waited the other's pleasure.

They all now passed through other gates that closed behind
them as had the first, and entered a spacious entrance hail, well
lighted with hanging lamps, where were still more men. As these drew
up in ranks, their chief took Wydale aside and questioned him.

"Where is your vessel?" he inquired.

Owen described the position as well as he was able, the other
listening with a pre-occupied air, as though scarcely hearing. But
at the end he nodded his head, and said

"Yes, yes; in the bay, at the western point of the island. What
size is she?"

"A brig, and her tonnage—"

"Aye, aye," the other interrupted, nodding again. "And you were
the only ones left on board—you four—the others all deserted you?"

Wydale almost started. He did not remember to have told him
how many had been left on board the vessel. However, he answered
quietly:

"That is correct."

"I assume," his questioner went on, "from your venturing thus
far unarmed into a strange country, that you had no arms. The
runaways stole all there were available?"

"Yes."

"You had not even a pistol to bring with you on an exploration that might be full of danger?"

"None, sir, else you may be sure I should have brought it."

"Yes. And amongst the cargo, had you none you could have got at before venturing abroad?"

This query seemed to be put, Owen thought, with a shade of anxiety in the tone. But he could only shake his head.

"I saw all the cargo stowed," he declared, "and it belongs to my friend who is with me, to myself, and another, jointly. We unfortunately know only too well that there are no arms of any kind on board."

"Ah! well. Now I will show you a nearer way back to your vessel."

And, with that, he turned and motioned to those who had first been with him to accompany him. They caught up lanterns that were standing at hand and went on in front, their chief walking behind with Owen and his companion.

Thus they passed out of the great entrance chamber, leaving behind them the armed men assembled there, and struck into a gallery that led off to the right. Here and there they came to other similar galleries, all of good height and width, and all brightly lighted with hanging lamps. They seemed to be well ventilated, too, and dry, for there was no trace of stagnant air or of damp.

After a long walk they suddenly emerged, through gates by which were other armed men on duty, into the open air, upon a hanging road or terrace that overlooked the sea. Here they caught sight of numbers of lights below, reflected in the water, and heard many subdued sounds and a distant hum as of a populous city not far away. But their guides waited not, and they were given no time to gain more than a passing glimpse here and there. Presently they turned again into an underground gallery in every way resembling those they had already traversed, and here they proceeded for a long distance, always in the same silence.

At last they came to a massive door, which was closed, and barred, and locked. And this, on being opened, gave entrance to an unlighted chamber, at the end of which was another ponderous door, which took some time to open. When, however, it swung back and they stepped outside, both the boy and Wydale uttered an exclamation of surprise; they could see at once that they stood on a ledge of rock overlooking the bay where lay the *Saucy Fan*.

By the aid of the lanterns they made their way down a rough path till they arrived in the centre of a dense mass of bushes, and here their conductor stopped.

"Take this lantern," said he. "With its aid you will see the way out. It will bring you to the shore, and the light will help you to find your way to your vessel and to get on board. To-morrow I will see you further. Now, good-night, and God-speed."

"Good-night, sir, and may heaven repay you for what you did for us to-day," Wydale answered gratefully.

"And, please, sir, may I thank you, too?" cried George impulsively; "and if you come to see us, we will all thank you, and my sister most of all, I know."

"Ah!" said the stranger, looking at the boy with kindly eyes, but in a half-dreamy fashion. "You have a sister here? Is her name Vanina?"

At this most unexpected and astonishing query both his hearers started in surprise. But he appeared not to notice it and turned, and, with a wave of the hand, seemed to dismiss them.

"May I ask a question?" Wydale begged of him. He had had much ado to make up his mind to the request, so curiously had the manner of the other impressed and awed him.

However, the stranger halted, and awaited the query.

"I only wished to ask," said Wydale, feeling very much confused—he knew not why— "whether you can tell me the name of the island—and—if you see no objection—your own name?"

"I am called Monella," was the answer, given in simple fashion and a quiet tone, "and this is the island of Atlantis. Good-night."

And so saying, the speaker turned and left them.

8
A Game of Bluff

For the first morning in what appeared a cruelly-anxious time, the four on board the *Saucy Fan* rose and sat down to their early meal in something like good spirits. It is not too much to say that they were, in a sense, quite different people—such creatures are we of the circumstances of the hour. The account brought back by Wydale and George of their adventures had changed all their thoughts, and fears, and hopes, and expectations, and directed their ideas into new and most unexpected channels. It was now clear that the island was inhabited, and by what appeared to be a friendly and a white race, one of whom, at least—and he evidently a man of mark—spoke English. From him and his followers it was clear they might look for honest treatment, and probably, if need were, for protection; for had he not already aided them in a most critical emergency? Moreover, though armed himself with only bow and arrows, he had scrupulously handed over to Wydale the revolver found upon the dead man, although he must have known its value. This went to show that they stood in no danger of having the ship plundered by the inhabitants. Their minds thus set at ease, they could now give them to the pleasurable excitement of anticipation and speculation as to the strange experiences that awaited them in their intercourse with this unknown, old-world people.

All sorts of incidents were conceivable in circumstances so unusual. Vanina and her brother indulged in almost every kind of surmise; the latter especially was full of irrepressible excitement. Wydale was, in fact, the only one of the four who did not altogether share in the elation of the others. The memory of the dead man's face, of the unaccountable horror—even terror—that had seized upon him the previous day, and his vague recollection of the terrible shape he had seen rise into the air from its horrible repast, and fly away with the departing mist—the memory of all this had by no means left him. Indeed it had haunted him throughout the night, and thrust itself into the foreground, even to the partial exclusion of what had happened since. He could not prevent his thoughts from dwelling on it nor help speculating upon the mystery of the deserted city. That the gruesome tragedy he had witnessed and the unknown horror had something to do with it he felt convinced. If so, the terror it inspired must indeed be great to cause a whole people to forsake their ancient city, and their gardens, and their pastures.

Then the crew of the brig. They might yet give trouble, for they would be desperate, and they were armed with rifles. Against those the two revolvers and the few cartridges he had recovered could do but little.

But, if he allowed his thoughts to dwell upon these doubtful points, he did so only as the prudent soldier calmly weighs and calculates the odds against him, but without permitting them to daunt him. Indeed, the spice of danger and adventure he foresaw was in itself a strong attraction, and how great that danger could be he already knew.

After the breakfast they discussed the programme for the day. Vanina wished to go ashore. She longed, she said, for a walk on the sands and under the trees, and was tired of being stived up on the vessel. But Wydale was opposed to it.

"You forget," he said, "that those scoundrels who deserted this vessel and left us to die—murderers they are, in intention, every one, skipper, mate, and all—are lurking in the neighbourhood. They have firearms—your own rifle, Dareville, among others—and are a desperate, utterly unscrupulous gang. One of them, at least—Foster—knows we are here, and will tell the others. Then think what a temptation the vessel and her cargo will hold out to them. Why, they would murder us all merely to get at the whisky to get drunk on. My advice is to stick to the ship to-day, until our friend of last night comes to visit us, as he promised. Then I hope things may assume a different aspect."

This advice was so well-judged that Sydney at once accepted it.

"Wydale is right," he said; "you had better defer your visit to the shore, Vanina. Confound those rascals; for the moment I had forgotten they were about."

"It's altogether an uncanny place, apparently," observed Vanina, with a little shudder, and in a disappointed tone. "Strange monsters about, both in the sea and on the shore. And, as though that were not enough, you must needs threaten us again with that hateful gang I thought we were well rid of. I declare you've chased away all the glowing expectations I had formed, and brought us back to the period of 'excursions and alarms'!

Wydale, to—or rather at—whom this speech was more particularly directed, laughed good- naturedly.

"I am sorry to seem to pose as a wet blanket," he assured her. "It's all for your good, you know, as mothers say to children; and it is, I hope, only for one day. After to-day, I trust there will be no further cause to place any, restraint upon your liberty. Your word shall be our law, even as though you were captain of the brig."

"Or Queen Boadicea," George put in slyly.

"Nay, someone more up-to-date, I hope," said she, the smile returning to her face.

"Well—say—ah! What do you say to Queen of Atlantis? Shall we dub you, Vanina, Queen of Atlantis?" George suggested.

And at this conceit he clapped his hands, and boisterously expressed approval then, lifting his sister's hand, he bowed over it and raised it to his lips.

"Thus does thy brother salute his sister and his Queen," he said, with mock solemnity. "N.B.—I got that out of 'The Pirate of the Gory Main,' that I was reading this morning before breakfast."

For answer he received a box on the ears, and an admonition to be more respectful to his sister than to mix her up with his "penny-dreadful-blood-and-thunder tales." Then he ran off to fish over the vessel's side. His sister followed him on deck, where, under the awning, she sat down to read a favourite book.

Wydale and Dareville sat a little apart cleaning and examining their revolvers, and counting up their cartridges. Of these there were, unfortunately, very few, and Sydney regarded them distressfully.

"We'll have to save these up," he remarked, ruefully, "for emergencies. Each cartridge here may prove worth its weight in gold."

"More," commented Wydale, tersely. "Each may save a life."

"Yes. And for that reason, even if the skipper and his following should come down on us, we must try to bluff 'em, somehow. A shot or two well aimed and timed may do a lot amongst a cowardly set like that."

"I have been thinking," resumed Wydale, "whether it is prudent to keep the vessel so near the shore. Wouldn't it be wiser to get her further out?"

"I don't see that it can make much difference. They're pretty sure to come in the boats. However, a soldier should never neglect a chance, and they might come, by land over the ridge and pop at us from behind those trees. So, suppose we slip the shore line and let her drift free. With this bit of breeze she'll swing out away from the shore."

This was soon done, the raft was hauled on board, and the brig slowly drifted farther out.

This had the effect of disarranging George's fishing lines, and he complained loudly when he pulled them up and found them in an inextricable tangle. But suddenly he ceased his lamentations, and stared at something in the distance.

"I say, what's that?"

Sydney took up a pair of glasses and looked. Then he put them quietly down.

"It's a boat," he said. "You two must go below. We are likely to have trouble."

Vanina stoutly protested, but was forced to yield, and retired with her brother to the cabin.

In consequence of the change in her position, the brig was now lying end on to the advancing boat.

"That may enable us to bring our cannon into play, if need be," Sydney observed. "Now don't let them come too near; and, if we have to shoot in earnest, I'll take the skipper and you the mate."

Wydale nodded, and no more was said. The two lounged over the bows and watched the boat—there was only one—through their glasses, waiting quietly till it should be near enough to hail. They could already make out the skipper, but Foster was not to be seen.

"That's near enough," said Dareville, presently. "Now, a hail and a command to stop, and I fire a shot across her bows, if she still comes on. Next shot I aim at the skipper. That's the programme, I take it."

Those in the boat took no notice of the hail; but when a bullet came splashing through the water alongside, sending quite a little shower of spray on board, they stopped at once, apparently in great surprise.

"Perhaps," suggested Wydale, "the mate hasn't yet got back, and their appearance here is accidental. If so, they don't know where these pistols came from, or what arms and ammunition we may have. You see Foster's not there."

"I fancy you're right. If so, we'll bluff 'em, if we play our cards with judgment." Then Durford, the skipper, stood up and shouted something that they failed to catch. However, its purport must have been deemed satisfactory by the speaker, for he sat down, and the boat, which had drifted round broadside on, began to move again.

"One for the gunwale this time, as a warning," Sydney muttered. "The next for his skippership in right earnest." And he fired.

The skipper, who had one hand on the gunwale and the other on the tiller, pulled the former hastily away, as a bullet crashed into the wood just alongside of it. They stopped rowing again, and seemed to be consulting.

"If we only had a good supply of cartridges, I would hurry up the rascals," Sydney grunted, discontentedly. "But we can't afford to throw a single shot away."

Durford again stood up. He made signs to those on the brig, pointed to the shore, and pulled out a white handkerchief. Then the boat was rowed towards the shore and grounded on the sand. Durford landed and walked alone along the shore to the nearest point that faced the brig, all the time busily waving the white handkerchief as a flag of truce.

"I've a good mind to kill him as he stands, flag of truce or no flag of truce," Sydney muttered through his teeth. "The murdering hound! It makes my blood boil to see him impudently standing there trusting to our honour, after the way he's treated us. However, as he's come for a parley, I suppose we must let him have his way."

"Brig ahoy!" now came from the skipper.

"On shore there, ahoy!" shouted back Dareville. "Who are you?"

This very unexpected question seemed to disconcert the flag-of-truce man, for he hesitated, and looked at the brig uneasily. After a pause, he began again; and the following colloquy ensued.

"Brig ahoy! Is that Mr. Dareville?"

"Shore ahoy! It is. Who are you, and what do want?"

"Oh, come, sir; you know me well enough. I am Joseph Durford, captain of the *Saucy Fan*."

"I know no Joseph Durford, captain of the *Saucy Fan*. I know a Joseph Durford, pirate, who abandoned his water-tight vessel in a calm; I know Joseph Durford, the rascally thief who stole our gold watches and rifles and revolvers, and I know Joseph Durford the would-be murderer of ladies and boys, who drugged our coffee and battened down the hatches, and left us to die in the Sargasso Sea; and whom I will lay by the heels and send to penal servitude, if I can catch him!"

Dareville said all this quite calmly, without the least show of temper. But it stung the other into a fury.

"It's all a lie!" he shouted, with an awful oath. "I never stole yer—watches; I've got a chronometer of my own, better'n both yours put together. If others stole 'em, I didn't. And, as to the rest, you was forgotten in the hurry—I thought you was in the other boat. One of 'em's lost."

"That will do. You may save your soul the sin of any further lies. So that's the fancy tale you had concocted, is it? Well, be off! You've no business here! If you or any of you attempt to come on board, we will shoot you down like the dogs you are."

"As to shootin', two can play at that game," retorted Durford, darting glances of hate from under his scowling brows. "An,' when the odds is about five to one, the largest number generally gets the best of it in the end. Anyhow, I am skipper of the *Saucy Fan*, and I am agoin' to take command of her. And, Mr. Dareville, you've alluded to a lady on board, your sister. I advise yer, for yer own sake and hers, not to get my men's blood up; yer don't know what men may do in the heat of—"

"Be off, you hound! I've had enough of this!" Dareville interrupted. "I have taken possession of the *Saucy Fan* in the name of

the owners, with whom I am a partner. Even on your own showing, you abandoned the brig—and we've salved her. I've appointed
myself skipper; and you've no further business here. Your very
presence is an insult. Sheer off! or I will put a bullet through you!"

"Then it's war to the knife, is it? You will regret this when it's
too late, Mr. Dareville."

"We're not afraid of you," Dareville returned, contemptuously.
"Now, see here! When you appeared in your, or I should say, *my*
boat—for it has been stolen from the brig—you interrupted a little
pistol practice I was enjoying. I want to go on with it; but you've
got your foot on the pebble I was taking for a target. Would you
mind moving your foot—thanks:" and a bullet from his revolver
struck the very pebble Durford had been standing on, just when
he raised his foot.

Evidently the feat impressed him. But he moved away slowly,
shaking his fist.

Dareville laughed. "I was sorry to waste the bullet," he said to
Wydale; "but am in hopes the hint may not be lost on him; and it
may save some lives."

"A good hint, too. I can see that you can shoot. Ah! What a pity
to be here without more ammunition."

"Yes; and the question now is, what arms and ammunition have
they got," responded Sydney, watching the boat somewhat anxiously through his glasses.

"If it comes to a long fight, they'll soon wear out our slender stock."

Durford had regained the boat in a towering rage, for he was
gesticulating violently. The craft was pushed off, and once more
headed for the brig.

"He seems to mean business this time." Dareville set his teeth
while he was speaking. "Mind! Leave Durford to me! I'll give him
what he deserves. But look out that they don't pot you."

The boat came on, but in a desultory fashion, as could be seen.
Men would pull, and then stop to look round apprehensively, when
a loud oath and threat from the skipper—audible even to those on
the brig—would start them rowing again.

Suddenly they stopped rowing altogether, and looked and
pointed eagerly at something on the other side of the vessel. Some

even stood up to look over the others, regardless of how they exposed themselves to the pistols of their antagonists.

"What are they looking at?" Sydney asked, suspicious of some ruse. "Look round and see. I'm not going to take my eye off that villain."

Wydale looked, and uttered an exclamation.

"It's a boat—several boats—a whole fleet of boats coming round the point!" he cried. "It must be our friend of last night."

It was as he said, a whole fleet of boats; and now that those on board of them had caught sight of the brig, they raised a hearty shout and blew loud blasts on horns and trumpets.

In his turn Wydale could not help shouting, "Hurrah! Hurrah!"

This brought George and his sister up on deck. At sight of the flotilla they joined in the cheer. It was heard on the strangers' boats, and immediately responded to by another outburst; while George actually danced round the deck in his excitement.

As for Durford and his crew, they evidently mistrusted the strange craft, for they turned their boat round and rowed away.

9
"Queen of Atlantis!"

The four on the deck of the *Saucy Fan* watched with ever-increasing wonder the advancing fleet, as more and more vessels kept appearing round the point, and those on board of them added their cheers and trumpet-blasts to the general clamour. And now that the first were nearer, and could be more clearly viewed, the spectators were altogether amazed at the richness of their mountings and the gorgeousness of the whole display. Every vessel had sails as well as banks of rowers. But the sails seemed intended rather for ornament than for use. They were of some material that glistened like silver, and on them were worked strange devices in brilliant colours. All were square sails, hung much as lug sails would be, and altogether appeared to partake of the character of banners. Certainly the vessels depended more for their means of propulsion upon their banks of rowers than upon these gorgeous sails; for they moved with the precision of machines, and appeared to be as completely under control as the engines of a steam launch.

The foremost vessels passed the brig for some distance, and then swept round towards the shore in a curve; behind them came five larger vessels—great State barges one might guess them—with one still larger and more superbly decorated in the centre. This vessel was the most richly fitted up and ornamented of all the imposing array. Its sides seemed to be of ivory, with a band of delicate turquoise blue running from stem to stern. In and out ran designs in gold and silver. The oars that appeared at the sides below the deck were gold-mounted, and the blades appeared to be of polished silver, and flashed in the sun each time they left the water.

The bow was shaped like the head, neck, and fore-part of the body of a stork or crane, with open mouth and outspread wings, the neck and head shooting high into the air.

A silver-spangled awning was swung above the deck, and upon the two masts that, like the oars, seemed to be worked in gold, hung banners or sails of wondrous workmanship, the silver sheen of the general groundwork dazzling the eyes as it caught and mirrored back the sunshine.

On the decks of the smaller craft were rows of men clad in polished armour, and armed with flashing spears and shields. And on the raised decks at stem and stern of the larger ones were officers in the most brilliant and varied suits of armour that perhaps have ever been seen; so, at least, thought those on the Saucy Fan, looking through their glasses at the different vessels, as each in turn came clearly into view.

When the five central vessels had arrived opposite the brig, the whole line stopped, and those behind them grouped themselves off the shore. Thus the *Saucy Fan* was in the centre of a glittering half-circle of the strange craft, all beautiful vessels as to design and decoration, yet small compared with the brig.

Then all remained motionless, while everyone on board sent up a deafening shout, the soldiers and their leaders lifting their swords and shields and other weapons again and again in the air, saluting.

"What on earth is it all about?" said at last the puzzled Sydney. "What a pity we didn't know they were coming. We'd have had the Union Jack flying, and we could have dipped it in proper style, you know."

"Couldn't we fire off the cannon?" suggested George. "There's only powder in it."

"A good idea, Georgy," Wydale answered, "but powder here is too precious to waste. No; all we can do, I'm afraid, is to shout back our loudest."

"If we could only get at some of the fireworks that are down in the hold, and let them off," sighed George. "That would fetch 'em."

And now from the principal barge a boat was seen putting off. In it were, besides the rowers, figures all clad in armour. One, a giant in stature, wore a coat of mail, with a white tunic underneath. George pointed him out to Sydney and his sister.

"That," he said, "is the one we saw last night; the man who called himself Monella."

Seeing their intention of coming on board, Wydale and Dareville hastened to the gangway, and replaced the ladder which they had hoisted in, in anticipation of the attack from the crew.

The ladder having been lowered, the commanding figure of Monella came over the side, followed by four others. A minute later the five new-comers stood in a semi-circle around the deck facing the other four.

A short pause ensued while the one group gazed upon the other, surprise and interest roused on both sides. And seldom, perhaps, in the history of the world—outside the realms of pantomime and comic opera—had there been seen a more extraordinary contrast.

The principal figure, towering head and shoulders above the others, was clad in a suit of mail—chain armour, all of gold. Beneath, was a white satin tunic, also embroidered with gold, precious stones being sewn or otherwise attached to it in such manner as to imitate the forms of birds. A white cloak with a scarlet lining hung from his shoulders, and round his left arm was a jewelled band as of some order or decoration, the centre being a diamond of extraordinary size and brilliancy. Upon his head was a helmet of gold, inlaid with silver, and by his side was a sword such as some could scarce have wielded even with both hands. So much for his dress. His face and figure were still more striking. Though his hair and full beard were iron grey, he showed no other signs of age. His figure was well-formed, supple, and muscular as that of a well-built man of thirty, and the perfect mould of the features intimated that as a youth he must have been handsome and well-favoured far above the average of mankind. The face was still supremely handsome, and one that attracted and retained the notice of all who looked upon it. But its greatest charm lay in its changing expressions and the penetrating glance of the steady, grey eyes. These seemed to be gifted with the faculty of charming or over-awing those upon whom they fell, according as they softened in tenderness, sympathy, or affection, or flashed in anger or contempt. But, whether they looked forth in stern rebuke, or in pitying interest, or lighted up with the fire of unflinching courage and high resolve, there was ever a touch of human sympathy that aroused and held the respect, trustfulness, and devotion of all around him. To these attributes—only seen now and then in the world, and never save in those born to rule their fellow-men—were added a graceful ease and nobility, even majesty of bearing, that of itself commanded homage.

Of those with him, three were in armour richly chased or damascened; while the fourth was habited in a coat of mail similar to Monella's, set off with an embroidered sash. All carried swords and daggers with jewelled hilts; but the last one's arms were of lighter make than the others. Opposed to these were the four in homely English garb of travel; certainly presenting as odd a contrast as can be well imagined.

Wydale advanced and warmly greeted the friend who had so opportunely come to his aid the previous evening, and Monella, in turn, spoke a few words of welcome to him and his friends, assuring them that the display of armed men in the vessels around was to be taken in a complimentary and not a hostile sense. A few minutes later, when he had become known to Vanina and Sydney Dareville, and had, in return, indicated the names of those with him, he, to Wydale's surprise, asked for a few words in private with "the maiden"—as in his old-world speech he designated Vanina—and her brother. As a consequence the three disappeared into the cabin, leaving Wydale and the lad on deck, confronted by the four strangers.

Of these, the one who wore the suit of mail now advanced and offered his hand. He was a man of perhaps forty-five years of age, with a clean-shaven face, good-natured in expression, and a figure that was inclined to stoutness.

"My name is Dr. Manleth," he began. "I am an Englishman, and am glad to welcome you and your friends on my own account."

And he shook hands with George.

"You look puzzled," he went on, with a smile, "and I don't wonder. I have been here five years, so am used to the place. But, when we first landed here—Monella and myself—it was more astonishing than I can well convey to you; especially as we, of course, did not then know the language; and it took a long time to understand it all."

"And how did you get here?" Owen asked.

"Shipwrecked; drifted here in an open boat; two others who were in the boat with us died of exposure and hunger and thirst. We were both nearly dead, too, when we got here. But they treated us well—handsomely, in fact—and Monella soon became their recognised leader—sort of Prime Minister, Commander-in-Chief and Archbishop, all in one. He is a wonderful man."

"But why all these soldiers? Whom is there to fight against? One would think you were at war with all the—"

"So we are; and very much at war, too, unfortunately. It has gone badly with us lately. But we managed as well as we could, and waited patiently, hoping that you were coming."

"That we were coming!" Wydale repeated, feeling bewildered. "How in the world could you guess that we were coming? And what help can we be to you? We have no firearms, I am sorry to say."

"So I hear; and, of course, we are sorry, too; and disappointed. But Monella seems in good heart about it, and that is everything, though I do not know what is in his mind. They all trust to him blindly, like a lot of children, sheep I had almost said. They are kindly, docile, well-disposed people, but haven't spirit. He's tried his best to infuse some of his own lion courage into them, but they have hitherto remained listless and wanting in enthusiasm while against us we have a horde of ruthless foes who are perfect devils for fighting and cruelty of all kinds. Hence, you see, Monella has been sadly handicapped, and any other man would have despaired. But that is a word unknown to him, I fancy. However, I hope we shall get on better now you have come. So we have all been hoping."

"*We?*" Wydale again asked in wonder. "What have *we* to do with it?"

"Hush! Here they come. Now we shall soon know whether the prophecies are to be fulfilled."

Vanina came first out of the cabin, followed by Dareville and Monella. She looked flushed, and her eyes were unusually bright.

Her whole manner and bearing, too, had changed—so Wydale thought, feeling each moment more surprised at her glowing face and sparkling eyes. Then he glanced at Dareville, and read there, too, signs that surprised and puzzled him. But no time was given him for speculation.

Monella stepped up beside Vanina, and addressed her.

"Let me now present to you, more formally, these gentlemen, some of the chief officers of State, This is the Lord Kandlar, High Chamberlain; this is the Lord Ombrian, the Admiral of our Fleet; this the Lord Selion, State Treasurer; and last, but not least, here is my good friend, Dr. Manleth, a scientist of no mean attainments and a good and worthy English gentleman. If I do not name him amongst our lords, it is from his own choice. He could be so ranked, if he chose, but has declined; he holds that a scientist should not seek worldly honours."

"Also," good-humouredly said Manleth, "a doctor cannot well be much of a fighting man. There must be someone to attend the wounded—and there have been many lately, you must know."

"Ah, yes," confirmed Monella. "And well it is for them that they have one like our friend here to tend them. And now, will you come on board our State barge?

"What are you going to do with this vessel?" Vanina asked.

"We shall tow her with us to our harbour and docks."

"Then," said Vanina, looking round, as Wydale, who was watching her, thought, with a sort of triumph, "let me stay on board and go with her. I will not desert the *Saucy Fan* for another vessel to make my entry amongst your people—no! not though that other vessel were the richest and grandest in the world."

"Be it so," replied Monella, inclining his head, as in approval. "I will now give the necessary orders."

He went over the side and spoke in a strange language to those remaining in the boat in which they'd come. These rowed at once to the brilliant barge and communicated their message to those on board, then hastened round to other vessels in turn. Then there was again much shouting and blowing of trumpets, and anon the barge moved round, and three of the larger vessels with rowers came near to take the brig in tow. The boat then came back, bringing six or eight native sailors—even these, Wydale noticed, were partly dressed in light armour—and under Monella's direction they manned the capstan and weighed anchor. Soon the *Saucy Fan* was once more on her way, moving majestically through the water in tow of a string of the native war vessels, amongst which she towered like a man-of-war amongst merchant craft.

The State barge came on behind her, and the remainder of the fleet fell into line, three abreast, some in front and some in the rear.

And, while they thus proceeded across the bay, from time to time mighty shouts went up from one end of the line of vessels to the other. And to Owen it seemed as though he could distinguish the word "Vanina."

"What is it they are saying?" he presently asked the doctor, who was standing beside him.

"They are shouting," the other made answer, "Hail, Vanina! Queen of Atlantis!"

10
"A Land of Strange Romance!"

Before Wydale could frame a reply or a further query in response to the astonishing statement of the doctor, the latter had moved away to speak to someone else. Thus left to himself, Wydale leaned over the taffrail, and gazed out on the scene before him with the air of a man too utterly bewildered to be quite sure whether what he sees is real, or only part of a fantastic dream. So, at least, he felt himself; and he had met with so many surprises in the last forty-eight hours, that he was now prepared for almost any unparalleled developments. Everything about him began to wear an air of unreality. Even his friends were changed; the very expressions of their faces were changed—so Owen thought—as they stood and talked with Monella and others around them.

Slowly the long array passed out of the bay, and began to round the point at the south-west end, and then there gradually unfolded itself before them another scene as unexpected as it was striking.

The coast-line ran off to the left—a long wall of high, precipitous, glistening rock, with three hanging terraces constructed one above the other on the face of the cliff. At intervals in these were small towers, and the roadways were screened off by battlements and loop-holed walls. Opposite to this coast-line, that is to say, to the right, and about half a mile away, another island rose out of this silent sea, looking, as it gleamed and sparkled in the sunlight through a slight haze, rather like a fairy creation than solid fact.

This second island rose steeply from the water, and upon it stood a mighty castle built of the crystal rock. In size, in height, it was colossal, and in design it displayed a massive grandeur that exceeded in effect anything Wydale had ever before beheld. Beyond it could be seen an extensive city, rising tier above tier in the background, with towers and minarets so lofty that they seemed to melt into the air above.

While Wydale was gazing in admiration upon this scene, the doctor returned to his side.

"That," he said, "is Dilandis, or 'New Atlantis,' though itself, I imagine, pretty old; and the island on which it is built is called Dilanda. The ancient city is situated in the other island, on the further side of those cliffs to the left."

Wydale nodded.

"Aye," he said, "I have seen the ruins. But tell me, why is it deserted? And why do you all go about thus in armour?"

"Your first question requires rather a lengthy answer," replied Manleth, "and I must leave it for another occasion, or for someone else, for, indeed, I am not quite sure that I rightly understand it yet myself. But, as to the second query, the matter is unfortunately all too simple. We are liable at any moment to attacks from our enemies. I say 'we,' because both Monella and myself have for some years thoroughly identified ourselves with the people here, who have been good friends to us. Their foes, the 'Karanites,' as they are called—from the name of their King, 'Kara'—are adepts with the bow and arrow, the sword, and the spear; hence you see that, in the absence of firearms, armour becomes a matter of necessity. All the armour which you see here is of very ancient make; they have quantities stored away. It remained unused, yet carefully preserved, for centuries; for this warfare is a comparatively recent trouble."

"I see. It all seems very strange—a little world in which one has to go back to antiquated modes of warfare. It seems like a dream, an impossibility in the nineteenth century."

"Ah, yes; it appeared so to us when we first came here. But we have grown accustomed to it, as you will after a time. I expect they will want you to join their ranks; and they will fit you out in a suit like all the rest. We had hoped you would have had some firearms with you in your vessel; that would have very quickly brought the war to an end. But we must now still struggle on as best we can without."

"That reminds me," observed Wydale, "you said that you expected us, and spoke of prophecies and other enigmatical outpourings. What does it all mean?"

Dr. Manleth gave a gesture of impatience. "I'm sure I can't explain. I do not understand myself," he said. "We live here in a half-real world, the rest is myth and superstition. Everything is more or less enshrouded in mystery, and though I have been here some years, there is much I cannot fathom. For instance, they insist that they were driven out of the old city by a race of vampires."

"A race of vampires! What does that mean?"

"They say that in the interior of the main island there are terrible, uncouth flying monsters. They call them 'Kralens,' which, in their language, signifies vampires, and declare that they not only attack and devour human beings, but have the power of fascinating them—holding them, as by a spell, before their own approach, thus preventing the victims from escaping. As a scientist one of course deems such a tale a myth."

"Have you encountered them?" Wydale asked.

"No. Our rulers won't let one venture there. But I have managed to slip through the guards once or twice, and have wandered about in the ruined city and its vicinity without seeing anything worse than my own shadow."

"But *I* have seen something more—only yesterday. I have seen—dimly through the mist—a monstrous flying creature which I can't describe; and I have seen its victim," and here he shuddered, "and I was almost stifled with an odour so supremely loathsome as to confuse your senses, and make you sick and dizzy, and unable to move, and to fill you with a deadly horror. I have such a vivid recollection of it that it will remain always rooted in my memory."

"You—you declare this to be true?"

"I do; solemnly. Upon my honour."

The doctor paused and ruminated for a while. Then said:

"It is very strange; but this is a marvellous land in which one scarce knows how much to believe and how much not. As to this monster's so-called fascinating power, I have a theory about it which you shall have another time."

"And your friend Monella; what does he say about it all?"

Manleth hesitated.

"Well," he said, "between ourselves, Monella is himself a living mystery. I met him first on shipboard when we were both 'homeward bound' on our way to England. At least, *I* was; he was on his way to South America. I have lived with him for five years, yet I know, in one sense, no more of him than I did at the end of the first week. I know not what countryman he is; he seems to speak every language known and unknown—and certainly one or two that must be almost pre-historic, I should think. When we arrived here he picked up the language with such ease that it seemed rather like recovering a once familiar tongue than learning one he had never heard. He appears to have been everywhere, to have done everything. Not that he is any boaster; far from it. This I do know— he is a right good fellow, a loyal friend, and an upright man, with a kindly, sympathetic nature; hard as nails, strong as a Hercules, bold as a lion, a wonderful fighter and leader, full of energy, of resource, of sound judgment and prevision. So much for the practical side of his very complex nature. For, with all that, he is a dreamer— 'a dreamer of dreams,' and a believer in dreams. A man with an unwavering belief in his own destiny that nothing can displace. He faces every danger with such reckless courage that we often remonstrate with him; but for answer he will merely smile and say, 'It is not my destiny to perish here,' or words to that effect."

"A strange man, from your description. Yet I can well believe all you say. I *felt* it, somehow, the first time we met."

"It is so with everyone; but his effect on all is not the same. Most love him, but some there are who fear and hate him. But all their dislike, and all they try to do, avails naught against him. He merely thrusts it aside disdainfully, and goes serenely on his way, like a man who brushes away a cobweb from his face."

"Have other people ever come here besides you two?"

"I have heard so, but cannot tell you much about them. But it is certain that many years ago a priest drifted here with some companions. They are all dead long ago, but they converted a portion of the islanders, and that's what all the row's about. It caused a split and a civil war, for the other section are idolaters. Their leaders are believed to be magicians. 'Tis an inexplicable land, in fact; a land of milk and honey, of practical, industrious people, and yet, withal, a land of dreams and fancies."

"Why do not more come here? Why is the very existence of the place unknown to the outer world?"

"That also is a puzzle; but it would appear that there are deep channels in the rocky shoals by which we are surrounded which, though they have undercurrents, are, on the surface, normally choked with the weed. At rare intervals, however, owing to some unusual combination of wind and tide and outside currents, strong surface flows set in along the channels, forcing aside the weed, and so making a clear waterway, that traverses all our inside seas, and finally finds a way out to the ocean on the other side. On such occasions the channels are free to navigation, and they remain so for a few days—seldom for more than a week. This may happen once or twice in a short time—a few years—and then it may not occur again for a century. So they say; I cannot tell you more."

"Then our chance of ever getting away is doubtful?" remarked Wydale ruefully. "Is that so?"

"I am sorry to say it is. But they have astrologers here—"

"Astrologers?"

"Yes; and they are said often to be able to foretell the time—at least, approximately. Certainly they predicted your arrival about this time, and, further, that your coming amongst us would bring victory and peace and happiness to the land for ever after."

"No wonder they have given us such a welcome, then, and shown such readiness to make the lady a queen," laughed Wydale. "But I'm afraid they will be very much disappointed. If we had firearms, it would be another matter. As it is, we are but a broken reed to lean upon. The question is, will they in their disappointment turn and rend us?"

"I trust not—I think not, from what I know of them. And they believe, too, firmly in Monella, and he, I know, will be a firm friend to all of us."

"Dreamer though he is?"

"Dreamer though he is," returned the doctor, laughingly. "But you will find that as a fighter—in warfare—he is no dreamer, but very practical indeed. It's fortunate he isn't on the other side."

Then Wydale entered into a brief relation of the adventures of himself and his friends. But soon the talk was interrupted, for they were getting near the fortress, and Owen found his attention taken up by all that he now saw.

Many small boats had come out to meet them, and their occupants, first adding their ringing cheers to those of the fleet, drifted past and fell in astern. And now Wydale perceived two lofty towers connected by a bridge high in air, with ramparts on the outer side, and beneath, great water-gates giving access to an extensive harbour. Through these gates, and through others again, the *Saucy Fan* moved slowly on, on all sides being seen fluttering flags, and people all waving handkerchiefs, scarves, or banners, and joining in the shouts of welcome. The masts of the brig went easily under the aerial bridges, and soon she was floating in the waters of the inner harbour, which was now crowded with boats of all kinds decorated in a hundred curious fashions. Here, while the vessel was being brought to a standstill, Monella and Dareville, who had been making their preparations, put a match to the carronade, and the loud explosion that ensued went booming across the water, repeated again and again from the rocks and walls like the thunder's roar, and dying away at last in a sullen growl.

At once a dead silence fell upon the crowd. They seemed stupefied, and gazed at one another in astonishment and alarm.

But Monella lifted his arms and addressed them in some words that Wydale could not understand, at the same time taking Vanina by the hand, as though to introduce her to the populace. Then the cheers rang out again still louder, and amidst them the brig was brought alongside a quay, and soon all was in readiness for landing.

"That was a good idea firing the little cannon," observed the doctor. "It will impress them. I heard you had a little powder; how much is there?"

"Only one small keg. It won't go very far even in royal salutes;" and Wydale shook his head.

"We must see whether we can't make some more," said Manleth cheerfully. "I am a chemist, and, with a sample to start with, I am not sure we could not manage it."

"Heaven send you may. From all I can understand it would be almost worth its weight in gold."

"More," said the doctor tersely. "They have more gold here than they know what to do with."

11
Princess Idelia

The party landed, and proceeded through the city, passing now through tastefully laid-out gardens, with glowing flowers, shady bowers, and cool, plashing fountains, and now through wide streets of noble buildings, making their way ever upwards towards a stately palace that occupied the highest point on this part of the island. As they mounted broad flights of steps that led from one terraced garden to another, views could be obtained stretching far over the interior of the island. Wydale saw that, as in the larger island, the interior formed a sort of basin, or crater, shut in from the sea by precipitous cliffs, but here and everywhere were signs of cultivation and successful agriculture.

Fields, meadows, parks, and groves, running streams and small lakes, were everywhere to be seen, with browsing cattle scattered amongst them. Overhead flew great flocks of birds, and the lakes and streams were full of water-fowl. Most noticeable of all were numbers of cranes that were to be seen on every hand, flying overhead, or walking in their solemn fashion, like dainty ladies, picking their way through the streets and gardens. Evidently they were privileged birds.

"What are all these cranes doing here?" Wydale asked the doctor, as they walked together behind the rest.

"They are tamed and trained to look after the other birds," was the reply. "And wonderfully they do it, too, as you will see another day. They are also good companions when you make friends with them. I have a couple that will follow me anywhere, if I but call them; and they are just as companionable here as dogs elsewhere. They will fish for you, catch the other birds for you, carry messages, and make themselves useful in a number of ways."

"And why is the other island so deserted, and this so thickly populated?"

"I have already stated that the people are said to have been driven away by certain terrible monsters, real or fancied. It is believed that these creatures, whatever they are, cannot fly high enough to pass over the cliffs that everywhere shut in the interior of the larger island. Therefore here—in fact anywhere outside—you are safe from them."

"But you have other gruesome monsters outside—gigantic cuttle-fish, to wit."

"Ah, you have heard of them?"

"Yes; more than that. We were attacked by them; that was our first welcome to the place."

"H'm; now that is odd! I know they are there, because our fishing-boats have abandoned that bay for no other cause. That is why you saw no signs of us when you arrived. The people will not venture there, for several boats have been attacked, and poor fellows dragged out of them and carried off. Yet when I and others have gone out to hunt for the cuttles, they never could be seen. From descriptions given to me, I think they are enormous calamaries. Only two known of exist, and, if we could capture them, we should do a good turn to our fisher folk."

"And where are we going now?" Wydale presently inquired.

"To the royal palace, which is also the royal observatory, where are the astrologers who watch the stars through telescopes, the size of which will astonish you."

"Ah, that reminds me; there are telescopes, as well as opera and field-glasses, among the cargo in our boat. I was thinking they would surprise the natives hereabouts."

"The glasses, yes; but telescopes, no. However, you will see later for yourself."

"And what are we to do at the 'royal palace'? and who lives there?"

"We are going to see the Princess Idelia; and, later, the grand old High Priest and Astrologer- Royal, Gralda, a seer said to be as old as Methuselah. You will like the Princess; she is a charming lady. But don't lose your heart to her, for she is engaged to Prince Rokta, whom we shall also probably see. She speaks English well."

"Speaks English? How comes that about? Who taught her?"

"We did, Monella and I. After our arrival here, and when we could speak their language well enough, I had classes; and now there are many at the court who can speak fairly well. You see your friends chatting with them now."

"That's been puzzling me for some time," said Wydale. "I *thought* they were conversing, yet could not understand how that could be. Hullo, Georgy! Are you deigning to take some notice of your old friend, or do you feel too high in the world amongst these grandees?"

This was addressed to the lad, who had thus far kept close to his sister.

"I say, Mr. Wydale," said George in answer, "isn't this just splendid? But," he went on, in a low and slightly anxious tone, "don't you think, if they call sister Vanina 'Queen,' that they ought to call me 'Prince'?"

This question was almost whispered, and Wydale could not help laughing at the conceit and at the serious air with which it was advanced.

But, before he could reply, they were at the entrance to the palace, where they were received by officials, guards, and footmen, all attired in striking and resplendent dress, whether suits of armour or liveries. Through these they passed on into a courtyard, then along broad corridors ornamented, some with statuary, others with frescoes on the walls, of exquisite colours and design; the marble floors covered in places with soft carpets cleverly worked in fashions and patterns that were altogether new to Wydale and his friends. At last they were ushered into a large chamber, in which about two dozen persons were assembled. At one end was a raised dais and a canopy that covered three seats or thrones of ivory and gold, beautifully carved and set with jewels. Over them, at the back of the canopy, was an artistic figure of a flying crane embroidered in gold on crimson drapery.

On one of the ivory seats was a fair young girl of about eighteen years of age. Her figure was slight and girlish, and her face was of that character of beauty that wins all hearts more by its air of appealing innocence than by its actual loveliness. She was dressed in a simple costume of a delicate lavender—a flowing robe drawn in by a girdle at the waist—with a golden coronet upon her head. Upon her breast was a figure of a bird in precious stones, and in the coronet blazed large diamonds of extraordinary fire and brilliancy.

At the entrance of the little party the young girl turned and gazed at the new-comers with friendly interest, and in the glance of the large, truthful-looking eyes could be seen, for a moment, a curious, perplexed expression. Then she smiled and, rising, advanced at once to meet Vanina. She took her hands in hers and kissed her on each cheek, then drew back, still holding her hands and regarding her with a tender scrutiny.

"And so you have come at last, Queen Sister!" she said, with a contented sigh. "And at last I see you in the flesh as I have often seen you in my dreams, and in—ah! you shall know that presently. And you see I have learned your language, so that, when you came, I could greet you and talk to you as a sister should. For we shall be sisters, shall we not?"

And, putting one arm round her visitor, she led her to the raised dais, and, leaving her there seated, returned to extend a kindly welcome to the others, whom Monella severally introduced.

George she kissed, laughingly saying, "We shall be brother and sister, you and I;" and to Wydale, as to the rest, her greeting was cordial and full of grace and dignity.

Monella then turned and addressed those assembled in the room, his words being interpreted to Wydale, in an undertone, by the doctor.

"Friends! ye all know how that, long before I came amongst you, there were ancient prophecies extant in the land, and known unto all the people, to the effect that in the hour of your utmost need a Queen should be sent to you from across the oceans to lead you on to final victory against your foes. Ye know, also that, whilst I and my friend have sojourned with you, we have done all that lay in our power to fight your enemies, and to give you the advantage of the greater experience that we have derived from our travels in the outside world. But for the want of those appliances that we

know have been invented, and are now employed in warfare in that
outer world, we could not help you all we wished. Our counsel, the
strength of our right arms, aye, and even our blood, we have freely
given; but victory has not as yet declared itself on our side. Now
to-day the ancient prophecies are fulfilled, for behold a gracious
Queen, stately and beautiful even as your own Princess, has come
across the seas to aid you; and her name is that which we were
told to look for—Vanina!" (At this there was a burst of loud applause.) "Yes, friends! the one ye looked for has arrived; the great
God has sent her at the moment of our greatest need. Let us do her
all honour, and accord to her a welcome worthy of this ancient
people and of the blessings and gifts Heaven has sent us at her
hands. For know ye that she brings with her many wonderful gifts
that shall not only aid in conquering our enemies, but shall prove
blessings to the land for long years after the final victory shall have
been won, and peace and prosperity shall have been secured. These
wonders ye shall shortly see for yourselves; they are stowed away
in the body of the great ship with the towering masts in which she
has sailed hither. Haply ye had looked to see her arrive in other
guise, attended by fleets and armies to fight your battles for you;
haply ye may feel some surprise that she should come to you in
such simple guise, and attended only by two or three of her kins-
men. But be not deceived; it is ever thus with the blessings Heaven
doth vouchsafe us—the greatest, the most precious, constantly
come to us in the most homely garb. Therefore I say, judge not by
outward pomp and show; for, if ye had any thought that Heaven
would send fleets and armies to fight your battles, then indeed have
ye been misled. In the countries we come from we have the proverb,
'God helps those who help themselves,' which means, to apply it
here, that God will help you to fight your battles, but will not fight
them for you. It is sufficient that all, henceforth, will fight with
bolder, stouter hearts, because we know that the hour of victory
draws nigh.

"And now, friends, your newly-arrived visitors are tired, and
need repose. They would leave you for a while for refreshment,
and to change the garments of travel for those of the country, they
come to aid. In a few hours' time they will join you again, and will

be pleased to receive further assurances of your welcome and un-grudging homage and support."

Having finished this address, Monella turned and spoke a few words to the princess, who invited Vanina and her friends to accompany her to another chamber and they passed out accordingly, receiving and returning on their way the respectful salutations of those present.

They entered a gilded saloon with couches or divans around, whereon were soft cushions, while here and there were little tables. The apartment opened on to a balcony, from which could be seen, in one direction, a broad expanse of smiling landscape; in the other the frowning, perpendicular wall of cliff of the other island, with its hanging terraces and castellated walls and towers.

Only George, Dareville, Wydale, and the doctor accompanied the princess and Vanina and Monella into this chamber, and the last-named suggested that the new-comers should first partake of some refreshment.

So, after a light meal, whereat were many curious dishes and strange but luscious fruits, mingled with wines of delicate and captivating flavours, during which there was very little talk on either side, the servants departed, and left the little party to themselves. Then Monella proceeded to tell what was in his thoughts.

"You must know," he said, addressing himself to Dareville and his friend, "that there have been abroad in this land, since quite ancient times, prophecies that in the time of the country's greatest trouble, in its darkest hour, and when its defenders felt themselves most sorely pressed, a ship should come across the sea carrying one bearing the name of Vanina; that this lady should become a ruler in the land, and should lead its defenders to victory, and restore peace and happiness to its inhabitants."

Here he waved his hand to Vanina, who was about to speak, to bid her keep silence for a while.

"Now," he went on, "the time of our sorest trouble seems to have arrived. This people has been driven from their ancient city—their homes in the island that belongs to them—by a section of their nation who prefer to follow idolaters and sorcerers and magicians, and a cruel, blood-guilty priesthood, who carry out revolting human

sacrifices to obscene monsters. But, although thus driven from
their homes, they have maintained themselves, for a long period
on this island—known as the island of Dilanda—by force of arms,
that is, by their superiority in fighting in their war vessels. Of late,
however, this has not been invariably the case; the fortune of war
has gone against us—for I identify myself now with them—and we
have received more than one grievous defeat. Emboldened by this,
our enemies have been occupying themselves, for some time past,
in the construction and fitting out of a great armada that is to over-
whelm our fleet, capture our city here, and give over the inhabitants into slavery—which means that many of them would be reserved as victims for their hideous sacrifices.

"This is not all, however; I grieve to say that a strange apathy
seems to have fallen upon the people, even upon my fighting men.
I cannot fully understand it. No doubt they have lost heart through
their recent defeats; that is but natural; but it does not wholly account for what I have remarked. And, having much pondered upon
the matter, I have concluded that it may arise in part from the reliance they are placing upon these old prophecies, for they are well
known amongst all classes. Their thoughts run somewhat thus:—
'If help is coming to us from over the sea, what is the use of our
striving and risking our lives meanwhile? And again, how can we
hope to succeed, since we know that the hour of our triumph is not
to be until our promised queen arrives?' Such thoughts, you must
perceive, are fatal to all enterprise, to all effort, even to manly courage itself; and the people I have led and have formerly found true
and brave, are, I am grieved and ashamed to confess, fast lapsing
into a race of cowards!"

The princess here uttered an exclamation of protest.

"Aye, aye, princess; I well know your kind heart, that likes not
to hear hard words said of your people; but, unfortunately, they
are true, and this is a time of difficulty and of threatening danger,
and it is not, therefore, a fit occasion for refusing to look facts in
the face.

"I feel assured," he went on sadly, "that, if what I hear through
my spies of this armada is anything like unto truth, then to face it
with our forces in their present mood will be but too surely to court

defeat. Yet do I know that my men are true and loyal and trustworthy; they lack only spirit, enthusiasm, that élan that alone can
lead men on to victory. At this critical time Heaven comes to our
aid with what seems to be a veritable miracle. Heaven has sent us
over the far seas a ship with a cargo of articles unheard of in this
country, and that will excite the wonder of our people. Many of
them will aid us greatly in our warfare. For the contents of this
welcome ship, and for their use, we are able and willing to pay those
in charge of her three—aye ten times the sum they are worth in the
outer world. But," glancing at Vanina, "that is only an item of the
miracle; for in this same goodly ship Heaven ordained that there
should come to us a maiden called Vanina, the name of her the
people here have been so long expecting.

"But the maiden hesitates to accept the destiny marked out for
her. She objects that in coming here she had no special thought or
conscious mission, that chance alone drifted hither the vessel in
which she came—as though there were such a thing as 'chance' in
the ordering of the world! In reply to her objection, I have urged
that each of us is bound to accept the position ordered for us, that
many, themselves unconscious of their fitness and the fact, are
chosen and deputed by Heaven upon special missions; and finally,
that it is her manifest duty to yield to its guidance so unmistakably displayed. For how can it be otherwise? Suppose, then, that
she refuse, are we to wait for another ship with another maiden
who shall bear the name Vanina? That would be waiting for a miracle in good sooth."

The Princess Idelia turned an appealing glance upon Vanina,
and laid her hand affectionately upon her arm.

"How now, my sister?" she exclaimed. "Surely it cannot be so?
Yours is the golden hour—the opportunity to do great good to all
of us, for which we shall be ever grateful. You hear what the good
Lord Monella, the leader of our forces, says. Out people want heart-
ening, they want enthusiasm. I, alas, cannot hearten them, partly
because I have no heart for martial deeds, partly because they look
to someone else. They believe our troubles will end only when a
queen named Vanina comes from across the seas to lead them on
to victory. And now that you have arrived at last, surely our trials

near their end. I gladly yield to you the place I know I can never fitly occupy. Therefore, why further hesitate?"

"But, dear princess," Vanina said, "how can I, a stranger, knowing nothing of such matters, take from you the place that is your birthright—the place to which you must have looked forward all your life?"

"Nay, nay, regard it not so, my sister. If you refuse, soon there may be no kingdom to be governed, either by me or you. Therefore, in resigning my throne to you, I give up to-day only what would most likely be taken from me by force of arms to-morrow. And, beyond all this, I am already tired and saddened by the life we have been leading, with its uncertainties and alarms and dreadful bloodshed. If, therefore, your taking my place will bring about an era of peace and happiness for our harassed people, then do I yield it you, not only without regret, but with a joyful heart."

"But still I see not how this that you expect can come to pass. You are making some great mistake," Vanina urged.

"Let us do what is our manifest duty in this life, and leave the rest to Heaven," interposed Monella Solemnly. "It is not for us to refuse because we cannot foresee the designs of Providence."

"And, finally, listen, sister. I have seen you again and again in my dreams. I know there is no other Vanina to delay for. I have seen, too, those you bring with you; and, to convince you that that is true, I can show you sketches I have made, for I can draw and paint a little. Come with me, all of you, and I will show you."

So saying, she rose and led the way into another apartment, at one end of which a curtain hung before the wall. Pulling this aside, she showed to the astonished company a large fresco, covering the wall, with nearly life-size figures of the four, and in the background the *Saucy Fan*. There was no mistaking those depicted, and the execution of the work was excellent. At sight of their surprise the princess clapped her hands, and laughed without restraint.

"See now how my visions were impressed upon my mind," she cried. "But indeed I was at first afraid to show you this, fearing you might laugh at my ideas of art, for I have heard that where you come from you have great painters."

"We will leave you alone for a while," said Monella to the princess and Vanina. "Do you talk upon this matter, and I doubt not you will arrange it as we wish;" and he motioned to the others to follow him into the chamber they had just quitted.

After some little time spent in desultory converse, Monella was summoned to the conference of the two girls, and presently the three returned together.

"We have arrived at an understanding," he informed the others. "By the laws of Atlantis, the king or queen cannot be crowned until after many ceremonies have been performed; and, further, until he or she has resided at least a year in the city in which the coronation is to be enacted. Seeing, therefore, that a certain period must elapse before the maiden Vanina can be formally installed as queen, it has been agreed that all proceedings to that end shall be postponed until a time of less general anxiety. In the meantime the maiden will take rank as Princess Vanina of Atlantis, and will reign jointly with the Princess Idelia. That, I think, my friends, will meet all our needs. The army will have their long-expected Queen Vanina before their eyes, to hearten them, if it can so do; and they will be informed that she refuses to be formally crowned until such time as they shall have proved that they deserve the favour by defeating her opponents. Is that not so, princess?"

Idelia clapped her hands in the impulsive fashion that belonged to her.

"That is well said," she cried. "Now have I indeed a sister-princess."

"I will take the necessary steps to call together the nobles and elders, and have the matter, as set forth, confirmed by law," Monella said.

"And what do you think of all this?" Vanina asked of Wydale and her brother, coming over to them and taking them aside.

"As for me," returned Sydney instantly, "I say, 'Go in and win.' We'll help you all we can." She looked at Wydale.

"You have known my opinion for some time," he said. "I said you always reminded me of a warrior queen. Strange that I should have had those thoughts and used those very words."

"And stranger still," she murmured dreamily, "that I seem to have been through it all before in the dreams and visions of the night."

12
Prince Rokta

When the conference described in the previous chapter broke up, the new-comers were led to apartments that had already been prepared for them, that they might rest and change their attire for costumes of the country. Of these a considerable wardrobe had been set out for them to choose from, many of the dresses being court suits of rich materials, ornamented with gold embroidery and precious stones. Dareville and Wydale found that their rooms adjoined, and the worthy doctor, who accompanied them thither, gave them the benefit of his own experience in the choice of vestments.

"We wear armour," he informed them, "only during the day, or when and where there is reason to fear attack. Here, in the town and in the palace, it is not needful. All approaches are watched and patrolled by scouts who would give timely notice of any descent in force upon the palace.

"This evening," he went on, after a pause, "there will be a grand reception in honour of your arrival. I should recommend you now to have a bath and take a rest, and when it is time, I will come again to fetch you."

That evening there was a great assemblage of the nobles and principal court functionaries, who thronged the Great Hall of Audience in the palace, and the adjacent galleries and terraces. Their court dresses—many of them of the brightest and gayest colours, yet tasteful in design and tone—sparkled with flashing jewels, as did the hilts and scabbards of the swords and daggers each one carried. They stood about in groups laughing and talking, or bustled to and fro exchanging a word here and there. Everyone seemed in the best of spirits, and the low hum and buzz of conversation, varied by occasional ripples of laughter that were good-humoured without being noisy, told plainly enough of the general feeling that the occasion was both an important and a happy one.

The interior of the palace was everywhere brilliantly illuminated with hanging lamps, and formed a striking scene. Viewed from the terraces and other points of vantage in the gardens, gleams of glowing light could be seen through the windows and entrances thrown open to admit the cool evening air. Without, also, amongst the statues placed every where about, were bronze figures holding braziers, from which lambent flames leaped up into the air, throwing around changeful, dancing shadows.

Amid it all came the soft, cool music of falling water from plashing fountains, both in the gardens and in the inner courts. But most curious of all was the fact that some of these in the gardens were themselves centres of light, their waters, thrown high in air and falling into basins below, being veritable cascades of fire. They threw dazzling, phosphorescent gleams around, which, mingling with the dancing shadows from the braziers, added a touch of weirdness to the picturesque features of the scene. Below and beyond could be seen the lights of the city, and those upon the watch-towers placed at intervals along the shore. Here sentinels paced to and fro throughout the night, many of them, doubtless, looking up with rather envious eyes at the edifice in which, as they knew, the great meeting was taking place, and which could be seen from all parts around like an illuminated fairy palace built high in the air. Each sentinel had beside him, upon his watch-tower, other braziers charged ready for instant ignition to give the alarm should occasion call for it.

Amongst the groups on the terraces, Wydale and Dareville strolled about, viewing with keen and lively interest all that was going on. With them were the doctor, Ombrian, the commander of the fleet, and Kremna, a young warrior, who was one of Monella's immediate followers or "aides."

He had been charged by Monella to attend the two young men. Ombrian was a tall, dark man of imposing mien, with hair and beard that had once been black, but was now just beginning to turn grey. Self-contained, he was little given to talk, and, when he spoke, his voice had a certain gruffness in it that, though at first unattractive, was not unpleasant to those who had grown to know and understand him. As to Kremna, he was a light-haired, blue-eyed young fellow, full of vivacity, energy, and chatter; but straightforward and brave, and devoted to Monella, and, as a consequence, ready at once to make friends with any friends of his chief.

Wydale inquired of the doctor the meaning of the "fiery fountains," as he called them. "We saw," he said, "cascades of the same character, in the bay when we first anchored."

"It is a sight certainly calculated to impress strangers; it was the case with us when we first came," the doctor replied, "and it argues, moreover, much ingenuity on the part of those, whoever they were, who originally thought out the idea. But they only cleverly took advantage of the fact that all the sea water about here is strongly phosphorescent, and throws out vivid gleams of light whenever stirred or splashed about. Over in Atlantis are extensive grottoes and subterranean galleries in the vitreous rock—they call them here the 'Crystal Grottoes or Caverns.'"

"Anywhere near the underground galleries I went through with Monella last night?" asked Wydale.

"Precisely; yes. You must have passed through some of the galleries which lead out of the grottoes. Well, the latter are partly lighted in a very ingenious fashion; the crystal columns left in hewing out the caverns—for they are mainly artificial—are hollow, and form conduits more or less transparent, for water which is pumped up into extensive reservoirs, above. The pumps are engines of no mean size and power, and they go on everlastingly, day and night, worked partly by the tides, and partly by the fresh water streams from the heights. The overflow runs away into the bay you speak of, and forms, at night, the phosphorescent cascades you saw there. The same principle has been applied here."

"I notice," Wydale presently remarked, "that the architecture, though fine, seems inferior to that which so impressed me over in the ruins, which, you say, are those of the actual ancient city of Atlantis."

"That is so. And you may notice the same thing to even a greater extent in the frescoes and mural decorations here. The statues and fountains you see around, too, are mostly old; they were brought, in fact, from the old town. The truth is that art, and, in a measure, craftsmanship, are dying out with us; probably for want of the stimulus of outside competition to keep them up to the mark. There are few artificers here now, save armourers; these have been kept in practice by the civil wars or internecine fights and struggles which have always, I understand, been more or less continuous."

"I wonder they have not exterminated one another long ago," commented Owen.

"It have done their little best in that direction, certainly," replied the doctor, with grim emphasis. "What with fighting and their human sacrifices."

"Human sacrifices!' Wydale shivered.

"Ah, yes; abominable and hateful rites they have—over in King Kara's country. There they still sacrifice human beings to their gods; and, I am told, also to feed the monstrous flying creatures you have seen. Formerly, too, there were feuds and fights with the 'Flower-Dwellers.'"

"What—who are they?" Wydale asked.

"In this group," replied the doctor, "besides those you know of, are some smaller islands, but only one of these is of any size. It is called Sylia, and is said to be inhabited by a terrible race—ferocious, merciless. Worse even, they say, than the Karanites, because more skilled in warfare and dark sciences. There are wonderful tales about these people; but, thank goodness—if the tales are true— they are willing enough to keep to their own territory, and not interfere with the dwellers in the other islands so long as they are let alone."

"But what a singular name— 'Flower-Dwellers!'"

This talk had taken place between Owen and the doctor while they strolled along in the wake of Dareville and his two companions. At times when they neared one of the groups that stood about, the conversation had been interrupted that the strangers might be introduced, and exchange a few words of greeting, and then pass on. Ombrian heard Wydale's last remark, and turned to answer him.

"The 'Flower-Dwellers,'" said he, in excellent English. "Ah! I have fought with them; or, rather, tried to. But you cannot; they do not give you a chance. They simply strike you dead; my men fell round me like saplings struck by the lightning. As for me, how I escaped I know not; only three of us came back."

"But what are they like?" Dareville put in.

"You cannot tell; no man has seen their faces, for they always wear masks," was the strange reply.

Further conversation was interrupted by a general move towards the central hall of the palace. Evidently some signal had been given that the hour for the audience had arrived.

When the hall was reached, a large concourse was to be seen standing or sitting round in ranks four or five deep. At one end, upon a raised platform, was a richly worked throne with high carved back in ivory and gold, and roomy enough for five or six persons to be seated upon it at one time. It was rounded in shape, forming a semi-circular background to the room. Close to it were conspicuous, standing on one side, Monella and another whose appearance at once arrested the attention of the strangers, and who was afterwards known to them as Gralda, the High Priest.

Gralda was an old man of imposing presence with fine features and bright clear eyes. His hair and beard were long, and white as snow; not so tall as Monella, he yet was of unusual height, and would have appeared still taller, but for a slight stoop. There was in the expression of his face a mingling of benevolence and world-weariness; and this was emphasised by his stoop. There was at once a likeness and a contrast between the two men, for while Monella's erect figure and great muscular frame, combined with the piercing eyes and usually alert, searching look, seemed to belong rather to a man in the very prime of life than to a grey-beard, yet at times there would come into his glance that same dreamy, world-weary expression that was more or less habitual to Gralda.

Something of this must have been passing in the mind of the doctor, for he said, half to his companion and half to himself, "I would give something to know which is the older of those two men."

The remark seemed to amuse his hearer, who was about to reply, when he caught Monella's eye, and read in it, and in a slight gesture that accompanied the look, an invitation to approach him.

Monella was very plainly dressed in a sort of tunic of white, with a belt of black, and a cloak of black and white. His attire was in marked contrast, in its simplicity and absence of all ornament, with that of those by whom he was surrounded. Gralda wore a flowing robe of a bright red, with a figure of a rising sun embroidered in gold and diamonds upon the breast. Upon his head he wore a narrow circlet, which had in the front a similar, though a much smaller figure. He received the two young men, when presented to him by Monella, with kindly courtesy, but, since he did not speak English, he said nothing beyond a few words of welcome, which were interpreted to them by Dr. Manleth.

And then there was first a stir, and then a general hush, and the new-comers, turning, saw entering the room a young man of striking appearance, very richly dressed, who came slowly towards the dais with an air that was careless and somewhat haughty, yet singularly courtly and attractive. In face and figure he was remarkably—almost wonderfully—handsome. He had the cast of features that we know as ancient Greek, with dark hair and eyes, a flowing moustache, and a supple, graceful figure that many sculptors would have been glad to be able to secure as a model for Apollo. This was well-shown off by a close-fitting costume of white and gold, adorned on the breast with the figure of a flying crane which, as the strangers had seen, was a common emblem in the country.

As he stepped up on to the dais, closely followed by two who seemed to be in attendance, the doctor murmured low

"Prince Rokta!"

Whether he of whom he spoke had heard the words, or that his turning round at the moment was accidental, was not quite clear. But so it was that he just then glanced in their direction, and, seeing the two strangers, regarded them with a peculiarly searching gaze.

Although there was nothing in the stranger's manner that was offensive, neither Dareville nor Wydale felt quite at ease; the former in particular, in the impulsive manner that belonged to him, felt tempted to resent it. But Dr. Manleth quickly introduced them; whereupon Prince Rokta greeted them in an easy manner, and with a smile, speaking a few words in very excellent English. Then going up to Monella and Gralda he inquired:

"What is this I hear the princess has done? Is it true that she has offered to vacate her place to put in it a stranger?"

"My son," said Gralda, "thou knowest it was so arranged. Thou didst offer no objection when it was suggested the other day at the meeting of our council. The Lord Monella, who was present, will remember it."

"The prince will doubtless recall," joined in Monella, "the announcement of the expected arrival of the strangers, and the fact that he gave his consent in the event of their appearance to what has since been done."

"Yes; *if*, my Lord Monella," rejoined Rokta, with some heat. "But little did I then think that what I regarded as a fantastic dream was actually about to happen."

At this moment Ombrian, Manleth, and two or three others approached, and joined in the conversation.

"It is not a question," began Ombrian bluntly, "who is to be princess here so much as whether shortly there will be an independent country to reign over. For my part, having heard the will of the people declared to-day, I adopt their views."

"It seems to me," said Monella coldly, "that the prince should have been present with us to-day."

"How so, sir?" retorted Rokta, "have I not been about my duties? Could I go round the island to inspect all the stations in less time?"

"Still," returned Monella quickly, "thou wert told—"

"Oh, a truce to your dreams and visions! Ever since I was a boy I have heard cackle of this sort! Thou knowest well, however, that I have no sympathy with such fancies; I am a soldier, a man of action, and of deeds, and not a dreamer!"

Before any reply could be made to this unlooked-for outburst, there was again a stir at the further end of the hail, betokening some fresh arrival.

This time it was the Princess Idelia, accompanied by Vanina, George, and several attendants; and there was much cheering and clapping of hands as the little procession passed up the room to the dais. As for Prince Rokta, when he caught sight of Vanina, he gazed at her with a glance that was full of wonder, mingled with very evident admiration. Certainly she looked very charming; and dressed as she was now, in a costume after the manner of the ladies of the court, but richer far than any of those about her, it was not surprising that she should rivet his attention. Evidently the Princess Idelia in welcoming her, and offering to give place to her, was resolved not to do things by halves. The richest dresses, the most precious jewels had been placed at her disposal; nay, she had herself insisted upon dressing her new friend, and choosing her ornaments, placing around her neck her choicest necklet, and upon her head a coronet like her own. She now advanced toward Rokta, and introduced him to Vanina with a gladsome pride that was very pleasing to behold.

"Behold, Rokta," she exclaimed, "my dear sister, our long promised Vanina; your future—"

Here Vanina put up her hand to stop further speech.

"Nay," said she, "let us not speak of the future; it will suffice just now to speak only of to-day. Let me, Prince Rokta, state to you my thanks for the kindly reception I and my friends have met with in this city."

Prince Rokta advanced slowly and took her hand, and, bending over it with that courtly ease which, it was plain to see, was with him a sort of second nature, he said:

"Princess, I am glad to hear what you say, and to add my welcome to that of the people of this country. Accept my apologies for having not been present when you arrived to-day. We have to be diligent and watchful, and I was away on necessary soldier's duties, making sure that all our guards were at their posts. Thus, I trust, my absence has not been without its advantages, since I have been doing my best to secure the safety of so fair a guest."

"Nay, Rokta," said Idelia laughing, "no guest at all; guests come and go, but Vanina, I trust, will stay with us for ever."

"I hope so, too," said Rokta, with another bow, and glancing while he spoke into Vanina's face with a look so full of meaning that she flushed and showed confusion.

But Idelia put her arm round her and drew her aside.

"Come and sit down," said she. "There are many waiting to be presented to you;" and she took her to the centre of the throne at the end of the room.

Meanwhile Manleth introduced George to the prince, who received him with much favour. He was soon engaged in animated conversation, the boy, quite at his ease, giving a lively narrative of some of his adventures.

Then, to the strangers' great surprise, there came into the hall a band of musicians. They were provided with harps and other instruments of novel design, but—as soon appeared—very effective and sweet in tone.

This orchestra played first some concerted pieces, the like of which none of the new-comers had ever heard before. In them the most tenderly-conceived melodies, full of a dreamy fascination, were intermingled with passages of such rugged harmony and weird, moving power, that those who heard them for the first time were astounded. Never, in the outer world, had they listened to such music; never would they have dreamed that anything so charming, so fascinating, Yet so different from anything they had heard before, could have been produced by such curious, almost uncouth-looking instruments.

When, after a little while, there came a pause, Vanina sighed.

"Wonderful! wonderful!" she exclaimed—and in what she said she expressed, besides her own, the feelings of Wydale and her brother. "I have never heard music that has so deeply moved me. Truly, you must have some great masters of the art here to be able to produce such music and such players."

Idelia laughed and clapped her hands, according to her wont, when pleased.

"Listen to that all of you," she cried, and she looked round. "In one thing, at least, then, we can both surprise and please our friends. But you shall listen to more of this another time. We go on now to the dancing. Let us see whether you will enjoy that too."

And she insisted, with friendly persistence, that her guests should join in the dances which ensued, notwithstanding that these were, of course, quite new to them. There was no lack of good-humoured assistance on all sides, and the strangers managed to acquit themselves fairly well, entering fully into the spirit of the entertainment. Vanina found a willing instructor in Prince Rokta, who danced with her many times that night.

Some time later, during a pause in the dancing, Prince Rokta went up to Monella, who was standing in the centre of a small group aside, and, extending his hand to him, he said:

"My Lord Monella, I have to express my regret, and to ask your indulgence for what I said a short time ago. Little did I think that your dreams and prophecies would end in bringing us such a gracious and charming visitor. I am sure she is, indeed, well worthy to be our queen, and I only regret that I was not one of the first to greet and to bow the knee to her."

Monella acknowledged this speech with a dignified inclination of the head and one of his curious half-smiles, but made no direct reply.

That night, after the festivities had ended, Wydale, walking slowly and alone to his apartment, met Monella, who laid his hand kindly on his shoulder, and, gazing at him keenly, said:

"My son, you seem unhappy and disturbed. This is not a good beginning for your stay amongst us."

Wydale glanced up at him, and something in the look he read there gained his confidence.

"I fear," he said sadly, "there is trouble in the air."

"Aye," said Monella, "there is trouble in the air; but when is there not? But keep up thy faith and courage, and leave the rest to a higher power. Remember, a battle is never lost till it is won. Goodnight; and God be with you!"

13
The Grottoes of a Thousand Lights

During the days that followed, the attention of the community into which the passengers of the *Saucy Fan* had so strangely drifted was chiefly occupied with the unloading of the vessel. This was a work of time and of some difficulty, for Monella, for some reasons that were not given, desired that the unloading should not take place where she then lay, but in the "cavern" opposite, where, it appeared, he had workshops. In order to effect this, the masts and rigging were first removed; the hull was then towed across the intervening space of water.

In due time various portions of the cargo were brought from the "cavern" back to the harbour and docks, and when they were landed on the quays and opened, the excitement rose to fever height. Vague rumours then flew from mouth to mouth concerning the wonderful "gifts" brought into the country, for the use and advantage of her people, by their heaven-sent queen that was to be.

Monella, furnished by Dareville with a catalogue of the cargo, was quick to appreciate the impression that could be made upon the people by these "wonders"—as they seemed to them—as well as the more solid advantage to which they could be turned.

"I had hoped for arms," he said, "but since Providence has sent us something else, it is for us to make the best of what has been vouchsafed us. It is fortunate that both the launch and the steam engine can be worked with petroleum, of which there is plenty here, instead of coal, of which we have very little. Formerly there were coal mines here, but they gave out ages ago. With the launch, the fireworks, the life-saving rockets, and the small cannon much may be accomplished."

"I should think so," rejoined Wydale, who with Dareville was assisting. "How would it be to fit the brig up as a great barge, to be propelled by oars? She could run down half your fleet at one crash, and scarcely feel it."

"A good idea, but there are difficulties. It was necessary to take her masts out in order to get her into where she now lies; but that does not matter, seeing that I had already decided to convert her into a fore and aft schooner; that is to say, to alter her to the rig of a schooner-yacht."

"Why so?" the two young men asked in surprise.

"Because, if the opportunity ever offer to get away from here, we shall be very short-handed, and our only chance of sailing her successfully to the nearest port would be to do away with the square sails."

"Ah, yes; I see. You look forward then to leaving here one day? You do not think we are to stay here for the remainder of our days?"

Monella gazed inquiringly at Wydale, who had put this question.

"Certainly, I hope to get away," he answered. "And I suppose you do, too. Those who have lived in the world beyond are not fitted to turn lotus-eaters, and lead a life of idleness in a place like this. I, at least, have work to do elsewhere."

"I feel you are right, sir. But who will navigate the vessel?" Owen asked.

"I will."

"And when?"

Monella passed his hands across his eyes, a way he had at times, and his glance wandered away dreamily into the distance, as though his thoughts had travelled far afield, and he had forgotten the subject of their talk. Then suddenly he seemed to rouse himself, and looked at Wydale earnestly; laying his hand upon his shoulder, he replied:

"That, my son, I know not; it is in the hands of Him by whom we were directed hither. I only know this—it will not be until the work for which we were sent here is completed."

Nor were Monella's expectations in other directions disappointed. The arrival of a vessel, that to the unsophisticated islanders

seemed nothing less than a marvel of marine architecture, bringing one who bore the long-expected name Vanina, created an enthusiasm that quickly roused them from their listless, almost despon-
dent, state. Drilling now went on daily, and both officers and men
began to show a zeal and alacrity and an interest in learning and
mastering the art of war, that were full of promise of success. So at
least the doctor thought.

"It is hardly like the same place," he declared one day to Wydale.

"Everyone goes bustling about with an air of business-like determination wholly different from the apathy that formerly reigned
supreme! All our fighting men are drilling and practising with a
will—and they need it to succeed—for they have of late been lamen-
tably lax and careless—especially the archers. Even Monella's wonderful shooting failed to imbue them with heart or emulation."

"That Monella is a good shot with bow and arrow I have had
ample evidence," said Wydale. "But how did he come to be so expert
at such an old-world exercise?"

"That has always puzzled me," replied the doctor. "When we
first came here the bows and arrows in use were very primitive
sort of weapons. Monella first made a mighty bow for himself—
one that no one else can draw—like Ulysses of old. He manufac-
tured arrows to match, and then showed what he could do with
them, to the astonishment of all, myself included. Then he set to
work to teach the people how to make like weapons for themselves;
or, rather, he taught the armourers to make them for the fighting
men. He has introduced many other improvements, too, in the arm-
ing and equipment of both men and boats; with the result that,
whereas our forces were before decidedly inferior to those opposed
to them, they are now nearly equal; or would be if the men had but
the spirit."

"And what are the 'enemy' doing now, do you suppose? And
why do we hear and see nothing of them?"

"For the reason that there has been between the two forces one
of these informal truces, or mutual cessation of active fighting, that
occasionally obtain in all long and tedious wars. This is why you
were unmolested; and it was fortunate that you arrived at such a
time. Otherwise, you would very likely have been captured, and

taken to their city to be given over to their priesthood, and your vessel would have been plundered."

"Then that fate may now befall the scoundrels who deserted us," observed Wydale, a little grimly.

"And when do you expect the next attack?"

"That, of course, we cannot tell; but Monella, who somehow gets to know something of what is going on, does not expect it at the moment. But he believes we shall have all we can do to repel it when it comes, for he has information that they are making the most strenuous preparations—fitting out, as he said the other day, an invincible 'armada.'"

"But if he has spies in the other camp, may they not also have spies here, and so get to know of our arrival and its results?"

"It may be so, of course; but I hope not."

Meantime, solemn councils of the nobles and elders of the people had been held, at which Vanina had been duly recognised as a princess, and their Queen-elect; her brothers being at the same time given the rank of prince, and Wydale the rank of noble, with a place high in command in the army under Monella.

All, too, were given uniforms and insignia and equipments appropriate to their rank; and the two young men were now accordingly—somewhat, it must be confessed, against their own wills—habitually dressed in suits of light armour. This was during the day, while moving about amongst the populace and soldiery, or crossing to the "caverns"; in the evening, when attending receptions at the palace, armour was exchanged for lighter raiment.

One day a party started, under Ombrian's guidance, to pay a visit to the "caverns" and underground workings in the main island that were still held by the inhabitants of Dilanda. The two princesses were of the number, which included all the new-comers, as well as the doctor and some of the Court officials and ladies in-attendance.

The trip across was made in one of the State barges, which was named *Princess Idelia*, after the princess, and it was escorted by five of the larger vessels of the fighting craft.

The day was oppressively hot. A tropical sun poured down upon a sea so calm that not so much as a ripple disturbed its glassy surface.

The light awning that was swung over the deck scarce sufficed to break the burning rays, and afforded but slight mitigation of the heat. The cliffs and hanging terraces of Atlantis were slightly shaded, and towered, murky and mysterious-looking, in a thin haze, it was not, therefore, until the strangers were quite close that they were able to make out that here, as on the other side, were great water-gates, through which their vessel could pass. But these gave access, not as in the other case, to a harbour, but to a gloomy tunnel in the solid rock, that led to great caverns within. The oppressive heat now yielded to an atmosphere that was comparatively cool, and the dazzling sunlight and blue sky were succeeded by a sort of twilight. After some ceremony, involving much blowing of trumpets, and hoarse challenges and signals from sentinels on guard, the great gates first opened, and then clanged behind them, with a noise that sent low rumblings echoing among the galleries. Then, at further trumpet blasts, other gates within swung slowly open, disclosing a considerable length of dark water channel, with a bright opening beyond. Finally, the barge came out into a scene that filled the visitors with surprise.

The narrow water-channel, cut through solid rock, opened suddenly out into an interior lake, in a vast cavern of such height that, though the whole extent was well lighted, the roof could not be seen. Here, around the borders of the water, were broad quays, and, beyond these, small caverns appeared in the rocky sides, in which were numbers of people busy with all kinds of work. The place was, indeed, a sort of underground dock with storehouses and workshops, lighted everywhere by great lamps and braziers, and ventilated by shafts that went up through the rock to the open air on the tops of the cliffs above. Here, reposing snugly upon the water, lay the *Saucy Fan*, dismasted, with many work people going to and fro, still engaged in unloading her.

At sight of the dismasted vessel, "Dear old *Saucy Fan*," Vanina cried. "How strange she looks—her masts and rigging gone, and laid up in so queer a place. What adventures she seems fated to go through! But why is this?"

"It is for the security of your vessel, princess," answered Ombrian; "that she may lie here in our safest retreat of all, beyond any possibility of mishap, till you require her. She could not have been got in here without taking down her masts."

"And," added Dareville, "Monella purposes to give her a lighter rig, and make some other alterations, I believe."

"Well, I should like to go on board and see how she looks in circumstances so changed," rejoined Vanina.

There was no objection to this, and, after a ramble over the decks of the brig and down into the cabins, the party continued their journey, now to be made on foot, through the galleries and caverns.

These rocky passages were intricate and extensive. At times the visitors ascended flights of steps and came out on the hanging terraces which overhung the sea below.

From these were to be had views of the opposite island, and of the city they had just come from, surrounded by fortified walls and rocks, with the great gateways and towers that protected the entrance to the harbour. To right and to left of the island could be seen only an endless expanse of sea choked with weed, with here and there dark rocks sticking up amongst it.

The heat was now intense, and all were glad to leave the terraces and plunge again into the coolness of the inner passages, even though many of them were dark and gloomy, and lighted only by the lanterns their attendants carried.

Here and there these galleries opened into a large chamber used as a guard-house, whence, through barred gates, could be seen views beyond of the interior of the island. Descending again, they came to the level of the water, and followed, but in a contrary direction, for a short distance, the side of a stream that ran into the lake or underground harbour wherein reposed the *Saucy Fan*. Then Prince Rokta stopped.

"We are now near," he said, "the great wonder of this underground place, *viz.*, the caves that we call the Grottoes of a Thousand Lights."

He opened a massive door of wood and iron that barred their further progress, and they entered the grotto.

Instantly the visitors became sensible of a delicious coolness, and the refreshing, swishing sound of falling water; then that the

whole place gleamed with a peculiar light. It was not the light of
the sun, for no rays could penetrate, nor of the moon, for she had
not yet risen; it was not the light of burning oil or gas, or of any
artificial illuminant that they had ever seen or heard of. It was prismatic, and scintillated in thousands—millions—of little shooting
points of every colour, that seemed to dart in and out, to and fro,
twinkling, leaping, dancing, ever in motion, and forming a combination that illuminated the whole scene with a soft and wonderful
radiance that, though brilliant, was still grateful to the eye. The
sides and the lofty roof were everywhere of a pure crystal as dazzling, wherever the light played upon it, as the diamond itself. Over
it all—in every possible direction—and down the crystal columns
which held up the roof—water played, running into tiny rivulets
that made their way into glowing pools in the arched recesses of
the place. And wherever the water touched, wherever it trickled,
or splashed or tumbled, it seemed to burst into coruscations reflected in every prismatic angle of the jagged crystal in iridescent,
opalescent sparkles. The whole place seemed to be filled with a
living light; a splendour, a lustre, that words cannot convey, or
thought conceive. And when one came to look farther, there could
be seen, on every side, sculptured forms of a thousand shapes and
subjects, all lighted up in this strange fashion, all glowing with
their own subtle fires.

The columns were carved in many ways; sometimes in flowers
and leaves that twined round them from the roof above to the floor
below. And so cunningly were they worked that the water ran in
and out amongst, and through, and under the flowers and leaves;
now a quarter of an inch or so beneath the surface of the crystal,
now over its face, and anon plashing against the outlines. Everywhere as it ran, tossed to and fro, backwards and forwards, in tortuous little channels, it burst into minute fiery points that were
reflected in the crystal in a hundred shades and colours. There were
statues of men in finely worked chain armour; and groups of women
in intricate lace robes that all scintillated with light; the hair and
features, and the whole of the figure, shimmering in the same
strange fashion. And there were ferns, and moss, and palms, and
plants, and shrubs, all delicately and marvellously carved; statues

of animals, of serpents, of other reptiles, every scale upon whose bodies glimmered with the same weird living light. In the pools were ships and boats, water plants, and fountains all thus lighted up; and finally there was a cascade that fell, a broad sheet of fire, from the roof into a basin below, sending out millions of sparkling particles on every side.

The visitors were full of exclamations of astonishment and delight, as they wandered in and out about this fantastic storehouse, ever finding something fresh to excite their admiration. And the Princess Idelia clapped her hands and laughed like a pleased child while she listened to them.

"You can wander about for a long space thus, and ever find something new," she told Vanina.

"But—who could ever have done all this wonderful work, and thought out so many clever little devices to thus utilise the shining, sparkling water?" Vanina asked. "Why—think how long it must have taken!"

"Hundreds of years, I have heard Monella estimate," the doctor answered. "He reckons this place one of the great wonders of the world. It is supposed that it was originally designed—long ages ago—by some great King of Atlantis, as an adjunct to his palaces and gardens, and that the work was continued and extended by his successors through many generations. You observe there are figures of animals from almost all parts of the world—America, Africa, Europe—proof positive in itself that those who formerly ruled here were acquainted with distant quarters of the globe. They must have brought these animals from the countries they inhabit, even as did the Romans in later times. You can see the same things in the frescoes that are still visible on some of the ruins of the old city. It is interesting to speculate on what strange assemblages, fetes, and festivals may have taken place here; what bygone peoples may have wandered in and out as we are doing to-day."

14
Monella Fights the Vampire

It was only with some difficulty, and after loudly expressing their admiration and their reluctance to quit the place, that the visitors were presently persuaded to turn their backs on the grotto, to plunge again into the gloomy subterranean passages. On their way back through the galleries they noticed barred gates that shut off other galleries.

In reply to their inquiry as to where these led to, Dr. Manleth said nobody seemed quite to know. They were mostly blocked with heaps of rubbish which prevented further exploration.

"I think our friend Monella knows more about them than anyone else," he added. "He had them explored, so far as was found practicable, and then caused the gates to be fixed to shut them off; for what reason I cannot tell you."

Presently they reached one of the guard-houses looking out across the interior of the island. It was much larger than the others, and consisted of two roomy chambers, each shut off by strong barred gates. Wydale quickly recognised the place as that outside which he had first met Monella.

At Vanina's earnest request, the gates were thrown open for them, and they were allowed to go out on to a narrow terrace beyond.

"It was from here," said Wydale, "that Monella sent flying to its mark the arrow which saved George and myself from that villain Foster. I wonder what became of the scoundrel after all!"

"Yes," George exclaimed. "See, Vanina! There, below, is the rock on which we stood, and yonder you can see the ruined city we came through."

The terrace upon which they were was in the shade, and the heat was less than when they had been upon the hanging terraces on the outer cliffs. There was now more haze, and, while the ruins could be plainly seen, the view did not extend very far beyond them; but in the dim distance could just be discerned what looked like a high and precipitous mountain; also, shimmering in the sunshine, the lake, reflecting their shapes in trembling, distorted forms. And from the lake ran a broad winding stream that disappeared almost beneath where they were standing.

"Those ruins," said Doctor Manleth, addressing Vanina, "are all that remain to-day of the ancient city of Atlantis, the chicf town of the extensive island (or maybe group of islands) called by that name, which, as some assert—and the statement is borne out by the ancient legends and traditions of the people here—was once the home of a mighty, conquering nation. A great power that, placed between the American Continent on the one side, and Europe and Africa on the other, actually, it is affirmed, held sway in all of them. Indeed—still according to tradition—the so called island must have been a continent in itself—even as we to-day call the great island of Australia a continent—and it was so placed that while its people could overrun the shores of the Mediterranean and other countries in the east, they could as easily reach America in the west. It is, in fact, declared that in those days Atlantis was the queen-city of the world."

"How I should like to see more of the fine old city!" exclaimed Vanina. "Cannot we walk over to it? It is not far; and the sun is still high."

Prince Rokta glanced inquiringly at Ombrian, who shook his head.

Idelia shivered, and so did George; nor could Wydale repress a shudder.

Vanina glanced from one to another in some wonder; then she looked out upon the scene that lay before them. All was still and peaceful; there was no living creature to be seen. The green trees that grew near the ruins and beside the water looked inviting; they were not far away, and one could walk most of the distance beside the cool-looking river, with trees here and there along on the road for shade.

"Come!" said Vanina, "you surely are not afraid to venture so short a distance. There is no one to be seen, and you have guards here who can keep watch and give us a signal, should they see anyone in the distance. You are all armed, too. Are you afraid—of—of—of what? Ghosts? Ghosts in the Sunlight?"

And she laughed.

"Sister, dear," said Idelia gently, "I have always heard that, in some places, there are evil spirits abroad in the sunlight, just as much as in the dark. Still, it is not spirits we have to fear. You speak of armed guards here; but not one of them would venture out to those ruins to save his life. And, as for watching and giving us timely alarm, they would be more likely, so soon as we had turned our backs, to rush in and close and bar the gates behind us."

"It is not safe to venture there," said Ombrian, with decision. "See, the haze is growing thicker. The mountain you could see but now has already disappeared. It looks to me as though a sea-mist might come up at any moment, and then—it is not safe. It is likely enough that we have been seen, and our presence here already noted. Our enemies have spies ever on the watch beyond the plain there; and of those who venture out far from here, many disappear; few—very few—return to tell the tale."

"Well," said Vanina resolutely, "one can venture a short distance, at least. Those who care to do so can accompany me, and *those who are afraid* can stay behind."

With these words, in saying which she laid a marked and contemptuous emphasis on the expression, "those who are afraid," she stepped forward, and, passing down the winding path, disappeared from view behind some rocks, before those around her had had time to make up their minds what they ought to do.

Wydale, after the terrible experience that had befallen him in that very place, would have wished to detain her by force, but was unwilling to suggest it. He had seen, and seen with sorrow, that Vanina had already somewhat changed, and not altogether for the better, since her elevation. True it was, she had not sought it; had, indeed, at first declined it, and had yielded only upon pressure. Nor had she shown any very marked alteration in manner towards him.

But gradually Owen had noticed, first in one little thing, then in others, that she was exhibiting a disposition to play the role of Queen-ruler of the country very seriously; and was disposed, at times, to show herself imperious and obstinate, and resolute to have her own way. Thus, though in the present instance he had the best of reasons for restraining her, even by force if needs be, he felt, with some bitterness, that to do so would only be to lay himself open to a sharp rebuke, and, possibly, humiliation. Of the others, Dareville had not passed through Wydale's thrilling experience, and did not, therefore, feel strongly enough upon the subject to care to take any action; while Rokta and the others stood still in doubt and hesitation, perplexed and dismayed at Vanina's hasty action.

But George, who, when he saw his sister disappear, had stood and stared after her in fear and alarm too great for words, now suddenly roused himself, and rushed down the path, loudly calling upon her to return. His terror moved Idelia greatly, who looked as though she were about to faint; and Wydale standing beside her, felt afraid to take his eyes off her, thinking every moment she would fall.

Just then Ombrian raised his hand to his brow and gazed fixedly, for a moment or two, across the country.

"See!" he then said, with what was for him unusual animation, "see! I thought so; the mist is coming up. We must all get into shelter. It is not well to be abroad here in the mist."

At these words, Wydale hesitated no longer. Hurriedly he called the attention of his companions to the princess, and followed down the path after Vanina and her brother.

He had scarcely gone, when Idelia, overcome by the hidden fears that oppressed her, fell forward in a swoon.

Prince Rokta caught her in his arms, while Dareville stepped back into the guard-house and called out one of the ladies in attendance. There, to his surprise, he came across Monella, who had just come up, and was asking hurried questions. On hearing Sydney's explanation, he went with him outside, saw that the doctor and others were attending Idelia, and then, addressing Ombrian, said:

"I will go after the maiden and her brother. Do you all go within and stay there and guard the gate; but keep a good look-out against my return. I fear there is danger; let no one follow me." With that, he snatched his great shield from an attendant, and disappeared down the pathway.

His last words had been spoken in a manner, and accompanied by a look, that impressed those around him with the conviction that he must be implicitly obeyed; and the two young men, who had already started to follow him, now hesitated. Ombrian held up his hand.

"See!" he said, "the mist is gathering around. There is no time to be lost. Look to the princess, first.'

Just then Dareville heard a call, and made out Wydale, on a ledge below, half supporting, half carrying George, and went to meet and help him.

The poor lad, remembering his former experience in the same place, and in deadly fear for his sister, was white and frightened-looking, and scarcely able to walk.

"I found him wandering about," Owen explained, "looking for your sister; neither of us could make out which path she had taken, and, while we were searching for her, Monella came down and bid me come back with the boy. He said we were not to fear; he would find your sister and bring her safely back. And in this mist, I fancy he is the only one that can."

The mist had now become so thick that to search further was impossible. Even to get back to the guard-house, near to it as they were, was no easy matter.

"Well, after all," said Dareville, with an attempt at cheerfulness, "there is no great harm in being out in a fog for a while—if—"

"Aye; if"—Owen returned, with a feeling of anxiety he could not disguise, "if there is no flying monster abroad here to-day. But, if there is, then God help our dear friend alone out there, if Monella fail to find her. And even if he do, heaven only knows how they may fare."

Hearing Wydale speak thus, Dareville, so soon as they had reached the guard-house, where all had now assembled—except Idelia and her attendants, who Were in an inner chamber—urged first that a search-party should be sent out, offering to lead it; then, that something should be done by shouting, or other signals, to assist the two outside to find their way back. But Ombrian only shook his head, and closed the gates.

"It is all useless, sir," he declared. "I have my orders and must obey them; besides, not one of my men could be induced to go out in this mist; and for you, as strangers, to go alone, is but madness. If there should be the danger we fear, there is only one man who may hope to face it and live through it; and that is he who has already gone in search of the princess, your sister."

Dareville was about to make reply, when a strange, unearthly, rushing sound was heard, and the words died upon his lips. For that had come to pass which those who knew the foundation for their fears had dreaded. The others also heard the sound, and those who heard it for the first, time opened their eyes and listened in alarm. Wydale and George both recognised it too well. They had heard it before in the mist, hard by that very place.

But none spoke; none, indeed, could speak; for now had supervened a foetid odour of such intensity that the senses reeled and succumbed to its loathsome power. All present fought strenuously against its deadly influence, but in vain; one after another yielded to a sort of physical paralysis. Looking back, afterwards, none could describe exactly the effect produced. They were conscious of a feeling of intolerable disgust—a disgust that grew into horror, as though they felt themselves in the grasp of some diabolical being inimical to man, whose form they could not see.

Dr. Manleth—perhaps the only one there who gave thought at the time to the analysis of his own feelings—afterwards attributed the physical paralysis produced entirely to the extraordinarily powerful and penetrating odour. Be this as it may—whatever the strange power or the secret of its action—there could be no doubt of the effect produced. For here were many strong men, mostly inured to war, men whose bull-dog courage and dashing bravery, in ordinary circumstances, were above suspicion—and among them one cool-headed scientist, entirely sceptical and self-observant—all conquered, rendered *hors de combat* without a blow, and by an enemy they had not yet even seen. It savoured rather of the supernatural, of the fell working of some weird spell of the legendary enchanter, than of a nineteenth century experience.

Meanwhile, the rushing sound came nearer, died away, and then returned. It was like that which might be made by some gigantic bird cleaving the air with great strokes of mighty wings, and circling round, returning again and again in restless, ravenous seeking for prey.

The mist outside grew denser, and the obscurity within the barred gates deeper, for no lamps were usually required in the guard-house by day; and no one there could move or call out to summon one of the guards in the inner chamber to bring a lantern. Indeed, from the cessation of all sound within, it seemed that all were in the same condition.

Suddenly a scream rent the air—a shrill, prolonged, appalling cry that made the blood run cold and the very flesh to creep. It was such a scream as might have been given by the two Gorgons when they awoke to find Medusa, their terrific sister, lying dead and headless at their side. A cry that was the embodiment of hoarse, stifling rage, of demoniacal fury, of superhuman savageness and hate. Soon came a deeper shadow without the gate, a shadow that was not steady, as of coming night, but flickered and wavered, and was accompanied by intermittent rushes of foul, nauseating air, and the sound of the beats of giant wings. Then some great mass hurled itself with a crash against the bars, seemed to seize them and shake them with a strength and will that threatened every moment to break them down giving vent, the while, to its blood-curdling screams which, in the confined space, sounded now like a thunderous roar, and reverberated sonorously in the rock-hewn gallery. Finally the apparition disappeared, the swishing of its powerful wings died down, and, for a space, there was a dull, heavy silence.

But this stillness was not of long duration. The rushing sound was heard again, but at some distance, and at the same moment arose a woman's shriek, followed by a confused medley of the sound of blows, smothered exclamations, and, again, the scream. But now a faint refreshing breeze was wafted in through the barred doors, and the mist began to clear away even more quickly than it had risen. The wind that now came sweeping through the galleries in-creased in force, bringing relief to the unfortunate occupants of the guard-house. Slowly the blood began to flow more freely in their veins; one by one they stretched their arms, yawned, as though just awakened from sleep, and inhaled deep draughts of the pure air that called them back to life, and restored energy to their stiff-ened muscles. Then each one, as he gazed around, glanced sheep-ishly at his companions, fearing looks of reproach or of contempt. But none could throw a stone against his fellow; all had succumbed alike to the insidious, baneful stench.

Then, amid an awkward silence, a call was heard from outside, and Monella appeared, blood-stained and dishevelled, bearing in his arms the unconscious figure of Vanina.

15
Vanina's Rescue

Monella carried his charge into the inner chamber, and delivered her to the attendants of Idelia. Attached to the guardhouse were living apartments occupied by the officers on duty for the time being, and their wives. It was into one of these rooms that Idelia had been taken, and she was only just recovering when Vanina was brought in. At once forgetting her own weakness, she insisted upon aiding in the restoration of her guest, and under her gentle ministrations Vanina slowly revived.

Outside, meanwhile, Monella briefly explained matters to the anxious inquirers who thronged round him, all talking at once in their eagerness to know what had happened. But his first explanation was somewhat brief, and left much of the curiosity of his questioners unsatisfied.

"The maiden is unharmed; she has only fainted. I also am unhurt save for a few scratches, which, with your permission, friends, I will now bathe in yonder stream."

All sorts of questions and remarks ensued. "But you have fought the Kralen?" "What was the result?" "Have you killed it?" "The first man that has ever been attacked and come back alive!" These and other exclamations of curiosity and astonishment resounded upon all sides, the while that Monella calmly strode across to a stream that fell from the rocks not far away, and there proceeded to wash, and, with the assistance of the doctor, to bind up his wounds. An attendant brought a bowl and linen cloths; and into the former Monella put a few dried leaves or herbs, taken from a wallet he always carried with him. These he bruised and mashed in water, then with the liquid bathed the places that had been bleeding, dipping into it also the linen with which he bound them up.

They may have been, as he declared, "only scratches," but some had a very ugly look, and seemed to be pretty deep. From the right shoulder every vestige of clothing and armour had been rent away, and it looked as though great talons had seized upon both arm and shoulder in more places than one. His helmet had been torn off; and his face was bleeding. But most eloquent of all was the scene of the combat when, a little later, his friends inspected it. For the air was now clear, and the sun was shining brightly, though near to setting; there was, therefore, no further danger to be apprehended from their uncanny enemy, which was never abroad, save in either darkness or thick mist.

When they came to the place of the encounter, one picked up Monella's shield, another his great sword, and the third the massive axe he carried in his belt. All bore marks of the contest; both sword and axe were notched, while from the shield pieces were broken away, as though by vicious bites from powerful jaws. The ground and herbage round about were trampled, and in places torn up and marked with scores. But nowhere was there any blood or other token that their enemy had been wounded in the fight. While examining his battered helmet, and endeavouring to adjust what had been bent and twisted, Monella, further pressed, now gave the following account of what had happened

"I heard the maiden's cry, and it brought me to her; for she was then not far away. And I was only just in time, for the Kralen was already hovering over her as she lay helpless on the ground, and slowly sinking through the air to seize her. I could but dimly see the creature through the mist; but its dark mass made a deeper shadow overhead, and the constant motion of the wings stirred the foliage around and blew about the maiden's hair. The movements of the monster were deliberate; it seemed in no way hurried, but hovered as though it felt sure of its prey, and was gloating over it in advance. So does the ichneumon fly hovering over the wretched victim in which it is about to plant the cruel sting that does not kill at once, but consigns to a long, slow agony, and a terrible death. I stood over the maiden and waited till the creature came well within reach, when I struck at it again and again with my sword, but alto-gether uselessly. The weapon glanced off from its skin as though it were covered with hard scales and it was much the same when I struck at the wings. But they were in such constant motion, and the light was so bad, it was impossible to get a fair blow in. So I did my best to injure the wings for flight, by tearing rents in their membranous covering with my sword; but with no effect that I could see, and, while I was thus striking at the wings, I was more or less exposed to attacks from the furious monster's teeth and talons. When I fended these off with the shield, it seized it in its jaws, and shook it as a dog shakes a rat, nearly wrenching it from my grasp, and actually tearing pieces from its edge. Meanwhile, its claws would strike savagely at my body, and landed more than once on my arm and shoulder. They even caught my helmet, and tore it from my head. After a space I began to realise that my sword was useless; that it was a fight in which strength and heavy blows alone would serve. So I threw away the weapon and attacked the beast violently with the axe. Twice did I beat it down to the ground with the rain of blows I showered upon it, and, while there, it tore viciously at the sand and herbage with its claws. But when I would try to rush in to end the fight, a wing would strike me in the face, and for a moment or two obscure my sight, and in that time the beast would recover itself, mount in the air, and come at me again with a rush."

Here Monella paused, and then went on slowly, with a grave shake of the head:

"How it would have ended, had the mist not lifted, I cannot tell you. I fear I should have fared badly; and, if so, then the maiden!—but that is too terrible to think of. By God's providence the fog began to clear; and, as it grew lighter, the effect was marked on my antagonist. I perceived that it was dazed by the growing light, its rushes were now so badly aimed that by merely jumping aside it was easy to avoid them. Evidently the creature, whatever may be its status in the scheme of nature, is one to which light is insup-portable—intolerably painful. It can live only in gloom and dark-ness, or in the semi-obscurity of mist and fog. As the air grew lighter still, the brute gave one final scream, full of baffled rage and spite, and flew off through the mist. I waited a short time to make sure it would not return; then I lifted the maiden in my arms and carried her up the path."

This short and simple narrative of what must have been a terrible encounter was told in a manner so modest and unassuming that it might have been supposed the narrator was merely describing a tussle with a savage dog. And the quiet acknowledgment at the end, that the hero of it could not say "how it would have ended" if the mist had not fortunately cleared, deeply impressed his hearers with a sense of their narrow escape from an awful tragedy.

Presently Wydale spoke.

"There is one thing you haven't explained to us: how is it you were not overcome by the paralysing influence of that awful stench that rendered us powerless even to move?"

Monella smiled, and drew something from his wallet.

"This is the secret," he replied. "Nothing very wonderful. Amongst the odds and ends in the cargo of the *Saucy Fan* I found some samples of this little contrivance. It is a sort of respirator-mask, so contrived that it fits over mouth and nose, and contains a little chamber in which can be placed cotton wool or tow satured with chemicals. Now, for a long time past, I have been experimenting with a substance which I conceived might counteract the deadly effluvium which I knew was given off by the Kralen, and which overcomes the senses of those inhaling it. I believed I had discovered the antidote, but had failed to find or make a suitable medium for its application, till this little contrivance came into my hands. I gather that it is a recent invention of a scientist to enable firemen to enter buildings filled with smoke. It was just what I had been wanting, and I resolved to try it on the first occasion."

Dr. Manleth took the respirator, and examined it.

"And now tell me," then he said, "what is this creature like? It seems to me it must be a kind of gigantic bat. If ever I heard a bat's scream, I heard it to-day in the cry of this beast—only magnified a thousand times."

"I think you must be near the truth," Monella answered, "and yet there was much in the creature that resembled rather a flying reptile than a warm-blooded animal, such as a bat. Bats, too, have not scales, as this gruesome brute seemed to have; I only say *seemed*—I could not see clearly."

"Just so. Still we know," Manleth went on, "that there are vampire-bats; and I may say that bats generally are about as hideous, and many species as savage and bloodthirsty, as any created beings. They are evil-smelling, too, to a degree, and fly abroad only in the dark or gloom; they cannot bear the light. It seems to me that, if we suppose some hitherto unknown species of colossal bats, the mystery is, in part, explained. There would still remain, however, the puzzle of its paralysing scent. It is almost on a par with the power of fascination, which legend formerly attributed to serpents."

"I see nothing in it that cannot be explained on quasi-scientific grounds," rejoined Monella. "There is scarcely any limit to be placed upon the diffusive power of scents. A millionth part of a grain of musk will make its presence known to the organs of smell, and it will affect a hundred persons simultaneously. But that, after all, may be nothing to the power of divisibility of other odours with which we are unacquainted. It may be possible to produce upon human beings, through the sense of smell alone, effects at which science, in our present state of knowledge, cannot even guess."

To this proposition the doctor could find no sound objection, especially since his late experience; and he turned and walked on in silence, as the party wended its way back to the guard-house.

"You have not told us, by the way," the doctor presently again observed, "how it happened that you came upon the scene so opportunely."

"There were two reasons. First, the approaching mist had been seen and signalled by our watchmen; and, feeling a little anxious, I came hither to warn you not to venture outside. Next, I had had notice of an attack to be made to-night on the barge *Princess Idelia*, on its return. I have altered the arrangements, therefore."

"Attack! An attack to be made on the barge!" cried Wydale. "Then we are now likely to see some fighting?"

"I have information," rejoined Monella, with a trace of sadness, "that our enemies are rousing up. I fear we are now at the commencement of another term of warlike operations. If so, we must do the best we can; but it is a prospect that I cannot view without regret, for I love not war and bloodshed."

"And yet," observed the doctor, in an undertone to Wydale, as Monella walked thoughtfully on in front of them, "he is a man whom nature surely intended for a warrior, and not a soldier merely, but a soldier-king, for he is a born leader of men; and, as for courage—well you will remember what I have told you before— and—we have all had a further example to-day. But it is true, all the same, that though he fights like a lion when in the thick of battle, he always goes into it with sadness and reluctance. I am quite convinced that warfare is abhorrent to him; but you would never think so, if you saw him in the midst of it."

"I like him none the less for that," said Wydale.

"Just so. And there's something else; when once the battle is concluded, no one is more ready and willing to help the wounded— even of our enemies. And," continued the doctor, in half-humor-ous perplexity, "I am compelled to admit that he often proves him-self a better doctor than myself. His knowledge of herbs is great. He spends much time, at intervals, in searching for them, and dry-ing and preparing them, and the wounds he treats with them heal in a fashion sometimes marvellous."

"And how were these signals given that warned him of coming fog?"

"By the heliograph. There is heliographic signalling apparatus at the various watch-towers along our line of coast, and the signal-lers are in constant communication with each other. Do you under-stand heliographic signalling?"

"Yes; it is employed continually in our little wars in Africa."

When they reached the guard-house they found the whole party standing at its entrance. Vanina, still pale, advanced quickly to-wards Monella.

"How can I ever thank you for your timely aid?" she exclaimed, seizing his hand.

But Idelia came forward too, and took his other hand.

"Nay, it is for me to thank the Lord, Monella," she declared, with a smile and manner full of grace and sweetness, though her face was wan, and she was trembling still. "He has preserved to me my dear sister; to our nation, their future queen. In my own

name, and in the name of our people, I thank him." Then she gave
a cry at the sight of his bandaged arm; and turned even paler than
before.

Monella was not one given to laughing. His nearest approach
to it was a smile. To-day, however, for a wonder, he laughed almost merrily at Idelia's expression of concern.

"Of a truth, princess," he said, "I am not hurt; and, if I were, I
believe we have done a piece of work this day well worth a little
pain. Look around over this fair landscape, over yonder ruins of a
once noble, happy city! All depopulated, desolated, turned into a
tangled wilderness, by your enemies, aided by unholy alliances with
unnatural monsters! To-day hath witnessed the first stand against
their foul ally. God helping us, it shall not be the last; but the beginning, rather, of the end. I shall not be content until I see your
people restored to their ancient homes, and yonder fertile country
smiling again with golden harvests and blossoming and fruitful
gardens."

A smile that was half glad, half frightened, lighted up Idelia's
face; then it vanished, and, raising her eyes solemnly to heaven,
she replied:

"I can only say 'Amen' to that, dear friend. But how came you
by your wounds? You have told us nothing yet of that; we are anxious to hear all about your wondrous fight."

Then ensued much talk, and many more questions had to be
answered and explanations given. The relics of the combat, the
notched sword, the broken shield, the battered helmet, were
handled and examined by each in turn, amid exclamations of
mingled wonder and dismay.

"These must be preserved," Idelia said at last, "as national memen-
toes of to-day's achievement. And now we would fain return. We
have seen enough to-day of this side of the water."

"That cannot be yet, princess," Monella answered to her surprise. And, in response to her inquiring look, went on, "There is
trouble abroad this evening. You must wait on this side for a while
until I have completed my arrangements. Then you may cross, I
trust, in safety. Meantime there is much still to be seen in our underground domains likely to amuse and interest our friends."

16
A Night Surprise

The series of caverns, grottoes, and underground galleries, called by the inhabitants by the general term, "caverns" or "grottoes," comprised not merely a town or community in itself, but far more. It was an arsenal, a dockyard, a fortress, an impregnable citadel or rocky fastness, and a manufacturing town. It had its workshops, its places of worship, its stores of arms and armour, its museums, its palace, and its marvellous "Grotto of a Thousand Lights," and other underground gardens and resorts. Its rocky passages, running backwards and forwards, often two or three, one over the other, extended several miles. How many miles no one seemed to know, any more than any could tell when, or by whom, the structures had been made.

Undoubtedly, they represented the untiring toil of multitudes of workers, carried on through countless generations with that persistence and stolid disregard alike of time and obstacles that form to-day our chief cause of wonder in contemplating certain ancient works—whether the rock-hewn temples and tombs of India, the pyramids of Egypt, or the mysterious "earthworks" of America. Amongst much that is conjectural, one fact stands out clearly enough about all these monuments of past ages; the workpeople employed upon them must have been reckoned—first and last—by hundreds of thousands, perhaps by millions; guided by a knowledge and skill sufficient to excite the wonder and admiration, and rival the ability of our greatest modern engineers, all the marvellous discoveries and appliances of modern science, notwithstanding.

Hence it was that Monella found no difficulty in amusing and interesting his visitors, until the time arrived when he deemed it safe for them to attempt the crossing back to the harbour. His "visitors," they might all appropriately be termed, since the "caverns" were essentially his particular domain. Throughout the period during which he had been "a sojourner in the land," he had made this curious retreat especially his own. There he had gradually gathered to himself everything he deemed essential to the government of the country and the supplying of its naval and military needs. There he passed most of his time, so much that many wondered how he occupied himself; the more so that, when there, he was invisible to all but a select few, who, whatever they knew, or did not know, gave no hint concerning it. As to this, there were many different theories amongst the people. Some believed that Monella regarded the outcome of the struggle then going on with doubt, and that he was making every possible preparation to fit the "caverns," in case of need, for a last retreating place, from which they could issue forth and harry the enemy, should he succeed in capturing their city and harbour. Others opined that he had discovered a mine of gold or precious stones, and was carrying on secret mining operations, and so on. But, though he did not give his confidence to many, there were very few who grumbled, or grudged him the right to act as he thought best. He had shown in a thousand ways his unselfish devotion to their cause. He was always on hand when wanted, ever ready to fight for them; certainly, therefore, he had earned the right to spend his spare time how he pleased. Gralda, their High Priest and Astrologer Royal, spent his spare time in an observatory gazing at the stars; why should not Monella, if it so pleased him, bury himself at times in the "caverns," gazing, maybe, down into the earth? So the people had grown used to it, and ceased to wonder.

It was nearly two hours after sunset when the state-barge, *Princess Idelia*, issued from the dark portals of the tunnel entrance to the caverns. In front of her rowed two light war vessels, as on their previous trip, and behind her, at some distance, came two more. The barge carried only two large lanterns, and they threw the light in such manner on to the upper deck as to show that there was no one on it. From the grand saloon below came sounds of voices and laughter, and from the port-windows beams of ruddy light. Below this again was another deck, where many rowers, lightly clad and armed, stolidly plied their long, heavy oars. In the phosphorescent waters no vessel could move at night without marking its course, every dip of its oars creating trails of light and for this reason, apart from the lanterns carried by the various craft, it was easy enough to see the procession from afar, though there was no moon and the night was dark.

Slowly, with monotonous lift and dip of the oars, the train of boats moved on, until about half-way across, they passed several vessels lying dark and shadowy on the water. These carried no lanterns; and so still was the surface of the sea, that no little wavelets even plashed against their sides to mark their position by their faint gleams.

Suddenly, just when the *Princess Idelia* came opposite to these dark shapes, the light shining through the port-windows of her saloon, and the sounds of laughter and of song floating from them out on the still night air, the space round the strange craft broke into sparkles of light, as oars dipped quickly into the water and brought their vessels alongside the barge. Silently, but swiftly, they closed round the bows and stern and made fast, then a minute later, crowds of heavily-armed men climbed up on to her deserted deck, and rushed to the stairways to make their way to the saloon. But the hatchways were all closed, and resisted for some time their efforts to break them open with their axes. Meantime, the two vessels that had preceded the barge put out their lights, and one rowed rapidly away into the darkness, while the other remained motionless and almost invisible. And the escort astern, instead of going to the assistance of the barge, turned and made off also.

The lights in the saloon and underdeck of the barge had died away, and below a strange silence had ensued. Only the noise of the hammerings of the assailants on the hatchways, and their savage curses at the delay in breaking them open could be heard, mingled at times with mysterious splashing in the water round about. At last the hatchways were forced open, and the triumphant assailants rushed tumultuously down the stairways only to find—

no one! Not a soul was to be seen; not one of the merry party whose laughter and song had been heard so plainly but a few minutes before. Astonished, the intruders rushed down to the lower deck, only to find that even the rowers had disappeared, and—most surprising of all—had even taken their oars with them!

Then there arose a tumult in the galleys the assailants had just left, and the latter rushed back on deck; they were too late. Their own vessels were in the hands of their enemies, the fastening ropes had been cut, and the galleys were now rowing away from them as hard as they could go.

Bewildered, amazed, maddened with rage, the three score men, who had boarded so triumphantly, stood about the barge in helpless fury. Without oars they were powerless to move the vessel so much as a single yard; and so they hung about her deck, some cursing and swearing, some quarrelling and indulging in mutual recrimination, some shouting to supposed friends in the distance to come to their aid; while others stared blankly out into the darkness, awaiting dejectedly developments. But they had not long to wait. The black shadowy boat lying silent and dark in front of them was joined by first one, and then another, till there were many, all equally dark and shadowy and silent. Nothing could be seen of them save the ripples of light upon the water; nothing could be guessed by the anxious watchers on the barge as to what these craft might be, or what their object. They could not even tell whether they were friends or foes. If the former, why did they not shout, and so declare themselves? If the latter, why did they hesitate to attack them in their present almost defenceless plight? Why did they not pour in broadsides of javelins and arrows?

But their suspense was not of long duration; the explanation of the riddle came when sounds were heard from the strange vessels as of much splashing of oars, and streaks and little showers of light appeared in many places at once, and the *Princess Idelia* began to move. Slowly, at first, but gradually increasing in speed, the barge forged ahead under the irresistible invitation of a dozen galleys with two or three score of stout rowers pulling at their oars, each galley attached to one or other of several stout hawsers that were fastened to the barge. Soon—very soon—the half-hundred or so of fierce warriors in the latter awoke to the almost incredible fact that they were being ignominiously towed, helpless and unresisting, straight into the harbour of their enemies, where in face of the odds they would have against them, fighting or resistance would, of course, be futile.

Then went up a howl of beast-like rage, as the unfortunates realised the situation. A few who had bows and arrows shot wildly in the direction of the rowers, but in the darkness they could see nothing at which to aim, and the arrows did no one any harm. Nor were there many of them, since the majority of the attacking party had left them behind, knowing they would be of little use at close quarters on the deck of the barge. Others, more sensibly, rushed down to cut the cables by which they were being towed, and, deeming the work easy enough, gave a crow of satisfaction at their own cleverness in thinking of it. But they soon found that the hawsers were attached to the bottom of the barge, far out of the reach of their swords or axes. Then good swimmers threw off their armour, and, each taking a sharp knife or dagger between his teeth, they plunged overboard and dived down to the hawsers, at which they cut and slashed as long as they could stay beneath the surface. But, to their astonishment, it was all in vain. The hawsers—there were more than one—as they soon discovered—though not very large, easily resisted all their efforts, and they only notched or broke their weapons. Again and again was this essayed, till, at last, the divers came up disheartened, crying, "Witchcraft! Witchcraft!" What had happened to their ignorant minds seemed a wonderful thing; but the simple explanation was that Monella, foreseeing this move, had taken the precaution to use some steel hawsers he had found amongst the cargo of the *Saucy Fan.*

As to the rest, the matter had been managed simply enough. The barge had carried, instead of the party who had crossed in her in the morning, a large number of men, all good swimmers, very lightly dressed, and armed only with short, sharp swords. These had been instructed in their parts, and imitated, sufficiently well, the songs and laughter of a careless, festive party returning home, unconscious of lurking foes around. No sooner, however, had the armed men in the hostile boats climbed up on to the deck of the barge, than the whole of her passengers, including the rowers, slipped noiselessly overboard, taking with them all the oars. Partly supported by these, they waited about while two or three expert divers managed to cut the lines by which the enemy's galleys were fastened, and the latter then partly drifted, and were partly pushed, little by little, farther and farther from the barge. All the armed men were now on her deck making an uproar in their endeavours to force the hatchways; and the only persons left in their galleys were the rowers, mostly unarmed, who sat watching their friends, too much pre-occupied to notice an occasional light swirl in the water round about them. Suddenly, on every side, men appeared who swarmed up over the bulwarks, and, one standing beside each rower holding a sword to his throat, ordered him to begin to row. The surprise was complete; the enemies' boats were thus captured and rowed away by their own people, while the headstrong fighting men they had brought were busy capturing a deserted barge.

Then other vessels, full of armed men, came up and chased away the two or three galleys of the enemy that had been left around as scouts; and finally, instead of troubling about the enraged foe-men, the barge was taken in tow, as has been described. But, perhaps, the most exasperating part of it all, to these captured ones, was the discovery—presently made—that it was their own galleys and their own rowers who, under compulsion, were towing them thus ingloriously into the enemy's port. When, therefore, they had shot their arrows in the dark, they had, in reality, been shooting at their own friends as well as at the foes who were compelling them to row.

And thus the discomfited warriors eventually reached the harbour. Here were lights, blazing lamps, braziers, flaring torches, and, on all sides, ranks of armed men, and archers with bows ready bent, and arrows aimed at the crowd on the deck of the barge; while upon the walls and towers, and over the archway, others held spears and javelins poised ready to hurl down upon them. The rowers then ceased their work, and the barge brought up alongside a quay.

Around the landing place, in a semi-circle, were drawn up a treble line of guards, and in the centre, at some little distance, could be seen a group that included, among many others, all those who had that day formed the party at the caverns. In the middle were Vanina and her brothers, and Idelia, the last shrinking back when the barge drew near. Beside these were Rokta, Ombrian, and other chiefs while Monella's towering form was conspicuous standing a little aside in converse with Wydale and Dr. Manleth.

When the barge came to a standstill, there was a great shout from the spectators, at which Monella advanced to the front and raised his hand for silence. He carried no arms; only on his left arm was a small buckler of leather and bronze. Ombrian and others stood behind him at a little distance. Standing within some thirty yards of the side of the barge, Monella now addressed the crest-fallen Karanites.

Manleth interpreted to Wydale, in a low tone, what followed.

"Men of Karandis," he called out to them, in a sonorous, ring-ing voice that even those farthest away could plainly hear, "we grant you your lives and gentle treatment. Lay down your arms; surren-der and fear nothing."

For answer, a rough-looking soldier on the deck hurled a spear with such deadly aim that it would have gone through the speaker's throat had it not been parried. But Monella deftly threw it aside with a quick movement of the buckler on his arm, and, when a great and savage howl arose from those surrounding him, again raised a hand for silence. He made no other movement, and showed no sign of anger. Only his eyes flashed, and, when he next spoke, his voice was stern and masterful.

"Men of Karandis," he said again, pointing now to the man who had thrown the weapon, "bind that man, and bring him to me! Ye all know ye can trust my promise, and that resistance is worse than useless. Ye know, too, how differently your king treats any prison-ers he may capture from us. I call on you to throw down your arms!"

For a space, those on board stared defiantly at Monella. A few more spears were even raised in air, and were about to be launched, when Monella turned his glance upon their holders, and, before that dauntless look, even the most militant dropped, first their eyes, and then their weapons.

Few even amongst that rough crowd seemed to care to endure and return Monella's glance. Either they would look down, or turn away, the while that some seized upon the man who had thrown the spear, bound him, and pushed him forward to the front.

"'Tis well," Monella said. "Once more, I say, throw down your arms; ye have my promise, and we want no senseless butchery here."

This time there followed a rattle on the deck, as every man obeyed, and cast his weapons from him. Monella nodded, and signed to some of the guards around to board the barge and bind the captives. Then, with a word to Ombrian, bidding him see that they were not ill-treated, he turned and walked away, heedless of the shouts and cries which greeted him, and rang again and again through the crisp night air.

A little later the captured warriors defiled in batches before Vanina, to whom Ombrian cried:

"Princess! future Queen of Atlantis! Behold your earliest captives! May this result of the first fight since your arrival prove an omen of the victories in store for us!"

And all the populace shouted themselves hoarse in frantic demonstrations of approval.

17
"Alarms and Excursions?'

After the events recorded in the last chapter, Monella's influence amongst the people became more marked than ever. He no longer had cause to complain of want of spirit or of patriotism. So far from that, he was almost mobbed, as he passed to and fro, by aspirants to military employment who begged and entreated to be allowed to enroll themselves under his command. Had all who offered been accepted, none would have been left to carry on the agricultural and other necessary work of the community. Even amongst the last batch of prisoners, a large proportion sent in a humble prayer to be allowed to serve under the man who had so cleverly entrapped them. And, since they were a source of embarrassment to their captors, Monella thought proper to accede, to some extent, to the request. He had them paraded before him, and, passing down their ranks, scanning them with his penetrating glance, he pointed to one here and one there, and so selected about three-fourths of their number. The others he would not trust, and ordered them to be closely confined and carefully watched. And it was afterwards a matter of common knowledge that no one of those he thus picked out belied his judgment.

Needless to say, a great impetus was given to drill and warlike exercises and manoeuvres. Emulation ran high between the several companies of the soldiers and their officers; and every day witnessed assaults of arms, whereat the members of the various troops competed for prizes and other honours. Dareville and Wydale were foremost, both in coaching and training those placed under them, and meeting all-comers in friendly rivalry. Even the

youths and boys were bitten with the warlike fever, and formed a
corps of cadets, of which George was made one of the chiefs. So
perseveringly, indeed, did he take to his new duties, that he speedily became one of the most expert among them in the use of the
bow and arrow, and in single-stick and other exercises. And it was
inspiriting to see his sister's pride when he proved himself the vic-
tor in competition with other boys of his own age.

Meantime, Monella's presage that a fresh era of warlike operations had set in, proved well founded. Almost every day the enemy
made demonstrations in one direction or another. The part known
as the caverns being unassailable, and the harbour and its defences
almost equally so, the Karanites divided their attention between
attempts to surprise and capture isolated boats, and landing parties at various points on the shores of the island in the hope of
finding a weak spot in which they could establish themselves, as a
base for fresh incursions. In the encounters that ensued, there were
many stubborn fights; and at times two or three would be going on
simultaneously at different points along the shore line. And though
in every instance the invaders were eventually driven off; the victories were by no means bloodless, as in the case of that which had
opened the campaign. On the contrary, many of them were san-
guinary and ferocious in the extreme. Many fell on both sides, and
still more were wounded. Among the latter were nearly all the leaders, including Monella, Rokta, Dareville and Wydale, and, curiously
enough in every case, the wounds were received in protecting
Vanina, who insisted upon joining in the conflicts, and herself en-
couraging the soldiers. Clad in helmet and breastplate, or light
chain armour, she went about amongst the ranks, now inspiriting
the fighters, anon kneeling beside the wounded to help bind up
their hurts, and speak words of comfort or of praise and thanks
for their devotion.

Small wonder that she speedily became almost idolised by the
soldiers, or that they were soon imbued with a deep conviction that
Heaven had indeed sent them a warrior-queen to lead them on to
victory. Sometimes, in the very height of the fray she would catch
Wydale's eye fixed upon her with a perplexed, inquiring look,
whereat she would toss her head, her eyes would flash, and her lips

curl into a smile in which a certain haughtiness and half-defiance were mingled with a flush, that showed she was not indifferent to the criticism his glance revealed. To Owen, at this period, her conduct was not only a constant puzzle but a source of pain; for, while he saw much he could not help admiring, he was also conscious of a gradual change in her demeanour towards him which filled him with foreboding.

In her enthusiasm, Vanina frequently exposed herself to danger with a recklessness which was perilous not only to herself, but to those around her who were ever watchful to defend her. In this Rokta and Wydale vied with her own brother and with each other; and each, in turn, as stated, was wounded, and compelled, for a while, to retire temporarily from the field. And, since they were not the only ones who owed their wounds to shielding her, Monella found himself at last compelled to interfere to put some restrictions on her actions. More than once, indeed, he himself had been constrained to rush into the thick of a hard-fought scrimmage and lay about him with his great sword or heavy axe to rescue officers, whose peril had been brought about by Vanina's rash though well-intentioned zeal. After that he decided that in future she must refrain from active participation in the fighting.

So the edict went forth, and henceforward Vanina had to content herself with watching "the battle from afar"; afterwards calling for those who had specially distinguished themselves, that she might praise and befittingly reward them. It was remarked with wonder that she herself had escaped without a scratch, for amongst their foes were many of savage instincts who would as soon have slain a woman as a man. Sooner, probably, in her case, in that they looked upon her as a witch. It was even said that some had sworn to give their lives to "kill the witch," believing that victory would not smile upon their side so long as she was alive to encourage her soldiers and support them with her sorceries.

Some two months passed in this desultory warfare, which at last became harassing and exhausting to all concerned. In the main the result was decidedly in favour of Monella's troops, thanks greatly to his generalship. As in the night surprise, with which the campaign had opened, he constantly gained the day by his strategy and resourcefulness. No matter what were the circumstances, he seemed ever ready with some new ruse to play off upon his opponents. One day, in feigned retreat, he led them into a quicksand that lay near the seashore, where their heavy armour quickly sank many of them beyond the help of those of their fellows who had stopped in time upon its brink. He built an outlying fort or blockhouse in an isolated spot beyond the fortifications, and put into it a garrison and stores. Soon the Karanites laid siege to it; then another troop of the Dilandians, as Monella's men were called, attacked the besiegers; but only to be driven off and chased. But when the Karanites returned from their pursuit, they found the garrison had slipped away in their absence. Thereupon they entered and took possession, and, finding good stores of wine and food, made preparations for a permanent stay, as a base for future operations. They sent for reinforcements, and more and more men crowded in; then the whole building fell with a mighty crash, burying three-fourths of them in its ruins; while the few who struggled out of the wreckage were set upon by their watchful foes, and killed or taken prisoners. For at the time of the building of the structure it had been undermined; and when the garrison went out of it, they left it upheld only by temporary supports hidden under the ostensible foundations; and these gave way under the increased weight of a more numerous garrison. On another occasion, when a party of Karanites, having effected a landing, were engaged with an equal number of Dilandians, in a fight which lasted for some time without advantage to either side, a number of Karanite boats were seen in the distance apparently with reinforcements. At that the Dilandians withdrew, pursued closely by their foes, who followed them some distance inland. But when the latter returned to the shore, after another profitless chase, they found their own vessels in the hands of Dilandians; for the supposed reinforcements had been one more of Monella's stratagems. He had utilised the vessels he had previously taken, and despatched them to the spot by a circuitous route, flying their own captured banners, and filled with Dilandians dressed in the purple uniforms stripped from captured prisoners. In this affair again, a considerable number of both galleys and men were taken with but trifling loss to the Dilandians.

In these and other ways Monella gained numerous small victories, until at last his enemies became either too wary or too much discouraged to trust themselves in further forays. And for a while there was again an informal truce or lull in the hostilities.

So far, Monella's policy had been almost wholly a defensive one; he had contented himself with keeping open communication between the caverns and Dilandis, and repulsing descents upon the line of coast. There were very few engagements on the water, and nothing was seen of the great armada. He had, however, utilised the time in preparing for a grand counter-attack, and he decided that the moment was now near when he could assume the offensive, and carry the war into the enemy's country with some prospect of success. The lull that ensued was, therefore, but the calm before another storm, and over the city of Dilandis there came a sort of hush of expectation. For, though Monella's plans were known only to himself and the two or three who were in his confidence, yet it was a matter of common knowledge that some kind of decisive stroke was about to be attempted.

Some there were who were disposed to think that Monella had too long delayed offensive action. They were all thereby, they objected, subject to constant harassing attacks, while their foes passed the time at home in peace, free from alarms, or raids, or invasion. Then again, there was little if any fish to be obtained, for no fisherman could venture far from the shore; and the Dilandians trusted in great part to fish for their food supply. These and many other trials and inconveniences were added to the hardships and suffering that fighting always must entail; and, after a time, they had induced some grumbling. Moreover, many, no doubt, were disappointed at finding that no particular advantage in the way of fighting had accrued from the many wonderful things that—as they had been told—had been brought in the "big ship" the strangers had arrived in.

As to this, even Wydale and Dareville sometimes wondered what use Monella proposed to make of some of the articles they had brought amongst the cargo of the *Saucy Fan*. There were the fireworks, the steam launch, the small cannon, the rockets, and so on; no use had been made of any of these. So far as their own revolvers

were concerned, they had reserved their small supply of cartridges
for grave emergencies. Only a few times had they brought their
pistols into use, and then it had been to save their own or some
other's lives; but then the effect on the enemy had been instanta-
neous and remarkable. On two or three occasions the use of the
weapons had turned the tide of battle when it had been going
against them, and sent their foes off in headlong panic just when
they had deemed themselves sure of victory. The moral effects, too,
were considerable, and in the end caused both the new-comers to be
regarded by the other side with an almost superstitious dread. But
the two, on their part, only longed the more for two or three rifles
and a few hundred cartridges; for then, as they were never tired of
saying, "the whole business could be ended, and King Kara brought to
his knees in a jiffy," whatever that period of time might precisely be.

One thing much surprised them in this connection; they heard
nothing of Durford and his companions; and they frequently wondered what could have become of them and of the rifles and other
arms they had carried off from the *Saucy Fan*.

As to social matters, all had made good progress in the language of the country; and come to know, and form friendships with,
many of the inhabitants. Their relative positions, however, had very
considerably altered—at least as regarded Wydale. For between
Vanina and Prince Rokta a close friendship had sprung up—one
that seemed daily to grow closer, while the relations between her
and Owen became proportionately colder. In Vanina's frequent
intercourse with the army or the hospitals, Prince Rokta was ever
her principal companion. She conferred with him upon all matters
in connection with the operations in which she took an interest, so
that they were constantly to be seen together. Wydale, as a consequence, seemed to grow more and more moody and discontented.
Indeed he was in worse case than that; for he was a prey to con-
tending passions, and had to chew, as best he could, the cud of
bitter disappointment. He had, from the first, fallen deeply in love
with Vanina; and, up to the time of their arrival in the place, had
had every reason to feel hopeful. But now she seemed to have no
further thought for him. Whether it was that her head had been
turned by the position into which she had so unexpectedly been

thrown, or that she had been smitten by Rokta's undeniably handsome face and figure, and his singularly graceful manner, Wydale
could not decide. He knew only that she had altered, and that his
chances of ever winning her seemed to be daily lessening even to
vanishing point. It was in vain he tried to console himself with the
reflection that she was a heartless flirt, and therefore unworthy of
a true man's love. The reflection did not help him to repress his
passion. And to do so was rendered ever more difficult by the fact
that in all other respects he was constrained to admit that he admired her more than ever. She had proved herself, in actual warfare, to be possessed of all those characteristics that he had dreamily attributed to her, in fancy, long before. Had he not said that
she seemed born to be a Warrior-Queen, one to lead men into
battle, and to hearten and encourage them in the thick of the fight
with her own rare courage? And had she not justified all this—and
had she not done so, moreover, without losing one jot of her womanly instincts? This had been shown and proved in many ways; by
her thoughtful care for the wounded, by her ready sympathy with
those dear to them—their wives, or sisters, or children. And at
home, at the court receptions, it was strange to see how completely
she could throw off the martial air, and become again the fascinating, though ever dignified and queenly woman, winning golden
opinions on all sides by her gracious kindliness to every one around
her. It was at these times, more than at any other, perhaps, that
Wydale would be sensible that he loved her more than ever; and
feel bitterly resentful towards Rokta, who—as he conceived it—had
deserted the beautiful, lovable girl he was engaged to, to enter his
(Wydale's) own particular "preserve"; to try to carry off from him
one which he had almost come to consider his own.

Meanwhile Idelia, who shrank from all association with fighting and warfare, save tending the wounded, secluded herself for
much of her time in her own apartments. She was even often absent
from the evening receptions and other functions; and when she
did attend them, everyone noticed that she appeared pale and careworn.

One day the smouldering feud between Prince Rokta and
Wydale broke out into an open quarrel.

Wydale, strolling aimlessly through the palace, and having nothing particular just then in the way of military duties to attend to, came across Idelia seated at a balcony that looked out over the city and the sea beyond the island. He was struck with the sadness that he saw written in her face and attitude; and, feeling in dismal mood himself, he sat down by her, and asked in a kindly way what was the matter?

Slowly she turned her eyes on him, and asked, in turn:

"Why do you suppose that anything is the matter?"

"From your manner, princess, and your face. I have been long enough here to be able to tell when you feel happy, and when distressed. We have all met with so much kindness at your hands that I should be ungrateful indeed, if I did not feel concerned when I see that you are unhappy."

"Who can be happy," asked Idelia, "in the midst of so much suffering? For such a long time now every day, every hour almost, brings us fresh affliction, news of the wounding or death of some of our people. I fear now even to look out from the palace, as I used to, over our country, lest I should hear suddenly the outcry and the shouts that tell that men are struggling to maim and kill each other. There is nowhere I can go, unless I shut myself up in some underground vault, to escape from all these troubles."

"All that I understand," returned Wydale, with a sigh; "yet I fancy, princess, it is not the sole cause of your growing melancholy. Affairs were much as they are now before we came; indeed, they were worse; for, at least, since we have been here, the position of your people in the warfare has improved."

"Yes, that is true; but—I had hoped, you see, that all this would have come to an end before."

"I know. I would say, however, that I think we are now near the end, and that a little time will see the finish. And yet, princess," Wydale continued, looking at her earnestly, "I fear the cessation of hostilities will not bring back the colour to your cheeks, or the merry laugh to your lips, that so charmed us all when we first came here."

Idelia glanced at him for an instant, but said nothing, and turned her gaze dreamily upon the distant landscape.

"I should be sorry to think, princess," Wydale went on, "that our coming amongst you had brought you trouble instead of the surcease of sorrow you had looked for. I should deem it a misfortune, indeed, if the time should come when you should wish in your heart that you had never seen the *Saucy Fan* and those on board of her."

At this Idelia buried her face in her hands and burst into tears.

"I don't like to say anything," she sobbed out, "but things seem somehow to be going wrong; and I do not know what to do to put them right. I have no father or mother to advise me, no friend—"

"No friend?" said a voice behind her; and the two looking round, espied Monella, who regarded them intently. "Say not, my daughter, that you have no friend while I am within call."

Idelia brightened up a little and responded:

"I know that, good friend. You must think me ungrateful to seem to have forgotten you, who have done so much for me and all our people. Yet you have so many things to think about, that I should be selfish to weary you with my troubles."

"Why so?" returned Monella, "if you can share them with newcomers?" and he looked at Wydale with so keen a glance that the latter felt embarrassed. "I hope, however," he went on, "that we have better times in store for us; and better times may bring more cheerful thoughts. In any case, keep up your courage, my daughter, and your faith, and all may yet be well." With that he turned and left them.

Wydale, to turn the conversation, took up a more enlivening theme.

"There is quite a refreshing breeze to-day," he said. "What a pity we cannot go for a sail."

Just then Prince Rokta, coming by, stopped when he saw the two together. His brow clouded; he hesitated, as though undecided whether to speak or to pass on. Then suddenly making up his mind, he said, with a laugh that was slightly forced:

"And what are you two discussing with such seriousness?"

Wydale looked at him calmly, and replied: "The weather."

Rokta flushed up and answered brusquely:

"I think not. People don't commonly discuss the weather in such serious fashion."

"Don't they?" returned Wydale coolly. "Perhaps you know best. But is it of the slightest consequence?" and with that he turned away, affecting to be interested in the view before him.

Rokta started, took a step forward, then swallowing his anger with an effort, walked away without further comment.

During this little episode Idelia had said nothing, and now made no reference to it.

Wydale had some further talk with her, chiefly about the prospects of the expedition Monella was then planning; but, finding that she was in no mood for conversation, he was on the point of rising to take leave of her, when Rokta returned.

"Still on the weather?" he asked sarcastically.

"No, indeed," replied Idelia, "not this time. We were discussing our prospects in the coming battle."

"It seems to me," said Rokta, "that this gentleman would do better to be in his place looking after his duties in preparation for that battle, than idling away his time with you."

Wydale sprang up.

"How dare you, sir?" he exclaimed. "I am not subject to your orders. Is it not enough that I have fought, aye, and bled, too, in your cause—a cause in which I have no personal interest—but that I must put up with insult in addition?"

"If you talk of insult," retorted Rokta hotly, "there are two sides to *that* question. Your whole manner and bearing towards me, for some time past, have been but covert insult."

"And what about yours towards me?" demanded Wydale. "How much longer do you suppose I shall endure your supercilious airs?

At this, Rokta put his hand on his sword and drew it; Wydale instantly did the same, while Idelia sprang up with a cry of fear.

18
A Great Naval Battle

Before the terrified Idelia could make up her mind what action she should take to prevent the duel that seemed imminent, Monella had again come into the apartment, and the princess stretched out her hands to him appealingly. He quickly gauged the situation and strode between the disputants.

"How now?" he asked, looking with unusual sternness from the one to the other. "Prince! Wydale! Have we, then, no longer foemen to fight, that we must begin to quarrel amongst ourselves? I never thought, prince, to see you draw your sword on one who is your guest, and your people's; who, moreover, has done such service against your enemies. And you, my friend,"—addressing Wydale—"is it fitting that you should thus attack one of the leaders of a people that have received you kindly, and treated you with honour?"

Both the hot-headed young men looked somewhat ashamed at this rebuke. But, when Monella inquired what the quarrel was about, they remained obstinately silent. Neither cared to avow what each knew to be the actual cause; while the ostensible one was too trivial—as they both well knew—to lay before Monella.

Since both kept silence, Monella turned to Idelia and inquired the truth of her.

"Indeed," she said, "there was no cause that I know of."

"Well!" Monella said, addressing the two, and with a touch of irony in his tone, "since there is no matter in dispute of sufficient importance to be imparted to the friend of both, I trust I may express a hope that matters will proceed no further."

Both sulkily sheathed their swords, Rokta addressing Monella thus:

"I have no wish to quarrel; but he knows how he has offended me. Let him say the word and the matter is at an end."

"I have neither said nor done anything that needs apology," responded Wydale; "the matter rests with him."

"Well, we can talk it over another time, my Lord Monella," concluded Rokta; and with that he walked away.

Idelia also went away; and Monella, left alone with Wydale, looked inquiringly at him, and shook his head.

"It is all very well to reproach me, as your looks appear to do," Wydale burst out, "but that man's manner to me lately has been more than I can bear. You know," he went on, with emotion, "how he is behaving. And you know, or guess, my secret. Before we came here I had ground for hope that—well—what does it matter what I hoped? It is all done with; and, of course, I have no right to interfere, perhaps even not to open my mouth. But, when I see Prince Rokta flirting, as he notoriously does, with one for whom I have a high regard, and see further what is plain to all, that he is breaking the heart of one of the most tender-hearted, sweetest women— when I see all this, and I remember that I am all the time fighting for his country, it is more than I can bear to take his insults patiently. In fact," he burst out recklessly, "I'll fight no more in such a cause." And, with that, he unbuckled his sword, took from his arm the armlet which was the insignia of his rank and the post he held as officer, and flung them into a corner. "Let them give me," he continued, "what is due to me for my share of the cargo of the *Saucy Fan*. With that I can keep myself, I suppose, in this country, until such time as we may be able to get away from it."

Monella looked at him and sighed.

"This is not well, my son," he answered, gently. "Have you then lost all faith in Providence?" "What would you have?" asked Wydale, moodily. "You cannot surely call upon me to go on fighting but to aid in my own undoing?"

"What I would suggest, my son," returned Monella, kindly, "is that, surely you will not let it be said that you shun the fight?"

"I tell you I will fight for him no more," Wydale rejoined, obstinately.

"Then fight for *me*," replied Monella, laying his hand on the other's shoulder. "If, as you say, we are ever to get away from here, there is much to be done; and you must help. Henceforth you shall be with me and help me alone. Surely you will not refuse me that?"

Wydale took the hand held out to him, and pressed it.

"I should be ungrateful, indeed," he said, "if I refused anything you ask of me. Command me always. For you I will even once more fight."

It is but fair to Prince Rokta to observe that, though he had refused to be the first to say a word to make up the quarrel, he secretly acknowledged to himself that he was somewhat in the wrong; and, from that time, was careful to give Wydale no further cause for offence. He was a well-disposed young fellow, with instincts such as we should term gentlemanly and straightforward. The only representative left of one branch of the ancient kings of Atlantis, as Idelia, a distant cousin, was of another branch, he had been brought up with somewhat exaggerated notions of his own importance, and was on that account inclined to be at times haughty and impetuous. Nature had endowed him with such graces that the wonder is that he was not more conceited than he really was. Perhaps the warfare in which he had been engaged more or less for many years had not been without some good effect; he had come to respect courage and bravery in others, and had learned that in hard fighting all are very much on an equality; that hard knocks are pretty equally divided between prince and peasant.

Therefore, it had come about that Rokta could not justify, even to himself, the line of conduct he had pursued towards Idelia and Vanina; therefore, also, he could understand Wydale's animosity. Once, too, in the thick of a fight, when Rokta had been hard pressed, and it had seemed impossible that he could come out alive, a bullet had come whizzing past and laid low his chief antagonist, just when the blow that would have slain him had been about to fall. And Rokta knew that Wydale had expended for him one of those cartridges which were more precious in that land than diamonds of the same size. Not that soldiers think much of such occurrences, or keep debtor and creditor accounts of the times they save each other's lives in battle. But Rokta had not forgotten; moreover,

at heart, he liked and admired Wydale for his quiet, sturdy courage, and felt inwardly sorry that he should have had good cause
for his feelings towards him.

"And yet," said Rokta to himself, by way of consolation or justifi-
cation, "admiring her, as I know he does, he can scarcely blame
me for having fallen under her spell." It was a lame excuse, as he
knew; and he endeavoured to make some amends after the quarrel
by behaving with what he considered magnanimity towards his rival.
He treated him, when they met—which now was seldom—with such
studied friendliness and courtesy that Owen, bitter as his thoughts
still were, could find no excuse for continuing the quarrel. And,
since neither he nor his rival said anything, and Idelia and Monella
preserved equal silence about what had happened, no one outside
those four so much as suspected that there had been any quarrel.

Even Sydney Dareville knew nothing of it, for Wydale, somehow, although on very intimate terms with him, shrank from making
a confidant of him as regards his feelings towards his sister. Sydney
had always seemed proof against the fascinations of the other sex.
Nor was he likely to interfere or remonstrate with his lively but
often imperious sister.

Probably, had Wydale laid his case before him, and solicited
his good offices, he would have been met with, "Fortune of war,
my boy; fortune of war. He who ventures on slippery ground must
expect a fall sometimes;" or some such comment. Moreover,
Sydney, for the first time, was said to have a little affair of his own
with one Inonia, a very bewitching lady of the Court, who had been
specially told off to attend his sister; thus, between that and his
military duties, he had little time for anything else. Indeed, some
went as far as to say that the dashing soldier, with his gay, mercu-
rial temperament, was such a favourite amongst the ladies of the
Court that this little flirtation was not the only one in which he
was involved.

One morning at daybreak, a great fleet of galleys and other vessels moved out of the harbour of Dilandis and proceeded, drawn
up in battle array, in the direction of Karanda, King Kara's capital.
The sides of the vessels had been raised by the addition of an upper
work of sheet iron, which formed a protection for those on board,

and almost hid them from sight. But for this, it would have been apparent not only that the vessels did not carry so many fighting men as usual, but that what they were wore scarcely any armour. Even their heavy shields had been left behind, the iron screen raised above the bulwarks being deemed sufficient for their protection. All sails and banners had been discarded, and the masts reduced in height to make the boats lighter and enable them to carry less ballast. The procession rowed slowly along the coast, here a great wall of precipitous cliff that rose almost perpendicular from the sea. At one point it attained the dimensions of a small mountain of crystal rock, that glittered and sparkled in the sunlight. Beyond this, the rocky wall continued as before, until there could be seen against the sky-line the towers and minarets that marked the city of Karanda, the object of their attack. From a distance the place was not unlike Dilandis. There were great water-gates, ramparts dotted at intervals with watch-towers, fortifications of stone running along for some distance on both sides of the harbour; while in the background rose hazy, purple mountains that soared up, steep and inaccessible, almost to the clouds.

Beyond the walls and ramparts could be seen the upper portions of stately buildings, temples of curious design built on a colossal scale, with mighty towering columns, palaces with pinnacles that glinted in the sunlight as though of burnished gold. From some of these ascended spirals of light blue smoke that drifted lazily away into the distance.

When the Dilandian fleet had approached within half a mile, the great water-gates swung open and showed within a swarm of vessels that at once came out to meet it. They issued forth with beat of drum and blare of trumpet, and amid the shouts and cheers of the crowds that had gathered to see them off. Emerging from the harbour gates, they spread out to right and left, adopting a crescent-shaped formation that extended farther and farther as more and more vessels poured out of the harbour and Pushed forward to the centre of the line.

All displayed sail-banners, richly worked in purple and silver, and hung on masts that glistened as though themselves of silver. The prows and sterns stood high out of the water, and on the former

were figureheads of dragon-like monsters, somewhat after the fashion of those on Chinese junks. The hulls were silver and ivory white,
with a broad purple band running from end to end and following
the shear of the vessel's build. The high ends were filled with armed
men, and the sunlight flashed and sparkled upon their armour and
arms, upon burnished helmet and breastplate, and polished spears
and shields. Overhead were pennons and streamers of varied
colours that were shifted constantly, no doubt signalling orders
and answering signs from one vessel to another.

This was the great armada of which there had been in Dilandis
so much talk and not a little fear, but of which nothing had till now
been seen. Certainly it made a glittering and imposing array, and it
outnumbered the Dilandian vessels by about two to one. The craft
themselves were also, on the average, larger and more massive-
looking; and they carried, in the total, probably three times as many
fighting men.

Altogether it looked as though the attacking fleet would stand
but little chance against the powerful force opposed to them. Apparently the Dilandians were of that opinion, for they no sooner
saw this armada advancing towards them, than every vessel put
about and headed for their harbour, the Karanite fleet following
them with shouts, and cries, and jeers.

It afterwards appeared that the readiness of the Karanites to
come out and offer battle was due to the fact that Monella had despatched to them, three days before, a notice of his intended visit.
He had sent back, in a small boat, two prisoners with his challenge.
The Karanites had at once decided to take it up, and had hastily
set to work to give the finishing touches to the armada they had so
long been making ready.

It looked as though the Dilandians, when sending their challenge, had under-estimated the force of their opponents, and that
now, having found out their mistake, they were anxious to regain
the shelter of their harbour and fortifications. At all events they
rowed away as if for dear life; and their antagonists rowed after
them with triumphant shouts. It was soon plain that the pursuers
were gaining steadily on the pursued; and, by the time the leading
vessels of the latter had come abreast of their harbour, the gates

were seen to be closed, as though those left in charge had either laid aside their usual vigilance, or had closed them in a panic against their friends. There being no time to wait for the gates to be opened, the Dilandians had only the alternatives of remaining to fight, and continuing their flight past their own city and round the island.

They chose the latter, and the triumphant cries of their pursuers became a frantic roar as they urged their boats along, vying with one another as to which should make the first capture of the flying vessels. Men armed with whips stood over the toiling rowers, and the cruel lashes cracked in the air and descended here and there upon the weakest and those who showed signs of flagging. And the perspiring oarsmen, thus urged, tugged and pulled at the long sweeps with savage energy; the oars made swirls in the water, and splashed it around, as they dipped into it with powerful strokes, and the vessels plunged forward with jerks that told of the frantic efforts that were being made. But in spite of all exertions, when they passed between the city of Dilandis, on the one side, and the caverns, on the other, the boats they were chasing, having far lighter loads to carry, now steadily kept their distance in front, and even began to draw away from their pursuers.

Suddenly—just when the last of the Karanite line had passed—the water-gates that shut in the entrance to the caverns opened, and there glided out a new antagonist, the sight of which filled with astonishment and fright those of the pursuers who were near enough to see it well. To them it looked like an uncouth and hideous monster, making its way, at an amazing speed, along the top of the water, without fins, or other means of locomotion. Its shape roughly resembled a great fish, and the part visible above the surface showed a body and back round and smooth as that of a whale's, large glaring eyes, and great jaws which kept opening and shutting with vicious snaps that could be heard hundreds of yards away. This appalling creature started in pursuit of the Karanite fleet, tearing through the water at a speed that threw up showers of spray in front, and left a long track of foaming, dancing waves behind it. It gained upon them rapidly, and when it came nearer, there could be heard, besides the fierce snap of the powerful jaws, another sound, as of a savage beast that panted and snorted with impatience to seize its prey. The Karanites in the rearmost galleys, when they saw this apparition rushing through the water after them, were seized with horror and affright. Some wildly fired arrows at it; but they only glanced off from its sides and fell into the sea. When it came nearer, others launched spears and javelins; but always with the same result. Then, when it was close astern, some hastily threw off the heavier pieces of their armour and leaped into the sea; others, more panic-stricken still, sprang overboard as they were, and sank beneath the waves to be seen no more. As to these timid ones, it must be remembered that they had in their own country the dreaded Kralen, and had therefore good reason for believing in the existence of all sorts of dreadful monsters. Others, of tougher fibre, stuck to their posts, and kept their weapons in hand, determined to attack the monster fiercely when it should close with them. But this it did not do. It swerved when it came nearer, and dashed past at a distance of two or three feet. Taking no notice of those in the vessel, it bit its way savagely through the oars, breaking them all off short; then it raced on to catch up the next boat, which it treated in the same strange fashion. In this way it overtook all the vessels of one line of the Karanite fleet, snapping off their oars on the one side; then, turning round, it returned down the line on the opposite side, breaking off the oars on that. Then, taking no notice of the fighting men on board, or the missiles they launched at it, it attacked the second line. At the end of half-an-hour every boat in the Karanite fleet had been crippled by the loss of its oars; and, when spare ones were put out, they also were snapped off. There being no wind to fill the sails, in less than an hour nearly the whole array were drifting helplessly and aimlessly about, unable to either move or steer. The exceptions were two or three stragglers that had managed to make their escape in time, and were not considered worth following up. It was thought desirable that one or two should take home news of the unexpected, terrible disaster that had overtaken the rest of the expedition.

Meantime, the Karanite fleet lay motionless and helpless upon the water. Those on board the different vessels chafed and fumed, and, no doubt, cursed and swore in Karanite. They looked around them in absurd dismay and helplessness, wondering what was to come next. But what was most humiliating, and drove them almost to the verge of madness, was the fact that the Dilandian fleet ignored them; or, at least, exhibited a deliberation and indifference which were as galling as unexpected. They merely surrounded the helpless vessels, keeping well out of bow-shot, and then rested on their oars. To the Karanites this was more exasperating than an attack, in which, at least, seeing that their boats were of greater weight and their fighting men better armed, they might expect success. But the Dilandians appeared to be in no hurry, and the two fleets remained for some time watching one another in very strange, unwarlike fashion. Then it became apparent that the Dilandians were waiting for some further development of their plan, for, though resting idly on their oars, they looked expectantly, but silently, towards the cavern gates, while the Karanites, lately so full of jeers and cries of triumph, sat equally silent and expectant.

And now came into view the cause of the delay the gates of the cavern opened, and there came forth, towed by three or four boats, the *Saucy Fan*, but no longer the *Saucy Fan* of old. Instead, there towered up a great mass, a colossal, mastless barge; and shortly great sweeps were thrust out from her sides, whereupon the towing boats drew off. To the smaller boats about her, the vessel appeared like a Triton amongst minnows. Taking her masts away had raised her much higher out of the water, since she now required little or no ballast to fit her for her new duties in the sheltered waters around Atlantis. And her actual height above the surface of the water had been further added to by a breast-work of loop-holed iron plates. Slowly, majestically, she approached the Karanite ships; the great sweeps that urged her forward worked with the precision of machinery; she carried no flags or colours, nor could a human being be seen upon her decks. But as she neared the foremost of her enemies, a tall form rose slowly into view above the bow, and Monella, looking calmly down upon the crowded decks of the galleys ranged in front of him, hailed them through a speaking trumpet.

"Men of Karanda," he called out, "yield ye! Yield ye now, and quickly, or take the consequences!"

For answer there came a shower of arrows, which he quietly threw off from his shield, then he disappeared. The desperate Karanites shot more arrows, and hurled their spears and javelins in vain against the iron-bound sides of the approaching vessel. Slowly, but relentlessly, she came on; and now shouts and howls went forth from the helpless

Karanites when they perceived and realised her object. But all their yells of rage and cries of terror and despair were useless. The *Saucy Fan*, advancing with irresistible power and weight, crashed into and rode clean over the smaller vessels in her path; and lo! nothing was left to mark her course but the tops of two or three masts and banners slowly sinking beneath the water, and struggling men, trying vainly to swim, but borne down by their armour. A few, indeed, had thrown it off in time, and now made desperate efforts to climb the sides of the *Saucy Fan*, or to force their way into the port-holes from which the sweeps ran out. But the sides of the vessel were as smooth and slippery as glass; the ports were too small to climb into; a few hung on in desperation to the sweeps, whereupon arrows and spears were hurled upon them from the deck, and they quickly sank to rise no more. The *Saucy Fan* passed on; and each time she came to a vessel, or a group of them, the same demand for surrender was heard, and, if refused, was followed by the same result. But one group of the Karanite vessels, being better provided than the others with spare oars, now came towards the *Saucy Fan*, and, in answer to the order to surrender, rowed round her and tried to shoot at the rowers through the port-holes. These vessels contained the elite of the Karanite fleet; all the principal officers were gathered there, and they had resolved to make one last desperate attack. But they met with even a worse fate than the others, for, instead of arrows, spears, and javelins, there now came hurtling over the bulwarks a storm of fiery missiles that filled them with astonishment and fright. They were, in fact, a shower of fireworks—crackers and fizzing squibs, fiery wheels and serpents, and plunging, hissing rockets, spreading panic and dismay amongst the crowded decks on which they fell. But worse even than this was yet to come, for now streams of petroleum were poured forth. Jets, thrown from hydropults, fell upon the blazing fireworks, and upon those standing near them; in a few seconds the boats took fire, and hapless creatures, with blazing clothes, leaped madly into the water. Two galleys made an attempt at a last savage revenge, purposely bringing their burning vessels alongside the *Saucy Fan* in the hope that she might be set on fire and perish with them. But this manoeuvre was easily defeated by the sweeps, which prevented their approaching her; and, when they frantically strove to break the sweeps up with their axes, they were found to be metal-covered, and to resist all their efforts. And still the *Saucy Fan* passed on, as though in dignified contempt, leaving behind her wrecks and struggling men and cries of despair and rage. The Dilandian galleys closed with the remaining Karanite boats, and the people on board them having, for the most part, no more fight in them, yielded without further struggle.

An hour or two later, a triumphant procession returned to Dilandis, bringing with them more than half of the Karanite fleet that had sailed out that morning, in such brave array. And their triumph was the greater, and the more welcome, inasmuch as it was an almost bloodless victory, so far as their own side was concerned. Thus ended the great and decisive naval battle.

19
King Kara

When, the following day, Monella's fleet once more sailed out
and approached the city of their enemies, they were met by a galley bearing on its mast a triangular flag, the three sides of which
were respectively purple, white, and green. This meant, in those
parts, a flag of truce, and signified that King Kara was desirous of
a parley. The galley brought, in fact, a letter for Monella; it ran
thus:

> "Since it has been written that thou wert to prevail
> against me, oh stranger chief! I fain would crave permis-
> sion to approach the rulers and council of thy nation with
> overtures of peace. I know that thou wouldst not trust thy-
> self in my capital, but I am willing to visit thine, if thou
> givest me thy safe permit. Send me thine answer, and, if it
> be well, expect me three days hence. Kara."

To this epistle a reply was sent acceding to the request, and
promising protection to King Kara and his chief officers during
their visit to Dilandis. And three days later, an hour before noon,
a small procession was seen approaching the harbour, and soon
afterwards King Kara and a dozen richly dressed followers landed
at the quay, and made their way through long ranks of the populace and soldiers, who had drawn up to see them pass to the palace.
In the dress, especially in the armour worn by these strangers, there
was a marked difference in style and workmanship from that prevailing in Dilandis. Their helmets were square at the top instead

of round; they were more richly damascened; the plumes that waved above them were of purple, and the prevailing colour of the dresses was also purple, relieved in some with black, and set off with precious stones worked into many strange devices. Certainly they made a brilliant show, all fine-looking, handsome men, but haughty in their carriage, and in some cases not too well-favoured, notwithstanding their undoubtedly attractive figures. In due course, they were received in the Hall of Audience, where Vanina, Gralda, Prince Rokta, Monella, and the other members of the Court were gathered.

Into this brilliant throng, King Kara walked with the air of a conqueror come to receive homage rather than of a defeated monarch sueing for peace. He was a finely formed man of upright build, with a face that had a curious, almost fantastic beauty. His age it was difficult to guess. He might have been a rather grave-looking man of thirty; or a hale and vigorous man of fifty. There was in his soldierly bearing a mingling of kingly dignity, with a consciousness of suppressed power. His demeanour was marked by unusual grace and polished ease; but perhaps his eyes were the most striking feature of his personality. Dark, piercing, glittering, they seemed to partake of a characteristic of the Romany race; to have the power of looking through, and beyond the person upon whom they fell, as though they could see there something undiscerned by others. In the glance with which he swept the room, and took in all around him, there was a suggestion of contempt. Yet when he smiled, his face took an expression that would have rendered him attractive, almost fascinating, in any company. His glance moved on until it rested on Monella, on whom it remained fixed with curiosity, and certainly with strange intensity, for perhaps half a minute. Then, with the slightest possible smile, he turned his look upon Vanina. She had been watching him with interest and sparkling eyes, her face flushed, and her bearing proud and full of queenly dignity. But at his gaze she paled, then shivered and drew back; almost, indeed, she seemed to reel as though about to faint. But he only bowed low, and thus addressed her:

"I have no need to ask before whom I bend the knee. There can be but one being called Vanina, and her I surely see before me!"

This was said in the language of the country, which Vanina now spoke and understood fairly well.

She was about to frame a reply when Prince Rokta, who was beside her, interposed:

"We are not assembled here to-day, King Kara, to hear compliments, but to listen to thy petition for peace. Thou hast sought this interview; say what thou hast to say as shortly as may be."

Kara looked haughtily at the young man, smiled slightly, and again there came into his eyes the suggestion of contempt.

"Truly I have come," he replied, "to sue for peace; but I see no harm if I express by way of preface my appreciation of the heroism and courage which, as I know, have been exhibited by this most noble lady, and to which, indeed, it is reported your people owe no small part of the successes they have gained. I have come to-day to propose a peace; I acknowledge that it will be of no avail for us to carry further these hostilities. Therefore am I ready to submit to reasonable and just terms of settlement. Doubtless you are already prepared with them. If you will state them, I will listen; and, if they should be just and reasonable, I will accede to them."

Here Monella and Gralda, who were seated a little apart, conferred together in a low tone; then Monella rose, and, addressing Kara, said:

"We have no wish, King Kara, to impose harsh terms. It would be in our power to demand a large indemnity, and to enforce it. We are in a position to carry fire and sword throughout thy realm, and retaliate upon thy people the suffering and misery that thou hast inflicted upon the inhabitants of this island. But we purpose to do no such thing; we desire only that there be no more bloodshed and to live at peace in future with our neighbours. Prisoners of war shall be exchanged, although we have many more of thine than thou hast of ours. We must have, in addition, full guarantees for thy good faith. There must be no possible ground for fear that thou wilt not keep to the terms of the bargain to be made. Further, we think we have it in our power to be of service to thy people, and to save them from that tyranny of thy priestly government which has called for a heavy roll of victims, and cast gloom and misery over the survivors. Therefore, we desire to know, art thou willing to undertake that all human sacrifices shall henceforth cease throughout thy land?"

At this King Kara hesitated; he looked at Monella, and from him to Gralda; whereupon the latter rose, and, with an air of grave dignity, addressed him.

"It had been our wish, oh King Kara," he began, "to impose on thee and on thy people conversion to the true religion of the one great God. And we have given much thought to the question of our duty in this regard. But, being justly of opinion that it becomes us not to force our religion upon others at the sword's point, but rather to induce them to embrace it by the force of our example, and the blessings they will see around us in their future intercourse with our country; we are willing to forego the immediate fulfilment of this our great desire. We are willing to confine our terms to those stated by the Lord Monella. If we cannot righteously insist upon your people changing their religion, at least we can, and do insist, that human sacrifice shall cease, and that thy people shall be free to come and go in thy land without being oppressed by the shadow of this great horror. Say, art thou willing to comply with this demand? If so, the rest is easy."

King Kara raised his head, and in a clear voice, that rang through the hall, replied:

"So far as regards myself, I have no wish that it should be otherwise. My difficulty will arise when I endeavour to enforce these terms. The power of the priests is great in my land, and a large section of my subjects might side with them against my will. But I will do my best; more than this I cannot promise."

Then followed speeches and arguments as to many points of detail; at the end of which, Monella, Gralda, and others of the chief councillors and officers of State, retired to consult together, leaving Kara and his attendants to await them.

In the council chamber there was a long and anxious conference. Monella had been strongly in favour of insisting upon the Karanites formally abandoning their heathenish religion. He pointed out that such a change would constitute the only true basis for a firm and durable peace. He feared, he said, that otherwise, ere very long, when the Karanites should have recovered from their

defeat, their priestly advisers would urge them on, and with success, to a fresh hostile outbreak. But the other councillors were
disposed to be satisfied with a cessation of human sacrifice; trusting that the rest of what they all devoutly wished for might be
brought about spontaneously.

Upon one point, at any rate, Monella insisted firmly, and that
was that King Kara should be required to give hostages for carrying out whatever terms might be agreed to. "Otherwise," said he,
"What security have we that he may not treacherously seize upon
some of our subjects unawares, and deliver them over to his priestly
friends, the first time he has reason to fear a hostile step from
them?"

When, therefore, a short time later, the councillors returned
to the Hall of Audience, bringing with them the written terms of
the proposed treaty, Monella, before handing it to King Kara, thus
addressed him:

"Here, oh king, are the terms upon which we have decided; but,
before I hand them to thee, let it be clearly understood that we
shall not be content to trust to thy word alone for their performance. We require *guarantees*; and these guarantees must take
the form of hostages approved by us. It is useless," with a wave of
the hand, when he saw that Kara was about to reply impatiently,
"it is useless to discuss this point. We are resolved, and if thou
wilt not comply, we are prepared, and firmly resolute, to take our
guarantee ourselves, by carrying on the war until we have taken
possession of thy city, and can dictate our terms in thine own palace.
Choose then, oh King Kara, between these alternatives."

During this speech, Kara's eyes had almost seemed to flash forth
fire, so furious was he. If looks could have annihilated, he would
certainly have slain the man who so addressed him then and there;
but of this Monella took no notice. Undoubtedly there had been in
his manner, during his address, that which clearly indicated that
he placed little reliance upon Kara's promises, and was assenting
to the moderate terms proposed against his own inclinations. There
was, to the bystanders, something almost of mystery in the looks
exchanged between these two. Kara glared at Monella, as might a
savage wolf at a lion, while the lion, on his part, looked back upon

the wolf with indifference, and as though he were almost beneath his notice. Many present wondered; for it was the first time, perhaps, they had ever seen Monella display such marked contempt towards anyone.

But whatever Kara thought, he managed to swallow down his rage, and, assuming an air of good-natured remonstrance, he replied:

"The great Chief Monella is pleased to speak with some discourtesy; he distrusts my kingly promise; it shall be seen in the future whether this is a just position to assume towards me. I will give you all reasonable guarantees, and hostages you can approve. In fact," bowing to Vanina, "if your Queen will receive her, I will send to your Court as hostage, among others, my sister the Princess Morveena."

At this there was a buzz of surprise throughout the hall, and Kara gave a glance at Monella, and then at those around him, that was full of a quiet triumph, as might a man who has scored an unexpected advantage in a difficult game. And the expression on Monella's face showed that the proposal was both unexpected and distasteful. Possibly he had reasons of his own for not wishing to see the sister of King Kara established at the Court, whether in a sort of honourable captivity, or otherwise. But the suggestion commended itself to the other members of the council; they looked upon it as an undeniable evidence of Kara's *bona fides*, and they intimated their willingness to accept it. Thereupon, the draft treaty was handed to King Kara, and he was invited to retire with his companions to an apartment in which they could discuss the details privately.

During their absence the assembly broke up into groups, and the buzz of conversation became general. Idelia, who throughout the interview had been seated beside Vanina, now rose, and drew her on one side.

"I do fear and distrust that man," she said to Vanina, with a shudder, "and, from what I have heard about his sister, I feel convinced I cannot like her. I hope she will not visit us on any terms whatever."

Idelia glanced inquiringly into the other's face but Vanina, instead of answering, gazed dreamily from the window; and Idelia turned sadly away. For a long time she had been depressed, not to say sad, in her intercourse with those around her; but towards Vanina she ever exhibited affection, though it might not be of so demonstrative a character as at first. Now, just when Idelia was walking away, Vanina suddenly seized her arm, and, pressing closely to her, said, in a tone and manner new with her.

"Do not go away, Idelia! Do not leave me! I, too, do not—oh! but what am I saying?" she broke off; "I know not exactly what is the feeling that has taken possession of me. I only know, dear sister, that I want you not to leave me now. There is something in your presence that imparts a sense of safety."

Idelia's large, truthful-looking eyes opened wide on her in innocent surprise. Vanina had spoken hurriedly, almost hysterically; the first time, probably, she had ever displayed emotion of the kind since her arrival. And Idelia marvelled while she walked beside her, and led her into another room, where they found themselves alone. There, to her astonishment, Vanina sat down, and, burying her face in her hands, broke into tears. Idelia, leaning over her, kissed her gently, and entreated to be told the cause of her distress. But Vanina for some time only shook her head and continued to weep. After a while, becoming calmer, she addressed Idelia:

"No doubt you are surprised to see me thus. You cannot be so surprised, however, as I am myself. Never before, I think, in my life, have I been thus affected; something tells me I have cause for fear of the unknown—a fear I know not how to fight against. And something whispers to me that, if I fear, it is because I am not *good* enough to resist an evil influence. If I were *good* like you, dear little sister, I should have no cause for this dread that is upon me!"

Idelia comforted her tenderly, and led her to her own apartment, where they remained long in confidential converse. And they were seen in the Court no more that day.

When King Kara returned to the Hall of Audience, the first thing he did was to glance round inquiringly, and a slight touch of disappointment in his face showed that he noted the absence of Vanina and Idelia. This did not escape the notice of Prince Rokta, who, throughout the previous interview, had eyed him keenly and even anxiously. Perhaps he was a little jealous of the other's physical gifts; for, undoubtedly, Kara's was an extremely attractive and even fascinating personality. Even Rokta's courtly grace and almost perfect figure lost something of their former charm beside the power of this new-comer. Rokta's graces became, indeed, but mere boyish beauty compared with the matured perfection of a man evidently born to please. And Kara seemed to be well aware of this, and comported himself accordingly, with an air of self-confidence that impressed the younger man, in spite of himself, with a feeling of inferiority.

The negotiations and discussions being presently ended, Kara now conversed freely with those around him, and this he did with a graciousness, and a sort of kingly condescension, that won on almost all about him. Only in the presence of Monella did he show any sign of being ill at ease; but Monella had left the Court, and appeared no more during the king's stay at the palace. But King Kara's advances towards Prince Rokta were received with such marked coldness that he turned away with an air of contemptuous indifference. Later in the day, the terms of the treaty having thus been settled, Kara and his companions were invited to a banquet as a pledge of mutual goodwill, and there he made himself popular amongst the assembled guests by his wit no less than by his *bon-homie*. Thus it came about that, when they went down to the harbour to re-embark, they were escorted by many of the notables with such evident friendliness that the populace caught the infection of the good impression he had made, and, good-naturedly forgetting all their grievances, gave him a kindly reception and a hearty send-off.

Thus ended King Kara's first visit to the Court at Dilandis, a visit that was fated not to be the last, and to be of supreme importance to all concerned.

Henceforward, Dilandis became a different city. Men put off their armour and returned to peaceful callings. The fishers took up their abandoned occupation, warehouses and bazaars were re-opened for the transaction of business and trade intercourse. Ploughs were started, men were set to work to clear and open up once more, for cultivation, tracts that had been given over to a rank growth of weeds.

Throughout the land industry was resumed on every side, and the people set themselves quietly to work to make up for all the time that had been lost, and the drain upon the resources of the country that the long war had entailed. Everyone became cheerful and hopeful, and turned his thoughts to peaceful work. Only a few vigilant men were detailed by Monella to watch the coasts, to make sure that they were well-protected against any treachery on the part of their late enemies.

20
Princess Morveena

In the days of peace and calm that followed upon the ratification of the treaty of peace, intercourse quickly sprang up between the two peoples so long at daggers drawn. Boats went to and fro between the harbours of Karanda and Dilandis, carrying goods and stuffs, making short stays, and bringing back cereals, provisions, live stock, and merchandise in return. The gates that led from the cavern were thrown open so far as to allow of a passage way into the interior of the island, and people passed freely to and fro, and wandered about amid the ruins of ancient Atlantis and in the "Grottoes of a Thousand Lights." But all other parts of the caverns were kept shut off, and closed to everyone save a few of Monella's chosen workmen.

Many an excursion was planned to the ruined city, and many a gay picnic took place amid the time-grown monuments of a remote and unknown past. Many a brilliant fête was held in the wonderful grottoes, which now often resounded with music and song, perhaps much as of old. Amongst those who most often visited the ruins were Wydale and Dr. Manleth, the latter especially seeming never to tire of studying the place and of trying to spell out the stories of past ages dimly revealed by the moss-covered stones. Here they wandered, frequently accompanied by George, upon the ground of their first meeting with the Kralen, but safe now from the fear of another such visitation. Steps were taken to reclaim the surrounding country, which had become overrun with a rich, tropical growth that, in many places, defied attempts to penetrate it even for purposes of exploration. Nor was rank vegetation the only

obstacle, for some parts absolutely swarmed with deadly snakes
and other noxious reptiles.

Wydale and the boy were also now able to revisit the bay in
which they had first anchored the *Saucy Fan*. Accompanied by
Idelia and others, they rowed along its shores, and told again, in
greater detail, their adventures on their first arrival.

And now often came over to the Court, King Kara, who avowed
his desire to do all he could in a friendly manner to cultivate the
confidence of his new friends. He soon became a familiar figure at
the receptions and other functions of the Court; and he so managed to ingratiate himself with his former foes that he became quite
popular. True, there were some who stood aloof, and watched this
new development with coldness. Monella, Gralda, Prince Rokta,
and some others, maintained a state of self-restraint; but Kara
seemed to take no notice of their evident luke-warmness, and
steadily to devote himself to proving that his professions were sincere. One of his first acts was to present some curiously wrought
pieces of jewellery ornamented with gems of extraordinary lustre
and value, to Vanina, Idelia, and many other members of the Court.
Marvellous specimens of the jeweller's art were they, such as won
the admiration of all who saw them. Vanina, indeed, so greatly
admired that given to her, that at once she hung it round her neck.
She regarded it, perhaps, as a sort of trophy or token of the triumph she and her friends had been so largely instrumental in pro-
curing. Idelia, on the other hand, received the one presented to
her coldly; she put it away, and it was no more seen.

Then there came a day when an appointment was made for King
Kara's sister, the Princess Morveena, to make her first appearance
at the Court; and to reside there for a time in accordance with the
stipulation that had been made. But matters had progressed so
rapidly that, though she came ostensibly as a hostage, she was, in
fact, received and treated rather as an honoured guest than as a
sort of honourable captive.

On the day of her arrival a festival was inaugurated, a gala day,
when every endeavour was made to mark the occasion as an auspi-
cious event. Once more the Hall of Audience was thronged with the
elite of the city; members of the Court put on their richest attire in

honour of the occasion. Once more Vanina, Idelia, Gralda, Prince Rokta, and others, sat in their chairs of state to receive the expected guests. And when King Kara appeared, leading his sister by the hand, cordial shouts of welcome were heard on every side, as she stepped forward and, falling on one knee, with a wondrous graciousness of demeanour, half-laughingly kissed the hands of Vanina and Idelia, "in token of homage," as she put it, "to those who had conquered her country and yet had shown themselves such kindly vanquishers." And then, when she drew herself up and looked proudly round, a buzz of admiration went up at sight of her queenly bearing and the remarkable beauty of her face and figure. There was a strong likeness between her and her royal brother; the same cast of features, the same flashing eyes, and the same dignity of carriage. Her beauty, indeed, was something to observe and ponder over; and even those who were least disposed to welcome her could not refuse a tribute of admiration to her outward charms and grace of manner.

Standing thus, gazing with an expression half-haughty, half-appealing, her glance fell upon Owen Wydale, who was standing observing her intently by the side of Monella, Manleth, and a group a little apart. When she looked at him she gave a slight start, and then, after shifting her glance for a brief space, turned to observe him a second time. But now Vanina rose and, descending from the dais, said:

"Princess, do us the honour to seat yourself beside me, that we may show you our welcome is sincere."

And as she led her to her seat, King Kara followed them with a peculiar expression that was remarked and wondered at by a few who were observantly looking on. Then he was invited to seat himself beside his sister.

That Morveena had made a great impression in this her first appearance at the Court of Dilandis was beyond a doubt. Everyone was delighted with her; her wild, picturesque beauty gained the homage of many hearts; and in the festivities, in the dance, and in the song, she gained fresh admirers. For she was gifted with a thrilling, magnificent voice of great power and compass, and remarkably well-trained. She had other gifts, too, which excited further approval and surprise; and she was soon even more popular than her brother. Sydney Dareville, in particular, did not conceal his admiration; even Prince Rokta, inclined as he was to be moody at the growing friendliness between King Kara and Vanina, seemed inclined to yield to her fascination.

But, during the dances and what followed, it somehow came about that she was frequently to be seen either dancing or walking about with Owen Wydale, to whom she was particularly gracious; so much so that Dareville subsequently rallied him upon the fact. This was when, the assembly having separated, they were walking together on the terrace, breathing the cool air that floated across the water, and watching the lights spread out beneath them.

"I never thought that you were given to flirtation, Wydale," he said, laughing, "but you have scored a success to-night. *I'm* not in it; nor anyone else that I can see. For once you have certainly put even Rokta's nose out of joint; and I could see that he was quite surly about it."

Wydale sighed.

"I wish, Sydney," said he, "that you would not talk in this strain; you must be well aware that there is no foundation for it. Certainly I cannot but see that this new star that has flashed upon us to-night is, in many ways, a wonder. She interests me, and I wish to study her; but it is a study of a kind that you do not understand. Probably you would not understand it any the more if I tried to explain myself; and, indeed, I don't know that I could."

At this Dareville laughed still more.

"All right, my friend," he said, "call it what you like. You may call it 'studying people'; *I* should call it downright flirtation, to say no more."

"I wish," Wydale went on gravely, "instead of talking in this frivolous fashion, you would help me to study her and her brother. I can't help thinking that they are here to play some game of their own. And unless I very much mistake, Monella thinks so too, though he keeps his own counsel and says nothing."

"All right, Wydale," assented Dareville, with another light laugh, "call it what you please! Study away as much as you like; I won't poach upon your ground." And with that, despite the other's protests against his suggestions, he went away, still laughing.

After that Princess Morveena remained at the Court, where she soon became a well-known character. Few there were who could resist her when she chose to make herself agreeable. With Vanina she speedily became great friends; but Idelia remained cold and unresponsive to her advances.

King Kara's visits were repeated; and frequently he and his sister and Vanina, with a few more, made up water parties, or arranged short excursions; and in the evening dances they were the most conspicuous figures.

During this time Dr. Manleth was able to give more time to the laboratory he had established than when his attention had been occupied with the wounded. It was said that he was engaged, amongst other matters, in trying to manufacture gunpowder. Indeed, he had produced small quantities, but so coarse and roughly made as to be of little use, except in the small brass cannon taken from the *Saucy Fan*. He managed, however, to manufacture some "meal" powder, with which, and the aid of other chemicals available in the place, he made some very passable fireworks to amuse the populace, and add to the entertainments at the evening fetes. In this work George took a lively interest; indeed, he showed such aptitude for chemical experiments that the good doctor took him into his laboratory and started him on a course of serious scientific training. Wydale also devoted a portion of his time to his tuition, saying it would be a thousand pities that he should be allowed to idle away his days. And so, between the two, the boy was making good progress in studies likely to be of service to him in his after-life.

One day something happened. King Kara came over to pay a visit, bringing amongst his attendants a stranger they had not seen before. He was dressed in an unusually gorgeous costume, with shining breastplate and a helmet surmounted by a blazing golden plume, and a visor that partly concealed his features. Wydale, from a little distance, observed him attentively; there was something incongruous about the man. To his mind the stranger's bearing was altogether out of keeping with his dress. There was an exaggerated swagger, mingled with a looseness of demeanour, that did not denote either the trained soldier or a man used to the ways of a Court. Moreover—at least, so it appeared to Wydale—he seemed to avoid his scrutiny; and, looking farther and more narrowly, Wydale was struck with the idea that they had met before. He mentioned his thoughts to Sydney Dareville, who happened to be near him, and who at once turned his attention to the new-comer, and for a short time watched him carefully. Then he drew Wydale to one side, and burst out laughing.

"Don't you recognise him?" he asked; and when Wydale stared in return, he added, "I've spotted him, I'll wager!"

"What on earth do you mean?" asked Wydale, in surprise.

Dareville laughed again; and then, bending over towards the other, said, almost in a whisper:

"It's Peter Jennings!"

Wydale started back and stared still more.

"Peter Jennings!" he repeated. "What! the ship's carpenter? One of the crew of the *Saucy Fan*?"

Dareville nodded.

"The same," he said. "That's Peter Jennings, late ship's carpenter in the crew of the *Saucy Fan*, and in the employ of the firm in which I claim to be a partner. But what in the world he's doing here, and in that extraordinary disguise, is more than I can even guess at."

Wydale thought a moment. Then a light broke in on him.

"Why!" he exclaimed, "of course, it is. How blind I have been! I knew there was something familiar about his cut; but, for the life of me, couldn't make out what."

"What we want to know," said Dareville, "is how it came about that he should have been one of the rascals who deserted us. I always had a better opinion of him."

"So had I," agreed his friend. "We must get him alone and question him, and see what he has to say for himself."

And this was managed a little later, and then they found it was indeed Peter Jennings. And very sheepish and foolish he appeared, when he took off the helmet with the golden plume, and faced the two young men. Despite the fact that they meant to question him severely about his share in the abandonment of the brig, they found it impossible to restrain their laughter when they looked at him.

Peter Jennings was a tall, thin specimen of a Deal boatman. He had a hard, tanned face, with grizzled hair and beard, and the straddling gait and lurching swing peculiar to his class. At one time he had been a boat-builder and shipwright; then a longshoreman; after that he had shipped on board various vessels, and seen much sea-service as ship's carpenter. Finally, he had drifted on to the *Saucy Fan* in the same capacity.

Imagine such a man, a thorough type of his class, dressed up in a suit that would have made him look ridiculous in a pantomime, carrying sword and dagger, and helmet with waving golden plumes, trying to give himself all the airs of a grand official of the king in whose service it now appeared he was.

"Hush, gentlemen!" he said, looking uneasily around, and with a comical look of apprehension on his face, and raising his hands in deprecation, "for the sake of heaven do not give me away. Mr. Dareville, Mr. Wydale, sir, as there is a heaven above, I swear I had no hand in deserting you. They gave me something to drink in my grog that sent me to sleep, and, when I woke up, I found myself in the captain's boat; and they told me as how you had shoved off in another."

"Well, Peter," rejoined Dareville, "we are willing to listen to an explanation; and shall only be too glad, if you can satisfy us that you were not an accomplice in that nefarious business. Still, as you can understand, it is a matter that does require an explanation; and a very clear one, too."

"For my part," put in Wydale, "I never had any reason to believe that you were a bad lot, Peter. Indeed, I do not forget that I should have fared badly, that day, out on the jib-boom of the *Saucy Fan*, if you had not given me your help."

"Aye, I be afeared you would, sir. Howsomdever, I don't take no account about *that*. I saw you was in trouble, an' I did my best to help ye out of it; an' very glad I was to see you come back safe and sound with the poor laddie."

"But how came you to be mixed up with such a rascally lot?" asked Dareville.

Peter sighed. "Ah, that be a long story, sir; but this I can say, that when I came to find out what they was like, I felt main sorry, and wished I were well out of it."

"But why," persisted Wydale, "if you were not one of their set, did they not leave you behind with us?"

"I scarce know myself, sir, unless it were that they thought I might be useful to 'em. I be handy, like, on board a ship, you see, sir."

Dareville nodded.

"Ah, yes; now tell us what you know about it."

"Well, you see, sir, it were like this—they carried me away, and, when I come to myself, we was off the island here. Then it come out there'd been a big mistake somewheres. I know now, from what I've learned since, that they had planned to desert the brig and row off to a ship what had been behind us all along—"

Dareville started.

"What!" he exclaimed, "that craft that was following us day after day?"

"You've just hit it, sir. That were the vessel."

"I told you," said Dareville to Wydale, "that there was something suspicious in that vessel's following us as she did. Now, Peter, what was she, and what was the plot between the two?"

"As I've learned since, sir, she were a sort of filibusterin' boat carrying arms and stores to some part where there were a row goin' on against the Government. Like enough it were Cuba, for all I knows. But the crew of the *Saucy Fan* was nothin' more nor less than a lot of rough fellows as was formerly in the slave trade, as I now knows, an' they was going out to join in with some insurgents. Mr. Blane, as I believes, begging your pardon, sir" (looking at Dareville), "had his own reasons for wishing to lose the *Saucy Fan* with all you aboard. So it was arranged that she should be left entangled in the Sargasso Sea, and that the crew should escape in the boats an' be picked up by the vessel that was following her. But it didn't come off; because they lost theirselves in a fog that come up quick, an', instead of making the friendly vessel, they drifted into a current that brought 'em here. Some on 'em had got at the liquor an' were very drunk, an' they managed to capsize one of the boats, an' lose everything they had aboard, including the rifles and arms they had brought with 'em from the brig. The men in the boat what upset managed to scramble on board the other one; but everythin' else was lost, except your revolvers and some cartridges which that bullyin' brute Foster had took possession of and put aboard t'other boat."

Dareville and Wydale nodded meaningly at each other.

"Then," said Sydney to Wydale, "when they came to attack us that day on the *Saucy Fan*, they had no arms after all "

"That were just it, sir," replied Peter, "and very much put out they was to find as you had pistols. I heard afterwards as you'd got 'em back from Foster; but they didn't know it then."

"I said at the time," laughed Dareville, "that it was a game of bluff on *our* part, and so it seems it was on their side as well as on ours."

"That it were, sir," assented Jennings. "It just upset their little game."

"But where are they *now*?" asked Wydale. "And where have they been all this time?"

Jennings lowered his voice, and almost whispered:

"In prison somewheres, sir, I don't rightly know where; but I've a notion as the priests are sort of fattening 'em up to make food for some dreadful beasts as they sacrifices people to."

"And how, then, was it that you escaped?" Again Peter looked cautiously around.

"Don't give me away, gen'l'men," he almost entreated. "You was talking just now about a game of bluff; well, I've tried a little game of that sort of my own. I made out as how I had built many a ship of war in my own country, and were a big man at it. So they took me on and made me—"

Peter hesitated.

"Chief Constructor of their Navy?" Wydale asked, much amused.

Jennings, holding his helmet in his hand, glanced round him to the right and to the left, and even up to the sky, to make quite sure that no one was within hearing, then he looked at the two, and gave what can only be described as a very comprehensive wink.

"It's just that, gen'l'men," he said, with a dry smile. "But you see they thinks a lot of me, and fancies that I was a great man when I was in England."

"A king in his own country," quoted Wydale, with a smile to Dareville. "However," he went on, "you haven't told us yet how you were captured."

"That were only too easy," Peter answered. "They pounced on us like eagles, and, as we had no arms, of course we couldn't make no fight of it. Howsomedever, I should have fared as badly as the rest, and been shut up in prison, if it hadn't been that their great astrologer, who is called Zanolda, somehow took a fancy to me. What 'as become of them I don't know. Very likely they are dead long ago."

"But why," asked Dareville, "should he take the trouble to pick you out from amongst the others?"

"Of course, sir, that puzzled me at the time, because I couldn't speak a word of their lingo, and couldn't make out what all their jabbering was about. But since then I've picked up the language a bit, and I've heard as how as he said that it was written in the stars that I should be useful to them, and that they were not to harm me. And, when I saw their boats, I made signs as how I could build bigger and better ones than any they had got. So they set me to work, and was so pleased with what I did that they gave me a fine dress to wear, and lots of people to work under me; and we've bin at it ever since." And he looked down with pride upon his gorgeous raiment.

"That accounts for the delay in bringing out their fleet to attack us, I suppose," commented Wydale.

"Jest so, sir. They thought they would have bigger and stronger vessels, if they could gain time. But they kept me in the dark; and I didn't rightly understand that it was you and your friends that I was working against."

"H'm! Well, it's a curious story," remarked Dareville. "I hope it's all right, and that you are talking honestly. Anyhow, for the present, we will give you the benefit of the doubt. We shall say nothing against you, unless we see good cause. But, if you are anxious to keep friends with us, you must do nothing further against us, should this peace not last."

"But why," suggested Wydale, "shouldn't he come over to us altogether? No doubt Monella would find something for him to do.

He is altering and refitting the *Saucy Fan*, and could always make use of a good shipwright."

Jennings eyed him earnestly.

"If you could manage that, sir," he said, "I'd serve yer faithfully. I've heard a lot about this gen'l'man, Mr. Monella. I've heard as how he's a great man, a fine fighter, an' a wise chief. I have heard that much, even over there," pointing towards Karanda, "amongst them as hates 'im. So he *must* be a downright good un; and I'd rather take service under him than where I am, and where, atween ourselves, gen'l'men," looking round cautiously again, "I don't feel none too safe. Not but what," he added reflectively, looking down again at his resplendent costume, "they've treated me very well so far, and I don't suppose," here he paused, gave another admiring glance at his get-up, and the helmet in his hand, then added regretfully, "I don't s'pose, you know, as Mr. Monella would—"

"Dress you up like *that*," said Dareville, bursting into laughter. "*No! That* he certainly would not. However, it is useless to talk further about it now."

Just then some people came strolling towards where the three were talking; so Peter at once put on his helmet, and, drawing himself up, swaggered away, with a grotesque attempt at a military salute.

One day a noteworthy incident occurred. Wydale and George Dareville were rowing in the bay in which the *Saucy Fan* had first cast anchor, when a rushing of wings was heard, and a large crane swooped down and perched itself on the bow of the boat.

"Why," said Wydale, "there is 'Dick,' our crane friend. Fancy his 'spotting' us over here! This is the first time he has ever followed us."

This crane was one of a pair with which they had made friends. In Dilandis, as has already been noted, cranes were made a sort of public pet of. They were trained for many purposes, and some were used as watch-dogs to guard and keep in order flocks of waterfowl of various kinds. And very wonderful it was to see them working. They circled round their charges, taking care that they did not stray too far, and bringing them all home at night, just as well-trained sheep-dogs do in the case of sheep. But there were others which wandered about in a free and easy manner "on their own." Now and then one of these would attach himself to a particular individual, as might a dog in search of a new master, following him or her about, and becoming a very faithful servant and amusing comrade. It was thus that two birds had attached themselves to Wydale, but they had not before followed him so far afield.

The bird now sat gravely on the bow making a curious figurehead, and looking about him with the air of superhuman wisdom characteristic of these birds. Presently the boat touched the sand, and the two prepared to go on shore, whereupon the crane hopped off into the water. There he immediately espied a dainty little fish. His long neck and beak went out like a flash and seized it; but, instead of swallowing it, he dropped it into the boat, and went off after more, which he brought back and dealt with in like manner. All this was done so sedately, and with such an air of friendly interest, that neither George nor Wydale could refrain from laughing.

"If we go on like this," laughed George, "we shall have a good fish supper indeed. What does he suppose we are going to do with them?"

"We'll see how long he'll be before he tires of this little game," said Wydale, "and what is going to happen afterwards."

But the bird gravely and tirelessly went on catching fish, dropping them into the boat until the two grew tired of watching him, and decided to go off on a hunt for oysters. At this the crane, appearing to know what they wanted, abandoned his pursuit and marched gravely at their side, now and then fishing an oyster out of the water and depositing it on the shore for his friends to pick up. Sometimes the bird stalked on in front, at others he dropped a little behind, and would come rushing up in ludicrous haste flapping his wings in ungainly fashion. Then, suddenly, apparently thinking he had caught enough fish for them for that day, he rose in the air, and soon all that could be seen of him was a small black speck in the distant sky.

After this the bird would often find them out in their excursions in the most unexpected manner, no matter which way they

went or how far they sailed. Sometimes he came alone and sometimes accompanied by his mate, and the two birds were always
ready to go a-fishing or oyster-catching for their friends, claiming
but a very small part of the catch for their own share.[1]

Meanwhile King Kara and his sister grew daily more friendly
with Vanina and others at the Court, until one day it was announced
that the Princess Morveena was about to return to her own city,
and that Vanina and her brother Sydney were going with her upon
a visit to Karanda.

Upon hearing this news, Wydale, in some inquietude, sought
out Monella, and questioned him upon the matter.

"The maiden is acting unwisely in thinking of going thither,"
was the reply; "but she is at present headstrong, and will not listen
to the advice of older and cooler heads. I like it not, and fear me
greatly that it will lead her into danger."

---

[1] An interesting instance of a crane's accompanying a hunter on
his daily expeditions is given in Anderson's "Twenty-five Years in an
Ox-waggon," a record of travel and adventure in South Africa. In some
parts of South America, also, it may be noted, cranes are made into
useful friends, and trained to look after the poultry and other feath-
ered denizens of the farm-yard. There they make their authority felt
like vigilant sheep-dogs, and keep order amongst those disposed to
be quarrelsome or to stray too far from home—Author.

21
The Last of the Great Cuttles

It has been said that that nation is happy, which has no history—*i.e.* (presumably), for the time being. If this is true, it applied, certainly, for some months to the group of islands which constitute, to-day, all that is left of "Ancient Atlantis." For during many months that followed the conclusion of the treaty with King Kara little occurred to disturb the peaceful relations of the erstwhile enemies. They traded together, they visited, and even intermarried; and the peace, concluded after so many years of incessant fighting, bid fair to be a lasting one. There was, in effect, free intercourse; everyone from one town was at liberty to wander over to the other, whether bent on business or pleasure, or mere idle curiosity; was free to stay so long as he liked, and to return to his own country when it so pleased him.

Between the two "Courts" the same relationship obtained. At first the announcement that "Queen" Vanina had arranged to visit King Kara and his sister made a great sensation. But when, in course of time, such visits had been exchanged again and again, and no untoward consequence had ensued, public curiosity in the matter died away.

Months passed, and still the relative positions of the two communities remained much the same. King Kara kept to the terms of the treaty, and the inhabitants of the respective islands were daily becoming more friendly, more intimate, and more given to the interchange of commodities. The plans for the reclamation of the country around the ruins of the ancient city of Atlantis were taking form, and projects with this object were considered.

Thus time sped on, and everyone in this little "shut-in world" passed it in various ways, according—like those, doubtless, in the great world outside—as their fancies, or their passions, or their interests dictated.

Between the two Courts, matters continued much the same upon the surface. But Vanina's repeated visits to King Kara's Court, at the instance of his sister, the Princess Morveena, and the growing friendship between these two and Vanina, which was so marked as to be obvious to all observers, was a source of profound grief to two or three at least of the silent lookers-on.

Needless to say, Wydale was one of these; but time sped on and he found himself, perforce, compelled to settle down into a world in which Vanina no longer filled his thoughts. He regarded her, indeed, as lost to him for ever, and endeavoured to find consolation in studious converse with George, his protégé, past and present.

It is a curious little fact in that complex mystery we are fond of generalising under the head of Human Nature, that if a human being, young or old, of generous instincts, once finds himself drawn into a position of protector of one weaker than himself, he cannot afterwards wholly dissociate himself from the role for the remainder of his life. The protégé may prove himself ever so unworthy; he may turn against his "protector" and offend him again and again, but the same generosity that prompted the stronger to help and protect the weaker will intervene, again and again, in favour even of him who has shown himself undeserving of it.

Thus it was that Wydale, having once, at the imminent peril of his life, befriended George, could never afterwards divest himself of a feeling that partook both of love and responsibility towards the boy. Hence his insisting upon his spending a portion of his time with him in study.

So matters went on. George, rejoicing in his youth, in the high position he held in the eyes of all the Dilandians in his rank of prince, and his place in the cadet battalion, in which he was one of the most skilful at single stick, fencing, and bow and arrow, nevertheless submitted himself dutifully to both Wydale and Dr. Manleth, and gratefully accepted the daily routine to which they subjected

him during certain days of the week. And even at other times,
Wydale was almost always his companion; the good doctor remaining immersed in his various researches.

And here it may be stated that his discoveries threw little light
upon the past history of Atlantis. Many different accounts did he
hear and read in ancient parchments that he unearthed, and many
ancient legends did he study. But the first origin of all was lost in
the mists of ages, and he never succeeded in getting beyond a general outline or theory, which may be summed up thus:—The greater
part of the great island of Atlantis had sunk beneath the waves,
the portion now left above water being what had once been the
highest parts—in other words, the tops of the highest mountains.
All the rest of what had once been a vast island continent had disappeared, carrying with it probably not one city, but many, including the real ancient city of Atlantis, the ruins still remaining being
those, he conjectured, of a hill station, or health resort that had
been built up amongst the former mountains of the land. Some
traditions affirmed that there had once been seven kingdoms, each
governed by a separate monarch, but all welded into one powerful
state under the general name of Atlantis. And the many hundreds
of square miles of rocky shallows which lay around the present islands, and amongst which the masses of Sargasso weed brought
down by the Gulf Stream had found a congenial resting-place, were
in reality the higher parts of the submerged continent.

As to the city of Karanda, it had also once, Dr. Manleth concluded, been a town amongst the mountains, and probably the
headquarters of a hierarchy, since it contained temples and other
religious buildings all designed upon a scale of great magnificence.
The doctor repeatedly visited Karandis to inspect these structures,
but was not permitted to see more than the outside; priestly big-
otry jealously guarded the interiors, and he was never able to get
beyond the portals. But, as in the case of the other towns and ruins,
he decided that they were, for the most part, comparatively modern;
rebuildings, that is to say, of structures that had been destroyed in
the great convulsion that had swallowed up everything save a small
portion of the high lands of the country. Then, surrounded by an almost impenetrable maze of rocky shoals, that became quickly

choked with the floating weed, the survivors of the catastrophe
became isolated from the rest of the world and had since so remained.

At rare intervals, some little-understood combination of oppos-
ing currents would force aside the masses of weed which normally
choked up certain deep channels of a steady stream, and would
then pour for a limited period round the group of islands, entering
on the south-west side and passing away through similar channels to
the south-east and north. This, with the movements of some undercurrents, probably due to differences in temperature between the
Gulf Stream and the colder waters of the Atlantic Ocean, prevented
the open water around the islands from becoming altogether stagnant.

Such is a brief outline of the story of Atlantis, so far as the doctor
could unravel it from the materials subjected to his observation.
But though the results may appear meagre and unsatisfactory from
an historical point of view, yet the opportunities his unique position afforded for study of the ruins and monuments, and still more
of the descendants of the people, were not wholly wasted.

For some eight months, only one event occurred that caused
any stir in the community; this was a fight with the great cuttle-
fish that for many years had haunted the waters of the bay in which
the *Saucy Fan* had first cast anchor. It was believed that these great
creatures had in the past been responsible for the otherwise unaccountable disappearance of many of the islanders who had gone
out fishing alone, and had never since been heard of. Their boats
had sometimes been found floating about, empty and deserted, yet
with nothing missing from them except their owners. Of course
these might, in some cases, have been captured by their enemies
the Karanites, but such an explanation could not always be made
to fit all the circumstances. And then, when men began to be afraid
to venture alone, and so went fishing in parties of two or more,
and taking care to carry heavy axes, and to keep them handy for
use, it was not long before reports were made of vicious and resolute attacks by these monsters, on the boats—attacks that had often
been beaten off only with considerable difficulty and danger.

From all accounts the creatures were as cunning as they were powerful and ferocious. They would lurk, motionless and unsuspected,

near the surface of the water, and if a boatful of fishers too strong
for attack approached, it would be allowed to pass; whereas a single
occupant in a boat would be seized and dragged out ere he had
time to let go his oars to defend himself, or could even cry out.

It so happened, however, that for a long period following the
arrival of the brig nothing was seen or heard of these giant cuttles.
Perhaps, after the adventure of the swordfish, and the attack on
those in the vessel—in which one, at least, of the two was known to
have been badly wounded—they became still more cunning. Or,
perhaps, they had made off, in their baffled fury, along the open
channel that then led out of the bay, and, when it became closed
again, could not immediately get back. But, whatever the cause, it
is certain that, after an interval of some months, during which they
were never seen or heard of, they suddenly reappeared upon their
old hunting ground—or rather, water—and signalised their return
by dragging a poor fellow out of a boat and making off with him.

The survivors came in and told their tale with loud expressions
of horror and affright; it was thereupon decided to make a determined attempt to destroy the monsters. From the statement made,
the attack had been so sudden that the occupants of the boat had
had no time even to attempt resistance, or to rescue their unhappy
comrade. Like a lightning flash, "something" had darted across the
bulwarks, twined round the victim, and dragged him over the side
before he could let go his oar, or could cling to anything in the
craft. Then the others had seen a great mass rise above the surface, long snake-like arms were raised twisting and wriggling in
the air, two great eyes appeared that glared at the boat with a look
that froze their blood, there was a mighty plunge, a swirl in the
water, and—nothing more. Then the survivors, seized with panic,
had rowed with all speed away, and returned to the harbour to tell
the terrible tale.

During the next three weeks an organised hunt was carried on,
but without result, till early one morning a boat came in with the
news that one of the creatures had been sighted on the shore,
amongst some rocks on a lonely part of the coast a few miles distant. Some ten or twelve boats quickly put out; most of those on
board wearing the armour that had now been long discarded. This

was to protect them from the crushing power of the long "arms" of the cuttle should they coil round them. Our friends, as well as the doctor, were included in the party.

When the party reached the spot, they saw on the shore a monstrous shape, from thirty to thirty-five feet high, not unlike a swaying balloon held down by gigantic ropes, slowly making its way among the boulders. Every now and then its body bent so far over as almost to touch the ground, then it would recover itself and rise upright again, just as does a captive balloon in a strong wind. On the lower part were two enormous eyes, nearly two feet in diameter, that turned a malevolent glare upon the approaching party. The creature was "walking" (if the expression may be allowed) among the rocks, supported, after the manner of its kind, upon the thicker parts of some of its great "arms," while the others played perpetually around it, reaching out and then withdrawing, on all sides, like hungry, writhing serpents. But these were far more dangerous than serpents, for serpents are armed only with one set of teeth, nor do they attack in groups, nor do we find land snakes of sixty or seventy feet in length, as were these twisting, wriggling "arms." Not only were they nearly three times as long as the largest known boa-constrictors or anacondas, but they were armed throughout their length with "suckers"—some as large as soup plates—each of which could seize its victim as surely as a serpent's teeth; and, in addition, there were great barbed hooks that would pierce the flesh and aid the suckers in retaining anything upon which they had once taken hold. And, as this monster gazed upon its foes, its glance was so suggestive of mingled ferocity, malevolence and strength, that those who looked upon it trembled. The whole swaying, balloon-like form was one mass of quivering rage; waves of irrepressible, inappeasable, overmastering fury seemed to shake it, and the membranous covering of the creature was ever changing colour, being now a dull, sickly green, then a cold ashen grey, giving way, in turn, to a deep violet. And all the while the great eyes that glared and watched had a look of almost supernatural cunning, as though planning some deep and well-nigh unimaginable atrocity that should annihilate its enemies. Such was the monster of the sea and rocks upon which the attacking party stood and gazed, some in perplexity, others in fascinated horror. Its hungry-seeking arms swept a circle of some hundred and twenty feet's diameter,[1] and within that circle none durst venture. Presently it climbed up on to a large flat slab of rock

[1] Naturalists have been constrained, during recent years, to admit the existence of gigantic cuttle-fish, or devil-fish, as they are in most places called by the fisher-folk. There are many different species of the cuttle-fish family, such as the octopus, the squid, the sepia, the calamary, etc., but they are all remarkable in that they possess no skeleton; and they have neither fins to swim with, like fish, nor legs upon which to walk, like crabs and lobsters. Instead, they have a number of trailing limbs, eight or ten in all, called by most scientists "arms," which resemble so many serpents, but are furnished with suckers with which to seize and hold their prey, and, in some species, with prehensile hooks as well. Creatures of this family have been captured, reaching from 25, 30, 40, 50 feet up to 80 and nearly 100 feet in length, and portions of these are preserved in great jars and tanks of spirits in museums in London, Dublin, St. John's (Newfoundland), Halifax, Yale University (U.S.A.), and other places. The largest ever found, up to the present time (1898), was captured off the coast of Florida in 1897. Here is a brief account of it taken from *Chamber's Journal* for August 28th, 1897 ("Science and Art" column): "Part of a large octopus, the proportions of which must throw all descriptions of such an animal by imaginative writers into the shade, was lately cast upon the beach near St. Augustine, Florida. Professor Verril, of Yale University, examined this curious derelict, and believed it to be a distinct species from all known forms, and he suggested that it should be named *Octopus Giganticus*. The part of the creature thrown up by the sea weighed six tons, and it is calculated that the living animal must have had a body with a length of 26 feet, and a girth of 5 feet, with arms 72 feet long, provided with suckers as large as dinner plates." Such a monster, "walking about" on the thicker portions of its arms, as is their fashion, would reach over 30 feet in height, and would present a picture exactly like that here drawn, its total length being, as stated, close on 100 feet. Such a creature, too, is quite sufficient to account for the stories of great sea-serpents. —Author.

some ten feet above the general level of the shore, and there remained, looking the while as if it meditated a spring upon its foes. These involuntarily retreated, doubting how best and safest to attack it. Meanwhile, another boat came up, bringing Monella with Ombrian, Kremna, and some others, amongst them Peter Jennings, who had resigned his position with the Karanites and taken service with Monella. He had resumed his former costume, and now appeared, thoroughly equipped and armed cap-à-pie, for the fray. Monella wore only his breast-plate by way of armour, but carried his great sword and axe by his side. It was a matter for serious consideration how, in the absence of firearms, this formidable monster was to be attacked. It is doubtful even whether firearms, short of a small cannon or an elephant rifle with explosive bullets, would have had much effect on it; for these creatures have no bones that a bullet might smash and so cause limbs to hang useless, and in their "pulpy" bodies ordinary bullets would produce no wound of any consequence. And for men armed only, with swords and hatchets to trust themselves within reach of those long, powerful arms would be an act of suicidal folly. So they hesitated, and consulted, and considered, the while that the creature remained watching them with its great, malignant, cunning eyes, the colours that kept coming and going on its body marking its continually changing passions; one moment full of concentrated rage and fury, the next, perhaps, apprehensive of attack, and desirous of safely reaching the water, where it would be far more formidable even than on land. There was something deeply impressive, almost awe-inspiring, in the creature's unbroken silence. Any land animal would have given vent to some kind of roar or raging scream; a serpent would have hissed, a crocodile have snorted, and perhaps bellowed. But this monstrous mass of quivering rage uttered no sound; only its eyes glared, and its snake-like arms twisted restlessly about hither and thither, seeking a victim to lay hold of.

Someone shot two arrows at it; these, although they caused no wound to speak of, seemed to enrage the creature beyond endurance. It sprang suddenly off the rock, and, almost before they had had time to note its action, was within seizing distance of those nearest to it. As it happened, these were George and the doctor; in an instant they were entangled in the deadly embrace of one of the far-reaching arms that had darted out like a flash to grasp them. It is impossible to give an idea of the agility this unwieldy monster now displayed. Its "arms" darted about so quickly that the eye failed to follow them; a lightning flash is really the only simile that seems appropriate.

Wydale, when he saw George seized, rushed, without an instant's hesitation, to his aid, and Sydney followed him, but only to be themselves enveloped in the same horrible embrace. Then Peter, who carried a hatchet in his hand, courageously ran to Wydale's help; others, fired by these examples, did the same, and thus a general *melée* was precipitated, the like of which has surely never been seen since the days of Laocoon and his hapless sons. The scene that followed was one of indescribable confusion; the monster lay upon its side with two of its limbs fastened for an anchorage to the mass of rock it had just left, while, amongst its other long writhing arms, men, fighting furiously, with loud and frantic cries and shouts, were mixed up in an apparently inextricable tangle. They were drawn hither and thither; two or three, perhaps, bound together—almost as in a bundle—found themselves suddenly dashed against a similar group; or they might be thrown headlong to the ground, while the powerful limbs that grasped them were so tough that, except near the ends, where they tapered off almost to the size of whip-cord, they were impenetrable by both sword and axe. It was one of these fine ends that had just managed to seize George and the doctor; and Wydale had cut them free before they could be drawn far enough for the creature to get a better hold. But, while doing so, he had himself been grasped by two other arms; and now there were perhaps two dozen of his companions in like case.

Suddenly Monella saw his opportunity; all the creature's limbs being busily engaged, he rushed in behind them and attacked the monster's neck. Holding his sword in both hands, with two slashing blows, he made a great gaping wound that laid the windpipe open, and instantly the hold of the "suckers" relaxed, the constricting arms fell away from those upon whom they had fastened, and lay upon the strand with but feeble signs of life. For in these strange creatures the holding power of the "suckers" has its centre in the force of suction in the gorge and body, and if the windpipe be either laid open or compressed, the "suction" immediately gives out. For the same reason the monster could no longer keep its hold upon the rock it had grasped for leverage, and thus, though it made efforts to turn and seize Monella—who continued to hack at the wound, making it, each moment, larger—it could only twist itself about slowly and convulsively, so that it was comparatively easy to avoid its nerveless attack. One last act of revenge, however, it still had within its power, and it made use of it. A great stream of inky-brown, evil-smelling fluid, was squirted over all within its reach, covering their faces, hands, and clothes, with a dark brown stain[2] that proved very difficult to remove, causing their eyes to smart and many to turn sick with the foul effluvium. But this was their enemy's last offensive act; a minute later it had been hacked to pieces.

So ended the last of the two great cuttles that had been for so many years a source of terror and danger to the islanders; for the other one was found lying dead high up on the rocks not far away. The cause of its death was not apparent; the islanders assigned it to old age, but it was noticed that two of its limbs had been amputated. These were the two that Wydale and Dareville had cut off when they had been attacked on board the *Saucy Fan*, and possibly this mutilation may have had something to do with the creature's ultimate death, though this would not necessarily be the case. For it is a fact well known to naturalists that limbs thus amputated frequently grow again in members of this curious order.

No one had been much hurt in the encounter, therefore the rejoicing at being rid of these two monsters was not dimmed by any cause for serious regret. A few flesh wounds, caused by the terrible hooks, were the worst that had to be attended to. But there is no

---

[2] This is the pigment known to artists as sepia, one of the most useful and durable of colours. We are indebted for it solely to members of the cuttle-fish family.—Author.

doubt some would have suffered severely, if not fatally, from con-
striction, had not their breast-plates partially protected them.

It seemed as though this unique fight—the battle with the
cuttle—was destined to be but the first of a series of stirring events,
for there followed quickly upon its heels two occurrences that
roused interest and excitement throughout the country.

The first of these was the announcement that Vanina was engaged to be married to King Kara; the second was the disappearance of her brother George.

The news of the first was brought to Wydale by Sydney
Dareville, who burst in upon him one day in a great state of excitement. Owen listened gloomily, but without apparent surprise. In
reality it was a great, a cruel shock to him, and he found it difficult
to hide his feelings.

"Do you approve of it?" he presently asked of Dareville.

"Honestly, no, my friend," was the emphatic answer. "But what
am I to do? My sister is headstrong—or infatuated—or something.
She will not listen to me. Can you not advise me in the matter?"

Wydale could only advise him to consult Monella; so they set
out to seek him, and presently found him in the "Technical School"
he had established in the town. During the past few months he had
started many schools, institutions, manufactories, and other useful works. Amongst them was a printing-office, and already he had
constructed an alphabet and grammar of the language, and had cast
founts of type to correspond; and now the printing press that had
come over in the *Saucy Fan* was at work printing, in the language
of the country, translations of many English works, including one
of the Bible. He and Dr. Manleth between them had devoted so
much time and attention to this, and to instructing some of the
most apt among their scholars, that there were now two or three
translators at work upon various English books.

Lathes, steam engines, and machinery of various kinds were
also at work. Dynamos for the electric light, electric batteries and bells,
quite a host of manufactures had been started, taking as patterns
one or other of the promiscuous cargo of the brig. And, finally,
new masts and other furnishings had been made ready to refit the
Saucy Fan as a fore-and-aft schooner, so that she might take the

sea at short notice, should an opportunity for leaving the island offer.

When they found him, Monella only shook his head, and said he could offer them no counsel at the moment.

"However," he said, presently, passing his hand across his forehead, as was often his habit, "perhaps Gralda can aid you here. He reads much that is written in the stars—which with me is a lost science."

So they consulted Gralda, who, in turn, consulted the stars; but the only result was to leave them even more anxious than before.

"The maiden," he said, dreamily, "is in grave danger. She hath fallen under an evil spell. But what the result will be I cannot see."

One of those most afflicted by this news was George. He burst into tears, and for many days went about sorrowful and depressed. He would not tell anyone his thoughts; but Wydale knew intuitively that the boy was sorrowing for him as well as for his sister; and it increased the love that had grown up between the two.

When therefore, a little later, it was found that the boy was missing, Wydale was the most upset of any. George had sought him out to ask him to come for a sail, as there was such a beautiful breeze;" but Owen had been engaged with Monella at the time, so the boy had announced his intention of going for a little sail alone. And, some time subsequently, he had been seen running before the breeze at some distance beyond Karanda; there all traces of him had been lost. Search-parties went out in all directions, and hunted for him wherever it was thought he would be likely to have strayed; but all returned unsuccessful; and two days and nights passed, and still neither did news come of the missing youth, nor was there any sign to throw light upon the cause of his disappearance.

22
"The Wood of a Hundred Deaths"

But to follow George.

His boat ran free before the wind, for Wydale had fitted her with a lug-sail, which George handled with dexterity. He passed the city of Karanda at some distance, and entered so fully into the enjoyment of the moment that he had left it a long way behind him before he was aware that he had passed it. He had, indeed, never before ventured so far in this direction, and now he saw, looming up before him, two or three miles away, the shores of another island. The sun shone upon a strip of tawny-coloured sand, and upon green woods that lay soft and inviting beyond the rippling water. While he was wondering at the sight, a strange object rose from the water near him, sailed along a little way above it, then dropped back into the waves. George caught a view of brilliant colours, but what the creature was he could not ascertain. It seemed to be half bird, half flying-fish; for, while its colouring resembled that of gorgeous plumage, yet it seemed to shine and reflect the rays of the sun as might the scales of a fish. Again and again it rose from the water and skimmed along in a wayward, erratic kind of flight; then it would settle once more upon the surface and remain quiet, merely rising and falling with the motion of the waves. Many times did George stealthily approach it, holding a large landing-net ready for its capture, but in each case it would rise lightly in the air just in time to escape him. Thus he chased it, as boys do a butterfly; and, indeed, the creature was a species of marine butterfly found in these regions, where it flits from one mass of Sargasso weed to another. They seldom roam far from the weed, and it was somewhat unusual to meet with one in the open water. At last it rose with a higher and longer flight than usual and disappeared altogether from view. Then George, looking round, found himself close to the shore he had seen in the distance, and a strong desire to land and look about it took possession of him. He thereupon hauled down his sail, ran the boat ashore, and, jumping off the bow, he took the kedge and fixed it in the sand at the end of the long painter. Having thus arranged matters so that the boat was safely fastened, yet so that he could catch up the kedge, jump on board and push off quickly, if occasion should arise, he proceeded to look about him. On each hand was a long stretch of sand, backed everywhere by a wood so thick that it seemed almost impenetrable. When he drew nearer to the trees, and inspected them more closely, he perceived that nearly all were more or less unknown to him. Some of the blossoms were absolutely gigantic; the fruits, too, were larger than anything he had ever seen or heard of. Upon some of these trees he noticed great thorns of enormous size; at least there were spikes that he supposed were thorns. He examined all these wonders with great curiosity, afraid to approach too closely, lest lurking enemies should rush forth upon him from the dense undergrowth. Presently, feeling somewhat frightened in the prevailing stillness, he went back to the boat and sat down upon it, half inclined to leave the place without further exploration. But the waves that came merrily dancing to the shore, and splashing with a cheerful, lapping sound against the side of the boat somewhat reassured him, for they seemed like light-hearted little friends in a lonely place. While thus seated he was seized with a new thought. Instead of walking along the shore, why should not he explore the place by coasting around it in the boat? That struck him as a good idea, and in a few minutes he was once more afloat; but this time he took out a pair of sculls, as being handier for his purpose than the sail. The wind had dropped almost to a calm, and the waves had become mere ripples, as he rowed leisurely along at a few hundred yards' distance from the line of coast. Every now and then he would pause and take up a pair of field-glasses, and carefully inspect the land through them; but still he saw no signs of life, save a few birds that flitted about from tree to tree, or rose for a short flight and

disappeared beyond their tops. But even these birds struck him as
new and strange. Presently he approached a rock that ran out some
distance into the water, and upon rounding this, he came upon a
little cove shut in at each end by rocks that jutted out into the sea,
and at the back by wooded cliffs. And there he saw something lying
upon the sand under the shade of two or three trees that here grew
by themselves not far from the water's edge. Looking carefully
through the glasses, he made it out to be a human being, apparently a young girl asleep. Thereupon he rowed very softly close in
shore; then he saw that she was a pretty little maiden about twelve
years old, dressed in the most extraordinary costume he had ever
seen. But though he carefully examined the surroundings, no trace
of anyone else could he perceive. And now, glancing again towards
the little maiden, he saw a sight that made him tremble. Creeping
stealthily towards her was a bright, orange-coloured snake, which
he knew at once to be one of the most deadly and aggressive of the
serpent family. He had already seen a specimen which an islander
had killed, and he had heard that some of the thick woods of these
islands were infested with them. They were like the fierce Hamadryad
of India, that ferocious, monstrous cobra that attacks with unrelenting fury every living thing that approaches it, even the serpent
tribe included; for it lives upon snakes, and snakes alone. But in
colour it resembled the "Lord of the Woods," of British Guiana, which
is equally deadly and equally to be dreaded, being the only really
aggressive snake of South America.

The Indians of that region regard it with the greatest dread,
and relate many wondrous tales about it; one being that it has a
sting in its tail, and that sometimes, when apparently retreating,
it suddenly darts backward and stings in a manner to cause death.
The Dilandians call this creature Vralpa, and dread it above everything, and with only too good reason.

Such was the reptile, which, with its bright, gaudily-coloured
skin, was distinctly visible even upon the tawny sand, and which
was slowly but steadily approaching the sleeping girl. Quietly the
boy ran his boat on the sand to which he was now close, and taking
his bow and arrow in one hand and the kedge in the other, dropped
softly into the water beside the bow, crept silently on to the sand

and pushed the little anchor into it, then knelt down and took careful aim.

It has been already said that, as one of the principal officers of the cadet battalion that had been formed in Dilandis, George had become expert in fencing and the use of the bow and arrow, and the latter arms he always carried with him, as well as a short sword. He was only a few yards from the reptile, yet the mark was no easy one to hit, for the beast, as it wriggled along, kept swaying its head to and fro; but its glittering, cruel eyes were fixed upon its intended victim, and it neither saw nor heard the enemy behind it. Almost with his heart at his mouth, George let the arrow go. It had a wedge-shaped, sharp, steel head, and it pierced the neck of the serpent, and, passing through, pinned it to the sand. Then, rushing up, trembling with excitement, and heedless of possible danger to himself, George drew his sword, and with one neat blow cut off its head before it had wriggled the arrow out of the sand, or could turn to defend itself from its assailant. And, now that it was beyond further power of mischief, the boy sat down on the sand, overcome with horror at the sleeping maiden's narrow escape, and with the perspiration pouring from his face, yet filled with a sense of quiet triumph at his performance.

In his excitement he had called out, and the cry awoke the sleeper, who sat up and rubbed her eyes. When she saw George she started up in a fright, but he rose and pointed to the decapitated snake. When she looked upon it, she first sprang back with another cry, then seemed as though she were about to run away. But there was nowhere she could run to, for the spot was surrounded on all sides by precipitous rocks. Indeed, when George looked round, it was a wonder to him how she came to be there at all, seeing that there was no path or other visible means by which she could have come. To reassure her, he spoke to her gently in the language of the country, telling her not to be afraid, since he was no enemy, and, indeed, had just saved her from the attack of the deadly reptile that had marked her for its victim. Then she seemed to gather courage, and, looking at him with large blue eyes, inquired, in the same tongue:

"Who are you, and what are you doing here?"

"I came in my boat," said George, pointing to it, "and seeing you lying asleep, and this snake creeping up to you, and well knowing that its bite was certain death, I landed, and was just in time to kill it before it sprang upon you."

She shivered and looked down again in horror and aversion at the mutilated serpent. Then there came upon her face a sunny smile that was full of friendly trust and confidence. She came up to him, and, putting her hand in his, and looking at him with eyes that were now soft with tears, she said

"You have saved me from a terrible death, and I thank you very, very much. I wish that my father were here; he would thank you far better than can I."

"Who is your father?" George inquired.

She drew herself up proudly, and said, eyeing him as though to watch the effect of her words:

"He is Loftra, chief of the Flower-Dwellers."

And at that George looked round with some uneasiness, for he had heard terrible tales of these strange people; of their ferocity, and their unrelenting hatred of all strangers; of the terrible power which it was said they had of dealing to all who approached them a death more sudden and sure even than that which followed the bite of the deadly reptile now lying harmless at their feet.

While thinking of all this, and continuing to gaze somewhat doubtfully at the little maiden, his attention wandered to the strange dress she wore. He could not think what it could be made of; it seemed soft as silk, and shone like satin, yet it put him in mind of nothing so much as a white lily with delicate mauve stripes. Certainly the girl was very beautiful, with her long golden hair and perfect childish figure; and her costume seemed to suit her charms. Of adornments she had none, in the ordinary acceptation of the word; that is to say, she wore no jewellery, but twined in her hair were exquisite little knots and chains of flowers, and yet flowers that were altogether of a novel kind. Indeed, she was altogether such an unusual, fairy-like creature that he began seriously to wonder whether, indeed, she was a little fairy, and whether he had somehow stumbled unawares into a modern fairyland. At last he spoke:

"How did you come here, and how are you going to get away?"

Then she glanced around, and the troubled look came back to her face.

"Indeed, I don't know how I am going to get away," she said, "for one of my wings is broken."

"One of your wings!" he exclaimed, astonished, thinking that verily his former surmise must be correct, and that she must be indeed a fairy. Still, he could see no trace of wings upon her shoulders.

She looked about her, and went up to some articles that were lying on the ground beside her, and picked them up. Then she opened them out, and he saw that they were two beautifully-formed wings, one of which was hanging as though broken.

"Yes!" she continued, looking down ruefully at what she was holding in her hand, "you see one of my wings is broken, and I couldn't fly any farther. I just succeeded in getting over those rocks; then I saw the water in front of me, and thought I should be drowned; but I managed to wheel round and alight on the sand without being hurt. And then I saw that I was in a place in which I was quite shut in, and from which I could not get away without my wings. So I had to stay; and I sat down to rest, knowing my people would send to search for me, and that I had only to be patient. But I got tired of waiting, and fell asleep under the trees."

George gazed at her perplexed.

"*Are* you a fairy?" he asked.

"Not I!" she returned, with a laugh; "only a little girl."

"Then why do you talk of flying?" he inquired. It was now her turn to show surprise.

"Can't you fly?" she asked.

"No; nor did I ever know anyone who could."

"Ah, now I remember. I have heard that the people outside our island do not know how to fly; so I suppose it does seems strange to you. But then, you know, we don't really *fly*; we can't go very high in the air, nor for very long at a time; and I couldn't have flown so high as to go over those trees and rocks, if there hadn't been such a strong breeze to-day. But it was so nice to soar up higher than usual against the wind, that I could not resist it. The others would not venture, so I went up alone to have a little flight all to myself. But," she added, sorrowfully regarding the broken wing, which she had dropped upon the ground, "it was very naughty of me, for I was warned that a great danger threatened me to-day; and so it has proved. And now I don't know how I shall get home again; and perhaps they will not think of coming here to look for me."

The boy's amazement grew. He picked up the wings and examined them intently; he was surprised to find how light they were. What material they were made of he could not understand; but they seemed very strong, yet so buoyant, that when he let go of one, it floated gently and slowly to the ground like a feather, instead of falling heavily at once, as one would have supposed from the size and apparent weight. He noticed that there were straps to bind them on the arms and shoulders; but his attention was diverted from them by the little maiden, who had seated herself on the sand and was crying bitterly; whereupon he went up to her to console her.

"There is nothing to cry about," he said; "if you want to get away from here and land on another part of the shore, you can do it easily in my boat."

She looked at him inquiringly.

"Go in your boat?" she repeated, doubtfully. "I should be afraid."

"Why should you be?" he said; "I will take you safely, and land you where you please."

For a space she made no reply, but seemed considering.

"But who are you?" she presently demanded. "And what brought you here?"

"My name is George," he replied, with some importance, "and I am a prince."

But if he thought that this announcement was going to over-awe her, he was quickly undeceived, for she eyed him curiously, and said

"A prince! Not a *real* prince? Were you *born* a prince?"

Now this was a home-thrust; one not at all to George's liking. He hardly knew, indeed, what to reply, when, seeing the cloud upon his face, the little maiden came up to him and said kindly:

"Never mind; if you were not born a prince, you can't help that, you know. In our country we have no princes or princesses, or kings or queens. My father and my grandfather are the chiefs of our people; and they, are very wise—far wiser than any kings."

To this assertion George was not disposed to give assent off-hand. He was about to argue the point when she went on

"Never mind that now; you have been very kind to me, for you saved my, life. Prince or no prince, you seem a nice, good sort of boy; and I will trust myself with you, if you will promise to take me round yonder rocks, and put me ashore farther along."

"That I shall be glad to do," was the boy's ready answer; and they walked together to the boat. But when they came towards it, he found it would be difficult to bring it near enough for her to step in. It was very shallow at this spot, and he looked from her to the boat, and from the boat back to her in some perplexity.

"It seems to me," he said at last, "that I shall have to lift you in."

"But then you will get wet," she urged.

"Oh, that's nothing! I jumped into the water just now, when I landed in a hurry to kill the snake."

So he took her in his arms and walked a little way into the water; but his surprise was great when he found how wonderfully light she was. She seemed to be scarcely any weight at all; and he lifted her over the side with so little exertion that he stood looking at her with astonishment.

"Why, how light you are!" he exclaimed, "you are no heavier than a baby."

But she was as surprised as he, and took no notice of his re-mark.

"How strong you are—for a boy!" she said. "No wonder you were not afraid to attack the vralpa. Are all your people as strong as you?"

"Not all; but, then, some are stronger," was the diplomatic answer. Then, with a sudden change he went on, "I say, what is your name?

"Myrla.

"Myrla! H'm; a pretty name. But Myrla what? What is your other name?"

She shook her head.

"I don't know what you mean," she said. "I have no other; nobody that I know has two names."

"*I* have two," George answered proudly. "My whole name is George Dareville."

She viewed him with a sort of languid curiosity.

"I have heard my people talk of King Kara and Prince Rokta, and others," she said; "but I never heard of even a king or a prince who had two names."

Now this was another home-thrust for George, though the artless maiden knew it not. He felt confused, and was relieved in consequence when she turned the subject by observing:

"Please bring my wings, and that horrid snake, too, that I may show it to my people."

He did what she asked him, lifting the remains of the reptile on two pieces of stick, and throwing them into the bow of the boat. Then he got in himself, pushed her off, and, taking up the sculls, set off in the direction she had indicated.

Soon they rounded the corner of the little bay, and came to a long stretch of sandy shore, backed by dense woods. But in one place could be seen an opening, and from this, just when they were rowing off it, emerged a group of men who wore black masks. At sight of them Myrla gave a cry, and George, who had his back to them, looked round and stopped rowing.

"Who are they?" he asked, uneasily.

"They are my friends," she said, "come to look for me, no doubt; but do not be afraid, for they shall not harm you."

But George recalled the stories of the Flower-Dwellers; he remembered having been told that they wore masks; and he began to speculate whether it would not be wiser to row away instead of landing his companion.

But she urged him to turn the boat ashore.

"They shall not harm you!" she said again, with emphasis. "Have no fear; I will take care of you. Besides you *must* come and see my father, and let him thank you for what you have done for me."

"I think," George hesitated, "you had better tell them to halt where they are; then I can land you and row away. I do not like the look of them."

"If you are afraid, I will," said Myrla; "but there is no necessity." And she called out to the approaching strangers in a language that George did not understand. Some talk ensued between them, and apparently some argument, but in the end the maskers withdrew for about fifty yards, when George ran the boat ashore. Myrla rose, and stepping lightly to the bow, sprang out clear of the water.

"Now throw on shore those pieces of that horrid snake," she asked him.

This he did; and she turned to go to meet the masked men.

"Don't you want these things, your—your—wings?" he called after her.

She looked round and answered:

"Yes; I will come back for them directly."

And she tripped lightly to her friends who advanced to meet her. She seemed to be disputing with them vehemently, for George, watching them closely, saw her make gestures of impatience and even anger, stamping her foot, and tossing her head. One of the men offered her a black mask, but she thrust it away, and again stamped her foot with petulance and heat and then ensued, apparently, more argument. In the end, however, she came back alone to him.

"It is all right now," she said, "you can safely land, and come with me. See," she went on, pointing to the strangers, "they have taken off their masks."

George noted that this was so; also that they were coming toward the boat with every sign of friendliness, and he eyed them with much interest. They were bearded men of middle height, apparently not very strongly built, but not ill-favoured. One fact, however, struck him, even at the first glance. It was that there was something unusual about the expression of their foreheads. But what it was he could not quite determine.

One of them came up, and looking first at the body of the snake, and then at George, he said, in the language now familiar to the boy, but with a slightly different accent

"We hear, young sir, that you have slain this vralpa, and so saved the life of the daughter of our chief. In that you have done us an inestimable service. It is against our laws, and against the orders of our chief, that strangers be permitted on our shores. But it is the earnest wish of the maiden that you should go with us, that her father should himself express his thanks to you. We doubt whether we are right in yielding, but since it is her wish, we have agreed to it; if we are wrong, and our chief do not receive you as she expects, you must not blame us. We take no responsibility for the result."

"But *I* know!" Myrla cried, imperiously. "And in this you must obey my orders; so let us be going."

"But what shall we do with the boat?" George asked.

"Oh, they will see to that," she answered. "They will draw it up and take care of it. And mind," she went on, addressing the group, "mind you bring my wings and the dead snake."

The men bowed with deference, and proceeded to haul up the boat, well clear of the water. Meanwhile, Myrla took George's hand, and led him away towards the opening in the woods.

The boy naturally doubted whether he was acting wisely in allowing himself to be persuaded to accompany her on a visit to a people of whom he had heard such ill reports. But the confidence exhibited by the girl, and the friendly looks and manner of the men, encouraged him. So they proceeded on their way, the others following.

Presently Myrla clapped her hands and laughed gleefully, as though struck with a happy thought. "What fun it will be!" she cried.

"What will be fun?" her companion asked.

"Why, when they see me returning with a stranger," she replied. "Never for many, many years—oh! long ages, as I have been told—has a stranger been allowed to enter our country!"

"Why do those people wear masks?" he asked, "and why did they want you to put one on?" She shrugged her shoulders.

"I am not sure," she said, a little seriously, "whether I may tell you. Perhaps you will learn all about it by and by."

They entered a steep, gloomy path that led into the depth of the wood, and mounted towards some lofty overhanging cliffs, and George looked about him with much interest, for the trees and shrubs and flowers, all the vegetation, in fact, were strange to him. The farther they went, the larger and more extraordinary became the fruit and blossoms to be seen on every side. One in particular of these strange flowers attracted his attention. It seemed to be a gigantic orchid, and it was so beautifully marked, the colouring was so vivid, and the scent, even at a little distance, was so delicious, that he stepped towards it with the intention of examining and perhaps plucking it. But, with a loud cry of fright, Myrla darted after him and pulled him back. He turned and saw that her face, but now flushed with pleasurable excitement, was white and pinched with fear.

"Oh, do not touch it !" she exclaimed, "for it will *kill* you. See," she went on, with a shudder.

And, taking from his hand the bow that he had brought with him, she held it out at full length, and, stretching out as far as she could, leant over and touched the lovely blossom, whereupon a bough above, armed with one of the long spiky thorns that he had noticed before, came down sharply upon the end of the bow with a blow like a hammer.

"See," she said again, and drew back, and caught his arm. "If you had been there that would have killed you."

George wondered greatly, and asked her to explain; but she shook her head and said only:

"You must touch *nothing* here, unless you are told you may. This is the 'Wood of a Hundred Deaths.'"

But she refused to explain further; and they walked on for a while in silence, when George's attention was attracted by a new wonder. This was a tree whose whole trunk was hollow and stood partly open, and in the interior could be seen what looked like a seat. Around, the sides were lined with a substance that resembled the richest velvet. It was of many lovely colours. George stepped forward to examine this fresh wonder, and again Myrla caught him and drew him back with a frightened cry.

"If you seat yourself therein," she cried, "you will never come out alive. That horrid tree would close round you, and nothing we could do would release you in time to save you. That is another of the many 'deaths' the unwary meet with in this awful wood!"

A little farther on they came to a similar tree. It was standing open as the other had been, but inside was something which George recognised as the huddled-up skeleton of a human being.

"Come along," urged Myrla, with a shiver. "That is some fool-ish stranger who had ventured into this wood, and sat down there for a rest."

Presently they came to an immense flower that hung, attached by a long trailing stem at each end, to a tree above, and formed a sort of swing, or rather hammock, beautifully shaped and coloured, and seemed to invite the tired wayfarer to lie in it, and swing to and fro in the shade.

"There," said Myrla, "is another deadly plant. If you lie down in that swing, it overpowers you with a drowsy scent, and then, while you lie asleep, closes over you, and you never come out alive. But after a time it opens again, and only your bones fall to the ground. See, look around beneath it."

And there, indeed, lying about, were many white-looking ob-jects that George saw were whitened bones.

He turned with a shudder and walked on, beginning to feel a sort of creepy horror of everything around him. But the girl beside him soon began chattering away gaily, evidently amused at the surprise and curiosity written in his face as he glanced from one new and strange botanic wonder to another.

And now he saw an opening in the path in front of him that indicated that they were nearing the margin of the forest. On their way through the wood he had seen many paths branching off and winding in and out, forming a veritable maze, through which Myrla picked her way, for the most part, without hesitation.

But once or twice she, even, was at fault, and waited for her followers to come up to point out the road, whereupon she would take George's hand and lead him on in front as before.

In this way they had first ascended rising ground to a consid-erable height, and then descended a little, and now, on their emerg-ing from the wood, an extensive view spread out before their gaze.

23
In The Land of the Flower-Dwellers

George found himself looking down across an extensive grassy plain that stretched away into the distance, and was surrounded on all sides by woods and groves of trees, for the most part of gigantic height and girth. The basin thus formed was dotted here and there with groups of smaller trees, amidst which flitted, in and out, what the boy at first took to be enormous swallows, but presently ascertained to be human beings skimming a little above the surface of the ground. Some of these flyers soon saw George and his companions and made their way to them, in long curved flights, skimming along a few feet from the ground, and mounting again when they sank low enough to touch it, a spring of the foot on the grass being sufficient to launch them upon a fresh swoop through the air. The resemblance to the flight of swallows, when these fly low, was very marked; or the motion might be likened to the long, graceful curves of skaters.

When the first of those who employed this mode of locomotion had come within twenty yards of George, they alighted on the ground and ranged themselves in a semi-circle, gravely scanning him. He found their silent gaze embarrassing, and stood waiting for what would happen next. Gradually the number of these strangers was increased, as others came skimming over the ground and brought up at the edge of the semi-circle. Then Myrla went forward and addressed them in a language George did not understand; and the four men who had been following them coming up, a long colloquy ensued. At the end of it some of the "flyers" set off, running along the ground before mounting in the air, and then, once fairly started, soon disappearing in the distance. The others turned to walk in the same direction, and Myrla, beckoning to George, they all set out together.

"They tell me my father and mother have been in great trouble about me," she explained to her young friend, as they went along. "I am very sorry; and I expect I shall get a scolding. However, it cannot now be helped. But I hope they will not be very angry."

George acquiesced, but showed more curiosity, just then, in the "flying" than in anything else; and he looked with great interest at the "wings" of those nearest to him. They resembled Myrla's, and were fastened to the arms and shoulders with straps and buckles that were quickly and easily adjusted, many unfastening them while they walked, and slinging them over their shoulders.

George felt greatly reassured by the demeanour of all he now encountered. Not only were they friendly, but there was an almost childish gaiety in their behaviour that very quickly won his confidence. In this respect they were very different from the masked men, whose serious and almost repellent air had, at first, rendered him somewhat doubtful of their intentions.

The little procession moved on across the plain; and, when it neared the farther end, they passed through groves of trees, amongst which were streams of running water, cascades and fountains, grottoes and shady arbours, and beautifully laid out gardens. Some of the groves they passed through bore fruit and flowers of such immense size that George gazed at them in astonishment, scarcely believing that they were real. And now from many of these great blossoms, as they swayed to and fro, some only a few feet above them, and others high in the air, little heads peeped forth, and wondering faces peered down upon them and asked what the commotion was about. From time to time some of these would emerge from their hiding-places in the colossal blooms, and throwing themselves, with outspread wings, into the air, would descend with a graceful sweep, alighting noiselessly and easily on the ground. Then, folding up their wings, they joined the crowd, eagerly asking questions of those near them.

Proceeding onwards, they came in sight of groups of buildings, one of which, from its size and style of architecture, George thought must be a palace or a temple. All its towers were shaped to resemble flowers or trees, and the ornamentation followed out the same idea. The material of the edifice itself was black and white marble, but the floral decorations were beautifully tinted to represent real flowers. At the top of a flight of steps that ascended to the entrance of this imposing structure, a group of people was collected.

"See!" cried Myrla, "there is my father, Loftra, and beside him, Felita, my mother; and on the other side you can see my grandfather, whose name is Zoreas."

And, with that, she ran forward and up the steps, and the next moment was caught up in her mother's arms. Then her father took her up and kissed her, after which there ensued some talk, which George, who remained at the bottom of the steps, could not hear. The men who had worn the masks now ascended the steps and threw before their chief the remains of the dead snake. These Loftra examined for a space, in silence, and then, coming down the steps, held out his hand to George.

"I have heard, my son," said he, "of what thou hast done for my child this day. Now is the mystery of the fate that hovered over her, of the veil we could not penetrate, cleared up. It was written in the stars that to-day a great danger threatened her; it hath been reserved for thee, by destiny, to avert that danger, and to be the first stranger that hath been admitted to our land for ages. Since, then, the great Spirit who directs all worldly affairs hath so ordained it, it is fitting that we recognise and abide by His will in this. Thou shalt find that we shall not be niggardly in our recognition of the service thou hast rendered us."

George felt a little confused at this somewhat stately welcome, and, being unused to making lengthy speeches, he contented himself with a smile and a modest, "Thank you, sir." Loftra then took his hand and led him up to his wife, who, without more ado, embraced and kissed him, whereupon Myrla clapped her hands, saying laughingly to George:

"There! I told you so. Did I not say my mother and father would receive you kindly, and love you for having saved my life?"

George was next presented to Zoreas, a fine-looking old man with flowing white hair and beard, who regarded him with kindly grey eyes, and addressed him with much dignity. At this shouts went up from the crowd around, who had been waiting only for a sign of the old man's approval to testify their friendly feeling.

"Now," said Felita, "the boy must be hungry, and must require refreshment; let him come with us to our table."

Then Myrla took his hand, and saying, "I will show him the way," led him through the portals into a courtyard, which they crossed, then passing through another gateway, they came out into a garden which George thought the most beautiful and the most wonderful he had ever seen. Here, under a large spreading awning, tables were laid out, upon which were golden platters and ewers and goblets, and a lavish display of cool, inviting fruits. And at this table, with the scent of the flowers around them, and the murmur of splashing fountains close at hand, George was soon seated before the most extraordinary banquet at which he had ever been a guest.

While eating, he had an opportunity of observing those around him. Loftra, the chief of the community, was a tall, handsome man of middle age, with fine, soldierly bearing; while his wife, though also middle-aged, yet had a wonderfully youthful air and look.

In fact, George now began to understand what it was in the expression of these people that had at first perplexed him; it was, he now perceived, the complete absence of wrinkles and other marks of age and care. There was in the brows, in the whole expression of their features, a calm repose, an absence of earthly passion, which, though he hardly understood it, yet he instinctively felt to be unusual, even if not unique. Zoreas, old man though he was undoubtedly, with his white hair and beard, and his bent figure, yet had the complexion and the bright eyes of a young man of thirty; not a crease, not a line, appeared upon his lofty forehead, and the whole cast of his features was instinct with good temper and benevolence. Yet at times there would pass over them a suggestion of severity which George noticed and even wondered at. Looking at others round about him, he noted the same general characteristics; all were handsome, calm, and free from even a hint of trouble; and all, moreover, seemed as full of gaiety as happy, careless children.

As to what he ate and drank at this unique repast, George had but a faint idea—at least with regard to most of it. There was nothing in the way of food but bread and fruits; but these fruits were of the most diversified description, comprising in their variety the flavours of everything under the sun, including even—so it seemed to him—the taste of meats of many kinds. For drink there were fruity beverages, cool, foaming, and of exquisite *bouquet*. Presently, Myrla, in response to his expressions of wonder, asked him playfully whether there was any fruit that he *did* know, whereupon George thought of grapes, and managed to make them understand what he meant. Myrla clapped her hands, and said:

"You shall have part of one with me."

This reply puzzled George not a little, but he opened his eyes still wider than before, when, a little later, there was placed before him what looked like one immense grape as large as a melon. From this Myrla cut two slices, one for him and one for herself, and when he had tasted it he found that it was indeed nothing else than an enormous grape. It was the same with many other of the fruits. Nectarines so large that only a portion could be placed on a dish, peaches and plums as large as pumpkins, and numberless others, all upon a scale that to the boy seemed like a dream of Brobdingnag.

Now when this function was concluded, and George had bathed his face and hands, and had rested for a while, he was led into an apartment in which only Myrla and her parents and her grandfather were present.

Here Zoreas was seated upon a chair of state, with Myrla's father and mother, one on each side of him. George stood before them, Myrla by his side, holding his hand, as if to give him courage.

"My son," said Zoreas, "it hath been delegated to me to decide upon what reward we shall offer thee for the service thou hast this day rendered us. By the will of the great Spirit, the Lord of the Woods and Flowers, whom we worship, it hath been given unto thee to perform this service; it is for us, therefore, to bow to what is here so plainly indicated. Doubtless, it hath been so ordained that we might render thee some special service in return. Say, then, what can we do for thee? If there is aught that thou desirest, that is in our power to grant, we will readily comply with thy request."

At this George felt embarrassed, and scarce knew what reply to make. He turned over in his mind all the articles that he would most wish to have. But then nearly all were such as it was not likely these people could supply, unless they were really fairies; but that he had by this time decided they were not. Probably his greatest wish, at the time, was for a repeating rifle and a good supply of cartridges; but that, he knew, they could not give him, and this applied to everything he tried to think of. While he hesitated, Myrla looked at him and smiled.

"You seem to have lost your tongue, Prince George. Shall I ask something for you?"

But George remained grave and thoughtful, and presently looked up and sighed, and then it was seen that the tears were in his eyes.

"There is only one thing, sir, that could really make me happy," he said, addressing Zoreas, "and that is, that my sister should marry Mr. Wydale, he who has been so kind a friend to me. I know that he loves her very dearly, and had quite hoped to marry her, but now she is going to be married to King Kara, a man I don't like at all."

"Thou thinkest, then," responded Zoreas, "that it would be better for thy friend and thy sister that he should marry her?"

"Of course I don't know, sir," George answered, modestly. "I'm only a boy, and have no experience of such matters. But when I see how sorrowful and depressed he looks, I can't help wishing that my sister would love and comfort him."

Zoreas eyed the boy for a space in silence; then he answered, kindly:

"Thy thoughts do thee credit, my son. They show that thy heart is well inclined. Now it may be that we can be of service to thee in this matter, for we know all that is going on in these islands, though we admit none of the other inhabitants into our domain. We have watched the actions of that strange chief, Monella, in his warfare against King Kara; and we know how that King Kara, having failed to gain his ends in open war, hath resorted to chicanery; how that he and his sister Morveena, by illicit arts and occult spells, have found favour in the sight of the rulers and counsellors of Dilandis, and have fooled them to believe in their good faith. For Kara is skilled in many hidden mysteries; he knoweth many of the secrets that belong to us, the Children of the Woods and Flowers; he and his priests and astrologers are learned, too, in the lore of the stars. But if they know much, we know more; we have secrets that Kara hath not yet penetrated, and that he would give much to have unveiled. Herein lieth our power to aid thee, and what we can do we will willingly."

At this George, who had been staring gloomily on the ground, glanced up with a cheerful smile. Then, stepping forward, he impulsively seized and kissed the sage's hand, and, bowing over it, replied:

"Oh, sir! if you think it possible, and can help me in this matter, then indeed will I be grateful, and shall thank you as long as I live!"

Seeing that the boy was crying, Myrla's mother drew him gently towards her, and bade him seat himself on a stool beside her; then pressing him to her, with her arm around his neck, she said affectionately:

"Poor boy! He has no mother, and only his sister to love and care for him."

At this George looked up in wonder.

"I have a brother, too," he said, "but how did you know I have no mother?"

Zoreas smiled.

"I have already told thee," he observed, "that we know many things that pass in the outer world. The present and the past are written in the stars; it is only the future that is hidden from us; and even as to that, we can at times read sufficient to be, to some extent, a guide to those who walk in darkness. Now, in order to help thee, it is necessary that we consult the stars. This will require at least one night; perhaps several nights. Rest here, then, in content, until we can discover what advice to give thee; then shalt thou return in more hopeful mood to thine own people."

"Thank you, sir," rejoined George simply. "But my sister and all of them will be so anxious about me!'

"No matter," returned the sage, gravely; "these things are of more importance to thee and to them than is their temporary anxiety. Besides, if necessary, if thy stay should be prolonged, I can despatch a message. We will see to-morrow. Meantime, I give thee over to the charge of my granddaughter, who brought thee hither, and who will find plenty to amuse and interest thee."

"But what about the boat?" George asked.

"It hath been safely hidden away, and will be well cared for."

Then George was led away by Myrla, but not before he had received another embrace from her kind mother.

"Be comforted, my child," she whispered, "for if we cannot aid thee, then none on earth can; and we will do all that lies in our power."

Outside, many of Myrla's playmates were awaiting her; and to these she introduced her new acquaintance, who quickly became at home with them and joined their games. They wanted to teach him to "fly," and tried to do so; but the attempt proved a failure though it gave them plenty of amusement. The fact was, as he subsequently learned, all these people were by nature very light-boned; and it was partly that, and partly long practice, that enabled them to skim along above the ground in the manner he had seen. There was also another reason, namely, that their "wings" were composed of a tenuous substance that grew upon certain trees in the woods about them. It possessed great buoyancy; so much so that the wings would almost float about by themselves, and even, with a puff of wind behind them, carry along a certain amount of dead weight attached to them. The most familiar illustration probably would be the puff-ball of the dandelion, only that this does not possess the same tenacity and strength.

But in this, as in everything else, as George soon discovered, this strange people pressed into their service all the flowers and plants about them. By some secret treatment they could render blossoms, no matter of what size, strong and durable, almost everlasting; and, in fact, they made of them materials for dress and other purposes. Thus George learned, with wonder, the secret of their unique garb, for they were all made from flowers; and when he had thought, on first seeing Myrla, that her dress resembled a lily, he had accidentally hit the truth.

In other matters it was the same. These people were the only consistent vegetarians he had ever met. They needed nothing more for their daily sustenance, or their existence, as a separate and isolated community, than that which grew around them. They had, after great and arduous botanical research, so cultivated, and in some cases altered the character of the shrubs and trees and flowers, as to evolve from them developments that would have caused astonishment in any other part of the world. After long ages of this cultivation, small blossoms had become gigantic; fruits that we think large were Lilliputian by comparison, and the giant blossoms their woods now produced could, by some process known to themselves, be rendered so lasting that they would, if desired, remain year after year unaltered on the tree on which they grew.

This was most clearly conveyed to George's mind later in the day. After the evening meal, Myrla said to him:

"There is a clear moon to-night; let us go out and play."

With that she led him out of the palace, under the trees of the groves surrounding it, and lo! most of the great blossoms that swung from them were lighted.

They swayed to and fro in the evening breeze like gigantic Chinese lanterns; and as the two passed beneath, Myrla would give utterance to a little cry, whereupon sleepy heads would pop forth from these giant illuminated flowers, and lazily ask what she wanted.

"We are going to play to-night," she said, "the moon will soon be up; and we have a stranger here who would like to see our games. He cannot remain with us for long, so come and play with him to-night."

George gazed wonderingly around; on all sides of him he could see long avenues of trees with their great flowers lighted up, showing off to great advantage their soft and varied colouring, and the more he looked the more he marvelled.

"Why," said he to Myrla, "do they stay up there in those great flowers, instead of living in the palace or in the pretty houses that I see around?"

But she only laughed.

"It is our nature," she returned, "for we are Flower-dwellers; and we love better to live in the flowers, where we can swing to and fro in the cool fresh air, than in stifling buildings on the ground. There are about us houses for all who desire to dwell in them; but it is our nature to prefer to sleep among the trees."

In response to Myrla's invitation, many little beings came floating down, in their graceful way, to the ground; some among them
carried in their hands small lanterns which gave them somewhat
the appearance, at a distance, of enormous fire-flies.

Presently it was proposed to take George for a flight, and when
the moon, which was nearly at its full, had risen high enough to
light up the plain, these laughing children were to be seen bearing
him up with what may be termed long skips of many hundred feet
in length above the ground; and thus did George get his first personal experience of their mode of flying. He found it a most delightful movement, especially after he had surmounted his first fear
that they would suddenly drop him to the ground. From the moment that he gained that confidence he found a great enjoyment
in the pastime.

Several days passed more or less in the same fashion; the while
that, for a space each day, Myrla's parents would walk with George
and gravely converse with him, and give him advice about his future.
They soon learned from him that he was an enthusiastic pupil of
Dr. Manleth's; also that the doctor was devoting much time to a
study of the botanical productions of the islands.

At this Loftra smiled.

"In that case," said he, "we can give thee some useful hints;
before thou leavest us, we will impart to thee some of nature's secrets that are known to us—enough, at all events, to encourage thee
in thine after-life. True it is that many of these secrets are connected with the special trees and shrubs that we have cultivated in
this island throughout long cycles; yet do we know that there are
other parts of the world also in which most of these are to be found
by those who diligently search for them, and this will set before
thee an aim for study. Thou wilt know that there are discoveries to
be made of which the outer world does not so much as dream!"

Five days passed thus, and still each morning George was told
that the stars were not yet propitious; but, in the meantime, he
was informed that a message had been sent to his friends advising
them that he was safe and would return shortly. This eased the
boy's mind, and allowed him to enter more fully into his surroundings, which, indeed, made an impression never afterwards to be

obliterated. And ever since, and for years to come, he has recalled and will recall again and again the days and nights he passed with this strange community.

Thus, in the evening, seated beside Felita, pressed affectionately to her, while Myrla sat at her other side, he would listen to an (to Myrla) oft-told tale the kindly matron would relate to him— the wonderful legend of the origin of the Flower-Dwellers; just as, in our nurseries, loving mothers tell their children tales of fairyland. All around him he could see through avenues of trees the arboreal dwellings of the inhabitants, most of them lighted up, and every now and then some of the dwellers in them, carrying their little lanterns, flitting down or skimming round hither and thither through the twilight, or in the deeper shadows of the night.

And this is the legend that she told:—

"In the beginning we were called Children of the Light, beings that flitted about upon the outside of the globe in an Elysium of delight. We floated to and fro upon the surface of the atmosphere of this planet, even as birds fly above the surface of the sea, and sometimes dive down into it. But on an evil day Alostra, our queen, fell in love with one of the Sons of God, who guarded the gates of heaven, and enticed him from his duty. And then a great curse fell upon us. We became heavier, and were doomed to sink down into the air, and there swim about like the birds, or as fish swim in the sea. But worse came than this, for Alostra remained obdurate, and would not petition for forgiveness, and so she sank lower and lower, and all those belonging to her, until at last they could no longer even fly in the air, but sank and grovelled on the earth, and became like the lobsters and the crabs compared with the fish that swim above them.

"Yet still," continued Felita, "we retained many of our former attributes as compared with the inhabitants that we found existing on the earth. We alighted upon what was then the highest land upon the surface of the globe, and that was the lofty peaks of the land called Atlantis, which then dominated the whole world. But that nation ruled it by cruelty, and bloodshed, and evil passions; and we, though we were cast out from our former blissful state, had no sympathy with what we found around us. And when we learned all this, and realised more keenly than ever all that we had lost, many amongst us shed so many tears, and of such concentrated grief, that they watered the whole of the ground around and where they fell they budded into the trees and flowers you see about us. In no other regions of the world—so we believe—do you find such wonderful vegetation as we have here, for, although some of the seeds have accidentally been carried to other lands, yet here are to be seen all the most wonderful of nature's secrets.

"And while Atlantis dominated the world, as at that time she did, we, by virtue of the secrets we discovered and the power they gave us, dominated her; for in her midst was our domain, a great unapproachable mountain, defended by woods that no man durst penetrate, except on pain of death. Through generations we looked down with disgust and pity upon the cruel passions by which those surrounding us were actuated, for all their conquests were achieved by hatred, and cruelty, and ambition. And, when the inevitable retribution came, and Atlantis, the mistress of the world, sank beneath the waves—all except the upper lands—we were unharmed, and looked on in serenity at what befell them. We felt no pity and no fear, for we knew that it had been written in the stars that we should not sink with them, and for their lost ambitions we had no sympathy whatever.

"Ever since, this little nation of descendants from the Sons of the Gods has maintained itself against the rest of the world, and has retained to-day many of the attributes of our ancestors. We are so light in weight that with very little assistance we can fly in the air; but ah! never again, until we pass through the gates of death, may we fly so high as we once did. Thus we came to be called Flower-Dwellers.

"And thus you can understand, my child," Felita added, "why we have preserved ourselves as a nation separate from the outer world. It is an inexorable law with us that none from it shall set foot here, much less intermingle with us. Death, quick and certain, is the fate of all who have attempted it. The very woods around us are full of traps for rash adventurers."

"Yes, I know," said George, and shuddered; "but still," with a sudden thought, "it seems to me strange that, with so much knowledge, you have not found a remedy for a serpent's bite."

This remark had been suggested by a talk he had had not long before with Dr. Manleth, who had informed him that not all the science of the world had yet succeeded in discovering an antidote for snake bite.

"Oh that is simple enough," replied Felita, smilingly. "That is one of the smallest of our secrets; only this child, situated as she was, could not obtain the antidote in time. We carry many of our simples with us; but we cannot carry everything."

"I see," said George. "I suppose, then, that you do not fear these serpents upon your own ground?" Felita shook her head.

"No, except that, of course, they are a nuisance; and sometimes they might bite young children unawares, who might die before we found out what had happened. For that reason we encourage the growth of trees that keep snakes away. None ever make their way here through the woods; they may approach our outer shore, but they never get much farther. Then," she added, looking at Myrla with ever so slight a touch of severity in her glance, but, at the same time, patting her affectionately on the head, "our little Myrla would never have been in danger, if she had not disobediently gone beyond the bounds that she knew she and her playmates are restricted to."

Then Myrla, half laughingly, half seriously, hid her face in her mother's lap with much show of penitence, and promised not to disobey again. And her mother, bending down to kiss her daughter's hair, replied

"I trust not, my child, for next time there will be no little friend George to rescue you."

Thus did some days pass, until, on the morning of the fifth, George was once more sent for for a private talk with Myrla and her parents. He had already learned that Zoreas had been the former chief of the Flower-Dwellers, but that, with increasing years, he had found the responsibility too great, and had resigned his position to his son. For Loftra, George had a high regard; he saw that he ruled his people with love and wisdom; and the ex-chief Zoreas was on all sides equally beloved, for he had been a wise and gentle ruler in the past. And George marvelled greatly, pondering these things, how it could have come about that this kindly, good-natured people could have gained such a terrible name with the Dilandians.

This riddle was now about to be, to some extent, explained to him.

"We have carefully considered," began Loftra, addressing George, "all that hath been revealed to us about thy sister, not only of her present situation, but of her past. She hath been led astray; but her heart is still full of kindly impulses, else would we not assist her. At this moment she stands in serious danger; what will be its outcome we cannot tell; we can only do what seems best to us to help you but that will be more than we have ever done before for mortal, so far as I know our history."

This was not such comfort to George as he had hoped for; he had looked for something more pronounced.

"Gralda told me so much," he almost wailed. "He said he could not help us. Can you, then, do no more than Gralda?"

"We can," was the grave reply; "but it depends upon the great Spirit, the Lord of the Woods and the Flowers, whether our efforts will be efficacious. Remember once more we cannot pierce the veil of the future; we can only peer into it, and dimly see vague disclosures that, to different eyes, take different shapes. It may be that the interpretations we place on these may be correct; but we can never be sure. However, we hope it may eventuate that our aid to thee may prove a fitting return for the service thou hast rendered us in preserving the life of our sweet child Myrla. I have heard that thou takest a great interest in all that appertains to science. Now, therefore, will I do two things for thee; I will give thee that which we have never yet given to a stranger, that which shall help thee in thy contention with King Kara. I will also show to thee some of the great prizes that lie before the successful worker in the sciences. I will show to thee, in fact, some of the great secrets of the 'Children of the Woods and Flowers.'"

24
Some Secrets of the Woods and Flowers

"Thou must understand," continued Loftra, "that I do not expect that thy young mind can fully comprehend all I now say to thee. Yet in the future thou wilt remember and perhaps better understand a part of that which now seems beyond thy grasp. For, if thou art a zealous worker in the cause of science, it will be a great help to thee to know the possibilities that lie before thee. I have already stated that King Kara is well-versed in certain of the secrets that belong to us; but all that he knows is small, indeed, compared with what we know. He knows, for instance, a subtle poison by which, with a mere scratch upon the skin, he can cause a trance so like to death that few can discern between the two. He can also quickly recall his victim from that trance, should he so wish. Further, he hath discovered another wondrous secret known to us, by which he can, in certain circumstances, control another's will. Now I know that he hath presented to thy sister a certain ornament which he hath persuaded her to wear round her neck. Is it not so?"

"Yes, sir " replied George, eagerly, "that is true." Loftra drew from a pouch attached to his belt a small disc or locket; it was made with perforations on each side, like those constructed to contain scented woods and other perfumes.

"Inside the locket that he hath given to thy sister," Loltra proceeded to explain, "there is something like unto this disc; and by this means he hath, with devilish art, controlled her will. Art thou listening, my son?"

"Certainly, sir," George answered. "And I think I begin to understand."

"Now I will illustrate the action of this curious talisman. Myrla, whisper to me something that thou desirest our young friend to do."

Myrla whispered something in her father's ear, and then laughingly stood aside as though awaiting the result.

"My son," Loftra then resumed, "my daughter hath desired that thou shouldst do a certain thing. I command thee to do it."

But George could only gaze at the speaker in inquiry; he did not guess what was required of him. But Loftra smiled.

"Thou seest," he said, "that at present I cannot command thy will. Now take this disc and hold it in thine hand."

George did as directed, and stood waiting for what would happen next.

"I now again command thee," the chief continued, to do what was just now in my mind."

George thereupon, like one walking in his sleep, went up to Felita, and, taking her hand, kissed it respectfully; while Myrla, bursting into childish laughter, and clapping her hands, exclaimed:

"That is what I asked my father to make you do."

"Now, thou seest," continued Loftra, "how subtle is the power that lies hidden in that disc. There emanates from it an influence that thou canst not detect. It has no odour of any kind, by which thou canst perceive its presence. For know," he went on with emphasis, and holding up one finger at the boy to point his words, "there are many gaseous elements in nature that can affect the brain without our being conscious of them through the senses. Our sense of smell is, at best, extremely limited. The animals, the birds of the air, and still more insects, are much more gifted in this way than human beings suspect. Animals and insects can detect scents altogether beyond a man's power of perception. And now I will give thee a further instance of this, which thou shouldst remember all thy life. Come with me."

Then the four proceeded for some distance through the woods, till they came to a bush on which were brightly-coloured blossoms. Each of his companions picked one of these in passing, but George, not being bidden to do the same, refrained. Passing on, they came to a curious-looking tree of a peculiar, deep, reddish purple tint;

the leaves, too, were purplish, and there was a small, deep-coloured fruit, not unlike elder-berries.

"Break off a twig," directed Loftra, "and hold it in thy hand."

George did as he was told; but no sooner had he done so, than he was seized with a deadly nausea. He could perceive no odour, yet he felt sick, and reeled with a death-like faintness. Indeed, he would have fallen had not Loftra caught him. Snatching the twig from his hand, he threw it far away, and fanned him with the blossom he had just plucked. Then George revived, and in a few seconds had quite recovered; yet was he conscious of no scent or odour from the blossom that had been waved to and fro before his nose.

"Thou seest!" observed Loftra, "that there are powers and agencies in nature of which thou hast, hitherto, never so much as dreamed; no, nor all thy scientific men. Hadst thou continued longer to hold that twig in thine hand, thou wouldst at this moment have been dead. It did not affect us, because we carry the antidote in our hands, and thou hast seen how quickly it acted as a cure in thine own case. Yet thou knowest that, from first to last, thy sense of smell was not affected."

"That is true, sir," George replied. "Ah! how I wish that you would show all this to my friend, Dr. Manleth!"

Loftra shook his head. "That cannot be; none of thy friends may enter here."

At this George would have entreated, but Loftra, with a wave of the hand that meant there should be no further argument, turned towards the palace. Arrived there, he again addressed the boy in the same serious strain:

"I have shown thee several wonders that have surprised thee. I could show thee hundreds; but it suffices only to convince thee of our great knowledge. Thou hast seen enough to teach thee what secrets nature has for those who seek her; enough to convince thee that in what I am now about to say I may be trusted. Now, here is a small disc like that I showed thee. Thou must take this, open the large locket that thy sister wears about her neck, and withdraw from it the disc thou wilt find therein. Thou must throw it into the sea, or where no one is likely to recover it. Thou must then put this disc in its place. If thou canst do this without Kara's knowledge, then shall thy sister recover the full control of her own will, and shall see Kara as he is, and not, as at present, with a dreamer's eyes. Now I will explain to thee how to open her locket."

And Loftra produced from his pouch a locket exactly like that given to Vanina by King Kara, and at sight of it the boy gave a cry of wonder.

"Yes," continued Loftra, who had divined his thoughts, "it is an exact counterpart; and now to show thee how to open it."

This done, he went and opened a cabinet, and took from it a beautifully carved ebony casket.

"Now," he went on, regarding the boy, if possible, more gravely than ever, "this is what we have never before given to a stranger, so far, at least, as I know our annals. This thou must carry carefully, and give into the hands of thy friend Monella, who will know how to deal with it. But first thou must give me thy solemn promise that thou wilt make no attempt to open it, for, if thou dost, the consequences will be disastrous."

"I promise solemnly," was George's answer.

"And I trust thee to keep that promise. And now that is the best that we can do for thee; and may the great Spirit whom we serve give His blessing upon the result."

He remained silent for a while, as though lost in thought; and then, looking straight before him, began again in dreamy fashion, as though talking to himself.

"Monella! Strange being who knows not himself, for he hath lost his memory."

"Lost his memory?" George exclaimed. "Why, he seems to know almost everything."

"Boy, I spoke not to thee," said Loftra, coming out of his abstraction; "but it doth not matter. Thou hast heard; perhaps some day thou wilt understand. And now to-morrow morning thou must depart. Some of my followers shall guide thee through the wood and accompany thee in one of our canoes to see thee safely within sight of Karanda. There seek thy sister, and manage carefully to observe my directions. If thou hasten on thy road, and tarry not by the way, thou shouldst arrive at an opportune time. So is it written."

George poured out his thanks, and would have kissed the other's hand, but Loftra turned and left the apartment before he could approach him.

The next morning George set out on his return. There was a tender leave-taking between him and those who had shown him so much kindness; and at parting Myrla whispered to her father, and then, coming shyly up to George, kissed him and ran away.

"Remember," said Loftra finally to the boy, "that thou must never return; nor must any of thy friends set foot upon our shores. If they do, certain death awaits them."

"But why," asked George regretfully, "why, after treating me with so much kindness, should you wish to kill my friends?"

"It is the law of our land, and is irrevocable," Loftra answered, with more sternness than he had yet shown. "If thou art wise, thou wilt so regard it. Farewell."

The men he had met on the shore on landing accompanied him through the woods. He passed, with a shudder, those deadly woodland wonders that had been pointed out to him, and saw again the bones of some of the victims lying whitening upon the ground. When they reached the shore, he found his boat awaiting him in charge of two men, who had also a canoe of their own. They had brought with them the ebony casket, which they had first carefully wrapped up, and then hidden away under a seat, and so they informed him. There was a fresh and favourable breeze, as Loftra had predicted. All then embarked, hoisted their sails, and were soon sailing towards Karanda.

On nearing the city, the men in the canoe gradually fell behind, and finally took down their sail, and watched him till he had arrived within a short distance of the harbour. Then, when he looked round, they waved their hands, turned their canoe, and paddled away.

Now when he arrived at the city, he found many persons assembled to receive him; they had seen him in the distance, and were curious to know what had happened to him in his absence. But he would tell them nothing, and, learning that his sister was at the palace, he made his way thither.

Kara's palace was a noble-looking edifice, standing upon a rock that rose from the sea. Perhaps of all the stately buildings in those islands, there was none more gratifying to the sight of those who could appreciate the beautiful. At each end great towers of fine proportions raised their heads majestically into the air, looking down in silent grandeur upon all about them.

But the sight was lost on George, who sighed while mounting the broad steps that led up to the entrance. He passed through the halls and galleries to seek Vanina. On his way he met many persons, who all questioned him, but he proceeded with but a brief word or two, till he came to the rooms Vanina occupied. Here he was stopped by some ladies in waiting, who informed him that Vanina was sleeping, and would have detained him till she awoke. But he remembered Loftra's words that, if he tarried not, he would arrive at a favourable moment, and he saw in the fact that she was asleep a fulfilment of the prediction. This was his opportunity; so, saying that he would go in to see her and stay with her until she should awake, he stole in softly on tip-toe, and was soon beside her.

Vanina was lying sound asleep upon a cushioned divan. Her chamber was one of the finest in the palace; its walls were exquisitely decorated, and one of the doors opened upon a balcony that overhung the sea, and commanded a view that extended to Dilandis. She lay with her head turned towards an open window, and a gleam of sunlight just lighted up her face and hair.

George hesitated but for a few seconds to assure himself that she was really asleep, and that there was no one near to watch him. Then, very softly, he opened Kara's locket, and there, as he had been assured, lay a disc exactly like that given him by Loftra. He made the exchange, closed the locket, stole to the balcony, and threw into the sea below the disc that he had taken out. Then he returned to his sister's side, and seated himself noiselessly, to wait patiently for her awakening.

And while he sat and looked at her, the boy was shocked at the change that he there saw. For Vanina was indeed greatly altered. She was pale and haggard, the rosy flush that had been one of her greatest charms had left her face. When awake, too, one could see that her eyes had lost their sparkling brightness, and her manner its old vivacity. She moved, and spoke, and acted like one in a dream; or as one who waits at intervals for directions or commands from some absent master.

George felt his eyes suffuse with tears; he recalled her as he had seen her but a few weeks ago, and he felt a rising anger against King Kara; he began to comprehend more clearly what Zoreas and Loftra had said concerning him, and the arts by which, as they declared, he had influenced Vanina.

Presently she woke up, and, seeing him beside her, uttered a startled cry. For a brief space she gazed at him, unable to decide whether she saw him in reality or was still dreaming. But he sprang quickly towards her, and the next moment was clasping her in his arms.

"I am so glad to see you back, little brother," she exclaimed presently, holding him at arms length, and keenly scrutinising his face to assure herself that he was well. "I thought I should have died with anxiety and grief, until your message came; and even then we knew not what to think, whether to trust to it, to believe you were really safe."

"I have been safe, dear sister, and with kind friends; so you need not have troubled so."

"But *where* have you been?" she asked, "and with what friends? And how can you have here kind friends who are unknown to us?"

"I may not tell you yet, dear sister," he replied, with a wise shake of the head. "Another time. But I must hurry away now; I have to see Monella; I have something I was strictly charged to hand to him."

"What is it?" she inquired.

"That also I may not tell you. Though, indeed," George added, "I do not know myself, beyond the fact that it is a small box."

She pressed him closely, but he adhered to his instructions, though he found it hard to do so, for, boy-like, he was almost bubbling over with the adventures he had passed through.

To turn the talk, he inquired about the others, and was told that all was well with them.

"And Mr. Wydale, is he well?" And he eyed his sister half-re-proachfully. He expected to hear her shelve this inquiry with some pleasantry; but for, perhaps, the first time in his references to Wydale, she looked confused. Her pale face flushed, and she avoided the boy's frank look.

"I fear he is not well," she murmured. "I saw him a few days ago. I went over to Dilandis on account of you. All there were searching for you, and he came to talk to me of you, and told me how terribly concerned he was. He is very fond of you. I remember his saying, when I begged him to do all he could to find you, 'I require no urging, for, if anything should happen to George, I should lose all I have left in the world to love.'"

She sighed and said no more. George viewed her thoughtfully. He felt half-resolved to tell her something of what was in his mind. Yet he doubted whether it would be prudent, and whether, too, it would be well received; for "grown-up people," as he was aware, do not listen very attentively to a boy's ideas upon such matters. And, indeed, a week or two ago he would not have ventured to say a word upon the subject, whether to his sister or anyone else. But that time seemed now long ago. He seemed to be much older—years older—now; for a few days of thrilling and altogether unforeseen adventure will often have that effect upon us all—and upon young people as well as upon their elders. At last George made up his mind.

"Sister," he began, and then he stopped, for his voice trembled a little, and he felt somewhat frightened. He knew Vanina's imperious spirit, and how she had often snubbed him when he had ventured an opinion that displeased her. But there came into his memory Wydale's sorrowful face, with its expression of world-weariness, and he suddenly took courage, and determined that, for his sake, he would now go through with what he had begun. "Sister, do you know why Mr. Wydale looks so ill and so sorrowful—or have you never given it a thought? Don't you remember when we first came here—on board the *Saucy Fan*—even the days when we first were anchored here? Ah, those were happy days. *He* looked happy, *you* looked happy, and *I* was happy too. But now," the boy concluded, with a sigh, "no one seems happy. I know Mr. Wydale is not; I am sure *you* don't look happy; and *I* can't be, seeing you two so different."

It was a long speech, and a difficult one for the boy to make, and he watched her anxiously to see the outcome, feeling that, if it failed, his little stock of eloquence would not hold out. But it did not fail, for Vanina burst into tears, and hid her face upon his shoulder.

"Do I recollect?" she sobbed. "Shall I ever forget? Why do you remind me now, when our happiness has gone from us, and can never be regained?"

"Why not?" George boldly answered. "Mr. Wydale is the same, and you are not yet—married—sister. Perhaps—perhaps—"

"Hush, George. It is too late. Do not speak any more about it. I see now—I seem to see more clearly to-day than I have seen before—that I have behaved badly towards my best friends. I seem to have awakened from a fevered dream, and now see everything in a different light. Why is this, I wonder? How strange that you should speak to me just when this new feeling has come over me. What does it mean?"

She rose and walked restlessly up and down the room, while her young brother regarded her in some perplexity. Had the new "charm" begun to work, as had been promised? If so, perhaps the less he now said or did the better, else might he say or do something to obstruct its influence. So he rose and prepared to leave.

"I was almost forgetting that they are anxious about me over there as well as here," he said, with affected cheerfulness. "Goodbye, now, sister. What message shall I give to Sydney and Idelia, and—Mr. Wydale?"

She advanced to him, and placing her hands upon his shoulders, and looking keenly into his eyes, made answer:

"Tell them, George, that I shall not be long behind you, and that, when I come, I return to stay amongst those I know to be my friends, and to come back here no more."

George fixed his eyes on her inquiringly, trying to read in her face whether this new resolve would be a lasting one; and, when he saw her flushing cheeks, and her eyes flash with something of their former light, his spirits rose.

"I will gladly tell them that," he said, "and I know they will all be overwhelmed with joy to hear it. And come quickly, sister dear.

I shall not be happy till you have returned to us, and I see you and Mr. Wydale good friends as you used to be."

And with that he left her, and, hastening to the harbour, regained his boat, more light-hearted than he had been for many months.

In due course he reached Dilandis, where he was warmly welcomed on all sides, and by Idelia as cordially as any. He remembered this afterwards, and recalled with gratitude her affectionate greeting when, next morning, terrible news spread through the land.

But now he sought Monella, and, first delivering the casket, proceeded to give to him and Sydney and Wydale an account of all that he had seen and done.

25
"Vanina Dead!"

"Vanina dead!" Such was the sad and startling rumour that was noised throughout the land on the morning after the boy's return. It is scarcely possible to give a notion of the impression everywhere produced. The whole community stood aghast; the daily routine of life was checked; men, women, and children alike had no heart to pursue their occupations. The fisher-folk stood idle, and their boats rocked empty in the harbour; with the tillers of the soil, the artificers, with the schools, the workshops, the printing-office— everywhere it was the same; work was suspended, and people hung about in groups discussing in low, hushed tones the dreadful news.

And this was only natural; for, though Vanina had not done much of late to endear herself to the Dilandians—had, indeed, by her engagement to King Kara estranged many former friends—yet now all thought only of the good in her. They remembered how she had come amongst them at a time of national despondency, and had, by her brilliant heroism, done much to inspirit their fighting men, and lead them on to victory. Then there was the cargo of the *Saucy Fan*, and the use it had been put to; the credit for this had been ascribed principally to her, and, when they thought of what they owed to her, a deep distrust arose of Kara, and a murmur that speedily became an insistent craving for revenge. For there was a general belief that Vanina could not have come fairly by her death, and treachery was suspected by the people. Only the day before, her young brother George had seen her, talked with her, and left her, to all appearance, strong and well; yet, but a few hours later, it was said that she was dead—had died so suddenly

237

that there had been no time to send for her brothers even. How could this be?

It was stated by King Kara and his friends that she had died of heart disease— "caused, probably, by the excitement of her brother's return." And her friends were invited to come and satisfy themselves that this was so. And it was difficult to controvert this statement, which had much of plausibility about it; and what ground was there for the feeling of distrust that was abroad? "Why," some asked, "should Kara do aught against the life of one who, in a very short time, was to become his wife? She had for some time said openly she meant to marry him; why, therefore, should he conspire against her life?" This was a difficult question to reply to, a perplexing fact to explain away. But the majority would not wait to explain or argue; they were suspicious, and began to call for "vengeance," and ominous rumours flew about of a renewal of the war. And in many places men were to be seen cleaning up their armour, sharpening their swords, and looking to their bows and arrows, quietly preparing for the outbreak which they believed inevitable.

It sufficed for them that the one they had regarded as their Warrior-Queen—though never actually crowned—had died in Kara's country in a sudden, mysterious, suspicious manner. For that there must be a reckoning with King Kara.

It was in this mood that Sydney Dareville found himself while he sat cleaning up his revolver and regretfully counting over the four or five cartridges he had left, and wishing, again and again, that they were hundreds or thousands instead of units. Wydale found him thus engaged when, heavy-eyed and gloomy, he sought him to inquire whether, and if so, when, he was going across to Karanda.

"Am I going there? Yes I am, Owen," retorted Dareville, savagely. "And I am going to make that scoundrel confess, at the muzzle of this pistol, what part he had in my sister's death, and then shoot him—and afterwards myself. Will you come and help me? Two pistols will be better than one in this affair; and you have some cartridges left, I hope?"

"I have three or four," said Wydale; "but, Sydney, it is not by the rash and murderous act that you suggest that we can best show our respect and sorrow for the dead. We have no evidence to go upon; and to shoot a man without clear proof is murder."

"I don't care," Sydney answered, biting his lips. "I told you I would make him confess; and, if I do that—and I have little doubt I shall—then it is no murder to shoot the cowardly scoundrel."

"What I suggest," said Wydale, "is that we take Dr. Manleth with us and demand to see her. Then let us hear his opinion as to the cause—of—her—death."

So overcome was he at this point, that he could scarcely conclude the sentence, and he was obliged to turn away.

Sydney remained silent for a space, and then said abruptly

"Where is George; how is he now?"

"He is with the Princess Idelia, and was sleeping when I left him. He had cried himself to sleep, poor boy, and she is watching him and tending him as tenderly as a mother. It is best for the present to leave him to her care."

"Yes; I think so, too. And I shall be glad if Manleth will go with us. Have you seen Monella? What does he say to it all? What advice does he give? But there,"—here Dareville broke off irritably— "what advice *can* he give? There is nothing to be said—only one thing to be done—and I mean to do it."

"I have not seen him," was Wydale's answer. "I tried to find him, but failed; and, since then, I have been all the time with George."

Later in the day the three started for Karanda, where they were received by the townsfolk with many marks of sympathy and good feeling. Vanina had made herself popular amongst them, and was now proportionately regretted. These people were altogether different from those by whom they were enthralled, *viz.*, the priests and their adherents. But of them not much had recently been seen; and all the other classes, almost without exception, had shown themselves to the strangers as well-disposed good-natured people. And there were now to be seen many signs of mourning amongst them, as the three passed by on their way to the palace.

Arrived there, they were received by Morveena and others who had been in attendance on Vanina; but of King Kara they saw nothing. They were told that he was prostrated with grief, and had shut himself up and refused to see a soul. At this Sydney glanced at Wydale, but said nothing, only set his teeth together harder.

Vanina was lying upon a raised bier at the upper end of a small hail in the palace. The daylight had been shut out with heavy curtains, and the palace was lighted with hanging lamps and many tapers. She was dressed in a simple white costume, the same that she had worn when George had seen her last, and lying on her side, with her face as though looking down the apartment, seemed to be calmly sleeping. Her eyes, indeed, were not quite closed, but the long drooping lashes so overhung them that this was scarcely noticeable. Dr. Manleth went up to her and took her hand; it was deathly cold and stiff, and, after a brief examination, he turned away.

Not much could be said in the presence of the dead; and Manleth presently led Sydney outside, Wydale staying alone with the marble-like form of the one he had so loved while living.

"So far as I can tell," the doctor said to Sydney, when they were alone, "there is nothing to show the cause of death. Of course a full examination might reveal more than is now apparent. The appearances are, however, quite consistent with death from heart disease. More than that I cannot say."

"She *is* dead, doctor?" Dareville asked, in a hot, low tone. "I ask that because I have heard such tales about this Kara, and his devilish arts and sorcerer-like ways, that really one does not know what trick he might play off on us."

But the doctor shook his head. So far as all appearance went, there was no possible ground for doubt.

"I wish Monella had been here," he said presently. "I should have much liked him to see her. But we could not induce him to come. I do believe he thinks it scarcely safe here for any of us."

"And I've little doubt that he is right," Dareville commented gloomily. "However, I have some bullets left for anyone who attempts any tricks with us. Only," he concluded, with a savage glance around, "I want to save them for Kara. I wish I knew where to look for him. I'd get at him somehow or other."

Manleth did his best to soothe and comfort him, and presently persuaded him to return to Dilandis. But when they sought Wydale and pressed him to accompany them, he refused flatly.

"I shall stay here—where my heart is—where my thoughts are," he declared. "Leave me to do as my heart dictates. Do you return and look to George, till I get back to him."

In spite of all their arguments, he insisted on remaining; and in the end they left him, promising to return next day. All that night Wydale remained in the hail in which Vanina lay. He was there alone, passing the time in prayer and silent communion with the dead; and in the morning when he came out from his vigil, he was hollow-eyed and haggard, and looked, said many, ten years older.

One of the first he encountered was the Princess Morveena. She invited him to have some breakfast with her, but he declined coldly, and asked where King Kara was.

"He has shut himself up away from all of us," she said, "and will see no one. He even refuses food."

"But *where* is he?" Wydale asked again. "I would speak with him."

She shook her head, and declared that she did not even know herself. He had given strict orders that he was not to be disturbed; and it would be as much as their lives were worth to disobey him.

The hours passed, and still neither the doctor nor Sydney came. At last Owen went down to the harbour to make inquiry, and then learned that the gates had been closed against all comers, just as in the time of war between the two communities.

"The Dilandians," he was told, by one he questioned, "are making warlike preparations, and threatening to come here to attack us; *that* we know. Therefore we are compelled to adopt counter measures."

And it appeared, from further inquiries, that Sydney and the doctor had that morning sailed across, and had been refused admission to the harbour; after waiting about for some time in their boat, they had returned to Dilandis.

"And by whose orders were they sent away?" demanded Wydale. "By King Kara's? Because I have been told he has shut himself up and will see no one."

But no one seemed to know exactly as to this; save that some thought the order had come, not from Kara, but from Malion, the high priest. Eventually, Owen retraced his steps to the palace. It was clear to him that he was now a prisoner within the enemy's gates, and though not yet under restraint, probably he soon would be. But the thought in no way troubled him. He felt too unhappy, and too listless, and cared absolutely nothing about what might happen to him.

He passed the day almost in a state of coma. For hours he would be alone in the hail in which Vanina lay; then he would lean on a balcony that overlooked the sea towards Dilandis, and there remain motionless as a statue, sunk in deep reveries, and noticing nothing that went on around him. Many passed and repassed, and some spoke, but none received an answer. And thus, too, he passed the following night.

In the morning he went early to the balcony, hoping he might see Sydney or others of his friends approaching, and that they might make some signs to him. But, disappointed in this, he returned to his solitary vigil before Vanina's shrine—as he now looked upon it; and here presently Morveena joined him.

"And why," she asked softly, "doth the Lord Owen thus shut his heart and close his ears to all his friends? I can understand that his grief is deep; for I know"—here she sighed deeply— "how much he loved our lost one. Still, it doth not become us to forget courtesy."

It had been the custom to speak of, and address, Wydale, in the language of the country, as "the Lord Owen." It was an easier name than Wydale for the islanders to pronounce. In like manner Dareville was styled "Sydney," in preference to his surname.

Wydale listened to this address in the listless manner that had never left him since he had received the news of Vanina's death. He did not even look round, when he replied, in a hopeless tone:

"If I seem to fail in courtesy, princess, thou must pardon me, and put it down to the anguish of my wound. For that I am wounded—aye, even unto death—thou must be well aware. I care not now to hide it;—even though others look upon my wound only to laugh at me," he went on bitterly. "I care not who knows *now* how I loved her. She is gone—so what can it signify? There is no harm in loving the dead! I know that, a little while ago, I durst not have spoken thus to human being, for—she was then promised to your brother. But now—she has gone from this world, and surely I may reverence her memory in peace. Wilt thou not, therefore, leave me?"

Morveena bit her lip, and hesitated for some minutes, during which Wydale fell again into his abstracted mood and took no further notice of her. Then she spoke again

"But listen to me, my friend. Thou art in great danger. In fact thou art a prisoner here. Thy friends have declared war against us—at least—" here she hesitated again, then went on— "they are preparing to make war upon us, and already we have felt compelled to adopt defensive measures. Therefore have they made thee a prisoner of war—only—"

"Only they are ashamed of their own treachery," Wydale interrupted scornfully, and with more spirit than he had yet shown since his arrival in the place. "A man came here, in time of peace, as a mourner at the bier of a dead friend—and he is to be treacherously made a 'prisoner of war.' Oh, most noble princess of a noble country! I congratulate thee upon reigning over such a land!"

"But I do not reign, or govern," she objected. And I came, in all good faith, to warn thee—and, if thou wilt, to aid thee. Is it a fitting return to treat me thus? I was about to say that, but for me, thou wouldst already have been seized, dragged from this place, and thrown into prison. I have insisted that thy grief shall be respected; I have insisted that thou shalt be free to indulge thy sorrow unmolested; and for me this has been granted. But consider, my Lord Owen, art thou making me a friendly return for this?"

Owen sighed. "If I have seemed discourteous, princess," he said wearily, "I ask thy pardon. After all, I care little now what befalls me, or how they deal with me."

She eyed him in silence for a few moments, then replied:

"Thou shouldst have more courage, more boldness, my Lord Owen, and—more belief in thy true friends. Now, I have seen ever since I did first set eyes on thee, how thou didst give thy whole thoughts to this lady who is dead—while she neglected thee—and how thou didst exclude all others from close friendship. Else mightst thou have seen—"

"Seen what?" asked Owen, noting that she hesitated.

"That there were some—*one* at least—" she went on, almost passionately— "who could have consoled thee for the loss of her thou couldst not lately even hope for."

Owen shook his head, and made answer, slowly:

"I thank thee, princess; I think I understand thy meaning. But it is well I should declare at once that, while I thank thee for thy proffered friendship, I can offer no such friendship in return."

"And yet," persisted she, "I hold a secret for which thou wouldst give all thou hast—aye," she exclaimed with sudden energy, "thy life, aye thy very soul itself, as I believe."

An inquiring look came into his eyes; then he returned calmly:

"Thou mistakest, princess. There is only one gift for which I would barter my life or risk my soul, and, that is beyond thy power to give."

"Be not too sure of that, my friend," she answered, with an air of triumph. "I know thy heart's desire; and I can grant it, if I so choose. It remains to ask, What wilt thou pay for it?"

But he regarded her almost with contempt, and said:

"Again thou mistakest, princess. My only desire is that the Princess Vanina should be alive again and restored to her friends. *That* is beyond thy power."

"But it is *not*," replied Morveena, coming close to him, and looking with her lustrous eyes straight into his. "It is just *that* I can do. What price art thou prepared to pay for its accomplishment?"

26
Morveena and Wydale

Owen Wydale gazed in a half-bewildered way back into the face that had come so close to his. There was in its expression a passion of such intensity as he had never looked upon before. Yet it failed to affect him with responsive feelings, for he only turned wearily away.

"Why dost thou mock me with proposals of impossible bargains?" he asked, in a disappointed tone. "*If* thou couldst do what thy words imply—*if* thou couldst bring the Princess Vanina back to life, and restore her to her friends, I would willingly remain here in captivity for the remainder of my days; nay, I would give my life itself—nor deem the price too high."

"I take thee at thy word, my Lord Owen," Morveena boldly answered. "Thou hast said thou wouldst gladly remain here in captivity, but in thy mind thou hast a sorrowful captivity. Say only that thou wilt remain a captive to *me*, and I will grant thee thy desire."

"Again I comprehend thee not, princess," he said. "Thou canst not restore the dead to life; wouldst that thou could, for then I would gladly give—"

"Wilt thou swear to that?"

"Right gladly. By what shall I swear?"

"Oh! I have heard," returned Morveena, "that thou dost believe only in one God; not in many, as do we. Thou shalt swear then by thine own one great God!"

"I do swear it!" Owen solemnly affirmed. "And now show me to what purpose thou hast led me on to this."

For answer, Morveena stepped up to him and said, almost in a whisper:

"Vanina is not dead!"

Wydale uttered an exclamation, but she laid her finger on her lip.

"Hush!" she said, "thou wilt call others hither, and bring down on me my brother's vengeance. Now I will show thee—but, remember, thou belongest now to me; thou art captive to me, as hath been agreed. Thou hast naught further with Vanina than to see her restored to life and to her friends!"

"Now," she continued, "stand thou where thou now art, and see what I shall do; but move not, speak not, and come not near her. If thou dost, I renounce the bargain."

"I promise," he declared, now roused to a high pitch of excitement and expectation.

Morveena mounted the steps, on the top of which was placed the bier upon which Vanina lay. She drew from a pouch or pocket something which she waved to and fro under the nostrils of the recumbent figure. And soon a flush suffused the deathly-white cheeks, the nostrils were distended, the lips parted, and the bosom heaved with laboured gasps; then the eyes opened and gazed at Wydale with an expression that he had never seen in them before. There seemed to be love, appeal, entreaty, all mingled together. He could not resist that look, and, forgetful of his promise, he rushed towards her and cried aloud, "Vanina! Vanina!"

But Morveena met him with uplifted hand and a flashing eye, and stepped forward to prevent him from approaching her; and thereupon Vanina sank back into her former death-like state.

"Thou hast not kept thy promise, my Lord Owen," Morveena said, almost fiercely. "Since I see I cannot depend on thee, I shall proceed no further with her restoration."

For a moment he almost glared at her. The thought came to him to seize her and force from her the secret that would bring his loved one back to life. But he recognised in time the futility of such madness, and stepped back.

"I was so astonished," he said humbly, "that I temporarily forgot my promise. Proceed; and I will not forget again."

"No!" she answered haughtily. "I will do no more to-day. I have shown thee enough for the time being. Thou knowest now that the Princess Vanina is not dead, but only in a trance from which she can be awaked at will. Thou hast agreed to certain terms; it remains to prove to me that thou wilt fulfil thy part of the bargain, if I do mine. And now," she added, in a softer voice, "now that thy anxiety is relieved—that thou knowest she is not really dead—there is no longer need for this sepulchral lack of gaiety. Thy friend sleepeth there in peace and quiet, and unharmed. Come now with me—thou art my captive, recollect—and let us see whether we cannot find some amusement to pass the time."

She led him, unresisting, out of the hail. He walked like one in a dream, feeling that he was beginning a new life—a life in which there would be no Vanina; and yet she would not be dead; she would lead *her* life amid other scenes, while he was leading his away from her. And, be it said, now that his great grief for her was assuaged, that he knew that she was not dead, it seemed but a small thing, after all, to sacrifice his future happiness. He rapidly balanced matters in his mind, and came to a conclusion which might be summed up somewhat thus:

"After all, I never declared my love to her—not since we came here—and she knows not that it still exists. She is to leave here free—if the bargain be kept—to love whom she pleases in the future; and I remain as the hostage of her liberty; but of that also she will know nothing. Since she has never loved me, she will not miss me; all that I have now to do is to make the best of the situation in which I find myself."

So he followed Morveena at her call, sat beside her at the banqueting table, and played his part with courtesy, if not with much enthusiasm, during the remainder of the evening. Morveena, her superb figure made the most of by her toilette, and full of triumph and satisfaction at the fulfilment of what she had long ardently desired, was not only gracious, but exerted every art for his bewitchment. So much so that Wydale, having once made up his mind that it was his duty to conciliate her, even found himself yielding to her compelling beauty and enchantment. And, when they parted for the night, she whispered to him, with sparkling eyes:

"Ah, now do I begin to believe in thy pledge to me! On my side I will keep mine, fear not; even in the very teeth of my brother Kara. Thou shalt see what pleasures we can taste together, and what it will be to rule with me this realm. But," she added abruptly, while a flash of distrust and menace swept across her face, "deceive me—rouse my jealousy—my anger—and then thou wilt find it were better thou hadst never been born!"

They separated soon after for the night, and Owen retired to a chamber that had been assigned to him; but, try as he would, and, notwithstanding that he had had no sleep for at least two days and nights, he could get no rest when he lay down. He lay and pondered over all that had occurred, and, the more he pondered, the more dissatisfied he became at having seemed to yield to Morveena's attractions, or blandishments, as he termed them to himself. And there came upon him a great remorse for every word and look that he had given her that night in token of his fidelity. The memory of it now brought to him a feeling of disgust. While in her company, the glamour of her great beauty had affected him beyond what he could have believed possible. Now the reaction had come upon him, and he felt more than sorry; he felt ashamed of himself. The fact that he had set out to go through it with good intent no longer sufficed to excuse him to himself. And as these thoughts came home to him, there entered into his mind a great longing to kneel again before the inanimate Vanina, to pour out to her deaf ears the story of his hopeless love, and to try to excuse himself—though she could not hear—for his seeming lapse, that night, from his love for her.

And, in the end, this craving so took possession of him as to become irresistible; and he abandoned further effort to contend with it. He rose, dressed himself, and stole softly through the silent and deserted corridors towards the ball in which Vanina lay.

He noiselessly entered the dimly-lighted hall, which he found empty, save for the death-like form he came to look upon; and, when he had gazed awhile upon the well-known, much-loved features, he sank upon his knees, and, half-unconsciously, poured forth, in murmured, broken words, his whole heart and soul.

"Oh, my dear one!" he almost sobbed, "you who never listened to my words of love ere this, and who cannot hear them now—to you, now, I may surely say what I durst not utter before—what I shall never address to you again. To-night I did seem to forget you, to be entranced by another's surpassing beauty; but it was not really so, beloved. Here, speaking to you for the last time, and in all earnestness and truth, I do entreat you that you forgive all that seems to be an offence to my great love for you. You will never know the sacrifice I have made to-day for your sweet sake—the sacrifice of the whole of my future life the hateful bondage to which I have given myself—ah—yes—but—still it is for your dear sake! You will never know! You will go forth—back to the old times—or at least to a new life in which I shall have no part; and perhaps you will think I was easily consoled for my loss of your love. Oh! dear one, think not that! That would be indeed the hardest of all for me to bear! I know you cannot hear my appeal to you; yet I cannot keep myself from praying to you never to have that belief about me—for—beloved—my heart—all my thoughts, my whole being, belong ever to you; and, as I have never loved any but you throughout my life—so—I solemnly swear, here, before your dear form that hears me not—I shall never have any love to give to another so long as life with me shall last!"

He rose slowly, sorrowfully, to his feet, and turned to retrace his steps to his sleeping chamber, when, to his astonishment, the room was suddenly filled with armed men, some of whom carried torches that lighted up the scene with a bright but flickering glare. In advance of them stood Morveena; but no longer the soft-eyed, languishing Morveena of two or three hours ago. In her place stood one who would have passed well for an incarnation of a Fury, or of womanly jealousy and hatred.

"Seize him!" she cried, with flashing eyes and scowling brows. "Seize the traitor who hath broken his oath to his own so-called God—seize and bind him, and carry him to the Hall of the Living-dead, and there let him meet the death that he deserves!"

27
In the Catacombs of the Living-Dead

In the centre or thereabouts of the island of Atlantis, about half-way, that is, from the "caverns" to the city of Karanda, the wall of perpendicular cliff that marked the shore line rose abruptly into a mountain of considerable height. It stood like a great tower at the point of junction with a rocky ridge that ran across the interior of the island, dividing it into two basin-like tracts of country. This ridge was the boundary line between the two communities; this mountain thus looked down upon both domains upon the one side and on the sea upon the other.

It bore several names. One was the "Crystal Mountain," for it was composed wholly of crystal rock. It had been hollowed out and formed in terraces; or perhaps it had been originally hollow, and thus required little work to adapt it for the purpose it was put to. In any case it was now an immense covered amphitheatre, with galleries capable of seating many hundreds of people, yet leaving a spacious arena in the centre. This was the Temple of the Goddess Kraldeema, the chief of the deities worshipped by the Karanites; and it was the abode of the mysterious monsters called "Kralens," otherwise "vampires," which were supposed to be under Kraldeema's special protection. For this terrible being was the goddess of death and suffering and cruelty; analogous, probably, to Devi or Kâli, the wife of Siva the Destroyer, that many-armed monstrosity worshipped by the Hindoos, known also formerly as the special deity and protectress of the atrocious Thug confederacy.

Another name for the Crystal Mountain was the "Hall" or "Catacombs" of the Living-dead. This referred to one part of it, where

250

an immense hail, carved out of the solid crystal, and shut off from all the rest, was given up to those unhappy ones who were destined to be sacrificed to the Kralens, and were here imprisoned awaiting their fate, all lying in the same state of death-like trance as that into which Vanina had been thrown.[1]

This formed a gruesome feature in the worship appertaining to the goddess. Its object it is difficult to determine; but it illustrates what would appear to be almost a general principle in regard to heathenish religions all over the globe—that they are chiefly to be distinguished from each other by some special form of cruelty invented for, and peculiar to, each.

One end of the "catacombs" opened into a garden, in which were fountains and perfumed flowers and shady walks; and it was part of the "preparation" which intended victims had to undergo that they should be occasionally roused from their torpor and made to exercise for a while—varying from an hour or two to a few days—in this garden. Here, shut in by walls of perpendicular rock that precluded all possibility of escape, they could look out through barred gates over the sea in one direction, and the interior of the island in another. The garden was placed in a high position, and parts of it were always more or less shaded by the overhanging rock; while cool and refreshing breezes often swept across it, entering through the great barred barriers at each end.

It was in this garden that Wydale found himself when he awoke to consciousness on the morning following the scene with Morveena. For some time he could not recall what had happened;

[1] A method of instantaneously producing this condition by a slight wound is known to the Indian tribes of British Guiana, who practise it on animals in their hunting expeditions by means of arrows dipped in some composition of which they possess the secret. An animal wounded by one of these arrows is instantly paralysed, and falls into a trance-like condition, yet it is not dead, and in this way the carcass can be kept in a hot climate longer than would otherwise be the case. See books of travel of the country by Mr. Barrington Brown and other explorers.—Author.

but by degrees recollection came back to him, though even then he
had only a confused idea of what had taken place.

He dimly remembered attempting to fight his way out of the
palace. He remembered that he had drawn his revolver, and shot
down the first two who had attempted to lay hands on him; that
this had so far frightened the rest that they had retreated and left
one entrance to the room free; but there he had been met by a fresh
crowd of soldiers, who, knowing nothing of the danger they ran,
had suddenly rushed upon him and borne him to the ground. He
had then but two cartridges left. These he had fired, when a stun-
ning blow on the head had blotted out the whole scene, and he
knew nothing of what happened afterwards.

He now rose, feeling somewhat dazed, from a couch upon which
he had been lying, and looked about him. He was in a sort of cell
that opened upon the garden, from which it could be shut off by a
thick door of wood and a barred gate. As the door was open, he
could see the garden through the gate, which he discovered was
unfastened, whereupon he opened it and stepped out into the sunlight, and for the next hour he was employed in exploring the place,
and speculating why he had been placed in it instead of in some
noisome prison. A prison, however, it was all the same. He soon
satisfied himself as to that. Round it, here and there, were narrow
chambers like that in which he had found himself. These were all
shut off, in similar fashion, by wood or iron doors and barred gates.
Sometimes the door was open while the gate was fastened, sometimes both were closed, shutting out all view of what was within.
At the farther end of each cell was another door, opening, probably, into a corridor. So far as he could ascertain, all the cells were
untenanted.

He wandered to the boundaries of the garden, and gazed out
through the barriers of open iron work upon the view spread out
beyond. But the place was so situated that he could see only what
was distant. Whatever was below was hidden from sight. Thus there
was no chance of his communicating, as he had at first hoped he
might, with some passing Dilandian boat. Nor was it possible to
climb up the bars, nor would it have been of any use could he have
done so, for on the other side was nothing but perpendicular rock,

so smooth that even a fly, one would have thought, could scarcely have walked upon its surface.

At one side, where the rock that shut in the garden rose sheer and overhanging—the opposite side to that on which the cells were placed—was a large opening, shut off in like manner, *viz.*, with a great door, that closed behind a barred iron gate. The door was open, and he looked in through the bars; but all within was gloom, only dimly illuminated by the light that came in through the gateway, supplemented by that of a few hanging lamps. From these came a peculiar aromatic scent, an odour as of incense.

Knowing nothing of the true meaning of the dim shapes he could but just discern within, Wydale turned from the place with little interest, and made his way to a seat under a shady tree that had been trained to form an extensive arbour. Here he sat down and listened for a while to the plashing of a fountain close at hand, thinking out all that had lately happened, and wondering at the position in which he found himself.

While thus ruminating, he heard a footstep, and, turning round, perceived, approaching him, a grave-looking man, with white hair and beard, dressed in a long, flowing purple robe, gathered in at the waist with a girdle. The stranger waved his hand as in salute, and thus addressed him:

"I am called Zanolda, and am Astrologer to King Kara. May I speak with thee, my son?"

Wydale received him doubtfully. The stranger's speech was fair enough, but Owen did not altogether like his face. It was smiling, but the smile was, to his thinking, too suave, too smooth. And there were lines about the features that betokened a disposition hard and stern at least, if not actually cruel.

"I knew thy countryman who stayed amongst us, and who hath now gone over to thy friends. Indeed, I may say that I befriended him."

Wydale suddenly called to mind Peter Jennings, and how he had related that Zanolda had saved him from imprisonment.

"I have heard of it," he therefore now replied, in a more friendly tone. "But why do you seek me? Do you bring me good news?"

Zanolda shook his head.

"I fear me not, my son; yet perhaps I have that to tell thee that thou fain wouldst know."

"Say on."

Zanolda seemed to hesitate, but presently proceeded:

"There is one in whom thou takest a great interest; indeed, as I know by my study of the stars, her fate and thine are closely interwoven."

"What of her?" demanded Wydale, with outward calmness, but with an inward eagerness he found it hard to repress.

"The decree hath gone forth that thou art to die together."

"Ah! *Whose* decree?"

"It is the decree of King Kara and of Malion, the High Priest."

Wydale remained silent for a space, and then rejoined:

"Well, I did not expect much else in such a country, so I am not surprised. We are in your power, and you can do with us as you will."

"It does not rest with me," was the reply. " I came but to warn thee; also to tell thee that perhaps a way of escape may even yet be found for thee."

"What way—the same that has been already offered?" Wydale asked, with such contempt that the other looked up in some dismay.

"Hush, my son!" he said, with a deprecating wave of the hand. "Pile not the fuel on fierce fires. Think of the maiden—of thy duty towards her."

It was a painful subject to discuss, and Wydale felt he would rather not pursue it. He trusted no one in that place; he felt convinced that he was surrounded on all sides by treachery, jealousy, and ruthless passion. What availed discussing anything with people whom one could not trust?

"Let us," he said coldly, "if you please, talk of something else— if there is aught else to talk about. If not, I pray you leave me in peace."

"Come with me," Zanolda said; "I have much to show thee. Perhaps, after thou hast seen, thou wilt be of a different mind."

He took from his girdle a bunch of keys, and, motioning to Owen to follow him, went towards the barred gate in the rock and opened it.

"In there," he said, "are the 'Catacombs of the Living-dead.' Here victims rest before they are given to the sacrifice. It gives them time for prayer and meditation—time to make their peace with the gods they have offended."

They entered a vast, vaulted hail, in which was a central walk partitioned off on both sides with bars, seemingly of gold, that were placed at intervals throughout its length. Behind these bars were vaults, open in front, and in each was a kind of altar, with tapers burning on each side; and in the centre was a raised slab, six feet or thereabouts in length. Many of these vaults were elaborately carved and decorated, and ornamented with gold and precious stones, that sparkled and flashed in the light of the lamps and candles; and some of the slabs looked like golden biers fitted for the lying-in-state of a dead king or queen or warrior chief.

And upon these biers were recumbent forms, lying and looking much as had Vanina. Under their heads and feet were jewelled cushions of purple and gold, while lighted tapers placed around them threw a dim, ruddy light upon the figures that lay cold and motionless as though dead.

"Thou seest!" said Zanolda. "These are all destined for the sacrifice. They are not dead, nor do they sleep in calm unconsciousness. They have no need for food or drink. All functions of the body are suspended, save that of the brain. They can *think* and *hear*, and that is all."

Wydale felt almost sick while he looked upon these hapless ones. There were both young and old, fair young forms and bearded men: all seemed to be calmly sleeping—but what, thought Wydale, must be their thoughts, if it were as Zanolda said?

Suddenly he started, and could not repress a cry. For there, extended upon one of the biers, was one he recognised. It was Joseph Durford, the rascally skipper of the *Saucy Fan*. Then he perceived close beside him, the mate, Steve Foster.

He stood and gazed upon these two with mingled feelings. Pity he could scarcely feel; yet their punishment was one at which his mind revolted. Still, but for these villains, he thought bitterly, neither he nor Vanina would now be in their present hapless situation. They might now have been happy in a mutual love; certainly they would never have been launched into these adventures that were ending so disastrously.

Zanolda observed the direction of his glance, and nodded in appreciation.

"Yes, yes, I see thou recognisest them. The others of their party have been given to the Kralens; but these two have lain here thus for many months—since, indeed, soon after they arrived here. I do not know what was thy quarrel with them, but I am aware thou lovest them not."

Owen shuddered.

"Truly I have no cause to love them," he replied. "Yet it is too great a punishment—to lie there day after day, week after week, and month after month, only to brood without cessation upon a wicked past and a hopeless future."

"There is worse in store for them," Zanolda responded, with grim emphasis. "More's the pity that thou shouldst court a like fate, when the road by which thou canst avoid it lies before thee. But now I am about to show thee our temple sacred to the goddess Kraldeema, the home of her dread ministers the Kralens!"

28
Vanina and Wydale

Passing through a low gallery closed at both ends with heavy and close-fitting wooden doors studded with bolts and spikes of iron, the two came out into the great amphitheatre that formed nearly the whole interior of the hollow mountain. At one end was a raised platform like a roomy stage, upon which was a throne of gold and silver, ornamented with jewels of great size and lustre. On each side of it were richly cushioned and ornamented chairs, evidently special seats for the priests and high officials. At the back was a cleverly-executed fresco in rich colouring of some great creature like a dragon.

All around, except at one end, were terraced galleries carved out of the solid crystal, rising tier upon tier almost to the roof. Some of these were of irregular width, running back, as it seemed, into side chambers, so that there were many dark recesses into which the light of the hanging lamps failed to penetrate. Flights of steps, cut out of the crystal rock, served for communication between these various galleries.

But the most noticeable feature of this uncommon "Temple" was a kind of cage which occupied the whole of the space not taken up by the galleries, thus enclosing a central arena of immense extent. The bars composing this cage were apparently of solid gold. They were strong and massive, and ran from the roof, sixty or eighty feet above, down to the floor of the arena, where they were fixed firmly in the rocky floor. At intervals horizontal bars ran round, knitting the whole together, these being from eight to nine feet, one above the other. The upright bars were about eighteen inches or two feet apart, leaving sufficient room for a person to pass freely through them into or out of the cage.

The cage followed the shape of the amphitheatre—that of a horseshoe—and was elongated at one end where there were no galleries, being carried right up to a perpendicular wall of rock. At this end of the floor was a ring of iron fencing, some forty feet in diameter, which appeared to be a guard-fence round a great well or pit. This pit was covered with a horizontal barred gate which shutdown over it in trap-door fashion. From this pit came a sound as of rushing or falling water. Immediately above the pit was a large oblong opening in the rock, now closed with a massive door of wood and metal. At times one was sensible of a sickly, foetid smell, but usually the prevailing odour was of incense diffused by the lamps and by numerous small braziers which flared around the lower galleries. These illuminated the place, so far as their light extended, with a weird, flickering glow that was reflected from thousands of minute points in the crystals above and below, and caused, in other places, fantastic, formless shadows that leaped and appeared and disappeared as the lambent flames danced up and down.

"This," said Zanolda, indicating the great space that was barred off, "is called 'The Golden Death-cage.' These great bars that reach from the floor to the roof high above us are all of solid gold. Yonder pit is the den of the Kralens. What is down there I know not; no man knows or hath ever known. We can tell, by the sound, that there must be below an underground torrent; but whence it comes and whither it goes we know not. Nor do we know what else may be below. Some say that there are great caverns there, extending far underground, and even under the sea. Certainly the subterranean river must communicate with the sea; and doubtless it carries thither the bones and other remains of the victims that the Kralens take down there."

"Take down there?"

"Why, yes; they seize upon their prey here in the cage, and carry it down to their dens below. The river must therefore carry off the bones, else would the place have become choked up long ago."

"You said just now," said Owen, thoughtfully, "that the sailors who deserted us had been given to these monsters. I thought that all such doings had ceased. It was so promised when the peace was made."

Zanolda shrugged his shoulders.

"It was so promised by King Kara," he replied, "but not by Malion, the high priest; and he governs here in all such matters. These ceremonies have gone on much the same, though the fact was kept secret from all but a comparative few."

"Then faith has not been kept with us! Another drop in the cup that Kara is filling for himself."

"A drop or two more or less can't make much difference to *him*," Zanolda rejoined, indifferently. "The cup was already nearly full," he added, dreamily, as though to himself. "So it is written among the stars. And it has been a gigantic cup, and has taken long in filling." Then, with an abrupt change of manner, he went on: "These braziers are fed with a certain herb that overpowers the effluvium given off by the Kralens, else could we not endure the place."

At that moment there issued from the pit a horrible, blood-curdling sound, half-scream, half-roar. Though Wydale had heard the cry before, yet he was wholly unprepared for the added force and power lent to it by the surroundings. The pit formed a gigantic speaking trumpet that magnified the shriek a hundred times, it was echoed again and again, reverberating from one rocky angle to another of the great domed roof, dying away, eventually, in low, sullen, muttering growls. Despite himself, Wydale started violently and shuddered; and, perhaps, had there been light enough, it would have been found that he had turned pale.

Zanolda regarded him with a peculiar smile. "Ah," he observed, "thou dost not like the sound of their cry? Few do."

"I have heard it before; but never like that," said Wydale.

"Let it teach thee the wisdom of avoiding them, my son."

Wydale was silent; a cold chill came over him, and he was seized with a great horror and disgust. "Let us go," he murmured hoarsely.

"But first let me explain—"

"Pray let us go from here; I feel sick and giddy."

Thereupon Zanolda led the way, and, without further talk, the two returned through the rows of "the Living-dead," into the sweet, fresh, perfumed atmosphere of the garden.

"What a contrast!" exclaimed Owen, inhaling a deep breath. His relief was great.

Zanolda eyed him with his enigmatical smile.

"Ponder it well, my son—what thou hast seen and heard—and think whether it would not be worth thy while to purchase immunity from this fate, and gain, at the same time, the smiles of an enchanting woman."

"Again that?" said Wydale wearily. "I thought the princess was incensed against me."

"She was; but she already repents her of her hasty action, and is ready to forgive thee—if thou wilt but ask her."

Wydale made a gesture of impatience, and Zanolda, seeing little hope of moving him, turned away.

"Think it over; I will see thee again to-morrow," said he at parting.

The next day he came again, and the next, and for several succeeding days. But Wydale remained of the same mind; and at last Zanolda grew tired and angry.

"I give it up; thou must meet thy fate," he said. "I shall come no more!"

For two days Wydale was left practically alone. Three or four times each day someone came into his cell bringing food and drink, without a word. But the prisoner scarcely tasted it.

On the third day since he had last seen Zanolda, he was taking his usual listless stroll about the garden, when, in passing one of the cells, he became aware that someone was within. The door was thrown back, and, on his trying the barred gate, it yielded. He pushed it open, and stood staring before him in amazement.

"Vanina!"

The figure he had been gazing at turned round, and he saw that it was indeed Vanina. She came towards him gravely, but without hesitation, frankly holding out her hand.

"Yes, it is I, dear friend," she said, with a look that was both sad and sweet. "It has been permitted me to come to see you that we might have a talk together." She sighed, then added, "Our last talk, probably, in this world."

And while Owen continued gazing at her, too surprised and bewildered to reply, she proceeded.

"Let us go out of this place, it is stifling. Ah!" she drew a long breath as she stepped into the garden, "this is a change indeed! I never thought to breathe the free air and look upon a scene like this again!"

Wydale, like one in a dream, led her to the seat beneath the spreading tree that had become his favourite resting-place; then, when she was seated, stood before her, gazing down upon her, still dumb, embarrassed and confused. He could not yet get over his bewilderment.

"Dear friend," Vanina recommenced, "our time is short, and there is much to be said. Seat yourself beside me, and let me tell you why I am here."

He did as she requested, still not knowing what to say.

"I have been sent here," she continued, with a sigh, "as a sort of ambassadress—on a mission to persuade you against myself—"

"Stop!" Wydale interrupted, almost fiercely. "Do you mean that you have been sent here with another message from that she—?"

"Hush," she urged softly. "Hear what I have to say—"

"I believe I know," he cried out, hoarsely; "and is this further insult to come from *you*? Have I not suffered enough through you? But—" He suddenly broke off, and went on in an altered tone, "perhaps it is your wish."

She put her hand appealingly on his arm.

"Listen to what I have to tell you first, and you will better understand."

She paused for a moment, then went on slowly, almost painfully:

"In any case we have terrible trials before us, and this is no time for false pride or misplaced sentiment. Unless—certain proposals be agreed to—we are both to die—by a dreadful death—on the fifth day from now."

"I know," Wydale assented, in a low voice. "Zanolda told me so."

"Then, dear friend, let us speak plainly to each other; let there be no misplaced reserve between us at a time like this. Let me set the example in being frank. My friend, I have been lying now for many days and nights powerless to move, yet unable to sleep away the time. My brain has been busy all the while, and I have seen the past with different eyes, I freely confess my own mad folly, and frankly own I thoroughly detest myself for my treatment of some of my friends, and, above all, of you."

Wydale made an impatient movement, but she went on:

"Do not interrupt me; let me go on while I have the courage, else may I break down. Now, let me tell you that in that state of trance in which I have been lying you can *hear* all that goes on around you, and, through half-closed eyes, *see* all that passes in front of them."

At this Wydale started; and a great thrill ran through his veins when he realised what all this meant. "Then," he exclaimed, "you heard—"

"Everything, my friend. I heard and understood the noble self-sacrifice you attempted for my sake—even while your heart was breaking in the attempt. I know, too, why it failed." She blushed slightly, then, looking down, she added: "And I thank you from the bottom of my heart—with all my soul—I thank you for what you then essayed in the hope of benefiting me, and for your good opinion. I did not know," she concluded, with a sigh, "there was such a man in the world; and it makes me feel the more acutely how unworthily I have acted."

Wydale caught her hand and tried to hold it in his own, but she withdrew it with gentle firmness.

"Vanina!" he exclaimed, "do not talk to me like this. You are breaking my heart!"

"I have done that already, I fear," was her reply; and I have lost your life as well. But for me, you would not be in the net in which you are enmeshed."

"Do not speak of that, Vanina. Life for me is worthless without you. If you think I have done aught to deserve your good opinion, tell me that you would have loved me if you could have got away from here."

She raised her eyes to him. She was calm and sad, and there was no affected shyness when she answered

"As I said, before, this is no time to conceal one's sentiments. I do not deserve your good opinion of me: still you shall have the truth. Owen, dear, true friend, I have loved you all along."

He sprang up and tried to take her in his arms, but she repulsed him in the same calm fashion, and bade him seat himself again beside her.

"Yes," she murmured dreamily, "at a time like this I may confess the truth, and you must know I would not now, with death staring me in the face, say to you what is false. But you will wonder why, if that was so, I behaved in the way I did. Truly," gravely shaking her head, "I know not myself. Let me say this, however. I began a half-flirtation with Prince Rokta more to tease you than for anything else. I was never serious in it, *never!* But when I found you seemed inclined to give me up to him so easily—"

"Vanina! How can you—"

"Hush! Let me go on. I had expected you to be bolder—more masterful—with me, and I was piqued at your seeming content to let me drift so easily apart from you. Well, that is all as to that."

"It was wrong—and cruel—cruel to me—and to that gentle girl Idelia."

"I know, I know, and heaven knows I have been sorry for it since; but *indeed* I never meant harm to any, and only afterwards saw my folly. Now, as to Kara"—here she shivered— "I know not what to say. Truly I do not like him, never have liked him; indeed, I detested him—I was afraid of him. But I seem to have been in a dream, and I awoke suddenly as from a nightmare that oppressed all my senses. I awoke, or seemed to—let me see—ah! I remember—it was the day George returned."

Wydale nodded. "I understand," he said, "and I believe you."

"That day, after George had left, Kara came in to see me, and he was more familiar than his wont, for he tried to take my hand—a thing he had never done before. Then I seemed to awake to the hatefulness of the union into which I had so nearly entered. I told him that it must be broken off, and that I should return forthwith to Dilandis; that I did not like him well enough to marry him, and never could. Then he flew into an awful passion—stormed and raved, and showed himself in his true colours. And the more he did this, of course, the more hateful he became to me, till suddenly he seemed to lose all self-control. He drew something from his pouch that glittered like a small stiletto, and I screamed out, believing he was about to murder me. But he caught me by the hand, and when I thought he was about to stab me to the heart, instead, he only slightly scratched the skin of my head amongst the hair. Immediately I felt sick and dizzy, and I know that I fell to the ground just when Morveena and others entered the room. Then they laid me where you saw me, and I have been there ever since till last evening, when Morveena brought me back to life, saying she wished to have some talk with me."

"And Kara? What of him? Where is he?"

"I know not. I have neither heard nor seen anything of him since the day on which we had our quarrel."

"I see," said Wydale, "that you still wear his locket."

Vanina put her hand up to her neck.

"This?" she exclaimed. "I had forgotten it. I will throw it into the sea yonder."

But Wydale stayed her hand. "Keep it, and wear it still for a while," he urged. "It has been the cause of your awakening from the spell that Kara had cast upon you; so we have been told, and I am bound, in the face of what has happened, to believe it."

And then he told her briefly of George's adventures amongst the Flower-Dwellers, and of his having exchanged the mysterious discs.

Presently they returned to the subject of Morveena.

"Well—you know now—what it is she has sent me here for," she said. "What answer am I to give her?"

"What answer you think well, Vanina. If it is your wish to save your life—I could perhaps even—"

"But it *isn't*," she answered, firmly; "I could never live out a life so purchased. Nor is it certain that she would—even, perhaps, *could*—keep her promise. The very air here is full of treachery and deceit and wickedness. No, Owen, I could not condemn you to such a life, even to free me; even if I could trust to her promise—I would rather die now and end it all—unless *you* wish otherwise."

"It is my decision also," Wydale answered, solemnly.

"But I cannot understand what Sydney and the others are doing all this time, that they seem to make no move on our behalf."

"They think me dead, for one thing."

"True; I had forgotten that. Oh, if we could only communicate with them! Five days, did you say? Oh, what could not Monella do in four days, if he but knew our situation, and that you are still alive."

"I fear he could not do much to aid us here," Vanina answered, sadly. "And there is no time—five days!"

"I don't know; Monella is so full of resource. Three or four days to him would be as good as three or four weeks or months with some. But," he added, gloomily, "I suppose it is of no use to speak of it. There is no possible way to let him know."

Presently they parted—a terrible yet tender leave-taking it was; and Wydale, believing that he would never see her again, abandoned himself, after she had gone, to grief; but now it was tempered by a sweet solace he had not known before.

But the next day she came again. She looked pale and worn, as though she had had no sleep and had been weeping all the night.

"She bade me come again, and make one last effort to induce you to accede to what she wishes," she said, sorrowfully. "And they have been doing and saying all sorts of things to frighten me and cause me to persuade you. What say you? Are you still of the same mind?"

Now, at that very moment, while they walked around the garden, there was heard the rushing sound of flapping wings, and lo! with two or three sharp circles, each smaller than the other, the crane that Wydale had made friends with, alighted on the path in front of him, and stood gravely regarding him, as though to say, "Where have you been to lately, and why do you never go out in the boat, so that I can come fishing with you?"

"Why," cried Owen, "it is 'Dick'! Dick the crane, you know. Our bird friend—George's and mine!"

Vanina glanced at the great bird almost affectionately.

"Perhaps it has seen George to-day, and our other friends," she said, with a sigh, "and come straight here from them. And it can return as freely. Oh if we could but do the same!"

"That gives me an idea," said Owen, in excitement. "If it can't take us back, it can take a message. If I tie a note round its neck, George will be sure to see it. I will write one; Heaven send the bird may not fly away before I can write it," he added, anxiously.

"Oh, Dick—dear Dick—good, nice Dick—come and stay with me! Do not go yet," Vanina pleaded, addressing the bird. Then a thought struck her she loosened a girdle she wore round her waist and handed it to Owen.

"Quick," she whispered. "Tie him for a few minutes with that. Be quick; if he opens his wings, we may lose our chance."

"Good!" Wydale commented, and, cautiously approaching the bird, he soon had him fettered by the leg, and securely fastened to the seat under the spreading tree. Then they both set to work to write short notes; for Wydale always had pencil and paper with him, and, like all fishermen, was never without a bit of string in one or other of his pockets.

He addressed his note to Sydney, and it ran thus:

"Vanina is not dead; I have seen and spoken to her, and she is beside me now while I write this, and she also will send a note. But we are prisoners, and are doomed to die in the Temple of the Kralens on the occasion of some great festival four days from this. Inform Monella at once. If any-one on earth can help us, it is he. If not, this may be our last message. God bless you all! Take care of George for the sake of
"Your unfortunate friend,
"Owen."

Vanina's notes, for she sent two—one to George and one to Sydney—were very differently worded; they were tear-stained and full of love and tenderness and regret for the trouble and anxiety she had caused. Nor did she forget to put in words concerning Wydale, telling how that his present plight was all through his de-votion to her. She ended with a very sad farewell, in case they should never meet again.

Then the notes were made into a little parcel and well wrapped up in other paper, and finally tied round Dick's neck in such a man-ner as to be conspicuous, after which he was released.

When he found himself free, the bird shook out his ruffled feath-ers, spread his wings, and soared up and away without more ado.

"He never said 'good-bye,'" said Wydale. "He is indignant at our chaining him up. I fear he won't come again. Heaven send, however, that he may be a faithful postman!"

29
In "The Golden Death-Cage"

There was a great gathering in the "Temple of Kraldeema" on the morning of the fourth day after the visit of the crane to Wydale in the garden. As he had feared, the bird came no more, and he had remained in doubt as to whether his message had reached its destination.

For some reason, he had been left unmolested in the garden; he had not been forced into a state of trance and placed amongst the "Living-dead," in accordance with the rule with those destined for the sacrifice. Perhaps Morveena had feared she might defeat her end, and thought it best to leave him free. Every morning his jailer asked him whether he had "any message for Zanolda," and, on his replying in the negative, left him without another word. Nor had he seen Vanina; and he assumed that they would meet no more. He now therefore passed his time in silent prayer and contemplation, and in preparing his mind for the terrible ordeal that lay before him.

In the Temple of the Crystal Mountain preparations were in progress for the coming sacrifices. It was the chief festival of the year in honour of the goddess Kraldeema, and none of her devout worshippers absented himself on such an occasion, unless unavoidably compelled. Kara was there in his robes of State, seated on the magnificent throne, and beside him, on one side, sat Morveena, and on the other, Malion, the high priest. Then there were Fralda, his assistant, and Zanolda; a long string of senior and junior priests; Kallenda, the commander-in-chief of the forces, and a number of his officers, with a large sprinkling of those amongst the townspeople who wished to display their zeal for their religion, or to curry favour at the Court; and all the flower of the priestly army. Of the townspeople generally, of the workers amongst the community, there were none. They had their duties to attend to; most of them, indeed, had now been impressed into service against the Dilandians in the new state of war that had arisen, and they were required to guard the harbour and its defences from any sudden attack that might be made whilst all their chiefs and rulers were absent at the festival.

Within the temple many mystic ceremonies had to be performed before the most important function—the devoting of the wretched victims to the Kralens—would take place. There were songs to be chanted, incense to be burned, processions to be formed that marched round singing, went through certain forms, dissolved, then reformed with further marching to and fro, and so on. And every now and then the voices of the chanters would be drowned in a thunderous, roaring scream that filled the whole place with its vibrations, and caused many to start and look around in nervous apprehension.

The "Catacombs of the Living-dead " were empty, for all there had been recalled to life, and, with a refinement of barbarity, had been turned out into the garden to taste again some of the sweets of life—the fresh air, the golden sunlight, and the perfumed flowers—before returning to that sombre, dim-lighted scene that was to be the witness of their dying moments.

Here, amongst the plants and scented blossoms, these doomed ones walked or sat about in a hushed silence, dazed with the unaccustomed sunlight, and filled with horror at the contemplation of their coming fate. There were exceptions, however, to these silent ones, and amongst them was Steve Foster, who passed the time in swearing and blaspheming audibly. Nor was Durford in much better mood; but he was less demonstrative, and it was only at intervals that he replied to Foster's ravings by an oath or a sudden denunciation of their gaolers.

Neither Vanina nor Wydale was amongst this crowd. The latter had been removed the night before and confined elsewhere; and in the morning he had been brought into the Temple by another way, and now sat on a seat apart, closely guarded by men with drawn swords, watching, apathetically, all that went on before him. He noted, dully, that many amongst the actors in the ceremonies at times seemed to turn sick and faint; they would reel and stagger, and almost fall; and every now and then he found himself in like manner affected. This was the effect of the foul vapours which rose from the Kralens' pit, and which at times proved stronger than the incense burned to neutralise their deadly power. He looked moodily up at the great window now closed and barred, that was placed at the end of the "cage" over the pit. And he now discovered that the Kralens sent out to desolate the country of the Dilandians, were prevented, by the high ridge that ran across the island, from devastating the territory of Karanda. The Crystal Mountain, being at the angle at which the ridge and the wall of sea-cliff met, looked down with its respective sides into both domains. Hence, when this window was thrown open and the barred trap-door raised, the monsters were free to sally forth, and prowl up and down the country of their enemies, while effectually shut off from their own.

Presently the time arrived for the Kralens to be let loose upon the earliest victims; and these were now brought in. They proved to be Durford and Steve Foster; and Owen could not repress a start of surprise on seeing them. Nor did they hide their astonishment when they noticed him. Since he was unbound, and appeared to be seated calmly at his ease, there was nothing to indicate that he also was to be one of that day's victims. The guards with drawn swords beside him might have been a guard of honour for all the two knew, and no one took the trouble to enlighten them. This crumb of comfort at least Owen had, that these men could not gloat over him, or rejoice that he was in like case to themselves.

They were bound and carried through the bars into the cage, and were laid down on the rocky floor; when those who had carried them in retired hastily outside the cage.

Wydale now understood why the bars of the cage were placed so far apart. It was that the attendants and assistants at these ghastly executions might be able to pass in and out without the opening or shutting of gates or doors, which, in certain circumstances, might be attended with danger to the spectators. For the

Kralens were powerful creatures that might force open an inse-
curely-fastened gate, whereas the bars, as they stood, were everywhere too close together for anything so large as these flying monsters to pass through.

Of the two wretched men now lying in the cage, Durford alone
seemed to retain his self-control. Foster had given way to abject
terror, and had made frantic appeals for mercy to those about him.
Now he lay motionless, with staring eyeballs, waiting for the end;
which quickly came.

For some little time the roarings that issued from the pit had
been increasing both in frequency and volume; and every now and
then there was a mighty blow against the under part of the barred
trap-door that shut the monsters in. Evidently they were hungry,
and they seemed to know that prey was ready for them; hence their
impatience. Then by some mechanism not apparent to the eye, the
great trap was raised, and the way made clear for them to mount
and seize their meal.

Upon what followed, Wydale gazed in fascinated horror, powerless to turn his eyes from the awful scene.

There was a loud rushing sound, the whirr of giant wings in
constant and violent vibrations, like those of a gigantic bee hovering above a flower. Then there rose slowly from the pit a shape of
such surpassing hideousness that it brought once more to Wydale's
mind the old legend of the Gorgons who turned people to stone by
their looks alone.

A scaly body, and legs armed with cruel-looking talons of startling length and thickness, were surmounted by a head scarcely to
be described in words. There was a huge mouth, whose upper jaw
curved over like the beak of a bird of prey, with large dilated nostrils, and a flat low forehead, if the term may be used in regard to
such a creature. There were details in its general outline that were
partly fish-like, partly human, and the mingling of the two was
inexpressively repulsive and disgusting. But the most frightful features of the monster were its eyes. These were large, fixed, and
fish-like. They seemed to see, and yet not to see, and withal there
was in their expression the most ghastly, horrible, mocking leer that
ever mortal eye could gaze on. To say that the creature's ugliness

surpassed anything ever seen is to describe it mildly. There was something in this frightful leer that was aggressive, exasperating, unbearable; a suggestion of triumphant malice, of satanic cunning, of smug satisfaction at its own outrageous hideousness, that seemed almost supernatural. The senses revolted at the spectacle; uprose in fury and repulsion; one longed to rush upon the creature, and with one's heel stamp out ruthlessly the life from a monstrosity so appalling.

This awful creature made its way forth from the pit, and slowly approached the two pinioned forms. There was in its movements—save for the ceaseless vibration of the wings—no trace of haste. It moved upon its prey with horrible deliberation, seeming to gloat over it with a sensuous complacency. But finally—almost to the relief of Wydale—it fastened upon the two, raised them in the air, and disappeared with them within the pit. The great trap-door closed on them with a clash, and at the same moment a woman's shriek rang out and echoed again and again from the sides of the rocky roof. Then Wydale turned and saw, not far from him, Vanina, who was swaying from side to side, as though about to fall. Instinctively he half rose to go to her assistance, but a heavy hand was laid upon his shoulder, and a voice whispered in his ear:

"Thou hast courted this, and must go through with it unless—"

It was Zanolda speaking.

Wydale made a gesture of disgust, and was about to reply impulsively, when he caught a glance from Kara, whose glittering eyes were fixed upon him with a look of devilish triumph. This had the effect upon his excited nerves of a sudden cold water douche; and at once he gathered together his somewhat scattered senses.

He returned King Kara's look disdainfully, and turned to Zanolda:

"Since it is to be, I have nothing to add to what I have already said," he told him, curtly.

Vanina, too, recovered herself, and now gazed composedly around, with much of her old imperious spirit. Kara regarded her a while in silence, and his brow darkened. Then he made a sign to Malion, the high priest, who thereupon stood up, and raised his hand as a sign for silence in the assembly.

He was an old man, with keen, dark eyes, in which ever lurked an evil look. His face was hard, and the lines of cruelty were to be traced upon every part of his furrowed visage. At first sight of him, Wydale had felt only detestation; nor were his feelings towards Zanolda much more friendly; for he felt repelled by his oily, unctuous, yet cynical speech and manner.

Malion now rose, and addressing Kara, said in a loud, clear voice:

"We understand, O King, that thou hast complaint to make against these two."

And he indicated Wydale and Vanina.

Then Kara rose, and, looking at Vanina with vindictive glance, returned:

"I do accuse them both: this woman, that she hath broken a solemn contract to become my wife; and this man, that he hath aided and abetted her therein."

There was silence throughout the place when these words were spoken. Then Malion addressed Vanina:

"Say, O woman, alien to our race! Thou hast heard what our great king hath stated. He declares that thou hast fooled him, first by pretending to engage thyself to join with him in marriage, and then by withdrawing and refusing to carry out thy contract. Say, is this so?"

"I scorn to deny it!" replied Vanina, resolutely. "I despise and hate him, and will die here to-day sooner than become his wife!"

"Enough! Thou shalt have thy wish," cried Malion. "We need no further evidence of thy traitorous thoughts and actions. And now as to thee"—addressing Wydale— "hast thou aught to say?"

Wydale shook his head, and looked down to avoid the burning gaze that Morveena had fixed on him. But he said nothing.

"One moment, my Lord Malion," burst out Morveena. "I fain would essay my humble influence on this transgressor. Perchance I may persuade him from the error of his ways. Let the woman meet her just doom; but let this man have space yet for repentance. Haply if I reason with him—"

"I refuse thy proffered offices, princess," Wydale answered firmly, almost rudely. "I decline to discuss this matter further with thee. Let it come to an end at once."

At this speech both Kara and his sister started up in ungovern-able fury. Her face was almost purple with rage, and her eyes flashed with an evil glare like a wounded tigress at bay.

"Be it so!" she exclaimed. "Then let him die, here, now, and the sooner the better. I would fain have given him yet one more chance. Let these two" —with scathing denunciatory gesture— "die to-gether. I will stay here and witness their death agonies; so only can my just anger be appeased."

But Kara made one last effort to persuade Vanina.

"Consider, maiden," he began. "I could, and I would, take thee by force. But it is written in the stars that—"

She held up her hand, and turned on him a look of such with-ering contempt that his eyes dropped before it.

"Peace!" she burst out scornfully. "I am willing to die, King Kara, but not to listen to thy insults." Kara essayed to reply; then, as though the attempt to answer almost choked him, he made a sign to Malion, which the latter quickly understood.

"Let the two prisoners be bound and placed in the cage," he said.

And the order was forthwith obeyed. The zealous attendants seized on them, and, with scant ceremony, bound them fast, and carried them through the bars into the cage, laying them side by side, almost on the same places that Durford and Foster had occu-pied but a little while before. Then they retired and left them.

"Farewell till we meet in the next world, beloved," said Owen softly to her.

"Farewell till then, dear friend," Vanina murmured, "and may Heaven forgive my sin in bringing you to this. For myself I can endure it; I have deserved it. But you—you die here to-day through my mad, wicked folly."

"Nay, dear heart, say not so. I do solemnly declare to you—"

He broke off suddenly, his attention attracted by a movement in the half-lighted galleries above them.

The trap-door had not yet been raised. Those who controlled the machinery only waited Kara's signal, but this the king, for some reason, delayed to give. It may have been that he hesitated at the last moment to devote so fair a being to so terrible a death, or it may have been that he purposely delayed the signal in order to prolong their agony. It was in this short interval that Wydale, turning his eyes wearily away from what he could see of the mouth of the pit, happened to look towards one of the deserted galleries above, and there he saw—just for an instant—George's face. But no sooner had he caught sight of it, and interchanged a look of intelligence, than it disappeared. But in its place remained two small hands, which were contorting themselves into many curious shapes.

Wydale quickly recognised that signals were being made to him in the deaf-and-dumb alphabet, which he and George had often practised together after the death of the latter's little deaf-and-dumb brother. And this is the message that the boy's hands—all that could be seen in the shadows above—spelt out:

"Take courage. Help is at hand. Do not give way. Tell sister."

"Vanina! Do you hear me?" Owen whispered.

"Yes, dear friend. What is it?"

"I have seen George up above there in the gloom, and he has signed to me that help is at hand, and that we are to keep up our courage."

But she only sighed softly, thinking that already his senses were leaving him, and that he raved. For how could George be there, and what help could possibly be at hand at such a pass? Even now the trap-door was lifting, and there rose slowly in the air that frightful shape with its maddening leer and its bloodcurdling scream.

But while it still hovered over the pit's mouth, a tall form came suddenly into view and passed between the bars into the cage. Both Wydale and Vanina caught a view of it as it stood over them for a moment, and then turned to confront the monster. It was Monella; and instantly a great hope leaped into their breasts. Was it possible that help had really come?

But this hope weakened when they saw that Monella was alone. He was not the leader of a conquering host that had suddenly stormed the city and swarmed up to the entrance of the Temple of Kraldeema. He was alone; and what could one man do against so many—and with the Kralen against him, too?

Monella towered above them, and a black mask he wore upon his face hid alike his purpose and his features. He was clad in a complete coat of mail; on his left arm he bore an immense shield; in his right hand he wielded a mighty war-axe, and in his belt there was another. Evidently, in remembrance of his former encounter with the Kralen, he had resolved to abandon the sword in favour of the axe; and, in view of possibilities, he had armed himself with two.

"Take courage," he whispered to them, quietly. "If God and my right arm fail me not, we shall yet save you."

But it seemed a hopeless task. Should he prevail against the Kralen, he would have all these armed men to face alone. And should he not prevail—well, then, he had sacrificed himself in vain. So it appeared to Wydale, while he lay eagerly turning over in his mind the possibilities of the situation. "And why," he thought, "now, while there was a pause, did not Monella cut the cords that kept them lying helplessly upon the floor?"

Then King Kara's voice was heard, ringing loudly through the hail:

"Seize him! Kill him! On to him, ye dogs! He is but one man, and has no followers. He hath ventured here; let him take the consequences. Seize him—kill him, I say!"

But Monella stood unmoved and calm. He did not even look to right or left, but kept his gaze upon the Kralen now preparing for a rush at this new foe. What mattered Kara's frantic orders? Well Monella knew that no one in that assembly would venture through the bars and into the cage while the Kralen was unloosed.

Kara himself, almost mad with fury though he was, soon thought of this.

"'Tis well," he said, concealing his chagrin that no one had moved to obey him. "Let him fight the Kralen—if he dares. The combat will afford us royal sport. He cannot conquer, for no man hath yet prevailed in open fight against the Kralen."

And now ensued a terrific combat between Monella and the monster. The creature seemed to know, by some fell instinct, that it had here a formidable foe to meet, and not merely its usual helpless, unarmed prey. At once it showed a serpent-like alertness and sagacity. It poised for an instant in the air, then made a sudden rush, trying to beat its enemy to the ground.

And it all but succeeded, for Monella was borne back and fell on one knee. He seemed to be assailed on every side at once. The great claws gripped at him, the beak-like mouth snapped at him, and the wings beat against him, closed round him, and with other claws at their extremities assailed his head and body. With a great effort, he aimed a heavy blow at the creature's body that drove it back, when he leaped again to his feet. At that the Kralen swept circling round, with piercing screams, and again swooped suddenly upon him, forcing him backward with its weight and impetus, and all but throwing him to the ground; but this time, as it passed over him, he dealt such a blow at one of its wings that a great rent appeared, and the limb was partially disabled. Quickly perceiving this, he was not slow to follow his advantage. He darted upon the monster before it could rise again beyond his reach, and, with a tremendous blow, broke off the greater portion of the wing he had already injured. Then the hideous beast lay flapping on the ground, roaring and screaming, and twisting helplessly, and whirring its uninjured wing, and snapping its jaws like a great steel spring trap, while it vainly strove to crawl along the ground to get at its assailant.

But Monella now took little further notice of it. He had to think about the human foes surrounding him. From these had gone up a wolf-like howl of rage when they had realised that the Kralen had been worsted. They uttered loud cries of vengeance, yet durst not yet enter the cage wherein the monster was still flapping about, and might, for aught they knew, recover itself. Nor did anyone there care to be the first to face that dauntless fighter whose figure was but too well known to many who had fled before him on the field of battle.

Just then another masked figure ran down one of the staircases and pushed its way into the cage. It bent down and cut the bonds of the two prisoners, while Monella stood in front of them, defying alike the wounded Kralen and the crowd of armed men outside the cage. Sydney Dareville—for he it was—after cutting the cords that bound the two, and whispering in their ears, proceeded to bind over their faces masks like those Monella and himself were wearing. Then he lifted Vanina in his arms and waited. Wydale had risen to his feet and stood beside them. Monella removed his mask, and, addressing those opposed to him, cried out in sonorous tones, that rang through the amphitheatre like the clang of a booming bell.

"Kara! Malion! All ye vile following of a cruel, bloodthirsty priesthood! Take from my hands the punishment that an outraged God hath sent you!"

He replaced his mask, and, drawing from a pouch what appeared to be a small crystal ball, he threw it on the ground some distance from him. There were heard sounds as of broken glass and a slight explosion, and that was all.

But the effect upon the angry, threatening mob outside the cage was magical, tremendous, awful. For the crystal ball and the masks formed the gift of the Flower-Dwellers that George had brought in the ebony casket; and when the little ball was broken, there spread around a strange and deadly gas that instantaneously seized upon every human being not protected by a mask. Its effects were altogether different from those caused by any other noxious gas or vapour known to science, in that it did not kill immediately, but produced first a paralysis of the lower limbs.

Each one affected by it became then as though turned to stone below the waist, the upper part of the body remaining for some time full of life, while the deadly numbness crept slowly upwards. None moved from his place; those who were seated remained seated, and those who had been standing kept their position. They did not even fall to the ground; it was as though they were glued to the spot by some terrible, irresistible power. Nor could they so much as guess at what it was that thus affected them; the death-dealing gas was colourless, odourless; no clouds of smoke or visible vapour spread abroad; no suffocating fumes attacked their nostrils.

The prevailing idea amongst these hapless wretches was that Monella, whom they had long learned to fear, was possessed of some fearful, diabolical power he had held in reserve, and now turned against them in requital of this their last act of intended wickedness towards his friends; and the majority gazed at him with dilated eyeballs, as on an offended god armed with resistless power. Two or three threw spears and javelins; but these he parried easily with his shield—but none could stir to advance against him.

Then Sydney lifted Vanina in his arms, and bore her up the staircase by which he and Monella had descended. This staircase and the galleries above were empty, all the crowd having found room below; there was no one therefore in their way when once they were on the steps. Wydale—all were protected by their masks—slowly followed, and last of all of this silent procession of living beings amongst the dying, walked Monella.

Meanwhile, in those left below, slowly—very slowly,—the deadly feeling crept ever upwards, till the arms ceased to gesticulate, and only the hands could wave, the heads turn this way or that, and the eyes roll in their sockets. Most awesome of all, perhaps, none cried out; probably the subtle gas had paralysed the voice as well as the limbs. And no more awful sight could be imagined than the despairing looks that these dying ones cast at Monella, as they turned their heads to follow him till he had reached the top of the ascent. Arrived there, he gazed down on them, then bowed his head as though he would salute the dying, and whispered within his mask, "God's vengeance is accomplished!"

Then he turned and opened a door in the rock, and, closing and fastening it behind him, made his way through an underground passage till, after passing other doors which he also closed, he found himself in a great cavern, where Sydney, Wydale, Vanina, George, and others, were awaiting him, all now without their masks. Then he removed his own.

"Is the maiden well?" he asked, alluding to Vanina.

Wydale seized his hand.

"Well and safe—both of us, good friend," he exclaimed. "Ah—" turning to Vanina, "did I not say that three or four days would be enough for Monella's help to reach us?"

"Thank God—not me," said Monella, solemnly. "Our enemies are all dead! The Flower-Dwellers' Gift hath done its work!"

30
The End

The following morning a fleet of boats sailed out of the harbour of Dilandis fully prepared to attempt the capture of Karanda by assault, and, should that fail, to lay siege to the place.

The steam launch—now named the *Queen Vanina*—accompanied them, and in it were to be seen Monella, Rokta, Ombrian, Dareville, Wydale, and others of the chief personages of the place.

The launch had been altered back to her original shape, and the steel shears which Monella had found in the cargo of the *Saucy Fan*, and been so effective in the destruction of the Karanite fleet, had been removed from her bows, and were now in more peaceful use in the little ironworks that had been established in the town.

But when they reached Karanda, it was quickly seen that there would be no fighting. The harbour gates stood open, and there were neither soldiers nor guards of any kind. The whole place was disorganised, the townspeople stood about in groups, talking in hushed voices, too utterly stunned by the calamity that had befallen them to think of organising resistance. They had not, indeed, a leader left. Every person in authority had perished in the dread catastrophe that had overwhelmed all those gathered in the Temple of the Crystal Mountain—either at the time or afterwards. For, as it presently appeared, some few of the chief officers to whom the defence of the city had been confided, while the rest were occupied at the festival, had, later in the day, incited thereto by vague rumours of disaster, left their posts to make inquiry at the Temple. And of those who had thus entered, not one had since returned; and when others had gone to seek them, they also had not come

back. Then a great awe and fear had fallen upon the town; no further attempts to approach the Temple had been made, and, as the
night passed and the morning dawned, and still none came forth
from that place of death, vague fears developed into absolute terror
and dismay.

It is scarcely, therefore, to be wondered that the Dilandians
were welcomed rather than repelled. The bewildered, frightened
populace were like a flock of sheep without a shepherd, and they
readily submitted themselves to their new rulers.

Monella entered into possession of the palace and the various
offices, and at once set up a government, and the people soon returned to their peaceful occupations, well contented with their lot.
The country was formally annexed to Dilanda, and incorporated
as a portion of that kingdom.

Meantime, it became a question, after order had been in some
degree established, what steps could be taken to remove and bury
the dead lying in the Temple of Kraldeema; but about this there
was a difficulty to be forthwith explained.

The ebony casket George had brought with him—the gift of the
Flower-Dwellers—and delivered into Monella's hands, had been
found, on examination, to contain six curiously-constructed masks
and a small hollow ball of glass or crystal. There was a scroll enclosed, which Monella managed to decipher, and which explained
that the ball was filled with a deadly gas which, even in the open
air, would kill everyone within a considerable distance of the spot
from which it issued, *except* those protected by the masks. This
was the great secret of the Flower-Dwellers; it was the explanation of their "Masked Men," and of the fact that they were able to
maintain themselves against all-comers and deal out death to all
approaching them.

Now it so happened that Monella had long been engaged in a
secret quest. He had discovered, amongst other ancient manuscripts and archives in one of the museums, a plan of the labyrinth
called the "caverns," from which he gathered that they had once
extended much farther than was now supposed, and had, in fact,
been connected with the "Crystal Mountain." He saw that, if he
could secretly find and reopen these lost passages, all cut through

the solid rock, they might one day afford a means of surprising the Karanites by an attack from an altogether unexpected quarter. With two or three assistants whom he knew he could absolutely trust, he had, therefore, long been engaged in opening up these passages, which had become blocked by falls from the roof, and in other ways. The quest had proved long and tedious; there were so many old passages and galleries which, after being emptied and explored, were found to lead in the wrong direction; and, in consequence, the workers were beginning to despair, when they stumbled upon the right one only a few weeks before. They were then able to penetrate into the Temple, for the passage they had discovered and cleared led direct into one of the recesses attached to the upper gallery of the amphitheatre. Here it was closed by a door of wood and iron, which, however, was old and rotten and rusty, and was left uncared-for by those in charge of the Temple, because the passage just beyond it was choked with debris. There were, indeed, many such old doors about the place, all leading into unused passages, similarly blocked, and it never occurred to anyone that this particular one was being industriously cleared with a view to using it against them if occasion should arise.

When, therefore, Monella became possessed of the terrible engine of destruction in the crystal ball, and was apprised by the message brought by the faithful crane of the peril in which Wydale and Vanina stood, he conceived it possible to effect their rescue almost single-handed. The chief difficulty lay in getting to them, so as to place the masks upon their faces, and this he foresaw could only be done while their enemies were kept at bay by the Kralen itself. Hence it was necessary he should once more essay a fight with the "vampire," and this he had not hesitated to do.

But, on returning from the expedition, having rescued the prisoners, and destroyed their foes in the manner that has been described, Monella had given the casket—in which were now only the masks—into George's care, charging him to deliver it to Dr. Manleth, who was curious to examine them to learn their secret. In shape and general design they were somewhat after the fashion of the one Monella had improvised on the occasion of his first fight with the "vampire"; but, almost necessarily, they comprised some further special secret, which the doctor was anxious to investigate. Unfortunately, George, while crossing in the boat, had, in his jubilation at regaining his sister and his friend—now, as could be easily seen, on the closest terms with one another—opened the casket to look at the masks, and the whole had slipped from his hands and gone overboard, and sunk quickly out of sight.

Thus the difficulty had arisen that no one could now go into the Temple to bring out the corpses.

"I was specially warned by the scroll that accompanied the 'Gift,'" Monella explained, "that, if the gas were employed in a closed place, its deadly effects would remain for years—it was stated, indeed—even for centuries. Moreover, the gas has the property of conserving the bodies of those it slays. It seems to me, therefore, that there is but one course to be taken, and that is to brick up all the entrances, and make the whole place one vast tomb. It is the only safe plan, for to leave it open would always mean danger to the living; many strangers, from curiosity, might make their way in, and so meet certain death. Even to build up and close the various openings will be a work of danger; but I think it can be effected without fatal results by strict vigilance and watchfulness on the part of those who overlook the work. The unique result will be that, owing to the preservative qualities of the gas, that hapless host will remain just as they died; and if the place were entered hundreds of years hence, they would all appear as though they had perished but an hour or two before!"

This work was duly carried out, and thus for years and hundreds of years to come this strange assembly will remain just as they were left by Monella and his masked friends—King Kara on his throne, Morveena, that unwomanly woman, by his side, with Malion and all the evil throng that followed him;—and, in their midst, in the golden death-cage, the slaughtered "Kralen,"—their faces turned, their open eyes all staring with that despairing look, their hands and arms pointing towards the top of the staircase from which Monella had looked his last upon them.

The unhappy beings crowded into the garden in which Wydale had been a prisoner, were released unharmed. Fortunately for them, the door of the "Catacombs" had been fastened against them while they were waiting for their death, otherwise, doubtless, many of them would have entered the place from curiosity, and would have perished.

Amid the general joy and congratulations, there was one deeply, disappointed man, and that was the worthy doctor. Not to be able to get at the body of the vanquished Kralen, and hold a post-mortem on the remains, and preserve the skull and other bones for scientists to examine and wonder at at the Royal Institution in London, was indeed a terrible disappointment to him.

Were there several Kralens, or only one? That is what he often wondered; and the point was never settled.

Besides the masks and crystal ball, the casket had enclosed something else—a prediction that the "channels" would be open at or about a certain date, then only a month ahead. And this agreed with Gralda's own reading of what was "written in the stars," as was the expression used in the country. So now was heard the sound of preparation for departure; for Monella was getting ready the *Saucy Fan*, and announced to all and sundry his intention of trying to get her out to the open sea. And it was soon known that Vanina and her brothers, and Wydale and the doctor, would accompany him.

"I have had enough of playing the role of 'Warrior-Queen,' or any other queen," Vanina said, with a faint smile, when pressed to stay and become, as had been promised, their ruler, or joint-ruler with Rokta and Idelia. "If there were likely to be further warfare, I might be of some good, and in any case would not desert my post, so long as I could be useful; but, happily for you all, there is no further fear of that, and Idelia is far better suited than am I to rule over your now peaceful country. I should like to stay long enough to see you married (Rokta and Idelia), but that, it appears, is impossible in the circumstances; so you must let us go without that happiness."

Perhaps the one who was most loth to leave was Sydney; he would have preferred remaining. But he could not well refuse to accompany his sister and brother. As to George, he cared only to follow Vanina and her lover, and was quite happy wherever they were.

The gentle Idelia showed in every possible way her regret at losing her friends, and her wish to testify her regard for them. She called a meeting of all the notables and councillors, and requested them to advise her as to what fitting tribute they should offer to their departing friends, and they advised her in no niggardly spirit. Since Vanina would not remain and wear the Crown jewels, they decided that she was, at least, entitled to her share of them, and this they insisted upon her accepting. And her share was worth a king's ransom. The others also were all recompensed in like princely fashion, so that Sydney and Wydale found themselves paid a hundred times over for the cargo of the *Saucy Fan*. Nor was Peter Jennings forgotten. He had also decided to take his chance in the *Saucy Fan*, and he was able to take with him enough to keep him comfortably for the remainder of his days.

Then the day of parting came. A small fleet of boats accompanied the *Saucy Fan* when, in tow of the launch, she slowly made her way towards one of the "channels"—not that by which she had come, but another, the current in which would flow out towards the open sea. To reach this it was necessary to pass near the island of the Flower-Dwellers, and there, upon the beach, George saw a group, and through his glasses could distinguish Myrla and her parents, and others he had known during his stay amongst them. And, as the procession passed them, they waved banners (made in the forms of giant blossoms) by way of "adieu."

"It's awfully kind of them to come down to see us off," George said; "I wonder how they knew? But there! they seem to know everything! If it hadn't been for them, we shouldn't have had you here now, you know, sis."

And Vanina gazed at the group with tears in her eyes, while she thought of all their help had done for her; and she kissed her hand to each in turn, as George pointed them out, one after the other.

Soon the island was left astern, and the *Saucy Fan* entered, in a little while, the "channel," which they found open. The current was gentle, though steady, and would offer no difficulty to the return of the launch. It had been arranged that this boat should be left as a present to the islanders (some of whom had learned to manage the machinery), and that it should tow back the other boats against the current.

In time, the open sea was safely reached, and there, in calm water, and with but a gentle breeze, the *Saucy Fan* spread out her white wings—the new ones that had been specially made to suit her altered rig. Loud were the cries of admiration from the Dilandians who saw her now for the first time in full sail; and long and hearty were the huzzas that followed the pretty vessel and those on board. And thus the *Saucy Fan* sped swiftly away, as graceful a craft as many a schooner-yacht in some of the crack yachting clubs.

She had scarcely passed out of sight of the boats and launch, when Peter Jennings, who was look-out man for the watch, espied a dark object on the waves, which turned out to be a boat with five shipwrecked sailors in it. They had been floating about, it seemed, for many days and nights, and were in an exhausted state. They were taken on board and kindly treated, and showed their gratitude by joining as crew, and proving themselves good sailors.

After a prosperous voyage, they arrived at Rio, where almost the first news they received on landing was that of the death of the Darevilles' stepfather.

"Then, after all, his rascally plot availed him nothing," was Sydney's comment. "Well, he is dead now; so the less we say about him the better."

Vanina was married shortly afterwards to Wydale, and, with George, went to live at her old home on the pampas. They keep the *Saucy Fan* as a pleasure yacht, and are often to be met with up and down the coast from Buenos Ayres to Georgetown in British Guiana.

Sydney went for a year or two's travel in Europe, and then married and settled down near his sister; and they often discuss together their adventures in the *Saucy Fan*. And, to amuse the children—for there are now several—Vanina will sometimes dress herself as a "warrior-queen,' in the dress and armour she wore when in the country, and put on her head the jewelled crown of Atlantis, which she brought away and has ever since kept intact.

George is studying chemistry, and declares he will persevere until he discovers some of those wonderful secrets of the Flower-Dwellers. Some think he will start off one day on another visit to the Island of Atlantis, and venture, once more, amongst the Flower-Dwellers; for it is said he has never quite overcome his liking for the winsome Myrla.

Dr. Manleth amuses himself still in the laboratory; but, being a rich man, has no need to over-exert himself; and he does not. He is looked upon, in a certain circle, as a harmless, but eccentric, scientific enthusiast, who believes in the existence of strange monsters, and fancies he once had some "Gulliver's travel"-like adventures amongst an unknown people somewhere in the Caribbean Sea.

And Monella! What of him? He remained for a while with Mr. and Mrs. Wydale, and then started off on the quest that had long been in his mind, namely, the search for the lost city of Manoa, or "El Dorado." He would fain have persuaded Wydale to accompany him, but on that proposal Mrs. Wydale peremptorily "put her foot." She had had quite enough, she declared, "of adventures amongst lost cities."

So Monella started on his mission by himself; and those who care to hear what followed, and the wonderful adventures that befell him, will find them faithfully recorded in the book "that bears the strange device" or title of THE DEVIL-TREE OF EL DORADO.

THE DEVIL-TREE
OF EL DORADO

A Romance of
British Guiana

Preface
Shall Roraima* be Given up to Venezuela?

Shall Roraima be handed over to Venezuela? Shall the mysterious mountain long known to scientists as foremost among the wonders of our earth—regarded by many as the greatest marvel of the world—become definitely Venezuelan territory?

This is the question that hangs in the balance at the time these words are being written, that is inseparably associated—though many of the public know it not—with the dispute that has arisen about the boundaries of British Guiana.

Ever since Sir Robert Schomburgk first explored the colony at the expense of the Royal Geographical Society some sixty years ago, Roraima has remained an unsolved problem of romantic and fascinating interest, as attractive to the 'ordinary person' as to the man of science. And to those acquainted with the wondrous possibilities that lie behind the solution of the problem, the prospect of its being handed over to a country so little worthy of the trust as is Venezuela, cannot be contemplated without feelings of disappointment and dismay.

This is not the place in which to give a long description of Roraima. It will suffice here to say that its summit is a table-land which, it is believed, has been isolated from all the rest of the world for untold ages; no wilderness of ice and snow, but a fertile country of wood and stream, and, probably, lake. Consequently it holds out to the successful explorer the chance—the probability even—of finding there hitherto unknown animals, plants, fish. In this

*The Indians of British Guiana pronounce this word *Roreema*.

respect it exceeds in interest all other parts of the earth's surface, not excepting the polar regions; for the latter are but ice-bound wastes, while Roraima's mysterious table-land lies in the tropics but a few degrees north of the equator.

Why, then, it may be asked, have our scientific societies not exhibited more zeal in the solving of the problem presented by this strange mountain? Why is it that unlimited money can, apparently, be raised for expeditions to the poles, while no attempt has been made to explore Roraima? Yet, sixty years ago, the Royal Geographical Society could find the money to send Sir Robert Schomburgk out to explore British Guiana—indeed, it is to that fact that we owe the discovery of Roraima—but nothing has been done since. Had the good work thus begun been followed up, we should to-day have been able to show better reason for claiming Roraima as a British possession. But, as the writer of the article in the *Spectator* quoted on page 3 says, "we leave the mystery unsolved, the marvel uncared for." This article is commended to the perusal of those interested in the subject, as also are the following books, which give all the information at present available, *viz.*—Mr. Barrington Brown's *Canoe and Camp Life in British Guiana*, and Mr. Boddam-Whetham's *Roraima and British Guiana*. Mr. Im Thurn's *Among the Indians of British Guiana* should also be mentioned, since it contains references to Roraima, though the author did not actually visit the mountain, as in the case of the first named.

As an illustration of the confusion and uncertainty that prevail as to the international status of this unique mountain, it may be mentioned that in the map of British Guiana which Sir Robert Schomburgk drew out for the British Government, it is placed within the British frontier. But in the map of the next Government explorer, Mr. Barrington Brown— "based," he says, "upon Schomburgk's map"—it is placed just inside the Venezuelan boundary; and no explanation is given of the apparent contradiction. Again, another authority, Mr. Im Thurn (above referred to), Curator of the Museum at Georgetown (the capital of the colony), in his book says that Roraima "lies on the extreme edge of the colony, or perhaps on the other side of the Brazilian boundary." These references show the obscurity in which the whole matter is at present involved.

Apart, however, from the special interest that surrounds Roraima owing to the inaccessible character of its summit,* it is of very great geographical importance, from the fact that it is the highest mountain in all that part of South America, *i.e.*, in all the Guianas, in Venezuela, and in the north-east part of Brazil. Indeed, we must cross Brazil, that vast country of upwards of three million square miles, to find the nearest mountains that exceed in height Roraima. Consequently, it forms the apex of the water-shed of that part of South America; and it is, in fact, the source of several of the chief feeders of the great rivers Essequibo, Orinoco and Amazon. Schomburgk, in pointing this out, dwelt strongly upon the importance of the mountain to British Guiana, and insisted that its inclusion within the British boundary was a geographical necessity.

Finally, Sir Robert's brother, Richard Schomburgk, a skilled botanist, who had visited almost all parts of Asia and Africa in search of orchids and other rare botanical productions, tells us that the country around Roraima is, from a botanical point of view, one of the most wonderful in the world. "Not only the orchids," he says, "but the shrubs and low trees were unknown to me. Every shrub, herb and tree was new to me, if not as to family, yet as to species. I stood on the border of an unknown plant zone, full of wondrous forms which lay as if by magic before me.... Every step revealed something new." (*Reissen in Britisch Guiana*, Leipzig, vol. ii., p. 216.)

Are our rulers, in their treatment of the question, bearing these facts sufficiently in mind? Are they as keenly alive as are the Venezuelans to the importance of Roraima? If they are, there is no sign of it; for while, in the Venezuelan statements of their case, there are lengthy, emphatic, and repeated references to the importance of Roraima, on the English side—in the English press even—there is scarcely a word about it.

From these observations it will be seen that there is reason to fear we may be on the point of allowing one of the most scientifically

---

* Mr. Barrington Brown says the mountain can only be ascended by means of balloons (see article previously referred to on page 3); and Mr. Boddam-Whetham came to the same conclusion.

interesting and geographically important spots upon the surface of the globe to slip out of our possession into that of a miserable little state like Venezuela, where civil anarchy is chronic, and neither life nor property is secure.

One of the avowed objects of this book, therefore, is to stimulate public interest, and arouse public attention to the considerations that actually underlie the "Venezuelan Question," as well as to while away an idle hour for the lovers of romance.

It has been suggested that, if it is too late to retain the wonderful Roraima as exclusively British—and to effect this it would be well worth our while to barter away some other portion of the disputed territory—then an arrangement might be come to to make it neutral ground. Standing, as it does, in the corner where the three countries—Brazil, Venezuela and British Guiana—meet, it is of importance to all three, and, no doubt, in such an endeavour, we should have the support of Brazil as against Venezuela.

With regard to the oft-discussed question of the situation of the traditional city of Manoa, or El Dorado—as the Spaniards called it— most authorities, including Humboldt and Schomburgk, agree in giving British Guiana as its probable site. We are told that it stood on an island in the midst of a great lake called "Parima"; but no such lake is now to be found in South America anywhere near the locality indicated. An explanation of the mystery, however, is afforded by the suggestion that such a great lake, or inland sea, almost certainly existed at one time in precisely this part of the continent; in that case what are now mountains in the country would then have been islands.

Indeed, most of British Guiana lies somewhat low, and it is estimated that if the highlands were to sink two thousand feet the whole country would be under water—the mountain summits excepted—and there would then be only "a narrow strait" between the Roraima range and the Andes. In this great supposed ancient lake the group of islands now represented by mountain summits might well have been the home of a powerful and conquering race—as is to-day Japan with its group of more than three thousand islands— and Roraima, as the highest, and therefore the most easily defensible, may very well have been selected as their fastness, and the site of their capital city.

Schomburgk thus states his speculations upon the point, in his book on British Guiana, page 6:

"The geological structure of this region leaves but little doubt that it was once the bed of an inland lake which, by one of those catastrophes of which even later times give us examples, broke its barriers, forcing for its waters a path to the Atlantic. May we not connect with the former existence of this inland sea the fable of the lake Parima and the El Dorado? Thousands of years may have elapsed; generations may have been buried and returned to dust; nations who once wandered on its banks may be extinct and exist no more in name; still, tradition of Parima and the El Dorado survived these changes of time; transmitted from father to son, its fame was carried across the Atlantic and kindled the romantic fire of the chivalric Raleigh."

As a natural sequence to the foregoing arises the inquiry, What sort of people were those who inhabited this island city, or who "wandered on the banks" of the great lake? Here much is to be learned from the recent discoveries of the Government of the United States who, of late years, have devoted liberal sums to prehistoric research. The money so expended has been the means of unearthing evidence of a startling character—relics of a former civilisation that existed in America ages before the time of its discovery by Christopher Columbus. The Spaniards, as we know, found races that were white, or nearly so; but these later discoveries go to show that long anterior to these—at a time, in fact, probably coeval with what we call the Egyptian civilisation—America was peopled with a white race fully as cultured, as advanced in the sciences, and as powerful on their own ground as the ancient Egyptians; and as handsome in personal appearance—if some of the heads and faces on the specimens of pottery may be accepted as fair examples—as the ancient Greeks.

It has long been known that America possesses extraordinary relics of a former civilisation in what are known as the great "earthworks," which are still to be seen scattered about in many parts of the continent, and which, as vast engineering works, challenge comparison with the pyramids themselves. But now discovery has gone much further; bas-reliefs and pottery have been found that set forth with marvellous fidelity many minute details concerning this pre-historic people—their personal appearance, and their ornaments and habiliments; the style of wearing the hair and the beard; and other particulars that can be appreciated only by inspection and study of the reduced fac-similes lately printed and issued by the Government of the United States.

Many of them relate to the custom of human sacrifice which, as most people are probably aware, prevailed largely in America when the Spaniards first landed there; though few, perhaps, know the terrible extent to which it was carried. Prescott tells us that few writers have ventured to estimate the yearly number of victims at less than twenty thousand, while many put it as high as fifty thousand, in Mexico alone! If we consider that the lowest of these estimates represents an average of some four hundred a week, or nearly sixty a day, such figures are appalling! And now we learn, beyond the possibility of a doubt, that the same practices obtained in America in times that must have been ages before the Spanish conquest, and, judging by the frequency of the representations of such things in these old bas-reliefs, as extensively. In these sculptures we can see the very shape of the knives used; the form of the plates or platters on which severed heads of victims were placed, and other such details; and in a certain series we are enabled to note the curious point, that, while the officiating priests always wear full beards, the victims appear to have usually possessed no hirsute adornments, or to have "shaved clean," as we term it. It may be added that these ancient white people seem to have been a totally different race from those the Spaniards found on the continent; and that between the two there is believed to have been a gap lasting for many ages, during which the country was overrun by Indian or other barbaric hordes; though how or why this came about is one of those mysteries that will probably never be unravelled.

In conclusion, I have to acknowledge my indebtedness to the writers whose books of travel I have named for the information I have made use of; as well as to express a hope that the writer of the review in the *Spectator* will regard with indulgence the liberties I have taken with his admirable article. I am sanguine enough

to believe, however, that I shall have the sympathy and good wishes
of all these in the endeavour here made to arouse public attention
to the real meaning and importance of the "Venezuelan Question";
and to add to the number of those who feel an interest in the future
status and ultimate exploration of the mysterious Roraima.

For the rest—if objection be taken to the accounts of the mountain and what is to be found on its summit given by the characters
in my story—I desire to claim the licence of the romance-writer to
maintain their accuracy—till the contrary be proved. If this shall
serve to stimulate to renewed efforts at exploration, so much the
better, and another of my objects in writing the book will thereby
have been attained.

Frank Aubrey

1
"Will No One Explore Roraima?"

Beneath the verandah of a handsome, comfortable-looking residence near Georgetown, the principal town of British Guiana, a young man sat one morning early in the year 1890, attentively studying a volume that lay open on a small table before him. It was easy to see that he was reading something that was, for him at least, of more than ordinary interest, something that seemed to carry his thoughts far away from the scene around him; for when, presently, he raised his eyes from the book, they looked out straight before him with a gaze that evidently saw nothing of that on which they rested.

He was a handsome young fellow of, perhaps, twenty-two years of age, rather tall, and well-made, with light wavy hair, and blue-grey eyes that had in them an introspective, somewhat dreamy expression, but that nevertheless could light up on occasion with an animated glance.

The house stood on a terrace that commanded a view of the sea, and, in the distance, white sails could be seen making their way across the blue water in the light breeze and the dazzling sunlight. Nearer at hand were waving palms, glowing flowers, humming insects and gaudily-coloured butterflies—all the beauties of a tropical garden. On one side of him was the open window of a sitting-room that, shaded, as it was, by the verandah, looked dark and cool compared with the glare of the scorching sun outside.

From this room came the sounds of a grand piano and of the sweet voice of a girl singing a simple and pathetic ballad.

At the moment the song ceased a brisk step was heard coming up the path through the garden, and a good-looking young fellow of tall figure and manly air made his way to where the other still sat with his eyes fixed on vacancy, as one who neither sees nor hears aught of what is going on about him.

"Ha, Leonard!" the new-comer exclaimed, with a light laugh, "caught you dreaming again, eh? In another of your reveries?"

The other roused himself with a start, and looked to see who was his visitor.

"Good-morning, Jack," he then answered with a slight flush. "Well, yes—I suppose I must have been dreaming a little, for I did not hear you coming."

"Bet I guess what you were dreaming about," said the one addressed as Jack. "Roraima, as usual, eh?" Leonard looked a little conscious.

"Why, yes," he admitted, smiling. "But," he continued seriously, "I have just been reading something that set me thinking. It is about Roraima, and it is old; that is to say, it is in an old number of a paper bound up in this book that a friend has lent me. I should like to read it to you. Shall I?"

"All right; if I may smoke the while. I suppose I may?" And the speaker, anticipating consent, pulled out a pipe, filled and lighted it, and then, having seated himself on a chair, crossed one leg over the other, and added, "Now, then, I am ready. Fire away, old man."

And Leonard Elwood read the following extract from the book he had been studying:—

"Will no one explore Roraima, and bring us back the tidings which it has been waiting these thousands of years to give us? One of the greatest marvels and mysteries of the earth lies on the outskirt of one of our colonies, and we leave the mystery unsolved, the marvel uncared for. The description given of it (with a map and an illustrated sketch) in Mr. Barrington Brown's *Canoe and Camp Life in British Guiana* (one of the most fascinating books of travel the present writer has read for a long time) is a thing to dream of by the hour. A great table of pink and white and red sandstone, 'interbedded with red shale,' rises from a height of five thousand one hundred feet above the level of the sea, two thousand feet sheer into the sapphire tropical sky. A forest crowns it; the

highest waterfall in the world—only one, it would seem, out of several—tumbles from its summit, two thousand feet at one leap, three
thousand more on a slope of forty-five degrees to the bottom of
the valley, broad enough to be seen thirty miles away. Only two
parties of civilised explorers have reached the base of the table—
Sir Robert Schomburgk many years ago, and Mr. Brown and a companion in 1869*—each at different spots. Even the length of the
mass has not been determined—Mr. Brown says from eight to
twelve miles. And he cannot help speculating whether the remains
of a former creation may not be found at the top. At any rate, there
is the forest on its summit; of what trees is it composed? They cannot well be the same as those at its base. At a distance of fifteen
hundred feet above sea-level the mango-tree of the West Indies,
which produces fruit in abundance below, ceases to bear. The
change in vegetation must be far more decided where the difference is between five thousand and seven thousand feet. Thus for
millenniums this island of sandstone in the South American continent must have had its own distinct flora. What may be its fauna?
Very few birds probably ascend to a height of two thousand feet in
the air, the vulture tribe excepted. Nearly the whole of its animated
inhabitants are likely to be as distinct as its plants.

"Is it peopled with human beings? Who can tell? Why not? The
climate must be temperate, delicious. There is abundance of water,
very probably issuing from some lake on the summit. Have we here
a group of unknown brothers cut off from all the rest of their kind?

"The summit, Mr. Brown says, is inaccessible except by means
of balloons. Well, that is a question to be settled on the spot, between an engineer and a first-rate 'Alpine.' (What is the satisfaction of standing on the ice-ridge of the Matterhorn, or crossing
the lava-wastes of the Vatna-Jokull, compared to what would be
the sensation of reaching that aerial forest and gazing plumb down

* Since then Roraima has been visited by two or three other
travellers; but their accounts have added little to our knowledge. They
entirely confirm Mr. Brown's statements as to its inaccessibility. (See
Preface.)

over the sea of tropical verdure beneath, within an horizon the limits of which are absolutely beyond guessing?)

"But put it that a balloon is required, surely it would be worth while for one of our learned societies to organise a balloon expedition for the purpose. No one can tell what problems in natural science might not be elucidated by the exploration. We have here an area of limited extent within which the secular variation of species, if any, must have gone on undisturbed, with only a limited number of conceivable exceptions, since at least the very beginning of the present age in the world's life. Can there be a fairer field for the testing of those theories which are occupying men's minds so much in our days? And if there be human beings on Roraima, what new data must not their language, their condition, contribute for the study of philologers, anthropologists, sociologists?

"One more wonder remains to be told. The traveller speaks of two other mountains in the same district which are of the same description as Roraima—tables of sand-stone rising up straight into the blue—one larger than (though not as high as) Roraima itself. It is only because of their existence, and because, for aught that appears, they may be equally inaccessible with Roraima, that one does not venture to call Roraima the greatest marvel and mystery of the earth!"

"What is that taken from?" asked Jack Templemore when the reader had put down the book.

"It is from the *Spectator*.* I say, Jack, what a chance for an explorer! Fancy people spending their money and risking their lives in exploring an icy, cold, miserable, desolate region, like the Arctic Circle, when there is a wondrous land here in the blue skies— yet no wilderness of ice and snow—waiting to be won; and no one seems to trouble about it! I do wish you would do as I have so often suggested—set out with me upon an expedition and let us see whether we cannot solve the secret of this mysterious mountain. You have the leisure now, and I have the money. Dr. Lorien and

* This article appeared in the *Spectator* of April 1877.

his son are now on their way back from near there; if they can undertake the journey, so could we. Besides, it is not as though we were
novices at this kind of travel; we have been on short trips to the
interior times enough."

Jack Templemore looked dubious. He was, it is true, used to
roughing it in the wild parts of South America. He had been trained
as an engineer, and, for some years—he was now twenty-eight—
had been engaged in surveying or pioneering for new railways in
various places on the Continent. His father having lately died and
left him and his mother very poorly off, he was now somewhat anxiously looking about for something that would give him permanent occupation, or the chance of making a little money. He and
Leonard Elwood were great friends; though they were, in many
respects, of very different characters. Elwood was, essentially, of a
romantic, poetic temperament; while Templemore affected always
a direct, practical, matter-of-fact way of looking at things, as became an engineer. He was dark, tall and sturdily built, with keen,
steady grey eyes, and a straight-forward, good-humoured manner.
Both were used to hunting, shooting, and out-door sports, and, as
Elwood had just said, they had had many short hunting trips into
the interior together. But these had been in previous years, since
which, both had been away from Georgetown. Templemore, as
above stated, had been engaged in railway enterprises, Elwood had
gone to Europe, where, after some time spent in England, during
which his father and mother had both died, he had travelled for a
while "to see the world," and finally had come out again to
Georgetown to look after some property his father had left him.
On arrival he had gone at first to an hotel, but some old friends of
his parents, who lived on an estate known as "Meldona," had insisted upon his staying with them for a while. Here he found that
his old friend Jack Templemore was a frequent visitor, and it was
an open secret that Maud Kingsford, elder of the two daughters of
Leonard's host, was the real attraction that brought him there so
constantly.

Now Jack Templemore, as has been said, was more practical-
minded than Leonard. He had not shrunk from the hardships and
privations of wild forest life when engaged upon railway-engineering

work, when there had been something definite in view—money to be made, instruction to be gained, or promotion to be hoped for. But he did not view with enthusiasm the idea of leaving comfortable surroundings for the discomforts of rough travel, merely for travel's sake, or upon what he deemed a sort of wild-goose chase. He had carefully read up all the information that was obtainable concerning the mountain Roraima, and had seen no reason to doubt the conclusions that had been come to by those who ought to know—that it was inaccessible. Of what use then to spend time, trouble, money—perhaps health and strength—upon attempting the impossible?

So Jack Templemore argued, and, be it said, there was the other reason. Why should he go away and separate himself for an indefinite period from his only surviving parent and the girl he loved best in the world, with no better object than a vague idea of scrambling up a mountain that had been pronounced by practical men unclimbable?

Thus, when Leonard appealed to him on this particular morning, merely because he had come across something that had fired his enthusiasm afresh, Jack did not respond to the proposal with the cordiality that the other evidently wished for.

"I don't mind going a short trip with you, old man," Jack said presently, "for a little hunting, if you feel restless and are a-hungering after a spell of wandering—a few days, or a week or two, if you like—but a long expedition with nothing to go upon, as it were, seems to me only next door to midsummer madness."

Leonard turned away with an air of disappointment, and just then Maud Kingsford, who had been playing and singing inside the room, stepped out.

Leonard discreetly went into the house and left the two alone, and Maud greeted Jack with a rosy tell-tale flush that made her pretty face look still more charming. In appearance she was neither fair nor dark, her hair and eyebrows being brown and her eyes hazel. She was an unaffected, good-hearted girl, more thoughtful and serious, perhaps, than girls of her age usually are—she was twenty, while Stella, the younger sister, was between eighteen and nineteen—and had shown her capacity for managing a home by her success in that line in their own home since her mother's death a few years before. The practical-minded Jack, who had duly noted this, saw in it additional cause for admiration; but, indeed, it was only a natural outcome of her innate good sense. She now asked what her lover and Leonard had been talking of.

"The usual thing," was Jack's reply. "He's mad to go upon an exploring expedition; thinks we could succeed where others have failed. It's so unlikely, you know. Now, if he would only look at the thing practically—"

Maud burst into a merry laugh.

"You do amuse me—you two," she exclaimed; at which Jack looked a little disconcerted. "You always insisting so upon being strictly non-speculative, and Leonard, with his romantic phantasies, and his dreams and visions, and vague aspirations after castles in the air. You are always hammering away at him, trying to instill practical ideas into him with the same praiseworthy perseverance, though you know that in all these years you have never made the least little bit of impression upon him. Your ideas and his are like oil and water, you know. They will never mix, shake them together as you will."

"But—don't you think I am right? Isn't it common sense?"

"Quite right, of course; and you are persevering; I'll say that for you."

"For the matter of that, so's Leonard," said Jack with a good-natured laugh. "He's as persevering with this fad of his as any man I ever met in my life. I do believe he's got a fixed idea that he has only to start upon this enterprise, and he will come back a made man with untold and undreamt-of wealth and—"

"And a princess for a bride—the fair maid of his dreams," Maud put in, still laughing. "We have not heard so much of her, by the bye, lately. He has been rather shy of those things since his return from Europe, and does not like to be spoken to about them. We began to think he had grown out of his youthful fancies."

The fact was, that, from his childhood, Leonard had been accustomed to strange dreams and fancies. These five—Leonard, Templemore, and Mr. Kingsford's son and two daughters—had been children together, and in those days Leonard had talked freely to his childish companions of all his imaginative ideas; and as they grew older, he had not varied much in this respect. Moreover, Leonard had had an Indian nurse, named Carenna, who had encouraged him in his fantastic dreamings, and who had, by her Indian folk-lore tales, early excited his imagination. Her son Matava, too, had been Leonard's constant companion almost so long as he could remember, first in all sorts of boyish games and amusements, and later in his hunting expeditions; and both Matava and Carenna had been always more devoted to Leonard than even to his father and mother.

But when Mr. and Mrs. Elwood left the estate they had been cultivating, to go to England, the two Indians had gone away into the interior to live at an Indian settlement with their own tribe. About twice a year, however—or even oftener, if there were occasion—Matava still came down to the coast upon some little trading expedition with other Indians; and at such times he never failed to come to see the Kingsfords and inquire after Leonard.

The Dr. Lorien, of whom mention had been made by Leonard, was a retired medical practitioner who had turned botanist and orchid-collector. He had been a ship's doctor, and in that capacity had voyaged pretty well all over the world. Since he had given that up he had travelled further still by land—in the tropical regions in the heart of Africa, in Siam, the Malay Peninsular and, latterly, in South America—in search of orchids and other rare floral and botanical specimens. The vicinity of Roraima being one of the most remarkable in the world for such things—though so difficult of access as to be but seldom visited by white men—it is not surprising that he had lately planned a journey thither.

From this journey the doctor and his son were now daily expected back. One of the Indians of their party had, indeed, already arrived, having been despatched in advance, a few days before, to announce their safe return.

Thus it came about that Templemore and Maud, while still talking, were not greatly surprised at the sudden appearance of Matava, who stated that he had come down with the doctor's party, who would follow very quickly on his heels.

Maud, who knew the Indian and his mother well, received him kindly; and, to his great delight, was able to inform him that his "young master"—as he always called Leonard Elwood—had returned to Georgetown, and was at present with them.

Matava had, indeed, expected this, for he had heard of Leonard's intention at his last visit to the coast some six months before. He was greatly pleased to find he was not to be disappointed in his expectation. Moreover, the Indian declared, he had news for him— "news of the greatest importance"—and begged to be allowed to see him at once. So Maud sent him into the house—where he knew his way about perfectly—to find Leonard; and then, turning to Templemore, she said, laughing, "I wonder what his 'important' intelligence can be? Some deeper secret than usual that his old nurse has to tell him, I suppose."

"I hope it's nothing likely to rouse a further desire to set off on this mad-cap expedition he has so long had in his mind," Templemore returned; "for," looking at her with a sigh, "if he should make up his mind to start, I am, in effect, pledged to go too, whether I wish or not."

"Why should you expect it? and how are you obliged to go?" Maud inquired with evident uneasiness.

"I know that Leonard saw Dr. Lorien in London before he came out last, and had a long talk with him. When he learned of the expedition upon which the doctor was then setting out, he was much annoyed at being unable to join him. He said, however, that he should be in Georgetown himself in a few months, and hoped to see the doctor on his return; and he particularly asked him to try to collect for him all the information and particulars he could concerning the best route by which to make the journey to Roraima. Dr. Lorien told me all this before he left us, adding that he felt certain Leonard's object in coming again to Georgetown was quite as much to arrange for an expedition as his ostensible one of looking after his property. And I know, too, from what I have seen since Leonard has been back, that his thoughts are full of the idea. You say he does not now talk much of it to you or to others?"

"No; and as I told you just now, we had begun rather to think he had given up his former romantic yearnings for adventure; and, when you have referred to them before him, I have thought that you were only teasing him a little about old times."

"Oh dear no; by no means. Whatever he may say, or leave unsaid to you and his general acquaintances, he is, in his heart, just as much set upon it as ever."

"It is odd, that," Maud observed thoughtfully, "because he used to be so fond of telling us about his dreams and visions and all the castles in the air and half-mystical imaginings he used to build upon them. But," she went on slowly, "I have noticed that, since his long absence from us, Leonard Elwood is very different from what he was as I remember him. He seems, at times, so reserved and distant, I almost feel inclined to call him 'Mr. Elwood' instead of 'Leonard.' And he is, in a manner, unsociable, too. He is so preoccupied always, so silent, and so wrapped up in himself, that you generally have to wait, if you speak to him, while he collects his thoughts—brings them back from the distant skies or wherever they have gone a-wandering—before he replies to you. Not that he is intentionally cool or distant, I think; and I am sure he is just as good-hearted as ever. Yet there is a change of some sort. Stella says the same. And, do you know, he sometimes gives me a sort of feeling as though he were not English at all, but of some other race, and that he feels half out-of-place amongst us, a fish out of water, as it were? I wonder whether he is in love!" And Maud gave a ringing little laugh.

Templemore shook his head.

"If he were, it would be with some young lady on the other side of the Atlantic," he returned. "And he would not be desirous of prolonging his stay on this side. No; I know what is the matter with him. He talks freely enough to me. And, now that he is expecting Dr. Lorien back, he is gradually working himself up into a state of excitement and expectation. He has quite made up his mind for some news or information—Heaven only knows why—and that is what makes him by turns restless and preoccupied. If, therefore, what Matava has to tell has anything to do with what I know to be so much in his thoughts, it may be the means of deciding him to go; and then I should have to go too."

"But why? I don't see what it has to do with you, Jack."

"It has this to do with me, dear Maud," said Templemore, taking her hand; "Leonard, some time ago, made me a very handsome—

to me a very tempting—offer if I would make up my mind to start with him on this vague expedition. He offered me £300 clear, he paying all expenses, and giving me, besides, half of whatever came out of it. Unfortunately for myself, I am not now in a position to say 'no' to such an offer. I have been, now, nearly a year waiting for something to 'turn up.' My mother has barely enough to live on, and depends upon me for ordinary comforts, to say nothing of little luxuries; and what I had saved up from former engagements is steadily getting less and less, and will shortly disappear. I do wish with all my heart I could get anything else, almost, rather than this wild-goose affair of Leonard's. Yet nothing has offered itself; so what am I to do? For your sake, for the hope of being able one day to provide a home for you—"

"Nay, Jack," Maud interposed, with a deep flush, "do not say for my sake. I would not have you set out on an enterprise of danger and difficulty for my sake. But I see clearly enough you must do it, if it be again offered, for your mother's sake. Yes, for hers, you must." The girl hesitated, and it was easy to see she found it hard to say the words, but she went on bravely, "So, I repeat, if it be again offered, you must accept it, Jack. And be sure I will look after your mother, and comfort her while you are away."

"That is spoken like my own dear girl," Templemore answered with emotion. "Yes, I cannot well refuse; and I know I may look to you to console my mother. You will comfort each other."

Just then they heard Leonard's voice calling out in excited tones for Templemore. A moment or two later he came rushing out of the house.

"Jack, Jack!" he cried. "Such a strange thing! Here is our opportunity! Matava has brought some extraordinary news!"

Leonard was so incoherent in his excitement, that it was some time before his hearers grasped his meaning.

His news amounted, in effect, to this. A white man had been staying for some time near the Indian village at which Carenna and her son Matava lived; and he had had many talks with both about a project for ascending the mountain of Roraima. It being an arduous undertaking, he sought the co-operation of one or two other white men; and Leonard's old nurse had urged him to communicate with

her young master, who would shortly be in Georgetown, assuring
him that he would be the very one—from the interest and enthusiasm he would feel—to join him and help him to achieve success if
success were possible. Matava, who knew of Dr. Lorien's presence
in the district, had suggested to the stranger to go to see him, and
a meeting had thus been brought about. The doctor would tell him
the result; but the main thing was that the stranger had sent an
invitation to Leonard to join him and to bring, if he pleased, one
other white man, but no more. The doctor was now at the Settlement, near the mouth of the Essequibo, transferring to the steamer,
front the Indian canoes in which they had been brought down the
river, his botanical treasures and other trophies of his journey. If
Leonard wished to go back with the canoes and the Indians who
were with them, he would have to let them know at once, and they
would wait. Otherwise they would be on their way back in a day or
two; which would involve the organising of a fresh expedition—a
matter of great trouble—should Leonard make up his mind to proceed later.

The enthusiastic Leonard needed no time to make up his mind.

"I shall go," said he. "It you will come too, Jack, I shall be only
too glad. But, if not, I may be able to find some one else; or I shall
go alone. So I shall send word at once to keep the boats and the
Indians."

"But," objected Maud Kingsford, "consider! You know nothing
of this stranger; he may be a blackleg, an escaped murderer or des-
perado, or all sorts of things."

"No, no! Carenna knows. She has sent word that I can trust
this man, and she knows. She is too fond of me to let me get mixed
up with any doubtful character. Dr. Lorien, too, and Harry have
seen him, and talked with him, and think well of him; so Matava
says. I shall know more when I see them in a day or two. Meantime, I shall keep the canoes and Indians, and risk it."

Then he rushed off to have a further talk with Matava, and, as
he said, see about getting the Indian "some grub."

Jack and Maud, left alone, looked at each other in dismay. It
had been one thing to talk vaguely of what they would do in case
Leonard should take what at the time seemed a very unlikely step.

It was quite another to be thus suddenly brought face to face with it.

Maud turned very pale and seemed about to faint. She felt keenly how hard it would be to see her lover depart upon an adventure of this uncertain character, the end or duration of which no one could even guess at. But she recovered her self-possession with an effort and, looking steadily at Templemore, said,

"What you said you would do for our sakes is to be very quickly put to the test, it seems. You—*will*—go, Jack?"

"Yes," he answered firmly; "since it is your wish."

"You must," she answered. "It is hard to lose you; it will be hard for us both. But go—and go with a good heart. Be sure I will be a daughter to your mother while you are away."

He took her hand in his and pressed it to his lips.

"For your sake, dear Maud, I shall go," he said. "For your sake and for my mother's; in the hope that some success may result; but not—Heaven knows—for the mere sordid hope of gain."

2
Monella

Two days later Dr. Lorien and his son arrived in Georgetown and, after taking rooms at the Kaieteur Hotel, went at once to call upon the Kingsfords. This haste was, in reality, prompted by Harry, whose thoughts were bent upon his hopes of once more seeing the pretty Stella; but the ostensible reason that he urged upon his father was somewhat different, and had to do with the message of which they were the bearers from the white stranger they had met in their travels. At the evening dinner the matter was discussed, Mr. Kingsford and his son Robert and the others being present.

The two travellers had much to tell of their adventures, which had been full of both interest and danger, apart from the matter of the stranger's message.

"And yet, I think," observed the doctor, thoughtfully, "our meeting with this stranger, and his behaviour, impressed me more than almost all else that happened to us."

"How so? What is he like?" asked Mr. Kingsford.

"In figure he is very tall; of a most commanding stature and appearance. I am not short."

"Why, you are over six feet!" put in Harry.

"And yet I almost think, if he had held his arm straight out, I could have walked under it with my hat on, and without stooping."

"I'm sure you could, dad," Harry corroborated.

"As to age—there I confess myself at sea. As a doctor I am accustomed to judge of age; yet he thoroughly puzzled me. If I could believe in the possibility of a man's being a hundred and fifty years old and yet remaining strong and hale and vigorous, I should not

311

be surprised if he had claimed that age. On the other hand, if one could believe in a young, stalwart, muscular man of thirty with the face and white hair of an old-looking, but not very old man, then I could have believed it if I had been told he was no more than thirty. In fact, he was a complete puzzle to me; a mystery. But the most remarkable thing about him was the expression of his eyes; they were the most extraordinary I have ever seen in my life."

"Wild—mad-looking?" Templemore asked.

"Oh no, by no means; quite the reverse. Very steady and piercing; but wonderfully fascinating. Mild and kind-looking to a fault; and yet changing to a look of quiet, almost stern resolution that had in it nothing hard, or cruel, or disagreeable. In fact, I hardly know how to describe that look, or convey an idea of it, except by saying that it was something between the gaze of a lion and that of a Newfoundland dog. It had all the majesty, the magnanimity, the conscious power of the one, with the benevolence and wistful kindness and affection of the other. Never have I seen such an expression. I really did not know the human countenance could express the mingled characteristics one seemed to read so plainly in his— all kindly, all noble, all suggestive of sincerity and integrity."

"You are enthusiastic! " said Robert, laughing.

The old doctor coloured up a little; then took out his handkerchief and wiped his face.

"I know it sounds strange to hear an old man of the world like me speak so forcibly about a man's appearance," he returned; "but, if it is true, I do not see why I should not say it. Ask Harry here."

"I couldn't take my eyes off his face," Harry declared. "He fairly fascinated me. I felt I should have to do anything he told me; even to taking my pistol and killing the first person I met. I do believe I should have done it—or any other out-of-the way thing. And he made you feel, too, as though you liked him so, that you longed to do any mortal thing you could to please him."

"What's his name?" asked Templemore.

"Monella."

"Monella? Is that all? No other name?"

"None that I heard. And as to his nationality, I cannot even so much as guess. I have been in Central Africa, in Siam, in India, in

China, in Russia, and have picked up a smattering of the languages of those countries; but this man jabbered away in all; additionally, he spoke French, German, Spanish and Portuguese, besides English. So much I know. How many more he speaks I can't say."

"Injun," said Harry.

"Oh yes, I forgot that. We had some of three different tribes with us, and he spoke to each in his own tongue."

"And what is his object in going in for this Roraima exploration?" asked Mr. Kingsford.

"He has a curious theory. He declares that the ancient island-city of El Dorado—or Manoa—was not at the lower end or part of the Pacaraima mountains, as some have surmised, but at the further and highest point of the range, which is Roraima itself. He holds that the great lake or inland sea of Parima once washed around the bases of all those mountains, making islands of what are now their summits; and that the highest and most inaccessible of all, Roraima, was selected by the Manoans for their fastness, and for the site of their wonderful 'Golden City.'"

"But that theory won't help him to get up there, will it?" Jack asked.

"Ah, but there is something else. He states that he was brought up by some people, the last members of what had once been a nation, but has now died out. They lived in a secluded valley high up on the slopes of the Andes. He has travelled all over the world, and went back to these friends of his, only to find that they were all dead, save one, and that he was fast dying. This survivor gave him an ancient parchment with plans and diagrams, by means of which, it was declared, the top of the mountain can be reached, where will be found whatever traces may be left of the famous city of Manoa or El Dorado. This man, Monella, has other old parchments which he can read, but I could not—he showed me some—and from these he declared his belief that there is almost unlimited wealth to be gained by those who find the site of this wonderful city."

All this time Leonard had been listening with sparkling eyes and flushed cheeks, though in silence. Here he glanced with a satisfied smile at Templemore, and said, "There's method in all that; at all events he is not undertaking the thing in a haphazard way and without something to go upon, that's certain."

Jack did not look hopeful.

"It is probably just as wild and hopeless an adventure all the same," was his reply. "What 'directions' or 'plans' or 'diagrams' can help a man to-day after the lapse of hundreds and hundreds of years—even if they were reliable, and the old party who handed them over was not mad—as he probably was?"

"As to Monella," observed the doctor, "I could see no sign of madness in him. He is one of the most intelligent, best-informed men I ever met. I cannot say anything, of course, of his informant."

"Has he any money, do you suppose—this man?" Robert asked.

"I don't know. But he pays the Indians well, and has got together a lot of stores, it seems; which must have been a costly thing to do. They have been brought over the mountains from Brazil. And he specially said you need not trouble to load yourself up with much in the way of stores—only sufficient to get to him. After that you will be all right. And he said nothing about money being wanted. But," and here the doctor hesitated, "he is very particular as to the character and disposition of those he purposes to work with. In fact, he subjected me to a long sort of cross-examination respecting our friend Leonard here. He had already gained a lot of information about him from the old Indian nurse, it seemed, and I was surprised at the details he had picked up and remembered. In fact, Master Leonard," continued the doctor, addressing the young man, "he seemed to know you almost as well as if he had lived with you for years. And your friend Mr. Templemore, too, he seemed to know about him, and to expect that he would join you."

"How could that be?" Jack demanded.

"Oh, from the old nurse and Matava, I suppose."

"To tell you the honest truth," Harry interposed, "I believe there's some hocus-pocus business about those two. She is reputed to be a witch, you know; not a bad witch, but a good sort. And I quite believe Monella to be a wizard; also of a good sort. And when those two laid their heads together, they could know a lot between them, I suspect. I should not at all wonder if he were not magician enough to lead you to the 'golden castle,' or 'city,' or whatever it is, and find its hidden stores of gold. I wish I had a chance to join him. But dad's wanting me somewhere else. So I am out of it."

"Yes," observed his father. "We have to go on to Rio, where I have some law business on. But we shall not be away a great while, and then we are going back to that district."

"Going back?" said Templemore in surprise.

"Yes, there is a lot to be done there. It is a wonderful place for my sort of work, and we really saw but very little of it after all. So we are going again when we return from Rio; but I cannot at all tell when that may be."

The doctor was a fine-looking specimen of a hardy, bronzed traveller. He was, as has been said, over six feet in height; his hair and beard were iron-grey, his complexion was a little florid beneath its tan, and his expression good-humoured and often jovial. His son, Harry, was somewhat slight in build, but wiry, and had been used to knocking about with his father. He was a young fellow with boundless animal spirits and plenty of pluck and courage. His ready kindness to every one made him a general favourite; and the lively, captivating Stella and he were special friends.

Mr. Kingsford asked the doctor whether any time had been estimated for the length of the expedition.

"That would be difficult," Dr. Lorien answered. "Apart from the long and tedious journey there, there is the girdle of forest that surrounds Roraima to be cut through. That may take months, I am told."

"Months!" The exclamation came from Maud who, with Stella, had been a silent but appreciative listener.

"Yes. It is a curious thing, but this forest belt is never approached even by any of the Indian tribes. They look upon it with superstitious awe and will not even go near it. Indeed, they all regard Roraima with a sort of horror. They declare there is a lake on the top guarded by demons and large white eagles, and that it will never be gazed on by mortal eyes; that in the forest that surrounds it are monstrous serpents— 'camoodis' they call them—larger far than any to be found elsewhere in the land; besides these, there are 'didis', gigantic man-apes, bigger and more ferocious and formidable than the African gorilla. Altogether, this wood has a very bad reputation, and no Indian will venture near it. Indeed, the mountain of Roraima and all its surroundings are looked upon as weird and uncanny. As a former traveller has expressed it, 'its very name has come to be surrounded by a halo of dread and indefinable fear.'"

"How, then, is the necessary road to be made through this promising bit of woodland?" asked Templemore.

"There has been Monella's difficulty," returned the doctor. "But for that, doubtless, he would not have troubled about any one else's joining him. But, though he is very popular amongst the Indians, they cannot get over their fear of the 'demons' wood', as they call it. They are, in fact, quite devoted to him, for he has done much that has made him both loved and feared—as one must always be to gain the real devotion of these people. He has effected many wonderful cures amongst them, I was told; but, more than that, he has saved the lives of two or three by acts of great personal courage. So that, at last, he even prevailed upon them to enter the 'haunted wood' with him. But they are making very little progress, it appears; he cannot keep them together, and they give way to panic at the slightest thing and make a bolt of it; then he has to go hunting over the country for them, and it takes days to get them together again—and so on. He is in hopes that the presence and example of other white men will inspire them with greater confidence and courage."

"A promising and inviting outlook, I must say," said Jack, eyeing Leonard gravely.

"Never mind," Leonard exclaimed with enthusiasm. "If he can face it, so can we; and if it is good enough for him to brave such difficulties, it is good enough for us. It only shows what sterling stuff he must be made of!"

At this Jack gave a sort of grunt that was clearly far from implying assent to Leonard's view of the matter.

There was further talk, but it added little to the information given above; and, inasmuch as Leonard had already made up his mind, almost in advance, and had to ask no one's permission but his own, he determined at once to set about the necessary preparations; and Jack Templemore—though with evident reluctance—agreed to accompany him.

"I have a list of all the things I took with me," remarked Dr. Lorien, "and notes of a few that I afterwards found would have been useful and that I consequently regretted I had not taken; and also some specially suggested by the stranger Monella. You had better copy them all out carefully, for you will find it will save you a lot of time and trouble."

Thus it came about that in less than a week their preparations were all made, and the two, with Matava as guide, were ready to set out. Matava had with him fourteen or fifteen Indians, who had formed the doctor's party, and these, and the canoes with the stores on board, were soon after waiting at the Settlement, ready to make a start.

Then, one sunny day at the beginning of the dry season, the Kingsfords, with Mrs. Templemore, and the doctor and his son, all took the steamer to the "Penal Settlement" (a place a few miles inside the mouth of the Essequibo river, the starting place of all such parties), to see the young men off and wish them God speed. When it came to this point the struggle was a hard one for Maud and for Templemore's mother; but they bore themselves bravely— outwardly at least. The three canoes put off amidst much fluttering of handkerchiefs, and soon all that could be seen of the adventurers were three small specks, gradually growing less and less, as the boats made their way up the bosom of the great Essequibo river—here some eight miles in width. Their intended journey had been kept more or less a secret; such had been the wish of him they were going to join. Hence no outside friends had accompanied the party to see them off. Those who knew of their going away thought they were only bent upon a hunting trip of a little longer duration than usual.

For two loving hearts left behind the separation was a trying one. For a few days Mrs. Templemore stayed on at "Meldona" with Maud, and the presence of Dr. Lorien and the vivacious Harry helped to cheer them somewhat; but, when the doctor and his son started for Rio, the others returned sadly to the routine of their everyday life, with many anxious speculations and forebodings concerning the fortunes of the two explorers.

3
The Journey from the Coast

The greater part of the interior of British Guiana consists of dense forests which are mostly unexplored. No roads traverse them, and but little would be known of the savannas, or open grassy plains, and the mountains that lie beyond—and they would indeed be inaccessible—were it not for the many wide rivers by which the forests are intersected. These form the only means of communication between the coast and the interior at the present day; and so vast is the extent of territory covered with forest growth that it is probable many years will elapse before any road communication is opened up between the sea and the open country lying beyond the woods.

Of these vast forests little—or rather practically nothing—is known save what can be seen of them from the rivers by those voyaging to and fro in canoes. There are a limited number of spots at which the Indians of the savannas come to the banks of the rivers to launch their canoes when journeying to the coast; and to reach these places they have what are known as "Indian paths" through the intervening woods. These so-called paths are, for the most part, of such a character, however, that only Indians accustomed to them can find their way by them. Any white man who should venture to trust himself alone in them would inevitably get quickly and hopelessly lost. Hence—save for a few miles near the line of coast—there are, as yet, absolutely no roads in the country.

Naturally, under such conditions, the forest scenery is of the wildest imaginable character, and its flora and fauna flourish unchecked in the utmost luxuriance of tropical savage life; for the

country lies but a few degrees from the equator, and is far more
sparsely populated that even the surrounding tropical regions of
Brazil and Venezuela.

Fortunately, however, for those who for any reason have occasion to traverse this wild region, there is no lack of water-ways.
Several grand rivers of great breadth lead from the coast in different directions, most of them being navigable (for canoes and small
boats) for great distances, leaving only comparatively short
stretches of forest land to be crossed by travellers desiring to reach
the open plains and hills.

Of these rivers, the Essequibo is one of the finest, and it was by
this route that the two friends, Elwood and Templemore, set out,
under Matava's guidance, to reach their destination. From this river
they branched off into one of its affluents, the Potaro, noted for its
wonderful waterfall, the Kaieteur, which they visited en route. Here
their canoes were left and exchanged for lighter ones, hired from
the Ackawoi Indians, who live at a little distance above the fall;
their stores and camp equipage being carried round. So far the journey had been uneventful, save for a little excitement in passing
the various cataracts and rapids; but the two young men knew their
way fairly well thus far, having visited the Kaieteur with Matava
some years before.

When, however, the journey was resumed above the Kaieteur,
the route was new to them; and, among the first things they noticed, were the alligators with which the river abounded. In the
Essequibo they had seen none, and not many below the fall; but
from this point, as far as they ascended the river, they saw them
continually. Once they had a narrow escape. They were making
arrangements for camping on the bank, and were nearing the shore
in the last of the canoes, when a tremendous blow and a great
splash overturned the boat, and they found themselves struggling
in the stream. An alligator had struck the canoe a blow with its tail
and upset it. Fortunately, however, it was in shallow water; and
the Indians, seeing how matters were, made a great splashing, and
thus frightened away the reptile. The contents of the canoe were
partly recovered, not without difficulty; but some were damaged
by the water.

As they proceeded up the river, the rapids and cataracts became more frequent, and the negotiation of them more difficult, till they reached a spot where further navigation was impossible, and they had to take to the forest, their stores and baggage being henceforward carried by the Indians.

This marked the commencement of the really arduous part of the journey. So long as the stores were carried in the boats, the Indians had been cheerful and docile, and easy to manage. But now their work was harder, and food was scarcer—for game is difficult to shoot in the forest.

Then, after two or three days, the gloom of the woods began to have an evident effect upon their spirits; they first became depressed, and then began to grumble. This would not have been of so much consequence, perhaps, but that Matava became apprehensive that they might desert. They were not people of his tribe, it seemed; they had come with Dr. Lorien from a different district; and when they began to understand that the eventual destination was Roraima, they became still more depressed.

All the Indian tribes who have heard of Roraima, in any way, have the same superstitious dread of it; and those now with the two young men were evidently not exceptional in this respect. Templemore and Elwood began to feel anxious and, to make matters worse, food ran short for the Indians. The latter live chiefly on the native food, a kind of bread called cassava, and, of this, a good deal of what they had brought with them had been lost or spoiled by the upsetting of the canoe.

In consequence, Matava advised that they should interrupt their direct journey to turn aside to an Indian settlement that he knew of, about a day's journey off the route they were pursuing; there they would be able to replenish their stores, he thought; and to this course a reluctant assent was given by the a two friends.

It turned out to be more than a day's journey, however; but they reached the place on the second day. It was called Karalang; there were not mo re than a dozen huts, and the people at first said that they no food to spare; but eventually promised to procure some if the travellers would wait a few days; and this they were perforce compelled to do.

This village was situated on a hill in a piece of open country in the midst of the great forest; and, during their enforced rest, the two friends were enabled to engage in a little hunting, and to see more of the wild life of the woods than they had seen before.

The first thing they did on arrival was to procure a couple of fowls for cooking, of which there were plenty in the village. But these were of no use as food for the Indians, who never eat them. Throughout the country this is everywhere the case; the Indians keep fowls, yet never eat them; and it is said that were it not for the vampire bats and tiger-cats, these would increase beyond all reason. Though, however, they object to fowls as a diet, they have no dislike to fish, and they were not long in discovering that there were some in a stream that ran near the village; and a supply was caught by their method of poisoning the fish in such a way that they float on top of the water as if dead, but are nevertheless palatable and wholesome as food. The poison is prepared from a root.

Amongst the miscellaneous stores the two had brought they had a liberal supply of firearms—five Winchester rifles, half-a-dozen revolvers and two guns, each with double barrels, one for shot and the other for ball. The extra weapons were in case of loss or accident, and Templemore had a good stock of tobacco, for he never felt happy for long together without his pipe.

On their way up they had had very little shooting. Jack had indeed killed an alligator, by way of relieving his feelings after the upsetting of the canoe; but there had been very little time to spare for sport. Every morning they had started as soon as the morning meal had been eaten, and had gone into camp at night only in time to cook a meal before it became dark. For in this part of the world night closes in at about half-past six on the shortest days of the year, and a little before seven on the longest. Practically, therefore, the varying seasons bring little difference in the length of the days. One cannot there get up at three or four o'clock and "have a good, long day," with an evening keeping light till eight and nine o'clock, as in summer-time in Europe. Hence the days seem short for travel and sport, and the nights very long.

"I think we've stuck to it pretty well," Jack observed in the evening, as he sat smoking by the camp fire, outside their tent—

for though the day had been hot the evening was chilly— "and we deserve a rest. So it is just as well. We will have two or three days' shooting, and a look round, before we go on to tackle 'the old man.'"

"The old man" was the one they were on their way to see—the one Dr. Lorien had met and described so enthusiastically. Jack was a little sceptical as to whether the good-natured doctor had not sacrificed strict accuracy to his friendly feeling for the stranger. Leonard, too, felt full of curiosity upon the same point.

"I can scarcely believe, you know," Jack continued, "that our friend will turn out all that the doctor pictured him."

"I shall be glad if he does, at any rate," Leonard made reply. "He would be almost worth coming to see for himself alone."

Jack laughed.

"That's rather stretching a point, I think. However, I am keeping an open mind on the subject. The gentleman shall have 'a fair field and no favour,' so far as my judgment of him goes. I won't let myself be prejudiced in advance, either one way or the other."

During the following days they enriched their stores by the skin of a fine jaguar, shot by Templemore, a great boa-constrictor—or 'camoodi'—twenty-four feet long, shot by Leonard, and many trophies of lesser account. Then, a fresh lot of cassava having been procured for the Indians, the journey was resumed.

In about three weeks from the time of their start, the party emerged from the forest into a more open country, where rolling savannas alternated with patches of woodland. Here the air was fresher and more bracing, so that the depressing effect of the gloomy forest was soon thrown off. They could shoot a little game, too, as they went along; there were splendid views to be had from the tops of the ridges and low hills they crossed. The ground steadily rose and became first hilly and then mountainous, till, having crossed a broad, undulating plateau, they once more entered a forest region, but this time of different character. The trees were farther apart; there were hills, and rocky ravines, and mountain torrents, steep mountains, and deep valleys. The way became toilsome and difficult; game was scarce, or at least not easy to obtain, owing to the nature of the ground; the cassava ran short, and, once more, grumbling arose and trouble threatened.

At last, one evening, Matava, with perplexity in his face, led the two young men aside to hold a consultation.

"These people," he said in his own language, "say they will not go any farther!"

"How far do you reckon we are now from your own village?" asked Jack.

"About four days. If we could but persuade them to keep on for two days more, we could fix a camp, and I could go on alone and bring back some of my own people to take all the things on."

"Ah! a good idea, Matava. Well, let us see what persuasion will effect. Any way, we had better get them to go as far as we can, and then encamp at the first likely camping-ground."

In the end the Indians were prevailed upon, by promise of extra pay, to go the additional two days' journey. Beyond that they would not budge. "They think that mountain over there in the distance is Roraima," Matava explained; "and I cannot get them to believe it isn't. And they are frightened, and won't go any nearer to it."

There was, therefore, nothing to be done but to adopt Matava's suggestion. It was agreed that the two friends would stay in camp and keep guard over their belongings, while he started next day for his village, to bring help.

The spot was a convenient one in which to camp for a few days, with a stream of water near. That evening, therefore, the Indians were paid, this being done in silver, which they knew how to make use of. The next morning, when Elwood and Templemore got out of their hammocks, they found they were alone with Matava. All the others had disappeared.

"Ungrateful beggars!" said Jack. "They might, at least, have gone in a respectable manner, and not like thieves slinking away. Let's hope they are not thieves."

But they were not. An examination showed that nothing had been stolen.

"The poor fellows were only frightened," Leonard observed. "They are honest enough."

Matava, meantime, was making ready to set off alone for carriers from his own village. When he was ready Templemore expressed a desire to walk a little way on the road with him "to take a peep over that little ridge yonder"; which is a wish common to travellers in a country that is new to them. But when they reached the ridge, there was only to be seen another short expanse of undulating savanna, whereupon Jack decided to return, leaving Matava to continue on his way.

Leonard, left to himself, finished the occupation he had in hand—the cleaning of his double-barrel—and, having loaded it, strolled out of the camp in another direction, to take a look round. He left the camp to itself, not intending to go far, and expecting that his friend would be back in a quarter of an hour or so. Not far away a "bell-bird" was ringing out its strange cry, that has been compared by travellers to the sound of a convent bell. He had heard these birds often in the forest since leaving the boats, but, in consequence of the density of the woods, had never been able to get near one. Here, where the trees were more open, there seemed to be a better chance, and he followed, as he thought, the sound. But soon he came to the conclusion that he had been in error; or the bird had flown across unseen; for the direction of the sound seemed to have changed. He, therefore, turned off towards where he fancied the bird now was; and this happened several times, till at last he became confused and found he had fairly lost his way. It is a peculiarity of the "bell-bird," as it is of many other birds of the forest, that their notes are often misleading; it is one of those cases of what has been termed by naturalists "Ventriloquism in Nature," many examples of which the traveller in these wild regions comes across. Leonard had arrived at the head of a small glen, and found himself on a grassy bank beside a little stream, sheltered from the glare of the sun by over-hanging branches. He laid down his gun and went to take a drink of the inviting limpid water, and then sat awhile on the bank looking down the picturesque ravine. It was very quiet and peaceful all around, and he fell into one of his daydreams. At such times the minutes pass on unheeded; and he sat for a long while oblivious of all that went on about him. But presently, behind him, a silent, cunning enemy crept up unseen and unheard till near enough for a spring; then there was a loud roar, and the next moment Leonard was lying on the ground in the grasp of an enormous jaguar.

For a minute or two the beast stood over him growling, but not touching him after the first blow that had knocked him down; while Leonard lay dazed and helpless, with just enough consciousness to have a vague idea that the best thing he could do, for the moment, was to lie perfectly still. Then, with another roar, the animal seized him by the shoulder and began to drag him down the slope towards some bushes. At that moment Leonard, whose face was turned away from the brute, saw, like one in a dream, the undergrowth through which he himself had come, part asunder and three figures appear. Two of them were Templemore and Matava, who stood rooted to the spot with horror-stricken faces; the third was a tall stranger who towered above the other two, and who also stood still for a second or two eyeing the scene, while the jaguar growled threateningly.

Then the tall stranger advanced, and the animal released its hold and was itself seized and pulled from over Leonard. In another moment he felt himself lifted in two giant arms, and, looking up, saw the stranger bending upon him a gaze in which there seemed a world of tender anxiety and compassion. Everything appeared to swim around him, and he knew that consciousness was leaving him; yet, for a space, the fascination of that look seemed to hold him chained.

"You—must—be—Monella!" he said, softly. Then he fainted.

4
The First View of Roraima

When Leonard came to himself sufficiently to see and understand what was going on around him, for the moment he thought himself once more in his days of childhood; for the first face he recognised was Carenna's, his Indian nurse, who was bending over him in much the same way and with the same expression as of yore. But, when he looked round, he saw that he was in an Indian hut; and slowly the memory of what had occurred came back to him.

Carenna, when she saw that he was himself again, gave a joyous cry; then, conscious of her indiscretion, put her finger on her lips to imply that he must remain quiet. He felt no inclination to do otherwise, and soon fell into a refreshing sleep, which lasted for some time.

When next he opened his eyes they rested on another pair, large and steady, and that seemed to have a wondrous depth and meaning in them. Then he saw that they belonged to the stranger who had pulled the jaguar off, and was now sitting alongside the mattress on which he lay.

"Keep thee quiet, my son," said he in a low, musical voice. "All goes well, and in two or three days you will be as strong as ever again."

There was something soothing in the mere glance of the eye, and in the very tones of the man's voice; and Leonard, reassured by them, remained passive for a while, till Carenna again appeared with a drink she had prepared for him.

When, later, Jack Templemore came in, and Leonard was able to talk, he found he had been ill for a week, and that he was then in the hut of Carenna at the village of Daranato.

"I've had an awfully anxious time of it," Jack said; "but Monella seems skilled in doctoring, and Carenna has been most devoted in her nursing and attention and would brook no interference; so I've had to hang around and pass the time as best I could."

When once Leonard had "turned the corner," as Jack called it, he recovered rapidly, and was able, in a few days, as Monella had predicted, to get about again. Nor was he any the worse for his mishap; for the beast's teeth had just missed scrunching the bone.

When he wished to offer his thanks to Monella, the latter put him off with a quiet smile.

"We think nothing of little incidents like that, my son, in a land such as this. Your thanks are due to God who sent me to you at the moment; not to me. Being there, I could not well have done otherwise than I did."

It appeared that Monella had come out from the village a day or two before to look out for them, and had fallen in with Matava. The Indian had led him towards the camp, near which they had met Jack, who was wandering about in search of Leonard. On learning that he was missing, Monella had proceeded to the camp and thence—by some method known only to himself—had tracked Leonard's footsteps—a thing that even Matava confessed himself unable to do—and thus had come upon him just in time.

"When I saw how matters stood," said Jack, "my very heart seemed to stand still. Neither I nor Matava dared to risk a shot, for the brute stood up nearly facing us and holding you in his mouth. But that wonder, Monella, quietly laid down his rifle and drew his knife, keeping the beast fixed with his eye all the time; then he walked up to it as coolly as though he were going to stroke a pet cat, put out his hand and caught it with such a grip on the throat that it nearly choked and had to let go of you at once. And presto! Before it could get its breath, whizz went the knife into its heart! And he lifted it up and threw it away from him, clear of you, as easily as one might a small dog. Then he picked you up and carried you to the camp, as though you were but a baby. The whole affair took only a few moments, and passed almost like a dream. It's fortunate he happened to come out to meet us. How could he possibly know we were coming?"

"I have always told you," said Leonard dreamily, "that there seems to be a strange sympathy between my old Indian nurse and myself. She tells me she 'felt' that I was in the neighbourhood, and sent word to Monella, who at once went to her, and then came on to try to intercept us. Only, you know, you never believed in those things. Yet here, you see, Monella must have believed her, or he would not have had such confidence in our coming as to wait about for us as he did."

"It's very strange," Jack admitted. "I confess I do not understand you 'dreamers.' I am out of the running there altogether.

"They say," he continued, "that from the top of yonder low mountain before us you can see Roraima pretty plainly. But I had no heart to go out to look for it while you were so ill, and, since you have been getting better, I have preferred to stay and keep you company. But now, I suppose, it will not be long before we set eyes, at last, upon the wonderful mountain that is to be our 'El Dorado'!"

When Elwood heard this, he became anxious to get a sight of the object of their journey; so, two days after, they started before dawn, with Monella, to walk to the top of the low mountain Jack had pointed out.

They reached the summit of the ridge just when the sun was rising, and there before them, like a veritable fairy-land in the sky, they saw the mysterious Roraima, its pink-white and red cliffs illumined by the morning sun, and floating in a great sea of white mist, above which showed, here and there, the peaks of other lower mountains like the islands they once were, but looking dark and heavy, in their half-shadow, beside the glorious beauty of this queen of them all, that reared herself tar above everything around.

It is impossible to give an adequate idea of the impressive grandeur of this mountain, which might be likened to a gigantic sphinx, serene and impassive in its inaccessibility.

Or it might be likened to a colossal fortress, built by Titans to guard the entrance to an enchanted land beyond; for the cliffs at its summit appeared curiously turreted, while at the corners were great rounded masses that might pass for towers and bastions.

In places, with the light-coloured cliffs were to be seen darker rocks, black and dark green and brown, worked in, as it were, with strange figures, as though inlaid by giant hands. And everywhere the sides were perpendicular, smooth, and glassy-looking. Scarce a shrub or creeper found a precarious hold there; but down from the height, at one spot, fell a great mass of water—like a broad band of silver sparkling and glistening in the sunlight—that came with one mad leap from the top and disappeared in a cloud of spray and mist two thousand feet below. Further along could be seen other narrower falls like silver threads.

There was no crest or peak as with most mountains. The top was a table-land, beyond whose edge one could see nothing. This edge was fringed with what looked like herbage, but, seen through a powerful field-glass, proved to be great forest trees.

Then, as the sun rose higher and warmed the air, the mist cleared somewhat around the lower part of the precipitous cliffs, so that far, far down could now be seen the foliage that crowned the great primaeval forest—the 'forest of demons'—that girdled the cliffs' base. Gradually the mist descended, and the full forest's height showed up like a titanic pedestal of green, itself floating in the haze that still remained below.

By degrees the mist rolled down the mountain's side, for below this extensive forest-girdle the actual base and lower slopes began slowly to appear, with waterfalls, and cascades, and rushing torrents and great rivers dashing and foaming in their rocky beds. Then other intervening ridges and patches of forest and open savanna gradually came into view, with the full forms of the surrounding smaller mountains, the whole making up a panorama that was marvellous in its extent and in the variety of its shapes and tints.

But scarcely had the sun revealed this wondrous sight to their astonished eyes, when a cloud descended upon Roraima's height.

Almost imperceptibly it grew darker, then darker still and yet more sombre, till the erst-while fairy fortress seemed to frown in gloomy grandeur. Its salmon-tinted sides, but now so airy-looking in their lightness, turned almost black, and seemed to glower upon the brilliant landscape. The forest also lost its verdant colouring and looked dark and forbidding enough to pass for an enchanted wood peopled by dragons, demons, and hobgoblins to guard the grim castle in its centre.

Then the cloud descended lower still, and castle and haunted forest passed out of sight, as swiftly and completely as though all had been a magical illusion that had vanished at a touch of the magician's wand.

Leonard rubbed his eyes and felt half inclined to think he had been dreaming. All this time not a word had been exchanged. Each had seemed wrapped up in the weird attraction of the scene; and the new-comers, even the practical Jack, had been astounded, almost overwhelmed, at the sight of the stupendous cliffs and tower-like rocks of the mysterious mountain, and its changes from gorgeous colouring and ethereal beauty to black opacity and shapelessness.

Presently Monella turned and led the way back to the camp, the others following, each absorbed in his own thoughts.

Templemore was more impressed by what he had just witnessed than he would have cared, perhaps, to own. Never before had he seen such a mountain, though he had crossed the Andes, and had looked upon the loftiest and grandest on the American Continent. To him there was something about Roraima that was wanting in all other mountains; a suggestiveness of the unseen, of latent possibilities. He could now understand why the Indians regarded it with fear and awe. It was, indeed, impossible to look upon it without believing that some wonderful story was hidden in its inaccessible bosom; some mysterious secret that it kept jealously concealed from the rest of the world. For, perhaps, the first time in his life, he was conscious of a feeling that bordered on the superstitious. What if that which they had witnessed were meant to shadow forth a warning; to be an omen! Did it portend that, should they gain the summit of Roraima, they would find there indeed a sort of earthly Paradise, but that it would turn—as suddenly and completely as the fairy-like first view had changed that morning—to the darksome solitude of a charnel house?

But Leonard, for his part, when he came to talk upon the matter, was only more enthusiastic than before; and Monella smiled with indulgent approbation when, with the ingenuous impulsiveness of youth, he enlarged upon his delight and expectations.

When they returned to the Indian village preparations were begun for a forward move to the place Monella had made his head-quarters;

not far from the commencement of the mysterious forest the Indians regarded with such dread.

During the march thither they had many more glimpses of
Roraima; finally they emerged upon the last ridge that faced it,
from which a full view of its towering sides and of the forest at
their base could be obtained.

Between them was a deep ravine, along which flowed a narrow
river dotted with great boulders. Having crossed this with some
difficulty and ascended the other side, they reached an extensive
undulating plateau, an open savanna with here and there small
clumps of trees. They were now almost under the shadow of the
great cliffs, and before them, three or four miles away, was the
beginning of the encircling wood.

Rounding the end of a thicket distant a mile or so from this
wood, they came suddenly upon a large and substantially built log
hut, and this, Monella told them, was his temporary residence. Near
it were several smaller huts roughly but ingeniously formed of
boughs and wood poles, which the Indians who worked with him
had constructed for themselves.

As they entered the larger dwelling Monella thus addressed
them:

"This, my friends, is where we shall have to live until our work
in 'Roraima Forest' shall be completed. Make yourselves as much
at home as the circumstances will permit; we are likely to occupy
it for some time."

And a fairly comfortable home it was; far more so indeed than
the young men had ventured to expect. There was rough furniture,
there were lamps for light at night, a number of books, and many
other things that took them altogether by surprise.

"It must have taken you a long time," said Jack Templemore,
"to get all these things transported here, and this place built and
its furniture made."

"It has taken me years!" was the reply.

The Indians who accompanied them, numbering about twenty,
were all of Matava's own tribe; altogether a different race from those
who had accompanied them nearly to Daranato and had been paid
off and gone home. When Monella had left his abode, temporarily,

at Carenna's request, to come to meet the two, all the Indians had gone with him, objecting to be left so near to the "demons' wood" without him. Now, however, they quickly distributed themselves among the huts, one acting as cook and servant in the house, and Matava attending to all other matters as general overlooker.

So far little had been said between the young men and their strange host as to the objects and details of their enterprise. The circumstances of their introduction had been so unusual that the discussion had been tacitly postponed until Leonard should have recovered sufficiently to take part in it. And even then, when Jack had broached the subject, Monella had remarked, "You had better wait till you have been to my cabin near Roraima, when I can better explain the nature of the undertaking. Then, if you do not care to join me in it, or we seem unlikely to get on well together, we will part friends and you will merely have had an interesting bit of travelling." So all farther explanation had been adjourned.

"I call this more than a 'cabin,'" said Leonard, when they had had time to make a sort of tour of inspection. "I think we ought to give it a better name. Suppose we call it 'Monella Lodge.'" And "Monella Lodge" it was henceforth called.

5
In the "Demons' Wood"

The following day, Monella led the two friends to the road he had begun to cut into Roraima Forest; but first he showed them two llamas that were kept in a rough corral near his dwelling.

"I brought them all the way from the other side of the continent," he said. "You know that there they are the only beasts of burden, and in this country there are none. They will be useful to us later."

As to the so-called "road," it was really but a pathway; and, in places, almost a kind of tunnel. The great trees of this primaeval forest were so high and dense that but little daylight penetrated to the ground beneath; and on all sides the undergrowth was so thick and tangled that almost every foot had to be cut out with the axe. Here and there one could see for a few yards between the giant trunks, and at these spots the path had been made wider. One curious thing Jack noted: the path did not start from that part of the wood opposite to "Monella Lodge"; nor even from the margin of the wood itself.

Asked why this was, Monella thus made answer:

"If in our absence others should come here, they might hunt up and down for the path a long time before they hit upon it—and very likely never find it. On this stony ground the tracks we leave are very slight and difficult to trace."

"But," said Jack, "your Indians know the way." Monella smiled.

"Not one of them would ever show another man the way," he replied, "let him offer what he might."

"But why all these precautions?"

"Later you will understand."

But, when Jack came to look round, his heart sank within him.

"I should not care to have a few miles of railway to cut through wood like this," he said. "It's the worst I ever saw. I do not wonder you have found it more than you could manage—only yourself and these Indians—and it's a wonder you ever got them to join at all, considering all the circumstances."

"Yes; that's where it is," Monella answered. "Many men would have despaired, I think. We have had trouble, too. Two Indians met with accidents and were badly hurt; though now they are re-covering. Then, some of the small streams that issue from the mountain became suddenly swollen once or twice, and washed away the rough bridges we had made across them; and we have met with many unexpected obstacles, such as great masses of rock, or a fallen tree, some giant of the forest that was so big it was easier to go round it than to cut through it."

That evening, Monella explained his project, and showed the young men the plans and diagrams Dr. Lorien had spoken of, and then went on to say,

"If you decide to join me, you ought to know something of the language in which these old documents are written. I both read and write it, and I speak it too. You will find it interesting to deci-pher them, and an occupation for the evenings."

Jack was not enthusiastic at this suggestion; but Leonard cor-dially embraced it.

"To learn the language of an unknown nation that has passed away will be curious and very interesting," he declared, "and will, as you say, help to pass the time. You may as well learn it too, Jack. You speak the Indian—why not learn this? Then we can talk to-gether in a tongue that no one but ourselves and our friend here can understand."

"And where did these ancient people 'hang out'?" asked Jack irreverently.

"Have you heard of the lake of Titicaca and the ancient ruins of the great city of Tiahuanaco; a city on this continent believed by archaeologists to be at least as old as Thebes and the Pyramids?" Monella asked.

"I have," Leonard answered, "though I know very little about them. But I believe I was in that country when very young, and had a curious escape from death there."

Monella turned his gaze quickly upon the young man.

"Tell me about it. What do you remember?" he asked.

"Oh, I do not remember anything; I was too young. But I have been told how that my father went somewhere in that district on a prospecting expedition, and, not liking to be separated from my mother, took her with him, and my nurse, Carenna, and myself. Whilst there they came across a small settlement of white people, as I understand, and remained with them some time. There was amongst these people a child of my own age, and so exactly like me, that my nurse grew almost as fond of it as she was of me, and used to like to take the two out together. One day, it seems, we both went to sleep on the grass, and she left us for a few minutes to gather fruit. When she returned a poisonous snake crawled hissing away, and she found the other poor little child had been bitten and was dead.

"That's all I know about it. Who the people were, and where the place was, I cannot say. I have always understood, however, that it was somewhere in the direction of Lake Titicaca. But Carenna could tell you more."

"And what about this ancient people of yours?" Templemore asked of Monella, who still gazed thoughtfully and inquiringly at Leonard. Templemore had heard of Elwood's early adventure many times before.

"High up on the eastern slopes of the great Andes is an extensive plain, as large as the whole of British Guiana," the old man replied. "It is twelve thousand feet above the level of the sea, and there, at that great height, is also the largest lake of South America, Lake Titicaca, over three thousand square miles in extent, on the shores of which was once a mighty city called Tiahuanaco. It is now in ruins; yet, even amongst its ruins, it boasts of some of the oldest and most wonderful monuments in the world. Two thousand feet above this again, are another large plain and another lake, little known to the outside world, being, indeed, almost inaccessible. It was there my people dwelt, and tradition asserts that they retired thither when driven out of Tiahuanaco by some invasion of hordes from other parts of the continent."

"Is it a very old language, do you suppose?" Jack asked.

"Undoubtedly one of the oldest in the world; and yet not difficult to acquire by those who know the language of Matava and his tribe—as you do. It has some affinity to it."

As regards the tongue spoken by the Indians, Leonard had learnt it from Carenna in his childhood; and Templemore had picked up a good deal from the same source, as well as on his hunting expeditions with Leonard and Matava.

When it came to discussing terms, Monella declared that he had none to make, except that on no consideration whatever should any other white man be invited or allowed to join them. As to the rest, he simply suggested that any wealth they might acquire by their enterprise should be shared equally between them.

"Suppose one of us were to die," observed Jack. "How then? Might not the survivors choose some one else to join them? Though," he added thoughtfully, "if it were you, we should not be likely to go on."

"I shall not die, my friend, until my task be finished," replied Monella with conviction.

"You cannot say," was Jack's rejoinder.

"No, I do not say I know, yet I can say I feel it. No man dieth till he hath fulfilled the work in life allotted to him by God," Monella finished solemnly.

The others already knew him, by this time, as a man with deep-seated religious convictions; though he made no parade of his beliefs. He seemed to have a simple, steady faith in an overruling Providence, and showed it, unostentatiously, in many ways, both in his actions, and in the advice he gave, on occasion, to the young men.

In the result, the bargain—if it can be so termed—was concluded. Elwood and Templemore formally enrolled themselves under Monella's leadership, and henceforth performed the duties he assigned to them; amongst other things assisting almost daily in the formation of the path that was to take them through the forest. When not so engaged, they would go out with some of the Indians on hunting or fishing excursions in search of food.

Monella had with him, amongst other things, a beautifully finished theodolite of wonderful accuracy and delicacy; with this he
settled the direction of the road from day to day. Often, obstacles
were encountered that made it impossible to go straight; these had
to be worked round and the proper direction picked up again by
means of Monella's calculations.

Another circumstance worthy of note and that caused the two
young men at first some surprise, was the fact that Monella had
with him some mirrors specially prepared and fixed in strong cases
for carrying about in rough travel, and intended for heliographic
signalling. They frequently took these out and practised with them
by sending messages to one another from the ridges of hills far
apart. Monella tried also to instruct Matava and some of the Indians in the work, but without success. They were indeed afraid of
the glasses, and looked upon it all as some kind of magic.

"Wouldn't it be simpler to go up the bed of this stream that you
seem to have been following more or less all the time, even if it be
longer?" observed Jack one day.

Monella shook his head.

"No use, my friend. It divides into so many branches; and then
again, in case of a rise of its waters, we should have all our road
submerged at once."

On Sundays they always rested. This, it appeared, had been
Monella's custom all along.

In his conversations in the evenings and during their Sunday
strolls, he would instruct and amuse his hearers with his reminis-
cences and adventures in all parts of the world, or with his intimate knowledge of the wild life around them. From his account,
he had undergone, at times, terrible and extraordinary hardships
and privations on the plains and in the forests of India and Africa;
of Australia; the Steppes of Tartary; the Highlands of Thibet; the
interior of China and Japan; the wilds of Siberia; of Canada; the
prairies of North America, and the pampas, plains, and rugged
mountains of South America—all, as Dr. Lorien had said, seemed to
be alike known to him. Nor was he less familiar with the countries
and cities of Europe; yet he spoke of his travels and experiences in a
simple manner that had in it nothing of boastfulness or ostentation,

but as though his sole object were to amuse and entertain his two young friends.

As they penetrated farther into the forest, their work became harder and the progress slower. This latter was unavoidable, since each day they had to walk farther and farther to and fro. Moreover, the Indians, who had displayed greater courage—so Monella had said—now that they had two more white men with them, once more began to show signs of nervous apprehension and fear.

This was doubtless due to the great difference in many ways— some definite enough, others indefinable and vague—between this forest and those generally to be found in the tropical regions of South America. Not only were the trees still more gigantic—making it gloomier—and the undergrowths more dense and tangled, but the birds and animals, judging from their cries, were unfamiliar to them. Many of the sounds usual to forest life in British Guiana were absent; the constant note of the "bell-bird" was not heard, nor was even the startling roar of the howling monkeys. Instead were heard other sounds and noises of an entirely novel and peculiar kind, unknown even to the Indians who had been used to forest travelling all their lives; sounds that even Monella either could not explain—or hesitated to. One of these was a horrid combination of hiss and snort and whistle, loud and prolonged like the stertorous breathings of some monstrous creature. Some of the Indians declared that this was the sound traditionally said to proceed from the great 'camoodi,' the monstrous serpent that is supposed to guard the way to Roraima mountain; while others inclined to the opinion that it was made by the equally dreaded "didi," the gigantic "wild man of the woods," that also had, as they averred, its special haunts in this particular forest. At times, a startling, long-drawn cry would echo through the wood, so human in its tones as sometimes to cause them to rush in the direction it seemed to come from, in the belief that it was a cry for help from one of the party who was in danger. This strange, harrowing cry, the Indians called "The cry of a Lost Soul"*; and they were always seized with panic when it was heard.

There were other cries and sounds equally mysterious and perplexing; and, so the Indians began to declare, strange sights too.

Of these they could give no clear account, but they maintained that, in the shadows in the darker places, or just before nightfall, while returning from their work, they now and then caught passing glimpses of vague shapes that seemed to peer at them and then disappear within the gloomy forest depths. And even Elwood and Templemore were conscious of the occasional presence of these silent unfamiliar shapes, and sometimes fired at them, though without result. These facts they made no attempt to conceal from one another, though, in their intercourse with the Indians, they put a bold face on matters, and affected to disbelieve the stories told them.

Monella alone was—or appeared to be—entirely undisturbed by all these things. If conscious of them, he gave no sign of it, but went about whatever he had to do as though danger were to him an unknown quantity.

There was, however, one unpleasant fact that could not be ignored, and that was the unusual number of "bushmasters" of large size in the wood. This is a poisonous snake, very gaudily coloured, whose bite is certain death. It does not—like most serpents—try to

---

* (Opposite) This strange cry is often heard in the depths of the forests in this region, and has never been accounted for, the only explanation given by the Indians being the one stated above, viz., that it is "the cry of a Lost Soul." It is alluded to by the American poet, Whittier, in the following lines:—

"In that black forest where, when day is done,
* * * * *
Darkly from sunset to the rising sun,
A cry as of the pained heart of the wood,
The long despairing moan of solitude
And darkness and the absence of all good,
Startles the traveller with a sound so drear,
So full of hopeless agony and fear,
His heart stands still, and listens with his ear.
—The guide, as if he heard a death-bell toll.
Crosses himself, and whispers, 'A Lost Soul.'

get out of the way of human beings, but, instead, rushes to attack them with great swiftness and ferocity. It is the only aggressive venomous snake of the American continent. It usually attains a length of five or six feet; but, in this forest, the explorers killed many of eight or nine feet, and two—that came on to the attack together—were nearly eleven feet long, with fangs as large as a parrot's claw. In consequence of the frequency of the attacks of these reptiles, so much dreaded by the Indians, and indeed by all travellers, one or two of a working party, armed with shot guns, had to be told off to keep watch; rifles being of no use for the purpose.

Templemore, as it happened, had had a bad fright when a child from an adventure with a snake; and this—as is frequently the case—had left in his mind, all the rest of his life, a great horror of serpents. He found, therefore, the presence of these "lords of the woods," as their Indian name implies, a source of ever-present abhorrence.

Besides the "bushmasters," there were the "labarri"—also a large venomous snake, but not aggressive like the other—and rattlesnakes. There were also, no doubt, boa-constrictors, or "camoodis," of the ordinary kind; but, thus far, only one had been seen, and that, though large, was nothing out of the way as regards size for that country.

Nor were serpents their only visible enemies; there were others of a kind new to the two young men. One day, while with the working party at the farthest part of the track, they heard the whole forest suddenly resound with a perfect babel of discordant noises. There were shrill cries and squeals, hoarse roars and growls, then a kind of trumpeting. The Indians retreated, throwing down their axes to pick up their rifles. As they hastily retired, four large animals sprang into their path, one after the other, with loud roars and growls. But Monella, who was behind Elwood, stepped forward and rolled two over with his repeating rifle, and Jack stopped another of the beasts with his. The fourth, apparently not liking the way things were going, leaped into the thicket and disappeared; though, judging from the sounds that came from the direction it had taken, there were many more of its fellows close at hand.

Gradually their cries grew fainter, until they died away in the distance.

Meanwhile, further shots had given the *coup de grâce* to the three that had been knocked over, and the victors went up to examine them. They seemed to be a kind of panther or leopard of a light grey colour, approaching white in places, with markings of a deeper colour.

Neither Templemore nor Elwood had ever previously seen any animal, or the skin of one, at all like these. They were, moreover, of different shape from either the jaguar or the tiger-cat; larger than the latter, and more thick-set than the former.

"These must be the 'white jaguars' that the Indians say help to guard Roraima," Jack observed, looking in perplexity at the strange creatures.

"Yes," said Matava, who had now come up, "and they are 'Warracaba tigers.'"*

"What on earth are they?" asked Leonard.

"Warracaba tiger," Monella said, "is the name given to a species of small 'tiger' (in America all such animals are called 'tigers') that hunts in packs, and is reputed to be unusually ferocious. They have a peculiar trumpeting cry, not unlike the sound made by the Warracaba bird—the 'trumpet-bird'—hence their name."

"They look to me more like light-coloured pumas," Jack remarked.

---

* A vivid account of an adventure with these formidable animals will be found in Mr. Barrington Brown's *Canoe and Camp Life in British Guiana*, page 71. Very little is known about them, but they are believed to have their haunts in the unexplored mountain districts, from which they occasionally descend into other parts. Mr. Brown states that the Indians fear them above everything; and, while comparatively brave as regards jaguars and tiger-cats of all kinds, give way to utter panic at the mere idea that "Warracaba tigers" are in their neighbourhood. It is said that nothing stops or frightens them except a broad stream of water—not even fire.

"No; pumas are not marked like that, and do not make the sounds we heard. Besides, you need never fear a puma, and should never shoot at one, unless it is attacking your domestic animals."

Both Templemore and Elwood looked up in surprise. "I always thought," the latter said, "that pumas were such bloodthirsty animals."

"So they are, to other animals—even the jaguar they attack and kill. But men they never touch, if let alone. I do not believe there is a single authenticated instance of a puma's hurting any human being, man, woman or child. In the Andes and Brazil—where I have lived long enough to know—the Gauchos call the puma 'Amigo del cristiano'—'the friend of man'—and they think it an evil thing to kill one."*

A few days after, they were attacked again by these furious creatures, and this time did not come off so well, for two of the Indians were badly mauled. But for Monella's cool bravery, indeed, matters would have been much worse; and Templemore had a narrow escape. Then, a day or two later, one of the Indians was stung by a scorpion; and Jack came near being bitten by a rattlesnake—would have been but for Monella, who, just in time, boldly seized the reptile by the tail, and, swinging it two or three times round his head, dashed its brains out against a piece of rock.

Indeed, upon all occasions where there was any kind of danger, Monella's ready, quiet courage was always displayed in a manner that won both the admiration of his white colleagues and the devotion of his Indian followers. Moreover, as Dr. Lorien had stated, and as Leonard had found by actual experience, he was skilled in medicine and surgery. To wounds he applied the leaves of some plant, of which he had a store with him in a dried state, the curative

---

* A very interesting account of the South American puma will be found in *The Naturalist in La Plata*, by Mr. W. H. Hudson. He states that the puma has a strange natural liking for, or sympathy with, man; that, though ferocious and bloodthirsty in the extreme as regards other animals, yet it never attacks man, woman, or child, awake or asleep. He quotes many authorities, and gives numerous instances, of a very remarkable character, from the accounts of hunters and others whom he has himself seen and questioned.

effects of which were reputed among the Indians to be almost marvellous.

But even these incidents were surpassed by a startling experience they had a short time afterwards. On going to their working ground one morning, two or three Indians in advance of the remainder of the party saw, lying across the path, what they took to be the trunk of a tree that had fallen during the night; and they sat upon it, indolently, to wait for the others to come up. Suddenly, one of them sprang up, exclaiming, "It's alive! I felt it move! It is breathing!" They all jumped up, in alarm, when the great snake—for such it proved to be—glided off into the wood. Most likely the others would have ridiculed their story, but that Templemore happened to come up in time to witness what occurred. And through the underwood, on both sides of the path, was plainly to be seen a sort of small tunnel that marked the place where the serpent had been lying asleep.

Matava and his fellows, of course, insisted that this was the great "camoodi," that Indian tradition had long declared existed in this forest—set there specially, by the demons of the mountain, to guard it from intrusion.

These constant dangers and adventures made the task of keeping the Indians from deserting doubly difficult, and rendered the work both harassing and tedious to the others. Only Monella showed no weariness, no sign of the strain it all involved; so far from that, these troubles seemed only to increase his vigilance, his power of endurance, and his determination.

And all the time they were cutting their way through vegetation that would have astonished and delighted the heart of a botanical collector such as Dr. Lorien. Not only within the wood, but in the whole district round, unknown and wondrous flowers and plants abounded. But the explorers had neither time nor inclination to take that interest in them they merited, and would, at any other time, have undoubtedly excited.*

* See extract given in the preface (page viii.) from Richard Schomburgk's book *Reissen in Britisch Guiana*.

6
The Mysterious Cavern

When the time drew near for the adventurers, if Monella's calculations proved correct, to reach the base of the towering rock towards which they were making their way with so much labour, a suppressed excitement became apparent throughout nearly the whole party. It was clearly visible in the Indians and in Elwood; and Templemore, even, showed signs of anxiety. Monella alone was imperturbable as ever, and, if any unusual feeling arose in his mind, there was no trace of it to be seen in his placid manner. Perhaps a close observer might have seen, at times, a little more fire in the gaze of his keen eyes; but it was scarcely noticeable to those around him.

Elwood did not attempt to hide the state of expectancy into which he had gradually worked himself; but while he, on the one hand, grew more excited, Jack Templemore, on the other, became steadily more pessimistic and moody. Since the adventure of the great 'camoodi' he seemed nervous and depressed, and he no longer troubled himself to conceal the discontent that now possessed him. The continued sojourn in that terrible forest was becoming too much for his peculiar temperament. Its gloom oppressed him more and more each day; and he had become silent and unsociable, often sitting for long intervals stolidly smoking and, if addressed, replying only in monosyllables. They had now been for some weeks in the wood, camping in it every night, and going back to "Monella Lodge" only for the Sundays. To this rule Monella rigidly adhered; but, since it took the greater part of a day to reach the edge of the forest from the point they had now attained, but little work was done at the path-making on Saturdays, Sundays, or Mondays. Hence their progress had become slower, and Templemore's discontent and impatience increased in proportion.

One morning, after breakfast, Jack was sitting on a log moodily smoking, while Elwood was busying himself clearing up after the meal recently finished. Monella and all the Indians had gone to the path-end, and were out of sight; but the strokes of their axes, and their calls one to another, could be heard distinctly, now and again, echoing through the almost silent wood. Very little else broke the stillness, but once or twice they had heard that weird sound, half hiss, half whistle, that the Indians attributed to the monstrous serpent. Presently, Jack took his pipe from his mouth and addressed Elwood "You heard what Monella said last night, that he hoped to-day or to-morrow would see the end of this work. Supposing, as I expect, that we find that we merely run against inaccessible cliff, I want to know what you intend to do. To attempt to work either to right or to left, along the foot of the rock, in the hope of finding an opening would be, I feel convinced, a mere wild-goose chase, and would lead us only farther into this hateful forest, and uselessly prolong our stay in it. Now, Leonard, is it agreed that the thing is to end when we get to the cliff? I've asked you again and again as to this, but you always put me off."

"I put it off—till the time comes for deciding about it; that's all, you old grumbler. What is the use of talking before we see how Monella's calculations come out?"

"If I grumble, as you call it, it is because I am anxious for others. I gave a solemn promise before I left my poor old mother that I would not rush into any obvious and unnecessary danger; any danger, that is, beyond the ordinary risks of travel in a country like Guiana. Now—"

"Well, what dangers have we courted that are beyond the 'ordinary risks of travel,' as you call them?" Elwood demanded cheerfully. "We have come safely through forests and plains thus far, and now we are in another forest—"

"Yes, but what a forest! I have been, as you know, pioneering in the furthermost recesses of Brazil and Peru; I know a little—just a little—you will allow, of wild life; but never have I seen the like of this wood! No wonder the Indians shun and fear it; indeed, it is a marvel to me how Monella ever induced them to enter upon this work, and it is still more wonderful how he has managed to keep them from deserting him. Heaven knows what we have experienced of the place is enough to try the courage of the best—the most ferocious 'tigers,' the biggest serpents of one sort ever dreamed of, and the more deadly and more fiercely aggressive venomous ones; strange creatures that one can only catch glimpses of and can never see; sounds so weird and unnatural that even the Indians can offer no explanation. That great serpent, alone, fills me with a continual cold horror. We never know where it may be lurking; it may make a rush at one of us at any moment, and what chance would one have with such a beast? What consolation, to think it would probably get a bullet through its head from one of us, if, while that was being done, it crushed another to a jelly?"

"Your old horror and dislike of serpents make you nervous, old boy. I wish you could get over it. In all else, you know, you are as bold as—as—well, as Monella himself; and that is saying a lot, isn't it? You must admit that, if our enterprise has its dangers, we have a leader who knows what he is doing."

"A splendid fellow! but—a dreamer—or—a madman!"

"A madman! He has method in his madness then! I admire him more and more every day. He is a man to lead an army; to inspire the weakest; to put courage into the most timid. I do not wonder the Indians are so devoted to him. I would follow him anywhere, do anything he told me! His very glance seems to thrill you through with a courage that makes you ready to dare everything! He is a born leader of men! He carries out, in every action, in his manner, his air, his principles, his extraordinary cool courage, and his gentle, simple courtesy, all my ideas of a hero of romance of the olden time—the very *beau idéal* of a great king and chivalrous knight. I can see all this; his very looks, his slightest motions are full of a strange dignity; never have I seen one who so excited alike my admiration and my affection! Yet, I do admit he is a mystery. One knows nothing—"

"Exactly," Jack burst in, interrupting at last the speech of the enthusiastic Leonard. "It is true, what you say, in a measure. He seems to have in him the making of such a man as you, I can see, have in your mind—a hero, a leader of men. Yet here is he, an unknown wanderer on the face of the earth, giving up the last years of his life to a fatuous chase after El Dorado, with a few Indians and a couple of credulous young idiots joining in his mad quest. I like him; I admire him; I believe—in his sincerity. But I say he is mad all the same, a dreamer; and for the matter of that, so are you. You suit each other, you two. Two dreamers together!" And Templemore got up and began pacing up and down, restless in body and disturbed in mind.

Leonard watched him with a half smile; but Templemore looked serious and anxious.

"We are surrounded by hidden enemies—many of them deadly creatures," he went on gloomily. "Already three of us have fallen victims, and we know not who may be the next. Even the most constant and watchful vigilance does not avail in a place like this; and the never-ceasing worry of it is becoming more than I can stand. One wants eyes like a hawk's and ears like an Indian's. One cannot feel safe for a single minute; you want eyes at the back of your head—"

Leonard went up and put his hand on the other's arm.

"All because you are so anxious about me and others, dear old boy," he said. "If you really thought of yourself alone you would never trouble; but you make a great affectation of nervous apprehension for yourself, while all the time you are thinking only of me."

Templemore shook his head.

"I don't know how it is," he returned, "but the thought of that great snake haunts me. I feel as if some terrible trouble were in store for us through it. A kind of presentiment; a feeling I have never had before—"

Elwood burst out laughing.

"A presentiment! Great Scott! You confessing to a presentiment! You who always deride my presentiments, and dreams, and omens! Well, this is too good, upon my word! Who is the dreamer now, I should like to know?"

Just then they heard a call, and, looking along the path, saw Monella at some distance beckoning to them.

"Bring a lantern," they heard him say, "and come with me, both of you."

"A lantern!" exclaimed Jack. He took one up and examined it to see that there was plenty of oil. "What on earth can he want with a lantern? Is he going to look for the sun in this land of shadow?"

When they came up to Monella they looked at him inquiringly, but no sign was to be had from a study of his impassive face. Yet there seemed, Jack thought, a softer gleam in his eyes when he met his gaze.

"I think our work is at an end," he said to the young men; "and," addressing Jack more particularly, "your anxiety may now, let us hope, be lightened."

Then he turned and walked on with a gesture for the two to follow. And Templemore felt confused; for the words Monella had spoken came like an answer to the thoughts that had been in his mind; so much so that he could not help asking himself, had this strange being divined what he and Elwood had been talking, and he (Jack) had been so seriously thinking, of?

However, these speculations were soon driven away by surprise at the change in the character of the wood. The trees grew less thickly, and the ground became more stony, the undergrowth gradually thinner; more daylight filtered down from above, and soon they found they could see between the trunks of the trees for some distance ahead. And then, in the front of them, it grew lighter and lighter, and shortly the welcome sound of falling water struck upon their ears. Then they came upon a stream—presumably the same that they had been, in a measure, following through the wood—rushing and tumbling in a rocky bed—for they were going up rising ground—and splashing and foaming in its leaps from rock to rock. The trees became still sparser, and the light stronger, till, finally, they emerged into an open space and saw, rising straight tip before them, the perpendicular flat rock that formed the base of Roraima's lofty summit.

It was here fairly light; indeed, a single ray of sunlight played upon the splashing water in the little stream, and the spray sparkled in the gleam. But still very little sunlight ever entered the place. The great wall of rock that reared itself in a plumb-line two thousand feet into the sky, overshadowed it completely on the one side; and on the other were the great trees of this primaeval forest towering up three hundred feet or more, and extending their branches above across almost to the rock, though below, the nearest trunk was quite fifty yards away. They stood, in fact, upon the edge of a semi-circular clearing that extended for a distance of perhaps a hundred yards, its radius being about fifty yards if taken from the centre of the exposed portion of the cliff. At each end of this space the trees and undergrowth closed in again upon the rock in an impenetrable tangled mass, denser, and darker even, than that through which the explorers had been slowly cutting their way.

Some of the Indians were grouped round the stream, two or three enjoying the luxury of wading in it, or sitting on the bank and dangling their feet in the clear cool water. Matava and the others were busy upon some kind of rough carpentering. Templemore and Elwood saw that the stream issued from a hole in the rock near one end of the clearing; and this was of itself a matter for surprise. They were, however, still more astonished when Monella, with a strange smile, pointed out another aperture in the rock near the centre of the open portion of the cliff. It was about sixteen or eighteen feet from the ground, and was not unlike a window or embrasure in a stone building of considerable thickness. Within—at a distance of eighteen inches or so—it seemed however to be closed by solid rock.

The two gazed in silence at this unexpected sight Elwood showing in his eager manner the hopes that it aroused, and Templemore pondering in silent wonder as to what it all meant. That Monella's 'calculations' had led them to a most unexpected result thus far—whether by accident or otherwise—he could not but admit. Of the fact there was now no doubt. But a clearing of this character, opposite to what looked like an opening in the rock, or entrance to a cave, was a fact too startling to be the outcome of a mere coincidence, or a lucky chance. He knew that a party of explorers might spend years—centuries, indeed, if they could live long enough—in a search for such a place in that forest and never find it, unless guided by the most exact information. Then the fact that the opening was so nearly in the centre of the clearing had a significance of its own; the question whether it was actually the entrance to a cave or merely a curious accidental hollow in the rock was thus answered, as it were, in advance. Besides, just below the "embrasure" a small stream trickled out, and, falling down the rock, found its way amongst the stones to the larger water-course beyond. Here there seemed presumptive evidence that the space at the back of the rock was hollow— was, in fact, a cave. But in that case the entrance must have been purposely closed by human hands. If so, by whom? and when? and why?

These thoughts revolved rapidly in Templemore's mind while he stood looking at the rock. He glanced around at the giant trees, and thought of the almost impenetrable character of the forest they had come through, and he felt that, if the ideas that had come into his mind were correct, it was impossible to suppose that such a cave could be the retreat say, of any unknown Indians living at the present time. Therefore, the puzzle seemed the greater. Who could have been there before them—and how long ago?

But Matava now approached the cliff bearing a sort of rough ladder that he had constructed under Monella's directions; this he placed against the rock just under the opening, planting the ends firmly in the ground. He had cut down two young saplings and, partly by means of notches, and partly by twisting some strong fibres to hold them, had fastened cross-pieces at short intervals, and so fashioned the whole into a very serviceable ladder.

Monella signed to him to hold it firmly, and proceeded to test its strength. Then, satisfied as to this, he quietly mounted it till he could insert his hand into the aperture. After a moment or two he called to Elwood and Templemore to assist in steadying the ladder; and, when they had come to the assistance of Matava and another Indian who was with him, Monella leaned over into the opening and, exerting all his great strength, pushed away the stone that was closing it, exposing to view a cavern beyond. After a brief look inside, he asked for a lighted lantern and a long stick, and, while these were being handed up, the expectations and curiosity of his companions became excited to a lively degree. The Indians, who had been amusing themselves in the water, came crowding round, half pleased, half afraid at this unexpected development of events.

"You're never going to venture into that place?" Templemore asked. "It may be full of deadly serpents. For Heaven's sake do not be rash enough to risk it. Send one of the Indians—"

Monella replied with a look—a look that Jack remembered for many a day after. His eyes simply flashed; and then he said quickly,

"Did you ever know me bid another go where I would not venture myself?"

Then he took the lighted lantern, swung it into the cavern at the end of the stick, and, having satisfied himself that the air within was not foul, he threw the stick in first and followed, himself, into the semi-darkness.

A minute after, his head and shoulders re-appeared, just when Jack was half way up the ladder to follow him.

"Wait a few minutes before you come up," he asked him. "I just want to give a glance round, and there is but one lantern. Or—well—suppose you come up and wait inside. But tell the others to keep to the bottom of the ladder, and be ready to hold it in case we should wish to beat a hasty retreat."

This seemed prudent counsel, and was carried out. When Jack got off the ladder into the opening, he was told to jump down inside; and he found there a level rocky floor about three feet below the aperture, which had thus a resemblance to a veritable window. By the dim light it gave he could see that he was in a cavern of considerable height and extent, and Monella, with his lantern, disappearing through an arched opening at some distance that seemed to lead to another cave within. He bad brought with him his double-barrel, one barrel loaded with small shot, the other with ball, and he gave a look at the revolver in his belt while he stood waiting at the entrance and gazing curiously about him. He saw that a small stream of water ran through one side of the cave; there were, in fact, two streams, for one ran in a ledge at some distance from the ground; but when it came to the opening they had come through, it fell to the floor and joined the other stream, the whole finding its way out through a fissure in the rock and running down outside, as has been before described.

Now the stone slab that had closed the "window," as Jack called the opening, had rested on a continuation of what may be termed the sill, and, on being pushed, had rolled off. It was a thin slab, roughly circular in shape; not unlike what one might suppose a millstone to be in the rough. Jack regarded it with close attention, almost indeed with awe; it spoke so plainly of human beings having inhabited the place, or, at least, of their having fashioned this method of closing the entrance to the cave. How long ago had they been there? And, when they went away, why had they closed the entrance so carefully?

Monella seemed a long time away; so long that Jack at last began to think of starting to look for him—they had already sent for another lantern in case it should be required—when he heard his footsteps in the distance, and shortly afterwards saw the gleam from his lantern. When he came closer, Jack scanned his face keenly, but, as usual, read nothing there.

"You can call Elwood," said Monella, "and I will take you to where I have been. You need have no fear; the place is quite free from reptiles."

When, however, Leonard was called, a difficulty arose; Matava and his fellows objected very strongly to being left alone outside; but it also appeared that they objected still more strongly to coming into the cavern. On no consideration whatever would they enter "the demons' den," as they had already named it. But, since they had to make a choice, they elected, in the end, to remain outside and wait.

When Elwood was inside and had had a few moments in which to get accustomed to the obscurity and peer wonderingly about him, Monella pointed out how the opening had been closed.

"I want you to notice," he observed, "that this stone was cemented, and this little stream of water that has accidentally found its way round here, has, in the course of time, loosened the cement; else I could not have pushed the stone away. We should have had to blast it."

"Yes," said Jack; "and it also shows that it was closed from the inside. Whoever last closed it never went out again—at least not by this entrance. Where then did they go to?"

"That's what we have to see about," returned Monella. "Now, follow me, and I will show you something that will surprise you."

7
The Canyon Within the Mountain

Monella, with the lantern in his hand, led his two companions through an arched opening into a second cavern which seemed to be larger and loftier than the first; and this, in turn, opened into a third, at one end of which they could see that daylight entered. Monella stopped here and, lifting the light high in one hand, pointed with the other to side-openings in the rock.

"They are side-galleries, so to speak," he said, "but do not appear to be of any great extent. I have been to the end of two or three. They all seem to be perfectly empty too; not so much as a trace of anything did I see, save loose pieces of stone here and there, that had, no doubt, fallen from the roof. Now we will go to the entrance on this side." And he turned and walked on towards the place where they could see the glimmering of daylight.

Quite suddenly they turned a corner and saw before them a high archway, leading out into the open air; and, before the two young men had had time to express surprise, they had stepped out of the gloomy cavern into a valley, where they stood and stared in helpless astonishment upon a scene that was as lovely and enchanting as it was utterly unexpected.

They saw before them the bottom of a valley, or canyon, of about half a mile in length, and nearly a quarter of a mile in width; its floor, if one may use the expression, consisted chiefly of fine sand of a warm tawny hue; its sides, of rocks of white or pinkish white fine-grained sandstone, with here and there veins, two or three feet wide, of some metallic-looking material that glistened in the sunlight like masses of gold and silver. In other places were veins of jasper, porphyry, or some analogous rock, that sparkled and flashed as though embedded with diamonds; other parts again were dark-coloured, like black marble, throwing up in strong relief the ferns and flowers that grew in front of them.

At the further end of the valley a waterfall tumbled and foamed in the rays of the sun which, being now almost overhead, threw its beams along the whole length of the canyon. The stream that flowed below the fall widened out into clear pools here and there, fringed by stretches of velvety sward of a vivid green. The water of this stream was of a wonderful turquoise-blue tint, different from anything, Templemore thought, that he had ever seen before; and he and Elwood gazed with admiration at its inviting pellucid pools. But most extraordinary of all were the flowers that nearly everywhere were to be seen. In shape, in brilliancy of colouring, and in many other respects, they differed entirely from even the rare and wonderful orchids and other blossoms they had come across in the vicinity of Roraima.

Of trees there were not many, though a few were dotted about here and there by the side of the river; and, in places, graceful palms grew out of the rocky slopes at the sides and leaned over, somewhat after the fashion of gigantic ferns. Though the valley was so shut in, and the heat in the sun very great, yet the amount of green vegetation on all sides, the blue water, and the light-coloured, cool-looking rocks, made up a scene that was gratefully refreshing after the gloom of the forest scenes to which the explorers had been so long accustomed. Moreover, by stepping back into the cool air of the cavern, they could look out upon it all without experiencing the drawback of the intense heat.

Elwood was in ecstasies. The triumphant light in his eyes, when he turned round and looked at his friend, was a thing to see.

"You confounded, wretched old grumbler," he exclaimed, "what have you to say now? Is not this worth coming for? Or is it that even this will not suit you? Perhaps it is all too bright, the water too blue, the flowers too highly coloured, or"—here a most delicious scent was wafted across from some of the flowers— "they are perfumed too highly to please you! You haven't found fault with anything yet, and we have been here nearly five minutes!"

Jack laughed; and Leonard noticed that it was more like his old, easy, good-natured laugh.

"I think you are too severe upon me, Leonard," he replied. "Don't you think so, Monella?"

Monella, the while, had been standing gazing on the scene like one in a dream. More than once he passed his hand across his eyes in a confused way, as though to make sure he was awake. When thus addressed, however, he seemed to rouse himself, and, without noticing the bantering question that had been addressed to him, and, extending one hand slowly towards the valley that lay before them, said,

"I praise Heaven that I have been led, after many days, to the land that I have seen in my visions. Now do I begin to understand why they were sent. And you too, my son," he added, looking at Leonard, "you have had your visions and your dreams. Tell me, does this not remind you of them?"

"Indeed it does," returned Leonard seriously. "Though, till you spoke of it, I had not thought of it. I felt so glad to think we had been successful so far, and that your expectations were being justified. It is all very strange."

"I am out of all that," observed Jack, with a comical mixture of offended dignity and good-natured condescension. "You dreamers of dreams have the best of such beings as I am. You are led on by visions of what is in store for you, as it would seem, while I have to work in the dark, and follow others blindly, and—"

"And think of nothing but how best you can serve and protect your friends," said Monella, looking at him with a kindly smile. "We are not all alike, my friend. It is not given to all to 'dream dreams,' any more than it is given to all to have true manly courage combined with almost womanly affection for those they call their friends. We three have little to boast of as between one another, I fancy. Would it were so more often where three friends are found grouped together or associated in any undertaking. But now to consider what is next to be done. It seems to me we could not have a better place for our head-quarters in our future explorations than this cavern. Here we have all we want: shelter from rain, and sun, water—pretty well all we could ask for. We must see about getting our things along here." He paused for a moment and then continued, "On second thoughts I see no reason why you should not remain here. There is no more baggage than the Indians can carry amongst them, and that is all we have to trouble about. I will go back, and you two stay here."

"That seems scarcely fair," Jack protested. "I have been lazy all the morning. I propose I go and leave you here—"

Monella shook his head.

"You cannot manage the Indians as I can," he answered. "Indeed, that is one reason why I think you would do better to remain here. When they find you do not return, and that they have to obey me or remain in the forest alone, they are more likely to do what we require. But I will ask you not to go far away, and not to fire off a gun or anything, unless in case of actual danger and necessity."

"You do not believe that the place is inhabited?" Jack exclaimed in surprise.

"Who can tell?" was the only reply, as Monella took up the lantern and turned away.

Left to themselves, Jack pulled out his inevitable pipe, the while that Elwood sought, and brought in, a couple of short logs from a fallen tree to serve as seats; and the two then sat down in the shade of the cavern-entrance.

Jack was very thoughtful; but his thoughtfulness now was of a different kind from his late moody silence. He, indeed, was ruminating deeply upon Monella, who was every day—every hour almost—becoming a greater mystery to him. He had been particularly struck with his manner and the expression of his face when they had stood together, looking out upon that curious scene. In Monella's words there had not been much perhaps, but in other respects he had strangely impressed the usually unimpressionable Templemore. There had been in his features a sort of exaltation, a light and fire as of one actuated by a great and lofty purpose, so entirely opposed to the idea that his end and aim were connected with gold-seeking, that Jack Templemore confessed himself more puzzled with him than he had ever been before. Too often, as he reflected, when a man sets his mind, at the time of life Monella might be supposed to have reached, upon gold-seeking, he is actuated by

sheer greed and covetousness. But by no single look or action whatever had Monella ever conveyed a suggestion that the lust of gold
was in his breast. Yet, if that were not so, what was his object? Did
he seek fame—the fame of being a great discoverer? Scarcely. Again
and again he had declared, on the one hand, his contempt for and
weariness of the world in general, and, on the other, his fixed intention never to return to civilised life. Jack began to suspect that all
his talk about the wealth to be gained from their enterprise had
been chiefly designed to secure their aid, and that for himself it
had no weight—offered no incentive. What, then, was Monella's
secret aim or object? What was the hidden expectation or hope, or
belief, or whatever it was, that had led him into an undertaking
that had appeared almost a chimera; that had so taken possession
of his mind as to have become almost a religion with him; that had
enabled him to support fatigue and physical exertion, privation,
hunger and thirst, as probably could few other men on the face of
the earth; and that had become such an article of faith—had made
him such a firm believer in his own destiny, that no danger seemed
to have any meaning for him? Neither storm nor flood, lightning
nor tempest, savage beasts nor deadly serpents—none of the dangers or risks that the bravest men acknowledged, even if they faced
them, seemed to have existence so far as this strange man Showed
any consciousness of them. Never had they known him to step aside
one foot, to pause or hesitate one moment, to avoid any of them.
He simply went his way in supreme contempt of them all; and, until
quite lately—till within the hour almost—Jack had attributed all
this either to madness, or to an inordinate thirst for riches for
riches' sake—which, as he reflected, would be, in itself, a sort of
madness. Now, however, his opinion was altering. The liking he
had all along felt was changing to surprised admiration. He remembered the calm, unwavering confidence with which Monella
had led them through all their seemingly interminable difficulties
and discouragements to their present success—for success he felt
it was, in one sense, if not in another. In the strange flowers and
plants before them, alone, there were fame and fortune, and what
might there not be yet beyond, now that they had in very truth
penetrated into that mysterious mountain that had so long defied

and baffled all would-be explorers? Monella, he still felt, might be a bit mad—a dreamer or a mystic—but, evidently, he was a man of great and strange resources. Few engineers, as Jack himself knew, could have led them thus straight to their goal from the data he had had to work upon. Yet he showed now neither elation nor surprise, and in particular, as Jack confessed to himself rather shame-facedly, no disposition to remind him of his many exhibitions of contemptuous unbelief. With these thoughts in his mind, and the remembrance of Monella's unvarying kindness of manner—to say nothing of the way he had exposed himself to danger on his behalf—Templemore began to understand better than he ever had before the affection that the warm-hearted Leonard entertained for their strange friend, and he became conscious that a similar feeling was fast rooting itself in his own heart. In fact Monella was now, at last, exercising over the practical-minded Templemore that mysterious fascination and magic charm that had made the Indians his devoted slaves, and Leonard his unquestioning admirer and disciple.

Presently, Leonard, who had fallen into one of his daydreams, woke up with a slight start and exclaimed, "What a paradise!"

Jack smiled, and said, "I wonder whether it is a paradise without a serpent, as it is without an Eve? But your dreams, Leonard, if I remember, were mixed up with a comely damsel; and there is none here. I fear we shall have to regard her as the part that goes by contraries, as they say."

Leonard looked hard at him, and there was evident disappointment in his glance and tone when he asked, "Do you then think this place is uninhabited?"

"I do," was the reply. "And I will tell you why. That stone that closed the entrance from the forest was placed there by some one, no doubt, and by some one inside. Yes; but how long ago? A very long time! Hundreds of years, I should say. It has taken quite that time for that stream of water to hollow out the little channel in the rocky side of the cave and play upon the cement until it has become loosened. The wood outside tells the same tale. It must be hundreds of years since any human beings made their way to and fro through the wood, to or from this place. Once there were many

people here; and they were not ordinary people either, I can tell
you. Not Indians, I mean, for instance. They were clever workers
in stone. That 'window,' as I call it, through which we came in, is
artificial."

Elwood gave an exclamation of surprise.

"Yes; I noticed it, though you did not. I have little doubt that
Monella noticed it too. The cavern was formerly all open, or, at
least, it had a large opening, and I am almost certain its floor was
originally level with the ground outside. If so, the present floor is
artificial, and there are probably vaults beneath. Outside, the stonework is so artfully done that you see no trace of it; it appears to be
all solid rock; but inside I saw distinctly traces of the joints. Then,
look at these archways, at the one we are now sitting under! They
have been worked upon too—to enlarge them, probably; to give
more head-room when the floor was made higher. See! here are
marks of the chisel!" And Templemore got up and pointed to many
places where the marks left by the tool were clearly to be seen.

"Well," said Elwood, "I suppose we shall solve the problem and
set all doubts at rest before many days are over. For my part I am
in a curious state of mind about it—half impatient, half the reverse.
If it is to turn out as you say, I am in no hurry to terminate the
uncertainty. This strange spot, the fact that we are really, at last,
inside the wonderful mountain—these things open such a vista of
marvellous possibilities that I—it seems to me—I would rather, you
know—"

"Oh, yes, I know, you old dreamer," Jack exclaimed, laughing.
"You would rather wait and have time to dream on for a while than
have your dreams rudely dispelled by hard facts. Now suppose we
go and take a look round in the shade over there. We need not go
out of sight of this entrance; so that Monella will find us immediately he returns."

The sun had now moved so far over that one side of the valley
was lying in shadow, and they strolled out to observe more closely
the new flowers and plants they had thus far seen only from a distance.

8
Alone on Roraima's Summit

When Monella returned about two hours later, the two young men had much to tell him of the wonderful flowers and plants they had found, of strange fish in the water, and curious perfumed butterflies that they had mistaken for flowers. There were many of these extraordinary insects flying about. In colouring and shape they resembled some of the flowers; when resting upon a spray or twig they looked exactly like blossoms, and upon nearing them, one became conscious of a most exquisite scent. But just when one leaned a little nearer to smell the supposed flower, it would flutter quickly away, and insect and perfume disappeared altogether. Many of the flowers that were scattered about the rocks were shaped like exquisitely moulded wax bells of all sorts and kinds of colours and patterns, white, red, yellow, blue, etc., striped, spotted, speckled. So distinct were they from anything the explorers had before seen, that they had picked some and brought them into the cavern to show Monella; but he could not give them a name.

The stream from the waterfall, they found, disappeared into the ground just before it reached the cavern. No doubt this was the stream they had seen issuing from the rock upon the other side.

At the further end the valley began to rise, following the stream, which came down in a series of small falls or cataracts. About this part they had found some other caves; but had not entered them.

"And most remarkable of all," said Templemore, "we have not seen a single snake, lizard, or reptile of any sort or kind. Yet this is just the sort of place one would have expected to be full of them. Nor have we seen either animals or birds."

Monella told them the Indians still refused to enter the cave. They all three, therefore, went to the "window," and assisted to get their camp equipage inside, the Indians bringing the things to the top of the ladder and handing them through the opening. They preferred, themselves, to camp outside, and had already made a fire to cook some monkeys they had killed with bows and arrows.

When all their things were safe inside, Leonard and Jack took some fishing nets and soon caught some fish in the pools of the stream in the canyon. They then made a fire just outside the cavern entrance, and cooked them for their evening meal. The fish seemed to be a kind of trout, but of a species they had never seen before.

Monella expressed his regret that all attempts to persuade the Indians out of their fear of "the demon-haunted mountain" had failed.

"They will neither come inside nor remain outside by themselves; that is, if we go away from here to explore farther. It seems to me, therefore, that we ought to have all our stores brought here before we start, and then let the Indians go back by themselves. We may be here for months, so had better get them to fetch everything we can possibly require from 'Monella Lodge.'"

Such was Monella's advice.

"It will take two or three days at least—possibly more," he continued, "to transport all our stores here. During that time we must be content to attend to nothing else, and postpone any further exploration of the mountain. Besides, when we once start, none can tell how far we may be led on. Better have our 'base of operations' settled and secure first. How far away are those other caves that you saw?"

"About a quarter of a mile," Jack answered.

"We will have a look at them in the morning," Monella said thoughtfully. "It may be wiser to hide some of our stores and belongings in different places, so that, if any accident should happen to one lot, the others may be all right. Eh, Templemore?"

"Just the very idea I had in my head when I spoke to you of those other caves," Jack responded. "We can take half an hour or so to explore them in the morning."

"Better take longer," observed Monella. "Better take the day, and do it thoroughly. Much may depend upon it hereafter. Suppose, therefore, that you remain here while Elwood and I return to 'Monella Lodge' and see about packing and bringing some of the 'belongings'? Then, if we find another journey necessary, you can go next time, and Elwood and I will remain here on guard. But we cannot get back to-morrow night. Do you mind staying here alone?"

"Not I!" said Jack, laughing.

"Very well then; we will arrange it so. We shall load up our two animals, and perhaps one journey will suffice after all. Any way, you hunt for the best and most secret hiding-places you can find. See that they are dry, you know. There are the three casks of powder—"

"What! Will you bring them too?"

"Certainly. We may have blasting to do before we have done with what we have in hand. The extra arms, too, we will divide, and secrete in different places."

"I see the idea," Jack assented. "Rely on me to do the best that can be done."

The three went back, after their meal, to where the Indians were camping just outside the "window." Matava looked grave, and shook his head dubiously, when Leonard told him of the arrangements come to.

"My heart is heavy, my master," he said in his own language, "at the thought of leaving you to fight the demons of the mountain. It is not good this thing that you are about to undertake. Doubtless the demons have left this place open as a trap to tempt you to enter their country. When you are well inside they will close it and have you securely captured and we shall never see you more. Alas I that my mother should ever have said aught to lead you on to this terrible enterprise. Better had she died first. I feel sure, if you go inside there, we shall never see you again!"

Elwood only smiled, and bid him be of good cheer.

"We shall return," he replied, "and, I trust, not empty-handed. And, if so, you and my old nurse shall share in my good fortune. But, if you think there is danger, why do you not come with us to help? It is not like a brave Indian to be afraid!"

The Indian shook his head and sighed.

"Matava is no coward," he responded. "His master knows that well. Against all earthly dangers Matava will help him to his last breath, but to battle with the demons of Roraima is but madness—and it is useless. No mortal man may brave them and live. Some one must take the tale to those left behind. It is not good that they should never know."

"That is a nice way of getting out of it, Matava," said Templemore, who had just come up and heard the last sentence. "But please don't take intelligence of our fate till you have learned it. Above all," he continued seriously, "do not alarm our friends in Georgetown by any wild, preposterous—"

"Oh, don't trouble as to that," Elwood interrupted. "Our friends know Matava and his superstitions about the mountain too well by this time. Besides, we will leave letters with him, to deliver, in case he returns before we get back."

It was now getting dark, and the three white men went back into the cavern to prepare their sleeping arrangements. First, it was determined to make a more thorough examination of the side-galleries, and this was soon done, for they were found to be of very limited extent. In passing the archway that led into the canyon, however, Leonard happened to glance out, and uttered an exclamation which called the others to his side. They also looked out into the valley, and were as much astonished as at their first sight of it that morning. It seemed to be lighted up!

On all sides, high and low, small lights were seen. They were of various colours, and hung, some singly, some in groups or clusters. Many drooped over the water, and were reflected in the pools below. The effect was extraordinary. The place seemed a veritable fairy land; and exclamations of astonishment and admiration burst from each of them while he stood and gazed upon the scene.

Then they went out to the nearest lights, and the marvel was explained. The bell-shaped flowers that had excited their curiosity during the afternoon all glowed with radiance. Inside each was a small projection apparently of a fungoid character, that was phosphorescent. It sent forth a light nearly as brilliant as that of a firefly; and this illumined the bell-shaped blossom, which then appeared of different hues according to its colouring by daylight. Even those that Elwood had picked, and thrown down at the entrance of the cavern, glowed with appreciable glimmer.

"I've heard of some kinds of toadstools and fungi being phosphorescent," Templemore remarked, "but never of such a thing in flowers."

"Yet," observed Monella, "if you come to consider the matter, there is nothing more remarkable in the one case than in the other."

The night passed without incident, and all were astir before dawn, making preparations for the day's work. After a light meal, all except Templemore set out on their way to "Monella Lodge," while Jack went out into the canyon to seek for caves and likely hiding-places for their stores, and to look about generally. He took with him his usual two-barrelled gun, a supply of cartridges, and some biscuits and other provisions. Water he knew he could get in plenty. He also took a lantern to enable him to explore the caves. Before leaving the "window," as he now always called the entrance by which they had found their way into the first cavern, he drew up the ladder, and then, with some difficulty, rolled the stone that had closed it into its place again. Most likely he could not have given any reason for this action if he had been asked; but probably a vague hatred of the gloomy forest, and satisfaction in shutting it out of view, were what chiefly prompted him.

"I will take all I want round to the other side," he said to himself. "I like that side best. It's a more cheerful outlook."

He thoroughly explored the caves, and decided that they were fairly suitable for the purpose they had in view. Then, quite accidentally, he came upon another that was so hidden by a tangled mass of creepers that its existence would never have been suspected. He fancied he had seen a small animal disappear behind a bush, and trying with a stick to see whether he could rout it out, he found what at first he thought was a large hole; but, on pushing back the creepers, which hung like a curtain across it, he found a large opening about eight or nine feet high. Inside was a roomy cavern with many recesses here and there, like high shelves in the rock, and many short side-galleries. Just the very place they wanted, he decided. Neither here nor elsewhere did he meet with any signs of his pet aversion—the serpent tribe.

He now began the ascent of the canyon, following always the course of the stream that came down it. In some places the way was easy and direct; indeed, as he could not but remark, there was every appearance that a well-defined, wide pathway, with steps here and there, had at one time existed. But in places it was broken away; the steps cut in the rock had crumbled, or trees growing in the fissures had rent them asunder. In other places masses of rock, fallen from heights above, blocked the road; and, occasionally, the trunk of a fallen tree. Then he came to a wayside cave, and was glad to rest in its shade from the heat of the sun, which began to pour down into the canyon with intolerable fierceness. He had proceeded so far that he imagined he must be half way to the top; and he looked up the canyon still beyond him and at the overhanging cliffs with curiosity, wondering how much farther he would have to go to reach its head, and what he would see when he arrived there.

While he sat quietly pondering this question, and enjoying a smoke following upon a light lunch, the idea grew upon him to complete the ascent that afternoon. He knew that, if he did so, it would be impossible to return that night, and this meant passing it in the open air. But that he did not at all mind; he was accustomed to it; and, since he saw no signs of serpents anywhere, there was an absence of the only thing that troubled him in such case. Monella and the others would not return till the following evening; he had plenty of time to do it in, and nothing else to occupy his time.

But would Monella like it? Why, however, should he object? He could do no harm in going to the top and back. It was not as though the place were inhabited and he might get involved in any adventures with the "natives."

The more he thus thought about it, the more strongly did the feeling grow upon him to make the venture. True, he had not much with him in the way of provisions; but he had enough for supper and breakfast if he put himself upon short rations. In the end he resolved to risk it.

Accordingly, so soon as the sun had gone across sufficiently to shade the path, he started off once more, and made his way still upwards. He encountered many obstacles that delayed his journey, but eventually, just when night was falling, he arrived at what he calculated must be the top of the ascent. It was a grassy plateau of a few hundred yards in extent, facing cliffs that rose still higher and shut out the view and were inaccessible. Down these the stream still flowed, though much smaller in volume than was the case below. What, however, caused him dismay, was to find that he was shut in on the other side by a belt of forest that seemed to be almost as dense and impenetrable as the hated wood below. It was too late to think of going back; there he must stay and pass the night. It was cold, too, up there, and he had no rug in which to roll himself. In fact, he began to wish himself back in the cavern, where he could have cooked himself a good supper and then rested comfortably. There was not even a view; he had hoped to have a glorious prospect and, having brought his field-glass, even that he might be able to look across the forest and savanna and make out "Monella Lodge"; possibly see his friends, who would now be nearing it. Instead of that, he was shut in upon a narrow ledge beside an unknown forest that might be full of wild animals of a dangerous kind.

Altogether Jack felt he had not acted wisely. He went a little way into the wood; but, finding it very dense, and fearful of losing his way in its dark recesses, he soon returned to the clearing. Finally, as it grew dark, being tired and drowsy after his exertions in climbing the canyon, he fell asleep.

9
Vision or Reality?

The following afternoon, a long train of Indians, with Monella and Elwood at its head, was making its way slowly along the tunnel-like road that had been cut through the heart of Roraima Forest. They all carried loads, and they had with them, besides, Monella's two llamas, which were also loaded with as much as they could carry. All looked more or less wearied from their long march, and cast many anxious glances ahead as they approached the end of their journey. When they reached the part where the path opened and the trees became thinner, Matava fired two shots, the agreed-on signal to Templemore; they were answered at once by one from him, and, shortly afterwards, he was seen making his way towards them. He relieved Elwood of a few things he was carrying, and inquired whether they brought any news.

"None," said Elwood; "and you?"

"First of all," returned Jack, "here's a very curious and awkward thing. I have come across a large puma that has taken a great fancy to me, and has become somewhat of a 'white elephant.' At the present moment it is looking out of the window, anxiously awaiting my return; and, though it has not yet learned to scramble down the ladder, I'm not at all sure it won't acquire that accomplishment shortly—or it may even risk the leap down. What I am thinking of is the animals you have with you—they might tempt it; otherwise, it seems tame and good-natured enough, and I do not think it will hurt either you or the Indians."

"Does it seem like an animal that has been tamed, then?" asked Monella. "And where did you come across it? Inside, I suppose?"

367

"Why, yes. But I'll tell you later. Meantime, can't we halt the animals here, and keep them out of sight for awhile? My new friend is as big as a lioness, and of the same sex—and would have one of them down in a moment, if she felt so inclined. You can't tie her up, you know, without a collar and chain, even if one cared to make the attempt. I tried to drive her away, but it was of no use; and I've been sitting there racking my brains as to what on earth I was to do when you came, and hoping against hope that the beast would take herself off." And Jack looked the picture of comical perplexity and bewilderment.

Meantime, the train had come to a halt, and Matava and the other Indians crowded round Templemore and examined him with great curiosity and attention. There were many strange Indians who had been induced, for a consideration, to accompany the party, and these were equally inquisitive. Some came and touched him, as though to make sure he was real flesh and blood. Since Jack seemed inclined to resent this, Leonard laughingly explained.

"They can scarcely believe that any man can have passed a night in the mountain and live to tell the tale," Elwood told Templemore. "Their idea is that you have been eaten up or captured by the 'demons,' who have sent back a ghostly presentment of their victim to lead on the others. So they are anxious to know whether it is really yourself or a spectral imitation. You may be sure, too, your 'lioness' will be a matter of serious speculation to them. She will be looked upon as a familiar spirit, to a certainty."

Monella had said little; but he now proposed to go on to the cave at once with Jack and Elwood, to see how matters really stood, leaving the others to await their return.

On nearing the "window" they saw, sure enough, the head and paws of an immense tawny-coloured animal that gave a cry—a sort of half-whine, half-roar—of recognition on seeing Jack. The ladder was lying on the ground outside.

"'There you are," he observed with a mixture of mock gravity and real anxiety; and he waved his hand towards the animal. "Let me introduce you to the 'Lady of the Mountain.' I only hope to goodness she will behave herself and receive you in a friendly manner; for, if not, I have no control over her. I disclaim all responsibility."

Monella and Elwood looked curiously at what they could see of the animal. It seemed, as Jack had said, nearly as large as a lioness.

"It is a puma," said Monella decidedly, "though a very large one. I never saw one anything near the size. However, there is no need to be afraid of it; you have heard me say you need never fear a puma."

"Yes," returned Jack, "and here is an opportunity of testing your faith in your own theory. I confess, if I did not already know she was well-disposed towards myself, I should think twice before I ventured upon going near her."

"Nonsense!" said Monella, taking up the ladder and placing it against the opening. "I will show you the creature is tame and friendly enough. I could see it at the first glance." And he ascended the ladder and entered the cavern, pushing the puma on one side as coolly as if it were a pet dog. Then he turned and called to Elwood to follow.

Jack also went after them, and found the puma already on friendly terms with both, much to his own relief; for he had had misgivings.

"The question now is what about the llamas?" he next said. "Do you think she is to be trusted there—and with the Indians?"

"With the Indians—yes—though they probably would object," replied Monella; "but, with the llamas, it is doubtful. So we had best be on the safe side, and keep them, if possible, out of her sight."

"She's wonderfully playful," observed Jack; "just like a great kitten. I've been playing with her with my lasso, and she will run about after it by the hour together, just for all the world like a kitten. If you want to keep her out of the way on the other side, all that need be done is for one of us to stay there and play with her."

"Let Elwood do so then," Monella decided. "He is tired; and you can come and help unload."

The animal had, in fact, already begun to show a liking for Leonard, and, when he went out towards the canyon, it followed him at once. Jack watched this with some surprise, and affected much disgust.

"Just like the generality of females," he remarked, "inconstant and changeable. Here have I been at the trouble of capturing the beast, and being worried with her all day, only to see her transfer her affections and allegiance to some one else at the very first opportunity!"

The unloading was then proceeded with, and before dark everything they had brought was placed within the cavern temporarily, to be moved on to other places, as might subsequently be determined.

When all had been brought in, the Indians set to work to cook their evening meal, while Jack did the same outside the canyon entrance. The hunters had shot an antelope, and with some of this and some fish a satisfying meal was provided; the puma lying down and watching the proceedings with evident curiosity, but with no more attempt at interference or stealing than in the case of a well-trained dog. Needless to say she was rewarded for her patience with a share.

When the meal was over, and Jack and Leonard took out their pipes, Monella, looking at the former, said, "You have something of importance to tell us. What have you seen?"

At this Elwood turned and regarded Jack with surprise. "Why, what is it?" he exclaimed. "You have said nothing about it all this time!"

Jack looked a little sheepish. He was somewhat taken aback, too, by Monella's direct question. It brought to his mind the query that had often arisen before—could this strange being read his thoughts?

"I scarcely know whether I have seen something or only dreamed it," he began hesitatingly; and seeing Leonard, at this, open his eyes, Jack went on desperately: "Well, yes! I may as well out with it and make a clean breast of it! I have something to tell you, and for the life of me, I cannot make up my mind whether I actually saw it, or dreamed it—whether, in short, it was reality, or only a vision!"

Leonard opened his eyes wider than ever, and gave a long whistle.

"You having 'visions'!" he exclaimed in unbounded astonishment. "You, the scoffer, the hard-headed, prosaic-minded derider of dreams and visions! Great Scott! Is the world then coming to an end? Or have the demons of the mountain in truth bewitched you as Matava declared they would?"

"Ah! I knew you would laugh at me, of course. And I feel I deserve it. However, if you want to hear what I have to tell, you will have to keep quiet a bit. I cannot explain while you are talking, you know."

"I'll not say another word; I'm 'mum,' but amazed!" Elwood answered. "Now go a-head."

"Well, yesterday, after you left, I pulled up the ladder and carefully closed the 'window' by rolling the stone back into the place, as we first found it. I thought to myself I would shut out the gloomy forest. Then I went up the canyon to explore the caves we spoke of, and soon, by accident, found a new one, so curiously hidden from sight, that it seemed the very thing we wanted; so there was no need to search farther. Then I thought I would stroll up the canyon a bit, and reconnoitre; and I found another cave about half way up, and, finding the sun getting warm, went in and had a rest. When it grew shady again, I thought, instead of coming back, I would go on to the top to see the view."

Monella uttered an exclamation.

"Ah! yes. I know you mean I ought to have kept below. However, no harm has been done, and I could see no objection to going up and taking a peep from the top. I had my glasses with me and thought I might even catch a glimpse of you on your way to 'Monella Lodge.' However, by the time I reached the top it was getting dusk, and, after all, I found myself quite shut in by yet higher rocks on one side that I could not climb, and a thick wood on the other. There was a grassy knoll of a few hundred square yards in extent, and there I had to make up my mind to pass the night. I was tired out; and, soon after it grew dark, I fell asleep."

Templemore paused, and glanced doubtfully at Monella, as if expecting him to say something; but he remained silent, and Jack proceeded:—

"I seemed to wake up after being asleep for an hour or two. I say seemed to wake up—I really cannot say—but either that, or I dreamed the whole thing. Well, I seemed to wake up, and fancied I heard distant shouts. I looked sleepily round and was surprised

and alarmed to see a very unmistakable glow in the sky through
the trees. It struck me at once that the forest must be on fire, and
if so, I thought, my position might be an awkward one. If the wood
were burning, and the fire travelling in the direction of where I
was, to have to retreat down the canyon in the dark would be anything but agreeable. After some consideration I decided to venture a little way into the wood, and climb a tree in the hope of getting a view of what was going on. I could hardly, I reflected, lose
my way, for, when I wished to return, I should only have to turn
my back on the direction in which the fire lay and march straight
back. Accordingly, I made my way into the wood; at first it was
very dense, but soon it grew thinner, and, encouraged by this, I
went straight on, when I emerged on to a high plateau, where an
extraordinary sight presented itself. I seemed to be on the edge of
an extensive sort of basin; I could see for miles; and in the centre,
as it appeared, there was a broad lake, and beside the lake were
lofty buildings lighted up on all sides, the lights being reflected in
the water. There seemed to me a large city; there were buildings that
looked like grand palaces; there were wide noble-looking embankments and promenades and bridges, all well lighted; and, on the
lake, boats, also lighted, were going to and fro, filled with people.
I could hear shouts and cries, though of what nature it was impossible to say; and through my glasses I could plainly distinguish
numbers of people moving about. It was as though some kind of
fete were going on. The large buildings towered into the air, and
their cupolas and turrets glistened as though built of gold and silver. In effect, it was a wonderful sight, and how long I stood watching it I cannot say; but, after a time, the lights went down and all
became silent and dark. I managed to find my way back to my camping ground, and, while thinking it all over in astonished wonder, I fell
asleep again, as I suppose. At any rate, when I finally awoke, the
sun was shining and this animal was lying on the grass by my side."

"What! the puma?" Leonard asked.

"Yes. I was rather upset at first sight of her, you may be sure.
To wake and find oneself in a wild place at the mercy of a great
animal like that is a startler for any one's nerves, I can assure you.
No chance to use one's rifle or anything, you know. However, while

I lay very still and watched it, not knowing what to do, I saw it must be a puma, though an unusually large one. Then I thought of what you, Monella, had told us—that we need never be afraid of a puma. And then the beast turned round and began licking my hand! It stood up, too, and purred, and put up its tail just like a tame cat; so I made friends with it and found it was quite disposed to be on good terms. After a bit my dream came back to me, and I went into the wood some distance, but could see nothing. The forest seemed awfully thick, and to get denser at every step; so I finally came away, thinking I must either have had a remarkably vivid dream or vision, or that I had really been the sport of some demons of the mountain such as Matava and his Indian friends so thoroughly believe in." And Jack paused, and looked at his two companions with an odd mixture of doubt and bewilderment.

Elwood's face, while he had been listening, had become lighted up with sympathetic enthusiasm. It fell a little at the end of the recital, when Jack made the suggestion about the "demons."

"Certainly," he said, "it sounds like witchcraft to hear you, our own matter-of-fact Jack, who never dreams, make such suggestions. But, either one way or the other, it goes to prove that there is something very extraordinary about this mountain."

Elwood looked at Monella.

"What do you think of it all?" he asked.

"I think," he replied, "that our friend ought, in future, to be less ready to deride those who may have to tell of strange things, whether dreams and visions, or out-of-the-way experiences."

"I admit that to be a just rebuke," Jack responded with a good-natured laugh; "but it does not tell us, all the same, what your real opinion may be." But Monella had already risen from where he had been sitting and moved away to speak to the Indians.

"I say, Jack," said Leonard, "can't you really say, straight out, whether you saw this or only dreamed it?"

"Truly, my dear boy, it seemed so natural that I should say it was real, only for the inherent improbability of the thing. Then, too, I could see nothing this morning to confirm it, you know."

"Surely," Elwood said dreamily, "the Indian tales of demons that can bewitch you cannot have any foundation? There cannot be an unsubstantial city of demons to be seen at night, that vanishes and becomes only plain forest in the daytime? That is taking us back to the Arabian Nights, isn't it?"

Jack shook his head.

"I am more bewildered and puzzled than I can possibly give you any idea of," he returned. "The whole thing is beyond me; the sight I saw, or dreamed; and then, again, the behaviour of this animal here."

"Ah," Elwood said, "this puma! Does it not behave as though it were a tame animal used to the company of human beings?"

"I must say that idea has occurred to me more than once to-day; but the more I think over it, the more hopelessly puzzling the whole thing becomes." And Templemore, for the time being, gave it up.

10
In Sight of El Dorado

The next morning Templemore, after leading Monella and Elwood to the hidden cave he had discovered, set out early with the Indians for "Monella Lodge" to bring in the remainder of the stores; and, while there, in the evening, he wrote long letters to his friends, to be entrusted to Matava to take to Georgetown. Amongst them, we may be sure, was one to the fair Maud, who, amidst all the excitement of his adventures, was never long absent from his thoughts. His letter to her was grave, almost sad in its tone. He knew he was about to set out upon a critical venture, the end of which none could see, and he warned her not to be surprised if nothing were heard of them for a long time.

When, the following afternoon, he and his party once more made their way back through the forest to where they had left Monella and Elwood, and had halted just out of sight, those two soon came to meet him in response to the usual signal-shots. The first glance at Elwood's face told Jack that he had some important news to impart. While Monella was greeting the Indians and giving directions for the unloading and camping, Leonard whispered to Jack, "We've been up to the top and have seen all you saw—It was no dream, old man, but simple reality. But don't let the Indians hear anything about it, or they would stampede straight away."

Jack stared in mute surprise, scarce knowing what to think, whether to be most pleased to have it established that he was not "a dreamer of dreams," or astonished at the almost incredible fact it conveyed—that the top of the mountain was, in very truth, inhabited.

"And the puma?" he asked.

"Is still with us. You had better go in and have a rest and take charge of her, while we see to the unloading."

This Jack was glad to do, and, on entering the cavern, he was welcomed by the animal with every demonstration of gladness at his return.

"Ah I you have not forgotten me then, old girl," he said, and he patted and stroked the creature. "You're not so very fickle, then, after all. Now come along with me for a while—I'm going to have a wash."

When all the fresh stores had been placed inside, and the Indians were engaged upon their evening meal, and Monella and the two young men were seated at theirs, Jack asked for further details of the wonderful news Leonard had briefly spoken of.

"It is substantially a repetition of what you told us," said Elwood, "save that we managed a little better in the morning than you did. That is to say, we did not go the wrong way into the wood, as I suppose you did; and thus, at sunrise, sure enough, we saw the wonderful city, which Monella avers can be no other than Manoa—or, as the Spaniards called it, El Dorado! We saw its palaces, and towers, and spires, glistening and glittering in the sun— a marvellous sight! So, Jack, old boy, you can be at ease; you are not yet 'a dreamer of dreams.'"

"But your intelligence, all the same, makes me feel quite dazed," answered Jack. "Are you really sure about it? Are you certain—do you feel confident that—er—well, that it won't all have melted into thin air by the time we get up there?"

"Scarcely. It is too substantial for that."

"Then it means this—that the mountain is inhabited after all," said the puzzled Jack. "If so, what sort of a reception are they likely to give us?"

"Well, that of course remains to be seen. But, meantime, it is certain that all your clever theories about the place 'not having been peopled for hundreds of years' are fallacious."

Jack presently asked Monella what he purposed doing next.

"We must put away our stores," was the reply, "and then arrange our plans for making our presence known to the inhabitants, whoever they may be, of the mountain."

"Yes, and then, if they speak the same language that you have been teaching me," Leonard put in, "Jack will have reason to be sorry he has not stuck to it a little more, I fancy."

Of late, Jack had practically dropped all efforts in this direction, particularly during the last fortnight; while Elwood had neglected no opportunity for using it in his converse with Monella. Elwood had, in consequence, got so far as to be able to speak it fairly well; but Jack was much behind him.

"By Jupiter! But I begin to think there is wisdom in what you say," was Jack's response. "I must do my best to make up for lost time."

The night passed without incident. The Indians stayed on through the following day, and Matava even yielded so far as to enter the dreaded cavern, and take a look into the canyon. Elwood managed to persuade him to do thus much, that he might take back to his friends at Georgetown a description of the scene. Matava was rather afraid of the puma, but the animal was quite friendly. The Indian evidently believed that Elwood and his friends were going to their destruction, and would never again be seen by mortal eyes. However, at Monella's suggestion, he made for them during the day a more substantial ladder, which the nails and tools brought with the stores enabled him easily to do. He also made some poles or struts to form bars to close the stone from within, and, with much perseverance, cut slots in the rock and in the stone to receive them. When completed, and the struts put in their places, the stone was firmly fixed and could not be moved from the outside.

Then Monella made another suggestion. He arranged with Matava a few simple signals that might be made from the mountain-top by flashing small quantities of powder at night, and that Matava could, in turn, answer from the plain beyond the forest, or, indeed, from "Monella Lodge". These signals were simply— "All well," "Coming down," "Not coming down." It was deemed best not to risk more than these, Matava's intelligence in such directions being limited; and, since he could not read, to write them down would have been useless.

When, on the last morning, the leave-taking came, the scene was an affecting one. The Indians were well pleased with the rewards given them for their services; but they were, one and all, in genuine distress at the thought of leaving the three adventurers to what they thoroughly believed would be a terrible fate. They even besought them to alter their minds and "come away from the accursed place"; needless to say in vain.

Matava, almost in tears, was loaded with messages to those in Georgetown, should he go back before seeing the travellers again; the understanding being that, if he found they did not return within a short time, he was to conclude they would remain for an indefinite period, in which case he would shut up "Monella Lodge" and return to Georgetown, and only expect to hear of them when he came that way again in the usual course.

At last, the Indians sorrowfully set out and disappeared in the forest, and Monella and his two companions set to work to distribute their stores and spare arms and ammunition. It was decided, after some discussion, to place the larger portion in the secret cave; leaving only a comparatively small part hidden in the cavern they were in, it being obvious that the latter was the one most likely to be searched, if any should be.

In the carrying out of the plan settled by Monella, the whole of the stores were divided roughly into two parts; two-thirds, and all the spare arms, ammunition and powder, being hidden in the secret cave; the other third, including most of their camping equipage, lanterns, store of oil, etc., but no arms, being stowed away in various remote parts of the cavern by which they had entered from the outer forest. This was in accordance with certain anticipations and eventualities that he had carefully thought out. Thus, if the people of the place should prove unfriendly, and they were forced to retreat at once to the entrance cavern, they had there, ready to hand, in addition to the arms, etc., they took with them, all that was really necessary either for a temporary stay or for the journey back to "Monella Lodge." On the other hand, if the inhabitants should turn out to be hospitable, and invite the travellers to stay with them, it might be a little while before they returned to the cavern at the entrance; in the meanwhile it might be entered and searched by others, who might carry off what had been left there. But in that case the loss would not be a serious one to the explorers, nor would the thieves find any arms or powder.

Early the next morning Elwood went out a little way into the forest to cut some short poles he was in want of, when the puma—apparently finding the new ladder more to her taste than the old one had been—scrambled down after him and disappeared into the wood.

"We had better leave the ladder and go on with our work," observed Monella, when told she had gone off and not returned. "No doubt she will find her way back presently."

But they saw nothing of her till the afternoon, when she came in, bearing in her mouth a good-sized wild pig, which she laid down quietly at the feet of her astonished friends.

"Why, Puss," exclaimed Jack—he had of late insisted upon giving her that name— "that is an accomplishment, and no mistake! You can go out hunting and get your own dinner, can you, and ours too? Well, after this we need not want for fresh meat, apparently, while we stay here."

The meat was not only a welcome addition to their larder, so far as they themselves were concerned, but solved the difficulty that had begun to puzzle them, *viz.*, how to find food for so large an animal. Up to now there had been enough left over from what the Indians had captured and brought in; but, since they had gone away, fresh meat had been growing scarce, and to feed Puss out of their limited stores of tinned meats was, of course, out of the question.

"You'll have to leave us and go back to your friends, whoever they are, Puss," Jack had said only that very morning. "We appreciate your society and all that sort of thing, and shall be sorry to turn you out of doors; but unless you can crunch up meat-tins and imagine they are marrow-bones, I really do not see where another meal for you is to come from." Whether Puss understood this speech or not, she had certainly settled the question in her own way, and very quickly.

"You shall go out again, to-morrow, on this sort of expedition, Puss," observed Jack. And she did; and next time brought back a small antelope.

This led to a discussion and a good deal of speculation as to whom Puss might actually belong to.

"I wonder who owns her, and whether they have missed her?" said Jack. "And I wonder too whether there are many more like her on the mountain? If so, why haven't we seen anything of any of the others?" Since, however, no answer could be given to these questions, the speculation remained a barren one.

After the stores had all been disposed of to his satisfaction, Monella decided to stay on another day before making the venture of showing themselves to the inhabitants; this was partly by way of a rest and partly to give them an opportunity of studying the plants and rocks in the canyon. Most of this day he spent in hunting for strange herbs and leaves; while Jack and Elwood were more interested, after the first feeling of surprise and pleasure in examining the flowers had passed off, in searching for signs of gold among the rocks. They found undoubted traces of both gold and silver, but in what quantity they might exist it was not possible at the time to form any opinion.

Every night the canyon was lighted up in the fairy-like manner of the first evening; and, during the day, two harp-birds had visited the valley and enlivened it with their dreamy music. The travellers also caught sight of two or three small animals; but did not obtain a sufficiently good view to make them out, and Monella particularly desired that they should not shoot at anything.

Of fish there was plenty; and bathing in the cool, limpid pools of "The Blue River," as Jack had named the stream, was a welcome luxury.

Finally, having completed all their preparations, the three, on the morning of the third day after the departure of the Indians, set out on their enterprise of visiting the mysterious inhabitants of "The Golden City."

They started at daylight, with just sufficient camping things for passing the one night, heavily laden with spare ammunition, and taking their Winchester rifles and revolvers, and one extra gun—a double-barrelled fowling-piece. After a midday rest in the cave that lay about half way up, they reached the summit, as before, at nightfall.

They assured themselves that the strange town was still in the same place—had not vanished into thin air as an illusive creation of the demons of the mountain. Then they settled down to sleep and were undisturbed during the night.

When they woke at dawn on the day that was to prove so eventful, they found that the puma had disappeared.

"Puss has deserted us," said Jack. "She knew she was close at home and preferred the kitchen fireside, I suspect, like a respectable tabby, to passing the night out here; and small blame to her. I shouldn't be surprised, if we happen to come across her when she is in the company of her own friends, to see her pass us by with her nose in the air with a 'don't-know-you' sort of look. You'll see, she won't know us! she would lose caste, I expect, if it were known that she had been away for a week hob-nobbing with a party of houseless vagabonds like ourselves."

11
Ulama, Princess of Manoa

The morning broke fine, and the sun rose with a splendour that was not often seen even in this land of gorgeous sunrises. As Leonard looked up at the sky above, with its tint of deep sapphire blue flecked with cloudy flakes, and cirri tinted with gold and pink and crimson, he thought he had never witnessed any effect to equal it. But, when they had quietly passed through the narrow belt of wood, and stood just within its cover, gazing down at the wondrous "golden city" that lay sleeping at their feet, the three friends remained silent and almost spell-bound. The scene was indeed one to which no description can possibly do justice. The sun was just high enough to light up the glistening towers and cupolas; and these, and the spangled sky above, were reflected in the glassy waters of the lake. Beyond and around all was haze of a rose-coloured golden hue, which gave to the centre picture the effect of a vignette. From the upper parts, which showed the clearest against this background of rosy mist, the various buildings grew less substantial as the eye followed their lines downwards, till the bridges and embankments seemed almost ghostly and unreal, yet strangely beautiful in their airy lightness. And the picture was so faithfully repeated in the lake that, but for the reversal of the images, the line that divided the reality from the shadow could scarcely be discerned; while the whole seemed poised, as it were, in the ruddy-golden haze like a mirage in mid-air. Just below them a rocky spur jutted out with clear-cut outline against the central scene, the palms and other trees with which it was crowned showing a lace-work pattern of feathery foliage through which naught could be seen but the golden mist. This part alone seemed real; the city, with its towers, its lofty buildings, its bridges, and its lake, seemed too fairy-like a creation to be indeed an earthly reality.

Of the three who were thus looking out upon this glorious sight, it would be hard to say, perhaps, which was most affected by its subtle influence. Templemore, notwithstanding his affectation of putting on ultra-practical glasses through which to regard and analyse everything, had, in reality—as is not infrequent with such characters—a deep undercurrent of appreciation of beauty, whether exhibited in nature or in the works of man. As an engineer, he could appreciate the rare grace and exquisite proportions of the buildings, and of the bridges, viaducts, and other such works, far better than could Elwood's less trained mind; and then, his was a naturally generous and unselfish nature, and—he was in love. Such a temperament cannot look upon anything that charms, that satisfies the senses, without wishing that the loved one were present to participate in the pleasure and gratification experienced. And the absence of that companionship must necessarily strike a chord of sadness and longing. He was one, at heart, deeply sensible of these emotions; so sensible, indeed, that he shrank from displaying them to onlookers; and thus it was that he half unknowingly hid them beneath a veneer of "matter-of-fact."

Elwood's younger impulses, on the other hand, bubbled up on all occasions unchecked and uncontrolled. He was of a highly imaginative and poetic turn of mind; he was not in love, and hence, the vague aspirations of his affections had as yet met with nothing upon which to rest, or, as it were, to centre themselves. He was filled with unformed hopes and shapeless expectations. The beautiful was not satisfying in itself; it was but a steppingstone, an enticing indication of something still more pleasing yet to be met with beyond, in the indefinite future. Thus he was always looking forward to an horizon that lay beyond his ken; while Templemore's hopes and longings, though they also turned upon the future, had found, in the being who had won his love, a settled, definite purpose in life. Not that the latter was altogether uninfluenced by that spirit of adventure which always actuates, more or less, young men of his age and character; though, in this respect, he might be swayed by somewhat more practical considerations than was the enthusiastic Elwood. In the breasts of the two, it could scarcely be but that there was some feeling of exultation and pride in the consciousness that what they had achieved was likely to bring them a high reward either directly or indirectly—in fame, or wealth, or both—even though no sordid, grasping greed mingled with the generous impulses natural to youth.

And Monella? With what feelings was he swayed while he silently surveyed the fair city that embodied the fulfilment of what he had been striving after for so many years? He was old, he had no children or other kin (he had declared) to interest himself in. Fame, power, riches, he despised—so he had uniformly given his two companions to understand. None of the motives that prompted the two younger men seemed to apply in his case; yet the fact was evident to them—had been all along, since first they met him—that he had been instigated by some overmastering idea that had become, as Templemore had phrased it, a sort of religion to him, a faith, a belief; that had urged him on unceasingly where success had seemed hopeless and the difficulties of his enterprise insurmountable. Templemore, at Monella's side, could not but reflect upon this now; as he had similarly reflected upon it when first they had found themselves veritably inside—so to speak—of the hitherto inaccessible mountain. But now, mingled with Templemore's admiring appreciation of all these things, there was a new element in his feelings towards Monella, which he could only define to himself as one of reverence. He felt inclined almost to take off his hat, and deferentially salute the indomitable, high spirit that had led them on to success, where success had seemed but a fallacious, impossible, fatuous dream.

But Monella seemed unconscious of all such thoughts. He gazed out on the scene before him with a countenance that expressed only a high and simple joy. His tall, commanding form had never seemed to his two companions so instinct with dignity and latent power as at this moment; and in his eyes, when he turned his glance, with a smile, to meet theirs, there were a kindness, a benevolence, a magnanimity even, that seemed to fill up the measure of the feeling of respect that was growing upon them—that made them wonder they had ever ventured to treat such a man as one of themselves. This strange emotion swayed both of them; they both felt it, though each thought it influenced himself alone. Afterwards they found this out by comparing notes; and yet again, in the time to come, they lived to comprehend that this vague idea had been something more than a fancy; it had been an instinct growing out of a solid, though then unknown, reason. It signified that the parting of their several ways, as between them and him who had been their comrade thus far, had commenced, had been already entered upon.

For a while they continued to gaze with swelling emotions upon the wonderful town. Bathed in the light of the rising sun, it slowly grew more substantial to the view, and its stately buildings gradually assumed increased solidity and reality. Their graceful outlines and proportions, their masterly design and bold execution, the novelty and originality everywhere apparent, impressed Templemore with astonishment, just as they delighted and satisfied the poetic fervour of Elwood. Templemore presently turned to Monella.

"Never have I seen the like of those structures," he exclaimed, "either in the places I have visited or in the pictured representations of the most celebrated cities of the world. Surely this people must be a nation of architects!"

"You speak truly, my friend," Monella returned. "I have travelled the world over and I have not seen the like elsewhere. But, as I have told you before—as I warned you I expected would be the case—we have here the chief town of an ancient people; a race so old that the oldest Egyptian records of which the world has any knowledge relate to peoples, and times, and things that are but as yesterday compared to the remote period to which these people can trace back their history. So is it written in my parchments."

"And is what we see, that glistens everywhere, truly gold—upon the very spires and roofs?" asked Elwood.

"I cannot say; but it may well be so, for these parchments of mine assert that gold is the most plentiful metal of any in these mountains. They say that the inhabitants used it for common purposes as other nations use iron; and that, in fact, iron and steel were far less common than gold and silver. But I think it is time we started down the slope to reconnoitre and await our opportunity."

The plan Monella had arranged was that, after concealing in the wood at the top the few camping requisites they had brought with them, they should move down towards the city through the clumps of trees, keeping within their cover, till they came to the point where the trees ended; that they should remain thus concealed for a time to see what sort of people passed to and fro, stepping out and making their presence known only when they saw any one who might be supposed to be a person of standing or authority.

Following out this plan, the three moved on through groves and plantations of trees bearing luscious, tempting fruits of a kind and nature totally unknown to them. Wonderful flowers, too, they saw on all sides, and many strange and curious birds; amongst them the harp-bird, whose enchanting notes came floating every now and then upon their ears. In due course they reached the farthest and lowermost clump, and here they were therefore compelled to pause. So far they had seen no one; but it was yet early morning.

The thicket within the shelter of which they now stood was upon a knoll that was not a great way from the lake. Looking across its waters of turquoise blue, they now made out that which had so puzzled them before. Moving on its surface were numbers of white swans of gigantic size; and it was these, as they subsequently ascertained, that drew the boats about which had seemed to glide here and there without sails or oars. They had seen these great swans through their glasses, but had believed them to be vessels fashioned in that shape; deeming them too large to be really living creatures.

Suddenly, Elwood gripped Templemore's arm, and pointed to some one—a youthful maiden seemingly—walking along the border of the lake in their direction. She came to within a few hundred yards, and then stood looking dreamily out over the lake at the towering, palatial buildings upon the opposite side.

"Great heavens!" Elwood exclaimed in a whisper. "The face, the form, the very dress that I have so often seen in my dreams! Can it be possible? Am I awake, or is this, too, but a vision from which I shall awake by-and-by?"

Monella put his hand upon his shoulder as a sign to him to be silent, and pointed to other forms approaching from the same direction. They all seemed to have come from a great pile of buildings near the water's edge some half-mile away. It was partially screened by groups of waving palms and other trees, which hid from view the entrances.

The new-comers consisted of a tall, handsome man, of a dark-hued skin, and richly dressed, and a following of a score or so of men, apparently a guard or escort. They carried spears that flashed and glittered in the sun, as did their burnished shields and helmets. These seemed to be of gold; they wore short black tunics and sandals. They halted—upon a sign from the one who seemed to be their leader—while he advanced towards the girl. Just then she turned and caught sight of him. At this she uttered a sharp cry expressive of surprise and fear; then walked quickly up the slope towards where the three travellers were concealed.

The man followed and overtook her when she was about a hundred and fifty yards from the edge of the wood. He seized her by the wrist; but she, wresting herself free, turned and confronted him, regarding him with a proud disdain, in which, however, fear was also plainly—too plainly—written.

Now that they were closer, the concealed witnesses could distinguish pretty clearly, through their glasses, the features of the two who stood facing one another, neither for a full minute uttering a word.

As to the maiden, she was in very truth a dream of loveliness. With skin as white and fair as the most delicately reared Englishwoman, glistening golden hair, large grey-blue eyes of entrancing and lustrous beauty, a perfect oval face, and a figure the very embodiment of grace, she appeared indeed more like the creation of a vision than an earthly being of flesh and blood. She was not exactly tall, yet of fair height for a woman. Her dress seemed of silk; it was rich-looking, but quiet in colour, and flowing in design. She wore golden ornaments enriched with glistening gems, and her hair, falling loosely over her shoulders, was confined by a broad gold circlet on the head and was cut short over the forehead. And in her face was an expression of exquisite sweetness—albeit now there were distracting emotions mingled with it. The clear-cut, pouting lip curled in scorn, though, the while, the eyes showed fear, as do those of the hunted hare. Timidly she glanced around, as if for aid; but not a soul was to be seen save those who accompanied the man she feared, and from them, it was clear, she could expect no help.

As to the man himself, he was, as has been said, of fine stature and handsome; but his was not beauty of a prepossessing character. His dark face expressed arrogance and cruelty; in his smile was cold, deadly menace; his haughty features wore a scowl; and his dark eyes fairly blazed with passion. Upon his head he wore a coronet of curious design in lieu of helmet or other covering. His tunic was of black material—silk apparently—with a large star worked in gold upon the breast. A belt as of gold was round his waist, and a short sword and a dagger were by his side. His hair, full beard, and bushy eyebrows were jet black; so far as one might judge he looked about thirty-five years of age. The tunic had short sleeves and was cut low so as to display his neck, round which was a kind of necklace; upon his bare arms were bracelets, and in all these ornaments there flashed, as he moved, sparkling jewels of large size and surprising lustre.

Then ensued, between the two, a hot discussion or dispute, though those within the wood were too far away to understand its purport. The man advanced again and again in a threatening manner towards the girl, who as often retreated a short distance up the slope; then, each time, turned and faced her adversary.

Suddenly, the man seemed to give way to a burst of fury; with a gesture whose murderous import there was no possibility of mistaking, he drew his dagger from its sheath, and tried to seize the girl; but she, eluding him, turned and ran farther up the slope. The man followed, and coming up with her, seized her by the wrist, and raised the hand that held the dagger.

At this moment Monella stepped out from the wood and called loudly to the assailant, at the same time holding up his hand in warning; but Elwood, revolver in hand, rushed forward in advance of him, and levelled the pistol at the moment when the blade was poised in the air and was about to be plunged into the bosom of the girl, who had now fallen upon her knees. He was only just in time; for the weapon had already commenced its fatal downward sweep when the report rang out; the murderer's arm gave a jerk that cast the dagger a distance of some yards, and the man himself fell backwards with a bullet through his heart.

Elwood hastened to the assistance of the girl, who swayed as though about to faint; but the sight of the strangers seemed to rouse her, for she rose to her feet and stood regarding them with wondering and evidently doubtful looks. Then she turned her glance upon the dead man, and shuddered at the thought of the death she had so narrowly escaped.

Looking once more at the three who now stood in a group a short distance from her—for Elwood had drawn back on seeing her rise to her feet—she drew herself up with a charming dignity and grace, and, to the surprise of the two young men, asked, in the language Monella had taught them, "Who are you?"

The words were intelligible enough. The inflection, the accent, or the exact pronunciation, may have been slightly different from Monella's, but the words rang out clear enough.

"Who are you?"

Monella stepped a pace or two towards her. His lofty form seemed to grow in dignity the while he bent his gaze upon her; and, looking up into his face, she could scarcely fail to read the true meaning of the glance she met. She felt its extraordinary fascination, and yielded to its influence, as so many had before. Her confidence went out to him at once; and her look, that for the moment had been proud and distrustful, softened into one of friendly interest. She bowed her head as though in involuntary respect—the respect a dutiful child might show to a parent—and spoke again; this time varying the form of her question:—

"My father, whence come you?"

"We are strangers from far countries, my daughter," Monella made reply. "We came here in peaceful and friendly intent, but fate has so ordered it that our arrival has been marked by the shedding of blood. Still, though of that I am deeply regretful in one way, I cannot pretend to be sorry, if, as I see reason to believe, it has saved your young life."

"Truly it has, and I thank you; and the king, my father, will thank you too; though I know not by what marvel it was accomplished, nor by what other marvel ye have come here, you who wield the lightning and the thunder, who hold men's lives in the hollows of your hands, and yet speak our language."

"Time enough to explain that, anon, my child," was Monella's answer. "For the moment we must know what yonder people are about to do. Their intentions seem scarcely to be friendly."

This referred to the small company of guards or soldiers, who were being harangued by one who appeared to be their officer, and who, when he had ended his speech, formed them into line, as though for a charge upon the strangers. The girl turned round and looked at them; and, doing so, her face grew pale.

"Alas, yes!" she exclaimed. "I had forgotten them for the moment. They are the special soldiers of Zelus whom ye have slain; and their officer will seek to carry you all before the father of Zelus, the dread High Priest. His vengeance will be cruel and terrible, if you fall into his power; but, if we could but get back to my father's palace, you would be safe; for he would protect you for my sake— for the sake of what ye have done for me today. But alas! How can that be? They are many and ye are but three. Ye have not even swords or spears—unless, indeed, ye can serve them as ye have served this one."

"Fear nothing for us, my daughter. We can truly serve these others in the same way, if the necessity unfortunately should arise. But we seek it not; we have come here, as I have told you, with peaceful intentions, and we have no wish to signalise our arrival by further bloodshed. Will you not, yourself, speak to these foolish people, and warn them not to rush upon destruction? Tell them we are powerful, and that, in your own words, we hold their lives in the hollows of our hands. If they will depart in peace, they may, and bear with them the body of their chief; but, if they dare approach with hostile intent, then shall they fall before us, ere even they have time to come a dozen paces, even as men are struck down by lightning. Tell them this, and urge them to be friendly; for we are not of the nature of those who take delight in slaying. To us, to slay is easy, but abhorrent."

The girl heard this with increasing wonder. She viewed the rifles (which all three were now handling) with a curiosity she did not care to hide. She took them for some sort of magic wands.

"I will perform your wish," she said, "but I doubt my power to stay them, for they are men used to working their own will, and now they seek your lives in revenge for this man's death. Indeed, they well know they go to their own deaths if they return to Coryon, the High Priest, and bring not with them those who slew his son."

She turned to go towards the soldiers, who were now standing in two ranks, with spears in rest, awaiting the word of command.

"Stay," said Monella. "If they listen to your words, they will want to come here to take up the body of their chief. We are willing they should do so; but it were better we did not meet, for I do not trust them, and they might plot treachery. See!" And he took his lasso from where it hung at his waist and laid it in a straight line on the ground about twenty feet from the dead body. "We will retire towards the wood; and let it be clearly understood that they must not cross that line nor touch that cord. If any man do so, he shall surely die then and there. Let them not think, however, that we retire from fear, because of their number. But now, my daughter, take heed lest they seize you. Be sure you keep near enough to avail yourself of our protection; but stand not between us and them, lest the lightning strike your own form in its course. Once launched, it goes straight to its mark, and blasts all whom it meets upon its path."

"I understand," she answered. "But you need have no fear for me, so far as these people are concerned. Their chief has dared more to-day than has ever been known before; but none of these would lay hand upon Ulama, the daughter of their king."

"Then," said Monella, "if you feel sure as to that, do not approach them, but go thirty or forty yards to the right, and bid them come near enough for you to address them from there. For the rest we will answer." And, with a sign to his companions, he walked slowly up the slope towards the wood they had left but a few minutes before.

12
A Preliminary Skirmish

The words that had been spoken on both sides in this conversation the two young men had followed fairly well; though they
had listened in silence and made no attempt to join in the discussion. On their way back towards the wood, Elwood was at first very
thoughtful; then he turned to Monella and said excitedly,

"How do we know she is safe, out there alone? And what will
her father, the king, say to us, if harm come to her? It seems to me
we are acting in strange fashion to leave her thus."

"Patience, my son," returned Monella quietly; "we must avoid
the shedding of blood, if it be possible. We have come here, as I
have already said, with peaceful motives. If violent acts be forced
upon us in self-defence, let us keep at least our conscience clear;
let us be in a position to show that they were forced upon us. Let it
not be said of us that we have come into a strange land to introduce dissension, and discord, and internal warfare; and all for no
other reason than the gratification of an adventurous spirit."

"But," said Elwood, "we have not introduced dissension and
trouble. It is clear enough that a terrible murder would have been
perpetrated had we not been here to prevent it. Surely, no one can
accuse us of commencing bloodshed; and, as to the rest, why, what
are the lives of two or three scoundrels like these, the infamous myrmidons—if we may believe what we heard—of a bloodthirsty 'high
priest'; what are the lives of two or three such wretches, compared
with the safety of this gentle, trustful girl, whom we are leaving
now almost at their mercy? In my view this is one of those cases in
which offence is the best defence. They are showing their intentions

pretty clearly; let us anticipate them by shooting one or two. That will frighten the remainder, and stop further hostile action; and, moreover, prevent their coming near this young lady, or princess, as I suppose she really is."

"I am bound to say I rather agree with Leonard," said Templemore. "I see, clearly enough, we are in for a fight, and shall have to kill two or three. Why not as well do it first as last? If, as she says, they are used to do as they please in the land, and if what we have just seen is a specimen of their style, pity is thrown away upon them. And, besides, is it good generalship, Monella? To attack first would be sure to scare them; but, if they make a rush, in absolute ignorance of the power of our rifles, may they not, some of them, charge home? And then we should have a hand-to-hand fight where they would be four or five to one."

Monella passed his hand over his face, and answered almost sadly,

"There is a time to be forward in attack, and a time to be forbearing. If the time come for the former, no man will ever see me flinch from it. But you know what has been said, that the shedding of blood is like unto the letting out of water, and that he who begins it is accursed. If these people begin it, we will not shrink; but at least we shall have clear consciences. Now listen to my plan. We must not enter the wood, or they will think we have fled. If they cross the line I have laid down, let each take the man opposite to him in the line, and bring him down. Then, if they still rush on, fire once more, and step back into the shelter of the wood. If they follow, you know what to do; your revolvers will suffice."

Meantime, Ulama, as she had called herself, had been addressing the soldiers. Their officer had advanced to speak to her, and angry talk had been exchanged, which those standing at the edge of the wood, with rifles at the ready, could not hear. But when, finally, she shook her head meaningly, and began to retire towards them, Jack Templemore set his teeth and said,

"I told you so! I knew it meant a fight! We might just as well have begun it, as let them think we are afraid."

"There is yet a chance," replied Monella. "They may hesitate to pass the line I have laid down. In any case, all we can now do is to wait and see." And, as Ulama came towards them, he signed to her to step aside, out of the line of fire.

The officer had returned to his men, and, after a short consultation with one who seemed to be next in command, the two ranks advanced, with the slow, measured tread of a well-disciplined troop, up the slope. On reaching the dead body they were halted while the two officers examined it. They had not understood how their leader had been killed; nor did they understand it now. They had heard the report of the pistol and had seen their chief fall, but the report had not been a loud one; and as Elwood had run forward at the time, for all they could see (Ulama being between them) he might have hurled a spear at Zelus. Yet the sound of the explosion had puzzled them, and stayed them from rushing instantly to the assistance of their leader. Altogether, they were perplexed. The dress of their opponents showed them to be strangers. They appeared to be unarmed, yet had they killed their dreaded master in the face of his guard. This argued conscious power; and it behooved them not to be too precipitate. After this fashion, probably, reasoned the two officers.

If so, the examination of the dead body could but add to their uncertainty; for they found there a wound they were quite unable to account for. It was not a spear thrust; it was not a wound from a sword or dagger. The scrutiny, in effect, yielded them no enlightenment; but the sight of the dead body of their leader and of the blood exasperated both officers and men, and murmurs were heard, and cries for vengeance. They probably began, too, to remember what Ulama had suggested—that if they went back with the dead body of their chief and without the slayer, their own lives would be forfeited. And all this time the strangers stood calmly regarding them, watchful of their movements, but offering neither to retreat nor to attack them.

After some further consultation, the one who seemed to be in command turned towards where the three strangers stood; flinging down his sword, he stepped forward and threw out both his hands, to signify that he desired a parley.

Thereupon Monella also advanced a few paces; then paused for the other to address him.

"Who are you? Whence come you? Why do you enter our land in this fashion by killing one of the greatest in the country?" asked the captain of the guard.

"The answers to your first questions are for your king's ear alone," returned Monella. "As to the last, we came in peace, but interfered to save a maiden from being murdered."

The other's face expressed an evil sneer, and he made answer:

"It is not usual, with us, for men to throw away their lives for women. For what you have done yours may be required. Still," he added diplomatically, "I am not judge nor executioner—unless you resist me. If, therefore, you will surrender like men of peace—as you say you are—and will come with me to tell your tale to my master, I promise you good treatment while in my custody."

Monella shook his head.

"You have had my answer," he said. "We seek your king. We will yield ourselves to no one else. And," he continued, with louder voice, "since you, my friend, dare to deride us for taking a woman's part, know that in the land we come from we are not accustomed to stand still and look on while women are being murdered. What manner of men are ye who dare openly proclaim so vile a doctrine? Soldiers of a High Priest? Guardians of a 'religion' that teaches things like this? The span that shall be left to such a being as ye serve is growing short. His power is waning, his days are even now numbered." He raised his arm, and extended it towards him he was addressing; then, with gathering force, and even passion, till he seemed like an inspired prophet of old thundering his denunciations against evil-doers— "We came here in goodwill and peace; we may remain to be a withering scourge to you and him you call your master. See to it, and take warning! There must—and there shall—be an end of such deeds as we have this day seen attempted by—as ye have no shame in avowing—the favoured son of your High Priest. Hence from my sight, ere scorn and anger overcome me! I have but to move my finger, and you fall dead before me!"

For the first time in their knowledge of him Templemore and Elwood saw their leader, usually so calm and equable, moved by a passion that was almost uncontrollable. They glanced at one another in surprise; and well indeed they might. For whereas, at first, they had felt almost impatient of his equanimity, and had feared he lacked the sternness to deal with those they were opposed to, yet now they thought only how to restrain his sudden and unlooked-for passion, lest it should embroil them further than was actually necessary.

But the fire of Monella's rage expired as suddenly as it had kindled.

"You have heard," he went on, coldly and disdainfully, to the captain of the hostile group. "I have warned you. I spare your life to give you time to do better."

But this contemptuous treatment, so far from having the effect intended, seemed to rouse the other's fury.

"Think not to impose on me by empty threats and vain-glorious boasting," he retorted. "I summon you to yield and come with me. If not, and we have to kill you in striving to enforce obedience, the consequences be upon your own heads."

"And I say that I have warned you," returned Monella quietly. He stooped and picked up a stone, then threw it to within three or four feet of the cord that lay between them.

"If," he said, "you but cross that cord so far as that stone, you die."

Instantly the other took up the challenge. He stepped back for his sword, then walked boldly forward, Monella meanwhile falling back in line with his companions; but the instant the other crossed the cord, Monella's rifle rang out, and the fatuous soldier fell prone upon the sword.

Then a tall fellow burst from the ranks and, brandishing his spear, rushed towards the fatal cord; he was followed by an adventurous comrade; but, even as they stepped across the line, they both bit the dust. Then all the others turned and fled; all save the second officer, who stood his ground, neither advancing nor retreating. He remained leaning on his sword, and looked, by turns, first at his flying men, then at the dead bodies that lay around him, finally at Monella and his companions.

Monella advanced and thus addressed him,

"How is it you stand thus in hesitation, friend? Are you in two minds, whether to fight or to fly?"

The second officer was a fine-looking young fellow with features that were not unpleasing. With a steady glance he looked Monella in the face and answered,

"I am no coward to run away, and no fool to rush to meet a thunderbolt. Whoever you are, it is plain that we are powerless against you. But indeed," he went on, with something almost like a sigh, "when I heard your words I felt no stomach to fight against you, if so be that they are true."

"I am well pleased to hear you say so, friend," Monella said, laying his hand upon the other's shoulder. "You have seen what it is in our power to do. I call upon you to be a witness in the presence of your king—of all your people—that we did not resort to force until all other means had failed."

"That will I gladly do," returned the officer, bending his head in courteous salutation. "Few would have been so persistent in their merciful intention. For myself, I know my fate if I rejoin my master; therefore, if you will accept my service, I would fain join myself to you. One can but fight and die; better to do so in the service of such a chief as you, than of him I have lately served"—and he seemed to shudder while he spoke.

Just then the maiden joined them, and he saluted her respectfully. She looked at him with sorrowful eyes.

"And is it Ergalon," she said, "that could stand by to-day and see another man raise his hand to slay the daughter of his king, and not move a step to hinder him? Has Ergalon indeed sunk so low as this?"

The words were said in pained surprise rather than in anger; and in the gentle eyes she turned upon him there was no sign of aught but mild reproach. But this seemed to cut him to the heart, when ringing words of accusation would, perhaps, have failed to move him. He fell upon one knee and bent his head.

"Alas! Princess," he cried, "I well deserve your scorn; yet knowest thou not how that against my will I have been forced into this service. Well I know that to ask pardon would be useless—the king will never pardon, should this reach his ears; still less will Coryon. Yet I care not if thou wilt but grant me thy forgiveness. If these strangers are thy friends, grant me to serve thee by serving

them; and should this service be even to death, it will content me
that thou shouldst say of me that Ergalon had done his duty, and
redeemed himself in thine eyes."

"Be it so, Ergalon," Ulama answered, her voice and manner
charged with a sweet graciousness that quite captivated the three
bystanders. Then, turning to Monella, she continued, "My father,
I owe you much for what you have done to-day. I shall try in the
future to repay you some measure. Meantime you will need
friends—accept from Ergalon this proffered service. I feel sure,
after what has happened, you may trust him—even to the death. I
know not who you are, whether immortals, or beings of like nature to myself, thus timely sent by the Great Spirit to my aid. But
this I know, that I may trust you; that you have come to be my
friends, and my friends from henceforth you shall be."

It would be difficult to convey an idea of the wonderful mixture of simple gentleness and queenly dignity with which these
words were spoken. Further, it would be hard to say which of her
hearers was most impressed. She had the art of winning hearts
without intending or desiring it; and few could long resist the fascination of her presence. Small wonder then if Leonard Elwood
had already fallen incontinently, helplessly, irretrievably in love.

"And now," she finished, "I invite you to my home, where my
father will bid you welcome."

"And these?" Monella asked, pointing to the dead bodies.

"Ergalon will know what to do," she answered; and moved away
in the direction she had indicated.

But by this time a small crowd was on its way to meet them.
Those forming it were, as it appeared, chiefly her maidens and attendants and a file of soldiers—her guards. They looked curiously
at the strangers, but, at a sign from her, fell in respectfully behind
the little party.

"Doubtless you marvel," she observed to Elwood and Monella,
between whom she walked, "how it comes about that with all these
people to attend and guard me, I was alone this morning. But for
that chance the dead Zelus had never found his opportunity of saying that he did to me. He must have been watching for it; perchance
had heard that I sometimes like to steal away alone for a little

ramble. One gets so tired of always having people around one," she added, with an almost childish wilfulness. "But this will cure me. For the future I shall be more careful."

Templemore, meantime, strolling along behind the others, found himself somehow placed between Ergalon and a dainty little damsel whose name, he afterwards found, was Zonella. She was Ulama's close friend, and was most busy plying Ergalon with questions about what had taken place. At the noise of the firing they had rushed out in alarm; then, missing the princess, had set out to seek her. In reply to her inquiries, Ergalon gloomily referred her to Templemore, and on this slender introduction the two soon found themselves in friendly converse, rather to the increase of their companion's moodiness.

It was well for Templemore that day that his affections were unalterably fixed upon a chosen fair one; else, inevitably, had he lost his heart either to the fair Ulama or to the dark-eyed, captivating Zonella. As it was, he was compelled to own that he had never seen two more fascinating maidens—save—save, of course, Maud Kingsford. In that reservation—and in that alone—lay the salvation of his heart. But this Ergalon knew not; and since he had long ardently—but vainly—sought the favour of Zonella, he was none too pleased to see her so quickly place herself on friendly terms with a total stranger.

But Templemore's acquaintance with the language was so limited, that his part in the conversation consisted more in listening than in talking; and his thoughts were more concerned in observing all that went on around him than in studying Zonella herself.

13
A King's Greeting

During the walk—which now more resembled a procession, for they had been joined by numbers of the inhabitants who had heard the rifle shots and had come out in curiosity or alarm to inquire into the cause—Jack Templemore had observed many pumas that, like tame dogs, accompanied the people who crowded round them. They were mostly smaller than the one that had followed him from the mountain top down the canyon, though a few equalled it in size. But he looked in vain for any sign of recognition from any of them; and it really seemed as though his own jesting prophecy were being actually fulfilled.

They now arrived at a colossal edifice that reared its soaring walls and towers high up in the sky. They passed between its open gates, that appeared to be of gold and iron, beneath an archway that, far above their heads, spanned the space between two lofty towers of pink-white stone. In the courtyard within were many other soldiers. These, when the party entered, seemed crowded together in some confusion; but, at sight of Ulama and her attendants, they quickly formed into lines, in obedience to hoarse words of command, shouted by officers in gorgeous blue uniforms, and with white plumes waving in their helmets.

The courtyard was large enough for two or three hundred men to drill and march about in. In the centre was a fountain that threw into the air a jet of water that fell back with a sound of refreshing coolness into a marble basin, from which rose curious-shaped green plants that showed in pleasing contrast to the dainty whiteness of the stonework. Here and there were marble statues, and, between them, large vases filled with flowering plants. Above, a broad gallery ran round the enclosure, and from this a number of richly-dressed people gazed down upon the strangers as they entered with Ulama.

The latter, making signs to Monella and his two friends to follow her, proceeded, through lines of soldiers and attendants who fell back respectfully before her, to an apartment at one side, outside which all remained save two or three whom she specially invited to accompany her. Around, were benches or divans and couches covered with richly embroidered stuffs; upon these she bade her guests be seated, begging them to await her while she sought out the king and solicited an audience.

When she had gone, a sudden silence fell on those she left behind; a silence that was the more noticeable, coming, as it did, after the confused hubbub and clank of arms that had filled the courtyard on the arrival of the strangers.

The scene was certainly a curious one. The homey, travel-stained dress of the new-comers contrasted strangely in its nineteenth-century plainness with the elaborate brilliantly-coloured costumes of Zonella and the half-dozen members of the princess's suite who had entered with her; with the luxurious carpets, rugs, and cushions everywhere around; and with the magnificence of the whole surroundings, that spoke more of the sumptuous luxury and elaborate decorations of a Moorish "Alhambra" than of what one would have expected in this isolated city of the clouds.

Monella stood, lost in thought, with bowed head and folded arms, his rifle, that that day had sent three human beings to their long account, resting against the wall beside him. Elwood, whose eyes had followed Ulama till she had disappeared through the inner door, also stood plunged in reverie, not noticing aught of his surroundings. Of the three,

Jack Templemore alone seemed alive to the interest and strangeness of the scene. His keen, steady eyes were making mental notes of every line of the architectural designs, as though with the object of afterwards constructing a like edifice from memory; and, from the building, they travelled to its furniture and decorations, and thence, finally, to the dress and appearance of those of the princess's suite who stood or sat around. Ergalon had remained outside with many more.

Presently, Templemore said quietly to Zonella, somewhat to her astonishment, "What is the name of this city?"

"What!" she exclaimed, "do you not know then that you are in Manoa? Where did you suppose you were?"

"Manoa! H'm. The same as 'El Dorado,' I suppose, as the Spaniards called it?"

"I know nothing of that, or of who you mean by 'the Spaniards,'" she replied. "Fancy your coming here and not knowing the name of the place! Where have you come from? I long to hear all about it. Are all the people there white like you and those with you? We have always been instructed, by our teachers here, that only black demons lived in the world beyond our island—at least we still so call it; though, of course; it is no longer an island; has not been for many, many long ages."

But when Jack attempted explanations, he soon discovered that he knew too little of the language to make things clear to his companion. He became hopelessly involved, his descriptions quite impossible, and, in the end, he had to give it up as hopeless.

"You must wait till I know your language better," he said with a sigh; "or else question my friends, who know far more of it."

"I will wait as patiently as I can until you can tell me yourself," she answered with an arch look. "I shall like better to hear it from you. I feel, too, a little afraid—of your friend there—the older of the two. He seems so proud and dignified."

Jack laughed.

"He is anything but that. He is as kind-hearted and good-natured a man as I have ever known. To-day he looks more serious than usual, perhaps. You see, we have had a disagreeable adventure, and do not yet know what may be its consequences."

"I think, all the same, he is a man of great pride and dignity," Zonella repeated. "He might be a great chief—a king—so far as one can judge from what one sees. He is not of the same race as you," she went on with decision. "He is more like one of my own people. Your younger friend, too, is not unlike one of our people; though I do not see the resemblance so strongly there, as in the case of the other."

This odd suggestion almost startled Templemore. Curiously enough, the same idea had struck him several times during the past half-hour; since, in fact, the opportunity had offered of comparing Monella's face and form with those inhabitants he had seen. Except that he was taller than any, there were many points in which there was obvious resemblance; and Jack began to ponder upon it as a strange coincidence. He was also surprised at the confidence with which the young girl had declared Monella to be of different race from himself. "You must be an unusually quick observer," he said presently, "to distinguish these things so readily. In my land young ladies do not much trouble themselves—"

Suddenly, Zonella laid her hand upon his arm and leaned forward with a look of fervid earnestness.

"Who is this man?" she asked. "What is his name, and what brings him here, and just at such a time, too?" This last seemed to be said more to herself than to her companion.

"He is called Monella," Jack told her. "I know of no other name; and, as to why he is here, I can no more tell you that than why you yourself are here. In some things he keeps his own counsel absolutely, and is altogether inscrutable—"

"Ah!" Zonella said this with a long breath. "Then, though he is your friend, and you are here together, you really know nothing of him. Is that what you mean?"

"Well," returned Jack slowly, "it's rather an abrupt way of putting it, but—well, I never thought of it in that light before—but—I really think you have about hit it."

"Yes! You and he have met by chance, and have agreed to travel together for a time. And you have let him bring you here, I suppose, without troubling yourself to ask him his objects?" Zonella went on, still with her glance fixed on Monella.

Jack opened his eyes.

"You have a very direct way of putting things, I must say," he laughed. "But again, I am bound to admit you are not far out."

"And your other friend—what do you know of him?"

"Oh, I have known him since he was a child."

"And yet," the girl persisted, "he is very different from you. Are you sure he is of the same race as yourself?"

"Quite," Templemore replied, laughing. "We are both of a nation that I suppose you have never heard of, but that makes no small amount of noise in the outer world, I can assure you. We are both English."

Just then a heavy curtain was drawn back, and Ulama entered, and with her an immense puma, larger even than their friend of the canyon, and behind it the latter animal itself!

"Why," exclaimed Zonella, "there is Nea, who has been missing for several days," and she called the animal to her. Great was her surprise to see it, after a brief acknowledgment of her greeting, turn to Jack and his two friends, with every sign of recognition and delight.

"Why, it's Puss, by all that's wonderful!" Jack cried. "At least, that's the name I gave her," he added, by way of explanation to Zonella.

"Do you know her, then? But how can that be?"

"She has been living with us for the last week; but she deserted us last night, and we wondered where she had got to."

"Then that accounts for it. We could not think what had become of her." And she began to chide the animal for its desertion of its home and mate.

"If Tuo had known you were off gallivanting with strange people, Nea, I fancy he would have come after you and marched you back." Then, to Templemore "But how odd that she should attach herself to you like that; you must have had some strong attraction for her."

"It was not what she got to eat, at any rate," said Jack. "In fact, I fear she was half starved. And at last she got so disgusted at what, I suppose, she thought our stinginess, that she went off hunting on her own account; and what she caught she offered, with a splendid lack of selfishness, to share with us." And he went on to tell how he first met the animal; Elwood, meanwhile, recounting the same story to Ulama; and they learned that the two pumas were named Tuo and Nea.

Presently, the princess gave a sign to her attendants, and they all followed her from the apartment, leaving the three strangers by themselves.

Elwood was the first to speak.

"We are to wait till the king is ready to receive us," he said. "I wonder what he is like, and what sort of a reception he will give us! What say you, Monella?"

The latter turned slowly, and seemed to wake as from a deep reverie.

"I know not what to say, my son; but I am full of pain at all that has happened to-day. My mind misgives me that civil war will come out of it; yet we can but try to do our best, and leave the rest to a higher power."

It was not long before the curtain was drawn aside again, and one entered who seemed to be a dignitary of the court.

"I have come," said he, "to conduct you to King Dranoa." And, with a ceremonious bow, he motioned to them to follow him.

They passed through many passages, across galleries and large halls, and up broad staircases covered with thick soft carpet that was noiseless to the tread.

On their way they saw many people of various costumes and appearance, who regarded the new-comers curiously, but not rudely. Presently they reached a heavy curtain before a doorway, where stood more soldiers and officers in brilliant uniforms. The curtain being drawn aside, they entered an immense hall, its sides lined with people, but the whole centre part unoccupied. They were ushered up this hall and there left standing, their conductor retiring to one side.

They found themselves confronting a high canopy, beneath which, upon a raised dais, a man, apparently somewhat past middle age, was seated; they had little doubt he was the king. He was a man of a fine presence, and seemed hale and vigorous, though his dark hair and beard were streaked with grey. His features were regular and well formed, his eyes steady and piercing; his expression was not unkindly; but his chin suggested weakness, a wavering and unsettled temperament. He was dressed in a long flowing robe, and large jewels sparkled upon his breast and shoulders, in the belt that girdled his waist and in the hilt of his short sword. On his head he wore a circlet that was simple in design, and scarcely to be called a crown; it was a band of gold with gems set as stars. Ulama was seated by his side; she, also, wore a golden

circlet in which gleamed, with softened radiance, one cluster of
large pearls. She had changed the simple dress in which she had
been clad when they had first seen her, and now appeared in a costume that was fairly dazzling in its richness, yet in exquisite taste,
and well chosen for showing to advantage her graceful figure.

At her feet Zonella sat, or rather half reclined, and other members of her suite were grouped around. Upon the other side of the
king stood his ministers and officers of state, and his body guard,
and, ranged around the hall were many others of both sexes, looking curiously and silently upon the strangers.

Over the canopy was an immense star wrought in solid gold.
Statues on pedestals were to be seen at intervals, and, most curious of all, on the walls were well-executed coloured frescoes depicting battle scenes.

The king rose and addressed them.

"Friends, I know not whence ye come, what brought ye hither,
nor how ye succeeded in passing the wood of black demons and
forced your way into our land. In ordinary circumstances it would
have been my duty to send ye away forthwith, or even to imprison
ye—possibly, still worse might have befallen. But my daughter hath
told me that ye have saved her life—a life doubly, trebly dear to me
in that she is my only child. But that ye came so opportunely on
the scene, she who is my heart's pride would e'en now be lying in
the cold grasp of death."

Here he paused, overcome with emotion.

"So," he presently went on, "it has been described to me. I understand, also, that, by some strange chance, ye speak our language,
and comprehend what I would say. We knew not that there were
people outside this land of ours who were white like us, and, above
all, could speak our tongue. But these wonders ye shall explain
afterwards at your leisure. At this moment not curiosity, but gratitude inspires me, in that ye have restored my child to me. There is
not one here"—his eyes travelled round the packed assemblage—
"who will not join with me in thanking ye for that which ye have
done. What say ye, friends?"—this to his people— "Ye have heard
in what dire peril hath my daughter been this day. Shall we not
give to those who rescued her a right good welcome?"

At this, the hitherto silent crowd burst out into acclamations. They cheered, they clapped their hands; they waved banners, they raised their spears and swords aloft and flashed them in the air; again and again the shouts went up, till they seemed in very truth to shake the walls. When, by a motion of his hand, silence had been restored, the king resumed,

"Ye hear! All greet ye, and *I* thank ye. Be assured of my protection an' ye have come in peace. But alas! I grieve to say I am not all-powerful. There are reasons for enjoining upon ye that ye be circumspect in your going to and fro, have always with ye the escort I shall give ye, and visit only places they shall indicate. This is not the time or place for further explanations, nor is it fitting I should now hear the wondrous things I doubt not ye can tell me. I only wish it understood that while I shall give ye my protection, and that of those devoted to me, ye must not hope too much from it; and it may fail ye, if ye observe not the conditions and limitations I have stated; the cause whereof I shall explain hereafter."

"While we return thee our thanks, O King," Monella answered, "on our part, also, let it be understood that we can protect ourselves. The cowardly assailants of the princess thy daughter fell before us like chaff before the fire. We could, an' we had chosen, have destroyed them all, even to the last one; but we spared some that they might noise the tale abroad and warn others of their kind not to raise their hands against us. Yet do I regret that it was necessary to kill any. We came in peace and goodwill, not to maim and slay, or to spread alarm and desolation through thy land. Yet this was forced upon us."

"It hath been so told to me. Perhaps, as ye say, ye can protect yourselves; and it hath been further told to me how ye wield the lightning and the thunder and blast your enemies, hurling them to the ground ere they can reach ye. For all that, if ye would go about in peace, and avoid the need for further exercise of your death-dealing powers, accept the guard I offer. If occasion arise, and they fail ye, and ye can help in your own defence—well, by so much the better will it be."

"Thou hast well said, O King. It shall be as thou hast spoken," Monella returned.

Throughout the interview the king had been eyeing the commanding figure of the man before him, not only with great intentness, but also even anxiously. Indeed, Monella, with his lofty stature and intrepid bearing, his nobly chiselled features, his bold, unflinching glance, would have made no unfitting occupant of the throne. And, possibly, this thought had struck the king, who once more spoke.

"And now I would fain know thy name, and what hath brought thee."

"I am called Monella."

"Monella! It hath a sound as of our own tongue," returned the king. "And thine end in journeying hither?"

"That is for thine ear alone, O King," Monella replied with decision, thereby arousing the surprise of all, the king included. Then, drawing from his breast a sealed roll of parchment he had brought with him, "But here is that which will in part explain." And he handed the document to the king.

The king unrolled the parchment, but, as the first words met his eye, he started; then, growing more intent, he read on. But presently, in evident agitation, he stepped down from the dais, placed his hand on the other's arm, and said in a voice that trembled with emotion,

"I will speak with thee alone. Follow me into my private chamber." And, looking neither to the right nor to the left, he passed down the hall, Monella following, the crowd opening out to give them egress.

No sooner had they gone, than confused murmurs of astonishment and curiosity burst out on all sides. Elwood and Templemore, as much taken by surprise as any one, looked each in the other's face inquiringly; but Zonella glided to their side and said in a low tone to Templemore,

"Said I not that thy friend was no ordinary man? Monella! Is it not like my name, Zonella? Methought, the moment my eyes rested on him, 'That man is a great man—a wondrous man—and he is one of our people!'"

14
Dakla

Ulama also left her seat and came forward to the two young men. "Your friend," she said, "has taken my father by surprise; else had he bidden you be seated. Nor did I know that he could not earlier have received you, or I would have sent my maidens to you with refreshment. Come now and sit near us, and I will point out to you my friends that they may be your friends; meantime Zonella will order fruit and wine for your sustainment. Anon you will be invited to our table; but meantime you will need something. We all do," she added, when they made gestures of dissent, "so you will not be conspicuous in partaking here of what we offer you."

Pages then entered bearing luscious fruits and tempting-looking foaming drinks; the former on massive salvers of pure gold, the latter in chalices of gold and silver set with gems. The fruits were all new to them, as also were the drinks; but, on tasting them, they found them to be all they looked.

The fruits were indeed delicious and refreshing; the drinks cooling and exhilarating: to Elwood and Templemore they were as nectar and ambrosia, and they said so, and asked many questions concerning them. But, seeing that the only information they received was a string of names that conveyed to them no meaning, they added little to their stock of knowledge.

They now talked freely with those around them; but found the questions showered upon them from all sides somewhat more than they could answer, so that Templemore said at last in an aside to the other, "Tell you what it is, Leonard; we shall have to give a public lecture—or perhaps a series—and invite as many at a time as the

Town Hall of the place will contain. Pity we didn't bring some magic lanterns and dissolving views to illustrate what we have to tell them. I would have done so if I had only known."

They, in their turn, were not less full of curiosity and interest in all they saw around them. The statuary, and, above all, the pictures amazed them.

"It upsets all one's notions of history and all that," said Jack quietly to Leonard, "to find this sort of thing in the so-called 'new' world. We might be back in Ancient Greece."

"Or Babylon, or Nineveh," Elwood answered. "It's like a dream—and, strange to say, I have dreamed much of it before. I keep thinking I shall wake up presently and find that this city, with all that it contains, has vanished."

"I trust not," said Ulama—to whom the last part of the sentence had been addressed—with a smile. "I should not like to think that I, myself, am but a dream. But, since you speak of having dreams of that which you find here, know that I have strange dreams also. All my life it has been thus with me. Of late they have been less frequent than of yore, and the memory of them is confused and indistinct; but I know that in them I have seen—aye, more than once your face, and the face of him you call Monella."

Elwood regarded the maiden in surprise, and she continued,

"Yes, it is true. Tell me, Zonella, have I not often described to thee those I had seen in my dreams; and did not some resemble these? As to face thou canst not know, but as to garb and other details?"

"'Tis true," replied Zonella gravely.

But the matter-of-fact Templemore found it hard to credit this; visions and the like were nothing in his way.

"Are you serious?" he asked.

"Quite," both said.

"And—me—a—I—myself, I mean; was I there too?"

Templemore's manner when he asked this question was so humorously anxious that Ulama laughed—a joyous, ringing laugh, the token of a soul innocent and free from care.

"No, indeed," she answered. "I never dreamed of you."

"And you?" he asked, turning to Zonella.

"No, never;" and she too laughed merrily.

"It really doesn't seem fair," said Jack, with an injured air. "Waking or sleeping, my friend has been a dreamer all his life; when we met with Monella we found he was one of the same sort; so those two were on terms immediately; but I—I am out of it all. Never had a dream in my life worth remembering. Not only that, but—as it now seems—I can't even get into other people's. I put it to you, Princess, am I not a little hardly done by?"

Thus they laughed and chatted, and time passed on, and still Monella and the king were closeted together. It was more than an hour—nearer two—before the king returned; and then alone.

"My friends," he said, "the audience is at an end. Affairs of state demand my earnest thought, and I must now dismiss you. But," beckoning the two young men to him, and taking in his own a hand of each, "once more let me commend these strangers to your care and friendship. They have rendered me to-day a service that is beyond price, and in rendering it to me, they have rendered it to us all. More I need not say, except to charge you to make their stay with us a pleasant one."

He withdrew, and, with his absence, the crowd began to thin; only those belonging to the court remaining. And now Ulama spoke.

"I shall hand you over to my good friends here," she said. "Doubtless you will wish to make a change in your apparel and—"

"Unfortunately we brought no change with us," said Jack.

"They will bring you a choice of vestments," she answered, laughing. "You will surely find something to your taste." She bowed courteously, and went out, followed by Zonella and her attendants.

They were now taken in charge by the high chamberlain, whom they already knew by name—Colenna. He, in turn, handed them over to his son Kalaima, a bright-eyed, fair, talkative young fellow with whom they quickly found themselves on pleasant terms. He conducted them to a suite of chambers which would be, he said, reserved to them. They found there various suits which he laid out for their selection, instructing them, with much good humour, in the way in which they should be worn. These were, so he told them, the distinctive dresses of a noble of high degree; and were presents from the king as a mark of his special favour.

Elwood laughed at Jack's expression while he turned over the various articles after Kalaima had left them to themselves, examining in turn the white tunic of finest silk embroidered with strange devices, the cap with jewelled plume, the heavy belt of solid gold, and the short sword and dagger; all ornamented with precious stones of greater value than they could estimate.

"Are you really going to deck yourself out in these things, Leonard?" he asked, with a rueful look. "Am I expected to do so too? Great Scott! What would our friends in Georgetown say if they could see us masquerading in this toggery?"

"When at Rome you must do as Rome does, I suppose," Elwood returned lightly. "After all, I don't suppose it will seem half so strange to the good people here as would our continuing to wear our present dress."

"There's a good deal, no doubt, to be said for that view," Jack said with resignation. "And, since it is intended as a compliment, I suppose we must e'en accept it as such. I only hope I shall be able to keep my countenance when I look at you—that is, before the king and others. At present I feel very much afraid that it may prove beyond my powers."

In their suite of chambers was a bath, with water deep and broad enough to swim in. A refreshing plunge, a reclothing in the unfamiliar raiment, and they emerged from their apartments dressed as nobles of the country. The attempts, honest, but too often futile, made by Templemore to preserve his gravity, caused him at times more personal discomfort than did even the strange garb but, since use accustoms us to pretty nearly everything the efforts required became gradually less and less.

But what sobered him, so to speak, the most, was his meeting with Monella, who was now attired in like fashion to themselves. The change seemed to have made an extraordinary alteration in the man. He looked taller and more imposing than ever, and in his gait and manner there were an added grace and dignity. It could now be seen that his form was supple and muscular as that of a young man's, graceful in the swing of the limbs and in every pose. His eyes retained their unique expression that seemed to magnetise those upon whom they fell; but his face had a greater gravity than

ever, and something of a majesty that awed Templemore when he
noted it.

"Of a truth," he said to Elwood, "that man seems to alter from
day to day even from hour to hour. He is just as kindly, as courteous, and as gentle; just as thoughtful—yet, I feel somehow that
there is a gulf deepening between us, and that it is widening, slowly
but surely. Yet not because one likes him less—that's just it, you
seem to like him and admire him more and more—but you feel you
do it from afar—from a gradually increasing distance."

And when, later in the day, they sat down to a banquet at the
king's table, and saw Monella seated beside the king, taking the
post of honour and accepting it with the easy dignity of one who
had been used to it all his life; not only the observant Jack, but the
less seriously-minded Leonard, felt, with increasing force, the feeling the former had described.

During this repast they learned that the Manoans were vegetarians; though their cookery was so skilful that such dishes as
the strangers tasted they found both appetising and satisfying. Not
only that, but, as they soon discovered, these dishes were fully as
invigorating and nourishing as a meat diet. This was due to the
presence of some strange vegetable or herb in nearly every dish;
but what this was they could not then determine.

At dusk, a new surprise awaited them; for, not only the palace,
but the whole city was lighted up by what they quickly recognised
as the electric light. They now could understand the brilliant aspect of the city as first seen by them at night from the head of the
canyon.

After the meal, Templemore and Elwood went out, with many
more, upon a terrace that overlooked the lake; where now boats
were going to and fro, some paddled by oars, some drawn by the
large white swans. But what at first puzzled the new-comers were
the antics of some who threw themselves into the water from considerable heights. Instead of falling almost vertically, as a diver
would, they swept down in a graceful curve, striking the water almost horizontally, then bounded up and flew through the air for a
short distance, till once more they touched the water and bounded
up again. Finally, when the impetus was expended, they swam back

to shore or were taken thither in a boat. Of course this style of bathing could not be practised *in puris naturalibus*, or in ordinary bathing dress; so they were furnished with a kind of divided parachute, or twin parachutes, not unlike artificial wings; with these they could descend from towers and great heights and with a long swallow-like sweep, striking the water and rebounding again and again. By practice some had obtained a wonderful dexterity in this amusement, and their evolutions would have deceived a stranger, viewing them from a distance, into a belief that they were actual flying creatures. Some of the children—who chiefly delighted in this pastime—were very expert at it.

While watching the gay scene before them—a repetition of what they had witnessed from afar—Kalaima came to say that the king requested their presence in his council chamber. Following the young man they entered a hall, smaller than that in which they had first been received, and found the king throned under a canopy as before, and Monella seated near him. Around the hall were ten or twelve of his chief ministers and officers, each placed before a small table, upon which were ink-horns, pens, and sheets of parchment.

Standing in the centre of the chamber was a man of swarthy skin and haughty mien, his expression cruel and deceitful. He wore a black tunic on which was worked a large golden star like that displayed by the ill-fated Zelus. Standing respectfully a short distance behind this man were two others, somewhat similarly attired.

The leader had just finished speaking when Templemore and Elwood entered, and he cast at them a scowl that was almost appalling in its malignity.

The king signed to the young men to seat themselves beside Monella; then, turning to the man who had just spoken, said,

"It avails nothing, Dakla, for thee to come to us with messages of this intent, and with presentments, void of truth, of what befell to-day. Here are the three strangers who, as thou sayest, opposed themselves to Zelus, the son of Coryon thy master. They slew him, it is true, and some of those who followed him, but it was to save my daughter from his violence."

"It is false, O King! They lie, if they say so! For our lord Zelus had no thought of violence!" This from Dakla.

"If thine errand here is but to charge with falsehood these three men, I'll grant thee audience no longer." The king's voice was stern, and his eyes flashed angrily, so that Dakla trembled, and there was less confidence in his tone when he replied, "But they are strangers whom the king knows not; wherefore should he accept their word before our trusted servants?"

"Because it is confirmed by mine own daughter, sirrah! And if thou darest again to say it is untrue that Zelus lifted his hand to take her life, thou shalt not return unpunished, be the consequences what they may!"

By the king's impressive manner, and still more by the menace he had thus let fall, Dakla seemed daunted. He had expected to be able to carry things his own way. He hesitated, then said in a milder tone,

"But even so, they should not have taken the life of our lord Zelus, but have brought him before thee."

"How could they do that when he had more than a score of men with him, and they were but three? Furthermore, there was no time for parley. An instant's hesitation, my daughter saith, and it would have been too late."

Dakla reflected; then he made a fresh suggestion.

"It will content us if the king remit to us for trial him who, with his own hand, did slay our lord. If, on due inquisition, it shall be found even as the king hath said, then shall he be returned unhurt."

The king's face clouded, and his lips curled with scorn as he replied,

"Out upon thee, with thy tricks and cunning snares! Thinkest thou we do not know thy master by this time? These strangers are my guests—under my protection! Hark ye! I say under my protection! If harm shall befall them, I will seize thyself, an' thou comest again within my reach, or any others of thy master's minions on whom I can lay hands, and their lives shall pay the forfeit."

"Thy words will grieve my master, King Dranoa," said Dakla, with a scarcely hidden sneer. "He careth only for the welfare of the king and of his people. But how shall there be safety for the dwellers in this land if such as these may go abroad and slay at will, and be protected by the king?"

"What safety is there now for any, when even the king's daughter cannot walk near mine own palace without assailment?" the king wrathfully demanded. "Hold thy peace, sirrah! and quit my sight ere worse betide thee!"

At this Monella rose, and, bending towards the king, said something in a low tone to him; the king, assenting with a nod, Monella slowly turned his glance upon the henchman of the priest, and thus addressed him,

"I have the king's permission to send a message of my own to Coryon, since the opportunity now offers. It is well that thou shouldst bear it, and better still if thou takest it to heart. I sent the same message by the murderous crew that followed at the heels of thy late shameful lord—as thou callest him—Zelus. It is this: that such things as he attempted will bring down vengeance and retribution on you all. Bid Coryon take heed and mend his ways; if not, his doom is fixed. We are but three; yet, if we chose, and the king so willed it, we could clear thee and thy master and his brood from off the land—aye, ere another sun has risen and set. And tell Coryon this, by the king's permission we are here, and, as thou hast heard, under his protection. For that protection we are grateful, but we need it not. If thou, or any of thy serpent brood molest us, we will hold you all to such a vengeance as shall repay the wrongs of others and rid the earth of you. I sent this message by Zelus's craven hounds, but my mind misgives me that in their flight they scarce remembered it; or, perchance, they feared to give it. Wilt thou now bear it to thy master?"

"Who art thou that dares to send a message of defiance to the great Coryon?" Dakla asked.

"One who can carry out his words; one who, as the ally of the king, will bring upon your heads that which has been so long deserved. One who, though he spared thy myrmidons to-day, will spare no more. Beware! Attack us, and we show no mercy!"

With each succeeding sentence he seemed taller, more imposing, and more menacing; until the last words were fairly thundered out, and his eyes flashed fire.

The countenance of Dakla fell before his gaze; he hesitated, panted, turned to go, then turned back, and finally, as one who

spoke against his will, he said, with no show of his former mocking insolence,

"Sir, I will bear thy message." Then, with an obeisance to the
king, he and his attendants left the place.

"I would give something to know what the king and Monella
talked about so long to-day," said Elwood to Templemore that
night, when they found themselves alone together.

"So far as I can gather," Jack replied, "there is a grand old feud
on here between these rascally old priests, on the one side, and
the king and his followers on the other; and Monella, I suspect,
has learnt enough concerning it to lead him to back up the king.
Well! So far as I am concerned, I am game to back him up, too,
against such a murdering lot as they seem to be. What say you?"

"You need not ask me," Elwood answered with some surprise.
"But I thought that you—well—that—"

"Would be rather more slow to get up enthusiasm, eh?" Jack
interrupted with a laugh. "Not at all. Fooling about in a dark,
gloomy forest, with no apparent end in view, was one thing; taking
part in an adventure of this kind to help a lot of people who have
received us kindly, is quite another; to say nothing of helping the
king, who's a regular brick, and his daughter, who's—"

"An angel!" put in Leonard.

And Jack laughed, but approvingly, and said goodnight.

15
Marvels of Manoa

During the following days Elwood and Templemore learned much of the strange land in which they found themselves; of its people, of their condition, and other details. But, since to give every separate conversation, incident, or other means by which they gained their information, would be tedious, it will suffice to cite some extracts from Templemore's diary that summarise the knowledge then and subsequently obtained.

"I am able now to jot down some account of this strange place and its inhabitants, so far, at least, as my limited knowledge of its language and other means of information go.

"The people seem to be amiable, fairly intelligent—considering, of course, that they know nothing of the great world outside—and generally well disposed. Although they maintain a small force of 'soldiers' or 'guards,' and drill and discipline them with as much assiduity as though they might be called upon to engage in warfare, yet, as a matter of course, there are no people with whom they can go to war; nor is there any likelihood of their having to fight, except amongst themselves. And this, unfortunately, has not been unknown; moreover, there are 'signs in the air' that it may not be unknown again.

"An unexpected discovery we have made is, that this mountain is connected with another close to it and called 'Myrlanda.' The connection is underground, and was made originally in the course of mining operations.

"Undoubtedly, once these people were a great nation. Their arts and sciences, their buildings, their engineering works, and their knowledge of mechanics, all give evidence of this; but, since a nation, isolated as this has been for ages, must necessarily either progress or retrogress, the Manoans slowly, gradually, but surely, have done the latter. They have numerous museums which are full of wonders of all sorts, pointing to lost arts, lost sciences, lost inventions, lost knowledge of all kinds. The fact that the demand has fallen off with diminishing population has led to the discontinuance of manufactures; though, in the museums, there are evidences that they once existed.

"This is the case as regards chronometric instruments. Their occupations being desultory, they have little need to know the time of day; so the use of clocks and watches has 'gone out of fashion,' and there does not now exist a person in the two 'islands'—as they still call these two inaccessible mountains—who can make a clock or a watch. Yet, in their museums they have many ancient specimens of clocks and watches of various kinds.

"Like remarks apply to many other arts and sciences and manufactures. The cause is likely to be found in the fact of their non-intercommunication with other nations.

"But the most wonderful thing of all, in this land of marvels, is a plant or herb they call the 'Plant of Life.' This, I am assured (though it seems hardly credible), if taken from time to time in certain forms, combined with other plants found here, induces great longevity in the recipients. The king, for instance, who looks between fifty and sixty years of age, I am seriously told is three hundred and forty! Yet that, even, is nothing out of the way here; for—assuming that they speak the truth—there are among the priesthood a few who have lived in the land one thousand, fifteen hundred, and two thousand years and more! I should scarcely take the trouble to write this down, were it not that I find it a matter of such common belief on all sides that it is impossible to avoid regarding it seriously. When first these statements were made to me I sought Monella and reported to him what had been told me, remarking that I thought it somewhat in bad taste on the part of my informants to combine together—as it seemed to me they must have—to palm off such tales upon a stranger. To my utter astonishment, he replied that he had reason to believe that there was truth in what I had been told! He had doubtless heard the same thing—and he is so quick to probe to the very root of whatever excites his interest, and a man so difficult to deceive, that, on receiving his solemn assurance (I asked for it) that he was not jesting, I felt bound to regard the matter attentively. I, therefore, set to work to get at all the facts as well as I could, and to see and examine the wonderful plant for myself. In this way I have arrived at the following data:—

"The plant, which is called 'karina' in the language of the country, is of a curious delicate, clear, blue tint—almost transparent in appearance, and in texture smooth and glassy-looking as to the leaves. It grows to a height of two or three feet, and is succulent in character exuding freely, when squeezed, a juice which has a very strong bitter-sweet taste. It is prepared in several ways—many having, it is believed, secret recipes which have been handed down from father to son from generation to generation; but they all relate more or less to a tea or infusion of the leaves, with or without the admixture of other herbs or drugs. To have the full effect it must be taken regularly, almost from infancy; indeed, it is so powerful that those not accustomed to it must take but very weak doses at first for a long time, till the system learns to assimilate it; otherwise, it may even act as a poison. Taken, however, regularly from childhood, it produces and maintains perfect health, defying all those usual fevers and diseases that afflict humanity in other parts of the world, and carrying the body unimpaired in all its functions—accidents, of course, excepted—into extreme age, without loss of vitality or strength.

"People do not, however, live for ever; there is one disease and only one that the 'karina' cannot cure. This is called the 'falloa'; there is also another name for it signifying the 'don't care sickness.' Those attacked with it gradually sink, and die painlessly and easily. This disease, no doubt, must come to all sooner or later; but it is generally believed that the priests—and they alone—are aware of some way of so preparing the 'karina,' that they can either cure even the 'falloa,' or keep it at bay for very much longer periods than other people succeed in doing.

"It is certainly a remarkable fact that throughout the land disease, in the sense in which we understand it, is unknown. Consequently, physical pain is almost absent, save in case of physical injury. Nor is it necessary to be continually taking the preparation of the 'karina.' When once the system becomes inoculated with it, as it were, it is sufficient, afterwards, to repeat the doses at long intervals; and a traveller, as I gather, might take sufficient of the dried plant with him on his travels to keep him in perfect health for many years in any part of the world.

"And when, at last, the 'falloa' attacks its victim, it causes neither pain nor suffering of any kind; only melancholy, and a distaste for life in general; while its approach is so gradual as often to be unnoticed.

"There is little doubt that the absence of ordinary diseases exerts a corresponding effect upon the physical development; and this alone is sufficient to account for a fact that is very noticeable here, viz., the beauty of the inhabitants. Both the women and the men are remarkable in this respect; and probably not in all the rest of the world put together could so many beautiful women and handsome men be found as one sees in this small, but strange country; and this applies to the old, in a measure, as well as to the young generally. Whether it also applies to the old amongst the priests, one cannot say, for they seem to keep entirely to themselves.

"As regards these 'priests,' there are two sects in the country, called respectively the 'Dark,' or 'Black,' and the 'White.'

"The religion of the 'White' priests, or 'Brotherhood,' resembles, in many respects, that of the Hebrews, save that for 'God' they use the term 'Great Spirit,' or 'Good,' or 'Almighty' Spirit. These have, however, now no influence in the country, and have been exiled to Myrlanda, where they confine themselves to a small 'domain,' have few followers and very little communication with the general inhabitants. The chief of these is named Sanaima.

"The chief of the 'Dark Brotherhood'—as they denominate themselves, and well they deserve their name, from all I hear—is called Coryon; and he and Sanaima are both popularly supposed to be more than two thousand years old! But, since both these millenarian gentlemen keep themselves shut up amongst their own immediate adherents, and seldom show themselves to the people, it would not be very difficult to keep up a tradition of this sort without a word of truth to back it. It may be urged in support of it, however, that we see many going about who, we are assured, are three, four, or five hundred years old; and these assert that they have not the true secret of preparing the 'karina'; this being known only to the priests.

"But whatever be the truth as to their longevity, the 'Dark Brotherhood' seem to be a set of bloodthirsty, licentious tyrants, ruling the people with a rod of iron, for the king, though nominally an autocrat, has but little real power; but his rule, so far as it extends, is mild, and his people appear loyal and well disposed towards him.

"The real ruler of the land is Coryon, the High Priest of the 'Dark Brotherhood'; a man who, though never seen beyond the limits of his own domain, makes his power felt everywhere. What I have heard of him and his chosen band sounds too atrocious to be true; yet I am assured I have heard only a part; the whole truth is of such a nature that men shrink from speaking of it to one another.

"It is said that they have many wives, whom they choose at will from amongst the daughters of the people; but what becomes of them afterwards no one knows, for they are never seen again when once they disappear behind the gates that shut in the domain 'sacred' to the 'Brotherhood.' Further, they lay a 'blood-tax' upon the population for 'religious sacrifices'; at certain intervals these victims are selected, it is said, by a sort of ballot, and from that moment vanish like the others, and their fate is never known; or at least no one professes to know. It is, indeed hinted, that it is too terrible to be published. One or two who have escaped back to their homes have, it is averred, died raving mad; their ravings being of so dread a nature that it could not be determined whether they referred to scenes actually witnessed, or were the offspring of their madness. What becomes of the children of these 'priests'—or at least of a large proportion of them—is also a matter for conjecture. They cannot well all live, or they would probably overrun the land. It is darkly whispered that all but a certain definite proportion are sacrificed. At any rate they are seldom heard of. Zelus, the one Elwood killed, was an exception, it would appear. He is described as the 'only remaining' son of Coryon; but what has become of his other children, if any, is not known. Zelus had set his mind upon taking Ulama from her father to make her, against her will, his wife— or one of them. Now it is generally understood that the king and his family, and the members of his household, are safe from molestation by the 'Brotherhood.' Therefore, in seeking to force Ulama, Zelus was offending against the strict law; yet, such was his insolent contempt for all law but his own will, that he not only designed to bear her off, but, in his rage at her resistance and the scathing disdain and scorn she showed in her refusal, he would have killed her. And it is quite certain that, had he succeeded, he would have been protected by his father, so that no punishment would have fallen on him.

"If, however, as appears from this, even the king's only child is not safe from these atrocious wretches, what must be the position of the common people? As a matter of fact, though they are by nature cheerful, contented and unselfish, yet over all there seems to hang the shadow of an ever-present dread, the overpowering, constant fear that to-morrow or the next day—this day, even, they or some of those they love, without the slightest warning, may be seized and borne off to an unknown fate. All the information vouchsafed in such a case is that the victim has been chosen by the so-called ballot; but it is hinted, and no doubt believed, that, if one of the priests, or one of their favourite adherents, happen to cast an approving eye upon a daughter of the people—be she maiden or wife— the 'ballot' is pretty sure to fall upon her before very long.

"This is the awful despotism wielded by these 'priests' in the name of religion. Needless to say, it is not confined to the particulars stated. If the priests themselves are not much seen in public, some of their emissaries and followers are continually about, and they domineer over the people and perpetrate many shameful acts of cruelty and injustice, in almost all of which they are supported and protected by those they serve. For, though these wretches are nominally amenable to the civil law, or to be brought before the king, few, even of the boldest of their victims, care to risk the after vengeance that they know would overtake them as the consequence.

"It was these miscreants that the king had in his mind when he insisted upon giving us an escort during our sojourn here. And,

though our firearms are undoubtedly our best protection, still, as
has been pointed out to us, we have made enemies who are treacherous and relentless, with fanatical adherents who mingle with the
people and might stab one of us in the back without warning, were
they allowed the opportunity of coming near us in the guise of ordinary well-disposed or curious citizens. We have thought it, therefore, only prudent to accept the proffered guard.

"Of the 'White Brotherhood' one hears little. Sanaima, their
chief, is reputed to be an upright, well-disposed man, who would,
if he had his way, assist the king to put an end to the domination
of the other sect and its human sacrifices and other evils and
abominations; but they do not seem to have the power, or, if they
have, they lack the resolution to take any decided or practical steps
to shake off the tyranny of Coryon. Nor could it be done without
plunging the country into a civil conflict that might last indefinitely and be productive of almost endless suffering; and the king,
as a kind-hearted man, shrinks from precipitating such a calamity. So Sanaima shuts himself up in his own domain and gives himself up, it is understood, to abstruse study.

"Turning to another noteworthy and surprising thing—the fact
that these people are acquainted with electricity and the electric
light—it seems that they collect and store it underground in some
way I do not yet understand. But upon all high rocks are placed
metal rods—lightning rods, in fact—and it is asserted that at all
times, day and night, but more particularly when there are clouds
around the mountain, a constant stream of electricity passes down
the rods and is retained and stored in insulated receptacles constructed for the purpose underground. The effect of this arrangement is that thunderstorms are unknown here. The armature of
lightning rods draws off all the electricity from the surrounding
atmosphere; and, though thunderstorms are often witnessed in the
distance—playing round other mountains, for instance—yet they
never burst over Manoa or Myrlanda.

"On this mountain—Roraima, as we call it—a name, by the way,
entirely unknown to the inhabitants—the city of Manoa and its lake
stand at one end of the great basin that lies within the summit. All
around are terraces of rock rising, one behind the other, till they

end in high wooded crags that form, in fact, the edge of the summit as seen from outside. Down these crags or cliffs pour numerous cascades that find their way, eventually, into the lake; whence they issue again as the great waterfalls that tumble from the summit—or near it—to the base of the mountain. For though, from a distance, these falls seem to start from almost the very summit, they, in reality, burst out from the level of the lake, more than a hundred feet lower than the highest rocks upon the top of the mountain.

"The rest of the top—apart from the lake and city—is a country of hill and dale, rocks and woods, very picturesque, and forming, in places, minor basins, or vales, of considerable extent and beauty, quite shut off from one another. I estimate the total extent roughly at a hundred square miles; but I believe Myrlanda covers nearly two hundred.

"None of the land in Manoa is given up to cultivation, save in the form of gardens, or orchards, and groves of fruit-bearing trees. The lower rocky terraces around the lake are beautifully laid out in this way. Here, are cultivated fruits of every kind. The trees are planted in such a way as to form shady walks and resting-places; beneath them are seats and fountains that are always playing, fed by the streams that rush down at intervals towards the lake. And across these streams are numerous bridges; some, where the torrents open out on approaching the lake, are necessarily of considerable width; those on the terraces above are small rustic structures—but all are ornamental, and some of exquisite design. Around the terraces flowers grow in profusion, partly wild and partly cultivated. Wonderful orchids, gloxinias, begonias; orange-groves covered with flowers and fruit; and gardenias with their deliciously scented blossoms; with many others that I have never seen before and have not yet learned the names of.

"The cereal and other crops required are grown in Myrlanda, which is principally devoted to agriculture; there also there are numbers of goats, and a kind of sheep, and large quantities of fowls. Pumas, which are kept as pets in Manoa, are not allowed in Myrlanda, for they would play sad havoc amongst the flocks and poultry; though, probably, they live upon them all the same; for the Manoans, being vegetarians, never eat meat, but give the flesh

of their animals to their pets. The latter include cats, of which there
are large numbers; some of most curious kinds. These two animals,
between them, it is said—the puma and the cat—have cleared the
land of all wild animals, including serpents; for there is no more
deadly enemy of serpents—even venomous ones—than the cat; and
the puma will attack and overcome larger non-venomous snakes.

"No one, to see these latter great animals playing continually
with the children of their masters—as may be witnessed here all
day long—would think they were naturally of such bloodthirsty
instincts. It has been said of pumas that, with the possible exception of some kinds of monkeys, they are the most playful animals
in existence. One can certainly see ample evidence of this in Manoa,
for the creatures, whether large or small, old or young, seem ever
ready to start a game of romps with whomever they can get to indulge them—whether little folk or their grown-up elders.

"The large swans that swim about on the lake, though very tame,
can scarcely be regarded as pets, though they are frequently to be
seen docilely drawing a small boat about; or a team of them will be
harnessed to a vessel of larger size. They get their own living among
the fish in the lake, and seem able to hold their own with the pumas.
I am told that this comes about from the fact that the young pumas,
being often foolish enough to attack them in the water, meet with
such treatment that—if they succeed in escaping drowning—they
ever afterward leave the birds alone. These swans make their nests
and rear their young on some islands that lie out near the centre
of the lake. Often, towards night, when the sun has perhaps set for
the day on the lake and the country surrounding it, these birds
may be seen in small flocks circling and whirling in the air, and
presenting a very beautiful sight as they rise out of the shadow,
and the rays of the setting sun light up their plumage. These are
undoubtedly the 'white eagles' that are asserted by the Indians to
be the 'guardians of the lake' on the top of Roraima.

"Myrlanda is honeycombed with mines, but hardly any are at
present worked, the demand for their products having practically
ceased; and such large stocks have accumulated from former workings that I am told they are not likely to be reopened for many
years. So far, I have only partially inspected the museums. They

are more surprising than even the people, for they speak plainly of a wonderful past history. Here are many strange inventions and machines, the very meaning and use of which are now but a matter of conjecture. They contain, too, stands of arms—spears, javelins, swords, daggers, shields, bows and arrows, etc., as well as suits of beautifully wrought chain armour—sufficient to fit out a small army. Most of these are mounted in gold, and many are ornamented with jewels. All are kept bright and in admirable order.

"The statues are surprising specimens of art, as are the bas-reliefs with which most of the buildings are embellished. Yet there are now no sculptors here, nor any painters. There are potters, but their work is inferior to specimens preserved in the museums. In many other branches of manufacture, also, the artificers of to-day are evidently unskilful as compared with those of former times.

"In the museums are also preserved manuscripts of great antiquity, and interesting as throwing light on the past history of the nation. Many of the nobles and chief people can write and read; but, printing being unknown, their opportunities of keeping up such accomplishments are necessarily very limited. The materials used for dress are mostly silk—obtained from silkworms—wool, and linen; the last being obtained from a fibre resembling flax. In the manufacture of these materials into fabrics the Manoans are particularly skilful; especially in working or embroidering upon them all kinds of new and quaint designs. Their boats, too, that float about the lake, are exquisite models; so that one can quite believe that the nation was once, as they declare, a maritime people, with fleets of ships, or, at least, large vessels of some kind. In the museums, by way of confirmation, are pictures—very cleverly executed works—of naval battles; and, in these, large vessels with two and three masts are represented.

"It is worthy of remark that in all these pictures representing battle-pieces—and these are many—none but white people are depicted. That different races intermingled in the fighting is indubitable; but the difference consists in dress and other details; not in the colour of their skins.

"It is a tradition of the Manoans that they formerly ruled over 'the whole world.' This may be taken to imply either the whole continent of America, or a large portion of it; but they knew nothing,

formerly, of black or red races; and their archives bear this out—
their pictures, perhaps, more forcibly than anything else.

"As regards the buildings, their architectural magnificence is
undeniable—almost, indeed, defies description. On many structures gold has been freely employed in the roofing, and for other
purposes where we should employ lead or iron. They say the gold
came chiefly from Myrlanda, and certain neighbouring 'islands'—
i.e., mountains—from which they are now isolated. Gold cornices,
and embellishments, of every conceivable shape and form, are commonly used for outside decorations; the very conduits to carry off
water being often of gold or an amalgam consisting largely of that
metal, and wrought into elaborate designs. Indeed, both iron and
tin—and lead also—seem to have been much more sparingly employed than gold and silver. Iron seems to have been used only
where extra strength and weight were required, and, in the form
of steel, for weapons, or for common utensils, tools, etc.; and of
copper there is very little anywhere to be seen. Silver, even, is less
common in heavy decorative metal work than is solid gold.

"Thus the tales that Sir Walter Raleigh heard of the splendours
of the ancient city of Manoa—or El Dorado—and that for many hundreds of years since have been regarded as fables, appear to have
been based, after all, upon actual fact."

16
Leonard and Ulama

"How I should like to see this wondrous outside world that you come from!" said Ulama dreamily. "The more you tell me of it, the more you whet my curiosity, and the more I long to see its marvels for myself."

"And yet," was Elwood's answer, "nowhere will you find so marvellously beautiful a scene as that which now surrounds us. I have travelled a good deal myself; and my friend Jack much more; and Monella, where has he not been? He seems to have visited every corner of the world! Yet he said to me, but yesterday, that he thought this the fairest spot on earth; and in this Jack agrees, so far as his experience extends.

"Since I first came here I have looked upon it from many points of view; from the water, as the boat drifts from one side to the other; from different places round the shore; from various spots on the rocky terraces above; and these different views I have seen under all the shifting effects of sunlight, moonlight, and in the mountain mist. Yet do I find myself unable to decide which I like the best. Whatever I do, wherever I happen to be, I see constantly some fresh enchantment, some new charm, some effect at once unexpected and delightful; till I strive in vain to make up my mind which I admire the most."

It was about a week after the arrival in the city of the three travellers; and Ulama and Leonard were seated in a favourite boat in which the princess was wont to spend a large portion of her time. It was, really, a small barge, of curious but graceful design and elaborate decoration. Over the after part was a white and light-blue awning; the bow ran up in the shape of a bird with out-stretched wings wrought in gold and silver, and the stern was fashioned like a fish with scales of blue and gold, its tail being movable, and running down below the water-line to form the rudder. Upon the sides provision was made for several oars; but this morning Ulama and Elwood had put off alone, content that the boat should drift wherever the slight air or current night direct.

Truly Leonard had not over-rated the beauty of the scene around them; scarce indeed would it be possible to do so. The water was a dazzling blue, yet so clear and limpid that it seemed more like a film of tinted air than water, so that the eye could pierce to great depths where many strange creatures could be seen. The sun, high in the sky, poured down its rays upon the buildings and the trees, in some parts lighting up only the tops and throwing purple shadows over the rest; in other places, touches of vivid green contrasted with the pink-white tints of the faces of the buildings; the whole quivering in the shimmering haze that conveys an idea of unsubstantiality in what one sees—a suggestion that it may be only a mirage that a passing breeze may dissipate.

Ulama was leaning in contented listlessness over the boat's side, her hand playing idly in the water. On the shapely arm, bare to the elbow, was a plain gold band in which was set a single diamond that even crowned heads might have envied. It flashed and sparkled in the sunlight with dazzling fire and power. A gold fillet, set with another matchless diamond, confined her hair, which fell loosely in wavy tresses round her shoulders. Her dress was of finest work, its texture thin as gossamer; pure white with here and there a silken knot of blue. It was gathered into her waist by a golden zone whose clasp was hidden by another and even larger diamond. No other style of dress could have so well set off the perfect symmetry and beauty of her figure. Thus, bending in unconscious ease over the boat's side, the young girl formed one of the rarest models of maidenly grace and loveliness that could that morning have been found amongst Eve's daughters.

Yet, probably, to most observers, the purity and sweetness that looked out from her soft, wistful eyes would have seemed the chief and most attractive charm of this radiant maiden of the "city of the clouds." And her gentle, lustrous eyes were the index of the pure and loving soul within.

No wonder, therefore, that she was, beyond compare, the best loved, the most honoured person in the land.

She was her father's chief, almost his only, joy. Apart from her he found but little that gave him happiness. At the same time he loved his people and honestly desired to do his best for them; and gladly would he have made great sacrifices to bring about their emancipation from the priestly tyranny that oppressed them. But he shrank from the extreme step of precipitating a civil war; yet the alternative of allowing things to take their course and continue in the old groove grieved him deeply; so much so that his distress had begun to take the form of settled melancholy.

His courtiers, who were devoted to him, noticing this, themselves became a prey to anxious misgivings, fearing in it the first symptoms of the sole incurable disease they knew—that which they termed the "falloa."

Leonard's last words had started a fresh train of thought in the young girl's mind, and presently she spoke again.

"Do you then mean that you would fain pass your life with us; you to whom the great world beyond is known, with all its endless interest? It seems strange that! Methinks that, were I in your place, I should deem life here but colourless and childish. For me, certainly, it has sufficed. I have a father who loves me dearly—dotes on me; my mother I never knew. She died when I was very young. I have kind friends around me whom I love, and who love me, and who seem to think far more of me than I deserve. And, were it not for the sadness in the land, I think I should be very happy; certainly I should be contented. Yet, now that you have told me of a spacious world beyond, full of all sorts of mysteries and unheard-of marvels, I confess I should like to see something of it."

"To do so would bring you no lasting pleasure," Leonard answered. "If we—if I—who have looked upon these things, have been brought up amongst them, if I am weary of them, and never care to see them more, and would spend the remainder of my life here, for you they would have no attractions."

Ulama glanced up shyly at him from under her long lashes.

"But are you—would you?" she asked with a slight blush. "Would you truly like to stay here all your life never to go back to your own land?"

"Yes! I *do* mean that!" And there was a fervid glow in Leonard's countenance. "All my life I have had a restlessness impelling me to seek—I knew not what—in distant lands. All my life I have had strange dreams and visions; not only in the stillness of the night, but also amidst the busy hum of day, and in all these one form was ever present; it hovered round me so that I could almost see and touch it. But—and now comes the strange part of it—that first day I set eyes on you, the moment you drew near, I saw in you the living image of her who had been the central figure of my waking visions, and held sweet converse with me while I slept. Then—when my eyes met yours—I understood it all! I knew then what had led me hither; what it was I had unconsciously been seeking, and wherefore I had been restless and unsatisfied at home. I knew that in you I had discovered all I craved for—the sweet fulfilment of my soul's desire. And then—then—I saw you in the grasp of one who would have slain you! And my heart stood still, for I knew that, unless my hand were steady and my eye unerring, in striving to save your life I might destroy it. Oh, think, think what must have been my anguish! Think, how—Ah! never will you know a tenth of what I suffered in that brief space; or my relief and thankfulness when I saw him fall, and you stand scatheless!"

The young girl looked shyly at him; then, noting the love-light in his eyes, and the glowing flush upon his cheeks, the while he had poured out all that he had felt for her, an answering blush stole over her own fair cheek; while a coy, dainty little smile seemed to flit airily around her mouth, setting into little dimples first here then there; in like manner as a ray of light, reflected from a mirror, will dance co-quettishly to and fro in obedience to the hand that moves the glass.

There was silence for a space, she gazing downwards at the water, but now and then stealing a shy glance at her companion.

Then another line of thought passed over her mind and shadowed her face for a moment.

"I wonder," she said with touching innocence, "what people see in me to like so much? I fear it is not always well that this should he. It was that which led Zelus"—she shivered at the name— "to thrust himself upon, and at last threaten me, and has placed you in danger for having slain him. It is very strange! To like, to love, should mean naught but happiness and loving-kindness and innocent delight; yet here it has led a man to attempt an awful crime, and has placed others in great peril."

"It was not *love* on that man's part," said Leonard, savagely, between his teeth. "At least, not the sort of love that urged *me* on, that has guided me—even as the unwinding of a clue leads the traveller through the maze—to the side of her I loved and worshipped in my visions. Mine is not the love that could ever do its object hurt; that could ever—"

He paused abruptly, seeing her glance up at him with a look of wonder on her face.

"You love me?" she exclaimed. "But that is past believing! 'Tis but a few days since you first saw me. You cannot know what I am really like! How then can you love me? I love my father because he has cared for me and loved me all my life; I love Zonella—and—and—other friends, because I have known them for so long, and they have been kind and good to me. How can you yet tell that you will love me? Perchance when you know me better you may even come to hate me."

"Oh! Ulama! What is that you say?" he said impetuously. "You cannot mean it! You are playing with me! But it is cruel play! The love I mean is not such as the slow growth of a child's affection for a parent or a girl-friend. It is a swift, resistless passion, that centres on one being above all others in the world, and says, 'This one only do I love; this one possesses all my heart and soul! From this one I can never swerve—my love will end only when my heart no longer beats; I cannot live without it.' Such a love bursts forth spontaneously from the heart, as does a tiny spring from the earth's bosom and that, when once it has found vent, for ever bubbles up fresh and clear and pure, and, commencing in a little rill, increases to a torrent whose force no power can stem. *That* is the love I mean; and 'tis such a love I bear for you, Ulama. Can you not understand something of all this?

"I know not," replied the maiden in a low voice, and glancing timidly at him. "You frighten me a little—or you would, but that I like you too well to feel afraid of you—but—I have no knowledge of such love as you describe."

"But, you have *heard* of a love that far exceeds mere friend-ship—far stronger than affection?"

"Y-es. I have *heard* of it; and—ridiculed it as fiction. Yet—if you affirm its truth, and in your own person have experienced it—I must fain believe you, for I know you would not say what is not true. But"—here she sagely shook her head— "though my ears receive your words, the time has not yet come when they have reached my heart."

Leonard seized her hand.

"But, meanwhile, I have not offended you, Ulama?" he asked entreatingly. "You will let me love you? Indeed, I am powerless to help it. And you will try to—to—like me—ah, you have said you do like me already. Will you not try to love me a little?"

"Nay," she frankly answered, "you would not surely have me *try*? What sort of love would that be that we had to *try* to bring into being—to force upon an unresponsive heart? You have said that it should burst forth spontaneously. I scarcely understand when you speak thus."

Leonard sighed.

"You are right, Ulama, as you ever are; and I am wrong; but my love makes me impatient. I will not expect too much of you. I will wait with such content as is in me to command until your gentle heart shall beat in unison with mine; and something in me tells me that one day it will."

Just then they heard the voice of some one calling to them, and, looking round, they saw Jack Templemore and Zonella, with sev-eral others, coming towards them in another boat.

When they were within speaking distance, Jack said that Monella had sent him to tell Leonard he wished to speak to him; Leonard accordingly took up the oars and rowed the barge slowly to shore. There he left Ulama with the party, and proceeded in search of Monella who, he had been told, was awaiting him upon a terrace that overlooked the lake.

Here Leonard found him seated with a field-glass in his hand. Monella turned and looked searchingly at the young man, who felt himself colouring under the other's glance.

"I love not to seem to spy upon your acts, my son," Monella began gravely, "but when I caught sight of you in yonder boat holding the hand of the princess, the daughter of the king, who is our kind and gracious host, I could not well do otherwise than seek a talk with you. I fear you have not well considered what you do."

At this rebuke Leonard coloured up still more, albeit the words were spoken with evident kindness. For that very reason, probably, they sank the deeper. It was the first time anything savouring of reproof to him had fallen from Monella's lips; and, up to that moment, its possibility had seemed remote; and now the young man deeply felt the fact that the other should have thought it necessary.

"I think I know what you would say," he answered in a low voice. "I feel I have been wrong—guilty of thoughtlessness, presumption, and seemingly of breach of confidence. I understand what is in your mind. Yet let me say at once that so far little—practically nothing—has been said, and nothing more shall be—unless—you can tell me I dare hope. But oh, my good friend, you who have treated me always as a son, and shown such sympathy and kindness towards me—who have known of my half-formed aspirations, and the ideas that led me on and ended in my coming here, and encouraged me in those ideas—who have learned that in the king's daughter I have found the living embodiment of the central figure of all my dreamings—you surely will not now turn upon me and tell me I must stifle all my feelings, and—give—up—the hopes—that had arisen—in my heart?" And Leonard sank wearily into a seat.

Then, for the first time realising his actual position, how next to impossible it was that the king would regard with favour his pretensions, he placed his hands before his face and groaned aloud.

Monella rose, and, going to him, laid his hand kindly upon his shoulder.

"I might bring all the arguments and platitudes of the 'worldly-wise' to bear on you," he said, "but I forbear; and I know they will not weigh with you. Moreover, it is undeniable that the circumstances are unusual and unlooked-for. But they do not justify you in forgetting what you owe to a kingly host and—I may add—to others; to us, your friends, for instance. You know, also, that our position here is critical; there is trouble brewing in the land. If the king should have reason to believe that one of us has abused his confidence in one matter, he may lose his trust in all, as touching other, and far more weighty matters—matters that may affect even his own personal security; to say nothing of our own lives, and those of many of his subjects. Therefore—"

Leonard sprang up and looked at him imploringly.

"For pity's sake say no more," he said, "or I shall begin to hate myself. I understand—only too well. Trust me—if you will; if you feel you can; if you have not lost confidence. You shall not have further reason for complaint."

Monella took Leonard's hand in his and pressed it affectionately.

"'Tis well, my son," he said. "I have full confidence, and will trust you. And you, on your side, must trust me. I may have opportunity to sound the king, and, if it so happen, you may count on me to say and do all that my friendship for you may dictate—and that will not be a little."

Leonard wrung the other's hand and tried to thank him, but a burst of emotion overcame him, and he turned away. When he again looked round he was alone.

17
The Fight on the Hillside

It had become the custom of the two young men to go every morning, when the atmosphere was clear, to a height at one end of the valley, from which a view could be obtained over the whole country surrounding that end of Roraima. The spot was a level table of rock under a picturesque group of fir-trees—for on the upper cliffs fir-trees were numerous—and from it, looking in the direction farthest from the mountain, the view was grand in the extreme; while, on the other side of them was the great valley or basin in which lay the lake and the city of Manoa.

It would be but labour lost to attempt to give an adequate idea of the prospect over which the eye could travel on a clear day, when one stood upon this giddy height. It extended to an almost illimitable distance; for, when one looked beyond the surrounding mountains of the Roraima range, there were no more hills to break the view till it reached the far distant Andes, had these been visible. Indeed, it was said that they were visible on a few days in the year; but, if that were so, it would perhaps be rather as an effect in the nature of a mirage than what is usually understood by an actual view of the far-away mountains. But nearer at hand, in other directions were mountain ridges and summits in seemingly endless succession, piled up in extraordinary confusion. From Roraima, as the highest of all, one could look down, to some extent, upon the others. Myrlanda was upon the other side, but Marima, and others of the strange group, lay before the eye, and one could see the woods and lakes upon their summits; but enough could not be seen to enable the spectator to decide whether they might be inhabited or not.

The beauty of the expanse of tropical vegetation immediately below was indeed marvellous. Here the explorers gazed down upon the tops of the trees of the gloomy forest that girdled the mountain (though not that part through which they had made their way with so much wearying, but dogged perseverance), and lo! it was a veritable garden of flowers of brilliant hue! For the trees beneath which they had crept, like ants among the stems of a field of clover, were gorgeous above in their display of blossoms, while shutting out the light from those who walked below.

Here and there, amid the green, the great cascades and torrents from the mountain side dashed impetuously from rock to rock; the streams that were in fact some of the feeders of the greatest of all rivers, the mighty Amazon; that river of wondrous mysteries, that pursues its course of four thousand miles through the plains of Brazil, and finds its way round at last into the Atlantic, there to hurl the volume of its waters with such force into the sea, that even the ocean waters are pushed aside to make a path for them hundreds of miles from land!

Here, upon the table of rock, in full view of one of the grandest and most eloquent natural panoramas it is possible for the mind of man to conceive, Leonard and Templemore stood the morning following the former's interview with Monella, looking out upon the scene. A high wind, of bracing and exhilarating freshness, blew in their faces, rushed with a roar through the branches above them, swaying the great trees to and fro, and then, seeming to tear off across the valley at one leap, continued its wild course amongst the trees on the heights that lined the further side. Leonard, on turning to look across the lake, saw Ergalon advancing up the slope and making signs to him. He drew Jack's attention to the signals, and they both descended the terraces of rock below to meet him. Here all was quiet; they were sheltered from the gusts of wind; the roar of the gale no longer met their ears.

All the time they had been in the city they had had a guard. It consisted of a file of soldiers with an officer, and they followed the two young men in all their walks, movements, journeys, never thrusting themselves on their attention, yet always ready to assist and defend them, if occasion should arise. Monella, also, had an escort whenever he went out. He had particularly enjoined on the other two never to stir abroad without their rifles, and this injunction, though they did not always see its necessity, they implicitly observed.

They had not seen much of Ergalon of late; he had attached himself more particularly to Monella, and had, in fact, become his particular attendant. Monella had trusted him so far as to explain to him something of the secrets of the firearms, and had instructed him in the loading of them in case circumstances should arise in which his assistance might be needed. Accordingly, when Leonard saw him coming up the hillside and signifying that he wished to speak to them, he at once called Templemore and left the ledge where they had been standing.

Soon they saw their guard approaching with Ergalon in advance of them, and, following them, Monella, who came on leisurely from ledge to ledge, occasionally giving a glance behind him.

The hillside was marked out in terraces, or tables of rock, most of them covered with greensward and fringed at the sides with belts of trees. Ergalon, who had taken his stand below, made signs to the two to come down to him, and, when they had descended within hearing, he addressed them.

"The lord Monella has sent me to warn you to await him here and to be ready for a contest. There is trouble afoot."

"But why wait here?" asked Jack. "We will go down to him at once."

Ergalon shook his head.

"No," he said. "He particularly desired that you would await him here."

"So be it; if you are sure you rightly understood him. But tell us, friend Ergalon, what all this means."

Ergalon explained that Coryon had unexpectedly dispatched a large force of his soldiers to capture the three strangers. They had hoped to surprise them without giving time for others of the king's soldiers to lend their aid. But he (Ergalon) had, through a former comrade who was still one of Coryon's people, attained intimation of the intended movement, and had been able thus to warn Monella.

"So the lord Monella," he explained, "sent on your guard in advance, and then himself walked up the hill towards you that they might see him. Thus he hoped to draw Coryon's people away from the palace and the houses to this place, where, he says, it will be better to make a stand and fight them, since thus no other persons Neill be injured in the encounter."

It was strange, but all who spoke of Monella, or to him, gave him some title of honour or respect. Ergalon called him "lord." Even Dakla, at the meeting in the king's council chamber—spite of his insolent swagger towards the king—had been awed by this man's look into addressing him by the equivalent in their language of "sir."

"How many are there of them?" asked Jack.

"Oh, a hundred—or perhaps more. But the lord Monella has said their number matters not; and he sent me to the king to beg that none of his soldiers should interfere. 'They would only be in the way,' he said. He sent these extra things for you. See." And he showed a parcel of cartridges he had brought with him.

"Good," said Jack. "He is quite right. That's all we wanted; we can answer for the rest. More soldiers would only be in the way; and some of them would be pretty sure to get hurt, if not killed outright—and all for nothing. I think I see Monella's idea. It is"—turning to Elwood— "to take up our position here and shoot them down as they come across this wide terrace just below us. Not a man of them will ever cross that stretch alive."

"Here are your guards," observed Ergalon. "The lord Monella desired that you should place them somewhere where they would be out of the way, but within call."

"Let them get on to this next ledge, then, just behind us. There they will have a fine view of everything. Did these people think to surprise us, do you think, friend Ergalon?"

"No doubt. Your habit of coming here of a morning has been noted, I suspect, and they had intended, I imagine, to creep round and get up through the woods unseen. But the lord Monella, being warned by me, went up on a high rock, where he could see them in the distance; when they saw they were observed by him, they gave up that plan and came straight on."

"I see. Well, we owe you something for having warned us, friend."

"It is nothing," Ergalon answered simply. "My life was forfeited that day, and you spared me; and through the lord Monella and the princess, I gained the king's pardon. I owe you all my service."

By this time the guards and their officer had arrived, and were placed by Ergalon on a terrace above and behind that on which the two were standing.

"We like it not, this mode of yours—putting us in the background, out of danger, while you stand up in front," observed the officer; "we consent only because the lord Monella so desires it. They are many, but we should not shrink; and others from the king's palace would soon come to our assistance."

"Yes, yes, good Abla. We have no misgivings of your courage. But you could do no good with so few men—they are more than ten to one, I hear—and your men would but impede us. Besides, it will give them a lesson for the future, if we deal with them ourselves, unaided."

Abla bowed and walked away unwillingly, as one who is bound to obey orders, but does so against his will.

Monella now came in view, and was soon standing by their side. After a few words of explanation, he said gravely,

"They thought to have surprised us all three up here; but, when they saw they had failed in that, they took a bold course and came straight on. Now that means, in effect, an open challenge to the king. It means," he continued with increased earnestness, "civil war. Civil war, you understand, has therefore broken out in the land—unless we nip it in the bud, *here*, *now*, as we can, if we show no untimely hesitation. These men are scoundrels of the serpent's brood; cruel, bloodthirsty tools of the human fiends behind them. They deserve no mercy, no consideration. Let none be shown to them! My plan is simply to shoot them down the instant they appear on that ledge below us. They must climb up in front; there is no way round it, nor any means of getting to the height above us. Therefore, they must cross that piece of open ground. One word more. The chief, Dakla, leads them. Do not fire at him. I wish to take him alive, if possible; he will make our best ambassador hereafter."

Under such conditions the battle could not be a long one. Monella had chosen his ground skilfully, so as to make the utmost

of the advantage firearms gave him. The black-coated myrmidons
of Coryon scaled the fatal terrace only to be shot down the moment that they came in sight. There were only four or five places
where they could climb up and, at these, not more than two men
could pass together. Those who reached the top and escaped a bullet,
turned back when they heard the explosions of the firearms, saw
the flashes and the smoke, saw also their comrades fall. Others of
those below who could see nothing of what was going on, swarmed
up in their places, only to fall or turn back at once in like manner;
till, in a short time, every man had been up and witnessed the
ghastly sight of the dead and wounded lying around, and had satisfied himself that not one could cross that level piece of rock to
come near their foes. Finally, the survivors were all seized with
panic when one of the last to show his head above the ridge came
back crying out that "the white demons were coming down after
them." At this, all those who were unhurt turned and fled. But many
had fallen, dead or wounded, and lay at the foot of the rock they
had climbed up only to be instantly shot down. Above, on the terrace
itself, but at one side, stood Dakla and one of his subordinates. These
had been amongst the first to appear above the ledge, and had moved
aside to let the men form into line up on the reek; but now they were
left alone, and, when Monella quietly descended from the rock
above, they had the mortification of seeing all their men who were
capable of running disappear in frantic terror down the hillside.

Then he who stood by Dakla made a rush at Monella with up-
lifted sword, thinking, since he seemed to be unarmed, that he
would fall an easy prey; but the man fell with a pistol ball in his
breast ere he had gone half way to meet Monella.

"Now yield, Dakla," Monella called to the other. "It is useless
either to fight or run."

"We will see to that," Dakla exclaimed savagely. "If thou be man,
and not demon, this sword shall find thine heart." And he too made
a sudden rush. But, before he had gone three yards, the sword flew
from his hand and his arm dropped useless by his side. Monella
had shot him in the arm.

"Thou see'st," he said coldly, as he now approached the crest-
fallen chief, "how ill-advised thou hast been not to give heed to all

my warnings. I could have slain thee earlier in the fight; I could have killed thee now, as I did thy friend there; but I have spared thy life. It is not for thine own sake, but that thou mayest bear a message to thy master, and witness to him of that which thou hast seen and warn him once more of the futility of warring against us, the allies of the king. Dost thou understand?"

The other cast a murderous scowl upon Monella, but made no answer for a moment. Then, after reflection, he said in a dogged, surly tone,

"So be it. But thou must give thy message quickly and let me go; for thou hast hurt me sore and the blood flows fast—"

"We will see to thy wound," Monella replied composedly. "Let me bind it up till we get to the king's palace; there it shall be seen to farther."

And Dakla, reluctantly, and with an ill grace, submitted to have his wound bound up by his enemy, who, before commencing, took away the other's dagger.

"I cannot trust thee with these playthings," he observed. "Thou art of the wolf tribe, Dakla."

Meanwhile, the officer and men of their guard had come down to the lower terrace, with Templemore and Elwood, and were looking in awe and horror upon the outcome of the fight—if so one-sided an encounter could be so called. On Monella and the two young men they gazed in wonder; and, gradually, they drew away from them in fear, from that moment treating them with even greater deference than before.

Monella despatched Abla to summon more soldiers from the king's palace to bring down the dead and wounded; and himself set about attending to the latter, first handing Dakla over to Templemore.

"Look you!" said Jack to his prisoner, "if you attempt to escape, I shall not kill you, but hurt your other arm; and, if that does not stop you, I shall hurt your leg, and I know that that will. Do you follow me?"

Dakla nodded a sour assent; then stood looking with evident surprise at the trouble Monella was now taking with some of his late enemies. Such singular behaviour he did not understand, and he shrugged his shoulders in contempt.

When, after a time, more soldiers, with some officers, arrived upon the scene, these were at once set to work to bear the dead and wounded down the hill. Monella followed with his friends and Dakla. The noise of the firing had brought out great crowds of people, who were now massed about the palace waiting to receive them. They had watched the precipitate flight of the survivors of the soldiers of Coryon, and rejoiced greatly at their defeat. But, when they saw the dead and wounded, and that Dakla was himself a prisoner, and heard that not one had been hurt upon the other side, their astonishment was complete.

The king himself, with some of his ministers and officials, came out to meet the victors; and his gratitude and emotion, when he noted all these things and greeted Monella and his friends, were profuse and heartfelt.

"Ye have indeed rendered us a service," he exclaimed, "and taught Coryon a lesson he will do well to take to heart. I feared me greatly that harm would come to ye, and that war would follow in the land."

"Nay, we have laid the dogs of war, I trust, at any rate, for the present," Monella returned, with a grave smile. "They will not attack us further, I opine, nor brave thee in the future in this rebellious fashion."

Then they entered the palace, and Ulama came forward to welcome them, with Zonella and many more.

"We have been in such trouble about you," she said, the tears standing in her tender eyes, "ever since they told us that over a hundred of Coryon's people had gone up the rocks to take you. And we heard the noise of the thunder-wands, and were in great fear, till they told us that your enemies were fleeing. Then we looked out and saw them rushing madly down the hill, throwing away their spears, and their helmets, and even fighting one another in their haste to scramble down the rocks. Then Abla came and told us you were all safe, and then—"

"Then," said Zonella, "you sat down and wept." And at that Ulama laughed.

"I fear it is true," she said.

18
The Legend of Mellenda

Monella's anticipations of what would follow the severe lesson
they had given Coryon's followers turned out to be well founded.
For when Dakla, with his arm in a sling, revisited his master, bearing a message from the king, the conditions offered were accepted.

Dakla had been straightly charged that these terms would have
to be submitted to; if not that his master and all his followers would
be starved into submission. They would be confined to their own
colony, supplies of food refused, and any of their number leaving
their retreat would be killed at sight.

The conditions imposed were that not merely the three strangers, but all the "lay" inhabitants were to be free from molestation
by Coryon's people; and that no more "blood-tax" was to be levied.

After many journeys to and fro, and much delay, Dakla at last
announced that Coryon agreed to the conditions for a time—for
four months. After that, their great festival would be coming on,
and—well, time would show.

"It is only a truce," said Monella, with a sigh, to his two young
friends. "I would it had been permanent; but it will give us time,
and the opportunity of shaping out our course. The people will have
a respite from the terrible fear that now is ever with them; and,
short of engaging in a protracted civil conflict, for which the people
are not yet prepared, I see not what better could have been arranged."

They were thus now able to move about more freely, and without a guard; their rifles, too, could be left behind when they went
abroad; though Monella had counselled that they should always

carry their revolvers; for he feared they were not altogether safe from treachery, or from some fanatical outbreak on the part of certain of the priests' adherents.

Thus Templemore and Elwood were now able to mingle more freely with the populace and to see more of their social life. And, wherever they went, they were well received, and treated with both confidence and respect. They visited the houses of people of all classes, from the palaces of the nobles to the dwellings of the peasantry, if so the lower classes might be called. There were, however, no poor in the country, in the ordinary sense of the word. The crops grown were supplied to all alike; every one had plenty to eat, and plenty of clothes to wear, and well-built houses to live in. And, beyond these requisites, there was little in the land to pine for. There were forests, and from these all were free to cut wood for fuel; the electric light was laid on to all alike. The water they required they supplied themselves with from the lake, or from one or other of the streams that everywhere gushed forth from the rocks above. Of shops there were none; but there was a market-place, and a sort of market or exchange was held there once a week. Even this, however, was falling into disuse. There was a currency; and there were many kinds of coins; but they were seldom used. They were of ancient make and were preserved rather as curiosities, seemingly, than for use. There was so little that the people wanted, either to buy or sell, that a simple system of barter sufficed for practically all their needs.

Elwood and Templemore, as they came to know all these things, and gained experience of the simple good-nature of the people, felt increased indignation and resentment against the priests. They saw that the horrible tyranny of these men had turned a land that might have been a realm of perfect peace and goodwill, into one where constant dread and hopeless misery and suffering had become so common, that all seemed helplessly resigned to it.

One day, when the two were in a boat with Ulama and Zonella, Kalaima, and others, Templemore, who had been talking of these matters, asked whether the state of things they had seen had been of long duration.

The reply came from Zonella.

"Ever since the time of the great Mellenda. So we are told. It is the punishment sent by the Great Spirit upon the people for their ingratitude to him."

"And who was Mellenda?" asked Elwood.

"What! You ask who was Mellenda? But I forgot; of course, you have not been here very long, and cannot know our history and legends."

"I have been prying about more in your museums than has my friend," Jack observed, "and I have learned something of Mellenda. But I know nothing of any legend. Pray let us hear it."

"Yes, tell us about it," Leonard urged. "I like fine old legends and tales of wonder."

"Ask the princess to tell you."

"No, no, Zonella," Ulama interposed. "You began it; you finish it. Besides, you are more learned in such things than I am."

"Very well," Zonella said resignedly. "I can only give it as I know it. If you want further details, you must go to the museum, or ask Colenna, the High Chamberlain, who is a very learned man. Only I do not wish you to ridicule it"—this to the two young men— "for, though I call it a legend, yet it is history; and all our people implicitly believe it. You could not offend them more than by treating it lightly or affecting to disbelieve it. I give you that as a caution, more particularly," she added, looking mischievously at Jack, "for I know that you are very much inclined to scepticism in such things."

"I will promise to be very good, and to make no frivolous remarks," was Jack's laughing answer.

"Then you must know," Zonella began, "that we deem Mellenda the greatest of our kings; that is, of our later kings. Our ancient line of kings before him had made Manoa the greatest, the most powerful, and the richest country of the world. These mountains that you have seen around us were all islands in a great lake—the lake of Parima. Its waters extended to the great mountains that we can sometimes see from the highest points about Manoa—far, far away. But over those, and over lands in every direction, our nation held sway. These islands were our chief fastnesses, and this one, Manoa, being the highest and the most naturally favoured of them

all, was the seat of government, and its city was the capital to which
were brought all the wealth and the most valued productions of
the other countries that formed part of its empire.

"But, after many mighty kings had lived and died, a weakness
seemed to fall upon the people. They were defeated in battle; provinces revolted, and many distant parts of the empire were lost,
passing under other kings. At that time, it is said, our kings and
nobles and chiefs among the nation were too much given to feasting and enjoyment; and, it is declared, they began cruelly to oppress the weaker of the people. And a change came over the religion. Up to then all had worshipped only one Great Spirit, who
was said to be a good Spirit—the great ruler of all spirits, in fact,
and his priests were called 'Children of the Light.' Their rule—what
they taught—was gentle; it is recorded that they were men of peace
and of great—very, very great—wisdom. But another religion had
been introduced, coming, it is believed, from some of the lands
that had been conquered; and this was the exact opposite of the
old one. Its votaries and high priests called themselves 'Children
of the Night'; they worshipped, not one God, but many strange and
terrible gods; their priests, also, were thought to possess great
wisdom, but of an evil kind. They taught that there was but one
way to escape the power of the Spirits of Darkness, and that was
by propitiating them by constant sacrifices; and they killed many
people at their festivals to give them to their gods.

"Then Mellenda came to the throne. He was the only son of the
last of the ancient line of kings. While young he had travelled far
and gained much knowledge in strange countries; and he had already, as general of some of his father's armies, defeated the enemies of the country, and regained some of the lost provinces. His
father was killed in battle, and Mellenda immediately set about
plans for reviving the old power and recovering the former empire
of the nation. He taught, too, that the White religion was the true
religion, and he made endeavours to put down the other. But he
was absent for long periods at a time, upon distant expeditions,
from which, it is true, he always returned victorious; but, while he
was away, establishing peace and order in some distant province,
the Dark Priests were craftily at work undermining his authority

at home. However, for a long time, nothing came of their plottings, and Mellenda reigned for several hundred years—"

"That's a long time," Jack interrupted, regardless of his promise.

"For several hundred years," repeated Zonella with a reproving look at the interrupter, "which was not very long, considering that his father had reigned for fifteen hundred years, and was then cut off, in the flower of his age, by an accident in battle. He (Mellenda) had restored peace at last throughout the whole empire; reformed the style of living, himself setting an example of great simplicity; and his wisdom and justice and kindness of heart had made him revered and loved wherever the name of Manoa was known. Then, finally, he married a princess he was passionately fond of, named Elmonta, and had four children, upon whom, they say, he lavished the most tender love. But some occasion arose for him to leave Manoa once more, to visit a distant part of his great empire. There was a treaty of alliance to be made with another monarch, or some such matter of importance. He sailed away and returned after a long absence, to find that Coryon—"

"Coryon!" exclaimed Jack, once more forgetful of his promises.

"Yes, Coryon, the same Coryon, as is believed, that we have here in the land to-day. He had seized upon the government and gained over a vast number of the most dissolute and discontented spirits to his side. He was then, as now, the chief of the Dark Brotherhood, or Children of the Night. All the crowd of idle, self-indulgent nobles and men of wealth, but of loose life, among the people, whom Mellenda had rebuked and curbed, broke out and joined Coryon's revolt; and they actually seized upon Elmonta, Mellenda's queen, and his children, and offered them as sacrifices to their gods. Coryon set up a king of his own choosing; and, when Mellenda returned, he found his wife and children dead, and the government in the hands of a puppet king controlled by Coryon, who threatened him with death if he landed and fell into his hands. Such was the message sent out to Mellenda when he arrived in sight of our island on his return, successful in the mission that had called him away, and impatient to get back to his wife and children. He had with him a great fleet of vessels; and, though the revolt had spread to the other islands, he could, perhaps, have found followers enough in other parts of the empire to have regained his throne, had he been so minded. But he was broken-hearted, and said that, since his wife and children were no longer living, he had nothing left to fight for, and cared not to take part in a civil war with his own people. Instead, he decreed that their punishment should be that he (Mellenda) would go away and leave them for many ages to suffer under the lash of the foul religion they had supported; till all who had sinned against him saw their wicked error, when he would return to punish finally the Dark Priests and those who still wilfully supported them. Then, and for ever afterwards, there should be peace and happiness and justice throughout the land for all his people.

"So Mellenda sailed away, and was never seen or heard of more. Not long after his departure came the great sinking of the waters, and the lake of Parima disappeared. This the better-disposed inhabitants left here regarded as a special punishment for their allowing Coryon to usurp the government and drive away the great, good, and wise Mellenda. And they rose up against Coryon and the king he had set up. But the crafty priest had obtained too strong a position for the movement to succeed. Moreover, he managed to pacify a part of his opponents in a strange way. He declared he had not put to death all Mellenda's children, and produced a boy, who, it is said, was recognised by those who ought to know as one of Mellenda's children. This child he promised to place upon the throne; and afterwards he did so.

"The nation, shut off from all the world, has much decreased in numbers, and is now unknown where it was once all-powerful. For centuries, it is said, the surrounding country was but a chaos of swamp and mud. By degrees there grew up vegetation, and finally trees that, in time, became thick, tangled forests that could not be penetrated. Thus, for long ages, we have been cut off from all the other peoples of the world. Some parties were sent out, hundreds of years ago, to explore the surrounding country; but some never returned, and those who did brought back such terrible accounts of awful woods haunted by fearful creatures, and of deserts beyond, inhabited only by black demons, that it was considered better to keep the country here entirely to ourselves. So I believe the only known way that led out into the woods was sealed up for good; and thus ended the lost attempt to communicate with the outside world.

"Many of the White Priests fled to Mellenda's vessels, and were taken away with him when he departed; but the others, including their chief, Sanaima, retired to Myrlanda, where they have ever since maintained themselves.

"That is the story of Mellenda, and of how he left us, and of what befell the proud city of Manoa after his departure. When he will come back we know not; but some old prophecies obtain amongst the people according to which the time of his return is very near, if it is not indeed overpast."

"His return!" said Jack. "You surely would not have us understand that you expect this venerable old fossil to return, in the flesh, to trouble himself about the present state of the descendants of his ungrateful people?"

Zonella stared.

"Why, of course we do!" she answered. "There is not a man or a woman—scarcely a child of a few years old—that has not been taught to believe in it."

"I should think so," Ulama exclaimed, almost indignantly. "We all know it will be so; we believe it absolutely."

"But," said Jack, "how long ago do you reckon all this took place?"

"About two thousand years," Zonella replied, after a brief, but apparently careful, calculation, counting up on her fingers.

"Two thousand years! And you—you two sensible young people—tell us you expect to see this badly-treated, but respectable, old gentleman turn up again, just much as usual, I suppose, after two thousand years!"

"Why not?" Ulama asked. "We have Coryon and Sanaima, both said to be older than that."

"Yes—but"—looking at Leonard— "I fancy that is like the Pharoahs of old, you know, where there was always a Pharoah on the throne, though kings were born and died. It would be easy to keep up a farce of that sort where, as here, the 'High Priest,' black or white, is so seldom visible—always in the background."

"But if the king is three hundred and forty, may it not be possible to live to two thousand, or more? I can point out many men of more than five hundred in the king's palace," observed Zonella.

The gentle Ulama, even, looked somewhat offended.

"We do not question the wonderful things you tell us about the world outside," she said. "Why should you question what we know to be true?"

"It seems to me," said Leonard, "that it all depends upon the virtues of the 'Plant of Life.' Now, if that herb, or plant, or whatever it is, really has the qualities attributed to it, why, the rest is easy enough."

"I admit that," Jack said, laughing. "When once that is conceded, a man may just as easily live to five thousand years. Only, even in that case, I see a difficulty. How would Mellenda get the necessary 'Plant of Life' away from here?"

"The White Priests who went away with him would not be likely to leave their secret behind," explained Zonella. "Besides, it is specially stated in our historical manuscripts—so Colenna has told me—that those who went out from the island for long periods— governors of distant provinces and the like—not only took a large supply of the dried plant with them, but seeds that they might grow it; and in some places they found the plant do well; though they kept its virtues a secret from the peoples they went amongst These things would be known to Mellenda and to the White Priests who went away with him; and, probably, they settled in a place where they knew the plant was being grown."

"Were that so, it would explain something of the former far-reaching fame and power of a small nation of islanders like these," said Leonard. "The secret of such a plant—the rapid increase of population when there were so few deaths in proportion—would of course give them a long pull over other nations."

"As to the question whether we seriously expect Mellenda to return to us," resumed Zonella, "in the large museum you will see one of his suits of armour, his banner, and a celebrated sword of his, all kept bright and ready for use and well preserved. They are kept there waiting for him."

"I saw them," Jack remarked. "He must have been a big fine man, if that suit fitted him. But, to go back to the son of this great king, said to have been saved after all, and then put on the throne; did he have any descendants?"

Zonella nodded.

"There have been five kings in the direct line since."

"I see. So that the present king is a great-great-great-grandson of the great Mellenda," put in Ulaina.

"I think it was rather fortunate you managed as you did when you came here," Zonella said after a pause; "for, if Coryon had been the first to know of you strangers being in the country, he would have striven in every way to have killed or captured you. They say he is a firm believer in the early coming of Mellenda, and is in mortal terror about it."

Jack was silent awhile, and then he observed drily, "Well, all I can say is that I should very much like to see the good gentleman, if he is still about; and I only hope and wish he will arrive while we are here. If he has been travelling around all these years, by this time he must know a thing or two! I wonder whether he will come in a balloon!"

19
Hopes and Fears

Amongst other advantages of the peace or truce that had been arranged with the mysterious Coryon, one was that Elwood and Templemore were free to visit the canyon and the caves where their reserve stores lay, and assure themselves that they were all safe. To do this they had to arrange to be away one night, since it was a day's journey each way. That night they passed in the cavern—which they had named "Monella Cave" in honour of their friend; the canyon itself they called "Fairy Valley"—and their camp equipage being all found intact where they had hidden it away, they had everything at hand for making themselves comfortable. They found, on examination, that the stone that closed the entrance was in the same position as when they had left it. Having removed the wooden bars, they rolled it to one side, and looked out into the gloomy depths of Roraima Forest.

From this outlook Templemore turned back with a shudder of disgust.

"How I hate that forest!" he exclaimed. "How miserable it seems out there! Verily it is wonderful, if you come to think of it, that we ever had the patience and perseverance to cut our way through to this place."

"We never should have done so, but for Monella's influence," observed Leonard. "How strange it all seems, doesn't it? Now that we are back here, we could almost think all we have been through a dream. One thing is certain; no other party of explorers would ever work their way through this wood as we did; they would get disheartened before the end of the first week. Nor could they possibly do any good by persevering, unless they had that to guide them which Monella had. What is that piece of white over there?"

And Leonard indicated a white patch upon a tree-trunk at the edge of the clearing.

Templemore took out his glasses and looked through them.

"It's a piece of paper," he cried excitedly. "Some one's been here! We must go out and inquire into this!" The ladder was quickly got out, and they hurried down it and across the clearing to the tree that bore the unexpected *affiche*. But, though the paper must have been purposely nailed in its place it was blank; on opening it, however, they found a few straight lines that formed a somewhat vague resemblance to the letter M.

"Matava has been here!" Leonard cried out. "All he can do in the writing line is to make some marks that mean M—his own initial, you know. Poor fellow! Fancy his venturing here to seek for us!"

The paper had been folded many times, the "M" being in the inside; and it had been nailed just under an overhanging piece of bark, as a protection from the weather.

"He must have executed this elaborate piece of penmanship at 'Monella Lodge'," said Jack, "and brought it with him in case his journey here should be in vain. He's a good fellow! Knowing, as we do, how he and all his tribe abhor this wood and the mountain, we can appreciate the devotion that led him to screw up his courage so far. And then to have come for nothing! It's too bad, poor chap! What a pity we could not have got down here and seen him! Plainly he had some hope we might return, or he would not have left this simple yet ingeniously contrived message for us!"

"His hope would be but a faint one at best," Leonard replied gravely. "Having been here and found the entrance fast closed, and after our failing to make any signals, as arranged, I fear he will carry back an alarming tale to Georgetown."

"I fear so too, Leonard," Jack assented very seriously. "They will be terribly alarmed about us; worse than if he had gone straight back without coming here."

That evening, after they had cooked their evening meal, they sat by the smouldering fire, both silent and both thoughtful. Jack smoked away moodily at his pipe; Leonard was absolutely idle, except that he turned his eyes, now on the glow of failing daylight overhead, then down at the scene around him.

Each knew what was in the other's mind; yet neither liked to be the first to speak of it. But at last Jack spoke.

"It's no use blinking the fact, Leonard," he began, "that this visit of Matava here and the account he is sure to carry back is a serious matter. Our friends will be more than alarmed; they will, perhaps, give us up for dead. This raises the whole question again, What are we going to do here, how long are we going to stay, and what about getting back? We can't stay here for ever—at least, I certainly don't mean to. I don't like the idea of going away and leaving you here. Where are we drifting to?"

Leonard was gloomy. He had been so more or less ever since that conversation with Monella about Ulama. For a few minutes he made no reply; then said, with a tinge of bitterness in his tone,

"You must wait awhile, Jack. I am not prepared to say yet, but—it may be I shall be ready to clear out soon with you."

Jack raised his eyebrows and gave a brief, but keen, glance at his friend. Then he smoked on stolidly for a while and ruminated.

"There's one who will never go back with us," presently he went on "and that's Monella. He spoke truly when he said he should never return to 'civilisation.' He seems to have resolved to make his home here for the future. He is now the king's right hand—his 'guide, counsellor, and friend,' with him constantly, except when he's away in the place they call Myrlanda, on some mysterious business. And, perhaps, the oddest thing of all is that he is the most popular man at the court—even with those he has, in a sense, displaced. You would think there would be all kinds of envy, and hatred, and jealousy, and counter-plotting, and general 'ructions,' when a stranger, suddenly come from goodness knows where, stepped upon the scene and became straight away the favourite and confidant and counsellor of the king! Yet, the more he takes that character upon himself, the more they all seem to like him!"

"Who can help liking him?" Leonard sighed. "Who can help loving him? Even where he reproves, he does it so tenderly you only love him the more for it. How can any one feel jealous, or angry, or

envious with a man who behaves to all as he does? For myself I do
not wonder; he was born to be a leader of men, as I said long ago;
he has that magnetic attraction that makes a great commander—a
commander who inspires such devotion that thousands and hundreds of thousands are ready to give their lives for but a glance of
approval or a word of praise. There can't be many such men at this
moment in the world; there cannot have been many since the world
was made. But, when such a man appears, he quickly spreads his
influence around him."

Jack gave a little laugh; but not an ill-natured one.

"You are as full as ever of enthusiasm for your hero," he remarked, "though he has been a sort of cold shower-bath to you
lately, eh?"

Leonard coloured, and shifted uneasily on his seat. "How did
you know that?" he asked.

"I guessed it, old man. In fact, I saw the 'cold shower-bath' in
his eye that day—you know."

"Yes—perhaps you are not far out, Jack. However, I promised
to leave things in his hands, and there they must remain at present.
Of his regard for me I have no doubt whatever—or for us both. If
he cannot do the almost impossible, I shall accept my fate, and try
to bear it as well as may be. Let us say no more about it now."

Jack, who for all his usual habit of appearing somewhat unob-
servant, could see most things, thought he could have told his
friend of some one else who was displaying signs of unhappiness
under Monella's "cold shower-bath" treatment—Ulama, to wit. She
had become very quiet and grave of late; and, indeed, the fresh,
childish gaiety she had shown during the first few days after their
arrival had disappeared. But Jack discreetly decided to keep these
thoughts to himself, and let events take their course. He knew that
they were in the keeping of a head wiser and more far-seeing than
his own—Monella's. Of late they had seen comparatively little of
him; he was most of his time either closeted with the king, or had
gone, it was said, to Myrlanda, to visit Sanaima, the chief of the
"White Priests." On these occasions he would be away for two or
three days together. Yet, whenever either of the young men chanced
to run against him—or, if they met at the king's table—they found

no alteration in his manner. Indeed, he showed, if anything, increased kindliness in both his words and actions, often going out of his way to do some little thing, in a manner all his own, to show, before whoever might be present, his cordial feelings towards them. For the rest, he had the air of one whose mind is charged with anxious and weighty thoughts, and both Templemore and Elwood felt rather than knew that he was occupied with fears of trouble in the future.

One morning, a few days after the visit to the canyon, Monella invited Leonard to walk out with him, and they went together to the place they had named "Monella's Height."

The day was clear and bright, and a slight breeze came sighing through the tree-tops. The scene around was full of soft repose, soothing and curiously satisfying to the mind. But Leonard noticed it not to-day; his heart beat fast, and his colour came and went, for something in Monella's manner told him that he was about to hear a statement of moment on the subject that was always uppermost in his thoughts. He tried to brace himself to bear the worst, if it must come; but his effort was not too successful.

"My son," Monella presently began, "I promised to speak with you, when I could, upon the matter we talked about one day. Is your mind still the same concerning it?"

Was it? Did he need to ask? Leonard impulsively replied. And he launched into a rhapsody that need not here be given at length. Monella listened in silence till the young man had finished, and then went on,

"Have you considered whether your wish is a wise—a final one? That, were it granted, you must remain here for good? Never to return to your own people?"

"Why, never?" Leonard asked. "In the future—one day, perhaps—"

Monella shook his head.

"You must clearly understand," he said, "that that cannot be. I have told you all along that I never expected to return from my journey here; and now I know that I shall never leave this place. And you and your friend—you will have ere long to decide either to stay here for good, or leave for good. If you elect to go, the king will send you away rich—so rich that you will no more need to strive for wealth; if to stay, he will give you posts of honour where you can profitably employ yourselves in helping me in the great task I have set myself—the teaching of the true religion of the one great God to these my people; for"—he continued, when Leonard looked up at him in surprise— "it is true that I am one of this nation by descent, and that I have, therefore, 'after many days,' only wandered back to mine own people. But I have seen too much of the world outside to love it; my people desire to keep to themselves, and I can only, from what I have seen and experienced, confirm them in that wish. I cannot find it in my conscience to do otherwise. Therefore, we are resolved that there shall be no intercourse between us and the great world beyond. It is useless to say more upon the subject; it is settled beyond all reach of argument or discussion. Hence, it will be necessary for both you and your friend to decide whether to remain and cast in your lot with us for your whole future lives, or to say farewell and return—but not empty-handed—to your own people. It is a serious and weighty matter for you to decide; therefore should not be settled hastily. Nor is there any need for haste; take as long as you please to think it over. Wait awhile, till you have seen more of the place, and have come to know the people better. Or wait until"—here the speaker's voice became impressive well-nigh to sternness— "until I shall have stamped out this serpent brood that hath too long held this fair land in its loathsome coils. Then shall ye see a new era here—an era of peace, and cheerfulness, and godliness—and ye shall see that it is good to dwell in such a country."

"I do not believe that any amount of reflection can alter my wishes in this matter," Leonard answered earnestly. "Painful as the thought of never seeing my friends again would be, yet it would be still harder to leave here and never look again on her my heart has chosen for its queen—aye, for years before I saw her. No! Now that fate has led me to her, nothing in this world shall part us—if the decision rests with me."

Monella regarded the young man fixedly, and there were both affection and admiration in his glance. Very handsome Leonard looked, with the light in his open honest eyes, and the flush upon his cheek. Then Monella's look waxed overcast as from a passing shadow, and he made answer, with a sigh,

"Youth, with its hopes and aspirations, when they come from honest promptings, is always fair to look upon; more's the pity that these aspirations all lead to but one end—sorrow, and disappointment, and weariness. Verily, all is vanity, vanity! We travel by different roads, but we all arrive at the same goal." He looked dreamily away across the landscape to the far distant horizon; then continued, as though talking to himself: "Yet youth pleases, because it desires to live in love—and love is God and Heaven in one. It is the principal of the only two things—it and memory—we carry with us in our passage from this life to the next. Love and memory are two great indestructible attributes of the human soul. True, we take with us our 'character,' as it may be called, but that counts little, unless it be founded upon love. And memory is the ever-living witness showing forth whether our life here has been influenced mainly by selfishness, or ambition, or hate, or cruelty, or—love. For only the love shall live and flourish again; all the rest shall wither and die. Ye hear of 'undying hate,' but there is no such thing. All hates, even, die out at last; love only lives for ever and can never die."

He paused, and remained for a space gazing into the distance. Finally, he turned again to Leonard.

"Come with me, and find your friend; I have that to show you that I wish you seriously to consider."

They walked together down the hill. Meanwhile he continued, "You say your mind is made up, if the decision rests with you. Well, nominally, it rests with the king, of course; but, in reality, I suspect, in this case with the maiden herself. The king is too fond of her—too anxious for her happiness—to desire to thwart her wishes. And he has remarked of late that she is not as she used to be; that she has fits of sadness and melancholy. Her state alarms him. I think, perhaps, he fears it may be the first sign of what is called here the 'falloa.' But," looking at Leonard with a half-smile, "I suspect there is a remedy for her disease, whereas there is none known for the 'falloa.'"

When Leonard heard these words his heart and pulses bounded, and he felt indeed as though walking upon air. Nor did he forget what he owed in the matter to his friend. His breast swelled with gratitude, and he poured out his thanks with a rush of words that stopped only when he caught sight of Templemore coming towards them.

Leonard ran to meet him, and somewhat incoherently explained what Monella had been saying, while Monella led the way to his own apartments in the palace.

When they were seated there he went over again most of what he had impressed on Leonard—for Jack had understood but little of Elwood's impetuous talk—and added,

"Now I want you to advise your friend and consult with him, lest he should decide too hastily; and that must not be. I also must speak further with the king. You see," he continued gravely, "this is a serious thing. The king's son-in-law will look forward to be king one day; therefore he must not be lightly chosen. Again, to choose one of an alien race is no small thing. For myself, I am free from any worldly prejudices about birth, and 'family,' and 'royal blood,' and all that vain, foolish cant. And the king is of the same mind, and wants only to choose for his child the one who pleases her, provided he is worthy. For that I have passed my word to him. I have lived long upon the earth and have consorted with many men; thus I have learned to judge of character and disposition. And I have met none to whom I would sooner trust a daughter of mine own, than to our friend here. On that point, therefore, I have been able to satisfy the king; and fate seems to have settled the rest beforehand. For, incredible as the sceptic may regard it, these two had met in visions long before they encountered one another in the flesh. Thus, in the present, as in the past, fate points the way, and so it will be in the future. For no one can escape his destiny. For good or ill, each has a destiny prepared for him, and that destiny he must perforce fulfil."

20
The Message of Apalano

The furniture in use in the city of Manoa, in material and style, was not unlike that found in Japan. That in the palace was of exquisite design and finish, much of it inlaid with gold and silver. It was such a cabinet that Monella now unlocked: he took from it a parchment roll.

"This," said he, "is the document I gave the king the first day he received us. Now, of course, it belongs to him; but I have borrowed it, temporarily, to show you. It was written by Apalano, the last descendant of those 'White Priests' who fled this country ages ago with the king Mellenda. In some of the old parchments in my possession it is described how those who thus went away found the empire going everywhere to pieces, and falling a prey to barbaric hordes of black or red or cruel white races; and how they eventually took refuge in the secluded valley high up amongst the peaks of the Andes, of which I have already spoken to you, and dwelt there through many centuries.

"They had brought with them, and succeeded in cultivating, the 'Plant of Life,' or 'karina'; but, notwithstanding—and albeit it made them all long-lived—the fatal disease, the 'falloa,' claimed them one after another, till Apalano and I alone were left. Then the 'falloa' laid its withering hand upon Apalano also; he lost his last child, and that affected him very deeply; for, before he died, he wrote this strange letter which tells all about myself that I know with certainty; yet hints, as you will see, at still more to be learned in the future.

"I will read it to you:—

"'To Sanaima, The Chief White Priest of Manoa. Or, if Dead, His Descendant or Successor. Or to the Reigning King of Manoa, Greeting.

"'I, Apalano, the last of the descendants of the White Priests who fled with the great King Mellenda, do commend to your care the bearer of this letter, he whom ye will know by the name of Monella. He is, after myself, the sole survivor of our race outside thy land of Manoa. Treat him with all courtesy, respect and confidence, for he is of royal descent, and the unsullied blood of thine ancient line of kings flows in his veins. Mark well his counsels, give heed to his warnings, and observe his rulings; for he comes to restore the true religion of the Great Spirit, and to bring peace and happiness to our land. Long years ago he did receive a grievous injury to the head in combat with a savage foe. This cast a shadow upon his memory of the past, so that he knoweth naught of what went before, and his former life is blank, save for some vague passing glimpses that, at rare times, come back to him in the guise of dreams and visions. We could have told him much of all that went before, but we have refrained;—first for that he might not have rightly comprehended what we had to tell, and next, in mercy; for he hath suffered much. It was deemed best that the recollections of his sufferings should sleep until the time for his awakening should arrive, when the work for which the Great Spirit hath appointed him shall lie before him and shall form his sorrow's antidote and comfort.

"'The memory that hath untimely been suspended—for we know that it may not be destroyed—perchance may be restored to its full power by such an accident as wrecked it; but, failing that, there is but one sure treatment—namely, to drink of the infusion of the herb called 'trenima' that groweth in Myrlanda and nowhere else. Let the stranger Monella, that bringeth this to thee, drink of 'trenima' in accordance with the rules I have laid down for him upon another scroll; let him, for some weeks, take of it sparingly even as I have written; then more frequently, and lo! all his past life, now hidden, shall be revealed to him, the sun shall light up the recesses of his memory, and he shall know himself and what lies before him.

"'And my dying eyes, though unable yet to pierce the future, still can see that his coming amongst you shall be in itself a sign of the truth of these my words. When he shall appear to you I know not; only that it will be at the time the Great Spirit hath appointed—not an hour sooner nor an hour behind that time—ay, not one minute. And herein ye shall read a message from the Almighty Spirit, and ye shall know that Monella's coming at that special time was marked out by the hand of Destiny. And ye shall find upon his body marks whose meaning will be known unto Sanaima, or to him on whom hath fallen his mantle.

"'With my greeting, I bid ye now farewell—ye unto whom this scroll shall be delivered—my first and last message to the land of my forefathers, and to those that now rule there. Through many centuries we, a faithful few, have kept your memory and our love for you green in our hearts; and I and those who have been with me had hoped, as the appointed time drew near, that the Great Spirit would have deigned to grant to us to see our ancient city and our native land. But it was not to be; all have gone save me and him who brings you this; but in him I send the blessing that we have preserved and nursed for you through long years of persecution and despair.

"'If ye would return our love and care for you, I pray you show them unto him we send. I know that he is worthy of them; and, further, that in his own breast he hears for you the sum of all the love we in our own persons would have shown, had we been spared to greet ye—I and those who have preceded me to the land of the Great Spirit.

"'Farewell!

"'Apalano.'"

When Monella had finished reading this strange letter, he leaned his chin upon his hand and fell into a reverie, Leonard and Templemore meanwhile looking on in silence. Presently Monella roused himself, and, with a deep-drawn sigh, passed his hand across his forehead with a look of pain. His action was as though he had half-caught some flitting thought or memory, that had, after all, eluded him; and that the effort to retain it had cost him mental pain. After a short interval he said, with one of his rare smiles and in the musical voice that captivated every one, so full were they of kindliness,

"Now you know as much about me as I know myself. I did not show you this before, because I had been charged to hand it only to those to whom it was addressed; and this is the first opportunity I have since had, for the king sent it to Sanaima, who returned it only a day or two ago. But, since you must now consider seriously the question of your going or remaining, it is right that you should know all I can tell you of myself. It is very little; yet sufficient to explain my present feelings. You can understand, now that you have read that letter, that I am now, with all my heart and soul, one with these people. I look at everything from their point of view; I consider only their interest, their welfare, their safety, their advantage. If you shall elect to remain with us—to become one of us—you shall find me ever a staunch friend who will do all he can to make you feel at home amongst us, and will place you in positions of great honour. If, on the other hand, you prefer to leave us, you shall not go without such marks of the king's favour as are beyond, perhaps, your dreams. These are the alternatives that lie before you. Take time to ponder them; there is, as I have already told you, no need for an immediate decision."

When, after leaving Monella, the two were once more alone together, Leonard burst out with the thought that filled his mind,

"I scarcely know how to express my feelings. I am full of sadness and yet of joy, and I know not which predominates."

"I know what it will be," said Jack gloomily. "You will stay, and I shall have to return alone. What excuse I shall give to people for leaving you here—dead to them and to the world for ever—or whether I shall ever be forgiven for appearing to have deserted you, God only knows. I wish you would think a little upon all this. For the rest, I congratulate you with all my heart. To be the future king of so ancient and remarkable a nation, is a piece of 'luck' that does not fall to everybody. By Jove!" he exclaimed with increasing earnestness, "upon my word I don't wonder at your going in for it—indeed, if—that is—well, if I had not already set my mind upon something else, I would chuck up the world in general and throw in my lot with you and be your—your Prime Minister—or State Engineer—or some other high functionary." And he laughed good-naturedly at the ideas the suggestion called up in his mind.

"Don't let us meet trouble half way," said Leonard hopefully. "The time of parting is not yet; who knows what may turn up? Monella may make us some concession that will meet the case. And now look here. I have been thinking of a plan for sending a message home."

Jack stared.

"How on earth?" he asked.

"It won't be much of a message, and perhaps it will never reach home; but we can try. Let us find a place where we can get a view in the direction of 'Monella Lodge' and watch at night for camp fires out on the far savanna. We must find a spot screened from observation on this side. Then we will bring some powder up from our stores, and flash some signals as Monella had arranged."

"But what good will that do? Even it they are seen it will only be by Indians who will not understand them."

"Never mind. If any Indians see them they are sure to spread the news about; and probably the first place to hear of it will be Daranato, the Indian village where my old nurse Carenna lives. Matava may have told her about the signals, or even other Indians. At any rate, she will be pretty sure to hear of them and let Matava know when he returns; or perhaps even send a message down by some one going to the coast, to say that signals had been seen that showed we were alive on the summit of Roraima."

Jack reflected.

"Yes!" he presently said slowly. "Yes. There is something in the idea. We will try it; it can do no harm. But, to be of any good, we shall have to signal frequently; once or twice would not be of much use."

"Precisely. Before long, Matava will be back from the coast, and will hear of them, and will come out on to the savanna at night to see them for himself. And he would watch night after night with an Indian's patience till he saw them."

"Yes; I suppose Monella won't object? We ought not to do it without his consent. But for that awful forest, we might even go farther; we might make an expedition for a week or two, and get to 'Monella Lodge' and leave a letter there; or even to Daranato, and leave letters to be taken to the coast by the first Indians going that way."

"No, we can't manage that, nor would Monella like us to be away so long. You never know what trouble might turn up here with these priests and their vile crew. And that reminds me of that letter Monella read to-day. What did you think of it?"

"An extraordinary letter! Really, I feel almost inclined to go back to my former idea that Monella and his friends were all mad together!"

Leonard stared aghast.

"What! You speak of that again?" he exclaimed, real indignation in his tones. "After the way everything has come out—after all Monella's kindness—"

Jack stopped him with a smile and a touch of his hand on the other's arm.

"Put the brake on, old man," he said. "I don't mean anything disrespectful. But if Monella, who already seems to have been about the world and to have seen as much as three ordinary men of three score years and ten—if the point to which his memory reaches is only a portion of his life—why, you see, he must be Methuselah, or the Wandering Jew himself, or some other mythical being. Already, he has puzzled me, times enough, with his extraordinary tales; at the same time you cannot doubt his absolute sincerity. So that if his 'complete' memory is to go back farther still, why—Heaven help us!—we sha'n't know whether we are on our heads or our heels."

After a short silence Leonard spoke.

"But, if they had this 'Plant of Life' with them—those he was with—would that not in part account for it?"

"It might; but it is making large demands on one's credulity. But what I really mean is this. I am inclined, at times, to think Monella a bit mad. He has a religious mania; he has persuaded himself—and evidently, from that letter, has been encouraged by others to believe it—that he has a religious mission to these people. Well, no harm in that, you say. No; and that he is honourable, upright, sincere, I feel very certain. Still, he may be self-deceived. He

seems to me to be one of those fervidly religious mystics who can
persuade themselves into almost anything."

"Yet he is no fanatic. See how mild and gentle he can be; how
slow to anger, how just in his discrimination between right and
wrong!"

"I admit all that. Still, I repeat, he might easily deceive himself."

That afternoon Leonard sought out Ulama and asked to be allowed to row her on the lake; and to this she smiled a glad assent.
When he had rowed the boat out a long distance from the shore,
he laid down the oars, and let her drift. A gentle breeze was blowing, and this served to temper the ardour of the waning sun.

"Do you remember the last time we were thus alone, Ulama?"
presently he asked her.

"Indeed I do," she answered, her cheek, that had of late been
very pale, now glowing with a rosy flush. "But I began to think you
had forgotten, and were never going to take me out again."

"Ah! It was not my fault, Ulama."

"Whose else could it be?" she asked.

"Well—I cannot tell you now. But, if you remember the occasion, do you remember also what we spoke of?"

The colour deepened in the maiden's face. She bent her head
and fixed her eyes dreamily upon the water; and one hand dropped
over the boat's side, as on that day of which he had reminded her.

"I then said," he went on, "that I loved you dearly, and asked
you whether you could love me in return. And you said you did not
understand such love as I described to you. Do you remember?"

"Yes; I remember," she said softly. "But then I said I could
scarce credit such sudden love for me; and that you might change.
And it seems you have, for, since then, you have never told me that
you loved me."

He seized her hand.

"No, Ulama," he cried passionately, "it was not so. I have not
altered. But I feared—that—well, that your father might be angered.
'Twas for that reason that I spoke no more to you of love."

"In that you did my father wrong," she answered frankly. "My
father loves me far too well to cause me pain and—"

"Ah! Then—would it pain you were I to go away from here and never see you more?"

She started, and a look of mingled fear and grief came into her eyes.

"You are—not—going away?" she faltered anxiously.

"Not if you bid me stay, Ulama. If you but whisper in my ear that you may come to love me—if only a little—then I will stay—stay on always—forget my country, my own people, my friends; give up everything, and live for you—for you alone, my sweet, my gentle Ulama; my beloved Ulama!"

Gradually her head sank until it rested on her hand; her colour deepened, she made no reply, but still gazed pensively into the water.

"Tell me, Ulama—am I to stay or go? Oh, say that you will try to love me!"

He still retained her hand, and now he passed his own gently over it, she making no effort to withdraw it. Thus answered, he pressed his lips upon it, and at this, also, she showed no resentment.

"I would have you stay," she presently murmured softly; "but indeed I fear it is too late for me to try to love you, for my heart tells me you have my love already."

And the boat drifted aimlessly in the evening light The sun had set, and the moon, the witness of so many lovers' vows—both true and false—had shown her silvery light above the surrounding cliffs; and still the two sat on and scarcely spoke, yet, in speechless eloquence, recounting to each other the old, old tale.

And, when the sweet Ulama left the boat, her heart could scarce contain the joy that filled it; and in her eye there was a light that it had lacked before, so that the king, her father, drew her affectionately to him and asked her what had wrought this wondrous change.

She shyly bent her head and answered him,

"To-morrow thou shalt know, my father." Then she hid her blushing face upon his shoulder. "I have a favour to ask of thee; but—I would fain not speak of it this evening."

Then, as though fearing that he would wrest from her the secret of her joy, she stole swiftly to her room, and from her window looked across the lake, now shimmering in the silver moonbeams.

For long she sat there motionless, dreaming youth's fond dreams; dwelling, in loving tenderness, on every word and look she could recall of Leonard while the boat had drifted here and there, and the lap, lap, lap, of the ripples against the sides had kept up a soft musical accompaniment to the rhythm of love's heart-beats.

21
The Great Devil-Tree

In pursuance of their design of making signals from the summit of Roraima, the two friends made further explorations of the northern side. And this led them into an adventure, one day, that had well-nigh proved fatal to them both.

On mentioning their intention to Monella, he had at first objected; but, upon Leonard's reminding him of the anxiety and distress Templemore's mother and fiancée might be, too probably were, in, he had given a reluctant consent.

"Your friends, Dr. Lorien and his son, talked of coming back again," he remarked. "Do you think they are likely to make the journey with Matava, and to be coming to seek for you?"

"Certainly they are coming into this neighbourhood, after orchids," Leonard replied; "and, now you speak of it—though I had not thought about it lately—the news Matava will probably take back may cause such anxiety that they may hurry to get here sooner than they would otherwise have been likely to, in order to make inquiry about us on the spot."

"Matava might lead them to the cavern, if they came to Daranato," said Monella thoughtfully.

"Yes; of course that is possible."

"And a very little ingenuity or a small charge of powder would force an opening; and their way would then be easy to get up here?"

"Certainly."

Monella's face clouded.

"That must not be; you must clearly understand that you must tell me in time if there seems any such probability. I wish not to

471

seem unfriendly towards your friends—and personally I liked them—but to allow them to come in here would be as the beginning of a flood, as the letting out of water. It cannot, must not be."

"Well, after all, it is only a supposition," observed Jack. "Time enough to deal with it, if the occasion actually arise. They were going on to Rio on some law business which was likely to occupy them some time; they might be detained there indefinitely, they said."

"Quite so," Monella answered decisively. "Only, remember, I rely upon you to inform me in time. And be very cautious and vigilant upon that side of the country, for, as you know, it is in that direction that Coryon and his people have their habitation."

In their walks they were often accompanied by one or both of Ulama's pumas, and on the day referred to the male one, Tuo, as it was called, came after them when they had gone a little way, and trotted quietly beside them; and this, as it turned out, saved their lives.

They came upon a place they had not seen before. Two great iron gates of highly finished workmanship, and picked out with gold, shut in a narrow opening in a high rock. They were such as might form the entrance to a public garden. A broad road wound round from the inside of the gates; but outside, where Templemore and Elwood were, the rocks rose up fifty or sixty feet, or even more, on either side; and though they followed them a considerable distance on both sides of the gates, the rocks still towered up precipitously for as far as they could see.

"This can scarcely be the entrance to Coryon's 'domain,'" said Jack, "or there would be some people about on guard. It must be some kind of public place."

"A cemetery, perhaps," suggested Leonard.

"I believe you've hit it. Well, there's a gate open, so I suppose there's no harm in our having a peep inside."

"Suppose some one were on the watch, and were to pop round and close and lock the gates when we were inside and out of sight," said Leonard suspiciously. "Monella warned us to be wary and to suspect traps."

"We have our revolvers; and, if the worse came to the worst, we could climb over these rocks."

In the result they went inside; then made their way to a wide terrace that ran round an extensive area of horseshoe shape, half natural, half artificial, as they judged. This terrace extended several hundreds of yards in both directions from the point at which they stood; but it narrowed off considerably on one side of the horseshoe. Above and behind it, cut out of the rock, were other terraces, like steps or rows of seats, but broad below and narrowing as they got higher. These went all round, almost to the top of the rocks. It was, in fact, a vast amphitheatre where many thousands of people could stand or sit. At the farther end it was open; and in the centre was a large arena sunk some fifteen feet below the main terrace on which they stood.

This arena opened out into a deep defile beyond, from the rocky heights of which there issued a rushing stream of water that flowed into a large, dark-looking pool below.

But what at once riveted their attention, almost to the point of fascination, was an extraordinary-looking tree that stood in the arena. This tree had no leaves, but branches only. In colour it was of a sombre violet-blue, tinged in places with a ruddy hue. The trunk was about thirty feet in height, and eight or nine feet in diameter. The branches, which were many—a hundred or more probably—drooped over from where the trunk ended and trailed about the ground. But what was most astonishing, these branches were all in motion. Though there was no wind, they waved to and fro, ran restlessly along the ground like lithe snakes, and intertwined one with another, at the same time making a harsh, rustling sound.

Straight in front of where they stood was a long pier of masonry that ran out towards the tree, which was not in the centre of the arena but was nearer to that part of the terrace where it grew narrow. In order the better to observe the object that had so roused their curiosity, the two young men walked across the terrace and some distance along the pier; and, when they had proceeded a little more than half its length, one of the long trailing branches—some of them appeared to be two hundred or three hundred feet in length—came up over the end of the pier, and, with a rustle, made its way swiftly towards them. It was within two or three feet of where they stood looking at it, when the puma, with a loud growl, sprang forward and bit at it. Immediately the branch curled itself round the animal's body and began dragging it along the pier towards the tree. Then two or three other branches advanced and went to the assistance of the first one, coiling round the poor puma and dragging it farther along, despite its teeth and claws and its desperate struggles. In succession, other branches crept up over the end of the stonework, and, just in time, Jack seized Leonard and dragged him back.

"For Heaven's sake come away, man!" he exclaimed in horror. "That tree is alive, and will drag us off, if once one of those branches touch us! "

They had stepped back only barely in time, for a moment after a trailing branch swept over the very spot on which they had halted. When assured that they were really out of reach, they stood fascinated, but filled with horror, while they witnessed the unavailing fight made by the poor animal that had saved their lives. More branches came to the aid of the others; they coiled round its mouth and closed it; round its legs and bound them; and soon, helpless, a mere bundle in the coiling, curling branches, as it were, it was drawn off the pier to the ground below. Then it was rolled on and on till it had almost reached the tree-trunk, where were shorter but thicker and stronger branches waiting for it. These, in their turn, soon coiled round it; then, slowly, they bent upwards, carrying the poor animal in their relentless grasp, and lowered it into a hollow in the centre of the top of the trunk, where it almost disappeared from sight. Then all the thicker branches coiled round it and shut it completely out from view, forming a sort of huge knot round the top of the tree and remaining motionless; while the longer and more slender branches continued to play restlessly about, seeking for further prey. Then, without a word, the two turned away; nor did they speak till they found themselves safely outside the great gates. Then they looked, horror-struck, at each other.

Jack was the first to break the silence.

"Great heavens!" he exclaimed. "What an escape! What an awful monster! What a frightful death! And that poor animal—that saved us both! What shall we say to the princess? Talk of 'traps'! If this gate was left open as a 'trap'—and it looks to me so—we have reason indeed to be thankful!"

"What is it?" Leonard asked at last.

"A 'devil-tree.' It is a carnivorous tree. I've seen a small one before; in a forest in Brazil that we were working through. One of the dogs got caught in it and was nearly killed before we cut it free with our axes. And then it was badly hurt, and so was I; a branch caught hold of my hand and tore some of the flesh off it. And where we cut this branch it bled! A dark crimson-blue liquid oozed out that stank! Oh, there, I can't tell you what the stench was like I I've smelt some bad smells in my time, but that beat anything I ever came across! But that was only a small bush. I had no idea they could grow into great flesh-eating monsters like this! Why, that thing must have been there a thousand—ah—two thousand years, I should say. Fully that."

"But," said Leonard, "why is it kept here? who feeds it—and—what—is—it—fed—on?"

He asked this last question slowly, and looked at the other in blank, horrified amazement.

"It can't live without food," he continued. "And it must want a lot too. Whoever can take the trouble to get it food of the only kind—as I suppose—that it would care for? And why is it there in the middle of that strange place? One would almost think it was kept there as a kind of show or curiosity; and yet—we have never heard about it all the time we have been here! And it is there, with the gate open, no fence to guard people, or notice to warn them. Well! It's a mystery to me!"

But if they had been astounded and horror-stricken at what they had seen, they were still more mystified and upset by Ulama's behaviour when they told her of their adventure; for she fainted right off and, when she recovered, seemed so overcome with terror as to be unable to say a word. No explanation would she give; save that now and then she murmured, almost in a moan, to herself, "Then it is true! And I never knew! It is horrible —too horrible!"

When Leonard expressed his sorrow about the puma, she hardly seemed to notice it.

"Ah yes! " she said once. "Poor Tuo! I shall miss him—and such a death, too! But oh, he saved you and your friend! And then, he was but an animal—but the others!"

At her express desire they promised not to speak to any one else about it. "I will tell you why—or you will know why—later," she added. "But you can speak privately to Monella about it; to no one else just now!"

When they found an opportunity of speaking to him about it, he looked very grave.

"You have had a narrow escape," he said. "Heaven be thanked you did escape. I cannot explain more to you now, but may be able to do so shortly. Meantime, please do as the princess says, and keep this matter to yourselves."

All this time Leonard's relations with Ulama had remained unchanged; they had not been placed on any settled footing. Monella had asked him to take time to make up his mind, and had intimated that nothing would be said or done meanwhile. Leonard had, however, been too impatient to put his fate to the test to be able to wait after the encouragement Monella had given to him. But, whether Ulama had spoken on the subject with her father, he knew not; for it so happened that he had not seen her alone since their love-scene in the boat.

And now she was evidently much discomposed about their adventure with the 'devil-tree'; though she did not refer to it again.

Naturally too, the recollection of it was very much in the minds of the two young men. Leonard asked Templemore, one day, what the branches of the one he had seen were like.

"They were covered with small excrescences," he replied, "that are suckers and piercers in one. They pierce the flesh and then suck the blood. The whole affair is a sort of gigantic vegetable 'octopus,' or devilfish, only that it has a hundred or more 'arms' or branches instead of eight, as the octopus has. I have heard of devilfish having been caught as large as eighty feet in length, on the coast of Newfoundland. But I never knew that its vegetable prototype grew to anything like the size."

"Of course I have seen devil-fish," said Leonard thoughtfully; "but they have a mouth—a great beak—to which their arms carry the food. Do you think it is the same here? You saw that the branches carried the poor puma up into a hollow in the top of the trunk. Do you suppose the thing has a kind of mouth there?"

"Goodness only knows! It must be an awful sort of affair, if it is so. The whole thing is monstrous and uncanny. Don't let us talk about it!"

But, as a result of this experience, they sought in another direction for a likely place from which to make their intended signals; and finally they found one convenient for their purpose. Then they made two or three trips to the canyon to bring up the requisite powder. They also brought back from the secret cave a number of things Monella wanted. From the first, at his suggestion, they had told no one except the king, Ulama, and Zonella, of the means by which they had gained access to the mountain; and these had promised to keep the knowledge to themselves.

"The place has evidently been so long unvisited," Monella had remarked, "that probably most of those who once knew of it have forgotten all about it. No need to remind them just now. Many years ago, as I have been informed, a project was started for filling it up."

"Filling it up!"

"Yes, and if you go to the other end of the canyon—that by which we entered—you will find, even now, in the thick wood that everywhere surrounds the top of the canyon, vast numbers of great boulders that were quarried from the surrounding cliffs and hauled to the edge in readiness to be thrown down. They lie, in fact, just over the cavern we came in by. There they have remained for a very long time, it seems. Had that intention been carried out, all our work in cutting through the forest and finding the entrance to the cavern, as you can see, would have been thrown away."

"And what stopped it?"

"It is said that the people threatened a rebellion. The belief in the eventual return of Mellenda—of whom you have heard—is deep-seated; and, though the people here are anxious enough to keep to themselves, they would not assent to closing irrevocably the only means by which their hero could gain admittance, should he ever come."

"Do they expect him to come with a host of followers—a conquering army—or do they expect the great lake to come back, and that he will arrive with a grand fleet of ships?" Templemore asked, with somewhat of a sarcastic smile.

Monella passed his hand across his brow in the half-dreamy manner that was his at times, as though striving to collect his thoughts, or to arrest and force into shape some half-formed conception that had flitted across his mind and escaped his grasp. For a minute he stared vacantly away into the distance and was silent. Then, with a look as though of pain at failing to catch the fleeting image, he turned away, saying simply, "I cannot tell you."

During the days that followed, Templemore passed much of his time in the museums; time that Elwood spent in a lover's dream of happiness with Ulama. In the relics of the former history of this strange people, Templemore took a deep interest; and in the archives and ancient manuscripts he found many evidences of the former existence of scientific and engineering knowledge that astonished and perplexed him. On the true meaning and import of some of these he sought the help of Monella, who would frequently accompany him in these visits, and, from his better knowledge of the language, was able to assist him to unravel their curious contents.

"These people must once have been great engineers and architects!" he exclaimed in surprised admiration on one of these occasions.

Monella smiled and made reply, "There is nothing so surprising in that, if you comprehend the true significance of the gigantic earthworks still extant in many places on this continent. Have you seen any of them?"

"No; but I have both heard and read of them."

"I have seen them; and I tell you your mind can form no idea of their extent, of the scientific knowledge and the prodigious amount of time and labour that must have been expended on them, unless you actually see them. They are of various forms, mostly geometrical figures upon a vast scale—miles in extent. The wonderful thing is that a certain figure is repeated exactly in different places hundreds of miles apart. Yet you shall take your cleverest engineers of the present day, give them the advantages—or supposed advantages—of all your modern discoveries and machinery, and scientific instruments, and, say, unlimited workpeople to do their building, and then it would tax all their skill to construct a work exactly similar to one of those great figures. Yet now, upon some of them, trees are growing that must be over a thousand years old!"

"And what were they for—what was their object?" Templemore asked.

Then there came over the other's face again that curious look as of one seeking for a lost recollection; but it seemed to evade him, and he answered somewhat as before,

"I think I ought to be able to tell you," he replied, "but I cannot now seem to remember."

It was while thus together one day that Templemore asked him for some further information concerning the 'Plant of Life.'

"You have told me," he said, "that your people, with whom you lived in that secluded valley high up in the Andes, had with them the 'karina' and cultivated it. Therefore I suppose you yourself have been in the habit of taking it?"

"Always. And in my travelling to and fro in the world I always had with me a good supply of the dried herb. I was accustomed to leave stores of it in certain towns, so that if I lost what I had with me by any accident, there was more within easy reach."

"I see. But what I am puzzled about is this: why, if the virtues of the plant are so great, do people ever die at all ? And why do some live longer than others?"

"As to the first question," Monella answered, "man was never intended to live on this earth for ever. The human frame must wear out sooner or later. As to the second query, some constitutions are naturally stronger than others, and these endure longer, just as is the case in the world outside where the plant is not known. The effect of the plant is simply to keep the blood pure, if originally pure. If, however, there is an inherited taint, that taint will make itself felt sooner or later and undermine the vitality of the system. In this case the plant will only result in ensuring a somewhat longer life than would otherwise have been the case. Sooner or later the vitality will fall off and gradual decay set in, although (the blood

being kept still pure) ordinary diseases are kept at bay. Lastly, there
is the question of the will."

"The will?"

"Yes; that has a most powerful influence. If a man who has inherited a constitution that is absolutely sound, from ancestors who
have possessed the same through many generations, and if he has,
in addition, a strong will, powerful beyond the average, he may
live longer—if he is so minded."

"I—do not understand you," said Templemore, somewhat
puzzled.

Monella gazed at him with a smile that was full of sadness.

"You would," he answered, "if you were old yourself; if you had
outlived all that made life worth having—your wife, and others you
love, your ambitions, your hopes. Then does the soul grow weary,
and restless as well; it is like unto a bird that is caged whose time
for migration has come. It will either fret or pine itself to death or
beat itself to death against the bars of its cage. Only two things
can then keep the soul from taking its flight; the will to live to complete some unfinished work, or a delight in a worldly, wicked life.
A nature superlatively evil, like Coryon's, may enable its possessor
to live on and on for an indefinite time; where better men take the
'falloa' and die. Or a man, not himself enamoured of life upon this
earth, may exert his will to carry out to its end some great work to
benefit his fellow-creatures, and he too may keep the 'falloa' at
arm's length for an unusually long period. In other words, the
'falloa' is a form of melancholia, of weariness with the world, of an
inward sense that life's work is completed. It is the result of that
feeling that we are told took possession at last even of him who
has been called the Wise Man of the World—King Solomon—whose
wisdom and riches and power only brought him to the same point
I have indicated—that at which the soul declares that all earthly
things are but vanity."

On another occasion, Templemore was accompanied by Zonella
and Colenna; and the latter took him into a gallery he had not before seen, the door being usually kept locked.

In it, to his surprise, were ranged hundreds of stands of arms
and military uniforms, helmets, spears, shields, swords, daggers,

and red tunics, all kept in splendid condition, as though for instant use. All the helmets had little silver wings at their sides, and
the shields were engraved in the centre with a strange hieroglyphic,
the same that he had noticed chiselled upon the fronts of many of
the principal buildings.

"There," said Colenna, "are the arms and uniforms of Mellenda's soldiers. Over in Myrlanda, in the great temple of the White
Priests, are hundreds more; all kept ready for use, as you see these
here. You see the silver wings upon the helmets, similar to those
on that of Mellenda's suit that stands in the other gallery. And that
figure upon the shields is the sacred sign that was engraved upon
his signet-ring. It signifies his seal or sign-manual. Wherever you
see that mark, it refers to him; on a building it implies that he designed or built it. His royal colour was red, as the king's to-day is
blue; and these red tunics are for his soldiers."

"When they come," said Jack, discreetly repressing the incredu-
lous smile that almost forced itself upon his lips.

"When he comes," said Colenna, lifting his hat reverently. "Yes,
when he returns to us."

"You don't believe in that, I know," interposed Zonella; "yet we all
do; and it is a good thing we do, I think, for I fear many in the land
would go mad under their dread of Coryon, if they did not believe
in a happier future for the country. But there," she added sadly, "it
does not matter to you. You have no interest in what may go on
here in the future. You intend to go back to your own country, and
care little for the sorrows or the fate of those you leave behind."

Colenna had walked away some little distance, to examine a
shield that he thought was not quite so bright as it should be.

"Not care!" Jack exclaimed, impulsively. "Why, how can you
say that? It is that thought that grieves me all the time I am here;
that makes me doubt how I shall ever be able to make up my mind
to leave. To leave behind one's dearest—"

Zonella turned to him quickly, with a heightened colour and a
bright look. This was so unexpected that he stopped and hesitated.

"Well?" she said. "You said your dearest—"

"My dearest friend, Leonard—of course," he answered, looking
at her in some surprise.

But Zonella's face paled, and she turned away.

"Let us go," she said with a shiver, as though a cold wind had blown upon her. "This old gallery is kept locked up so much it gets to smell musty, and makes one feel quite faint."

22
Smiles and Tears

One morning, Monella sought Leonard and reverted to their former conversation about Ulama. "You have well considered all the words I spoke to you, my son?" he said. "Are you still of the same mind?"

"I had hoped that you knew me too well to think it necessary to ask the question," Leonard said earnestly. "Since I first looked upon Ulama, my love for her has been given past all recall. I have never wavered in my resolution to remain here for her dear sake, if I may hope to gain the king's consent."

"Then," returned Monella, "the king would talk with you concerning it. Let us go to him."

And, without further preface, he led the young man into the private chamber of King Dranoa, where he left him.

The king, Leonard thought, looked ill and careworn; but he received him with great kindness, and in a manner that quickly reassured the anxious lover.

"It has been no secret to me for some time," said Dranoa, "that thou hast looked with affection upon my child. She, too, hath spoken to me; I see that she hath set her heart upon this thing, and I love her too dearly to desire to thwart her wishes, unless for some weighty reason. Here I see no such reason; for, though thou art a stranger, yet thou art worthily recommended by one upon whose judgment I have learned to place reliance. He that led thee hither is not a man to act lightly or without full consideration in a matter of such paramount importance; if thou hast gained his confidence and esteem, I doubt not that there are good reasons for it. He hath

the unerring eye that pierces to the very heart, and that no hypocrisy, no cunning, can deceive. Were it the case that my dominions
were to-day the great empire over which my forefathers held sway,
I would seek such a man's advice in the appointment of my generals, my ministers, my governors for distant districts. Therefore do
I feel that I can rely upon his judgment, even in a matter so mo-
mentous as the choice of one to espouse my child and to succeed
me on my throne. And knowing, as I do full well, that the 'falloa'
hath laid its hand upon me and that my days in this my land are
numbered, it is grateful to mine heart to feel that my child will be
comforted, when I am gone, by one whose affection for her is pure
and wholly hers, and who will have at his side a friend and counsellor who will guide his youthful steps in the path that I would
have him follow. This conviction hath lifted from mine heart a
grievous trouble, and hath enabled me to bear without sorrow or
regret the knowledge that the fatal sickness hath taken hold upon
me. For the fact that I shall now soon quit this earthly life I care
nothing in itself; it hath been the fear of what would then befall
that hath filled me with forebodings and with fear. But, if I see—as
I hope to see—the power of the Black Coryon broken and destroyed
for ever; my child wedded to one worthy of her love and honour;
my successor aided and advised by one so competent to guide as is
thy friend, then indeed I shall feel I can lay down the burden of
life with thanksgiving, and take my way to the great unknown of
the hereafter without fear, without regret, without a sigh; but, instead, with the great content of one who feels he hath nothing more
to wish or hope for upon earth. For know, my son," continued
Dranoa with grave emphasis, "no man wisheth to prolong his life
for that which it hath yielded, but rather for that which he is hopeful it may yield. The proof of this is easy; no man desireth to live
his life over again; therefore he is, at heart, and from actual experience, dissatisfied and wearied with life; not charmed with it. Yet
do many cling to it, fatuously believing, in the face of all their own
actual experience, that it shall yet, in the future, afford them joys
and gratifications they have never found in the past. These, my
son, are the words of one who hath lived long enough to gain the
wisdom that teacheth how to sift the wheat from the chaff."

Dranoa paused, and remained silent awhile. Then he resumed, with a change of tone,

"But I wish not to weigh down thy young imaginings with the sober knowledge that belongeth not to thine years but to mine. It will be sufficient to give thee counsel that is more suited to the circumstances. Therefore I say this to thee: thou hast a good heart and good instincts—trust them, follow them honestly; and leave the rest to the Great Spirit that ruleth over all. And now I have but one more thing to say; it were better for the present that this that is between us were not known openly. Personally, that will not concern thee. When the time hath come, I will myself announce it to my people. Meanwhile, thy mind will be at rest with the knowledge of my approval of thy suit."

Leonard gratefully poured out his thanks to the kindhearted king; then went to seek Ulama.

He found her sitting alone in an apartment that overlooked the lake, so deep in thought that she did not hear his coming. She was leaning on the window-sill gazing pensively upon the beauties of the scene that lay outspread before her.

But Leonard thought, as he caught sight of her and played his steps upon the threshold, that she herself was the fairest creation of all, posed as she was with that unconscious grace and charm that seemed with her to be innate. For a full minute he stood in silence; then, still without moving towards her, he softly called her name, as though fearing to approach her till he had permission.

She turned her head towards him with no surprise, but with a look of sweetest pleasure in her gentle eyes.

"I did not hear you," she said dreamily, "and yet—I know not why—I was looking for your coming."

"And what were you thinking of so profoundly, sweet Ulama?"

"I was thinking," she replied, "how much more beautiful our lake and its surroundings have seemed to me of late. I scarce noticed them before; I suppose because I have known them all my life. Yet, now that you have pointed out some of their beauties, I not only feel and appreciate them, but I note many others on all sides that I never saw before. It is very strange! I wonder why it is?"

"It is love, Ulama," Leonard said, coming quietly to her side and laying his hand lightly on her shoulder. "Love can make the plainest works of nature beautiful; small wonder then if it makes those that are really so display new and unsuspected charms. It is because love has taken up his dwelling in your heart that you now see new beauties in these familiar scenes."

But Ulama shook her head sagely, and smilingly made answer,

"You know you told me that the first time you saw our lake you deemed it the fairest spot on all the earth. And you did not know me then, so could not love me. How then can what you say explain it?"

Leonard laughed and took her hand in his.

"You forget that I had seen you in my dreams and had loved you long before," he said. "Perhaps some instinct told me that here I should find the abode of her who already had my heart. Or, if that explanation does not please you, here is another. Love and sympathy are inseparable; you admire, now, things that you thought little of before, because you see that I admire them."

"Yes; that may be," Ulama admitted, with a thoughtful look. "But then, it does not explain why you should see beauties where I did not. I think you must have a quicker appreciation of the beautiful in nature than is given to me."

"It may be so; and that in turn explains how it came about that I was so quick to realise the beauty of the fairest daughter of Manoa!" And Leonard's look was so tender, so full of loving admiration, that it brought a rosy glow to Ulama's cheek. "And it also reminds me that I sought you here to tell you something of importance, something that has brought joy and gladness to my heart. I have just been talking about you with the king."

The colour in the girl's cheek grew deeper; and now she turned her glance again upon the landscape that lay sleeping in the morning sunlight.

"Dear love," continued Leonard, "think what it means to me—to both of us, I hope—when I tell you that the king has given me permission to ask you to give yourself to me! Ah! Not only has he done that, but he has done it in a manner—accompanied it with kind words of trust and confidence that have filled my whole heart with gratitude. He speaks as though I had already proved that which I can only hope to show in the future—my true desire to make myself worthy of your love. His kindness and many marks of friendship towards one who is but a stranger here have overwhelmed me. I feel the whole devotion of my life to you and him can scarce repay such generous, ungrudging proofs of his confidence and favour."

"You have a good friend in Monella," Ulama said quietly. "He never fails to speak well of you when occasion offers. And he is one of our own race, and has had great experience of the world outside, of which we know nothing; and my father knows he can rely on his opinion."

"Yes, I know that is true, dear love, and my heart burns with gratitude to him too. And now, beloved"—and he put his arms round her and drew her to him— "may I not think of you as all my own? Let me hear you say with those dear lips that you know now what love is, that it has sprung up unforced in your pure heart; let me hear you say, 'Leonard, I love you!'"

And, as he drew her closer to him and her head nestled upon his shoulder, a whisper, that seemed but a faint sigh, breathed softly the words so sweet to hear for the first time from a loved-one's lips— "I love you!"

Later in the day Leonard told Templemore of his interview with the king; and, as he did so, a look came over his face that, as his friend expressed it to himself, "did one's heart good to see, even if but once in a lifetime!"

"In your happiness I too feel happy, dear old boy," he said. "And I should have little concern, for the time being, if only those at home knew we were alive and well. As it is, the thought of their anxiety troubles me unceasingly."

"Let us hope our signal flares were seen and will be reported," Leonard answered. "I think they must have been seen; and, if so, Carenna is sure to hear of it, and will find some way of sending word."

This referred to what they had done to carry out Leonard's suggestion. After some perseverance in watching from the spot they had selected, they saw, one evening, camp fires far out on the savanna. At once they made their signals with small heaps of powder, and these they repeated several times. No response whatever came; nor did they expect any. There was nothing for it but to wait patiently in the hope that their signals had been seen.

Then ensued a time, lasting many weeks, which was almost uneventful. To Leonard and Ulama it was one uninterrupted dream of blissful happiness. To Templemore it was pleasant and interesting, for he found plenty to engage his mind. He studied the designs of the chief buildings; of the bridges that spanned the streams that fed the lake. In the arches and general construction of these he formed engineering ideas that were new to him. He visited often the great waterfall that formed the outlet of the lake, and declared that the sight of the vast body of water shooting out in its leap of two thousand feet, its deep, thundering roar, and the play of colour when the sun shone into the mist and spray, made up a combination that threw Niagara itself—which he had seen—into the shade.

One day, when Ulama and Zonella were alone together, the former thus addressed her friend, "Sometimes of late I have fancied there has been some unpleasant passage between you and Leonard's friend. I myself am so fortunate, so happy, that I like not to see those about me otherwise. I would have all my friends as happy as myself." And she took Zonella's hand and rubbed her face affectionately against it "Tell me, Zonella, have you two quarrelled?"

For a moment Zonella's face, usually so pleasant to behold, looked hard and almost fierce. Then it softened, and, with a loud cry, she threw her arms around Ulama; she hid her face in the gentle bosom, and burst into a torrent of impassioned tears.

It was some time before Ulama, greatly surprised as well as pained and puzzled, could understand the meaning of this outburst; but presently Zonella, growing somewhat calmer, sobbed out, "Ah! You—you little know, little think what I have suffered. He cares no more for me than he does for you—perhaps less. His heart is elsewhere; he is set upon going away from our land, and only his regard for his friend delays him."

Ulama's beautiful face bent over Zonella's, and her tears fell upon the other's cheek as she pressed her lovingly to her bosom.

"Alas! Alas! My poor Zonella! And is it possible that love, which has been so sweet to me, should bring to you but pain and suffering?

I almost fear for my own happiness; that my selfishness in yielding to it has blinded me to what was going on with the others. But it never occurred to me that love that is to me so wonderful in the joy and pleasure it confers, could also be the cause of misery and sorrow. And yet," she added thoughtfully, "you are not without one to love you. Poor Ergalon has long been faithful to his love for you. Oh, how strange and contrary it all seems! Poor fellow! Perhaps you have made him suffer even as you yourself have suffered. Can his love not console you? I know so little myself that what I say may be only foolishness, yet—"

Zonella smiled faintly, and shook her head. Then she kissed the other tenderly.

"Let us say no more, my dear," she said. "I am sorry I gave way as I did; but you took me by surprise. Perhaps, too, your implied advice is wise. It might be better to try to love the one you know does truly love you, than to fret your heart out after one who loves you not, and who is beyond your reach. At least, as you say, there is one in the world who loves me."

Thus the time sped on. Monella was much away; sometimes for a week together; so the young men saw comparatively little of him. Templemore, on one occasion, expressed a wish to visit Myrlanda with him, but Monella said there were difficulties in the way.

"It is better you two should remain here for the present," he declared. "At a future time, let us hope it may be different."

But one day Monella came to him with a look of gravity that at once aroused his interest.

"It is time," he said, "that I should show you something of the truth, that you may understand what lies before us. Can you brace up your courage and your nerve to stand a severe trial?"

Templemore opened his eyes in astonishment.

"Need you ask?" he answered. "Have you ever known me wanting in courage?"

"Ah, no. But this that I refer to requires courage of a different sort. Yet it must be faced. But I warn you it will be a shock. Make up your mind to a test that will tax all the nerve you can summon to your aid."

"And Leonard too?" Jack inquired, wondering.

"No. Say nothing to him. Let his dream be happy while it may. Be ready to come out with me to-night, when Ergalon shall come to seek you. And bring your rifle."

23
The Devil-Tree by Moonlight

It was about ten o'clock when Templemore, with Ergalon as guide, came out from the king's palace by a side-entrance that was little used, and the door of which the latter now opened with a key. Outside, at a short distance, they found Monella pacing up and down.

Before leaving, Templemore had told Leonard just so much as would explain his absence; then had managed to slip away unobserved by their friends of the king's court.

The night was fine but chilly, and all three were muffled up. In the sky overhead the moon shone calm and clear, lighting up the valley with great distinctness; but across its face wild-looking clouds were scurrying, showing that a strong wind was blowing up above, though little of it was felt below. Only now and then an eddying gust would sweep down the hillside and stir the trees around them, then die away with a rustling sigh or a low moan.

Ergalon led the way; skirting the town he took a roundabout road that Templemore soon saw led to the neighbourhood of the scene of their adventure with the devil-tree, though they were approaching it from a different direction. Finally, they entered a thick wood that covered a steep hill; and now Templemore's companions made signs to him to observe strict silence and to proceed as quietly as possible. When they had reached the summit of the slope, and stood on the ridge within the shadow of the trees, which here ceased abruptly, Templemore uttered a half-smothered exclamation. Instantly, he felt Monella's heavy hand upon his shoulder grasping him with a grip of iron; and it brought to him the recollection of the caution he had received.

"Whatever you see or hear," Monella had rejoined, "you must remain absolutely quiet and utter no sound; do nothing that might betray our presence."

What had excited Templemore's surprise was the fact that he found himself looking down into the great amphitheatre in which stood the well-remembered tree. Its long trailing branches were still moving about swiftly in their strange, restless fashion; but most of the shorter and thicker branches were curled up at the top of the trunk in the same kind of knot as they had formed after carrying thither the body of the puma. Viewed in the bright moonlight, the tree was a hideous monstrosity that had yet a certain terrible fascination which attracted and retained the sight while it revolted and repelled the mind. The coiled branches upon the top reminded one irresistibly of the snakes entwined round the head of the Medusa; they formed a kind of crown, of a character suitable to the frightful monster whose formless head, if one may so term it, they encircled. The appearance of the whole thing was repulsive, ghastly, ghoulish. There was that in the mere form and outline of this gruesome wonder of the vegetable world that instinctively aroused aversion. Its naked branches—that in ordinary circumstances could belong only to a dead tree—its colour—half funereal, half of a deep blood-tint almost unknown amongst botanical productions—its never ceasing movement, so suggestive of an everlasting hunting after prey, of an insatiable craving for its hateful diet of flesh and blood, of sleepless hunger, of tireless rapacity and relentless cruelty—all these made up an unnatural creation that appalled the instincts and chilled the very blood of those who looked upon it. This had been the feeling, or combination of feelings, that had made itself felt in Templemore's mind when he had first seen the spectacle by daylight; it impressed itself much more strongly now that he saw the tree in the cold moonlight—now standing out clear and well-defined, now plunged into semi-obscurity, as the hurrying clouds chased each other across the sky above and threw their fleeting shadows beneath.

From the spot where the three men stood a clear view was presented of the opposite side of the enclosure—i.e., of the side nearest to the tree, which was there sufficiently close to the main terrace for its branches to sweep over it; but the terrace was here protected by a covered-way or verandah formed of metal gratings, the interstices in which were small enough to keep the dreadful writhing snake-like branches from pushing through them. When Templemore had seen the place before, this part of the terrace had been open; for the metal screens, or gratings, were, in reality, sliding shutters that could be withdrawn into grooves in the rock beyond. Here, at the end of the covered-way, was a gateway that formed the entrance to the labyrinth of caverns and galleries in the cliff in which Coryon and his adherents lived.

These sliding screens were movable at the will of those within the gateway. They could be either moved along in their grooves and thus protect those traversing the covered-way, or withdrawn, so that the branches of the fatal tree, in that case, guarded the entrance most effectually; for no man might then venture to approach the gateway and live.

Underneath, there were cells in the terrace, also within reach of the tree; and screened off, in like manner, by sliding grated doors. Through these gratings came faint beams of light.

Templemore noted all these things; yet, while his gaze wandered to them, each time the tree itself attracted it again and seemed to hold it spell-bound; and he waited—waited, hardly daring to breathe; waited for he knew not what; waited as one expectant and oppressed by a dim unshapen foreshadowing of some new and nameless horror.

Nor was it without reason; for, slowly, the coiled "crown" unfolded, and something came little by little into view. Gradually the something rose out of the hollow in the trunk, was carried up clear of it, then lowered over the side towards the ground. In shape it was cylindrical, and of a colour that could not be discovered in the fitful moonlight. Soon it was deposited upon the ground, and the branches that had lowered it released their hold, and it remained for a brief space untouched. Then other branches crept up to it with tortuous twistings and, coiling round it, raised and swung it to and fro, then quickly dropped it. Anon, yet other branches would do the same; only, in their turn, to drop it or to hand it on to others. Thus was it passed about; now lifted high in the air by one end, then by the other, anon dangled horizontally in mid-air. In time it made the circuit of the tree; but each branch, or set of branches that laid hold of it, rejected it eventually, as though, by some fell but unfailing instinct, they knew there was nothing left in it to minister to their hateful appetite. And all the while the shadows came and went, and the moon looked down between them and lighted up the hideous scene.

Meantime, from out the dark and filthy water and thick slime of the large pool a few hundred yards away, crawled uncouth monsters the like of which Templemore had never looked upon, save, perhaps, in some fanciful representations of creatures said to have existed in pre-historic times. These mis-shapen reptiles were from ten to twelve feet in length. They had heads and tails like crocodiles, and in many other respects resembled them; but in place of the usual scales they were covered with large horny plates several inches in diameter; and in the centre of each plate was a strong spine or spike, thick at the base but sharp at the point, and four or five inches long.

These creatures crawled up to the fateful tree; and it was quickly evident that they came to claim their share in the foul repast—the dry husk and bones from which the tree had sucked the rest. Their armour made them safe against the tree; for the branches no sooner touched their bodies than they recoiled, baffled by the sharp points they everywhere encountered. Two or three of these horrid reptiles began to drag the dead body towards their haunt, and finally carried it away, but not without several tussles with the twisting, curling branches which seemed loth to relinquish their prey; or, perhaps, wished to play with it a little longer, as a cat might with a mouse.

Monella had handed his field-glass to Templemore, still keeping a hand upon his shoulder. The young man placed it to his eyes, and in an instant gasped out, "Great heavens! It is a human body!"

Yes!—if that may be so called which was but the mutilated husk of what had once been a living, breathing, human being! But now there was little left beyond a shapeless form!

Templemore felt sick, and almost reeled; but Monella's grasp up-held him, and was a silent reminder that he was expected to master his emotions, however strong and painful they might be.

"It is no time to give way," Monella whispered in his ear. "Wait and watch!"

It was, however, almost more than Templemore could do. He felt like Dante led by his guide to witness the tortures of the damned. But here, as it seemed to him, was a scene that rivalled in horror, if not in agony, even the scenes in the "Inferno." He set his teeth and clenched his hands; his breath was laboured, and his heart almost stood still. But for Monella's hold upon his shoulder he must have fallen.

But now there came out of the covered-way two figures; they stood on the terrace and bent their gaze upon the scene, silent and motionless. They were dressed in flowing robes of black, or some dark colour, that were emblazoned on the breast with a golden star.

Grim, weird figures were they; their dark forms showing sharply against the light-coloured rocks behind them, the while they gazed with cruel composure upon the ghastly contention between the loathsome reptiles and the tree.

When it was ended, and the beasts had disappeared with their prey into the dark waters of the pool, one of the figures on the terrace put a whistle to his mouth, and a low piping sound reached the ears of the concealed watchers.

Immediately a rumbling noise was heard; and one of the sliding gratings beneath the terrace rolled back, thereby disclosing a cavernous cell, in which was a lighted lamp on a rough table. Then a figure seated by it, his face buried in his hands, sprang up with a loud cry, and retreated into the thick gloom beyond. But the terrible trailing branches swept in after him, twined round his legs and threw him down, then quickly drew him out feet foremost. Vainly he shrieked, and clutched at this and that; at the table, at the edge of the sliding door; relentlessly, inexorably, he was dragged from one futile hold to another, upsetting the lamp in his struggles, till he was outside. Other branches swooped down upon him, coiling round him in all directions, and stifling his cries as, slowly, with an awful deliberation and absence of hurry, or even of the appearance of effort, he was hauled high into the air and disappeared into the hollow of the fatal tree. The great branches silently arranged themselves into their knot-like circle; at another sound of the low whistle the sliding door returned to its place with a sullen rumble, and the two dark-robed spectators turned and left the place.

Then Monella and Ergalon also came away; and it is no disparagement of Templemore's courage or 'nerve' to state that they had almost to carry him between them. When they had got to a safe distance, Monella placed him on a boulder, and held to his lips a flask containing a strong cordial. Templemore, who had been on the point of fainting, felt revived by it at once; the liquid seemed to course quickly through his veins, and the feeling of deadly sickness, after a time, passed away.

Monella, meanwhile, contemplated him with compassion and concern, but said no word. Presently Templemore gasped out,

"What horrors! What frightful, cold-blooded atrocity! What a race of foul fiends! Great heavens! To think such things go on in this fair land—a land that seems so peaceful, so contented, so free from ordinary pain and suffering!"

"Ah, my son," replied Monella, and there was an indescribable sadness in his tones, "now you can understand the great horror in the land; that which has oppressed it for many long ages; that casts a gloom upon people's lives; that turns to gall and bitterness what, but for it, would be a life of innocent enjoyment."

"But why?" Templemore exclaimed almost fiercely; but the other checked him.

"I think I know what you would say," Monella went on. "You would know two or three things, I think. To the first question (as I read it) I reply that the reason you have not heard of this thing from other people is that they have learned, from long habit, never to refer to it, even to one another. Almost incredible, you think? Not more so than are many things that happen in your own life, in your own country. I could name many known to all, yet alluded to by none—often wrongly, as I hold. Still, there is the fact. It is the same here. This horror in the land broods over, enthrals the people; yet, because they hold it in such dread, they make an affectation of pretending not to know of its existence; perhaps, in mercy to their children.

"Next, it surprises you that I have not told you sooner. The answer is simple. You are not like myself; I am one of this people;

you are but a sojourner in the land—a visitor. I had the desire to make your sojourn here as pleasant as it could be; that your interest in the many curious things you see about you should not be lessened, nor your stay here rendered unhappy by the knowledge of that which you have seen to-night—the earlier knowledge of which could have done no good to any one.

"Lastly, you naturally desire to know why, in that case, I have now chosen to enlighten you. For this reason: the time is approaching when certain plans of mine and of the king's will be completed, and when I devoutly hope we may be able, with God's help, to end this thing for ever. In that I shall ask you to help us—I hope you will aid us all you can."

"I will," said Templemore impetuously. "Against such a hellish crew as that I am with you heart and soul. I think I begin to understand—"

"Yes, I never doubted your readiness to take part with us. But it was necessary to give you absolute proof of what goes on, that you might understand those with whom we have to deal. You have now seen for yourself—"

"Ay, I have seen!" Jack shuddered.

And will now understand that, when the time comes to extirpate this serpent brood, there must be no hesitation, no paltering, no half-and-half measures, no mercy. It will be of no use to kill the old snakes and leave the brood to grow up again, or eggs to hatch. Do you take in my meaning?"

"Yes, and think you will be right and well justified."

"Good. If you wonder why, knowing all this, I have done nothing heretofore, it is that the king's plans could not sooner be matured. Meantime we have stayed the horror for a while."

Jack uttered an impatient exclamation.

"Oh, yes," Monella declared, "we have, and you have helped to do it. These wretched creatures you have seen sacrificed to this horrible 'fetish-tree' of theirs, are their own soldiers—those who escaped from us by running away. They deserve no pity. They themselves have given many an innocent victim—even women and children—to that tree—"

"I know that to be true," Ergalon interposed.

"The truce we forced on Coryon," resumed Monella, "has had this effect at least—it has saved the lives of numbers of poor creatures who would have been seized and sacrificed during the time that we have been here. Instead of that, however, the arch-fiend Coryon has had to content himself with making victims of his own wretched myrmidons by way of punishment for their running away from us. They are as bad as he—very nearly. At any rate they are not worth your pity."

"Well, I am glad to hear that, at least," said Templemore. "It takes away a little of the load of horror that turned me sick. Truly, of all the diabolical atrocities that the mind of man in its depths of cruelty and wickedness ever conceived—"

Ergalon shuddered now in his turn.

"I can look on at the sacrifice of victims such as these," he said gravely, "because I know that every one of them has deserved his fate by acts of cruelty; but when it is a case, as it has been in the past, of women, young girls, and poor little children—"

"For Heaven's sake say no more," Jack entreated; "I begin to feel sick again at such suggestions! I will fight to the death against such wretches. As it is, for the rest of my life I shall see before me in my dreams what I saw to-night. Surely no wilder phantasy, no more outrageous, blood-curdling nightmare ever entered the most disordered brain. And now it will haunt me to my life's end!"

24
Trapped!

One day the king announced his intention to fix a day for Leonard's formal betrothal to Ulama according to the usage of the country. Immediately the people began preparations to do honour to the event; and congratulations and marks of friendship and goodwill were showered upon the young couple by all those who were well affected towards the king.

In the opposite camp, however, as might be expected, the announcement was differently received; and, indeed, the crafty Coryon took advantage of it to sow dissension among some of the people, and to suggest opposition to the proposal. His adherents had certain supporters in the land; people who bought their own security by aiding Coryon secretly against their neighbours. This was why the king had shrunk from pushing matters to the extreme against the priest. He knew that these half-hearted or doubtful ones were quite as likely to side with Coryon, at the last moment, as with himself, and that thus a civil war would be inaugurated.

Monella, since he had come into the country and espoused the king's side, had thrown more energy and method into the cause than had been previously bestowed upon it. Through the Fraternity of the White Priests, and their covert friends and sympathisers, and through Ergalon, who had secretly gained over some of Coryon's people, an active work had been carried on amongst all classes, and with satisfactory results. But Coryon, on his side, had been busy too; though hitherto with less success. Now, however, he found a useful aid in the objection many felt to seeing the king's only daughter wedded to one who—as it was cunningly suggested to them—was a stranger, an adventurer, come from no one knew where, and unable to show such evidence of descent and other qualifications as should entitle him to seek alliance with the daughter of their king.

But Coryon's emissaries worked silently and unseen and there was nothing outwardly to show that two undercurrents were gradually gaining strength and approaching that point whence the slightest accident might bring them into active opposition.

Indeed, in announcing the proposed betrothal, the king had, for once, acted directly against Monella's advice. The latter had counselled that the matter should be kept secret until the contest with Coryon—now in abeyance—had been finally decided; for he foresaw the use to which Coryon would put it.

Leonard and Ulama were too much taken up with each other and with their own happiness to trouble themselves about the "pros and cons" that had weighed in the minds of Monella and those who thought with him. That the effect of the proclamation would be to hasten his marriage was, of course, sufficient to commend it to Leonard; and he left all the rest to others.

Templemore knew not sufficient of what was going on around him to have any opinion upon the subject. Since the night when the real use to which the great devil-tree was put had been revealed to him, he had been very unhappy. He felt as might one who had been slumbering peacefully in sight of a terrible peril, to whose existence he had suddenly been awakened. Not that he had any fear for his own safety; yet he was filled with a nameless dread, a vague sense of horror and distrust, of unreality, in the life about him. He could not but realise that there would be no real peace, no security for life or property, until an absolute end had been put to Coryon and his atrocious crew, and their abominable fetish-tree destroyed. But when would that be? he wondered. His sense of disquiet was increased by having to keep from Leonard the knowledge he had gained, and being thus debarred from discussing matters with him. Not, however (as he acknowledged to himself), that that would have been of much advantage; for Leonard was too much absorbed in "love's young dream" to be likely to discuss such things coolly and critically.

Three days before that fixed for the ceremony of betrothal, which was to be marked by a still grander entertainment, the king gave a preliminary fete. There was much feasting for all and sundry; boats, gaily decorated with flowers and banners and coloured streamers, glided to and fro upon the lake; the young people skilled in diving from great heights into the water with their parachute aids, contended for prizes, and there were many other forms of gaiety and festivity.

Leonard and Ulama, seated upon a terrace, looked upon the scene, and waved their hands in frequent recognition of friendly faces and signals here and there amongst the crowd. Ulama's lovely face was radiant, and the soft light in her gentle eyes, her pleased acknowledgment of the tokens of affection and the good wishes she received on every side, and her grateful smiles for all, were charming to behold. Her wondrous grace and beauty seemed, if possible, enhanced by her half-shy, half-proud glances, and the flush that mounted to her cheeks when she turned her eyes with love on Leonard. Never before, even in that country where the charms of the daughters of the land exceed the average, had such a vision of lovely maidenhood and such rare beauty been beheld. And yet all those who knew her, loved her as much for the innocence and sweetness that beamed ever in her face and guided all her thoughts and words and actions, as for the physical perfection that compelled their admiration.

She stole her little hand into her lover's and sighed quietly.

"I am so happy, and yet my eyes are full of tears. And I feel half frightened too; frightened lest my happiness should be too great to last. Is it wrong, then, to be happy, think you? It almost seems so, when I know so many others are unhappy."

Leonard fondly pressed her hand, and gazed deep down into her eyes.

"If you feel happy in your love, dear heart," he answered, "it is because you love so much; and surely to love cannot be wrong, or to take pleasure in it. Besides, in that you think so much of others you but show your sweet unselfishness. Therefore, trouble not yourself about the regrets for others that accompany your love. For, if today they sorrow, they have had their times of happiness in the past, or may have them in the future."

"It may be so," replied Ulama. "I doubt whether in all the world there is another maiden who loves as I do, and therefore who could know the dread that weighs me down. But as for me—ah, I tremble at my own great joy, and fear it is too great to last. And every one is so kind to me and seems so rejoiced to see me happy—that—that I can hardly keep from crying."

And for a brief minute the gentle-hearted girl placed her hands before her face to hide her tears—tears that were born of the great gladness of her love and her tender sympathy for others.

And so for these two the day passed, like many that had gone before it, in a blissful dream; but it was a dream from which they were soon to be roughly awakened to the dark knowledge of what wickedness can achieve.

For, amid the feasting and among the revellers, were evil beings who had plotted in their black hearts to kill the joy of the gentlest-hearted maiden that ever with her sweetness brightened this sorrow-laden earth; wretches that even then were spinning around her the treacherous web designed by the fell Coryon to end her dream of happiness for ever.

When Templemore woke up the next morning he gazed about him in surprise. He was not in his usual sleeping apartment; but, instead, in some room that was strange to him. It was small, dingy and ill-lighted, and the couch upon which he found himself was not that on which he had lately slept. He sprang up and, in vague alarm, looked round for his clothes and his arms; the clothes were there, but there was no revolver, and his rifle was nowhere to be seen. Even his sword and dagger, that formed part of his usual dress, had been removed.

Dressing himself hastily, he rushed to the door, but it was fastened.

"Great heavens!" he exclaimed, "I am a prisoner; my rifle and pistol have been taken away in my sleep. Oh, what, what has happened to Leonard? What can it all mean?

He hammered at the door, but no answer came. Then he tried to look out of the window, but it was too high for him to be able to see anything through it but the sky. There was nothing to be done but wait; so he sat down upon the bed, a picture of misery and bewilderment, and forthwith began to formulate all sorts of theories and ideas to account for what had happened to him.

When, after a long interval, the door was opened, a man entered whose dress showed him to be one of Coryon's black-tunicked soldiers. He brought in some food, and a pitcher and a mug, which he deposited upon a small table, and was turning to go, when Templemore sprang up and addressed him. He felt so incensed at the sight of this emissary of Coryon's that he could indeed scarcely refrain from hurling himself upon him, despite the fact that the man was armed. But just outside the door, as he could see, were other soldiers; he could hear, too, the clank of their arms, so he knew that to attack the one before him would be worse than useless.

"What is the meaning of this?" he demanded.

The man, who was just on the point of going out, turned back for a step or two, and then said in a low tone,

"You are the prisoner of the High Priest Coryon."

"But how, and why, and where?"

The man shook his head quietly. He was not an ill-favoured fellow, and regarded his prisoner in a half-friendly manner, Templemore thought.

"You are still in the king's palace," he continued, "but your friend and the princess have been taken away to Coryon's abode."

"Taken away to his place? Great God help them and help us all, then!" Jack moaned, as the picture of what he had seen there that well-remembered night rose up before his mind. "And how has all this come about? and where is Monella, and where is the king?"

"I may not talk to you," the soldier answered. "I have disobeyed orders in telling you thus much. But Ergalon was a friend of mine and I know that he is a friend of yours." And he went out, closing and fastening the door behind him.

Here was terrible news! Leonard and Ulama prisoners of Coryon; perhaps immured in one of those awful dungeons within reach of the terrible tree, where the very sight of what went on beyond those barred and grated doors was enough to drive the bravest mad; and where, at any moment, that whistle—a door run back—and then—!

"It's too dreadful—too horrible to think of!" Templemore exclaimed. He sprang up and began pacing restlessly up and down. "I shall go mad myself, if I dwell upon such thoughts."

The hours dragged slowly by till evening, when, just when it was growing dark, the door was once more opened and the same man came in and, looking at Templemore, made a sign to be silent. Then he returned to the door and led in a muffled figure, and, without a word, retired. The figure threw back a hood that covered the head, and Templemore, with glad surprise, saw that it was Zonella.

He ran forward and took her hand in his.

"Zonella!" he exclaimed. "This is surprising, and gladdening too. It does one good to see your face after all that I have been imagining. Tell me—what does it all mean?"

She laid her finger on her lips and said in a hushed voice,

"It means that the cunning, treacherous Coryon has played a trick upon us all, and made you prisoners. Your friend and our beloved princess have been carried off, the king himself is kept a prisoner in his room, and so are many of his ministers."

"And Monella and Ergalon?"

"Monella was away in Myrlanda, as you know, and so has escaped; and Ergalon—who is free too, but in hiding—has sent a trusty messenger to warn him."

"And you?"

"I am virtually a prisoner too. That is, I am forbidden to leave the palace. But I am free to go about within it. The whole place is full of Coryon's soldiers."

"Can you tell me how it was managed?"

"The 'loving cup' was drugged. All who partook of it fell into an unnaturally heavy sleep. You remember almost every one throughout the palace drank some, in honour of your friend and our poor princess. Alas! alas! My dear, my loved Ulama!"

She sobbed bitterly, while Jack marched excitedly up and down the place.

"Is there no hope—nothing to be done?" he exclaimed despairingly.

"There is only one thing," was answered in a low, hesitating tone.

"What is that?" he asked eagerly.

"I have come to try to aid you. If you wrap up in this cloak and go out quietly now, while it is half dark, you may get clear out of the palace unobserved. One of my maids is waiting for me without, and will show you the way. I warned her of my plan, and she is to be trusted."

"What! And leave you here in my place to suffer Coryon's vengeance? Why, Zonella—dear, kind friend—what must you think of me?"

"I can think of nothing else," she answered simply. "And for me—I care not. Whatever may befall me, you will be able to get away; perhaps even to serve your friend."

Jack took her hand in his, not noticing that she seemed to shiver under the touch.

"Such an offer is too kind, too much, my dear, good friend," he said. "It cannot be; we must try—"

"For my sake, then," she exclaimed impulsively. "I would rather die myself than see you carried off to yonder dens. Or"—she paused confusedly, and then went on— "for your friend's sake. Think! Consider! Do you refuse merely from any thought about me? Think what you might be able to do for others—for your friend, for Ulama!"

Templemore passed his hand over his face; the tears were coming into his eyes. When he tried to speak again, he felt half choking.

"You are a noble girl, Zonella," he answered with emotion; "and when you appeal to me on their behalf you cannot know how hard it is to me to stay on here, knowing that I have the chance just the chance—of saving them. But it cannot be, dear friend, it cannot be; but—I thank you. My whole heart thanks you." He pressed her hand, and turned sorrowfully away.

Presently, she spoke again, this time in a different tone; indeed, her voice sounded hard and strained.

"Then Ergalon shall risk his life for you," she said. "I know that which will induce him to attempt what to-day he said could not be done. I will seek him at once. For now, good-bye; do not go to bed, but be ready, if you hear some one at the window. You can reach it, if you stand up on the table." And, without further explanation, she left him.

Templemore sat for long pondering upon this strange interview, and wondering too what she had planned; and the time seemed to drag wearily while he waited for some signal at the window.

It was about midnight, as he judged, when there came a tap, tap from the outside. He sprang on to the table; then by the dim light that came through the window he could discern the upper part of a man's body swinging on a rope.

"Is that Ergalon?" he whispered.

"Yes," came back the answer. "If I send you in a short rope and you wait till I have gone down, you can then pull in the rope I am on, get on to it, and come down yourself. Do you dare try it?"

"Yes."

"Then here it is. Now wait till you find you can pull this one in."

Templemore felt about and caught hold of a small cord that was hanging inside the window—which was open to the air—and he pulled lightly at it till he felt the strain upon the rope to which it was attached, relaxed. Then he pulled harder, and a portion of a thicker rope came inside. By its means he was able to climb up on to the sill. With some trouble and manoeuvring he got outside and was soon sliding down the rope, which Ergalon steadied from below. It was very dark, and he descended amidst some trees where it was darker still. When he touched the ground, at first, he could see nothing; but Ergalon turned on the light of a bull's-eye lantern. It was one of those Monella had brought with him, and lent by him to Ergalon.

A voice, that he knew to be Zonella's, whispered,

"That has been well done. Now what do you propose to do?"

"I must get down to the canyon by which we came into the mountain. There we have left spare weapons.

"But I can't get down in the dark; not even, I fear, with the lantern."

"There will be a moon later; perhaps that will help. Let us go in that direction."

"What! you, too?" Jack asked in surprise.

"Yes, why not? I shall be as safe with you as in the midst of Coryon's hateful minions, and I may be of service."

"You couldn't climb down that place and up again," Jack reminded her.

"Then I can wait near the top, and Ergalon can go with you to help you carry what you want."

"But we shall be a long time, all day to-morrow."

"No matter, I will manage."

Then the three made their way with much difficulty, owing to the darkness, to the top of the canyon. Here they sat and talked in guarded voices till the moon had risen high enough to light the hazardous descent.

Templemore learned how Coryon's plans had been carried out; how Ergalon's escape had been due to his absence from the palace, awaiting the return of a messenger from Monella. At a late hour, on his way back to the palace, he had been warned by a friend amongst Coryon's people. On this he had sent on the messenger to Monella to inform him of all that had occurred. The man had been only just in time to get through the subterranean road before Coryon's soldiers took possession of it and closed it.

Templemore's escape had been planned by Zonella. She had smuggled Ergalon into the palace and up to the roof disguised as one of her own maids; and in this she had been aided by one of his friends amongst the soldiers of the priest. Ergalon had at first objected strongly, conceiving that the attempt was foolhardy and could not succeed, that he would only lose his own liberty and, perhaps, his life, and that Monella might be displeased. In short, he had considered himself bound to do nothing that was in any way risky until Monella had communicated with him. But Zonella had contrived, by some means, to persuade him; and had herself stolen out and steadied the rope for Ergalon in his perilous descent.

From his friend in the opposite camp Ergalon had learned one very important thing—that nothing was likely to be done to Leonard or Ulama till the day that had been named for their betrothal. That day Coryon had fixed upon, with cruel irony, for the holding of a sort of trial, the result of which would be a foregone conclusion.

"Therefore," said Ergalon, "if you can get back by the morning of to-morrow" (it being then already morning) "you will be in time;

though I fear you will find it difficult to effect much good alone, and I cannot yet tell when the lord Monella may be able to get through the subterranean passage to come to your assistance."

"We will try, anyhow," said Jack, setting his teeth with grim determination. "And, if I fail, we will die together. One can but die once. I think it is possible to get back with a couple of rifles and pistols and the necessary ammunition by the morning. If human effort can do it, it shall be done; and I can then put a pistol into your hands, too, my good friend."

25
In the Devil-Tree's Larder!

Leonard awoke from a deep sleep, on the morning after the fete, to find himself, like Templemore, in a place that was strange to him.

So profound had been the slumber induced by the drug that had been mixed with the drink, that he had been carried all the way to Coryon's retreat in absolute unconsciousness. When he at last woke up, he was in one of the cells under the terrace within the reach of the great flesh-eating tree.

No words can describe the horror and anguish that filled his breast when, by degrees, he realised the dreadful truth. Not only did he shudder at the thought of his own too probable fate, but the fear that his sweet Ulama might share the same awful doom drove him almost to the verge of madness. He cursed the false sense of security that had led up to this terrible result. A few simple precautions would have frustrated this treachery! But it was too late!

Through the grated door he could see the great devil-tree, hear the swishing of its long, trailing branches, watch them come up to the grating and search about over its face for some opening large enough to penetrate, even trying to wriggle in through its small slits and perforations. In the centre of the cell was a block of wood fixed in the ground to serve as a table. A small stream of water ran down from a pipe above and fell into a channel in the floor, and a pitcher stood beside it. For chair there was a smaller log of wood; the "bed" on which he had found himself was simply a bag of straw whereon were laid two or three rugs. An iron door shut off the back from an interior gallery, and the cell was partitioned off from others, on each side, by grated screens, like that in the front. The occupants of adjacent cells could, therefore, see each other.

As Leonard looked round in astonishment and alarm, and exclaimed, involuntarily, "Where am I?" a discordant peal of mocking laughter rang out from the cell upon his right.

"Where is he! He doesn't even know where he is!" a harsh voice cried out. "He—one of the gods that wielded the lightning and thunder! After all, caught by Coryon, and brought here like the rest of us! Ha! ha! ha!"

Leonard, shocked and amazed, went to the side whence the sounds proceeded, and there saw, peering through the bars, a horrible face that grinned at him with hideous sneers and wild-looking eyes. The hair and beard were matted and dishevelled; the face and figure, so far as he could make them out, looked gaunt and thin. He was dressed in the black tunic with gold star that denoted one of Coryon's soldiers.

"Ha! ha! ha!" laughed the mocking voice. "You don't know where you are, eh? I'll tell you, my lord, son of the gods, that can kill us soldiers with a magic lightning wand, but can't keep yourself out of Coryon's clutches—you are in the 'devil-tree's larder'!"

"The devil-tree's larder!"

"Yes, my lord; the devil-tree's larder. That means that they have put you here to keep you cool and in good condition, before they hand you over to be food for their pet out there." And he pointed to the tree.

Leonard shuddered, and the awful truth of the man's statement forced itself upon his mind, in spite of his wish to believe it too atrocious to be possible. He went up to the door in the front and examined it. He saw that it ran in grooves at the top and bottom.

"Ah," said the mocking voice behind him, "that's right. You see how it's done now. They run that back from inside, sudden-like, some time when you don't expect it; and in come the twisting branches that lay hold of you, and out you go to make him a nice meal. Ha! ha! ha!"

Leonard turned and stared in helpless horror. Was it possible that there was such cold-blooded, fiendish cruelty in the world? Yet—he remembered the fate of the poor puma. He trembled, and turned sick and faint; while the one in the next cell continued to jeer and mock at him.

"Where is your lightning-wand, my lord? Why have you not brought it to try it on the tree? You managed to get me brought here; and now you've managed to get here yourself!"

"I got you brought here? How? What then are you doing here?" Leonard asked, his surprise overcoming his disgust.

"What am I doing here? Why, the same as you—waiting in 'the devil-tree's larder' till I'm given to him for a meal—as you will be. And it's all through you; because you killed some of us and we others ran away; this is what they do with us."

Leonard shuddered again, while the man went to the stream of water that, as in Leonard's cell, was pouring down from a pipe above, and, filling the pitcher, took a long drink.

"Makes you thirsty, this sort of thing," he said, with another jeering laugh. "You'll find that water there mighty handy if they let you stay here long enough. Ha! ha! ha!"

The man was evidently in a state of high fever. The place was full of fetid odours given off by the foul tree; and, apart from that, the want of sleep would superinduce fever, if, indeed, it did not drive mad the wretched occupants of the cells; for who could sleep for more than a minute or two at a time in one of those dens, where, at any moment, the door might be run back and the miserable prisoner delivered over to the fatal branches? It was this constant, ever-present dread that banished sleep, and must inevitably end in madness for the victims, provided they were kept there long enough.

Then the thought flashed upon him that Ulama also might be an occupant of one of these awful cells; and at that such a burst of grief and agony came over him that he hid his face within his hands and groaned aloud.

"Yah! don't give way like that, my lord. Being here's not so bad when once you're used to it! Look at me! You don't see me worry and cry like a great girl. I take it quietly; I've been too used to seeing others here. Many's the time I've had the pulling back of these doors and have seen a man or a woman hauled out squealing and kicking like an animal going to be killed; and I've laughed at them.

I thought it such fun! And now those who used to help me and laugh with me, they're waiting to see how I like it; and they will laugh at me, too, just the same. But I don't care. What does it matter? It's nothing, I tell you, when you're as used to it as I am."

The wretched creature thus trying to delude himself with boastful talk and jeering at his fellow-captive, was himself, it was easy to see, worked up into the highest state of nervous dread and fear. The least sound made him start and look with straining eyeballs in the direction from which it came. He kept going to the pitcher for draughts of water, and never remained still for a single instant. If he sat down for a short space, the twitching of a foot, or leg, or hand, spoke of agitation within that would not be controlled.

Leonard turned from the sight with mingled feelings of disgust and loathing and, going to the other side, looked through the grating of the adjoining cell, to see whether it was occupied. And, looking, his heart seemed to come up into his throat when he saw a silent female form seated with its back to him. The exclamation that escaped him caused the form to turn, when he saw that the woman was a stranger. Her face was pleasing in its features, and good-looking, but had in its expression such a burden of unspeakable horror and despair that he shivered as he met her glance. At sight of it, for the moment, he almost forgot his own misery, and he asked gently,

"And who then are you?"

For a few seconds there was no reply; then, in a voice that had in it the suggestion of much sweetness, albeit now forced, and unnatural,

"I scarcely know. Once I was a happy young girl; then a well-beloved and loving wife and mother; now I am only something with which to feed yonder monster."

"Yes," continued the woman dreamily, "I was once good-looking, they said. Certainly, my husband thought so; and that was enough for me. But it was my curse, alas! for Skelda, the chief of the priests next to Coryon, thought so too. He stole me away from my home and my children and forced me to become one of his so-called wives. And now, because my sorrowing and pining have seared and furrowed my good looks, even as they had eaten into my heart, he has tired of me, and has sent me to the fate that, sooner or later, we all come to here—all of my sex, at least, as well as many of the other among those who are not priests. Yet," she added, "it is but five years since they brought me here. What I look like now you can see for yourself!"

Leonard looked at her with pity; and there came into his mind the remembrance of Ulama's words of the day before— "It seems almost wrong to be happy when I know so many others are unhappy"—and his own light rejoinder. And he reproached himself in that he had been content to bask in love and self-enjoyment while, close at hand, there were such abuses, such direful sufferings. True, he had not actually known their whole nature and extent; but he had known of the so-called "blood-tax"; and had heard enough to make it certain, had he given the matter due consideration, that there were evils in the land that cried aloud for remedy.

Then his thoughts reverted to Ulama, and he asked, "Do you know aught concerning the Princess Ulama?"

"I know that she was to be brought to this place, and that she was to be put into the cell I occupied before they brought me here yesterday. It is underground; a long way from this part."

At least, then, the poor child, Leonard thankfully reflected, was not in one of the cells in sight of the dreaded tree.

Presently he asked the woman whether she had known Zelus, the son of Coryon.

"Ah yes! Who did not in this land?" was the reply. "The monster! A great spasm as of relief and joy came upon us all—all the women, I mean—when we heard of his death. He was the worst of them all, though one of the youngest. No one was safe from him. Even the princess he sought to bring here to treat as he had treated so many others!"

"I know. I killed him when he was in the very act of raising his cowardly hand against the king's daughter," said Leonard quietly.

The woman turned and looked at him with more of interest in her manner than she had yet shown. She scanned him closely.

"Then," she said, "you must be one of the strangers of whom we heard. But you are young, and not, as I have been told, of our race. We heard of one older, one who, it was said, belonged to our people. And when we heard that, we all rejoiced; for surely, we said, he brings us tidings of what all have been expecting. Therefore, we who were held here in a bondage that is a daily, hourly torture, a never-ceasing degradation, we welcomed your coming as a sign that the Great Spirit had at last brought our long punishment to an end. I, even I, dared to hope I should escape the fate that has befallen all others, and should live to see again my husband and children before I die. But, alas! it was but a dream—a delusive, passing hope, a thing too good to come in my time. Four months have passed and nothing has occurred, though ye smote the hated Zelus quickly; and even Coryon was filled with fear and dread. Why have ye failed to do more, and, instead, fallen victim to Coryon?"

Ah! why? It was a question that now sank deep into Leonard's soul and tortured him with vain regrets and self-reproach. For he had a heart that swelled with kindness towards his fellows, and a tender conscience; and the more he thought things over, the more difficult he found it to feel that he was without blame. He had been too selfishly wrapped up in his own personal feelings, he now acknowledged; too little interested in those very matters that, as the king's future son-in-law, should have taken, if not the first, at least a prominent position in his mind. And then, to be ignobly trapped, at a time when there was nothing but feasting and amusement in their minds! Their arms taken from them—they who could have kept at bay all Coryon's soldiers and dispersed them, had they but been vigilant and wakeful! It was a cruelly humiliating thought—it was worse; for the child-hearted, innocent Ulama, who had a right to rely on his protection, had been sacrificed also to his self-abandonment and want of watchfulness.

Thus did Leonard reason, now that his opportunities had vanished. He knew not what was the true explanation of the position in which he found himself; but a vague, half-formed idea crept into his mind that Coryon would hardly have ventured upon such a daring stroke unless he had felt he could rely upon the support, or, at least, the indifferent neutrality, of a certain proportion of the people. And if he, Leonard, had shown more interest in the affairs of the people over whom he was one day to be kink he might have gained so firm a hold on their confidence and affections as would have rendered Coryon's schemes hopeless from the very start.

But such thoughts, whether well or ill-founded, came row all too late. Here he was, caged, and at Coryon's mercy. His relentless enemy had but to give the signal and he would be consigned to an awful death.

He had some further talk with the woman, who told him terrible tales of indescribable barbarities and iniquities perpetrated by the priestly tyrants under the covering of their "religion"; tales that made the blood within him boil, and filled his soul with savage, though helpless, indignation. Then he asked the woman's name, and was told it was Fernina.

At last, he asked the question that, though often upon his tongue, yet he had shrunk from giving voice to.

"And what do you suppose will happen—here?"

She sighed and shook her head, hopelessly, despairingly.

"Only what always happens," she answered, in a dull, listless tone. "None that are once placed here ever escape the fatal tree; except that sometimes they are carried up above and laid on what they call 'the devil-tree's ladle.'"

"'The devil-tree's ladle?'"

"Yes; it is a contrivance on wheels; a kind of long plank shaped at one end like a great spoon. Those who are to be given to the tree are laid upon it, bound so that they cannot move, and then pushed out along the stonework till they are within reach of the branches; those who push the plank at the other end being far enough away for their own safety. It is part of the system of terrorism and torture here," Fernina added, "to place some of us, at times, in rooms that are in the rock above, and that overlook this place, and to keep us locked in there for days and nights, that we may be cowed and frightened at the scenes that are enacted here. Often, a hateful fascination compels you to become an unwilling witness; in any case, you cannot avoid hearing the shrieks and moans; imagination supplies the rest."

Leonard turned away, not caring to hear more, and sat down to brood, eating his heart out with keen regrets, all now unavailing. The jeering of the half-mad wretch in the other cell had ceased;

he, too, had fallen into a sort of brooding lethargy, and so was quiet; but a constant tap, tap, tap, of one foot on the stone floor told he was not asleep. Thus the hours dragged by in silence, save for the intermittent, stealthy rustle of the branches outside, as they came prowling over the face of the gratings in their sleepless seeking after the prey they seemed to scent within.

Once, a small grating at the bottom of the door of each cell was opened, and a platter with coarse food upon it was pushed in; then the space closed up again. The sounds made them all, for the moment, start; then they relapsed again into the stupor of despair. None touched the food or even noticed it. But the man in the further cell had now seated himself near the little stream of water and, every now and then, he roused himself to take long draughts.

When it grew dark, a lighted lantern was pushed under the door into each cell, as the food had been. Leonard felt drowsy and longed for rest; yet was afraid to lie down or to close his eyes. Now and again they even closed against his will in a short doze; but it was never of long duration, and each time he woke it was with a renewed sense of the horror of his situation.

He had just roused from one of these brief snatches of sleep, and had had time to remember once more where he was, when a low rumble made him spring up and look around. Then the man in the next cell gave an awful cry—a cry that rang in Leonard's ears for many a day—and at the same moment the grated door of his prison slowly began to move. In his demented terror he banged himself against the partition between the two cells, tried to get his fingers into the slits that he might cling to it; then climbed up on to the wooden block in the middle of the cell. But the rustling branches neared him, sought for him on every side, and soon mounted the log and caught him in their deadly embrace. Slowly, but irresistibly, while he never ceased his cries or his vain struggles and clutchings, the coils around him tightened and dragged him out into the darkness, where his cries gradually became weaker, and were finally heard no more; and when they ceased, and he heard the door rolling back, with dull rumbling, to its place, Leonard tottered to the pile of rugs in the corner of his cell, and fell upon them in a swoon.

When he returned to consciousness a bright light was shining through the grated door. He got up and, like one who is but a help-less on-looker in a fevered dream, he went to the bars and gazed out. It was bright moonlight outside, and there he saw the same ghastly scene repeated that Templemore had witnessed a short time before. He saw the dead body of the latest victim of the tree's insa-tiable thirst for blood dangling amongst the branches; caught up, now by the neck, and now by the feet, and passed on from one branch to another in what seemed a new dance or sport of death; and finally carried off by the great crawling reptiles that had come up to claim their share in the repast.

While the scene lasted, Leonard seemed incapable of volition; his limbs refused to obey the will of his reeling brain and to bear him away from the sight. But, when the creatures had disappeared, he turned and made his way once more to the low bed, where he remained in a state of torpor till the day was far advanced.

After what seemed a long interval, he sat up and rubbed his eyes, after the manner of one just awakened from the horror of a nightmare. Then he saw the woman who occupied the next cell standing with her eyes fixed on him; and, when she found he was once more awake and conscious, she addressed him.

"I am sorry for you," she said. "Even in my own misery I am not so blinded but that I can see that your burden of sorrow is a heavy one—more than you can bear. Yet methinks, were I a man, I would not thus give way to it. I am but a woman, but my greatest wish—since nothing else is left me—is that I may see Coryon once more—stand face to face with him—and show him that all his cal-culated cruelty and subtle ingenuity of torture have not subdued my spirit, nor the scorn that a heart conscious of having done no wrong can feel for such as he. I would give him back look for look, hate for hate, as I have before to-day; and make his wicked eyes quail before mine with the consciousness that the spirit of one he has unjustly oppressed can show itself greater than his own. But with you—he will but laugh at you—for I feel, somehow, you will be taken from here to meet him. I suspect he has sent you here first to crush your spirit with the sight of the horrors that are per-petrated here. He—have you ever seen him?"

"No," Leonard answered, staring at her in amazement.

"Ah! then you know not what he is like. I tell you," the strange woman went on, her eyes lighting up with unexpected fire, "he is a man whose mere glance strikes terror into the souls of ordinary men. There is that about him that makes you shrink as from some unearthly incarnation of all the powers of evil; and in that he delights, yea, more, even, than in torturing his victims."

Here she broke off abruptly; then resumed, in a different manner.

"I have been wondering whether you are he who was to have wedded the princess?"

"Alas! yes. You have divined aright," Leonard answered sadly.

"Then," said the woman, with increasing warmth, that gained as she went on an energy that was almost fierceness, "then, the greater the reason you should throw off this weakness and gird up your strength to meet the haughty tyrant and show him that your spirit is equal to his own. In all his ill-spent time upon this earth— and they say it has been a very long one—it is his boast and his pride that scarce any can meet his glance without quailing under it. Think! Think how he will triumph over you—how he will point the finger of scorn—turn the look of cold contempt upon the one who aspired to be the future king of this country—and that means to stand on an equality with himself—and yet, as he will declare, is but a weak, puling, or ordinary mortal. Ah! would I were in your place! You can but die. But I would make him feel that I had a heart, a spirit, more dauntless, more unconquerable than his own. Ay! I would die knowing that for many and many and many a year to come, the remembrance that he had met one spirit he could not intimidate or master would be to him an instrument of defeat and shame, eating into his proud heart, even as the suffering he has caused to me has gnawed into my own."

The woman spoke at the last with a force that almost electrified her hearer. Leonard felt roused as, perhaps he had never been roused before.

"You are right, my friend!" he exclaimed, "and I thank you. As you truly say, he who aspires to high things should show himself worthy to achieve them, and not even the shadow of a dreadful death and cruel sufferings should have the strength to cow his spirit in the presence of this most cold-blooded and revolting tyrant. If I have shown weakness, it was not from personal fear, but from thought of the suffering of one dearly loved, and my self-reproach for having been the unintentional cause of it. It is well that I met you; for you have taught me how I should meet this Coryon!"

"And," said the woman, "if you want one unerring shaft to launch at him—one that I know will pierce the armour of his pride and drive him to the verge of madness—tell him you know one woman whose spirit more than matches his; tell him that she is called Fernina."

26
Coryon

At sunrise on the morning of the day that was to have witnessed Leonard's public betrothal he was sitting staring gloomily, through the grating of his cell, at the never-resting branches without, when the sounds of drums, on which a long tattoo was being beaten, broke on his ear.

The sounds cane from both near and far, some half-muffled in the galleries and caverns of the cliff, others echoing from one side to the other of the rocky enclosure till they died away in the far distance.

Since the previous morning nothing further had occurred; the woman was still in the cell on one side of him; no new victim had been brought to occupy the other.

The roll of the drums caused Leonard to start up and look about him. He was haggard and worn from want of sleep, but his step was firm, and his face was stamped with a look of quiet resolution that showed he had taken to heart his fellow-prisoner's advice. When he rose up she spoke.

"It is as I thought," she said; "they are to have one of their gatherings to-day, when the tree will be given its meal in sight of all who are summoned to be present. That is why one of us was not given to it last night, no doubt." And she gave a short, hard laugh, that was far from pleasant to hear.

"No doubt it is your turn," she went on in a softer tone. "You must summon all your fortitude. Be brave! If one must die, one needs not show such craven fear as that half-mad wretch exhibited the other night."

"You speak well, my good friend, and what you have said to me has braced me up. Would that, before we part, I could say or do something to serve or comfort you."

"That cannot be; only remember what I told you—if you want a taunt to hurl at the tyrant's head, a taunt that will stab him through his self-admiration, you know now what to say. Soon they will be here for you. Ah!" here she broke off, as though a new thought had come to her. "On these days they are all assembled outside—all the men. Only the women and children are left within their dens. Oh, if I could but get free for half an hour! I know some of their secrets, and could play a trick upon them that would go far to square accounts between us. But, of course," she added mournfully, "it is foolishness to think of it."

Overhead could now be heard the scuffling of many footsteps, and, anon, more drum-beating, with much blowing of horns and trumpets. Next, there were shouting and cheering, followed by what appeared to be a speech from some one; but the words were not intelligible to the two anxious listeners.

At one time the noise had brought a faint hope into Leonard's mind that it might portend the approach of friends; but the words Fernina had just spoken quickly dissipated any such idea.

Presently, steps were heard in the gallery outside, a key was inserted in the lock, and two of Coryon's black-coated soldiers entered. They were both armed with drawn swords; and one of them, addressing Leonard in gruff accents, said,

"You are to come with us." Then, turning to his comrade, he asked, "Have you the cord?"

"No," was the reply, "I thought you had it."

"And I thought you were bringing it. Go, get it." The man went out.

Then he who had remained, raising a warning hand to Leonard, addressed him in low, guarded tones.

"The lord Monella," he said, "is hastening to thine aid with many armed followers; but he has been detained in the underground pass. Whether he will arrive in time, I know not; if not and thou be harmed, thou wilt be avenged."

"Who art thou, then?" asked Leonard.

"A friend of the lord Monella's."

"And my other friend—what of him?"

"He was a prisoner, but escaped, and has gone—I know not whither."

"Heaven be praised for that! Ah, I can guess where he has gone!" Just then a sudden thought came into Leonard's head.

"See, friend," he said earnestly, "canst thou not turn the key in the lock of the next cell and give the poor creature there one little chance for liberty?"

"I do not know, but I will see. If the key fits, I might."

"Quick, then, ere thy fellow returns."

The man hastily took out the key and tried it in the lock of the woman's cell; it fitted, and he unlocked the door; then withdrawing the key, he replaced it in the door of Leonard's cell.

"Roll that log to the door to keep it close till you think it safe to venture out," Leonard advised the woman. She had but just done so when they heard the steps of the other soldier in the gallery.

"What is thy name, friend?" Leonard asked him in a whisper.

"Melta," the man answered; and then, when the other made his appearance with some cord, he began to rate him for having been so long.

Leonard was bound in a loose fashion, just sufficient to prevent his free use of either arms or legs, and led away. On his way out he said a kindly word to Fernina.

"The Great Spirit help you," was the reply. "I have no fear for you now; you will die with courage, if it be so fated. A heart that can feel and think for a stranger in the midst of such distress as is yours to-day is the heart of a brave man. But we may yet meet again."

Leonard shook his head sadly.

"I have no false hopes," he answered. "I do not expect that help can now come in time. I may be avenged; that is the most I can hope for."

"Yes!" said the woman in a meaning tone; "you will be avenged; and so shall I."

The man who had been sent for the cord laughed jeeringly at the woman when she said this, but took no further notice of her;

and the three proceeded along the gallery till they came to some steps at the end. Ascending these they entered a broader gallery or corridor above; then, turning back, they passed out through the gateway and along the covered-way, finally emerging on the main terrace of the great amphitheatre.

Round the sides of the enclosure a large number of people were gathered. Among these were black-coated soldiers to the number of, perhaps, two hundred; the others, of whom there were from four to five hundred, also carried arms of some sort, spears or swords. When Leonard cast his eyes around and noted them, the heart within him sank, for he saw how difficult would be a rescue, even with the armed followers that the man Melta had said accompanied Monella.

In the centre of the great terrace, upon a high chair carved and emblazoned, and with a great banner waving above his head, sat the dreaded Coryon. Round him were grouped, first his nine priests in black robes, and Dakla and others of his chief officers; then, ranks of soldiers and, among them, some of the king's ministers and chief functionaries, all bound as Leonard was. But the king himself was not there; nor was Ulama; and Leonard, when he had assured himself of this, turned his gaze on Coryon.

It was well that he had been warned that he would need all his courage to enable him to look upon this man unflinchingly. Even thus prepared he found it barely possible to keep down the emotion the sight excited in his breast.

He saw before him a man of great height and powerful frame, clad in a black robe with a star on the breast worked in virgin gold and set with jewels. His grey hair and beard were unkempt and long, his skin of a dark swarthy hue, his forehead, albeit broad, was receding, and furrowed, and wrinkled into a sinister scowl, and his lips were parted or drawn up in a set snarl that disclosed teeth more like a wild beast's fangs than a human being's teeth.

When Leonard first caught sight of him, he was standing with one arm extended as though he had just finished some harangue; but, when Leonard was brought up, Coryon sat down. Then he slowly turned his glance upon the prisoner. And beneath that glance a feeling of cold horror stole into Leonard's breast; he felt as though an icy hand were about to seize his very heart and wring it in a grip of iron. It was the nameless dread that a man may feel in the presence of something that his instincts tell him is a deadly enemy, yet of which he cannot discover the form, or size, or nature; whether earthly or supernatural. Here, certainly, the outward shape was that of a man, but in the eyes there was something suggesting that their owner was not a man at all, but a living incarnation of depravity—a demon with eyes, for the moment quiescent as with the cold glitter and deadly malignancy of the serpent, but instinct with suppressed power, and ready to flame up with terrible, relentless, overwhelming energy. Mingled with the snakelike glitter of malevolence there were lurid flashes that darted forth perpetually, causing the beholder to recoil as though from actual darts. At sight of him one thought of some nameless monster coiled up and meditating a spring upon its prey; a monster that was the implacable foe of the whole human race, that embodied, in human form, all the power, the attributes, the cruelty, of an arch-demon from another world.

From such a being the soul shrinks with a horror that is less earthly fear than the natural loathing of evil things that is implanted within the breasts of all endowed with pure and holy instincts; and this was Leonard's feeling while he stood, half sick and faint, enduring and returning Coryon's fixed look.

But just when it came upon him that he must either shift his glance or drop helpless to the ground, the thought of all the childlike, innocent Ulama must have suffered through the shameless treachery of this fiend in human shape came into his mind; and, with the thought, forth from his heart rushed out the blood, bursting through the icy grip that had all but closed upon it, and coursing through his veins in a leaping torrent, like one of those great waves of fiery indignation that sometimes, for a while, gives to one man the strength of ten. With a sudden impulse that forgot everything but his righteous anger, he put forth such an effort that he broke the cords that bound him; then, rushing impetuously upon Coryon, before any one could interfere, he actually had him by the throat in a clutch that, spite of the other's own gigantic strength, would have ended his vile life if, for a few seconds longer, his assailant had been left alone. But a dozen hands laid hold of him and pulled him back, bruised and panting, to the custody of the men he had escaped from. But, though baffled and injured in the struggle, there was in his eyes a light almost of triumph when he turned round and faced his enemy once more.

"Aha!" he shouted. "Coward! Hateful murderer of women and children and unarmed men! Thou darest not come down and meet me man to man! Though thou art near twice my size, I had choked the foul life out of thee, had we been left alone!"

At first, Coryon made no answer, except to glare at his late assailant with his evil eyes; but they fell away under the other's dauntless look, and he put his hands to his throat as if in pain.

"This will cost thee dear," at last he said, in a harsh, croaking voice; but Leonard replied with a cold smile, "Thou canst but kill me; and I would not beg mercy from such as thou. Why dost turn thine eyes away, coward Coryon? Dost feel at last that so foul a thing may not endure the glance of an honest man?"

Coryon sprang up and stood for a moment with his hands extended towards his prisoner, his fingers closing and opening convulsively as though he half intended to accept the challenge in the other's words and looks. Then he managed to control his passion and sat down again, first addressing a few words in a low tone to a priest who stood beside him.

27
On the "Devil-Tree's Ladle"

When Coryon sat down, a kind of buzzing or hum or talk in low tones broke out on all sides. Exclamations and expressions of astonishment were heard, for never had such audacity been known in a prisoner standing thus on the very brink of death and almost within reach of the clutch of the fatal tree.

Leonard was now bound again, and Dakla sent two or three of his subordinate officers to stand beside him. But, even while they bound him, the guards, as he could hardly fail to see, treated him with a measure of involuntary respect; and well they might, for there was not one amongst them that durst look the evil Coryon in the face.

Then was brought out the contrivance called the 'devil-tree's ladle'; it was simply a long plank widened out at one end, and mounted, in the centre, on wheels. An irrepressible shudder passed through Leonard when he saw this grim apparatus. But there was little outward sign of his emotion, and his eyes were soon again fixed on Coryon, who rose and thus addressed those present,

"Friends, ye all see here a confirmation of that which I have already explained unto you this morning. Yonder stands one of the strangers whom the king hath admitted to his friendship; the man he was about to honour by alliance with his royal house. Ye can see for yourselves the untutored passions by which this youth, who was, forsooth, to have been your future king, is swayed, and his lack of seemly behaviour in the presence of one like myself, who hath for so many years held a high position in the land, and hath conferred so many benefits upon it. Not the least of these, my friends, is that which I have just achieved—only just in time. I have, with the joint help of those powerful gods whom we all here serve, been able to defeat and overcome even the magic with which these men were armed. Ye all know, or have heard, how they came provided, by some enemies of our race outside the country, with magic wands that brought down lightning and thunder and death upon those opposed to them; and to their seeming power the king weakly yielded, and allowed these strangers to assume high stations in the land. Zelus, my well-beloved son, early fell a victim to their lawless intrusion into our domains, as did many of my people whom I sent to capture them. But in the end I have prevailed against them; I have taken from them their magic wands, and now they are, as ye all can see, but ordinary men. But a punishment hath fallen upon the king, for he is sick to death, and that is why he is not here to-day. He hath not long to live, and soon the country will be without a king. Now it seemeth to me certain that the people are averse from accepting this young stranger as the successor to their dying ruler, and that they desire one of their own race. This hath caused me much anxious thought, but I have at last, I think, discovered a solution of the difficulty. I will espouse the Princess Ulama, and become the king's son-in-law; thus will your minds be set at rest; for ye will know that whenever the king dieth he will be succeeded by a ruler who is not only of your own race, but hath served his country long enough to satisfy all objectors as to his experience, or his ability, or his solicitude for the welfare of his native land."

While uttering these words, Coryon looked with a hardly-veiled smile of malice at Leonard, who, listening to the infamous proposal wrapped up in such unblushing hypocrisy, started as though he would have rushed again upon the speaker; but he was held too firmly by those who now surrounded him. He could scarce keep from groaning aloud at what he had just heard.

Coryon marked with evident satisfaction this effect of his announcement, and proceeded, in an unctuous voice, and with an affectation of great resignation, "In doing this, good friends, I have, I assure you, no thought, no feeling save the welfare of my country. I had not thought ever to take to me another wife; though I had looked with favour upon the desire of my son Zelus to ally himself with our king's daughter. But, since this young stranger hath rendered that impossible by slaying treacherously mine only son, I will accept the necessities of the situation, and sacrifice my own feelings for the general good. Perhaps, after all, it is as well; for in me ye will have, as ye all know well, one who thinks always only of his people's weal. For long ages I have guarded the land from outward foes by making friends of the powers of darkness. This, and this alone hath protected us from invasion by the hordes of wild men that we know exist beyond our borders. The powers, whose High Priest I am, have guarded us through many centuries, and have planted around the limits of our island a forest impenetrable and filled with terrible creatures for our protection. True, they let these strangers through, but only as a warning of that which might befall if we forgot, even for a moment, our religion, or rebelled against the sacrifices it requires and that our gods look for from us and will insist upon. True, we have to sacrifice some of those we love to our sacred tree, but what is that compared with the benefits and advantages that the rest receive? We have peace, prosperity, contentment, freedom from invasion, from wars, from enemies and dangers of all kinds; and, compared with these, the price that hath to be paid is, after all, but small. Henceforth, too, there will be a stronger guarantee for peace throughout the land, in that your king and the head of your religion will be one. And you, my faithful followers, who have served me well," continued the arch-hypocrite, casting his eyes around, "will no more be called upon to reside in the rocky fastness that has been so long our home; for I shall take up my abode in the palace of the king and there shall ye all follow me." At this a loud cheer went up from all. "And now to more immediate duties. I have condemned this murderer of my son to death; he shall end his life befittingly as a sacrifice to the gods whose power he hath defied in coming here—defied only to his own doom. So shall perish all who brave me; and so shall perish this man's friends, his murderous abettors who, too, are in my power. And now, sirrah, if thou hast aught to say, thou hast just a minute. If thou hast aught to ask me, now is thy final opportunity."

When he ceased speaking, Coryon sat down, first casting at Leonard a hideous glance of triumph. Leonard saw the sneer and

knew that his enemy's desire was to excite him to a farther display
of useless anger; but the knowledge only served to calm him, and,
when he spoke, it was in a voice that had in it neither bitterness
nor passion, but only a great sadness. He did not wish to gratify
Coryon by exhibiting anger; and thus he spoke,

"It is true I have something I would say, but it is not to thee, O
Coryon, but to those who are not Coryon's degraded servants, but
free agents, who have been misled into supporting him here to-
day. To you, good people, I address myself." And Leonard cast his
eyes around upon those who were not wearers of Coryon's uniform.
"I have much to say and much to ask. Know that the power of this
boastful tyrant who declares with mock humility his wicked purpose to force the youthful daughter of his king into an alliance that
revolts her—know, good people, that his power is almost at an end,
and that he will never enter into that palace, in which he has promised to find place for his credulous followers. He may kill me if he
will, but my death will naught avail; a few hours hence he will be
either a prisoner in the hands of those who came with me, or hiding
in his underground haunts like a hunted animal that dares not show
its face above the ground. But the end will be the same. He will
quickly be hurled out, and a terrible punishment will be meted out
to him and to all those who abet him—every one, that is, who shall
support him. Therefore I say this to you, when my friends come—
as come they will—do not help Coryon's myrmidons against them.
They will come armed with a fearful power that you can scarce conceive; you shall see the very rocks fall away before them in crashing thunders as they hunt these rats out of their holes. If you fight
on Coryon's side, they will mow you down like grass before the
scythe. On the other hand, if you side not with these doomed ones,
but, instead, ask for mercy, you shall find it; for we came not to
this land to teach cruelty and murder, but to deliver it from the
tyranny that has so long oppressed it. That is my advice to you;
what I would ask is that you tell your fellow-citizens that I am sore
distressed in that I have done far less than I might to win their
affections and their confidence. That I have made a terrible mistake,
that it has led me to this situation, I now see. But my error I shall
expiate with my life; when I am dead, and you see the benefits my

friends will shower on the land, then tell all that I was of the same mind, and was full of naught but kindly feelings. But—my great—love for one so fair—as your young—princess—took up my thoughts, perhaps, more than should have been the case." Leonard's voice almost failed him here; but by a strong effort he recovered himself and went on. "That is all that I would ask; let them remember me and think kindly of me. You will see in those days who has spoken truly—whether I, or Coryon. You will know how false has been every word he has said to you to-day. Even what he says about my friends is false; they are not in his power, nor has he deprived them of their magic power, as you will all quickly see. To say that by his atrocious so-called religious rites he has guarded and advanced this country is a lie—"

"Silence!" exclaimed Coryon, who had all this time been moving restlessly in his seat.

"I come from a land—the greatest on the earth—that has an empire upon which the sun ne'er sets; we have no such wicked murders called sacrifices; yet we are safe against our enemies, and—"

"Silence, I tell thee! What think'st thou we care about thy country or thyself?" Coryon burst out.

"I say," Leonard went on, disregarding him, "that every word this man utters is a lie. He cannot say one single sentence without uttering a lie—"

"If thou sayest more, I will have thee scourged as well as killed," Coryon cried, in growing rage. "It speaketh well to these good people for my patience that I have let thee have thy say thus far. Never, for many a year, has mortal dared to flout me to my face as thou hast done."

"O Coryon!" Leonard exclaimed, turning and facing him, "truly did I say that thou could'st not speak one single sentence without uttering some lie, and now thou art convicted. For I know of one, at least, that has flouted and dared thee to thy face; one whose spirit thou couldst not quell; and she but a woman—her name Fernina!"

At this a perfect howl of rage escaped from Coryon's lips. He sprang up and clutched at the air, and gasped; and, for a moment, Leonard half thought he would have a fit. But he recovered himself, and shouted, in a screaming voice, "Seize him! Gag him! Lay

him on the feeding-ladle of our sacred tree! We will see how he
fancies its embrace!" Then, turning round and addressing some
one near him, he cried out, "Bring forward the princess, that she
may witness this my act of justice towards the murderer she would
have taken to her bosom. Let my future wife look on. Ha! ha! ha!
My future wife! How dost thou like the title, murderer of my son,
and would-be king?"

His rage was something fearful to behold; many even of his own
myrmidons trembled, and they made speed to do his bidding.

Leonard was seized and bound to the wheeled plank, and, after
trying in vain to turn his head to take one last look at Ulama, he
closed his eyes and resigned himself to prayer. At the same time
Ulama, looking but the mere ghost of her former self, was led to
the side of Coryon's chair between two women, and forced to look
upon the dreadful scene. At the sight of Leonard bound to the fatal
plank, and the grim tree with its restless branches ever twisting in
avid hunger for their prey, a look of stony horror came over her
face; she gave one gasping, sobbing cry, and fell back unconscious.

For some moments Coryon paused; he was inclined to wait till
Ulama should be restored to consciousness, for he wanted to prolong the torture of the lovers somewhat before finally consigning
Leonard to his fate; but his fury mastered him, and he gave the
signal to the two men holding one end of the plank to push it out
along the stone pier.

They had just begun to move it when a shot was heard, and one
of them fell to the ground; and Leonard, turning his head, saw
Templemore, high on the rocks above, kneeling with his rifle at
his shoulder.

Coryon saw it too, and, with a shout, and many threats, urged
the other man to push out the plank; but, instead, he started back
in terror, and only just in time to escape a second bullet that came
singing past his ears and wounded a soldier standing near.

Coryon, mad with rage and disappointed malice, snatched a
spear from a soldier beside him, and ordered others in front of
him to seize the plank and push it out, prodding at them with the
spear to force obedience; but one, who stepped forward at his bidding, fell before he could reach the plank. Meantime, Templemore,

followed by Ergalon and the brave Zonella, had come leaping down
from ledge to ledge, threatening all who barred his way, and shooting down one or two who tried to stop him. He now stood, a revolver
in each hand, at the end of the plank, and there he kept a circle
around him, while Ergalon cut the cords by which Leonard was
bound, released the cloth that had been tied round his mouth to
gag him, and helped him to his feet. Immediately he rushed to
Templemore.

"Give me a rifle, Jack! Let me shoot down that son of Satan
and rid the earth of him for ever."

Ergalon was carrying three rifles, the one Templemore had been
using and two spare ones; one of these he handed now to Leonard.

But, in the interval, Coryon's chief officer, Dakla, had taken in
the situation; and having already had experience of the weapons
with which he saw Templemore was armed, had advised Coryon to
retreat into the covered-way.

"It is useless to stay here, my lord," he said. "Thou wilt surely
be killed! Haste to the shelter while there is yet time! There I think
thou wilt be safe. If not, thou canst retreat within the gates."

"Dost think the danger is so great, good Dakla?" Coryon asked,
incredulously.

"I am sure of it, my lord. Haste thee—and take some soldiers
with thee and keep them between thee and thine enemies, or thou
wilt never reach the shelter alive. I will leave some men here and
take others up on to the rocks above, whence we can hurl down
great stones upon them. Haply, if no more come, we may yet prevail against these."

Coryon and his priests and immediate followers hastened away,
accordingly, leaving the still unconscious Ulama, in charge of the
two women, behind his chair. He was only just in time, for a soldier he forced to walk beside him fell by a shot from Leonard's
rifle a moment before they gained the shelter of the covered-way.

Leonard saw the women beside Coryon's chair, and, though he
knew not that Ulama was lying there unconscious, he guessed she
was near the spot; therefore he feared to fire more shots in that
direction; while he knew it would be useless to fire at the iron-
work of the covered-way. For a space, therefore, there was a pause;

but soon Dakla's men appeared on the rocks above them and began to roll down stones and boulders.

The position of the little band was now becoming critical. To retreat, leaving Ulama in the hands of Coryon, was not to be conceived. Yet they could not advance, for a compact body of men stood ready to receive them; and at these they durst not fire lest they might hit Ulama or one of her attendants. Yet every minute they stayed where they were increased their danger. Great masses of rock, started by persons above who showed only an arm or hand above the ridge, came crashing down and shooting past them. And, when a head was raised above it here and there to take a hurried aim, it was seen only for a second, and gave little opportunity for a shot.

They had had two or three narrow escapes, and had avoided injury only by leaping out of the path of the rocks that came crashing and bounding down. Jack urged Zonella to go back, but she stoutly refused; and he was at his wits' end what course to take, when loud shouting was heard in the direction of the entrance of the enclosure. Soon, a rush of armed men in red tunics came along the roadway at the rear of the black-coated soldiers standing around Coryon's chair. Instantly Coryon's men gave way, and rushed across the terrace towards the covered-way; while the red-coated men poured in and spread themselves out on either side.

And now could be seen men carrying flags and banners, and amongst them two of mighty stature; one of them, the taller, dressed in the coat of mail and the helmet with silver wings that had been preserved so long in the museum and that was said to have belonged to the legendary Mellenda. He wore, too, the great sword that belonged to the suit, and it seemed, upon his towering form, to be of no more than usual and proportionate size.

As this majestic figure came more closely into view, accompanied by Colenna and some others of the king's officers, Leonard and Templemore's astonishment were great at recognising no other than their friend Monella!

28
Rallying to the Call

To make clearer the events described in the previous chapters, it should be stated that, when Templemore and Ergalon had returned from their journey down the canyon in quest of arms and ammunition, they found with Zonella, who was anxiously awaiting them, a messenger from Monella.

It was not yet daylight, and the two who had made the descent and ascent of the difficult path under conditions of considerable hardship, were very much exhausted. They were therefore glad, though surprised, to find that, in their absence, Zonella had provided both food and wine for them.

"How pleased I am to see you I need scarcely say," she exclaimed. "But first, eat and drink, while I talk. I have much to tell, and there is yet time to spare. Therefore, rest and refresh yourselves, while I relate what has been made known to me.

"Your friend, Monella, has done wondrous things. It seems—as Ergalon here no doubt has been aware—that he has long been quietly making preparations for some such crisis as the present. Coryon, it is true, by his treachery, has stolen a march upon him, but he is being gradually and surely enmeshed in the net that the lord Monella has drawn around him. For a long time Sanaima has been secretly drilling numbers of his followers in Myrlanda, where he has a large store of arms, and he and Monella have gained over many of Coryon's men; in particular, some of those sent to close the subterranean pass. When, therefore, the two, with many armed men, presented themselves at the entrance to the pass and found the gates closed against them, instead of making a desperate fight of it in which many must have been killed on both sides and the news of it have been carried to Coryon's ears, they waited for their friends inside to act. Soon, those of them amongst the soldiers who guarded the approach, seizing their opportunity, fell upon their fellows in their sleep, bound them, and opened the gates. The same thing has occurred in the palace; all Coryon's soldiers really devoted to him have been quietly made prisoners, and the palace is now in the hands of Monella and Sanaima and their friends; and Coryon knows it not.

"Now, when Monella found that you had escaped, he divined whither you had gone, and sent messengers here to await your return; and I sent them back at once to tell him I expected you here ere long. And now another has arrived with instructions, in case you should return in time to put them into execution, as—the Great Spirit be praised!—you have. Monella has sent two or three of Coryon's own people to him with various messages to allay his suspicions; and Coryon quite believes that you are still a prisoner, and that Monella is still in Myrlanda, unable to get through the pass. Others of Monella's men, dressed in black tunics taken from the prisoners, are now placed at intervals on guard at all the approaches to Coryon's retreat; where already, by this time, nearly all his followers and his adherents amongst the people are assembling. There will be some hundreds altogether; all hostile to you and your friends. But, when they are all assembled, Monella will gather together also many hundreds from the people outside, and march them to the amphitheatre and so surprise Coryon and all with him."

"But how," asked Templemore, "if Coryon gets to hear of it?"

"He will not. No move will be made till all are gathered in the amphitheatre; after that, any stragglers going thither from the town, and any messengers sent thence by Coryon, will fall into the hands of Monella's disguised soldiers, and will be quietly seized and bound."

"I see. And now what is to be done to make sure of the safety of our friends?"

"The directions are these. You are to go quietly, through the forest, to the wood at the edge of the amphitheatre where—"

"I understand," broke in Ergalon. "It is the place,"—turning to Templemore— "where we stood and looked down upon the great devil-tree that night. I can take you by a route that leads through the woods all the way, and thus we shall not be seen."

"Yes, that is right," resumed Zonella. "When you get there, you are to remain concealed, and watch all that goes on, and, unless compelled, do nothing till the arrival of Monella and his friends. But, if it should be absolutely necessary to interfere before that to save our friends, why, then, of course, you must do the best you can."

"I only hope we may be in time to save them," said Templemore, with a sigh. "I am terribly anxious. Let us be going; it is already getting light."

The three then started—for Zonella insisted on accompanying them—and the messenger was sent back to inform Monella. When they approached the amphitheatre, four black-coated soldiers suddenly sprang up before them from among the bushes, where they had been lying concealed. Templemore drew a pistol, but Zonella stepped in front of him, and said something in a low tone to the soldiers, who at once gave way and let them pass.

"What did you say to them?" asked Templemore.

"I gave them the pass-word," she answered quietly.

"And what is that, if I may inquire?"

"It is a word you do not regard with the same feelings as ourselves," she answered gravely. "But in Manoa it has always been a word to conjure with, and, so it is today—it is 'Mellenda.'" And, while she spoke, she looked at Templemore half defiantly.

But he made no reply, and they walked on in silence, and now with all caution, to their destination.

Meanwhile, so soon as the sun had risen, messengers were hurrying hither and thither amongst the populace, knocking at doors, and summoning all friendly to the king and the princess, to assemble in the great square where stood the large museum. And, in reply to excited questionings, they often only gave the magic word, "Mellenda," or said, "Mellenda calls you."

Most of the population were early astir that morning, restless with anxiety and fear for the princess and her betrothed, who had, they were told, been carried off by Coryon. As stated, by the great mass of people their princess was much beloved by the people; and Leonard, if he had not gained their affection, had the sympathy, for her sake, of all loyal subjects, and they were many. Indeed, all they wanted was a leader; they were too cowed to take action for themselves.

No wonder, then, that when such a leader came, announcing himself as the long-expected, legendary Mellenda, the whole population, outside those who were gathered around Coryon in the amphitheatre, rallied to his standard, and clamoured to be armed and led against their oppressor. That there were plenty of arms in the museum all well knew; and, when the messengers ran to and fro, spreading the news of the return of their hero-king, all the men who heard the tidings left at once whatever they might have in hand, and hurried to the museum. There they found Sanaima with a number of followers already equipped in the well-known red tunics and winged helmets; and Colenna and others engaged in giving out arms and uniforms to many more.

And when, shortly after, Monella appeared at the top of the wide flight of steps, clad in Mellenda's coat of mail, with the well-known banner floating above him, and wearing at his side the mighty sword, every man and woman and child amongst the crowd below gave a great shout and knelt before him. Then Monella drew the mighty sword, that an ordinary man could hardly wield, and, flourishing it in the air as easily as though it were but the lightest cane, addressed the kneeling people in sonorous tones that were heard by all, and were delivered with an air of exceeding majesty and dignity, "Yes, my children! I have returned to you! After many days the Great Spirit hath led my weary steps back to my beloved country, there to finish my life's work, and end a long and troublous journey. My pilgrimage through the ages hath been a punishment to me, even as the same dreary time hath been a punishment to you; a punishment to myself for having placed too high a value, in the times that are long past, on power and conquest and dominion; to you, for that your forefathers forsook their faith—the worship of the one Great Spirit—and embraced the religion of the powers of darkness, and supported the atrocious Coryon in a rebellion against their lawful king, and in the murder of those near and dear to him. For that, the punishment hath been that they should be oppressed and cruelly ill-treated by him they thus supported, through many generations. But, at last, the anger of the Great Spirit is appeased. He hath led me hither to deliver this fair land from the horror that broods over it. I come to you, not with great fleets of ships, with armies and generals, as of yore; but as a simple wanderer returning to his home. Yet in my coming the Great Spirit sent you all a sign; for I arrived but just in time to save her who is the child of Manoa's ancient race of kings and—my own descendant. This was the sign—this and the death of Zelus at the same time; which was a warning to Coryon that he heeded not. But time presses, and I may not say more now. The princess and our friends are in great peril, and I go to save them. I go to break Black Coryon's power for ever, and to punish him as he deserves. Then will I bring again to this fair land peace, and happiness, and security for all."

Then, amid acclamations, and shouts and cries of delight, Monella—or Mellenda, as he now called himself—moved off towards the place where Coryon, in fancied security, was boastfully proclaiming his intention to espouse the princess, and to live henceforth at the palace as supreme ruler of the country.

Those of Sanaima's followers from Myrlanda, who had been instructed in their duties, took charge, as officers, of ranks and companies of the newly-recruited men They were assisted by many officers of the king's guard who had been held prisoners in the palace, but had been released, and had now changed their blue uniforms for the red tunics and winged helmets in the museum.

Some, however, remained behind, to equip and despatch reinforcements as men continued to arrive asking to be enrolled. Thus, if trouble should arise with Coryon, Monella would have at his back, eventually, an overwhelming force. And as the men kept marching off in companies, the crowd of women and children and old men collected in the square in which was the museum stood about in anxious groups, awaiting news; hardly daring to hope for what all so fervently desired—the final downfall of their ruthless tyrant.

29
'Thou Art My Lord Mellenda!'

To return to the scene in the amphitheatre. Monella, and those with him, advanced with measured tread; but suddenly his eyes fell on Ulama. For a few moments he bent over her, then he came slowly to the front and looked around him, and in that rapid survey he seemed to take in everything.

Beckoning to Leonard and Zonella he said, when they had joined him, "The princess lies there in a dead faint. This is no place for the poor child. Bear her tenderly outside. My people will protect you." Then he turned again to look around.

In their surprise at the unexpected inrush, those on the heights had ceased hurling down the rocks, and now they gazed in wonderment at Monella and those with him. Beside him stood a tall man in a white robe upon which was worked a figure of the sun in diamonds that flashed and sparkled as he moved. His long hair and beard were snowy white, his forehead, high and massive, was clear, and curiously free from lines and wrinkles. It had the impassive look of one who suffers few earthly cares to trouble him. His features were pleasant and benevolent in expression, and the clear grey eyes were open and candid in their glance.

Like Monella, he was far above the usual height; and, like him, was of imposing presence and stately mien. Altogether, one would say of him that he was a good man, a man to be trusted and respected; he had at the same time the air of one deeply engrossed in intellectual pursuits, or leading an ascetic life. He lacked just that touch of tender human sympathy that made Monella's mere look so fascinating to those with whom he came in contact, and that bound so thoroughly to him those who yielded to its subtle influence.

Ergalon had already whispered to the others that the stranger was Sanaima, the ancient chief of the White Priesthood; and Templemore regarded him with interest and curiosity.

Above their heads waved great red banners with strange devices and elaborately carved standard poles. At a sign from Monella, Coryon's banner, that floated above his chair, was pulled down and trampled in the dust; then the largest of the red ones was hoisted in its place.

Next, Monella quietly seated himself in Coryon's chair and gazed around the enclosure, his features set and stern, and his steady, piercing eyes seeming to read the very heart of every one upon whom he turned his gaze. The king's ministers and other prisoners had been unbound, while Templemore had been hastily explaining, to the best of his ability, all that had taken place.

Presently Monella rose, and, waving his hand towards the people not clad in Coryon's uniforms, he thus addressed them, "How comes it, that in this place of evil deeds and heinous crimes, I find many of the king's peaceful subjects—or they who should be peaceful—ranged round and calmly looking on at acts of cold-blooded cruelty against the king's own child and those he calls his friends? What have ye to say in excuse or extenuation? Choose the highest among ye for a spokesman, and let him come forward and explain this shameful thing, if so he can. Else I may include ye all in the punishment I am here to mete out to these evil-doers."

At this there was a great hubbub and commotion. Some of Coryon's companions in the covered-way turned in a panic to make their escape into the interior gallery; but found, to their dismay, that the gates were fast closed and barred against them from within. And when they glanced out at the rocks above, they saw red-coated soldiers, who now lined the heights and kept still arriving in ever-increasing numbers. Dakla and his principal officers had withdrawn at their advance, and now stood, with the priests, crowded together just inside the covered-way. Outside the iron screens the long, trailing branches swept up from time to time, as though seeking to get at those within.

After a hurried conference among the people, one of their number stepped down on to the main terrace and placed himself before Monella.

Templemore stood on one side of Monella's chair, rifle in hand, with Ergalon close by holding the spare rifles, all ready loaded. He watched with growing wonder the continual arrival of red-coated soldiers on all sides of the rocky ridges. "They all carried spears, or swords and shields, and wore the curious helmets ornamented with little silver wings that he had seen in the museum. And now, amongst them, were to be seen many citizens in ordinary dress. But all kept a space between themselves and those who had been there on their arrival; their manner towards these was evidently unfriendly and threatening; and, since the newcomers outnumbered the others, including all Coryon's people, the position of the latter was growing anything but comfortable. And still the red-coated men kept coming, pushing those in advance of them into positions lower down and farther round the terraces of the enclosure.

There was a general hush when the one who had been chosen spokesman came forward and stood in front of Monella, who asked curtly, "Thy name?"

"Galaima," was the reply, given in a clear, unhesitating voice. "I have been chosen by those whom thou didst but now address, to speak in their name. Seeing that punishment hath been spoken of, we desire first to ask what authority thou hast to speak in the king's name; by what right thou dost threaten us; and who thou art?"

"You have the right to ask those questions," returned Monella coldly. "Know then that I am King of Manoa—thy king, and the king of Coryon, and of all in this country."

"King of Manoa!" echoed Galaima in surprise, while similar exclamations broke forth around. "But, my lord—I speak with all respect—how can that be?"

"The King Dranoa is sick even unto death. His illness hath been hastened in its course by acts of base treachery perpetrated by Coryon—with whom I shall deal anon. Finding himself dying and unable to lead his soldiers to the rescue of his child, he hath abdicated in my favour, for me to hold the post so long as I think fit in the interests of the nation. Here (taking out from his bosom a roll of parchment) is his sign-manual duly sealed and executed in the presence of the High Priest Sanaima and others who are with me; and here is his sceptre of office, and this is his signet-ring—these being given to me by him in token of my authority, and also in the presence of Sanaima and many others you see around me. Is it not so, friends?" Monella demanded, turning to Sanaima and the others near.

A loud shout went up in confirmation; then, at a wave of Monella's hand, there was again a deep, expectant silence.

Coryon had come out from the covered-way on hearing the unlooked-for and unwelcome news, and now stood, a little in advance of his own people, an attentive listener and observer of what was going on.

"Thou hast heard," resumed Monella, in the same cold, stern tone. "I come duly armed with authority to punish, and I have the power. Do thou and thy fellows yonder desire to take part with the traitor Coryon, and fight against us; or do ye disavow him and throw yourselves upon my mercy?"

"My lord, with all respect, I ask for the reply to my last question. We came hither—of a certainty I and my immediate friends so came—to protest against the king's choice of a son-in-law. We were unwilling to have thrust upon us, as our future king, one who is of a different race—who is a stranger in the land—and who, so far as it appeareth, hath no claim to royal dignity. Now—with all respect, I say again—for all we know, those same objections apply to thine own case. If, however, I am wrong in this, and thou canst convince us that thou hast reasonable claim to the dignity the king hath conferred upon thee, then we are ready to submit ourselves as loyal subjects."

"Thy logic is good," observed Monella with bitter emphasis, "for thy present purpose; but it faileth to explain how it came about that, instead of making known your sentiment in a petition and awaiting the king's friendly explanation, as befitted faithful subjects, ye supported Coryon in his treasonable acts—in kidnapping the king's daughter and his friends. Further, ye were all proceeding, at Coryon's mere suggestion, to put to death this stranger, without giving him either time or opportunity to afford the information ye now profess yourself so anxious to obtain. However, thou shalt have thy question answered—and, that done, let me warn thee that I am in no mood to suffer further trifling. King Dranoa's good-natured weakness, and my own misplaced leniency, have already wrought too much misunderstanding. Ask thy question of the lord Colenna, the king's High Chamberlain."

Then Colenna stepped forward, and, in a loud, sonorous voice, that resounded throughout the vast amphitheatre, cried out, "Know ye all, by the command of King Dranoa and the unanimous assent of his ministers, that the great lord Mellenda, who hath been hitherto known amongst us as Monella—which in ancient times had the same signification as the word Mellenda—hath made himself known to his people, and hath assumed the office of ruler of the countries of Manoa and Myrlanda."

At this extraordinary announcement Coryon moved back into the covered-way with unsteady and almost tottering steps; while Monella rose and, with another wave of the hand, signalled for silence. Turning to Sanaima, he asked, with quiet dignity, but in a ringing voice that all could hear,

"And thou, august head of our religion, faithful through so many years of persecution and despair, who dost thou say I am?"

The Sanaima raised his hands to heaven as though to invoke a blessing, and said, solemnly, "In the name of the Great Spirit whom I serve, I recognise and welcome thee, my lord Mellenda!"

But still Monella waved his hand for silence; and, raising his voice, he cried, "Come forth, Black Coryon! I command thee! Come forth!"

And Coryon came forward, and stood before him; but he durst not meet his eyes.

Monella slowly raised his arm and straightened it, pointing his finger at his enemy.

"And who, foul Coryon, who dost thou say I am?"

For the space of a few seconds Coryon looked his questioner in the face. There was a brief struggle to hold his own and to repel with proud defiance the glance Monella turned on him; then, bowing his head, he murmured humbly,

"Thou art my lord Mellenda!"

Then a great shout went up. Again, and again, and yet again it was repeated. "Mellenda! Mellenda! Mellenda!" It rang out from far and near. It was taken up by a crowd of women and children without the gates, and thence it travelled back and echoed from one side of the rocky amphitheatre to the other.

When, once more, there was silence, Galaima dropped upon one knee and begged for clemency for himself and friends.

"Lay down your arms, each one of you, and go!" the answer came. "Let me not look upon your faces again yet awhile."

Then Monella, turning to Coryon's soldiers, commanded them also to lay down their arms and surrender themselves prisoners.

Here Coryon showed the first signs of resistance he had yet exhibited, and his officers, who had stood watching for a sign from him, withdrew in a body into the entrance to the covered-way, seeing in it the best opportunities for a last desperate fight.

"My lord forgetteth," said Coryon, "that he hath given no assurance that the lives of my people and servants will be spared."

"I can make no terms with thee or with thy minions. I came here to punish the evil-doers, as well as to save my friends," returned Monella with grave meaning. "Thou hast been warned again and again since I came into the land; I sent thee word that, if I came to thee, I would bring retribution in my hand."

"But surely," urged Coryon, in the smooth, oily manner he could put on at will, "if we submit, my lord will require no more? Thy friends are safe; no harm hath been done to them. May it not be that I remain here with mine own people, within mine own domain—the domain that hath been mine for centuries—in friendly alliance—"

"What!" exclaimed Monella, turning wrathfully upon the crafty hypocrite with a blaze of anger in his eyes, as might a lion turn upon a snapping cur. "Thou darest to speak to me of alliance! Alliance with thee! With a thing so foul, so loathsome, so detestable as thou! Shall the eagle ally himself with the carrion crow? Enough!" He broke off, in indignation at the insult, and, turning to the officers of his own party who stood near, cried,

"Seize them and bind them! Every one! Let not one escape! But take them alive, if possible."

A large number of the red-coated soldiers, led by their officers, now advanced upon the crowd of Coryon's people gathered at the entrance to the covered-way. Many of the latter came forward at once and threw down their arms; while others stood irresolute. Coryon, himself, made no effort to escape, and was seized by a couple of men, who quickly bound his hands behind him. But Dakla and all Coryon's priests and some half-dozen of his lieutenants and a few soldiers—perhaps those who felt themselves most guilty—stood defiantly some little distance within the gallery, determined to resist capture to the last.

30
A Terrible Vengeance!

Of all the spectators of what had occurred in the amphitheatre, no one, probably, was so utterly astonished and helplessly bewildered as was Templemore. At Monella's assumption of the royal office he felt no great surprise. It seemed almost a natural thing, taking all the circumstances into account, that the king, finding his daughter stolen away and himself too ill to pursue and punish her captors, should delegate his authority to the man in whom he had of late reposed such confidence. But at Colenna's announcement that in Monella he recognised the long-expected, legendary Mellenda, Templemore was, as may be supposed, considerably startled; and his perplexity was increased when Sanaima, in his turn, subscribed to Colenna's declaration; but when Coryon himself affirmed his belief in the marvellous assertion, Templemore's ideas became so hopelessly confused, that he knew not what to think or what to make of it. In other circumstances he would, no doubt, have quietly settled matters in his own mind by deciding that all present had become victims to a passing fit of madness or transient delusion; but the grim realities of the strange drama that was being played before him made it impossible to explain things by any such hypothesis.

It was in the midst of the conflict thus proceeding in his mind, that Dakla and his fellows took up their attitude of defiance; so Templemore promptly decided to postpone further thought upon the matter. It was sufficient, for the moment, that there was the prospect of a fight in which his friends would need his help; and he began handling his rifle significantly, glancing while he did so at Monella.

The latter had laid his hand upon his shoulder as though to stay him until he should have had more time to study the situation, when a rumbling noise was heard, and an iron door shot out from the inside wall a little distance from the end of the covered-way, completely closing it and shutting out from view the men within. So suddenly had this been done that Dakla was almost caught by it, and would have been jammed against the iron pillar into which it fitted, but that he had managed to withdraw himself inside just in time to escape it.

The impression upon the minds of those outside was that this unlooked-for obstacle that intervened between those within the protected gallery and their enemies, had been purposely made use of to gain time to force open the interior gates and thus assist their escape into the labyrinth of passages beyond.

The first effect was to dishearten those of Coryon's adherents who were still outside in a state of indecision. Seeing themselves thus, as they thought, incontinently abandoned by their leaders, they threw down their arms without further ado, submitted to their captors, and, in few minutes, were pinioned and marched out of the way.

It now became a question what steps were to be taken to follow up those who had so cleverly escaped, temporarily, at all events, from their pursuers. These were, after Coryon himself, the most guilty of the whole atrocious confederacy; and Templemore turned to Monella with a look of inquiry.

"What say you," said he, "shall we try whether that door is bullet-proof?"

But Monella again laid his hand upon the other's arm, and gazed, as though in expectation, first at Coryon—who was standing out in the centre of the terrace, guarded by two soldiers—and then, from him, to that part of the covered-way nearest to the rocks that ended it. His quick eye had noticed that Coryon seemed as much taken by surprise as all the rest, and that there was, in his face, no trace of that triumphant satisfaction that might have been expected if this manoeuvre of his chief friends had been looked for. Instead, there was a fixed look that was momentarily changing from surprise to terror.

Templemore, following Monella's gaze, noted all this—and so did others. A hush fell upon all present; every one looked at Coryon, and, from him, to the length of grated iron screens, over the face of which the branches of the fatal tree were playing with busy sweep, evidently aware, by some unfailing instinct, that there was plenty of prey for them within. And it was now noticed that the larger number of the longer branches had gathered themselves upon that side.

Gradually, the look on Coryon's face changed into one of absolute horror, the while he stood staring at the outside of the covered-gallery.

To make what follows clear, it is necessary to describe this covered-way a little more in detail. It has already been explained that it formed the approach to an opening in the rock—closed by gates—which was the principal entrance to Coryon's retreat. When unprotected by the sliding gratings at the side, it was so near to the great devil-tree that the longer branches could sweep its whole width for some distance in front of the gates. At the side was some masonry, above which the rock rose steep and almost over-hanging. At the end, above the entrance, the rock rose also abruptly, and then followed the line of the arena, shutting in the latter at this part by a rocky wall that rose perpendicularly some fifty or sixty feet. But the part within reach of the tree was roofed over by iron gratings, forming a sort of verandah, which, in turn, could be rendered safe from the terrible branches by sliding grated doors or shutters that could, by machinery within, be moved forward in telescopic fashion along the whole length accessible to the tree, and a short distance beyond. Thus, when the side "shutters" were withdrawn, the entrance-gates were very effectually guarded by the tree itself. When they were extended, they, in conjunction with the roof, constituted an efficient protection to the covered-way. But herein lay also a cunningly-devised and deadly trap; for, just within the entrance of this covered-gallery, was another iron door that could be moved across the passage so as to imprison any one caught between it and the gates at the other end. This door came out of a scarcely noticeable slot in the masonry at the side; and it was situated far enough along to place those thus caught within reach of the tree, if the side shutters were withdrawn.

Doubtless, many had fallen into this frightful trap. Thinking the gallery well protected they would walk unsuspiciously along it towards the closed gates, when those watching from within could close the gallery behind them and open the sides; and their fate would then be sealed.

This was the only part of the main terrace within reach of the tree. Round the remainder of the amphitheatre it was far removed from it, and was of ample width. Only at this part, and upon the stone pier that jutted out towards the tree from the centre, or down in the arena itself, was there danger to any one moving about within the vast enclosure.

At a point in the cliff, high above the covered-way, was a small grated door in the rock. This was another entrance to Coryon's fastness; but it was sufficiently protected by the nature of the steep and narrow path by which alone it could be reached.

While those gathered around the enclosure, following Coryon's fixed gaze, were watching the outside faces of the sliding doors or shutters, these doors began to move; and, amidst a hush of awe-struck expectation, they disclosed a gap which gradually widened, and through which the fatal branches quickly darted. Then, from within, arose a fearful and appalling cry, as the miserable prisoners caught in this trap of their own contriving began to realise their situation. The gap grew wider, and, anon, another opened farther on, and into this the searching branches likewise entered, hungry for the prey within. And, as the gaps grew wider, they disclosed to view an awful scene. Some dozens of terror-stricken wretches could be seen fighting and struggling with the writhing branches and with each other, amidst a deafening din of screams, and shrieks, and yells; the officers and soldiers using their swords, and the priests and others their daggers, in a hopeless contest with the twisting branches that kept coiling around them. In their mad struggles and desperate efforts the combatants fought with one another, the stronger striving to push the weaker in front of them; the latter, in turn, stabbing backwards at those who thus tried to make use of them. Three or four, in headlong terror, leaped from the terrace on to the ground beneath, where they fell with dull thuds, and probably broken limbs; but, ere they could rise, their legs were entangled in the ubiquitous branches and escape became impossible. Dakla was seen, with a sword in one hand and a dagger in the other, at one moment slashing furiously at the branches that assailed him, at another striving to hold in front of him Skelda, the next in rank to Coryon.

Two of the priests were seen engaged in a hand-to-hand struggle, apparently unmindful of the coils that gradually encircled them and presently dragged both out, locked together, and still frantically fighting with each other. They were carried up to the top of the tree, and disappeared, still fighting, within the cavity. But, though the rapacious tree had now as much as it could, for the time, dispose of in this way, it had no intention of giving up its hold upon the others. These it grappled in its toils, dragging them about hither and thither, dangling them now this way and now that, but never giving one a chance of escape—evidently bent on saving all up for future meals—perhaps days hence. It was a gruesome scene that shocked and sickened the spectators, for all they were so incensed, and justly so, against the victims.

Meanwhile, the iron door in the rock above had opened, and a woman was seen hurrying down the dangerous path. Her hair was streaming loosely about her shoulders, her eyes were wild and fierce, and she laughed and gesticulated in a fashion that made those who watched her think her crazy. She made her way to where Coryon still stood, a silent witness of what was going on before him; and she then paused and surveyed the awful scene with a smile that was almost devilish.

Just then Skelda leaped out of the covered-way on to the ground beneath; then, rising to his feet, looked round despairingly, and, glancing up, he met the fierce gaze and cruel smile of the woman he had so shamefully betrayed. She pointed her finger at him.

"Ha! ha!" she cried triumphantly, "this is my work, Skelda! I closed the gates and shut you all in with the outer door. My love to you, my—husband!" This last word was hissed out at him between clenched teeth. "My love to you, dear friend." And she mockingly threw him a kiss on the tips of her fingers. Then, when the wretched Skelda's feet were dragged from under him by a branch that had coiled round his legs, she addressed herself to Coryon, who had now fixed his eyes upon her, his evil face twitching convulsively with the fury he could not suppress.

"See, great Coryon! Mighty Coryon! All-powerful Coryon! See my handiwork! Yes, mine! See what a woman's wit hath done for thy precious friends. What a day to live to see! I saw thee in the clutch of thy prisoner; heard thee called 'coward' to thy face. It was sweet that; and sweet to see thy prey escape thee! And this is sweet too! Look at thy great friend Skelda; see how he kicks and shrieks! Think of it—all my doing! See how Dakla glares! Now he and Palana are fighting one another! Oh, but it is a brave sight to look upon! Fit even for the gods ye have served so well! I think I am almost avenged; but the sweetest of all is yet to come—when I see thee given to the tree, as I shall!"

Coryon struggled, but vainly, to get at her. She shrugged her shoulders and turned her back upon him, then slowly approached Monella; the look of triumph died away, and an expression that was partly of sorrow, and partly of hard determination, took its place. Arrived in front of him, she threw herself humbly on her knees.

"My lord," she cried, with clasped hands, "I crave justice at thy hands, I demand it! In the names of the countless women and fair children whom yonder monster hath given over to the same awful death that hath now overtaken his own creatures; in the name of my own bitter wrongs and sufferings, I demand that this loathsome being shall not escape his just reward. I ask that he be given up to that tree to which he has consigned so many; and that first he be confined in the same cell from which I have escaped. I will lead thy officers to it. Let him be kept there till the wicked tree, with recovered appetite, shall be ready to devour him! Let him there endure the tortures he hath inflicted upon me and countless others!"

"Who art thou, daughter?" asked Monella gently.

She shook her head mournfully and replied, much as she had to Leonard, "I am called Fernina, lord. Once, I was a joyous-hearted wife and mother; but Coryon stole me away from my home to give me to his friend Skelda. What I am now I scarcely know; misery and suffering, and shame and infamies unutterable have made me— alas, I know not what!"

"From my heart I pity thee, my daughter. Thy wrongs cry out for punishment, and thy prayer is just. Show my officers the place. Coryon shall be the last meal of the accursed fetish he has fed with the blood of so many victims."

"I will go back by the way by which I came," Fernina answered, "and will make safe again the covered-way; then will I open the gates, that thine officers may take him in that way."

By this time the covered-way was empty; every occupant had been dragged or had leaped out and was held in the toils below. There was, therefore, nothing to prevent its being used again. Fernina went up the path and disappeared from view; then soon the sliding shutters were seen to move back in their places; and, shortly after, she appeared at one end of the covered-way and beckoned to those in charge of Coryon to follow her. He was led down and placed in the same cell she had occupied, and there shut in and left to himself, and to look out, if he chose, at his friends in the tree's tenacious arms outside. Some of them were so close he could have spoken with them.

After Coryon had been removed, Sanaima turned to Monella; then raised his hands and eyes towards heaven.

"Let us thank the Great Spirit," said he solemnly, "that hath, at last, delivered our enemies into our hands, and that without the loss of a life, or so much as a wound upon our side!"

And Monella added a heartfelt "Amen."

"Of a truth," he added reverently, "the wicked have been caught to-day in their own snare. At last, we may truly rejoice that the curse hath been removed, for ever, from the fair land of Manoa. But this is a fearful sight; let us hasten from it. But ere we do, Sanaima, send kindly and trustworthy people to care for the poor woman Fernina and the other women and children who are somewhere within. I cannot now stay longer; I must look after the princess and return to the palace."

"I will remain and look to them myself," answered Sanaima. "Now that the Great Spirit hath at last given them into my charge, it is a trust that belongeth to me, and to me alone."

During the foregoing events, several messengers had passed to and fro delivering messages, in low tones, to Monella or some of his officers, and speeding away again with their replies, or upon other errands. In this way Monella had learned that the princess had recovered from her long swoon and expressed a strong desire to return to the palace to her father, and he had sent back word to Leonard to accompany her.

When, therefore, Templemore, with Monella and many more, reached the great gates on leaving the amphitheatre, they found Ulama and all those with her gone, and they now hastened to the palace after them.

31
'The Son of Apalano!'

On leaving the amphitheatre, Monella and his followers formed a long and imposing procession. Only a few had been left behind to guard the prisoners. These last were immured in cells pointed out by Fernina, who was well acquainted with the interior arrangements of Coryon's retreat. For within the rocks was an almost endless series of passages and galleries opening, at the further end, on to an extensive hanging terrace on the very face of the great precipice that formed one end of Roraima's perpendicular sides. Even those of Coryon's followers who had gone over secretly to Monella, were only partially acquainted with the interior of this fastness; hence Fernina's assistance was found of great use by Sanaima and those who remained with him.

It can scarcely be said that the procession, as it left the great gates of the amphitheatre, exhibited, at first, many signs of having just been engaged in a victorious and successful expedition. Those who formed it were, for the most part, silent and preoccupied; for the scenes they had witnessed—and that, as they knew, were still in progress—were of too horrible a character to be readily dismissed from the mind. But, as they proceeded on their way, they met and were joined by fresh bands of red-coated sympathisers; and these, not having the same for repressing their elation at the result of the day's proceedings, broke out into cheering as they passed the groups of people who were now coming out to meet them. For messengers had gone on in advance to tell the news, and the crowds who had been waiting so anxiously in the city, soon learned that Coryon's downfall was an accomplished fact. They had already heard the good tidings of the rescue of the princess and her lover and friends, and were only waiting for this last crowning announcement; when it came, they became almost delirious with joy, and soon poured out to meet the victors and give them an enthusiastic welcome.

Thus the procession that started so quietly—almost in sadness, as it seemed—from the dismal amphitheatre, became at last, as it entered the city, a veritable triumphal pageant, meeting on all sides, and returning, cheers and shouts of joy and exultation. And when Monella, with Templemore, Colenna, and others came into view in the centre of the long array, every head was uncovered and every knee bent. Then, when he had passed, the excited crowds rose and shouted again louder than ever. And well might they do so; for they—and only they—knew the full meaning of the horrors from which they had that day been delivered.

By the time they had neared the king's palace, the crowd had grown so dense that it was with some difficulty that space was cleared for the passage of the principal persons into the building. At the entrance, under the great archway, Leonard, looking pale and anxious, awaited them. Running forward to meet Monella, he said, "I have heard the news and congratulate you all. But I am in sore distress about the princess. We had much ado to bring her here, and I fear she is very ill. Let me entreat you to go and see her at once, and then let me know what you think about her."

"Certainly will I, my son," replied Monella kindly, and hurried away; while Leonard turned and greeted Templemore and the others with him. Then they all entered the palace and went up one of the great staircases and on to a terrace overlooking the open space where the crowd was assembled, and there awaited Monella's return.

Presently he came to them.

"The princess is weak and much depressed," he said, "and will require care for awhile; but I see no cause for anxiety. Naturally, the poor child is terribly upset. She grieves, too, about the condition of the king her father, and wishes to help nurse him, but this she has not strength for at present. Patience, my son. Be patient and of good heart." He looked with pity and concern at Leonard's haggard face with its hollow, dark-ringed eyes and its worn-out look. "You have suffered—cruelly—I can see," he added, placing his hand gently on the young man's shoulder. "You have been sorely tried."

"Ah!" returned Leonard with a heavy sigh. "You cannot imagine what I have been through! My thoughts still dwell upon the horror of it; my eyes still see the sights I gazed upon! I feel as though I shall never be my old self again. And Ulama! Though I do not yet know how much she saw or knew, I sadly believe she shares my feelings."

"You are both worn out—exhausted, my son. Wait but a space—while I speak to the crowd and dismiss them—and then I will give you a cordial and refreshment; after that you must lie down and have a long sleep."

"I fear even to sleep," said Leonard, shaking his head sadly. "I dread the thought of sleep, for I know but too well what my dreams will be."

"Nay, my son, have no fear. I will promise you dreamless, restful sleep," Monella answered, and moved away to the front of the terrace.

At the sight of his commanding form and upraised hand the shouts and noise and all the subdued roar that till now had been continuous were hushed. Then, as with one accord, all uncovered and fell upon their knees. He spoke a few brief words and then dismissed them, pointing out that his friends were in need of rest and quiet.

The crowd, in respectful obedience, quietly dispersed, and Monella, motioning Elwood and Templemore to follow him, led them into his private apartments and there mixed and administered to both certain drinks that had an immediate and wonderfully revivifying effect. These potions had also the advantage of stimulating their appetites, so that they were the better enabled to take the nourishment he pressed upon them. Then he accompanied them to their sleeping chambers and bade them lie down and take the repose they so sorely needed. None of the three had had any sleep or rest—for Leonard's swoon in his cell and subsequent state of torpor could scarcely be so called—for the past two nights,

The two young men were not only worn out, but in that excited state in which the brain seems to insist upon going over and over and over again the events of the previous troubled time, in that ceaseless, monotonous whirl that makes all efforts at sleep so useless. But Monella—who alone showed no sign of the strain all had undergone—sat down by the side of each in succession for a short time, and talked to him in his low, musical tones. What he talked of, or what he did, neither could afterwards remember; but the effect was magical. As Leonard afterwards expressed it, a soothing, delicious sense of drowsy rest crept over his senses; a rest that was not sleep, for he could still hear the usual sounds around, but gradually growing hushed and muffled. Then came a sensation as of being lifted and wafted away by a gentle wind; and in the sighing of the breeze there seemed a delightful strain of music, a dreamy lullaby that carried with it a restful peace sinking imperceptibly into untroubled repose.

The strangest thing, perhaps, is that even the unimpressionable Templemore was affected in the same way, as he afterwards admitted. Nor was that all; for, on awaking, he was conscious of having had the most delicious dreams, though he could not quite recall their subject. For some time he lay in a state of blissful ease, striving to recollect the dream that had left sensations so delicious, and afraid to rouse himself for fear the remembrance should vanish altogether. He could hear the usual sounds going on in the palace, the tramp of armed men, and clashing and jingling of arms; but he was only half-conscious of them. Then he heard his name called in tones that seemed to come from the far distance, and, opening his eyes, he saw Monella standing beside his couch and regarding him with a grave smile.

"Wake up, my friend," he said. "It is time you roused yourself. I wish to have some talk with you and Leonard. You have slept for eight-and-forty hours!"

Templemore sat up and rubbed his eyes.

"I feel as if I had slept for months," he answered in a half-dazed way. "And I've had such curious dreams, or visions; I feel quite sorry to be awake again. It's a strange thing for me to talk like that, I know," he added with hesitation.

"What did you dream of?" asked Leonard, who had entered in time to hear the other's concluding words.

"That's the strange part of it," returned Templemore, looking perplexed and somewhat sheepish. "I've had a most extraordinary dream of some kind, or a vision or something—that I know, yet I cannot remember what it was. All I can now tell you is that it was something so extremely pleasant that it has left the most agreeable sensations behind it. My very blood seems in a warm, delicious glow from it. What can it be?" he added, looking in a bewildered way from one to the other.

But Monella made no comment, and went away.

"It's been just the same with me," said Leonard, in a low voice, that had an expression almost of awe in it. "Monella woke me about half an hour ago and I felt much like what you have described."

"It's very odd," Templemore returned thoughtfully.

"It must be the drink he gave us. Do you remember what Harry Lorien said of him? That he believed Monella was a magician? I begin to think him a wizard myself. But, dear boy, how much better you look!"

"So do you, Jack; and he tells me Ulama is the same—and it's all his doing, you know. He is a wizard; and that's all there is to be said about it."

"The question is," Jack went on, "what was it he gave us? Here it has made us sleep nearly forty-eight hours; and it seems, has done us, in that time, as much good as one would have thought would have taken a week or two to accomplish, and yet it has left no dull, drowsy, listless feeling, such as opiates generally do. I can't make it out." And, shaking his head gravely, Templemore went to take his morning plunge.

When they sought Monella, he bade Leonard give him the particulars of all that had occurred to him. Leonard recounted them.

"It seemed very terrible to me," he said when he had finished, "at the time; and truly I thought I should never get over it. Yet—now—it seems such a long while ago—so far off."

"That is well, my son," returned Monella. "For it has been a sore trial. I have heard about you," he continued, turning to Templemore, "from the lady Zonella and from Ergalon."

"I owe a great debt to her—to him—to both," Templemore replied. "Without their aid I fear things would have gone badly with Leonard, and myself too."

"Yes, Coryon had ably laid his treacherous schemes, and we all have reason to be thankful for their failure," said Monella solemnly. "Things came to a crisis just then. I had just matured certain plans that Sanaima and I had laid out; and only the day before my long-lost memory returned to me, and I remembered, all in a flash, as it were, the whole of my former life."

"That you were—that is—are—" Templemore began; but stopped and looked confused.

"Yes, that I am indeed Mellenda," was the reply, given with an air of grave conviction. "I know the statement sounds incredible to you; you are of that nature, have been brought up in that kind of school, that makes such a thing sound impossible. But if I myself feel and know that it is true, and if my people around me know it and not only admit it but rejoice in it, then, for me, that is sufficient."

"Certainly," Templemore assented, feeling very uncomfortable under the other's gaze.

"Still—to you—let me be, while you remain here, simply what I have been before—your friend Monella. I am the same being to-day that you have known and, I hope, liked—that you have joined with in facing danger and adventure—I am the same! The mere fact that I remember things now that I had forgotten before makes no difference to me or to our friendship."

This was said with a look of such kind regard that Templemore felt his own heart swell with responsive feeling. It was true he had a strong inclination to regard the other as a sincere, but self-deceiving mystic; but, apart from that—apart from this strange delusion, as he deemed it, about Monella's being the legendary Mellenda—Templemore looked upon him with feelings of the greatest admiration, affection, and respect. And he had never been so conscious of those feelings as at this moment. He took the hand that the other extended to him, and bent his head respectfully.

"Sir," said he in a low tone, "no son could respect and reverence a beloved and honoured father more than I do you. No one could feel prouder of the love and esteem you have been kind enough to show me; no people, I feel satisfied, could have a worthier, a more disinterested, or exalted ruler. If I find it difficult to realise the marvel that you have related, if I have the idea that, perhaps, you are mistaking your own dreams for actual realities, it is not from any doubt of your sincerity or veracity—only that in that way alone can I bring myself to explain the wonder."

"And I, on my side, respect the honesty that will not allow you to pretend what you cannot feel," was the reply. "To you let me be simply Monella, and let us continue on our old terms of mutual friendship and esteem. And now I am going to rouse your wonder and surprise with yet one other unexpected statement. Your friend Leonard here is not the son of the parents he has all his life supposed himself to be."

Leonard sprang up with an exclamation.

"I will explain how. You have already told us"—this to Leonard—"how that your supposed father and mother, with yourself, and your Indian nurse, once stayed some time with a strange people in a secluded valley among the peaks of the Andes. I was not there at the time, but they were my people."

"Your people!" Leonard repeated with astonishment.

"Yes, my son, my people! Apalano, and two or three others of whom you have heard me speak—all, alas, now dead! I was informed of your visit when I next came back to them, for a while, from my wanderings. I heard of it and what had happened; how Apalano's little child—his only one—had been killed by a venomous serpent."

"The child of Apalano!" Leonard repeated in amaze.

"The two children," Monella continued— "Mr. Elwood's child and Apalano's—were wonderfully alike, and your nurse, the Indian woman Carenna, was very fond of both, and was in the habit of taking them out together. She was out with them thus one day, and left them both sleeping in the shade of a clump of trees while she went a few yards away to gather some fruit. She returned (so she says) in a few minutes; then, thinking one of the children had a strange look she picked it up in alarm; at the same moment a serpent glided out from under its clothes and went away, hissing, into the wood. But the child was dead; and it was the child of the Englishman. Then Carenna, frantic with grief, and afraid to tell the truth to her master and mistress, exchanged the clothes and ornaments of the children. The trick succeeded; for the dead infant was swollen and discoloured; and Apalano mourned the death of his only child, when it went away, in reality, with the strangers and their Indian nurse."

"Then," said Leonard excitedly, "I am—"

"Ranelda, son of my well-beloved friend! Ah," said Monella, sadly, "it was a cruel thing to do. It preyed upon the mind of my friend, and, I truly believe, brought on the fatal sickness. But for that he might have lived, haply, to see at last the land of his fathers—might have been one of us here to-day."

Leonard felt the tears come into his eyes at the picture called up by this suggestion; and he said in a low tone,

"Alas! My poor father! It was cruel—very cruel!"

"It seems so," Monella returned with a sigh. "But God so willed it. And He has also willed that you should be led back to your own nation—that, after many days, you should join with me in the work that I had set myself."

"It's very wonderful. Yet it seems to me to explain those strange dreams and visions that were ever urging me on to attempt the exploration of the mysterious Roraima! I suppose, when Carenna found out who you were, she confessed?"

"Well," answered Monella, with a half-smile, "I made her do so. People find it difficult to hide anything from me. I saw she had some secret, and compelled her to divulge it. But, since she was so afraid to confess to others, and especially averse to your knowing it, I made her this promise, that, if you desired to return from our adventure, you should do so in ignorance of the actual facts. I was only to tell you in case you freely elected to stay here permanently. That is why I have kept it back thus far. I had intended to announce it to you and to the people at the time of your public betrothal. Then they would have received you, with one accord, as one having a right to rule over them. And now you can understand why I have regarded you with such affection from the first; and how glad I was to find, in Apalano's son, one so worthy of my love and confidence.

Your father was allied with my line, and you are, therefore, akin to me. Worthy son of a worthy father! Let me join with you in thankfulness that you have, after all, come into the heritage that is yours by right! The young eagle was bound to find its way to the eyrie for which it was best fitted." And Monella stood up and laid his hand affectionately upon the young man's shoulder. Leonard reverently bowed his head, and the other pressed his lips upon his forehead.

There was silence for some seconds. Then Templemore took Leonard's hand.

"And let me too congratulate you, Leonard," he said fervently. "It is good news for you—this; for, since you have elected to pass here the remainder of your life, it will be a great comfort and advantage to you that you have such good claims and qualifications for the position."

"I am thinking about my poor father who died of heartache and disappointment," rejoined Leonard; and in his tone there was a note of genuine sorrow. "And I can scarcely forgive Carenna—fond of me as I know her to have always been—for her cruelty to him."

Presently Templemore turned again to Monella, saying, "Did Carenna then believe this mountain was inhabited, that you would find here the people you came to seek? Did you yourself think that?"

"As to myself, I can scarcely tell you," was the answer. "'Reason said that the hope of finding here the people of whom Apalano had so often talked to me—for that was all I then knew—was chimerical; yet Apalano's dying wishes, and some strange sentiment or instinct within me, urged me on. Then, when I met with Carenna, I found she quite thought it might turn out true."

"Carenna thought it?"

"Why, yes; but that is not very surprising, for, according to the Indian ideas, it would not be the only instance in this country. There is a belief amongst the Indians in several parts that some of the unexplored mountains are inhabited by strange and unknown races. This applies to those—and there are many; Roraima is not the only one—that are surrounded by the curious belts of almost impenetrable forest. The Indians believe that, if these forests could be passed, strange peoples would be met with living on the mountains thus encircled; and they say that on clear nights the lights from their fires may often be seen.* Therefore Carenna was quite prepared to believe we might find Roraima inhabited."

"I see. Then she, at least, will not have been so very much surprised at our not returning, and may not have given us up for dead?"

"Yes; that is probable enough."

"And if she has heard of the signal flares we made when some Indians—as I suppose they were—were camping in sight of the mountain, she would look upon that as a sign of our being up here alive?"

"I think that is very likely."

"There is the suggestion of a little comfort in that," said Templemore; "for, otherwise, those I left behind, and who are dear to me, must have given up all hope and be now mourning me as dead. With Leonard it is different. He stood alone in the world and has no one to grieve for him more than as an ordinary friend."

* Mr. Im Thurn, referring to this belief amongst the Indians, states that he has himself seen, from a distance, strange lights on the Canakoo Mountains for which he was quite unable to account. See *Among the Indians of British Guiana*, p, 384

32
The Tree's Last Meal

"And now," said Monella, "I have some other news to give you; for you have slept for nearly two days, and in that time much has been done. While you slept we have been busy."

"Do you never sleep—yourself?" Templemore asked.

"Yes; but not for long at a time. However, the long rest you have taken is no reproach to you, for it was my doing. I saw that it was needful to restore your strength and good spirits. You are the better for it; the princess, the lady Zonella, and others have also had long rests and are the better for it, as I have already told Leonard. The king Dranoa, too, is better—in a sense; for he has now no mental trouble, and with his sickness there is no physical pain nor suffering nor distress of any kind. But he is very wishful now that the marriage of his daughter should take place as soon as possible; for only then, he feels, will he be able to die happily. In deference to his earnest wish I have settled for it to be solemnised at the end of a fortnight; and, in view of the fact that the state of his health cannot but be a source of sadness to his people, I have deemed it better to order that it shall be a quiet ceremonial, and not a great fete, as had been planned. This will not offend your feelings, my son?"

Leonard looked up with a bright smile.

"After what you have told me," he said, "I feel, with gladness and gratitude that it is not without reason that you have so often thus addressed me—as your son. Now, I may indeed claim you as a father."

"You may indeed," Monella assented; "I take the place of my lost friend."

"Then you have no need to ask whether what you think best pleases me. If you will be my father, choose for me and instruct me; for I feel I have need of your help to enable me to take up, and bear worthily, the position I owe to you. I felt this," continued Leonard, with great earnestness— "I felt this very strongly when I lay in that foul den that the poor demented wretch called the 'devil-tree's larder.' I made then a vow that, if it should please God to deliver me from the peril that threatened me, I would thenceforth devote my life to the good of the people I had come amongst. I repented sorely that I had given my thoughts too much to selfish— albeit innocent—enjoyment; and I vowed I would not be guilty of that selfishness in the future, if the chance and the choice were offered to me. And now that they are, help me—instruct me, my father, I pray you, in all that may enable me to fulfil that vow."

Monella gazed long and fixedly at the young man; and in his eyes there was a glistening as of a tear. Then he rose and went to the window that looked out over the lake, and stood awhile, with a far-off vacant look that told his thoughts were wandering to distant scenes or persons. It was some time before he looked round.

And, when he again turned to speak to the young men, they were both conscious that some indefinable change had taken place in his manner. His face expressed unmistakably a great and exalted joy; and the eyes, that at all times had had so strange a charm in them, had taken on a new expression. For a little while Templemore strove in vain to ascertain in what the change consisted; but presently it seemed to him that they had lost that half-sad, half-wistful expression he had so constantly remarked; and that they now conveyed, instead, a sense of contentment and repose.

"That which you have now told to me," said Monella, walking slowly up to Leonard, "is as sweet to me as water to the thirsty in the desert." With grave deliberation he placed both hands upon the young man's shoulders and looked into his eyes with fatherly affection.

"Know, my son Leonard—or rather Ranelda, as you rightly should be called—know that in these words you bring to my soul the message it has been awaiting—sometimes in hope, too often, alas! in doubt and in despair—through the long ages. Yours is the hand—the—hand of the son of Apalano—that bears to me the key of my fetters; and yours are the lips that announce my coming freedom! My work, then, nears its end, and soon—ay, soon—I—shall—be free!"

While uttering these last words Monella raised his hand, and with upturned face looked rapturously above him, as if his sight, piercing the marble ceiling overhead, perceived some far-off scene that, while invisible to his companions, filled him with the most intense delight. Presently, he turned away with a regretful sigh, as though the vision he had been gazing at had vanished, and added, with an absent manner, "Now, when I leave you, I shall feel—"

He stopped; in his eyes there was a far-off look; and Leonard, who had been looking on with wide-open, wondering eyes that comprehended little, if anything, of his discourse, exclaimed in anxious tones,

"Leave me—leave us! What mean you, my father?

"You surely do not think of leaving the people you so love, to become again a wanderer?"

Monella shook his head; and, appearing to rouse himself, he replied in quite a different voice, "You misunderstand, my son; I speak of when I shall be called away—called from this earthly life."

"But that will not be for a long, a very long time yet," urged Leonard, looking with confidence at the stalwart frame, and remembering the many feats of strength the other had performed.

Monella turned his eyes on Templemore.

"Do you remember," he asked, smiling, "a conversation we had one day in the museum; when I explained to you that no 'Plant of Life' or other specific—no power, indeed, of earth—can keep in its earthly cage the soul that feels its work is done, and that, therefore, frets itself against its prison bars?"

"I remember," answered Templemore in a subdued tone, and avoiding Leonard's questioning eyes.

"Ah! then you understand me. And now"—this with a gesture that enforced obedience— "now let us go back to that which we were speaking of. I was saying that King Dranoa desires that you and Ulama should be wedded without delay. To spare the feelings of the maiden, and give her time, so that the matter may not come upon her too suddenly, I have named a day two weeks hence. There will be no pageant, no public fete; only the necessary ceremony, quiet and solemn."

"I should prefer it so," murmured Leonard.

"Then that is arranged; and it will take place in the great Temple of the White Priests that has been closed for so many years. Workmen are engaged upon it, and it is now being cleansed and renovated. It will be ready in time.

"The next thing I have to tell you is that Coryon has suffered his punishment, and is dead."

"Coryon dead?" the other two exclaimed in a breath.

"He is dead," Monella repeated solemnly. "It seems that during the night after we left, there were dreadful scenes in the amphitheatre. Those large reptiles—they are called 'myrgolams' here—came out of their pool and attacked the half-dead wretches entangled in the tree. But the branches tried hard to retain their victims, and so—well, you can almost imagine what took place. The creatures carried off the miserable beings in scraps; tore them piece by piece from the clutches of the branches till nothing was left!"

He paused for a moment, and his listeners shuddered.

"Thus it came about that the greedy tree was, after all, baulked of most of its intended victims; all, indeed, save three or four; though the deaths the others met with were not less horrible. Yesterday, finding the monster had no victims in its grasp, I ordered the separating door to be withdrawn. In a moment, Coryon was seized and carried up into its awful gorge. With that, the tale of this terrible tree must end. I have no heart to devote more criminals to it; though there are some among the prisoners who are scarcely less guilty than was Coryon. But these Sanaima will deal with; he will punish them as seems best to him; and I have set men to work to dig a mine from one of the cells so as to get underneath the tree. Then it can be blown up with gunpowder. And I designed to ask you to superintend the work for me," turning to Templemore.

"That I will gladly do. And—the—reptiles?" Templemore was doubtful of the name.

"Kill them off, if you can, with bullets. And now, to turn to your own affairs. Think not I have forgotten them; I know you are anxious and will be getting restless and unhappy. As I said to you before, when you go away, you will not go empty-handed. On the contrary, you will carry with you such riches as will place you beyond the need of toil for the remainder of your life. I need not say, 'Do not therefore be an idle man,' for I know that you will never be. Whenever it pleases you to go, some of my people shall escort you through the wood to 'Monella Lodge,' as we called it, and there await you while you go on to Daranato and bring back such Indians as you require. Then, do you, in turn, with your Indians, re-escort my people to the cavern; for, you must remember, they are not used to forest life; nor can they, if left alone, protect themselves against wild animals. Will that please you?"

"Yes, truly it is all I can ask or wish for," Templemore responded.

"I shall wish to know—that is, all here will wish to know," said Monella, "that you get back in safety to 'Monella Lodge.' With the heliograph mirror which you will find packed away at 'Monella Lodge' you can send us back a message to that effect; then, with the one we brought here with us, we can reply, and send you a 'God speed you' to start you on your way. Shall it be so arranged?"

"Gladly," responded Templemore with emotion. "But must I then resign myself to the thought that I shall never see Leonard or any of you any more?"

"You must," Monella answered quietly, but firmly. "Leonard—or Ranelda, as I prefer to call him—has asked me to guide him and instruct him; and my first and last advice to him is, and will be, to keep his people to themselves. Now let us consider this question from what you yourself would term a practical point of view.

"The term 'El Dorado' has come to be a synonym in the outside world for a sort of earthly paradise, has it not? Originally handed down from actual facts and history relating to this, the celebrated island capital of Manoa—the Queen City of my once powerful and extensive empire—with the tales of its wonderful wealth and the virtues of the Plant of Life; its memory lingered through the ages long after the waters had receded and left it isolated and unknown. And the Spaniards called it 'El Dorado,' which has ever since been but another expression—as I have said—for 'Earthly Paradise,' or 'summit of every man's ambition.' Is it not so? And seeing that the great curse that so long lay upon the land has been removed, can you say that now it does not deserve the term? Have we not here a veritable 'Earthly Paradise'—an actual realisation of what you in the outside world understand when you use the expression 'El Dorado?'"

"Truly I believe it."

"Ah yes! It is so now—or will be henceforth, when those who have had such sorrows here shall have outlived them," said Monella with impressive emphasis. "But what I would put to you, is this; you have, perhaps, seen something of frontier settlements, or miners' camps, and gold diggings—at least, I have—and you have heard of them. Now, you know well enough that the only people who would care to brave the hardships of the journey hither would be those led on by the lust and greed of gold. Supposing things were reversed, and you were in Leonard's place, and had here your wife—as he will have—your friends, your own people—all that was dearest in the world, with ample wealth, would you care to allow him, or any one else, to lead people hither, to turn this 'El Dorado' into a 'Gold diggings,' a 'Miners' camp,' with all their hideous associations, their gambling and drunkenness; their rowdyism and their debauchery, their shootings and murders?"

"No!" said Templemore thoughtfully, "you are right there. Still—surely, between that, and forbidding intercourse altogether—forbidding me even to come to visit my friend—"

Monella smiled and gravely shook his head.

"You think that, between the two extremes, there should be some middle course possible," he rejoined. "Unfortunately—or fortunately—there is none. You will have no need to come here seeking for wealth. You would not be likely to undertake the expedition alone. Those who accompanied you would do so from self-seeking motives. Then, again, you will have other ties; you will have your wife, children. You do not contemplate dragging them hither through trackless wastes to greet friends they have never known as you have? They would not like it, again, if you, a man of wealth, able to do as you pleased, were to leave them for a long space while you made the journey hither alone! And, finally, the thing is not practical or feasible for another reason. You will have much ado to find your way out from here. You know that in these regions vegetation spreads rapidly unless—as in the canyon we came up, or in the clearing immediately outside around the cavern by which we entered, or out on the savanna—there are special causes that check its spread. Should you come back in a year's time, you would not only find the road we cut out impassable—you could not even trace it. The spread of the undergrowth, the fall of great trees or branches, the hurling down of rocks from the heights above, floods from the streams and watercourses—all these, and other forces of nature in this wild region, will, within a few months, have combined to block up or obliterate completely the path we cut with so much difficulty. Is it not so?"

"I fear you are right, though it had not occurred to me," Templemore admitted with reluctance.

"Then, again, with the wealth you will take back with you, you will not care to remain in Georgetown. You will wish to travel with your wife; in any case, it would be years before you would be likely to think of undertaking another journey."

"If ever you do, though, dear old Jack," Leonard burst in impulsively, "if ever circumstances should arise to make you wish to communicate with me, you can always do so by the heliograph, you know, or perhaps by balloon, if I'm still alive."

But, though Leonard put on a cheerful tone, it was easy to see that both he and his friend felt deeply the severance that too clearly lay before them. Yet, after Monella's argument, they saw no alternative.

"I am as sorry as you can be," Monella wound up kindly; "but your duties call you away from us, even as Leonard's call upon him to stay. And now I must leave you, for many are waiting to see me. First, however" —this to Leonard— "I will lead you to the princess."

Leonard followed him from the apartment into another, where Monella left him; and presently Ulama entered, looking radiant, lovely, beautiful—so Leonard thought—beyond belief.

At the sight of Leonard, she threw herself upon him with a joyous cry; with her face upon his shoulder, she sobbed and laughed by turns.

"Oh, my darling! my darling!" she murmured in gentle accents, "if you only knew how glad I am to see you! I've had such dreams—dreams about you—dreams that frightened me so! They were only dreams, were they not?"

She looked up anxiously, and fixed her glorious eyes upon his face, and closely scanned it. Then she gave a sigh, the token of relief, and once more she nestled her face upon his shoulder.

"Yes!" she said softly, "after all 'twas but a dream! For you look well, and your eyes are bright and happy-looking; and in my dream you were looking dreadful! Your poor face looked so thin, and so different, and your eyes so sunken, and they had dark rings around them, and oh! their terrible, despairing look! But it was only a dream, or you could not look well again so soon, as now you do. Yes, 'twas but a dream, my darling! But oh! an awful dream. I thought there was a great tree—like that you said you saw one day; and it was a tree that fed on human beings, and you were lying bound and they were going to give you to that dreadful tree! Oh, Leonard, my love, think what a dream that was for me! Think, for a moment, what I felt! And there were other dreadful, awful things!" She shivered and cried softly for a space.

"Yes, my darling," Leonard answered soothingly. "But, as you say, 'twas but a dream!"

"Ah, yes! And now it seems far off; for, after it, came other dreams, that were happy and delightful, so that the bad one receded ever farther. Just when I seemed even at the very point of death from horror, a cool hand pressed tenderly on my brow, and brought me peace. It seemed to cool the fever that had made me think my very brain would burst; and a voice said—oh so kindly— 'Be at rest, my daughter, I bring thee peace, and surcease of thy sorrow.' Then I opened my eyes and saw a strange form leaning over me. It was dressed in a warrior dress, just like that which stands in our museum and which is called Mellenda's. Helmet, sword, everything the same. Then I felt secure and happy, for I thought the great Mellenda had come to deliver me in my trouble. But—and this seems so strange—when I looked up at his face, who do you think he was? Ah! you would never guess! But the countenance was Monella's—your friend Monella's! Was not my dream a strange one?"

"Strange, indeed, my dear one," said Leonard tenderly.

"From that moment," went on Ulama, "everything was changed, everything was lovely. It seemed to me that you then came to me, and led me from that scene of horror. Where we went I know not; but, hand in hand, we wandered on, till you led me home. Then once more things became confused—I can scarcely remember — but I'm nearly sure Mellenda seemed to come to me again. And— yes—I remember, he repeated, 'Rest, my child; I bring thee rest and peace.' Then he left me, and we wandered on—you and I, my Leonard—through the loveliest, the most entrancing scenes; among places, people, strange to me, yet all delightful; and, oh, it all seemed so sweet, so restful, so grateful, after the horror of that first awful dream! At last I wakened, and they tell me I have slept through two whole nights and nearly two whole days! Did you not wonder that you saw me not the while? Tell me how you have passed your time without me?"

And thus the gentle, loving girl talked on with childlike inno- cence, Leonard at first evading her inquiries, averse to mar her happiness by telling her the truth.

Indeed, it was not for some days, and then only by degrees and carefully guarded words, that he revealed the truth about her "dreams."

33
The Last of the Great Devil-Tree

Templemore did not find the occupation of directing the operations for destroying the great devil-tree a very agreeable or engrossing one. His memories of the amphitheatre filled him with disgust and loathing both of the place and of the vegetable monster it contained, and he never went near them without reluctance; for all that, he stuck conscientiously to the task now that he had undertaken it. But there was neither excitement nor interest in it to keep his thoughts engaged, and to prevent their brooding upon his desire to get back to those dear to him. Now that everything was settling down peacefully in the land, and there was nothing specially to keep him, he felt he was not justified in prolonging further unduly his friends' suspense. He saw comparatively little, too, of Leonard, who was continually engaged with Monella and others in councils and consultations that naturally had little interest for Templemore; though, no doubt, they would have been glad enough of his company and assistance in their deliberations, had he chosen to offer them.

As a consequence, he wandered about a good deal alone; and took to haunting the spot from which he and Leonard had made their signal flares, and whence he could, with his glasses, just distinguish "Monella Lodge" and the adjacent open country. Here he would sit by the hour together, wistfully gazing out over the vast panorama spread beneath him, and moodily watching for the slightest sign of life in the far distance.

Sometimes Nea, the puma, offered herself as a companion in his walks; at such times, when he went to the amphitheatre, he

was always in some concern to keep her out of the reach of the
fatal tree, lest she should meet the fate that had befallen her unfortunate mate.

It had been arranged that he would wait till Leonard's marriage, since it was so near. But he had determined not to delay his
going more than two days beyond it; and he now awaited the event
with something akin to impatience. At the same time, he knew that
the journey back to Georgetown would be anything but easy or
agreeable. It had been arduous, difficult, wearisome, and dangerous enough on the way up, when he had the company of Leonard
with his exhaustless boyish enthusiasm. What would it be like, he
asked himself, going all that weary road again alone, for he would
be alone in the sense of being the only white man amongst a number of Indians. Then again, he must return with very little to show
for all the time, and trouble, and danger he had incurred. Monella,
it was true, promised him "wealth"—and no doubt would keep his
promise in the form of a selection of precious stones. They were
numerous and comparatively cheap in the country; so Templemore
had no scruples about accepting such a present. And, when he
reached Georgetown, they would mean wealth. That was all satisfactory enough; but there was much, very much more he would
have liked to carry away with him; things of much less intrinsic
value, but of greater scientific interest. Of these there were more
than could be catalogued in a few lines; vessels of gold and silver;
wonderful antique jewellery, specimens of their armour, swords,
etc., were some; dress-fabrics also; an endless number of curious
botanical and zoological specimens, for others—these form only
the beginning of a long list of things he had in his mind, and would
have liked to carry with him. But well he knew the impossibility;
the difficulties of transport were insurmountable. In a country
where it was difficult to get carriers even for the bare food required,
it was obviously useless to dream of carrying back with him a "collection" such as he would have wished to take.

There was natural disappointment in all this. It is hard for an
explorer to face danger, hardship, discomfort; to separate himself
from civilisation and from those he loves, and to risk illness, fever,
wounds and death, and then, having achieved success, to have to

resign himself to returning without those trophies he would have delighted in exhibiting to an astonished and wondering world. But just, perhaps, when he had convinced himself, by dwelling morbidly upon such thoughts, that he had good cause for dissatisfaction, his good nature would assert itself and remind him of the other side to the picture. Was it a little matter to take back with him wealth enough to make his mother's future secure and comfortable; to marry the girl of his heart, and to be henceforth a man of means and affluence? And if his part in the expedition ended in such result, had he any just cause for complaint? Did he not rather owe a debt of gratitude to those who had urged him on, in spite of his own scepticism, to share in their enterprise? At this thought a rush of gratitude would come into Templemore's mind; then he would torment himself in turn, with misgivings as to whether he was not guilty of ingratitude in now feeling impatient to get away from—to leave for ever—the friends who had thrown such good fortune in his way.

And thus Jack Templemore felt anything but happy in the days that preceded Leonard's marriage. And, of course, he was in love, and felt home-sick; so, perhaps, it is not much to be wondered at that he was restless and changeable and ill at ease.

Yet, had he been in a different mood, his stay in the place might now have been very enjoyable, and of surpassing interest. He was free to go where he liked and do as he pleased. The people were not only friendly and willing and anxious to please, but showed pride and pleasure, if he but spoke to them. The story of the rescue of Leonard and the princess had been noised abroad and told and re-told over and over again, and the part that Templemore had taken in it was well known. Then, again, it had also now become known who Leonard really was; and the people felt that what Templemore had done for his friend had been done for them, inasmuch as it had saved for them the life of one who was of their own nation and whom they now valued highly. Thus Templemore was regarded as a hero, second only to Monella (or Mellenda). The people were quite ready to credit him with qualities he did not possess; for was he not the close and trusted friend of their own great hero? If Mellenda had chosen this one from all the people of the outside world—for they knew by this time that there was a great world, outside their mountains, peopled with white races—must it not have been for some very good reason? Must he not be a great man, a hero, a wonder, for the great Mellenda to have chosen him as his friend and companion on his return to Manoa?

Thus reasoned the simple-hearted people; and, since it was also known that he was going away from them for ever—going back to the outer world that was his home—it created a sort of mystery about him. Must he not be some very great man in that world that could not spare him even to stay and enjoy the friendship and favour of their own great hero-king?

So they regarded him with an interest and curiosity almost amounting to awe. Mothers would bring out their children to look at him as he passed, bidding them remember, for the remainder of their lives, that they had once seen the wonderful stranger, the great friend of their own great hero.

Meanwhile, Ulama had given herself up zealously to joining with Leonard in the work he had set himself among the people. She had been gently and tactfully told the story of all that had occurred; she knew now that her 'bad dream' had been only too true. The knowledge cast for a while its shadow upon her fair face, and she seemed to lose some of her childish gaiety and to become more staid under its influence. But it also called into play all the womanly tenderness and sympathy of her nature. When she heard of unhappy women and children needing care and comforting, she eagerly desired to assist in the work in company with Leonard and Sanaima; and thenceforth she devoted to it all the time she could spare from attendance upon her ailing father.

Amongst those in constant attendance on the princess might now be seen Fernina. She had been brought to the palace by Sanaima, who had discovered that her husband was no longer living. The meeting between her and Leonard was affecting; he presented her to Ulama and commended the poor woman to her kindness. Ulama knew now the particulars of the terrible time the two had passed together in the dread cells within reach of the great tree, and received her with a heart filled with compassion.

Fernina's gratitude and pride at the kindliness of her reception were such that they went far to assuage her sorrows. Her two children also were well cared for, and, by degrees, the old look of dull misery in her face gave place to a softer expression that promised to bring back, in a measure, her former beauty. It was understood that Fernina would in the future take Zonella's place; for it had been announced that the latter would shortly be married to Ergalon.

One day Templemore informed Monella that the mine had been completed, that he had placed the cask of gunpowder in position, and laid a fuse.

"And the reptiles?" asked Monella.

"I have left them alone—and for a reason. It seems to me they are inclined to attack the tree; have done so, in fact. They are getting hungry and have nothing else to attack, and, being well penned in, they are beginning to feed on the only thing within their reach. After all, the 'flesh'—if one may so term it—of a 'flesh-eating' tree may quite possibly form an acceptable food for these ugly reptiles when they are starving. If, when we have blown it up—or down—they are disposed to devour it and so clear it out of the way, it may save some trouble."

Then a day was fixed for firing the mine, and a large crowd of the citizens assembled to witness the destruction of their enemy; but many, whose memories of the place were sad, remained away.

When the explosion took place, a long tongue of flame shot up into the air with a thunderous roar, the great tree seemed lifted bodily up, swayed, and then fell with a mighty crash full length on the ground, disclosing a rent in the trunk from which a thick, noisome stream of dark-coloured fluid slowly flowed. This gave off an odour so offensive and over-powering that none could stay in the enclosure; so the crowd quickly dispersed, with loud expressions of wonderment and admiration at all that they had seen. But Templemore remained long enough to see, from a distance, that the foul reptiles had approached the tree, and were greedily drinking up the liquid that flowed from the wound in the trunk. And, visiting the place next day, he found that they had torn the rent still further open, and were busily tearing the trunk to pieces, the branches now showing but feeble signs of life. In the end they fulfilled his expectations and devoured every scrap of the monster. Thus ended the existence of the terrible, horror-laden devil-tree!

It was shortly after he had completed the destruction of the hated tree that Templemore made a discovery that filled him with grave uneasiness. He was wandering about among the heights that lay at one end of the canyon—that immediately over the entrance-cavern—when he found himself amongst huge blocks which had been quarried out (as Monella had one day mentioned) with the idea of precipitating them into the canyon to block it up impenetrably. On examining the quarry from which they had been taken, he observed with alarm that some masses of overhanging rock seemed almost on the point of giving way. A sort of partial land-slip had already taken place, and there were fresh-looking cracks and fissures that threatened shortly to loosen the overhanging masses and set them free to fall into the canyon below. He spoke to Monella about this, and he at once accompanied him to the spot, and his opinion confirmed his own. This made Templemore busy himself in earnest with his preparations for departure; for he feared that, if these rocks actually fell, the entrance to the cavern might be so blocked up as to take long and arduous labour to clear it.

It being now within a day or two of Leonard's marriage this was all he could do in the matter. But Monella sent men down the canyon in charge of Ergalon—since the latter now knew the road—to carry in advance and deposit in the cavern some of the things Templemore desired to take with him. They returned on the eve of the wedding, Ergalon stating that all they had taken down had been duly stored as desired, ready for Templemore when he went down.

That evening King Dranoa was much better and insisted on presiding at the evening meal. He even hoped, he said, to be able to be present at the wedding. Ulama's joy at this, and the sweet delight that lighted up her face, were alone enough to infuse happiness into those around her. She looked at Templemore, too, and smiled and nodded her head in a mysterious way that roused his curiosity; and, later, an explanation came.

At the very end of the repast a mysterious-looking dish or tray, whose contents were hidden by a golden cover, was brought in with a good deal of ceremony and was placed before the king. Then Ulama glanced shyly at Templemore and clapped her hands. At this the king lifted the cover, and displayed to view—not some new eatables, as

Templemore had anticipated, but—a beautifully fashioned belt, and several exquisitely-worked purses that all sparkled and flashed with the little diamond and other stones that were worked in patterns into the silken netting. And, when Templemore looked inquiringly at Leonard, that young man only smiled and nodded mysteriously like the others.

Then King Dranoa thus addressed him:

"My friend, thou hast already heard, I believe, that we do not purpose to allow thee to depart hence without begging thine acceptance of some little testimony of our appreciation of what thou hast done for us. I say we, for all here—all in the land indeed—are deeply in thy debt. Without thy courageous help and unselfish devotion my dear daughter would not now be here happy and joyous as she is to-night, and my kinsman and son-in-law that is to be would, I fear, only too probably have met a dreadful fate. Therefore, we have all joined in subscribing to these presents, of which we beg thy acceptance. The princess hath worked this belt, and inside it are some of her own chosen jewels that thou hast often seen her wear. The lady Zonella, and others of her maidens, have worked these purses—they are for thy friends—and we have all contributed to their contents. I know naught about thy world outside, but understand that what is in these satchels will be of far greater value to thee, and those dear to thee, than to us here. I truly hope it may be so; else I should hesitate to offer them, as being but a poor return for what thou hast done for us. If, however, they can purchase for thee, in the future, any surcease of toil, of trouble, of anxiety, then, and only from that point of view, may they be worth the offering. Take them, my friend; and may the blessing of the Great Spirit go with them, and accompany thy footsteps throughout thy life."

Then Ulama took the belt and poured out its contents upon the tray—a magnificent, glittering heap of superb precious stones. Then she emptied each purse in turn, making other sparkling but smaller heaps. And each purse had a little label with a name to it; and Templemore looked on in wonder as the contents of each were revealed and the names read out by Leonard. There were three large purses, one for his mother, one for Maud, and one for Stella. Smaller ones for Mr. and Robert Kingsford, Dr. Lorien and his son;

and two, still smaller, for Carenna and Matava. No one had been forgotten.

Templemore looked from the one to the other, his heart filled with emotion. Even more than the overwhelming value of the jewels, he felt the loving-kindness that had thus taken thought and trouble for those dear to him.

"But—Dr. Lorien and Harry—and—the others" he said, hesitating. "I don't see—"

"The good doctor," Monella explained, "will be sorely disappointed that he cannot come to see us and take back to the world some of the botanical rarities we have here, and which, to him, would be great treasures. These are to console him. As to the others of your friends—this is the least we can do to show our regret for the sorrow and anxiety they will have borne on your behalf, through us. That is all."

For some minutes Templemore was silent.

"It is too much—a great deal too much!" he got out presently. "I don't know what to say—"

"Then say nothing, dear friend," Ulama interposed, with a merry laugh. "Now let me put them back and show you how they all fit nicely into the belt. You see, while you were working for us at that horrid old tree, we had not forgotten you. Keep the belt always for my sake, and think of us all lovingly in the future, as we always shall of you. Now I want you to take me out on the terrace."

34
A Marriage and a Parting

In the ancient Temple of the White Priests Leonard and Ulama were solemnly made man and wife according to the custom of the country. King Dranoa was able to be present at the ceremony, and nearly the whole population may be said to have assisted, for they thronged in crowds to the great building where in ages past their kings had all been married; though comparatively few of the populace could find room inside the Temple. The remainder filled all the surrounding open spaces, and waited patiently to greet the bride and bridegroom on their way back to the palace.

Templemore had a place of honour in the assemblage, and watched the function with curious interest. Sanaima, with an array of white-robed priests; Monella, with his commanding form, conspicuous by his noble bearing; the beautiful Ulama, all suffused with blushes; and her handsome bridegroom; the kindly, dignified Dranoa, looking weak and pale, yet well-pleased and content; and the brilliant crowd of spectators, officers in gleaming armour, and courtiers in gorgeous dresses—all combined to form a noble pageant. The building, whose interior Templemore now for the first time saw, was a magnificent structure, and helped to add grandeur to the imposing spectacle.

At the conclusion of the ceremony, the procession, on its way back to the palace, was greeted with excited and enthusiastic cheers and cries that seemed almost loud enough to shake the towering buildings past which it slowly filed.

In the evening there were general feastings and rejoicings. These were continued till the night was far advanced; and it was morning ere the city again subsided unto rest.

The following day, Templemore was busy completing his preparations, and going round to bid farewell to those he knew. But, towards the afternoon, he was surprised to see a large crowd outside the palace; and still more astonished on learning that the people were gathered in his honour. The good-hearted citizens, it appeared, liked not the notion of his going away without some public mark of the esteem in which they held him; so, somewhat against his will, he was called out on to the terrace that overlooked the place in which the people had assembled. Monella, Ulama, Leonard, and all the members of the court and of the king's household, stepped out with him; and the first two each took him by the hand, and led him to a spot where all could see him. Then a great shout went up, and he was cheered again and yet again, till the strange feelings called up by the unexpected warmth of the welcome he received made him go red and white by turns.

"They have come for a sight of you, and a word of farewell ere you leave us," explained Monella. "Will you not give them a few words?"

Templemore was unused to oratory, and he would fain have excused himself; but he saw that to do so would disappoint his friends. So he made them a short speech, assuring them of his appreciation of their friendly feelings.

"The unexpected warmth and kindness you have shown in thus coming here to-day," he said, "I shall always gratefully remember. If, in company with the friends who led me hither, I have done aught that seems to you to call for commendation, I will only ask you, in return, to keep for me a tender corner in your memories when I have left you. If, when I have gone, you will but think as kindly of me as I shall of you, then indeed I shall be well repaid."

Then Monella addressed them in his sonorous tones.

"My children, I am well pleased that ye should have thus gathered here to-day, and of your own accord, to show to my friend that you are not unmindful of his part in the events of the past few months. I am glad and proud that he should receive, before he leaves us, this proof that my people are not ungrateful to one who hath done so much for them. A great work hath been accomplished in the land since we three, as strangers to you all, arrived some months ago. At the last, its prompt completion was due in no small measure to your quick response to my urgent call, at a time when hours were precious—and even moments. When I left you in the times long past, I sailed away with fleets and armies; when returning I was a simple wanderer. Yet ye gathered gladly at my summons, and no voice was raised to question my authority. This was well, and helped me to achieve success; yet might we have been too late to save the well-beloved of your princess had not our friend here kept all Coryon's vile following at bay till we could come to aid him. If the dread devil-tree exists, to-day, no more, and all the wickedness and cruelty that went with it have been trampled out for ever, if now your minds are all at peace, and your daughters and your other dear ones are secure—ye owe much of this to our friend's ready courage and devotion; and I am rejoiced to see that ye have not forgotten it!

"Now will my friend know that he bears away with him the love and the good wishes of us all. We wish him all happiness in his future life; our sole regret is that he cannot stay and spend that life with us!"

At this there were shouts and roars of applause, and other tokens of assent.

"And now, my children," went or, the speaker, "I have somewhat else to say to you. The ancient Temple of the Great Spirit is once more open; see that ye neglect not to there offer up your thanks for the blessing that hath been vouchsafed you. Give heed to the teachings of the worthy Sanaima. See that ye take to your hearts the precepts that he will expound to you. So shall the good work that I have begun be continued and consummated after I shall have left you."

Loud murmurs of surprise and objection were here heard.

"Nay, let not that which I have said arouse your grief, my children. Remember my long life and weary wanderings to and fro upon the earth; these have been a punishment to me, even as events, during this same time, have been to you. Ye would not wish to keep me here when I tell you that my task is done, and my tired soul is seeking rest—rest not to be found on earth, but only in the great domain beyond the skies. I may not linger here now that the work that I was sent to do is finished. I have freed you from the curse that did oppress you; have brought you one to govern you who combines within himself the blood both of your ancient White Priests and of our kings; and in Sanaima ye have a wise counsellor and guide. Seek not then to stay me; when the Great Spirit calleth, weep not and repine not, for then is the hour of my deliverance. Then shall I be united, at the last, to my well-beloved queen, my Elmonta, and my children that have gone before!"

When Monella ended, he raised his hands and face towards heaven, and stood gazing upwards like one inspired. His face seemed transfigured and was lighted up as by, a thrilling joy; and, as on the occasion of his talk in the palace with Templemore and Leonard a few days before, he appeared to see something invisible to those around him, but the sight of which filled him with supreme content. Then he dropped his arms, looked around him as though he had just awaked from sleep, and, with bent head and tardy steps, walked silently away.

Ulama caught Templemore by the arm.

"Oh, do you think it can be true—what he says?" she exclaimed in anxious tones, almost a sob. "It cannot be that we are about to lose him? Do you think so?"

"Nay, I see no cause to apprehend it," was Templemore's reply. "Our friend seems as robust and as strong as a man can wish."

"Yes! So think I, and yet—he has spoken in this strange fashion several times of late. His words fill me with foreboding."

She looked at Templemore with such sorrow in her gentle eyes that he scarcely knew what to say to comfort her. And just then he was obliged to leave her to return the salutes of the people, who were now separating and returning to their homes or their various callings.

The next morning, shortly after sunrise, Templemore stood at the top of the hillside, not far from the entrance of the canyon—the spot from which he had first seen the "Golden City"—looking his last upon the fair scene outspread beneath, and saying the last words of farewell to his friends. Once more the people had assembled to do him honour, and they now crowded the slopes on every side.

Already some of the little party who were to accompany him to "Monella Lodge" had started and were on their way down the canyon, and Ergalon, under whose charge they were, stood waiting for Jack Templemore. The latter was surrounded by a little group, of whom the chief were Leonard, Ulama, and Zonella, who seemed as if they could not make up their minds to let him go. Monella, his arms folded, stood apart, gravely looking, first at the group, and then out over the landscape with dreamy eyes, his noble figure, outlined against the dark foliage, the centre of a half-circle of officers and courtiers who stood respectfully a short distance from him. Templemore was dressed in the same clothes he had worn on his arrival; beneath them he had buckled on the precious belt with the jewels it contained; his rifle was slung across his shoulder.

Amongst those around were to be seen Colenna and his son, Abla, and others who had been amongst Templemore's first friends; and all showed by their demeanour genuine sorrow at the parting. As a last and special gift—one more token of his remembrance of his boyhood's friend—Leonard had that morning handed to Templemore a deed of gift making over all his property in the "outer world" to Maud Kingsford.

"It is nothing to give, since it is no longer of any use to me," he observed, with a quiet smile. "But, since I must convey it to some one, let it be a dowry for Maud in addition to the purse the others send."

It would be difficult to say how many "last handshakes" were given, or how many times Ulama, with tear-dimmed eyes, pleaded for "a minute longer—just a minute," Zonella, with sorrow in her looks, seeming mutely to second the appeal. But the parting came at last, and, amid loud huzzas, and the waving of hands and scarves, and other tokens of good will, Templemore turned away and, with Ergalon, disappeared into the thicket.

Little was said by either as they made their way down the rough path, and, even when they rested in the shade of the half-way cave, neither seemed disposed for talk. Almost in silence they ate the refreshments with which the forethought of their friends had loaded them, and drank cool draughts from the rocky shallows of the stream.

Suddenly, while they sat within the cave, waiting for the sun to move so far that the path should be in shade, a heavy booming detonation like the firing of cannon burst upon their astonished ears; and they started up together and stood listening anxiously.

"What on earth can that be?" exclaimed Templemore. Ergalon gravely shook his head.

"Falling rock, I think," he answered. "If so, it must be farther down the canyon."

"Let us hasten," cried the other, a vision rising before his eyes of the entrance-cavern blocked, and his being forced to return. "This is what I have been fearing."

Despite the sun, he started off at a rapid pace down the path, Ergalon following and striving, as well as he could, to keep up with the other's impetuous movements. During the remainder of the descent they heard two or three other similar noises; and at each of these Templemore hurried on still faster.

When they reached the bottom, they came upon the little party who had preceded them; they were standing in doubt and alarm, looking along the valley, which was already partially blocked by fallen rocks, while more continued to fall at intervals, crashing on to those already fallen and sending up clouds of dust. With the group, looking on at the scene in a sort of mild surprise, stood Nea the puma.

"The stars be praised," Ergalon exclaimed, relieved, "it's all at the other end."

"What do you mean?" asked Templemore in surprise.

"Why, the rocks have not fallen near your cave," was the reply. "All is clear there," and he pointed to the hidden cave.

Then there were explanations, and, to Templemore's dismay, it now appeared that Ergalon had mistaken his instructions and placed all the things in the wrong place. He was not really to blame in the matter; for he only knew of the one cave—that to which he had accompanied Templemore when they had come down to fetch the spare weapons. He knew nothing of any other cavern, and Templemore had not remembered this.

The situation was a trying and terribly disappointing one, and Templemore found himself in a grave dilemma. If he hesitated, it was plain his way would soon be totally barred. If he went on, and risked being crushed by the falling rocks, he must go alone; leave behind him everything he had intended to take with him, save what he had on his person, and make up his mind to face the dangers of the gloomy forest by himself! Even now it was almost folly to risk death or serious injury by making for the cavern.

Templemore hesitated, the while that more boulders came crashing down. Then he thought of what it would mean for him were he to be shut up in the mountain for an indefinite period. He looked up keenly and saw enough of what was going on to grasp the fact that the whole sides of the canyon were crumbling and falling in, and it looked a sufficient quantity to make it likely that the reopening of the road would be a work of years. As that conviction dawned upon him, with a brief word of farewell he dashed away from the group, and, despite their startled endeavours to stay him and the entreaties they called after him, he ran swiftly along the valley towards the entrance-cavern. After him bounded the faithful puma; he had no time to give to the attempting to send her back, and the two went rapidly on, dodging the great masses that now crashed down faster than before. A massive boulder rolling down seemed about to crush them, but they escaped it and disappeared in a cloud of dust from the view of the spellbound witnesses of their hazardous race.

Just when they reached the cavern a great stone pitched upon one already fallen and, splitting into several pieces, sent heavy fragments flying around in all directions, like an exploding bomb-shell. One of these fragments struck Templemore in the back, smashing his rifle, and throwing him, stunned and bruised, upon the floor of the cavern.

35
Just In Time!

At sunrise, one morning, a fortnight after the events recorded in the last chapter, a party of travellers, consisting of three white men and a number of Indians, set out from the Indian village of Daranato, making their way in the direction of Roraima.

The three white men were Dr. Lorien, his son Harry, and Robert Kingsford; and among the Indians was Matava. As they toiled along the rough path it was easy to see that the travellers were, for the most part, travel-worn and weary; they moved forward in a half-listless fashion, scarcely looking to right or left, and showing but little interest in the scenes that lay along their route. Only when they came to the ridge from which the first view of Roraima is to be obtained did any of the party exhibit curiosity. Here a halt was made, and they all gazed for some time silently at the great mass that raised itself high above the surrounding landscape. This morning, clouds hung over it and it appeared sombre, dark and threatening, and gave no sign of the fairy-like lightness and beauty it sometimes assumed when seen from this same spot.

Robert Kingsford had come up from the coast, in the company of the doctor and his son, bent upon solving, if possible, the mystery that surrounded the fate of the two friends who had left Georgetown, nearly nine months before, to join with an unknown stranger in the exploration of Roraima. All that had since been heard of them was the strange, almost fantastic account that had been brought back by Matava, according to which they had actually found a way into the mountain, and thenceforth had disappeared. The very entrance by which they had made their way through the solid wall of cliff had been afterwards found fast sealed; and no trace or clue to their fate had been left behind. This had been Matava's account, and he had not hesitated to express his belief that the three adventurers had been captured by the demons of the mountain, and either eaten up then and there, or kept as prisoners and slaves in durance vile.

This story, however, did not satisfy the minds of the others, and Robert Kingsford, seeing and compassionating the deep sorrow of Templemore's widowed mother, and the still more passionate grief of his own sister Maud, determined to investigate matters for himself. Dr. Lorien was detained longer in Rio than he had expected; but, when at last he returned to Georgetown, he readily joined the other in the proposed expedition of inquiry.

They had a very arduous and difficult journey up from the coast. It happened to be a season of exceptional drought, and cassava, and food of all kinds, were extremely scarce. The sun had been unusually fierce, and the heat abnormal; hence, by the time they reached Daranato, even the sturdy and seasoned doctor—a very veteran in tropical travel—was nearly worn out; while the other two were in still worse plight.

Add to these trials the fact that they had little, if any, hope of succeeding in their quest, and felt, in reality, that the expedition was, at best, but a sort of forlorn hope; and it will be understood why they had started from Daranato dispirited and depressed.

Thus, when they obtained their first view of the mysterious mountain, the cause of all their trouble, they were not inclined to regard it with any very friendly feelings; and its gloomy, forbidding look this morning was reflected, so to speak, in their own minds. "There is our enemy," they felt. "There is the fascinating, sinister chimera that has bewitched, and lured away from us, our dear friends, and caused us all this anxiety and useless trouble." And so, as Roraima frowned upon them, they frowned back, and returned in kind its gloomy and unfriendly greeting.

But frowns and angry looks could do them no good; so the travellers, with a very few words of comment, continued their route towards "Monella Lodge," where they arrived towards evening.

Here, a mile or so from the "haunted wood," and almost, as it seemed to them, under the very shadow of the mighty towering walls, they set about making arrangements for a stay of several days. They found everything in the cabin much as Matava had led them to expect; the place, indeed, just as Templemore had left it at his last visit. Many things had been left there that the travellers now found useful, and that seemed veritable luxuries after the discomforts of their long journey.

Kingsford's thoughts were intent upon his missing friends; and, indeed, this was also the case in only a slightly less degree with the other two. All were oppressed with vague suspicions of the Indians, even of Matava. Might these not have murdered the three travellers for the sake of the things they had with them—articles and stores which would be as priceless treasures to Indians; therefore which might quite conceivably have offered a temptation too great to be resisted?

However, amongst the tribe at the village, they had seen no signs of "white men's" belongings to any unusual extent; and, now that they saw what a number of things had been left undisturbed in "Monella Lodge," their suspicions were very considerably lightened. For all that, they found it difficult to believe implicitly the fantastic tale Matava had told about the three adventurers' disappearance

The Indians gathered wood and lighted fires, while the white men made a careful and interested inspection of the contents of the habitation and its surroundings (the two llamas had been removed to the village, where, however, they had both since died). Inside, they found a lamp and a small cask still partly full of oil, which was a discovery they appreciated when it grew dark.

After their evening meal, the three friends sat for some time smoking their pipes and discussing the strange situation in which they found themselves. They were now within reach of their journey's end. If the tale told by Matava were correct, and the road through the forest were still fairly clear, they ought to be able to reach the mysterious cavern the next day; when they were determined, if requisite, to blow open the entrance with gunpowder. In addition to that which they had brought with them, they had found a considerable quantity at "Monella Lodge." This surprised them; for in this country gunpowder is more valued by Indians than almost anything else.

The three friends were sitting talking, and were thinking of retiring to rest for the night, when Matava came rushing excitedly into the place.

"Come quickly, my masters," he exclaimed. "Come! Come and see the light on the mountain!"

Somewhat languidly those addressed rose and went out. They had so often heard the usual stories of lights seen at night on unexplored mountains that they attached but little importance to them. They had treated in like manner a statement by Carenna and Matava that some Indians, camping out on the savanna a few months before, had seen strange and unusually bright lights, that they took to be signals, on Roraima's summit. The Indians had been scared and broke up their encampment at once, fearing the lights might have been placed there to lure them into the power of the demons of the mountain.

When, however, the doctor stepped outside, and looked up towards the top of the stupendous precipice, he saw a brilliant flame that had all the appearance of a signal beacon.

"It doesn't look like a forest fire," he said to Kingsford, while they were examining it carefully through their field-glasses. "And now and then I almost fancy I can make out human forms passing in front of it."

The others had the same impression, and Harry Lorien declared he could see flashes of light, as though the beings round the fire were dressed in clothes, or carried something, that reflected the firelight.

"Let us try burning a little powder," the doctor suggested, "after the fashion Matava says was arranged between him and the others, but which they never carried out."

So they sent Matava for the powder, and told him to fire it in the manner that had been settled between him and Monella. It is true none of the three messages agreed upon would be applicable to the present occasion—but that they could not help.

Presently, three tongues of flame leaped up into the air, then suddenly died out, leaving those around temporarily half-blinded by the glare. Then they stood for some time anxiously watching through their glasses.

What seemed a long interval ensued; when, suddenly, three brilliant gleams flashed out on Roraima's height, in exact imitation, as to the intervals between the flashes, of the signals they had themselves made.

"Try another," Doctor Lorien cried, in growing excitement. "Arrange the three differently this time."

This was done, and the answering flashes came back, again in exact imitation; and this time with scarcely any delay.

Doctor Lorien seized Kingsford by the hand.

"Heaven be praised for this!" he exclaimed, his voice half-choked with emotion. "It begins to look, indeed, as though Matava's account were true; as if our dear friends may be alive after all!"

Words cannot describe the delight with which the travel-worn party hailed these signs, that so unmistakably pointed to the conclusion suggested in the doctor's words. There was one thing, certainly, they could not understand; none of the signals agreed upon between Monella and Matava had been given from the mountain; but they were inclined to attribute this to Matava's having, after the lapse of time, forgotten or mixed up what had been arranged. Only the thought that their supply of powder was not unlimited restrained them from continuing the signalling; but they were reluctantly compelled, as a matter of prudence, to discontinue it.

"Now," said the doctor, "we can attack the "haunted wood" with a good heart. Surely, our friends will come down to meet us, now that they know we are here!"

Before daylight they were all astir, and set off at once on the journey through the forest, Matava guiding them. The road, or track, was followed with difficulty, and was almost blocked at times. Only an Indian's instinct, indeed, could have made it out. In places the rough temporary bridges that had been made over water-courses had been washed away, but, the water being very low from the long-continued drought, this caused no serious difficulty. They met with some adventures by the way, which were, however, suggestive of the dangers that lay around them rather than important in themselves. At last, towards evening, Matava told the doctor they were getting near the cavern. And now he begged him to proceed with caution. He could not get over the fear that the "demons of the mountain" had eaten up or captured their friends, and were now awaiting more victims whom they had lured on by imitating and answering the signals of their murdered friends.

This theory did not find much favour with the doctor; for all that he so far yielded to the entreaties of the Indian as to send him on to scout in advance, while he, and the others of the party, walked in silence behind. And, since Matava now moved with especial care, they made slow progress.

As it happened, however, Matava's caution was in a measure justified; for just when they came to the part where there was an opening in the trees, and they could see ahead of them the light that came down into the clearing round the cavern, Matava stopped and raised his hand.

All stood still, except the doctor, who moved up to the Indian's side and looked whither he was pointing.

For a moment or so he could see nothing to account for the other's behaviour. To the right the stream that came out of the rock was now plainly in sight; and ahead of them was the clearing. The entrance to the cavern was as yet hidden by intervening trunks, but the light-coloured rock could be seen between the trees. Matava slowly raised his rifle and took a careful aim; then, as though dissatisfied, he lowered the weapon and stood with up-lifted hand enjoining silence upon those behind him. To make sure, he turned round and, with many gestures, impressed upon them all to keep motionless and silent; then, having satisfied himself that they understood and would obey his signs, he faced round and again raised his rifle.

And now, Doctor Lorien, following the line of the Indian's aim, became conscious of a slight movement among the trees in front of them. Presently—the Indian still waiting his opportunity to fire— he saw that a great hanging mass was swaying to and fro, passing and re-passing the space between the trunks of two trees. At first he thought it was a large mass of hanging creeper, but, remembering that there was no wind to cause the movement, he looked more closely and saw that it was the head and part of the body of a gigantic serpent that was depending from a branch above. Suddenly, Matava's rifle rang out, and a moment after an enormous mass fell to the ground and writhed and twisted about in horrible contortions.

Then a loud, hoarse roar was heard, echoing through the forest. The startled travellers looked about on every side, but could see nothing to explain the sound; then it came again and again, while the colossal folds in front of them, half hidden by the trees, continued to rise and fall, lashing against the trees and shrubs with blows that seemed almost to shake the ground.

Matava advanced and fired other shots into the struggling monster; then, watching his opportunity, made a rush and dexterously cut off the creature's head with a blow of his axe.

And now, looking towards the rock, they saw the "window" entrance to the cavern, and the head of the big puma from which had proceeded the loud roars they had heard; and by the side of the puma was a pallid, thin, haggard face that they had some difficulty in recognising as Jack Templemore's!

"You have come only just in time," he said, in a weak voice, with a poor attempt at a smile, when the doctor had come near. "We were almost done for; at least, I know I am. I scarcely know whether I have strength enough to get the ladder out for you."

They tied two lassoes together and threw one end in; this he fastened to the ladder, and, thus assisted, it was got out. Immediately the puma sprang down it and disappeared into the forest. Then the doctor, followed by Kingsford and Harry, climbed up and entered the cavern, to find Templemore lying on the floor unconscious.

He was suffering from a sprained ankle and a badly bruised arm, and was exhausted from want of food. It was some time before he could explain matters to his rescuers; and they, meantime, were anxiously wondering at finding him thus alone, with no sign about of his two friends. When he had briefly accounted for their absence, he told how he had been kept prisoner for more than a week by the great serpent that, all that time, had relentlessly watched and waited outside. But, apart from this, he could scarcely have got through the wood in his crippled state.

"Still," he said, "but for that serpent, Nea, the puma, would have brought in some fresh meat. As it is, I have had to share with her even the small amount of tinned food we happened to have left here."

The flying pieces of rock that had injured him had broken his rifle; and he had only a few cartridges for his revolver.

"It's all been unfortunate," he said. "They put all the things in the wrong cave, and, when I came to myself after my desperate race between the falling rocks, I was in darkness and the puma was licking my hands and face. With much difficulty I found my way to the front here and pulled the stone away; then found a lantern and some oil, and got a light. The entrance to the canyon I found was all dark—buried—and I could still hear rumblings as of further falls of rock; but they sounded distant. I imagine, therefore, that the valley must be buried pretty deep. I set about making myself as comfortable as I could; and, when I put the ladder out, Puss, as I call her, went out hunting while I bathed my ankle and arm. Several days she went out and brought in something pretty regularly, and I thought I should be able to nurse myself up and get well enough to struggle through the wood alone. But, one morning, she refused to go out; that day I had a visit from a pack of 'Warracaba tigers'; another time when she stayed in, looking out myself, I saw that awful serpent hanging from a bough; and there it has been day and night ever since; Puss refusing to venture forth. I fired all my cartridges, except two, at it without any effect. It kept ceaselessly swaying its head about, and my arm pained me and my hand trembled; and, unless you can put a bullet through its head, it's of no use firing at a creature like that, you know. If my rifle had been all right, the thing would have been easy enough. I kept two cartridges in reserve—one for poor Puss and the other for myself—and I think you came only just about in time to save us both." And Jack's voice shook, and he felt a choking sensation in his throat. It was clear he had given up hope and had been making up his mind to face death alone.

Robert Kingsford's gratification and delight in the fact that his journey had, after all, turned out to be the means of rescuing his friend, the lover of his sister, may be imagined. Nor were the others less pleased; only the good doctor's satisfaction was clouded by his inability to get out into the wonderful valley to obtain any of the botanical treasures that lay so near at hand. But his chagrin disappeared when Templemore, as some consolation, showed him the purse of gems that had been sent to him.

"We'll give up orchid-collecting after this, lad!" he exclaimed to his son. "No need to wear out my old bones any longer in toilsome wanderings, when we've got enough to live on comfortably without."

Presently, Puss came back with a wild pig, and great was the rejoicing over the meal that followed.

Then all, save Templemore—who could only look on from the window—went out to examine the reptile monster they had killed and to gaze in astonishment at its huge proportions. The Indians had already begun to skin it, but had not finished the operation when the time came for making their preparations to pass the night.

These were complete—the four white men sleeping in the cavern and the Indians bivouacking outside—when strange cries were heard echoing through the forest. Instantly there was a great stir among the Indians. With one accord they started up, exclaiming, "The tigers! The tigers are coming!" Forgetting their fear of the "demons' cavern," they cried out piteously for the ladder to be put out for them; and no sooner was this done than they scrambled up it with all speed into the cave, and pulled it in after them.

In reply to the amazed inquiries of the others, Matava explained that they had recognised the distant trumpetings of "Warracaba tigers," those fierce animals that nothing—not even fires—can stay or keep at bay. Soon, in fact, the animals could be heard on all sides around the cavern, though but little could be seen of them in the darkness. Their growls and roars and squeals were answered by hoarse roars of defiance from the puma that were deafening as they reverberated through the galleries of the cavern. Outside, the "tigers" made frantic efforts to leap up and get in at the window, while those within had much ado to keep the puma from leaping out amongst them. They also fired a few shots at them, but in the darkness—for the fires had burned low—they were fired at random.

"Why," said the doctor, "I should think there must be a hundred of them! What an awful place this forest must be! I know that wolves hunt in packs, but I never before heard of 'tigers' doing so.

Wolves can't climb trees as these can. It's awful, perfectly awful!"
he added, the while he listened to the diabolical noises going on
outside. It was, indeed, as a former traveller has expressed it, 'like
a withering scourge sweeping through the forest.'*

It was hours before the din died down; and then, just when the
tired travellers were falling asleep, the most appalling, human-like
cries broke forth, sounding first quite close at hand, and then dying
away in a long-drawn wail or shriek.

Again the new-comers started up in alarm; but Templemore,
smiling feebly, bade them take no notice.

"It is only the 'lost souls'," said he.

"The 'lost souls'!" exclaimed Kingsford. "What can you mean?"
He began to think the other must be raving.

"I know no more than you do," was Templemore's reply. "So
the Indians account for those sounds, and that is all I can tell you.
Since I have been here they have serenaded me thus every night—
even sometimes by day—and at times I have thought all the 'lost
souls' from the Infernal Regions must have been let loose for my
especial entertainment—or to frighten me to death or drive me
mad—I know not which. I really think, if I had not had the company of this faithful beast—she always roars back defiance at
them—I should have gone mad."

Towards morning the sounds ceased, and sleep became possible for two or three hours. But when, at daylight, the Indians
rose and ventured out, they found the great snake had been almost completely devoured. Only some bones and a few bits of skin
were left.

* See Mr. Barrington Brown's *Canoe and Camp Life Among the
Indians of British Guiana*, p. V. He says these animals hunt in packs
of as many as a hundred or more.

36
The End

Templemore was carried, with much difficulty, to "Monella Lodge," where an attack of fever supervened, and it was nearly two weeks before the doctor pronounced him out of danger.

Carenna came over from her village to nurse him, and tended him as devotedly as she had Leonard. In the height of the fever he raved constantly of the great devil-tree, of gigantic serpents, of Monella, and of "lost souls"; and, mixed up with all, were a number of names strange to those who listened to him; for he had been too ill when found in the cavern to give more than a brief idea of the adventures he had passed through.

While he lay upon his bed of sickness, anxious friends watched from the mountain top for tidings of his fate, but received no intelligible answers to their signals; for none of those now with Templemore knew how to reply to them. Thus it was not till he was convalescent and well enough to be taken out into the open air, that any interchange of messages became possible.

Those below, looking up, day after day had seen little flashes of light, of which they could make nothing; but now Templemore explained their meaning.

A search in the cabin brought to light the mirror Monella had thoughtfully packed up and hidden carefully away; and Templemore was thus able at last to open communication with his Roraima friends.

His first signalled message to them brought back the reply:—

"Heaven be praised! We are all so thankful! We have mourned you as dead! And we are in great affliction, besides, for Monella, the great, great-hearted Mellenda, is dead! He died peacefully the day after you went away."

Then, presently, when Templemore had sent back a message of sorrow and condolence, another came.

"The whole valley at the bottom of the canyon is half-filled up. It would take years to clear it. And we pictured you as lying dead beneath it all!"

Many messages passed to and fro during the remainder of the travellers' stay; and then, after a time, Templemore having thoroughly recovered, preparations were made for the journey back to the coast.

Both Carenna and Matava were grieved at the thought that Leonard had remained on the mountain for good, and that they were never likely to see him more. Carenna, alone, however, expressed no surprise. She told Templemore that the deception as to Leonard she had practised upon the good people who had received them so hospitably in their lonely mountain retreat had, all her life, been a sore trouble to her. It was some consolation to her, therefore, to know that he had, after all, been led back to his own people. She at first refused the valuable present Leonard had sent her, saying that to receive forgiveness was in itself more than she had hoped for. But, needless to say, Templemore persuaded her into accepting it. Matava's delight with what had been sent him was unbounded; especially when Templemore told him what treasures he could purchase with it: rifles, pistols, unbounded supplies of powder, and unlimited tobacco, and other things that Indians prize.

Meanwhile, Doctor Lorien and his son had been assiduous in collecting specimens of all the botanical and zoological treasures with which the neighbourhood of Roraima abounds; and, when the time for starting came, they had good reason to be satisfied with the result. They might have done still better, perhaps, if they had gone more into Roraima Forest; but this they could not make up their minds to do. Indeed, they could not venture far without an Indian guide; and this they could not get. Neither Matava nor any one of the other Indians could be prevailed upon to go into the wood again; and even the doctor was not very pressing. All had

had quite enough of the "haunted wood." For it now came out, too, that Templemore had become a believer in the "didi." He declared that more than once during his imprisonment in the cavern he had seen, either at early morning or at dusk, strange human-like shapes—gigantic apes—standing watching within the shadow of the trees.

Nothing, he said, would induce him to enter that wood again. And he felt certain that only the fact that the entrance to the cavern was so high from the ground had enabled him to escape with his life.

Nea, the puma, alone showed no fear of the gloomy forest. She went hunting there daily, and nearly always returned with something to reward her enterprise.

When all was ready for the start, two or three last messages passed between the travellers and their friends upon the mountain.

"Heaven keep you and all those dear to you! Your memory will always be cherished by all here," came from Leonard. To which Templemore replied "Long life and happiness to you and your dear wife and all your people."

"God bless you, Jack!"

"God bless you, Leonard!"

Thus they finally parted; and a few hours later the homeward-bound friends looked their last upon Roraima from the ridge near Daranato. The mountain was lighted with the red rays of the setting sun and towered up in glowing splendour. The greens of the wood at its base, varied and vivid in colouring, as they were, contrasted with the pinks, and purples, and reds of the precipitous walls above, that now looked again like a fairy fortress in the clouds, smiling, and fascinating in its light, aerial beauty.

"What a pity the city does not show!" said Harry. "What a glorious sight it would make!"

"At least you have conquered the secret the mysterious mountain has so long and so well concealed," Doctor Lorien observed to Templemore.

The latter gazed on the mountain gloomily. His mind went back to the morning when he saw it first and the vague forebodings that had then come into his mind.

"I don't know," he said doubtfully. "I have not brought away with me the most wonderful secret of all—the 'Plant of Life.' When I think how I was cheated out of that, by the mountain itself, as you may truly say—for its very rocks came crashing down to prevent my escape, or to kill me if I persisted; or at least, to insure my leaving nearly everything behind—when I think of this, it seems to me that Roraima has guarded most of its secrets pretty effectually, and I am almost persuaded there is something uncanny about it."

Harry laughed at this; the more so that it came from Jack.

"That's very fanciful—for you," he returned. "If it had been Leonard, now, I should not have been surprised."

"I am afraid my ideas of what is precisely practical and what is fanciful have been a good deal modified," Jack confessed. "So would yours, if you had passed through my experiences."

"Well, after all, perhaps you haven't lost much," Harry returned. "A small bundle of dried plants wouldn't have been of much use, and as to the seeds, if, as I understand you, they only thrive high up on the mountains, I don't see what you were going to do with them. Moreover, very likely they would have been eaten up by insects, or lost, or got wetted and spoiled, or something, before you got back or could have planted them in a likely spot."

Then they continued their journey, staying that night in Daranato, where the great puma at first created a scare among the dusky inhabitants, but, showing friendliness towards all, she was soon the object of unbounded wonder and interest on every side.

Some two months later there was again a little dinner party at "Meldona," Mr. Kingsford's residence, and the same faces were gathered round the hospitable board—all but Leonard Elwood's. Maud looked charming and happy as she glanced, now and again, first at Jack Templemore's bronzed face, and then at her brother, listening, not for the first time now, to her lover's wondrous tale.

She and Stella had shuddered before at the accounts of the great tree and its victims, and of the horrors of the "haunted wood"; and had talked of Ulama and Zonella, and wondered, again and again, what they were like.

"Poor Leonard! I am sorry to lose him," Maud said. "Yet, I suppose, he does not need pity; for he is to be envied in many ways.

Fancy his dreamings—about which we used to tease him so—coming true after all!"

"It is just a year ago to-day," observed Mr. Kingsford to the doctor, "that you were at dinner here and first told us about that wondrous stranger, Monella. We've had an anxious time ever since."

"I have never known a happy moment till you all came back the other day," said Maud sadly. "I am so thankful that the cruel suspense is ended at last. I have often recalled the words Dr. Lorien used about Roraima; that 'its very name had come to be surrounded by a halo of dread and indefinable fear.' I can truly declare that it has been so with me. I, too, had come to hate and dread the very name. It has seemed to me like a great, remorseless ogre that had swallowed up two of our friends, and, as I feared, was going to swallow up my brother and two more. Yet," she added, looking at Jack, "had I known how things really were, had I known of your lying lamed, and ill, and alone in the den in that horrible forest, I think I should have gone mad! What a comfort to you this dear, faithful animal must have been!"

Nea was by her side, and she put her tear-stained face affectionately down to the animal's head. The big puma had already established herself as a favourite with every one in the house.

"Truly," returned Jack, "such thoughts occurred to the while I was cooped up there. I couldn't help going over things in my mind; and, when I considered how the mountain itself, and all the horrors of the forest, seemed to have combined against me to prevent my escape, I was seized with a sort of hate and detestation of the place. And, ever since, my sleep has been disturbed—and will be for years to come, I feel convinced—by nightmare dreams of the sights and sounds that haunt my memory!"

"I feel that I have a grudge against it, too," the doctor avowed. "Consider all the wonderful things you have told us that are to be found inside! Then, just when I got so near, to be shut out in that way! That 'Plant of Life,' too! I'd have given a good deal to have some specimens of that, and some seeds. I would have got them to grow, somehow, if the thing could be done!"

"I'm precious glad, then, that you didn't," the irreverent Harry put in. "I'm hoping to be a physician—one day—remember! And

what chance would there be for me and the rest of the profession, if you taught people how to live for hundreds of years without so much as an illness?"

This very unexpected view of the matter from the vivacious "budding doctor" had the effect of turning the thoughts of the others from the somewhat gloomy channel into which they seemed to have drifted.

After dinner, the belt, and the purses, and their glittering contents, were brought in and spread out to view.

"Whatever else may be said," Mr. Kingsford declared, with emotion, "there is not one here who will not have cause to remember the stranger Monella, and Leonard, and their friends, with grateful feelings. And you, Jack, above all; for, if I am any judge of the value of your share of these things, you are a millionaire. And that brings back to my mind the thought that is now constantly perplexing me, Who was this wondrous Monella after all? I really cannot bring myself to believe he was—what was his name?—Mellenda, you know."

"No," assented the doctor. "As a man, I have the greatest liking and respect for him; but, as a scientist, I am bound to disbelieve in that part."

"Since I have no claim yet to be considered a scientist," said Harry, "I suppose I am free to believe what I like. So I go the whole ticket. I believe he was what I first pronounced him to be—a magician—and—I swallow the Mellenda legend—whole! So there!" This very emphatically.

"Oh dear, yes!" Stella exclaimed, her blue eyes opening wide at the doubting ones. "Why, of course, it must be true. It is so much more romantic and poetic, you know!"

Robert shook his head gravely.

"No!" he said, very decidedly. "I honour and respect the man, and his memory, from all I have heard of him, but—I cannot accept that wonderful part of it."

"Well, I do," Maud exclaimed, looking round with a pretty air of defiance, more particularly directed against Jack. "So that makes opinion even, so far—three for, and three against. Now," to Templemore, "of course, I know you will side with the others."

To every one's surprise, however, Jack also shook his head.

"I don't know that," he answered, with a comically bewildered air. "I've really had all my old notions so mixed up and blown about, that I honestly admit I really cannot make up my mind. The whole thing is an enigma that I cannot solve as yet—probably never shall. So you may put me down as neutral—undecided—whatever you like to call it,"

Maud clapped her hands; and upon that the puma gave a loud roar, evidently signifying her assent and approbation, "Three for, three against, and one neutral," Maud cried. "That's better than I hoped for!"

The doctor laughed, and his good-natured eye twinkled.

"You've all but beaten us," he said good-humouredly. "But, going away from that part of the subject, I feel truly sorry to think that he should have died so soon after he had accomplished the work he had had so much at heart."

"There again I am inclined to differ," Templemore answered slowly. "I honestly believe that nothing could have happened to please him more. All his later talk clearly showed that. He said he was utterly weary of life, and anxious to be 'released,' as he called it; yet his love for his people was so great, he let no sign of this appear till he felt sure all had been finally achieved. It was the fear that that work might be upset after he had gone—and that alone— that made him so anxious to shut out all future communication with the world outside; of that I feel convinced. It was that that influenced him too, I have no doubt, in making me promise to keep my adventures there a secret from the world in general. But, just at the last, almost when I was coming away, a doubt seemed to come into his mind, and he said to me, 'I release you from that promise, if circumstances should arise in which you conscientiously believe it would be conducive to the good of my country to tell the story of your sojourn here.' What he meant I cannot conceive; I only tell you what he said. Possibly time may show. He seemed to have the 'gift of prophecy' to some extent in those days; certainly, everything went to show that he foresaw, or expected, his own approaching death."

This was all some years ago.